KAY ARTHUR

ISRAEL
My Beloved

HARVEST HOUSE PUBLISHERS

EUGENE, OREGON

Scripture quotations in this book are taken from the New American Standard Bible, 1960, 1962, 1963, 1968, 1971, 1972, 1973, 1975, 1977 by the Lockman Foundation. Used by permission.

Psalm 42 on pages 74-75 is taken from the King James Version of the Bible.

Maps illustrated by Lynda Adkins.

Cover design by Koechel Peterson & Associates, Minneapolis, Minnesota

Interior design by Left Coast Design, Portland, Oregon

ISRAEL, MY BELOVED

Copyright © 1996 by Kay Arthur
Published by Harvest House Publishers
Eugene, Oregon 97402

Library of Congress Cataloging-in-Publication Data

Arthur, Kay, 1933–
  Israel, my beloved / Kay Arthur
       p. cm.
    ISBN 1-56507-403-3 (Cloth)
    ISBN 1-56507-624-9 (Trade Paper ed. 1997)
    ISBN 0-7369-0370-4 (Trade Paper ed. 2001)
    I. Title.
  PS3551.R764183 1995
  813' .54—dc20

                                                                95-30366
                                                                CIP

Printed in the United States of America

18 19 20 21 /BP–LCD/ 17 16 15 14

A historic epic…
crossing the borders of time.

Israel, My Beloved is the story of a nation, a people chosen by G-d, for G-d. Sarah, the main character of *Israel, My Beloved,* is the embodiment of this nation. The prophet Ezekiel describes a child discovered abandoned in a field, taken as the adored wife of G-d only to play the harlot with many lovers (*Yehezquel*/Ezekiel 16). Sarah portrays this child.

This is the story of her adultery, her husband's judgments, and His everlasting love that moves nations as He relentlessly pursues her, seeking to woo her back to Himself.

Based on true accounts recorded by Jewish historians, Israel's story is told, beginning from 586 B.C.E. and continuing onward into the near and certain future. It is the story of the fulfillment of biblical prophecies played out over the centuries, some now complete, others yet to be fulfilled.

The characters of this book tell the story of

…the Diaspora (*Devarim*/Deuteronomy 28:63-69)

…Israel's return to the land, never to be cast out again (*Yehezquel*/ Ezekiel 36)

…the final period of Jacob's trouble, the great day of the Lord (*Daniyyel*/ Daniel 12:1; *Yirmeyahu*/Jeremiah 20:4-7; *Yo'el*/Joel 2:1-2), and

…the ultimate triumph of the remnant, who come through the fire, refined as silver, tested as gold when the Lord will be king over all the earth (*Zekharya*/Zechariah 13:7-9; 14:9).

Sarah's story transcends time and focuses on the events of her history. Like no other, Israel is an everlasting nation, the indestructible "wife of G-d."

Those who know the Scriptures will recognize her, those who don't will learn about her…and those who listen carefully will know that because God keeps His covenants, Israel will always be beloved of G-d.

This is a story—an epic—that will impassion your heart…enlighten your understanding…and give you a glimpse into the very certain future just beyond the horizon with the dawning of a new day.

It is a story I lived as I wrote it, and my life will never be the same.

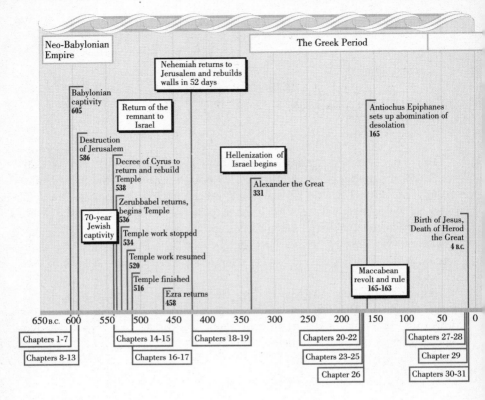

Neo-Babylonian Empire

The Greek Period

Nehemiah returns to Jerusalem and rebuilds walls in 52 days

Babylonian captivity
605

Return of the remnant to Israel

Antiochus Epiphanes sets up abomination of desolation
165

Destruction of Jerusalem
586

Decree of Cyrus to return and rebuild Temple
538

Hellenization of Israel begins

70-year Jewish captivity

Zerubbabel returns, begins Temple
536

Alexander the Great
331

Birth of Jesus, Death of Herod the Great
4 B.C.

Temple work stopped
534

Temple work resumed
520

Temple finished
516

Ezra returns
458

Maccabean revolt and rule
165-163

650 B.C. | 600 | 550 | 500 | 450 | 400 | 350 | 300 | 250 | 200 | 150 | 100 | 50 | 0

Chapters 1-7

Chapters 14-15

Chapters 18-19

Chapters 20-22

Chapters 27-28

Chapters 8-13

Chapters 16-17

Chapters 23-25

Chapter 29

Chapter 26

Chapters 30-31

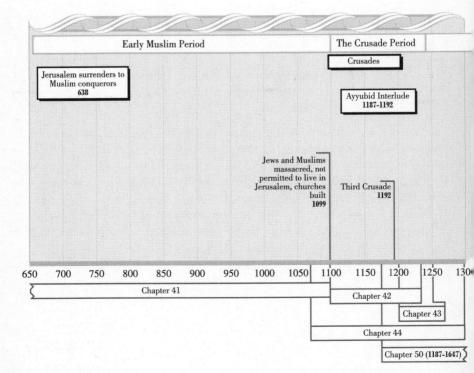

Early Muslim Period

The Crusade Period

Crusades

Jerusalem surrenders to Muslim conquerors
638

Ayyubid Interlude
1187-1192

Jews and Muslims massacred, not permitted to live in Jerusalem, churches built
1099

Third Crusade
1192

650 | 700 | 750 | 800 | 850 | 900 | 950 | 1000 | 1050 | 1100 | 1150 | 1200 | 1250 | 130

Chapter 41

Chapter 42

Chapter 43

Chapter 44

Chapter 50 (1187-1647)

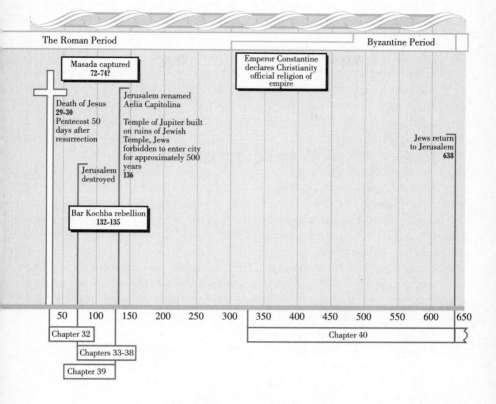

The Roman Period · Byzantine Period

Masada captured
72-74?

Emperor Constantine
declares Christianity
official religion of
empire

Death of Jesus
29-30
Pentecost 50
days after
resurrection

Jerusalem renamed
Aelia Capitolina

Temple of Jupiter built
on ruins of Jewish
Temple, Jews
forbidden to enter city
for approximately 500
years
136

Jews return
to Jerusalem
638

Jerusalem
destroyed

Bar Kochba rebellion
132-135

50 100 150 200 250 300 350 400 450 500 550 600 650

Chapter 32

Chapters 33-38

Chapter 39

Chapter 40

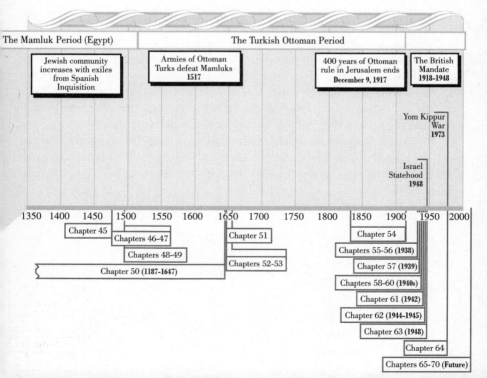

The Mamluk Period (Egypt) · The Turkish Ottoman Period

Jewish community
increases with exiles
from Spanish
Inquisition

Armies of Ottoman
Turks defeat Mamluks
1517

400 years of Ottoman
rule in Jerusalem ends
December 9, 1917

The British
Mandate
1918-1948

Yom Kippur
War
1973

Israel
Statehood
1948

1350 1400 1450 1500 1550 1600 1650 1700 1750 1800 1850 1900 1950 2000

Chapter 45

Chapters 46-47

Chapters 48-49

Chapter 50 (1187-1647)

Chapter 51

Chapters 52-53

Chapter 54

Chapters 55-56 (1938)

Chapter 57 (1939)

Chapters 58-60 (1940s)

Chapter 61 (1942)

Chapter 62 (1944-1945)

Chapter 63 (1948)

Chapter 64

Chapters 65-70 (Future)

Thus says the Lord GOD to Jerusalem, "Your origin and your birth are from the land of the Canaanite, your father was an Amorite and your mother a Hittite.

"As for your birth, on the day you were born your navel cord was not cut, nor were you washed with water for cleansing; you were not rubbed with salt or even wrapped in cloths. No eye looked with pity on you to do any of these things for you, to have compassion on you. Rather you were thrown out into the open field, for you were abhorred on the day you were born.

"When I passed by you and saw you squirming in your blood, I said to you while you were in your blood, 'Live!'...

"Then you grew up, became tall, and reached the age for fine ornaments; your breasts were formed and your hair had grown....Then I passed by you and saw you, and behold, you were at the time for love; so I spread My skirt over you and covered your nakedness. I also swore to you and entered into a covenant with you so that you became Mine," declares the Lord GOD....

"I also clothed you with embroidered cloth, and put sandals of porpoise skin on your feet; and I wrapped you with fine linen and covered you with silk. And I adorned you with ornaments, put bracelets on your hands, and a necklace around your neck. I also put a ring in your nostril, earrings in your ears, and a beautiful crown on your head.

"Thus you were adorned with gold and silver, and your dress was of fine linen, silk, and embroidered cloth. You ate fine flour, honey, and oil; so you were exceedingly beautiful and advanced to royalty.

"Then your fame went forth among the nations on account of your beauty, for it was perfect because of My splendor which I bestowed on you," declares the Lord GOD. But you trusted in your beauty and played the harlot because of your fame, and you poured out your harlotries on every passer-by who might be willing.

"And you took some of your clothes, made for yourself high places of various colors, and played the harlot on them, which should never come about nor happen. You also took your beautiful jewels made of My gold and of My silver, which I had given you, and made for yourself male images that you might play the harlot with them....

"You built yourself a high place at the top of every street, and made your beauty abominable; and you spread your legs to every passer-by to multiply your harlotry....

"How languishing is your heart," declares the Lord GOD, "while you do all these things, the actions of a bold-faced harlot. When you built your shrine at the beginning of every street and made your high place in every square, in disdaining money, you were not like a harlot.

"You adulteress wife, who takes strangers instead of her husband!"

—EZEKIEL 16:1-8, 10-17, 25, 30-32

Chapter 1

*S*arah wouldn't look back. That she had determined. And when Sarah made up her mind, that was it. She was a strong-willed woman, to say the least—stubborn as a donkey.

Her husband, who watched from their bedroom window, knew her intent. The straightness of her posture, the rigidity of her thrown-back shoulders might seem like nothing more than good poise to a passerby. But he knew his wife. Her determined defiance was more than practiced posture. It was her final statement to him. Sarah wouldn't turn around for one last look even if her life depended on it. Although she had come crawling back after the last several flirtatious encounters, he knew this time it was different. She'd never return of her own accord.

"I know he's at the window watching," Sarah muttered as she walked briskly. "It's just like him. He won't take no for an answer!" Her words were tainted with a bitter haughtiness. "He always thinks he's right. He thinks he knows everything. Well, if he does, he ought to know I'm sick of being married!"

The issue was settled in *her* mind. This was it. No more. The thrill, the joy, and the happiness Sarah felt in the early years of their marriage was gone. What had once shone brilliantly had, with the passage of time, become lackluster. The daily routine of married life had dulled the sense of anticipation and wonder she experienced when their relationship was new. The awe of being married to someone more than capable of meeting her every need had turned to complacency, then to dissatisfaction.

He, however, had remained the same—loving, devoted, consistent, never-changing. Sometimes it made Sarah angry that he was *so* perfect.

"I've changed," said Sarah firmly, keeping up her quick pace. "I tried, my husband, I really tried! But there's too much out there in that wonderful world— too much that I want to know, taste, touch, experience." Somehow hearing the adamancy of her words justified and strengthened her actions. Their passion stirred her own passion.

"I want to mingle with Assyrians, Egyptians, Babylonians. I want to know how they live, how they worship their gods. I want to walk through their lands, taste their food, sing their songs, sleep in their beds. And I don't want a narrow-minded husband warning me of their ways—preaching the dangers of such liaisons. I want to make my own choices and not feel condemned. I want to be free to roam. And free I will be! Free to live, free to love . . . whom I want, when I want."

Presently her love was Meshach—wonderfully sensual Meshach. A seductive smile came across Sarah's lips as she pondered this Chaldean's reckless zest for life. The very thought of his touch awakened feelings long dormant. Meshach loved life; he lived without the restriction that rules bring. "I'm determined," he said, "to taste life to the fullest before death extinguishes all feeling and my body returns to dust." She thought that strangely poetic.

The tinkling of Sarah's ankle bracelets—an effect she had learned by mincing her steps—matched the tingling of her body. The sound brought attention to her long olive legs—legs Meshach often commented on. As she hurried her pace the merry tinkling increased. In her mind, the sound somehow distanced her from her husband's watchful eyes, which felt like guilt nipping at her heels.

As Sarah drew nearer to the high places of Jerusalem, where she would meet Meshach, the splendor of the home her husband had built blazed before her mind's eye instead of diminishing behind her back. Sarah knew she'd never live in a house like that again. Even the most extravagant of the homes lining the path of her exodus could not compare with what she was leaving. Nothing she had ever seen could compare.

"Enough of this . . . enough! What difference does a home make when you're not happy?" Sarah stopped abruptly, shut her eyes, and shook her head. She didn't want this moment spoiled by the vision of what she was leaving. After taking a deep breath and renewing her resolve, Sarah picked up her pace again.

"A house I can't take with me," she rationalized. "These I can," she said aloud as she reached down, patted the bag hanging from her shoulder, and tucked it under her arm to relieve the weight of its heaviness. It was filled with jewelry lavished on her by a devoted husband. "Nothing but precious stones of the rarest quality set in the purest of gold and silver are suitable for your adornment," he had said. She winced as a spasm of guilt unexpectedly tore at her conscience.

"With these I can buy anything I want . . . anything!" Sarah said, spinning her deluded web of rationalization, talking to her husband as if he was just a few steps behind her instead of standing at the window watching her become a speck on the horizon of her new venture. "It's only right that I take these with me. They're mine. I earned them as your wife. Besides, if I left them, they'd just be a painful reminder of me every time you look at them."

Sarah knew her husband would never sell the jewelry. He needed no money. A slight pout brought out the fullness of her lips as she reasoned, "They'd just go to waste—unappreciated, tucked away in a box waiting for someone who is never coming back. The cattle on these thousand hills are yours. What are these jewels to you other than painful reminders of me?"

At that moment, in her rebellion, Sarah despised his faithfulness. "You don't need these. You don't need anything. *You* are self-contained. Why then do you demand such total devotion? Why do you want me? Why won't you just let me go? Why do you have to be so grieved—so hurt that I'm leaving?" she said with a mix of anger and sarcasm. "I hate it!"

The anguished look in his eyes. The remembrance of his words. She hated them both! Sarah's back stiffened even more, making her appear a few inches taller. She was going to have what *she* wanted for a change. She would be like the women she had heard about—the royal women of Egypt. She didn't want to be set apart from the nations; she wanted to be part of them.

As Sarah quickened her pace, purposely looking down at the road, she noticed her shadow wasn't running before her. Could it be that the heat on her back was from the burning of his eyes rather that the warmth of the sun? Sarah didn't want to know. She wasn't going to look. She began taking longer strides, eager to increase the distance between her and her husband—distance that would put her out of his sight.

If Sarah had turned back for one last parting look, she would have seen his shadow half hidden in the window. A shadow that belied the true strength of her husband. Tears rested on his strong cheekbones as he moved back the curtain a little more and watched the love of his life walk away.

His heart was heavy; the pain in his chest crushing. His words, unheard by his wife, resonated with omniscience. "Oh Sarah, I know where you are headed. I've known it from your youth, and I have loved you anyway. How I wish you had listened to me, believed me. I wish you had been content with my love. This rebellion, my love, is going to cost you more than you can ever imagine."

He paused and sighed deeply. "Someday, you'll come back. But until then you will walk through the fires of hell . . . fires that will threaten to consume you."

He blinked, trying to see through his tears. Sarah was out of sight, yet he continued to look out the window. The linen curtain, caught by the breeze, flicked at his face and stirred his attention back to his surroundings. As he reached up to catch the curtain and bring it back inside where it belonged, his eyes fell on the palm of his right hand. The curtain, like a veil, covered the covenant mark in his hand—a mark he had put there to reassure Sarah of his unconditional love. He looked up again at the deserted road. Then, leaning out the window, he shouted into the wind, "The day is coming, Beloved, when you will say that I have forgotten you . . . forsaken you. But I won't. I won't. I can't. I've engraved you on the palms of my hands. . . ."

Chapter 2

He had to get off his feet. The emotion of the moment drained him. Reclining on his couch, he closed his eyes—not to sleep, for sleep was impossible. He closed his eyes to shut out the present. He wanted to permit himself some reverie, to think about the past, to relive the days when he first saw her.

Then he heard the soft, familiar pat of his servant's feet on the marble floor. He opened his eyes and a faint smile appeared on his lips as he turned his head without lifting it. He remembered he was not totally abandoned in his palace.

"It's getting dark, Master. I thought—"

"Yes, Elieazar, yes. It is dark, so very dark." He raised his head and motioned with his hand. "Put down the oil lamp, but please, for now, I beg you to leave me alone . . . my faithful one." He spoke the words gently. He and Elieazar had been together for so long they had become much alike. Elieazar moved quietly in the background, anticipating his master's desires and carrying out his wishes almost as if they were one.

Elieazar reluctantly moved to the door and hesitated for a moment as if he wanted to speak. The soft light cast by the oil lamp illuminated a face kindly etched with lines that spoke of character, experience, and wisdom. His skin looked soft, almost translucent. His face was framed by a radiant white beard and head of hair curling softly to his face and neck. His eyes were filled with compassion and concern. What troubled Elieazar's master troubled him. He, too, had seen Sarah leave. As his master watched from one window, Elieazar had watched from another. He also knew that this time Sarah would not be back. Elieazar loved Sarah because his master loved her. But right now he was angry about the way Sarah had treated her husband. He wished he could give her a good verbal thrashing to bring her to her senses.

His master looked at him but said nothing. Elieazar knew his master didn't want to talk—not now, at least. So he pushed open the door and left.

Once again alone in the room, Sarah's husband leaned back on the huge soft pillows covered in Sarah's favorite colors—purples and reds. Then he closed his eyes and began to reminisce in a hushed tone, almost a whisper.

"I remember when I saw you for the very first time, Sarah. You were lying in a field. A baby unwanted, abandoned by the mother who gave birth to you. She had not washed you, nor rubbed your little body with salt as is the custom."

He spoke as if Sarah was in the room, resting her head on his lap as he ran his fingers through her long, dark hair. How she loved to be touched in those days, to have him brush her hair with his fingers. They had often spent whole evenings that way, so close a whisper would do.

"You didn't know that you were abhorred on the day you were born. Your mother was a Hittite; your father an Amorite. And neither cared for you. They left you lying in a green field sprinkled with flowers, not even bothering to cut your cord or wash you." His voice was filled with the same tender compassion he felt the day he found her. "No one wrapped you in cloths. No eye took pity on you until I came along. But when I saw you I was filled with compassion." The flickering oil lamp caught a smile filling in furrows ploughed by sorrow.

"I determined that you would live. Live, not die! And live you did. I watched you grow. The years passed quickly. . . .

"Then, Sarah, you became a woman; your breasts were formed. It was time for love and you became mine. I spread my skirt over you. Do you remember?"

Suddenly he arose from the couch and walked over to the window. Spreading his arms the width of the window, he gripped the opening with his hands until his fingers and knuckles turned almost white.

"Oh, my Beloved," he cried out. "As you go to meet your lover on the road, remember how I covered your nakedness, how I bathed you, how I clothed your beautiful body and anointed you with the purest of oil!"

"Remember that," he pounded the ledge with his fist. "And remember the night when I cut a covenant with you—a solemn, binding oath swearing my fidelity to you, a guarantee of my faithfulness to my promises. Remember that when someday you think I will never take you back."

His rising voice hurled across the night like a falling star—as if somehow Sarah might hear and take notice. "I promised you children—descendants—like the stars of the sky, like the sand of the sea. I promised you land—land that would be yours for an everlasting possession. The land you have lived in all these years. Children . . . land . . . unconditional love . . . sealed in a covenant ceremony. What more could you ask for?

"When your lovers are finished with you, when they break their promises, remember that I keep mine. My covenant is unconditional—a binding agreement that I will never, ever go back on. Remember the blood of the covenant shed as I split the animals in two . . . the three-year-old heifer, goat, and ram. Each half laid opposite the other . . . the pigeon and the turtledove."

He turned from the window and rested on the ledge, revisiting in his mind's eye the event of so many years ago. "That's why I woke you from sleep. I wanted it etched in your memory forever. You were terrified by the darkness, yet you had to see me pass through the halves of those animals with that flaming torch in my hand. I was determined that you would always know—always remember."

He turned back to the window and leaned out again, even farther, the sleeves of his garment outlining the form of his strong arms. How she had once relished their strength, the security she felt when he held her tight as they walked through the shadowed valleys from Egypt to Canaan.

"Remember, Sarah," he shouted into the wind. "Remember the days when we first loved one another. Remember them, and compare them with this heat of passion that drives you to seek the arms of other lovers!"

Had Sarah been there, she would have heard the rancor . . . the fire of jealousy blazing in the blackness of the night.

Chapter 3

here was a light tap on the door as it eased open.

"Master, I heard your voice," said Elieazar, who had been standing by his window contemplating the changes Sarah's departure would bring. "I thought you were going to bed. Were you calling for me?"

"Come in, Elieazar, come in." His words were weighted with weariness. "You're always concerned about your master, aren't you, my loyal one." His was a loyalty to be treasured. "Elieazar, I cannot sleep nor even slumber. My beloved is gone. She has forsaken me. She's walked away for good this time. And I'm grieved, Elieazar. Deeply grieved."

A sigh escaped his lips, causing his enormous chest to heave. Elieazar looked at his master's chest—a chest that had enveloped Sarah often. How his master loved to hold her in his arms—to take her into him and hold her tight, to have her cradle her head in his all-sufficient breast.

Elieazar looked at him, saying nothing. He was dumfounded. How could anyone—any living soul—ever want to leave the security, the presence of his master? How could anyone walk away from so pure, so selfless a love as his? Surely there was no one like him in all the earth. Of course he was strong and unbending, but he was never unloving. Certainly he was righteous and just, but he was also filled with lovingkindness and compassion.

Elieazar not only loved his master, he also feared him. That's what Sarah lacked—a fear of her husband. A healthy fear born of respect, of trust. That was why she continually disobeyed him . . . why she didn't listen to what he said. It grieved Elieazar. He, too, had tried to talk to Sarah and explain this master he had served since what seemed the beginning of time. But Sarah thought she knew it all. To her, Elieazar was just a servant who was to remember to keep his place.

Elieazar knew his place. He was there to do the master's bidding without question. His master need not be questioned; he never made a mistake. He seemed omniscient. Elieazar also knew that disobedience would bring consequences. What the master said, stood. He never changed his word. He expected obedience and always made known beforehand the cost of disobedience. Wasn't that what he had overheard his master telling Sarah—that punishment would be in accordance with her deeds? If his wrath came, it would be just—and only for a moment. His mercy and compassion were always waiting the next morning.

15

Awe filled Elieazar's eyes. As he stood looking at his wearied master, he thought, *He can be trusted because he's always the same yesterday, today— and I believe—forever.*

Elieazar then remembered the reason he had come. "If you are not going to bed, then let me light the wood," he said kindly. "A fire will keep you warm."

"Yes, yes, light the fire. I'll spend the night here," he said as he seated himself on the edge of the couch. He rested his elbows on his knees, rubbed his eyes, yawned, and put his chin on his hands. He looked vacantly into space for a moment. Then he covered his eyes with his hands as he waited for Elieazar to leave. He didn't want company. He wanted only to recall their past, to remember as if she were there listening, cradled safely in his arms.

After the familiar sound of Elieazar's shuffling footsteps faded down the hall, he uncovered his eyes and stared pensively at the fire. "You followed me through the wilderness as I led you from Egypt. Day in and day out you trusted me to provide everything you needed. Oh, there were times when you complained," he said with a little chuckle, "but you learned your lesson. Sometimes the hard way, but you learned. Then we finally arrived in the land I promised you—the land that I swore would be yours forever."

He rose from the couch and went to the fireplace. He felt cold. *Probably,* he thought, *because I feel so alone.*

"It was then—at Mount Nebo just before we crossed the Jordan—that I warned you that this could happen. You could choose to disobey me, to serve the gods worshiped by other people. You could choose another lover.

"Oh my Beloved, remember . . . whatever you are doing now, remember the devotion of your youth—the love of your betrothal. How I wrapped you in fine silk, in the loveliest of embroidered cloth. Remember the gold, the silver I gave you.

"You've taken your jewels; I saw them under your arm. When you adorn yourself for your Chaldean lover, remember who gave them to you and how you used to adorn yourself for me. If you dance for him, may your heart remember how you danced before me—the delightful jingle of your jewels, the coins, and the ankle bracelets!

"And as you make love under every green tree, remember where you are lying down. In *our* city—*our* Jerusalem. The city I built for you. *My* gift to you. A city you are desecrating with your adulteries."

He pounded the mantle with a clenched fist. "How could you descend so low! How could you desecrate Jerusalem, violate the purity of love by cutting trees in the shapes of sexual symbols? How could you embrace such sensuality? I warned you where all that would lead. Now you want another lover!"

He paced back to the window, almost as if he expected to see Sarah coming up the road. "Am I not enough? Haven't I satisfied you . . . your need for love, your every desire? Can your lover provide what I have given you? Remember the splendor of the temple I built for you. It is *my* name you engraved there. Is it not engraved on your heart also? Your name is engraved on mine!"

His voice became hard—almost threatening. "If you continue your harlotry I cannot defend you. I *will* not defend you. I cannot protect a faithless wife from the consequences of her own deeds. I cannot go against who I am and what I stand for. Not even for *you*."

He turned away from the window. His stride kept pace with the impassioned words spilling loudly from his mouth.

"What of our children? When they see you neighing after this foreigner, will they not follow your example? Think, my love—consider your ways! Our children have always watched you carefully, doing as you do. What is to stop them now?"

Periodically, almost rhythmically, his hands flew into the air punctuating his speech. The pacing continued, only more rapidly.

"You're going to follow your lovers. Your mind is set. If you take one, you'll take another. And our children! What of our children, Sarah? Will they not become adulterers just like their mother?!

"Beware, Sarah. The lovers you trust will strip you naked and carry you to their land. And what will you do then? You cannot even speak their tongue! Their language will be a babble to you. You'll be the foreigner!"

Now he was shouting. "Do you think they will treat you kindly like foreigners are treated in our land? No! You will be despised!"

His voice took on the didactic tone of a irate teacher. "That always happens with illicit affairs. You'll be a reproach to those who see you. They'll think of you as nothing more than a bold-faced harlot. A harlot like no other, for instead of receiving money, you will pay your lovers—with the gifts I gave you! I tell you, Sarah, you will be hated. When it is evening you will wish it were morning. And when morning comes you will wish it were evening. You will live in dread. Your life will hang in doubt. For what is a harlot worth?"

He walked the floor, silent for a while as if pondering his own words, the tragedy of Sarah's destiny.

Then, once again he had to verbalize the pleading of his heart. "Oh, my Beloved, when it happens—and it will—remember our temple. Remember Jerusalem, our city. . . ."

With that he went to the window and flung open the shutters that the night wind had closed. Leaning out, he shouted, "Remember, my name is here. Remember, my Gomer." He shouted even louder, "Remember! Humble yourself, Sarah. Call for me; turn from your wicked ways. I will hear you. . . ."

Abruptly his shouting turned into sobs. "I will hear you. I will hear . . . and I will forgive you. . . ."

Drained of his energy, he left the window and collapsed face down on his couch. For a few moments, his arms were his pillow. Then, rolling over on his back, he lay there staring at the shadows dancing in the dim light of the oil lamp.

The last words he uttered before dawn were spoken with sober confidence. "I love you, Sarah, with an everlasting love. And with lovingkindness I *will* bring you back."

He never went to sleep. Perhaps his watchful vigilance would stir Sarah to remember the words he had spoken to her—words that could repel her lover, words that could rein in her passions if she would remember them: "Oh Sarah, Sarah, put me like a seal over your heart, like a seal on your arm—for love is as strong as death... jealousy as severe as Sheol."

Chapter 4

*S*arah felt she was going to drown in the passion of the moment. She ached with desire. Every fiber of her being longed to know him—every fiber but one: her mind. Her thoughts forbade surrender.

Mustering all the strength she had—emotionally and physically—Sarah pushed Meshach away.

"I can't . . . I just can't. Not right now, at least. . . ."

Meshach was more startled than angry. Never had he found it necessary to force himself on a woman. They always yielded. It was part of the sweetness of conquest.

Although his passions were ignited to a red-hot heat, he would not allow passion to overrule his principles of conquest. Despite his disdain for rules, Meshach did have principles—principles both in love and war. In battle he never allowed human emotion to constrain him when dealing with his enemy. The enemy was always the enemy and would never be dealt with compassionately. Compassion might cost him his life one day—or the lives of the men under his command.

Just as compassion would never rule Meshach in war, so also would passion never rule him in love.

He would not force himself on someone who did not beg for him. When Meshach said, "I want you" to a woman, he wanted her to plead to be taken. Nothing less would ultimately satisfy him. Some of his fellow Chaldeans told him he was a fool.

"What does it matter," they asked, "as long as you are satisfied?" But they didn't understand. To Meshach it was a matter of conquest—not just of a woman's body, but also her soul. He wanted them both. Then, having conquered her, he could do with her as he pleased.

Meshach rolled over onto his back. Tonight would not be the night. He knew he had more work to do.

For a moment they were silent, both looking up at the stars peeking immodestly through the branches of the trees. Meshach had intended to take Sarah to his quarters outside the city, but they had progressed no farther than this grassy knoll. He hadn't minded, for it was a perfect night and a perfect setting. Not conventional, but romantic. There was just enough light from the moon to see the longing in Sarah's face, the outline of her body under her shimmering silk gown. A warm gentle breeze rustled through the grass on this high hill that was closer to the stars and farther from the city. All around them were groves of trees cut for the gods and their followers, who nestled together for occasions such as this.

Meshach turned on his side and leaned on his right arm to face Sarah. He pulled up a blade of green grass and ran it through his lips. "Talk to me," he said. He knew women loved to talk. If that's what it would take to win her, he would listen.

Sarah stayed on her back, which pleased him. With his eyes he could follow the outline of her supple body and conjure up all sorts of fantasies while she talked. The sport of it all—even the waiting—Meshach found tantalizing. Sometimes he wondered if anticipation was not more exciting than realization.

"I . . . I feel a little foolish." Sarah smiled, hesitated, and began again. "You see, I was so certain this was what I wanted. I had thought it through and was sure that I didn't want to be restricted to one man."

Her eyes left the little flower she was twirling in her hand and looked straight into his. "Other women do what we are doing. Why, it's even part of your culture, isn't it? Your gods do not tie you down to . . ." she dropped her eyes just for a moment as she carefully chose her words, ". . . to knowing, to loving, to having only one man or one woman."

With that she turned on her side and looked him right in the eye—not with a brazenness but with an honest, almost childlike curiosity. "Don't you go to your temples and make love with the temple . . . uh, temple . . ." Sarah hesitated. Should she call them prostitutes?

"Prostitutes." He said it for her and laughed. He found her naiveté surprising in light of her strong sensual drive.

"Well, do you?" She laughed with him. "Is that part of your worship?"

"Yes, my little Israelite, it is part of our worship. Our gods are not as restrictive as the one whom you call the one true God. Our gods understand us; they understand our passions. Even our preferences. There are chambers next to our temples—chambers where you'll find men as well as women. So you can have your choice. If I want a man, even that is all right—"

"But," she sat up abruptly, "you wouldn't, would you?" There was alarm in her voice.

"No, my love," he said as he reached over and ran his hand over the outline of the moon on her body.

He drew back his hand. "Men are not my taste. You are the vineyard, the sweet wine I desire."

Her words came slowly. "Grapes must first be picked and crushed before they give forth sweet wine. . . ."

"When they're ripe, my love. When they're ripe. . . ."

"And how does one know when they are ripe?" Her voice deepened.

He smiled. He wondered how often she had played this game. He loved the anticipation it bred. Had he been able to take her at the moment he would have been disappointed. He wanted to prolong the mounting pleasure, which heightened his senses, his desires.

"One knows when the fruit is ripe by. . . ." Meshach's words trailed off as he slowly took the blade of grass from his mouth and reached over with it to—

"Don't!" Instantly Sarah moved back and her countenance changed.

"What's the matter?" asked Meshach.

"I just don't want you to do that."

"Do what? I didn't do anything! You don't know what I was going to do because you stopped me."

Meshach was frustrated. He felt like a man about to take a long drink to quench his overwhelming thirst only to have someone knock the wineskin out of his hand just before it reached his lips. The drink was spilled. His thirst had not been quenched. He knew women; they were responders. He had to be gentle. Careful. He could not react. He had to stay in control.

"Forgive me," said Sarah. "It's just that when you moved toward me with that blade of grass, I . . . well, to be honest, I'm . . . a little tormented by the thoughts that keep nagging at me. You see . . ." she paused, waiting for his reaction.

"Go on, my love." His words were gentle. "I want to know what little foxes are spoiling our vineyards."

Taking Meshach at his word, Sarah began talking slowly, very matter-of-factly, but without hesitation. It seemed as if Meshach's display of concern had unleashed her tongue. "You have to understand that I married early. When I reached womanhood, my husband took me for his wife. I became his," she said, not uttering his name. His name held such respect, such fear that she felt she could not desecrate it by speaking it aloud in the setting around them. She wished it didn't bother her, but it did.

She went on. "I've never fully known another man. There have been occasions when I've been with other men, but never have I. . . ."

Meshach was surprised by Sarah's hesitancy in talking about all this, and yet delighted by the revelation of what a prize he would capture. There were more than gleanings awaiting him in this vineyard!

"My husband has always been good to me. Without him I would never have attained what I have. He found me as a newborn baby abandoned in a field. No one wanted me but him. He protected me as I grew up, and then . . . when I became a woman—when it was time for love—he loved me and I loved him. At least, I thought I loved him."

Sarah paused for a minute. It seemed disparaging to talk of loving him when she longed for the arms of one who was the antithesis of her husband.

"I followed him . . . trusted him. He took care of all my needs—even when I murmured or complained. He cared for me even when I lashed out in anger and disappointment because I wondered how he would provide for me. He didn't give up on me even when I stomped my feet and told him I wished I were in Egypt again—a desire that I now realize was absolutely ridiculous."

Sarah laughed as she reached over and touched Meshach's chin. "But he was patient with me, even as you are being patient with me now. I remember what he did one time when we were traveling through the wilderness. I grew tired of just eating bread; I wanted meat. So he sent me quail. He sent so much it made me sick. He's like that . . . able to provide everything and anything I want. He's patient. Longsuffering."

Sarah sighed and ripped some grass—roots and all. She looked at it, shook off the dirt, and tossed it beyond her feet. "Sometimes I get bored with all that. Yet, as I said, everything I am and everything I have came from him." Sarah's voice softened. "And that's why I asked you to stop when you whispered in my ear that you wanted me. Even though he gave me everything, I wanted you. But he won't share me with you . . . or anyone."

Meshach smiled. If he had any doubt before, it was gone now. He knew eventually he would have her. But why hadn't she surrendered tonight? His curiosity got the best of him. "Why, then, may I ask, did you stop me . . . push me away if you wanted me? I assume that when you said you wanted me you meant *want* in every sense of the word?"

"I stopped you because all of a sudden I could hear my husband's words: 'Drink water out of your own well.' They were almost audible."

In a modest move, wrapping her dress around her legs, Sarah drew them up and rested her chin on her knees. She rocked ever so slightly. "He always told me that whenever I was thirsty, I was to come to him. He would satisfy my every desire if only I would let him. Then he warned me: 'Any other place you go to have your needs met or your thirst satisfied will only turn out to be a broken cistern.'"

"Oh," he exclaimed, "are you telling me that I am a broken cistern?" He rolled on his back, threw out his arms, and pounded them on the ground. "I'm a broken cistern—a dry well!"

Then he turned back on his side, swept his left arm the whole length of his body, and said, "Look at me. What do you see that is broken?"

Sarah frowned. "That's not what he meant. He meant broken cisterns don't hold water. So if I drink from one, eventually the water that quenches my thirst will dry up. And I wouldn't be satisfied."

She paused, then reached over and gently took his hand. "Do you understand? My husband's words trouble me, Meshach. What if he is right? If he is, then I'm making a big mistake."

Sarah's voice became adamant. "Suppose there is only one true God! Suppose what your gods permit you to do or even . . ." Sarah hesitated, almost as if in pain, "what they ask you to do isn't right?"

Sarah hesitated as if the answer was relevant to her personally.

"Suppose there really are consequences to my behavior? My husband says I will reap exactly what I sow. He set two paths before me: one leads to life, the other to death. Although he loves me and wants me to choose life by loving him with all my heart, soul, strength, and mind, he says the choice is mine. I can choose my *way,* but not the *consequences.*"

Sarah grasped his hand and laughed, momentarily changing the tone of the conversation. "That's why I couldn't. At least right now. It's my mind and—" she grew sober again, "a somewhat troubled heart. I have to think about it, Meshach. I must be sure. Don't you see? If I didn't know these things, if I hadn't lived by them, if I hadn't heard them all my life, then it would be easy to give in to what you want . . . what I want."

Sarah paused for a moment and continued thoughtfully, "Do I want you even if the consequences are what he says they will be? Are you worth it?" Sarah bowed her head. "Meshach, I did something awful once—not too long ago. I went against my husband. I listened to others. I can't get the horror of it out of my mind. I don't want to do something like that again and have to live with it, sleep with it. . . ."

"Do you want to tell me what it was?" Meshach's voice was tender.

Sarah paused and shook her head.

She's a tough woman . . . a determined one, thought Meshach.

"I just want to know my husband might not be right. Do you understand? I've rambled on and on telling you all this. Do you think he's right?"

Meshach smiled. He knew women liked to be understood. "No, Sarah, he's not right. And yes, I understand. I don't want you if you don't want me— body, soul, and mind." He then reached over and gently ran his hand down her forearm and over her hand. "I am not going to force you, Sarah. It will be your decision."

Sarah smiled. She was relieved. Meshach did understand. In her anxiety, she didn't want to lose him. After all, she had walked out knowing where she was headed. She had no intention of turning back. At least, not now.

For the first time that evening, the two sat in total silence...feeling neither awkward nor uncomfortable. Both were absorbed in their own thoughts.

Sarah sighed. She wished her husband was as tolerant, as broadminded. That seemed to her such a noble quality—to understand that people were different and that they had different standards and beliefs. She felt that people should be accepted just as they were without insisting there was only one right way, one path for life.

Finally Meshach broke the silence. "I have an idea. Why don't you come and see how other people—Israelites like yourself—worship other gods? You can see that right here in Jerusalem." Meshach rolled on his side, looked at her, and grinned. "You know, a person can't have too many gods!"

"And," he said with smugness because of a new strategy that had just occurred to him, "haven't I heard there are prophets in this city who disagree with what your husband believes?"

"Yes, there are prophets like that."

A grin broke over Meshach's face. He had hit the mark. He listened with satisfaction as she continued.

"I've heard them. In fact, they made me wonder if my husband was really right. When I had some of the gardeners of our city cut the trees into various shapes—shapes such as—" she hesitated out of embarrassment. *How can I name the parts of a man's body?* she thought to herself. *Harlots talk that way!* "Well, the prophets said it was all right to trim the trees that way. They said that my husband would probably become angry, but that he'd get over it and still love me. I was afraid he'd banish me from Jerusalem or the temple. But the prophets assured me he'd never do that. 'You belong to him; disaster will never come to you. His reputation rests on your well-being.' And you know what. . . ."

She's off and talking again, he thought. *So much for this night.* Meshach laid back on the cool grass, closed his eyes, and let her talk.

" . . . the prophets were right. My husband was angry—absolutely furious.

But he didn't banish me. He told me to cut down the trees and burn them. But I said nothing. And I didn't cut them down. People in the city enjoyed them. They helped their . . ." Sarah stopped momentarily, choosing her words carefully, " . . . they helped their intimate relations and they helped mine, too. I would think about those symbols and," her voice took on a seductive heaviness, "you know. . . ."

Meshach smiled involuntarily. He was learning a lot. There was no end to the stimulus he could provide! Wait until he took her to the high place of Baal and Astarte! At the spring festival, virgins would shave their heads and surrender their virginity. They'd watch the celebration of the season as men and women acted out a sacred marriage—an act that not only insured the fertility of the earth, but also served as an aphrodisiac for the spectators. In the worship of Baal, Sarah could watch all sorts of sensual orgies and images.

As Meshach lay there, he searched his mind for other ways he could weaken Sarah's walls of resistance. *Maybe I'll let her see the sacrifice of a child.* Those sacrifices eventually took on a sensual nature. He shuddered involuntarily.

"Are you cold, Meshach?"

"No, no. Go on."

"Of course there is another prophet . . . a strange one. I believe his name is Jeremiah. He had the nerve to confront me face to face in the marketplace. He told me to go home and listen to my husband, not to false prophets who proclaimed their own visions and dreams. I thought, what makes this man so confident that he's right when he is so outnumbered? How could all those other prophets be wrong? They prophesy peace; Jeremiah predicts destruction. Who wants to hear about destruction? Yet Jeremiah wouldn't stop. He warned me that if I didn't listen, cut down the trees, and stop dabbling in idolatry, I'd be uprooted from my husband, my land, and from Jerusalem. If I didn't repent, he said, I'd be the reason our temple would be destroyed! He was just trying to scare me. My husband would never let that happen no matter what I did! If I could do so, I would have Jeremiah thrown into leg irons, locked up, and dropped in a cistern."

"Let's do that, Sarah. Let's find that prophet who's trying to rob us of life!"

Suddenly she jumped to her feet, put one hand on her hip, and with her other hand pointed at Meshach. She laughed. "I almost forgot! He warned me about you. He did—he really did!"

"And what did he say, my little Israelite?" he asked.

"He said if I didn't listen to my husband, then you would become God's judgment upon me! Can you imagine? *You!* Are you God's judgment? Such a judgment I should have!" She laughed as she reached down to take his hand.

With that, he grabbed her hand and pulled her down.

Enough talk for tonight, he thought. *Let me remind you of what I'm going to give you. But not tonight. You're going to come begging, my Israelite.*

Then he rolled over with her several times in the grass. Sarah began laughing and cried, "Stop! Stop! You're crushing me. . . ."

Meshach jumped to his feet and pulled her tight against him. "Grapes are meant to be crushed," he murmured, his lips seeking hers. "Without the crushing there's no wine . . . no intoxication. . . ."

Chapter 5

*S*arah leaned toward the mirror for one last look at her eyes. *Painting them with kohl definitely makes the white of my eyes appear even whiter!* She smiled. She looked beautiful and she knew it. *As beautiful as any other woman in this city,* she thought, *and maybe even more!* Turning for a side view, Sarah adjusted her belt to gather the silk in just the right places so as to get the shadowy silhouette she desired. *Enough to entice his imagination!*

Her hand went to her neck. She had forgotten her jewels! With a lighthearted laugh Sarah walked across her bedchamber to where she kept her treasures. Handwoven silk carpets from the Orient lay strewn across the floor of her new home. The floors were beautiful mosaics, but Sarah couldn't bear to walk on cold floors in the winter. Her bed was set in the corner, far enough from the fireplace to keep her from becoming unbearably hot and yet close enough to keep her warm during the chilly Jerusalem evenings.

The bed, veiled with sheer linen dyed the color of pale amethysts, was strewn with pastel pink rose petals. Intricately carved chests inlaid with ivory and onyx served as stands for elaborately worked gold candlesticks. Her room was a study in seduction, a creation of her hands. Oil lamps were placed strategically to get the desired effect—light that would flatter her no matter where she was in the room. Two beautiful couches with matching embroidered silk and linen, overflowing with huge down pillows, invited visitors to sit in the corner opposite her bed. Between them there was a low table. Ornate glass bowls filled with grapes, delicious little pastries made with a variety of cheeses, dates, and sweets sat on the table beside two beautifully sculpted jars. One for white wine, the other for her favorite sweet red wine. Fresh flowers fragranced the room. There were so many varieties that they appeared to have been gathered from all the gardens of the world.

The couches were next to a small balcony. On some evenings Sarah would open the shutters to invite the breeze to catch her gown, wrap it around her thighs, and then release it while the setting sun or bright moonlight etched her body with its light. The depth of color cast by the evening sunlight played with a man's imagination as it danced on the rubies, emeralds, and amethysts nestled between her breasts, in the goblet of her navel, and at her slender feet.

With the utmost detail Sarah had prepared her way to seek love.

Her bedroom was her masterpiece—a canvas prepared for her living portrait. Even the idols placed on the white marble columns proclaimed their own message. Although unsure of what she really believed about them, they amused her. At times she even talked to them. Tonight was one of those nights. As Sarah crossed the room to get her jewels, she ran her fingers over their strange little bodies—some carved of wood, others of stone.

Isis, the goddess of life and healing, a gift from her Egyptian lover, and Thermuthis, the serpent-shaped goddess of fertility and fate, were acquisitions obtained during her most recent trip to Egypt. "What strange little gods you are. You have eyes but you do not see, ears but you do not hear, a mouth but you never talk to me. You are fashioned after humans or animals. Some of you are half animal and half man. You're short, squatty, tall, big breasts, big—" she trailed off and laughed. "Yet I like you. You and I don't hide our bodies." Sarah picked up a goddess with many breasts and flippantly kissed her head. "You, my dear, don't make me feel guilty that I am a woman. As a woman you understand my desires, yet you are among the gods! Heaven needs to have a queen!"

Sarah picked up her box of jewels and went back to her mirror. After draping several necklaces around her neck, Sarah chose the amethyst. *Purple is for royalty and I feel like a queen!* As she leaned forward to fasten the clasp, she noticed what happened under the folds of scarlet as she lifted her arms. *I must remember to remove my own necklace at times!*

Standing before the mirror, Sarah ran her hands delightedly down her sides and over her hips. She had known love—in delicious shapes, forms, and expressions. She had tasted it all and craved more. After Sarah finally yielded to Meshach, her curiosity was piqued. She couldn't shake the thought there was something more she needed to experience. So she traveled the Nile and there drank the waters of pleasure with Ramses, an Egyptian.

Now why am I thinking of him? Is it because of Isis, the goddess of Egypt? No, it's the dress! Ramses had been taken with her scarlet dress—so taken that he pleaded with her not to wear it for anyone but him. It had to be his dress. *Well, my Egyptian, it's not going to be yours tonight!*

Sarah's thoughts drifted back to her first encounter with Ramses. It had been a night of ambivalent emotions. The moment he took her in his arms, all she could hear were her husband's words: "Woe be to those who go down to Egypt." She hated his nagging woes; they hung like a curse over her pleasure. Sarah raised her hand to her forehead. *Why am I thinking of an Egyptian when I'm going to see Meshach? Why do I think of my husband when I've left him? What's the matter with me? I have everything I want. My jewels pay for it all!* Sarah put her hands on her forehead and rubbed it for a minute. She had a headache.

With time to spare, Sarah lay on the couch and closed her eyes. She thought about Meshach. Of all her lovers—Assyrian, Egyptian, Chaldean—she enjoyed Meshach the most. All the way back from Egypt she had planned her reunion with him. That had helped to take her mind off the cadence of the camel strolling its way across the Judean wilderness. Somehow the rhythm of the camel's footsteps kept tangling with her thoughts. Then there was her husband's worrisome refrain: "Woe be to those who go down to Egypt. Woe be to those who go down to Egypt." Sarah was sure that if she hadn't forced herself to think of other things—to plan every last detail of her reunion with Meshach—she would have gone mad. Especially in the suffocating dryness of the desert.

Sarah had thought often of Meshach while she was in Egypt, but she never regretted making the trip. The Egyptians treated her like royalty. Of course she was royalty in their eyes! The Egyptians knew nothing of her separation from her husband. Why talk about it? The world need not know! Besides, she and Ramses were most discreet as she spent time in his palace on the Nile.

"Mistress! Mistress!" shouted the young woman running into Sarah's room.

Sarah bolted up out of her couch. "Pellopia!" she screamed at her intrusive servant. Sometimes Sarah wondered why she put up with the girl. It didn't matter if her family was poor and they depended on her earnings. If Pellopia couldn't remember not to barge into a room unannounced, why keep her? But Sarah did.

"What in the name of the gods do you want?" Sarah yelled. "I told you I wasn't to be disturbed! You are to knock before you enter. Knock, Pellopia! Knock. I don't like having people surprise me or walk in on me. Have you got that straight? Do you hear me?"

Pellopia stopped immediately, plugged her fingers in her ears, and squeezed her eyes shut.

Sarah stormed over to Pellopia and grabbed her hands. "Quit squinching your face like that and get your fingers out of your ears. Open your eyes. Look at me when I talk to you. How many times have I told you not to do that?"

Sarah's head still hurt and she was hot. She paced the room, periodically waving a hand into the air. "I will talk the way I want to talk in my own home. And I won't have you putting your fingers in your ears every time I . . . I swear by the gods," she sneered. "I don't know why I bother with you. It's only because I like your mother and father. I want to help them. But you, *you* are another story!"

Although Pellopia was slight of body compared to Sarah, she refused to fear her mistress above her newfound faith. "I can't help it," she responded. "I hate it when you blaspheme—calling on gods like those . . ." Pellopia pointed toward the idols, " . . . those wretched little idols of stone and wood." Pellopia hesitated for a moment and wondered if she dared to be as brazen as the prophet Jeremiah. "And the way you behave. Being who you are—seeing this . . . hearing you . . . upsets me. How can you—"

Pellopia's eyes grew wide with fright. She had gone too far. Sarah flew across the room, hand open wide, fire in her eyes. Pulling her arm back as far as she could, Sarah swung and knocked Pellopia to the floor.

Pellopia looked up at Sarah, her eyes welling up with tears and her nose bleeding. Suddenly Sarah felt guilty. Ashamed of herself. What was happening to her? She had never slapped a servant in all her life. Of course, no servant had ever spoken so brazenly to her. . . .

"Get up . . . and understand this. It is the last time I will ever say it. I will not have *you*—a servant—talking to me like that. You had better watch out. Family or not, if you don't change, you're going to find yourself out in the plaza again, begging. Now—by the gods!" Sarah glared at Pellopia, "tell me why you came in and interrupted me."

Pellopia could not wait to tell her. She delivered her message slowly. She didn't want her mistress to miss a word: "There's a man who wants to talk with you," Pellopia said, watching with delight as Sarah's eyes lit up. She knew what Sarah was thinking.

"Meshach has come?"

Pellopia stood quiet and stony faced.

"You know, the Chaldean?"

"No, mistress, this man is a prophet. Jeremiah. He's waiting below your window. He won't come in, but he says you are to open your window and talk with him. He has a message for you."

"Get out of here. Get out of here right now!" Sarah shouted.

Instinctively, Pellopia covered her ears again. When Sarah screamed, she hit a note that hurt Pellopia's ears. Pellopia hurried out, leaving the heavy carved door ajar. In a moment Sarah slammed it shut.

Pellopia ran down the corridor trying to remember where the closest window would be. She wanted to hear what the prophet said to her mistress. Pellopia had been fascinated by Jeremiah's preaching. She liked the stormy old man who wept as he proclaimed the word of the Lord; she had heard much about him. Everyone had an opinion. Most of the other prophets did not like Jeremiah, nor did they agree with him. The people of the city called him a prophet of doom. They preferred prophets who prophesied peace. Jeremiah came with the message that he had been sent to Israel and to the nations to pluck up, break down, destroy, and overthrow. The other prophets said that God would never do those things—especially to his own people. The gossip was that even the priests didn't like Jeremiah. He had accused them of ruling by their own authority rather than the Lord's.

Pellopia wondered what Jeremiah would say to her mistress. Had he come to condemn Sarah's lifestyle, a lifestyle like that of so many people in Jerusalem? Had he come to warn her? Although she didn't know much of the Torah—being a woman, a Gentile convert, and a servant of the lowest sort—Pellopia had a healthy fear of the blessings and cursings given by Moses in the book of Deuteronomy. She had determined she would live accordingly no matter what the cost. In her simple understanding it made sense that if God was really God and men were mortal, then there ought to be a blessing for obedience and cursing for disobedience. All these thoughts ran through her mind as she searched for the best place to listen without being seen.

Sarah cautiously opened the shutters and peered down at the street below. Sure enough, there was Jeremiah—plainly robed in sackcloth and standing a short distance from her home. With the movement of the shutters, Jeremiah looked up and raised the staff in his hand. The blackness of the sackcloth shadowed his face but not the glimmer of his steely eyes. In brokenness and tears he cried, "Sarah, what were you doing on the road to Egypt? Were you going down to drink the waters of the Nile? You have forsaken your husband, the one who is your fountain of living waters. Why do you hew out broken cisterns that will never hold water? You'll never satisfy your thirst apart from your husband. Your own wickedness will reprove you."

Sarah didn't want to listen. She wanted to scream at Jeremiah just as she had screamed at Pellopia. She wanted to slam the shutters, squinch her eyes, and put her fingers into her ears. But she didn't. She stood there and listened.

"What injustice did you find in your husband that you have gone far from him? You are walking after emptiness and will become empty. You're a harlot with many lovers; you have polluted the land with your harlotry and wickedness.

"Yet your husband implores you, 'Return, faithless wife. I will not look on you in anger. I am gracious. Only acknowledge your iniquity. You have transgressed against me. You have scattered your favors to strangers under every green tree. You have not obeyed my voice.'"

Pathos and pleading filled Jeremiah's words. "Return, Sarah. Return to the husband of your youth. The one who brought you out of Egypt through the wilderness to this land—a land promised to you as an everlasting possession."

As Sarah looked at Jeremiah with his hand and staff outstretched, she could see her husband with a flaming torch in his hand passing between the pieces—cutting a covenant—guaranteeing that which would be her possession forever.

Sarah closed her eyes and leaned her head on the cold stone. It still ached.

"Amend your ways and your deeds, and he will let you dwell in this place. If you will only listen and repent—if you will put away your idols— he will turn the Chaldeans back and spare Jerusalem. But if you do not, Nebuchadnezzar and the Babylonian army will cut down your trees and cast up a siege wall against Jerusalem. Your city will be punished!

"Do not listen to your prophets, your diviners, your dreamers, your soothsayers, or your sorceries, who speak to you saying, 'You shall not serve the king of Babylon.' For they prophesy a lie to—"

Sarah's eyes opened with alarm. Had she heard Pellopia scream? Leaning out the window, Sarah saw Pellopia's white, thin hand closing the shutters of a nearby window.

Why had Jeremiah stopped speaking? Sarah wondered. Craning her neck, Sarah looked down at the street and saw Jeremiah on the ground with two men hovering over him. It took a moment for her to realize what was happening. They were dragging Jeremiah away by his feet. His head bumped mercilessly against the rough stones. Another man now stood in Jeremiah's place beneath her window.

"Sarah, I am Hananiah, the son of Azzur, the prophet who was from Gibeon. Hear the word of your Lord and husband. Do not fear, Sarah. The yoke of the king of Babylon has been broken. The vessels Nebuchadnezzar took from the Lord's house during his first siege will be brought back from Babylon within two years. And the exiles will return. Peace, Sarah, peace. . . ." With that, Hananiah swirled his elaborate shawl—with its wide blue borders and long tassels—over his shoulder and hurried in the direction Jeremiah had been taken.

Then, seemingly from nowhere, a harsh wind came up and slammed the shutters violently.

Sarah thought she heard a voice—a cry. She forced the shutters open again. She wasn't sure whether it was the wind or her imagination. Then it came again, with a fierceness borne on the torrent of the wind: "Repent—"

Shaken, Sarah bolted the door of her room and hid herself under the covers of her bed.

Chapter 6

When Sarah finally woke up, her headache was gone. The potion had helped. She walked to the table, poured a glass of wine, and sat down on the couch. Jeremiah's words still rang in her ears. Her mind was a whirling kaleidoscope of questions. What had they done to Jeremiah? Where had they taken him? Where had the other prophet come from? Who was really telling the truth? What should she do? Was this some kind of an omen, a sign that she shouldn't go to Meshach?

Was her husband playing a trick on her? Had he discovered what she was planning? But how? Only she knew of the reunion she had planned now for several weeks. Her astrologer had consulted the stars and told her this was the most propitious of nights to go. He even told her where they were to make love. Had her astrologer gone to her husband? No . . . that's ludicrous, *My husband has decreed the death of every astrologer, every spiritist!*

Sarah swirled the red wine round and round in her cup as she contemplated the whole situation. *Two prophets . . . one of doom, one of peace. First doom. Then doom was dragged away. Peace was proclaimed. Is there something . . . some message in this sequence of events?* Sarah was slipping deeper into superstition.

Jerusalem destroyed? My husband would never allow Jerusalem, his beloved Zion, to be taken by an enemy. He could easily crush his enemy at will. . . .

Sarah undid her sandals. Sliding her legs beneath her, she leaned back against the pillows. She was weary. *It was two to one,* she reasoned. *The astrologer set the day and the place of my reunion with Meshach. Until today everything has gone according to plan. Even Hananiah's prophecy canceled out Jeremiah's prediction of doom. The astrologers knew the mysteries of the heavens, the movement of the stars in their orbits. Why, Egypt was full of astrologers! And aren't prophets spokesmen for the one who rules the heavens?*

"I'll go!" Sarah spoke aloud with resolve. As she fastened her sandals she said, "I'm ready and I'll go! And I'll take Meshach a gift!"

Hastening to her dresser, she searched for her thickest chain of gold. From another drawer, she took out a money bag. Then Sarah headed for the door. *I'll deal with Pellopia later.*

Stepping outside, Sarah found her spirit lifted by the lingering beauty of the day as the sun reluctantly slipped away. She loved saying good night to the day, tucking it away in the darkness.

She walked the streets of her beloved Jerusalem with a renewed energy. The gentle breeze felt soothing on her back after her headache. Although Sarah left earlier than she had planned, it was good to be out.

Because there was no reason to hurry, Sarah strolled in and out of the shops in the marketplace. Each shop had its own personality, familiar smells, and scents. Spices from the orient and herbs dangling by their stems wafted their fragrance on the soft evening breezes so common in this city. The aroma of roasting meat hung in the air and mingled with the luscious smell of the last batches of bread coming out of clay ovens on large flat paddles. Some of the meat and bread would still be warm when it was taken home that night for the last light meal of the day. Voices called out the closing bargains of the day. Men bartered and debated. Giggling children chased one another in the streets. The noises of the marketplace helped deafen the troublesome words of Jeremiah, which periodically echoed in her mind and brought a certain heaviness to her spirit.

The streets were especially crowded now. Because tomorrow's sundown would begin the Sabbath, people were shopping for the meals that must be prepared before the setting of the sun. Tomorrow would be a day of cooking. And the marketplace would be chaotic and unbelievably noisy as shopkeepers tried to outshout and outsell their competitors, ridding their stalls of perishable merchandise.

Nothing would be sold on Sabbath. *At least openly,* she mused. No buying, no selling. No gathering of wood, no kindling of fire. The Sabbath had been Israel's way of life from generation to generation, though now some people questioned its importance. Some brazenly declared the Sabbath a bother. Personally Sarah loved it, but probably for the wrong reason. As much as she enjoyed the sound of Jerusalem, Sarah treasured the wonderful quiet the Sabbath brought to her city. That's when she could hear the birds sing; their unhindered melody soothed her nerves.

"Sarah! Mistress Sarah!" shouted a voice over the din.

Sarah turned to see who was calling her. Near the middle of the marketplace, Sarah caught a glimpse of Elieazer waving, beckoning her to wait for him. With the exception of her husband, he was the last person she wanted to see!

Sarah dropped her head, covered it with the veil that had been draped over her shoulders, and made her way out of the market. She headed in the general direction of the high places just outside the walls of Jerusalem. She didn't want to get caught; Eliezar was a sweet old man as righteous as her husband and absolutely devoted to him. How would he react if he saw her painted eyes and scarlet dress? She didn't want to find out. Though of gentle spirit, Eliezar would probably describe her as a bold-faced harlot!

Sarah made several sharp turns through the streets and didn't slow her pace until she was sure Eliezar wouldn't pursue her. She looked at the sky. She hadn't realized it was getting so late. It was propitious that Eliezar had called to her; Sarah had wanted to be at the high places before dark. Although her astrologer assured her Meshach would be there, Sarah wasn't overly impressed by this pre-diction. Finding Meshach there would be logical because this was the place their friends usually gathered for their evening trysts. It was here that they relished their wine, discussed with friends and strangers the happenings of the city, and had their philosophical debates. Then finally, couple by couple or sometimes group by group, they'd wander off to worship the gods of the high places—high places built by Solomon for his wives. There they would do what the gods did!

Sarah felt a comforting security as she walked through the city of David past the walls fortified by Hezekiah. She had heard Jeremiah's predictions of destruction, but the solidity of the walls—strengthened by their depth—stood rigidly against his words. *Jerusalem destroyed? A desolation and an object of hissing? Never! Jewish mothers and fathers eating the flesh of their sons and daughters? Impossible!* Sarah almost laughed at the absurdity of these warnings. *Only heathens eat their own in the days of famine. No Chaldean is going to besiege us! Serve in Babylon as slaves for seventy years? And all because we did not give our land its Sabbaths? Never!*

Jeremiah is out of his mind. He should have taken a wife. She would keep him sensible and at home—not running loose like a madman babbling in the streets. Although Nebuchadnezzar has brought us into subjection twice, he allows us to have our kings. We pay him tribute! Why would he ever want to destroy Jerusalem? If that were Nebuchadnezzar's intent, would not Meshach tell me?

These thoughts swirled in Sarah's mind as she walked.

My husband loves this city; our temple is here. Sarah was counting on that love—a love that would close his eyes to what he deemed iniquity. *He'd never allow someone to conquer it.*

Sarah looked at Mount Moriah, where Abraham went to sacrifice his son Isaac long ago. The gold of Solomon's temple gleamed in the last soft pink glow of the evening sky. *That temple is my assurance. Granted, a little idol worship goes on there at times, but without the temple we couldn't celebrate our annual feasts. Where would we make our sacrifices?*

Sarah's thoughts turned to the sacrifices as she reasoned the need for the temple. *On the Day of Atonement the goat of Azazel carries our sins into the wilderness …and the blood of the other goat slain on that day covers our sins for the year. This means, of course, that I am covered, as are the people,* Sarah rationalized. *And if the temple is destroyed as Jeremiah predicts, how will we worship without it? My husband would never allow his magnificent temple to be ransacked! That's absurd! Ridiculous! Why, its vessels alone are worth a fortune—let alone all the gold covering the interior.*

Sarah eased her mind with her twisted logic. *Jerusalem can never be taken! It is mine forever. That was my husband's promise. After all, the city is part of the land he gave me. Because he sealed it with an unconditional covenant, he'll never go back on his pledge. Not he! Misfortune will not come on us. And we will not see sword or famine. The prophets said it, and I believe it!*

Although Jeremiah said these prophets were wind and God's word was not in them, Sarah found that rehearsing their words of peace helped to dispel the storm clouds threatening to overshadow the joy of seeing Meshach again.

Not he. Misfortune will not come on us. And we will not see sword or famine. The words became a refrain in Sarah's mind, repeated step by step as she made her way up the hill to find her Chaldean.

"Sarah! Sarah! Over here!" Ritza waved her arm vigorously. Ritza did everything with vigor.

"Ritza, how good to see you!" Sarah liked Ritza. Though she was hard and coarse, she was entertaining to be around. Ritza had lived a hard life. Her mother died when she was young, and her father left her more or less to fend for herself. Sarah thought maybe it was the circumstances of Ritza's life that had made her a little hard on the outside, a tease. They had become friends—introduced to each other by Meshach. Although Meshach had been intimate with Ritza in the past, Ritza never seemed to resent his relationship with Sarah.

Ritza could tell that Sarah's mind was elsewhere. "Sarah, is it so good to see me that you don't even look me in the eyes? So good that you scan the landscape to see who else is here? Where have you been, Sarah? I've missed you."

"Egypt," Sarah's eyes continued their search. "Ritza, have—"

"Egypt, no less! My, aren't you something! Was it wonderful? Tell me, what are the men like?"

Sarah brought her gaze back to Ritza. "Forgive me. I don't mean to be rude. May I tell you about Egypt later? I want to find Meshach."

"Meshach! Meshach? You mean you don't know, Sarah?"

"Know what? Is he all right? Has something happened to him?"

"You really care about that Chaldean, don't you? For some reason I thought you had grown tired of him. I started to make a play for him again myself. I thought you wanted new pastures and figured maybe that's why you went to Egypt. I knew where you had gone. Meshach told me. He said something was bothering you."

"Enough, Ritza. Enough. Tell me what happened to Meshach."

Sarah's obvious irritation wasn't setting well with Ritza. "All right, all right. It's just that—"

"Ritza, please. I'm upset. Tell me what you know."

"Meshach left. He's gone back to Babylon. At least, that's what we think."

"Babylon!" Sarah exclaimed. "But he didn't tell me . . ."

"He didn't know. His orders came suddenly. I think he was to leave this afternoon, maybe this evening."

"This evening! When did you last see him? Maybe he hasn't gone yet." *Maybe he was coming to my house. Maybe I passed him on the way.* Sarah felt sick. She wanted to turn around and run home. Maybe she'd find him. Maybe it wasn't too late. She had to go back.

"Sarah, I saw him a day ago. But I know he's gone. One of his friends walked with him out the city gates. His friend came back and told me. You won't find Meshach in the city, so don't rush home. Believe me, Sarah. As much as I hate to tell you, he's gone."

It was as if Ritza had read her thoughts.

"Did he leave me a message? Say anything?"

Ritza sighed and looked down. *She really cares. This woman really cares about the man. What will I tell her? That he never said a word? That he never mentioned her name? Never said, "Tell Sarah . . ."?*

"Did you see him before he left? Did he tell you where he was going?"

"Yes, Sarah, I saw him. But he was . . . well, he seemed preoccupied."

A new thought entered Sarah's mind, and suddenly she was overwhelmed with jealousy. "Was he seeing someone else? Was he with another woman?"

"Sarah, you know these men. They have to have a woman—"

"Ritza, look at me. Tell me the truth. I want the truth, curse you!"

"Sarah, you don't have to curse me. You know I'm your friend. It's just that—"

"Forgive me, Ritza. I know you don't want to hurt me. It's just that . . . well, I'm disappointed and I've had a hard day. I've had a bad headache. That's all. . . ."

Ritza looked at her and contradicted, "You know that is not *all*. I'm not just listening to your words, Sarah; I'm watching you. You care. It's all right, Sarah. You don't have to pretend with me. Meshach had been seeing this girl; she was with him and that's probably why he didn't give me a message for you."

"Ritza!" Sarah put up her hand. She didn't want to hear another word. She was afraid she'd burst into tears—uncontrollable tears. The events of this day were too much. What a fool she had been to consult an astrologer! What did he know? Maybe astrologers *should* be put to death. Sarah bit her lip.

"I'll talk to you later. . . ."

"Take care, Sarah. May the gods go with you."

"What else?" Sarah replied sarcastically as she walked away.

No gods went with Sarah as she made her way back to the city alone. Back to her empty house, her empty bed, and the ominous cloud of Jeremiah's words.

Chapter 7

$\mathcal{S}$arah was stunned. Another woman Sarah could forgive; after all she had another man. But her relationship with Meshach went beyond a tryst under a green tree. How could he leave without a word?

Sarah wept all the way home. She felt rejected. Used. And she was angry!

As Sarah approached her house, all was dark except for a small light flickering through the shutters of her bedroom balcony. *Pellopia must have gone to bed. At least I don't have to face her...look at her questioning eyes.* Sarah still remembered the shaming look Pellopia gave when she saw her bed strewn with rose petals. Just her look, apart from all her impudence, was enough for one day. Pellopia would be dismissed in the morning.

Sarah made her way up the steps to her bedroom. She didn't bother to carry an oil lamp; light would betray her emotions. Nor did she want to risk waking up or running into Pellopia. As she pushed open the door to her room, her sandaled foot hit a light object on the floor and sent it rolling. What it was, Sarah didn't know and didn't care. Pellopia could find it in the morning.

Her strength gone, Sarah fell on her bed. Her whole body ached. She wanted one thing: sleep. That would help shield her from the realities of this day, and perhaps bring dreams of life as she wanted it to be.

But sleep would not befriend her. Her back was in a knot and so was her mind. Sarah got up and walked to her balcony. She stood there looking at the sky and feeling as black as the night. She felt so very alone. How different this evening had been from what she had planned. Leaving the balcony doors open, Sarah dropped onto the couch, yawning as she locked her fingers and stretched her arms. She sat there swinging her legs and watching the moonlight play on her olive skin.

For a moment her mind was totally blank. Then she remembered the object she had kicked with her foot. *I wonder what it was?* She twisted her feet some more; her body felt nervous.

"It was a scroll!" Sarah jumped up. "That's what it was! It rolled!"

She wanted to laugh, to sing. Her achiness vanished as joy washed over her soul. She grabbed the little oil lamp and headed for the bedroom door. *Meshach did let me know. He just couldn't say anything to Ritza in front of that woman!* Sarah reasoned.

Upon entering the hallway, Sarah got down on her hands and knees and used the little oil lamp to search for the scroll. "Where is it? Where did it go?" she muttered as her hand groped under the table. Then her fingers touched the soft parchment. Sarah gave a sigh of relief as she retrieved the scroll. Hugging it to her chest, she hurried back to her bed, confident it would bring her the reassurance she so desperately needed.

Crawling in among the rose petals, Sarah curled up in bed ready to savor every word. Suddenly her appetite was back; she hadn't eaten all day. Bounding from the bed, she ran across the room and grabbed an apple and a sweetcake. *That stupid astrologer sent me to the wrong place! Don't astrologers and soothsayers know anything?* It seemed so logical, now that she could reason it all out. *If Meshach had to leave, my bed was the perfect place to bid each other farewell. That's why he came here! And why he was with that woman when he couldn't find me! I wonder what Pellopia said to him?*

Sarah chastened herself. *Why did I go down to Egypt? If I hadn't gone this never would have happened. Maybe this is my woe for going.*

Settled on the bed cross-legged, Sarah put the apple in her mouth and held it with her teeth while she picked up the scroll. As she slid her hand down the side to find the seal, the light of the oil lamp illumined its impression. The apple fell from Sarah's mouth as her eyes widened in disbelief. Furious, she picked up the apple, hurled it across the room, and collapsed on the bed in a heap. Sarah wept bitterly until she fell asleep, the scroll beside her, the seal unbroken.

She didn't know if it was the early morning light or the crowing of a rooster that awakened her. She didn't care. *What right has the sun to shine when life is so dark?*

Sarah rolled over, hoping to go back to sleep. But sleep abandoned her to the reality of day.

The scroll lay on her bed. Sarah went to the washbasin, splashed the tepid water on her eyes, and looked in the mirror. Her face was a mess. Clumps of kohl stuck to her eyelashes. Black matter had gathered in the corners of her eyes, which were swollen and puffy from crying so bitterly. Her scarlet dress, like her face, was stained with kohl. *Probably ruined, but who cares?* Sarah thought as she crawled back into bed.

How could he leave without even telling me? The how and why of the whole situation weighed heavily on her mind. Sarah felt used. *No, misused!* She had trusted in a man whose flesh had been her strength and joy—and now her strength and joy were gone. *I've been abandoned—abandoned like a land of salt without inhabitants, a bush in a desert, living in stony wastes in the wilderness.*

A shiver ran through her body. Wrapping a silk shawl over her shoulders, Sarah slipped out of bed to light the wood in the fireplace. For a moment she stood there watching with fascination as the small twigs quickly caught fire only to surrender their existence so the logs might take on their flame.

Sarah's thoughts were morbid. *They die a slow and lingering death just for the sake of heating a room.* She was like a twig, wood to ignite her lover's fire—burning to warm one who walked away before her love was spent.

Sarah went back to her bed. She had no strength to face the day. Lying on her back, she listlessly ran her hand over the covers trying to find the scroll. It would take too much effort to sit up and look for it.

Finding the scroll in the covers, she raised it above her head and found the seal. It was the seal of her husband. Sarah sighed. *This must be why Elieazar tried to stop me in the marketplace.* For a few moments she simply looked at the seal. Finally, her curiosity got the best of her. Mustering up the energy to sit up, she scooted to the head of the bed. She broke the seal, unrolled the scroll, and began to read.

Beloved,

> *My heart is breaking because of your adulterous ways. Therefore, I am writing to you one last time.*

Sarah could see him sitting at his writing table, quill in hand. His hands were large and strong. Sarah remembered how, when he rolled up his sleeves, she had marveled at the strength and power of his arms. Sarah knew that as he wrote there would be tears in his eyes, but a firm set to his jaw. She had a husband who was a strange mixture of lovingkindness and righteous indignation. He had a strong, unyielding sense of justice.

> *I thought perhaps if I wrote to tell you again of the calamity that is coming, you might reconsider what you are doing and return, my love. My heart is in anguish at what I am about to do. . . .*
>
> *But first I want to assure you again that I love you and always will. I chose you above all others. I could have had anyone for my wife, Sarah; I looked the whole world over but I chose you. I love you, Sarah. I love you with an everlasting love. Nothing can alter that, my darling—not even you! I will love you no matter what you do. I loved you from the day I found you in the field and I have never stopped and never will. However, my love cannot negate the words of my mouth and the righteousness I require.*
>
> *Therefore I must, one more time, attempt to tell you that if you will amend your ways—if you will return—I will forgive. I will forgive your iniquity and we will start anew, Sarah. Anew. Think, my Beloved, what that could mean . . . what that could be.*
>
> *Oh Sarah, I groan and shudder to tell you what I will be compelled to do if you do not listen and do not return. This you must know. If you will not return, then I will abandon Jerusalem and allow our temple to be destroyed. If you are saying, "No, not us. Calamity will not come on us," then you are forgetting what you know about me—what I have taught and told you all these years. You are not thinking clearly or rationally.*

When I warned you time and again about the consequences of infidelity, of disobedience, I meant what I said. I must judge iniquity simply because of who and what I am. To allow it to go unjudged would be to violate my righteousness and justice. I must and will watch over my word to perform it—not only its promise, but also its warning and judgments.

Don't you understand? Your actions have far-reaching implications. Sin is never isolated or stagnant. Yours has not stood still. Because of you, others have turned their backs to me and not their faces. Following your example, they have gone after Baals. They have trooped to the harlot's house like well-fed lusty horses, each one neighing after his neighbor's wife. How do you think this makes me feel? The purity of my eyes recoils and flies shut when I behold this evil.

And our temple, Sarah—how long has it been since you've visited our temple? Have you seen the idol of Jealousy at the north gate of the inner court? My heart cannot help but be jealous when my love is scorned. You and others have turned to idols fashioned in the hands of man and prefer them to me, who fashioned every good thing on earth for your enjoyment. Every form of creeping things, beasts, and detestable creatures along with the idols of the house of Israel are carved on the wall. Women weep for Tammuz, and others go to the entrance of the temple, turn their backs to the Holy of Holies, and prostrate themselves to the sun. To the sun instead of me—the light of life!

Oh Sarah, you have lost respect for me. You have disdained me, my words, my works, my very being. Do you know what that does to my heart? To be relegated to second place, third place—no place. To be forgotten, rejected, and then disregarded altogether. To be looked down upon instead of looked up to. And what is worse is that others have followed your example. There is no fear of me—no respect, no trust—before their eyes. Consequently our people do wrong to the widows and the fatherless. They oppress the alien. They do not and cannot trust one another. They lie, steal, and murder. They despise what is holy. They profane the Sabbaths, slander, ignore the law. They do not uphold justice. Fornication and adultery have become a way of life—with you, and thus with them.

You have been to the high places. You have lain under their green trees. How do you think I feel knowing where you are and what you are doing? You belong to me. You once vowed you would follow me anywhere and love me always.

Sarah winced at what she was reading.

And there is perversion. Men with men, women with women, incest. Immorality rarely stands still; it has an unquenchable appetite, wanting more and more, doesn't it, my wife? Another partner, another thrill of a different kind. These are abominations in my sight, and you know it.

Sarah's heart turned cold—calcified, almost like stone. For a moment she simply stared at the scroll, then she spoke aloud as if her husband were present: "You call it perversion worthy of death. I call it a matter of preference—even though men are my preference. That's why our marriage will never work. We don't see things the same way, and never will. It's no use; I have gone after other lovers and I am going to stay gone."

Feeling agitated, Sarah rose from her bed, walked over to the fruit bowl, and picked up a knife. She went back to her bed and cut off the first part of the scroll. Then she walked over to the fireplace and haughtily dropped the piece into the fire. Having done that, she got back into bed, pulled the covers around her neck, and tried to sleep. But sleep eluded her. So she just lay there with her eyes closed . . . wondering where Meshach was, what he was doing, and if he was alone.

There was a light knock on the door. *At least she knocked,* Sarah thought. "Go away, Pellopia. Go away. I'll call you when I want you."

"But mistress—"

"Go away!" Sarah shouted angrily.

Sarah sat up in bed, drawing a cover over her. She could hear the patter of Pellopia's feet going down the stairs. Then she picked up the remnant of the scroll and began to read again.

> *They have taken bribes and shed innocent blood. Everyone is greedy for gain, from the prophets to the priests. They have turned Jerusalem into a bloody city and the blood of the innocent must be requited. And you, Sarah, have not restrained them by your righteousness; rather, you have excused them in your unrighteousness! You have continued to walk in the stubbornness of your heart. You heard the voices of the prophets, the true and the false, and you have chosen to believe only what you want to believe.*
>
> *My adulterous wife, if you will not repent, then I must refine and assay you as silver. Judgment begins with those closest to the throne. I will put you in the crucible of affliction. You have left me no other recourse. I will do what I must do to turn you around and to bring you back. Therefore, I am going to scatter you and our people among the nations—nations whom neither our people nor their fathers have known. Then I will send the sword after you all until I have annihilated you. Only a remnant will survive.*
>
> *Sarah, if you are not going to listen and return to me, then go into the streets of Jerusalem and call the mourning women. Let the voice of wailing be heard in Zion. There's an army coming even now—an army I can still turn back. The Chaldeans. . . ."*

Sarah's eyes locked on the word *Chaldeans.* A Chaldean army coming? *Meshach! Was that why you left? No, no—that doesn't make sense. My husband is just trying to scare me. He's talked of judgment before. It's been his constant threat.* Sarah didn't realize she was twisting truth to her own destruction. *He loves me too much to do anything like that. Judgment will never come. It hasn't yet; why would it now?*

"You're simply trying to bring me into line," said Sarah, "and I'm not going to budge. You sent prophets who cried out judgment long before Jeremiah but it never happened. Besides, if you bring the Chaldeans, I'll have one there to protect me!" Of that Sarah was confident . . . or so she thought!

Sarah sighed. She was weary of reading. She'd read no more. Not now, nor later. She walked to the fireplace and dropped the rest of the scroll into the flames, forcing a smile as she watched it curl in the heat. The flames slowly licked up the last remnant and final words of the parchment—words she read as the fire devoured them line by line:

> *How can I give you up?*
> *How can I surrender you?*
> *My heart is turned over with me.*
> *All my compassions are kindled. . . .*

Nothing but ashes remained in the fire. Yet the words smoldered in her heart.

Sarah went back to bed. What reason did she have to stay awake?

Had Sarah taken but a moment to look out her window, she would have seen another fire burning in the distance. It was the fire of an army camp—Nebuchadnezzar's army.

Zedekiah was twenty-one years old when he became king, and he reigned eleven years in Jerusalem. And he did evil in the sight of the LORD his God; he did not humble himself before Jeremiah the prophet who spoke for the LORD. And he also rebelled against King Nebuchadnezzar who had made him swear allegiance by God. But he stiffened his neck and hardened his heart against turning to the LORD God of Israel.

Furthermore, all the officials of the priests and the people were very unfaithful following all the abominations of the nations; and they defiled the house of the LORD which He had sanctified in Jerusalem. And the LORD, the God of their fathers, sent word to them again and again by His messengers, because He had compassion on His people and on His dwelling place; but they continually mocked the messengers of God, despised His words and scoffed at His prophets, until the wrath of the LORD arose against His people, until there was no remedy.

Therefore He brought up against them the king of the Chaldeans who slew their young men with the sword in the house of their sanctuary, and had no compassion on young man or virgin, old man or infirm; He gave them all into his hand. And all the articles of the house of God, great and small, and the treasures of the house of the LORD, and the treasures of the king and of his officers, he brought them all to Babylon. Then they burned the house of God, and broke down the wall of Jerusalem and burned all its fortified buildings with fire, and destroyed all its valuable articles.

And those who had escaped from the sword he carried away to Babylon; and they were servants to him and to his sons until the rule of the kingdom of Persia, to fulfill the word of the LORD by the mouth of Jeremiah, until the land had enjoyed its sabbaths. All the days of its desolation it kept sabbath until seventy years were complete.

—2 CHRONICLES 36:11-21

Chapter 8

*I*t was the month of Av. The days in Jerusalem were hot and the sun lingered too long in the heavens—increasing the people's thirst and reminding them they had once eaten at least three times a day. Now when night came it was no longer a friend bringing rest. The hunger of famine kept them awake as if it were day.

Famine racked people's nerves—testing the genuineness of love and the priority and value of relationships. The inhabitants of Jerusalem were in a viselike grip, pressured beyond measure from both sides. The visible enemy without, seen by the eyes of man. The invisible enemy within, the determination to survive at any cost. The walls of the city, built to keep out the enemy, now shut them in to famine. There was no going outside the city walls to forage for grass, for roots, for anything to fill the empty, echoing cavern inside. And there was no living inside the walls.

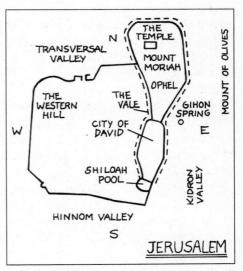

Sarah's house was a tomb with only one ghost—the shadow of a woman who roamed its deserted halls. Pellopia was gone. Whenever Sarah felt she had to see another living soul to keep from going crazy, she joined the women with whom she used to make raisin cakes for the queen of heaven.

Sitting and talking with them helped shorten the interminable span of the day. Although the queen of heaven no longer got her cakes—in times of famine even the gods had to suffer if they didn't heed the entreaties of their worshipers—the women still poured out their sacrificial libations to other gods. Even though the offerings were but a trickle, they were afraid not to. If the Almighty One refused to come to their rescue, where else had they to turn but to their idols? Yet these idols did not seem to be listening either. The desperation in the city grew proportionately as the Babylonians' siege wall mounted ever higher.

Although Sarah wasn't particularly fond of the women, they helped her to maintain her sanity. They sat huddled together talking in low mournful tones. People were mysteriously disappearing and security was found only in numbers. Oftentimes, people who were passing through the streets could smell the strange fragrance of roasting flesh.

The women were mere shadows of what they had been. They looked so different. With the fullness of their flesh gone, their bones gave them new and grotesque shapes covered by skin that took on the appearance of animal hides in the drying process.

As Sarah scrutinized the group she noticed how the color of everyone's skin had now become a dismal grey—all except for Hannah and Meshullemeth. Their skin was almost black—indicating the extremity of their starvation. Sarah was scared about Meshullemeth, the youngest of their group. She looked so terribly weak and seldom said anything. *Maybe it takes too much energy to talk; maybe she is giving all her food to her children.* Sarah looked at everyone's eyes; they were lifeless—brown pupils encircled by a sickening yellow pallor protruding from bony sockets. Gone was the spark, the glimmer— glazed over with sorrow.

Their clothes were filthy and foul smelling. There was no water for washing. Every now and then, one of the women would reach for the edge of her veil or the sleeve of her robe to wipe away her tears as she remembered a better time. Reality was appalling in its nakedness. How could a nation that was chosen above all other nations to be the Almighty's special possession ever experience such a tragedy? It was utterly incomprehensible!

When the women lacked something to talk about, there was always Jeremiah. He was still around and as vocal as ever. For a while he had disappeared, and the rumor was that he had been lowered by ropes into the cistern of Malchijah because the rulers were weary of hearing him say the city would be given into the hand of the king of Babylon.

Hannah, the oldest woman in the group, spoke up. "They say Jeremiah told King Zedekiah if he would go out to Nebuchadnezzar's officers then our city would not be burned and Zedekiah and his family would survive."

Another woman, not much younger than Hannah and not wanting to be outdone by her, spoke the obvious: "But if Zedekiah refused, Jerusalem would be burned with fire. And Zedekiah would not escape and—"

Burned with fire! Sarah recalled how the fire had curled the last fragment of her husband's scroll until it was nothing but white ash. The scroll was made of animal skin. What would it be like if her city were on fire? How could their flesh survive the searing heat? Would their leathery skin curl in the flames?

"They say," Hannah's voice took on a pompous tone as she gave her interrupter a stern look and reclaimed her seniority among the group. It was Hannah's story; she was going to tell it! Respectfully they waited as she licked her lower lip, exposing yellow scraggly teeth. "They say Zedekiah wouldn't listen to Jeremiah because of the Jews who had already gone over to the Chaldeans. Zedekiah was afraid the enemy would turn him over to the defectors and they would abuse him. He simply didn't believe Jeremiah nor did the other officials of the city." Hannah punctuated her words with an affirmative nod as if she had been in the presence of Zedekiah when he said it.

Jedidah, a woman younger than Hannah, spoke up. She lowered her voice for effect; it was a pleasant change after Hannah's high-pitched rasp. "People are tired of hearing Jeremiah. He never prophesies anything good. Remember back when Jeremiah reminded our officials, court officers, and priests of the time when they and all the people of the land made a covenant before God?"

Encouraged by the attention she had gained, Jedidah continued, pleasantly surprised that Hannah hadn't cut her off. "Jeremiah reminded them that when the officials and the people cut the calf in two and passed between its parts they were entering into a solemn, binding agreement. An agreement bound by death. That's why they stood between the pieces of those slain animals and said, 'God, do so to me and more if I break this covenant.'"

Several of the older women sighed and motioned with their hands as if to say, "Is she telling us anything we don't know? Covenants we know!"

Hannah rolled her eyes.

Jedidah continued, ignoring Hannah's look and hand gestures. She wasn't about to give up the stage. "Jeremiah told them they had transgressed this covenant. However, he also said there was still time to repent, but . . ." Jedidah drew out this last word for effect, "if they did not, then the Almighty would not withdraw his judgment. They must turn from their harlotry!"

Guilt gnawed at Sarah's already famished stomach. It did every time she heard about Jeremiah reminding the people of their adulterous ways. She could not help but remember her husband's words—words not consumed by the fire. They were etched not only on the scroll, but on her conscience. She wondered if repentance and a return to him would make him send the Chaldeans away or provide an army strong enough to defeat them. Sarah hadn't heard a word from him since the night she burned his scroll. Now she wished she had kept the scroll and finished reading it.

Hannah's raspy voice brought Sarah back to the matter at hand. "Some of the people asked Jeremiah, 'Where should we go?' and he answered,

'Those destined for death, to death;
And those destined for the sword, to the sword;
And those destined for famine, to famine;
And those destined for captivity, to captivity.'"

Sarah could not help but wonder: *If his words are true, where will I go? Will I die of famine or*— she could not stop the thought, which came swiftly, like the thrust of a sword—*will I die because someone is famished?* The situation in Jerusalem was so desperate people were ransacking homes, beating the occupants, stealing whatever they had, and sometimes doing worse. It wasn't safe to be out in the evenings, let alone in the blackness of the night. She had heard chilling stories of women who ate their children, fathers who killed and ate their sons, and sons doing the same to their fathers. If they did this to their own flesh and blood, what would they do to strangers?

Sarah shuddered as she thought of what famine brings—of the insanity of hunger. She remembered the days of the famine in Samaria, when Ben-hadad, king of Aram, besieged that city. A donkey's head sold for eighty shekels of silver and a fourth of a kab of dove's dung for five shekels. She also remembered—and wished she hadn't—the woman who cried out to the king for help because another woman said to her, "Give your son that we may eat him today, and we will eat my son tomorrow." And that's what they did. However, the next day, the other woman hid her son so he wouldn't be eaten.

Now it was Sarah's turn to wipe her eyes on the sleeve of her robe as she questioned herself. *What if I hadn't burned the scroll? What if I had returned to my husband—love him or not? Was the love—the lust for one man—worth the destruction of our nation? Why didn't I listen before it was too late?*

Sarah felt sick . . . and scared. Scared that she had passed the point of no return.

However, the Babylonians were still outside the city. Had Sarah run to her husband and confessed her sin, he would have listened, forgiven her, and healed her brokenness. He would have healed the brokenness of their people. Unfortunately, Sarah had forgotten the character of the one she was married to. He wasn't like her. He wasn't like Meshach. He was in a category all his own; all she would have had to do was take him at his word—literally. Instead, Sarah sat there feeling doomed—irreparably doomed. *He has given us poisoned water to drink and drink it I must. But it would be better to die by the sword than by famine.*

The thought of famine wouldn't leave Sarah's mind. Why didn't the army attack and get it over with? If they were doomed, then let the doom come. And come quickly. Sarah didn't want to die a slow death. She didn't want to have her skin turn black and to be able to count her bones. To watch her abdomen swell while the rest of her body diminished into a skeleton. To be so weak she wouldn't have the strength to cry for help.

When the army comes, will my Chaldean be with them? If he is, I know I will not die. I don't want to die; I'm too young. I have not yet begun to live. Maybe I am destined for captivity. . . . The thought became a fragile thread of hope.

But what would life in Babylon be like? Surely it wouldn't be bad; Sarah and Meshach would have each other.

Sarah's thoughts sapped the last of her strength, as did the talk of the women. She needed to get up and move around. She dismissed herself and began to walk.

She walked for more than thirty minutes. Or was it an hour? She lost all sense of time as she wandered the streets thinking about her husband, her children, her lovers, her Chaldean, and Jeremiah. How long have Nebuchadnezzar's armies been camped outside our walls?

For a moment Sarah gazed at the city walls. The departing sun silhouetted the forms of the watchmen standing on top of the broad walls. *If the walls around Jerusalem are broad enough for two chariots to ride side by side, surely they are strong enough to withstand the battering rams of the Chaldeans.*

Before Sarah realized it, the sunset had given way to night, and she was yet some distance from home. A curtain of fear dropped over her heart. She was alone, and people were hungry enough to kill. Who would protect her? Someone could simply grab her, carry her away, kill her, and eat her. Who would know? Who would come to her defense? These questions clawed away at her sanity.

Sarah rummaged through her money purse to find the red thread she carried to ward off evil. Unable to find it, she began to panic, feeling around her neck and checking her wrists. *Where was it?* Sweat broke out on her forehead. Then she discovered it in her hand. *I must have gotten hold of it when I felt among the coins at the bottom of my bag.* Relieved, she clutched the thread tightly in her hand and hurried down the narrow streets, her body trembling uncontrollably.

Suddenly, light loomed behind her and cast her shadow on the wall of the building in front of her. Sarah became frightened. Whose shadow was it? Hers? Or someone else's? Who was behind her with a lighted torch? How close was he—or was there more than one person behind her? Should she turn to see who was following? Should she face her attacker, or scream and run?

Sarah screamed—involuntarily. Hands pushed open the shutters above her. Faces followed hands as people leaned out their windows and cried with fright. Sarah turned in the direction that everyone was pointing.

The Temple Mount was ablaze . . . as were the houses around it! Flaming missiles propelled by Babylonian archers cut through the sky like meteors—fascinating the children but igniting terror in the men. People began to pour through Jerusalem's narrow streets not only to flee the fire but also the soldiers wielding swords sated in blood.

The Chaldeans had come over the city wall and were marching through Jerusalem in seemingly endless ranks. They descended like locusts, devouring every home with fire and striking every man, woman, and child in their path with their swords. No enemy eye took pity; no one was spared. Innocent babies—their little bodies impaled on Chaldean swords—were mercilessly paraded through the streets with shouts of victory only to be tossed aside when a new victim was discovered.

Those who prophesied peace had lied! The words on my husband's scroll were true.

Now the truth was known, but it was too late. Those destined for the sword were joining those destined for famine. Sheol was continuing to enlarge her borders.

Was Sarah destined for sword or captivity? She tore through the streets, pushing, shoving, stumbling, crying. "Let it be for captivity . . . oh, please let it be for captivity!"

A calloused hand caught her flying hair. Another caught her dress. "No! No! Noooo! Don't!" Sarah screamed then pleaded, sobbing hysterically. "Please don't . . . oh, please—" He laughed as he held her by the hair and then smothered her cries with his brutal, hungry lips. His sword dropped at her side as he forced her to the ground . . . .

Chapter 9

A huge clay bowl thrown from a high window shattered at Sarah's feet. Cowering in the dust and whimpering in pain, she looked at the remnants of the bowl. Apparently the soldier looting the house didn't want it because it was not silver.

Smashed against the ground and raped, Sarah felt worthless like the broken clay bowl. Jagged fragments of her pride, rebellion, womanhood, and self-respect lay in the rubble of Jerusalem's carnage. Now the broken bits would be trampled into the dirt by Babylonian sandals as soldiers went through the razed city gathering those destined for captivity. In years to come the clay fragments might be unearthed and pieced together again into a vessel once shaped on the wheel of history by the hands of the Divine Potter. But for now those potshards were totally unnoticed by anyone but Sarah.

Finally getting her trembling under control, Sarah weakly pulled herself to her feet and for a moment leaned on the wall of what appeared to be the only house still standing in the vicinity. She could feel the uncleanness in her skirts as she surveyed a city hardly recognizable. Staggering through the devastation and destruction, all she could think was, *There's nothing to live for; there never will be. I've been ruined for life. What was left of my hope has perished in these streets.* Because Sarah could not see beyond her immediate pain and brokenness, she wished from the depths of her soul that she had been destined for the sword.

Besieged with bitterness, her husband's promises would not come to her rescue. Her pain, her shame, her own sense of worthlessness, the hurt—the memory of it all—so cluttered Sarah's consciousness that she couldn't find her footing on the bedrock of the unfailing truth that she had a husband who loved her with an unconditional love and that her future with him was as certain as the rising of the sun and as never-ending as the seasons of the year. Spring would follow the deadness of winter, awakening the root and bringing forth shoots of life—the flowers of spring. And with certainty summer would follow and bring an abundant harvest beyond her imagination—a harvest that would satisfy every imaginable longing of her soul, which now seemed dead. And all that would happen simply because she was *his* wife. He was jealous for his reputation. But Sarah did not know that.

"Sarah! Sarah!" The cry was weak, like that of a lost baby kitten. Thankfully Sarah heard it. Her thoughts were now diverted from her own pain to that of another.

Hannah, the senior maker of raisin cakes for the queen of heaven, lay twisted under a huge wood beam. Rough stones, dirt, broken pottery, and shiny fragments of glass were her mattress. The bony arm that reached pitifully toward Sarah looked like a taut clothesline draped with a wrinkled, blackened rag of ancient flesh.

"Oh Hannah!" Sarah wept as an alien tenderness overwhelmed her heart. It was a tenderness she never dreamed she would feel for someone like Hannah, of all people. *Do I feel this way because I too have been pinned to the ground in the debris of a man's unbridled lust? Because I was helpless with no one to rescue me?*

Sarah didn't know where the tenderness came from. She only knew she had empathy for another person in pain . . . and it felt good. "Lie still, Hannah. I'll get us help."

Looking around for the first strong helper she could find, Sarah grabbed the arm of a young man headed toward the Valley of Hinnom. "Help me!" she pleaded.

"Help yourself," he snarled bitterly as he pulled his arm from her grip and continued on his way.

"No! No! Come back! It's an older woman, please—" she said as she tried to follow him. Stepping gingerly through the rubble she continued to plead, breaking into tears and sobbing hopelessly. "I can't do it by myself . . . I'm not strong enough. Have you no mercy, young man?"

The young man broke into a run, leaping like a gazelle over the ruins.

"Sarah!" Hannah's voice was weak.

"Oh, Hannah!" Sarah turned, pushing herself every step of the way until she reached the woman. Falling to her knees, she cradled Hannah's head and shoulders in her arm. Wiping the dirt from Hannah's face as best she could, Sarah bent down and kissed her on the forehead.

Hannah's wizened old face softened, releasing some of its deep wrinkles to a faint smile. Tears filled her yellow eyes. "Lie still," said Sarah. "Someone will come and help me. And if not, I will find the strength to move the timber myself."

Sarah looked at the weathered piece of wood. She was afraid to try and move it for fear that she'd slip or find it too heavy and drop it back on Hannah. *It must be the threshold of someone's door.*

She leaned down again and whispered, "I won't leave you, Hannah. Don't worry. . . ."

In the midst of all the devastation and despair, it felt so good to hold someone and be gentle, loving, caring. Sarah felt within herself a tenderness she had not felt in years—a tenderness, she reasoned, that came from caring more about someone else than yourself. It made her realize how hardened and how self-centered she had become. Once again she bent down to kiss Hannah's dirty but now precious forehead.

"Sarah," Hannah's voice was barely above a whisper, "why are you so concerned abut me?" Hannah broke into a weak grin. "You're different. You never cared before. . . ."

"Oh Hannah, I'm so sorry. I didn't—" Sarah broke out sobbing. She could not talk. She just held Hannah in her arms, stroking her coarse gray hair and wondering what she was going to do.

Sarah never heard the approaching footsteps and wasn't even aware that someone was present until she felt the gentle hand on her shoulder.

"I've come back. I'm sorry. I was scared. Please forgive me."

There were tears in his young eyes. They were beautiful eyes—blue like the blueness of the Great Sea just beyond the shoreline in the summer sun. Sarah thought, *Eyes like—*

"How old are you?" she asked.

"Fourteen. Why?"

The tears began to spill again. She rolled her lower lip over her teeth and bit down, trying to keep control of her breaking heart. "I had a son with eyes the same color as yours. That's unusual, you know, with Israelites."

"Did he die?"

Sarah nodded.

"Now? In this?" There was alarm in his voice, as if her son's doom might mean his.

"No, it was years ago . . . when he was five." Sarah took a deep breath. "But now, come; help me get this beam off Hannah."

"You keep holding her and pray. I think I'm strong enough to move it myself."

"You look strong. And older than fourteen, but be careful; don't let it slip."

"You just hold her and don't let her move."

In but a moment the beam was removed. Sarah tenderly moved Hannah's head to her lap. Her body ached from holding Hannah in her arm for so long.

The young man stood before Sarah. "Can I go now? I'm looking for my family."

"Of course. I hope you find them. I can't thank you enough for coming back."

"I had to. I couldn't leave you like this." He then leaned down and awkwardly kissed Sarah's upturned forehead. "I'm sorry about your son."

She looked at the young man's blue eyes, and without taking her eyes off them, nodded and said, "Thank you."

As the young man left, Sarah turned her attention to Hannah. Hannah's head was rolled to one side and her wide-open eyes did not move. Blood trickled from her gaping mouth. Hannah was dead.

Sarah gently closed Hannah's yellowed eyes and her mouth. Wiping away the blood with her dress, Sarah leaned down and caressed the wizened old face with her fingers. Then she kissed Hannah on the forehead for one last time.

"You shall not die. You shall live."

Sarah looked up, startled. The voice sounded like her husband's. It was the same voice he used when they sat together on the couch, her head in his lap, and he told her the story of when he found her abandoned in the field.

There was no one in sight.

Sarah smiled as the tears flowed again. She thought of Hannah's last words: "You're different." *Can I ever be different?* Sarah wondered. She wanted to find out. *I want to live, even though I am destined for captivity.*

Chapter 10

*S*arah could not believe that Meshullemeth, as frail as she was, had survived the sacking of Jerusalem or made it this far into the journey. They had traveled northward parallel to the coastline of the Mediterranean Sea, past Hazor, Damascus, Riblah, and Aleppo. Then they headed east following the path of the Euphrates River—a river of life leading them to Babylon, which was not far in the distance.

Sarah and Jedidah had helped carry Meshullemeth all the way from Jerusalem. At first the three of them walked for days without saying much, conserving what little strength they had for the journey. When Meshullemeth spoke it was usually to ask about her lifeless little girl, Michal, whom Jedidah's son and daughter alternately took turns carrying. Or, it was to thank Sarah and Jedidah again and again for their mercy and kindness.

Meshullemeth and her two-year-old daughter Michal were all that survived of their family. Meshullemeth's son, Shallum, had been wrenched from her arms and carried away screaming on the horse of a Chaldean soldier during the invasion. Meshullemeth survived by falling to the ground, as if dead, and covering Michal with her body. When the massacre had ended and the rape and killing had subsided they had staggered out to join the ranks of the captives waiting to be taken to Babylon. Now Sarah wondered if mother and daughter would ever make it to Babylon.

Moving unobtrusively among the seven hundred-plus captives, Sarah and Jedidah had been careful to shield Meshullemeth from the Chaldean soldiers accompanying them on the journey. The Babylonians were to bring home only the strongest of the spoils, and Meshullemeth was anything but strong.

Neither Sarah nor Jedidah—nor Jedidah's children—could bear the thought

55

of seeing Meshullemeth or little Michal thrust through by a soldier's sword or left by the road to die. In fact it was this determination, this goal, that increased the little band's strength for the journey.

Jedidah's daughter, Dinah, turned to her mother and said, "Imma, I think Michal is stronger today."

"Michal's stronger?" Jedidah asked aloud, wanting to make sure Meshullemeth overheard this encouraging bit of news. "What makes you think that, little Imma?" Little Imma—little mother—was Dinah's new name, although Dinah wasn't little and was in fact blossoming into womanhood.

"She's smiling more. And several times she even lifted her hand and tried to pinch my nose." Dinah had truly been an Imma to Michal. Jedidah was grateful. She didn't know how she could have cared for Meshullemeth and the baby also. *Baby?* she thought. *She's two years old but looks half that.* Even in weight, Michal felt like a one-year-old.

Jedidah wanted Michal to live. How could Meshullemeth survive another heartbreak after losing her husband and son? Also, Meshullemeth was more broken in health than all of them because during the siege she had given all her food to her husband and children.

"You're such a good little Imma, Dinah. That's why Michal is gaining more strength," Sarah said as she reached over to caress Dinah's cheek and Michal's. Dinah's eyes brightened with the compliment; she had always wanted a little sister to care for.

As they walked Sarah's eyes constantly surveyed the faces of the other captives who were struggling on this seemingly endless journey to a land unknown, to a people whose language they did not understand. Sarah wondered if the young man with the blue eyes had survived. She had thought about him when she saw the blue-green of the Mediterranean Sea where it met the setting sun just off the shore. Then she thought about her own son and his blue-green eyes . . . the look in his eyes as he walked into the Valley of Hinnom. But the thought was not allowed to linger. Sarah would not permit her mind to take her down that fiery, nightmarish tunnel of despair.

Although the women had agreed not to talk about the devastation of Jerusalem in front of the children, Sarah permitted her thoughts to return to the ninth of Av, vowing it would be a day she would never forget for as long as she lived. It was the day they destroyed her temple. Sarah never made it home after that fateful ninth of Av.

She thought again of what her eyes recorded as she huddled against the wall where she had been violated. Unbridled panic rode through the streets, refusing to be reined in and sweeping through the populace like the fire and soldiers that had ignited it. People ran every which way screaming and crying out for their loved ones. Some sat forlornly rocking back and forth while holding a dead body. Others simply sat on the ground and stared numbly into space.

The enemy—magnificently dressed horsemen girded with belts on their loins and flowing turbans on their heads—had prevailed. They had walked through the city foraging for treasures they had not earned, looking at the survivors with scorn, forgetting their humanity.

As if physical torment wasn't enough, it seemed the soldiers had to take verbal revenge for all the months they had spent laying siege to Jerusalem. Clapping their hands in derision, they'd hiss and shake their heads. With mocking laughter they'd ask, "Is this the city of which it was said, 'The perfection of beauty, a joy to all the earth'?" Gnashing their teeth at the pitiful remnant they boasted, "We have swallowed up Jerusalem! Surely this is the day for which we waited. We have reached it! We have seen it!"

In the aftermath of it all, young virgins lost their virginity in pain, shame, and horror—never to know the joy of bestowing their purity in sanctity, pleasure, and honor. Princes were hung by their hands in the city. Elders who had long been respected were mocked and mistreated.

Sarah recounted how some people had sat desolate in the streets and on the hillsides beyond the ruins of the walls. Others had wandered about confused, wondering why they survived and others died. All were waiting to see what would be done with them. Those who had successfully hidden some of their treasures now used them to buy bread—giving their precious belongings for meager rations. Little children would toddle a short distance and then simply faint from hunger. Infants sucked frantically on dried-up breasts only to find them barren. Languishing in their mothers' arms, their tongues cleaved to their mouths because of thirst. No longer could they cry and flail their little arms and legs in frustration as they did just months earlier when they couldn't get to the breast soon enough. Their strength was gone. Listless from their last expenditure of energy, they whimpered like kittens.

Once-beautiful women clothed in purple, the color afforded only by the wealthy, now wore the blackness of famine and embraced ash heaps. Their skin had so shriveled on their bones that many of them were no longer recognized by those who knew them. Some were deranged, stumbling around either babbling or saying nothing. These formerly compassionate women had boiled their own children for food. They forgot that in rescuing their bodies from starvation they also spared their minds—minds that would not forget the onus of their hunger.

Skin that was as hot as an oven because of famine could find no refuge under the shade of a tree. The beautiful trees of Zion and her surrounding hills had either been cut to build the siege ramps and weapons of war or had burned to the ground when Jerusalem was set afire.

Yet the most devastating sight of all was that of the Babylonians carrying out the gold, the silver, and the precious articles before they torched the temple. The smoke of its burning ascended into the heavens, and the glory of Israel was wiped to the ground.

In all Jerusalem there was only one sound—the sound of mourning. There was no music, no humming of psalms, no sound of the lyre or the harp. Dancing had been replaced with mourning. The crown had fallen from Jerusalem's head. Majesty had departed from the daughter of Zion.

Sarah remembered . . . she would never forget.

Noticing that the children were walking a short distance ahead of the three women, Meshullemeth turned to Sarah and Jedidah. "If I don't live, will one of you take care of Michal for me and raise her as your own?"

Before Sarah could say a word, Jedidah answered, "Meshullemeth, you are going to survive. I know you will. Jeremiah said some people were destined for famine, others were destined for the sword, and still others—a third of us—were destined for captivity. Why you lived only the Almighty knows! I thought that you, of all people, would never survive. When you would come and sit with us, so weak from giving all your food to your loved ones, I thought to myself, 'Meshullemeth is destined for famine.' But you survived! It is the will of the Almighty! Aren't I right, Sarah?"

Sarah smiled. "You are right, Jedidah."

"You know, when the soldier grabbed my son, little . . . little . . ." Meshullemeth's voice was trembling as she fought for control ". . . Shallum out of my arms, I realized I was helpless and so were the gods we had sacrificed to. Even the queen of heaven could not help us. And in that moment I saw the awfulness of what I and others had done. We had turned our backs on the Almighty One, and . . . and. . . ."

Meshullemeth was sobbing. Sarah and Jedidah stopped for a minute, releasing her from their arms while she covered her face and wept remorsefully.

Dinah happened to look back at that moment and saw Meshullemeth crying. She hurried back, holding Michal in her arms, and asked Jedidah, "Imma, Imma, what's wrong? What's wrong with Meshullemeth?"

Sarah put out her hands to take Michal from Dinah's arms. She looked admiringly at this growing young woman. Signs of blossoming gave a softness to the shape of Dinah's robe. Her tall young body had survived the famine well. The luster was starting to come back into her brown-black hair, which she habitually combed straight back with her fingers—leaving it to fall and swirl around a face taking on the dignity of womanhood. The chubbiness of childhood had departed quickly with the famine. Now her high and prominent cheekbones framed her straight nose classically set between her dark, intense eyes. Already she was a very attractive young woman.

Sarah drew Michal to her breast and for a moment remembered her own daughter.

"Sarah, may I have Michal back?" asked Dinah.

"Wha . . . what?"

"What are you thinking about, Sarah?" asked Dinah kindly. The children all liked Sarah and had adopted her as their aunt. "It seems like your mind was in another place."

"I'm sorry, Dinah. I—"

"No need to be sorry," Dinah responded. "Imma says I'm always off somewhere else, too. I understand. May I have Michal back now?"

"Of course. I just wanted to hold her for a moment."

"Imma's motioning me to go away. I guess all of you are talking privately. Is everything all right? I noticed Meshullemeth crying."

"Yes, she's all right. She's just telling us something that is very precious to her. Now run along."

Dinah turned to head back toward her friends when Sarah suddenly called to her again.

"Wait, Dinah! Where's Jotham?" Sarah asked. "I haven't seen your brother all day. In fact, I haven't seen him for two days."

"He told Imma he was tired of seeing the same people every day. He wanted to see who else survived before we got to Babylon. He's seeing if he can find any other boys his own age."

With that Dinah separated herself from the women and caught up with another girl carrying her little brother.

"I'm sorry I held us up," Meshullemeth sniffed as she regained her composure. "It's just that I want to tell you what took place so that if anything happens to me, you can pass this along to Michal when she is old enough to understand. I want her to know and remember the lesson her Imma learned. I truly believe it is why I, of all people, survived the famine and the sword."

Meshullemeth looked at them anxiously; she wanted to make sure they understood the gravity of her request. "You'll remember? You'll listen? Carefully?" Jedidah and Sarah nodded. They were curious to hear what she would reveal.

Reassured, Meshullemeth straightened herself, took Jedidah and Sarah by the arms for support, and continued her story as they walked. "Anyway, as I was saying, when Shallum was snatched from my arms, I suddenly saw the wretchedness of what I had done to the Almighty. I had exchanged him for other gods. Suddenly I could hear Jeremiah's words, his condemnation of what we had done—almost as if he was right next to me. I fell to the ground in remorse, wrapping Michal's tiny body in my arms and taking her to the ground with me. There I put my face in the dust and ripped the front of my dress in sorrow and repentance, covering Michal with my body as I cried out for forgiveness and mercy. I stayed in that position for a long time, confessing every sin, every transgression I could remember. I also groaned over all the abominations that had been committed in our land. Finally, when I couldn't think of another thing to confess, I cried out for another opportunity to serve the Almighty in holiness and righteousness, even if it were but for a day, a week . . . whatever he wanted in his mercy to give me."

Jedidah stopped and looked at Meshullemeth with sorrow. Sarah took

Meshullemeth in her arms and whispered, "I, too, deserved to die by famine or sword. But because of his lovingkindness I, too, survived."

Jedidah put her arms around both of her companions and said, "I can't believe it. Just like you, I repented and cried for forgiveness for all the times we disparaged Jeremiah's words and refused to listen. Oh Meshullemeth! Sarah! Could this be why the three of us and our children survived?"

Chapter 11

She died! She died! We're almost there and . . . she died! I can't believe it!" Jedidah was crying hysterically on the ground, holding Meshullemeth in her arms and rocking her back and forth. Sarah stood there covering her eyes. *Why, why did she have to die? Why couldn't she raise Michal . . . know some joy . . . have a chance to live righteously even longer?*

A crowd gathered around, discussing among themselves what they knew, what they didn't know, and what they thought they knew—passing the information on to other spectators who were joining on the outer fringes.

Suddenly Jotham was pushing his way through the crowd. Dinah, who was sheltering Michal in her arms, directed her brother. He had another young man with him. "Imma, Imma! What's wrong, Imma?" Jotham asked, fear in his voice. Sarah looked up, shocked. There, next to Jotham, stood the young man with the blue eyes—the one who had helped her with Hannah. He, however, didn't see Sarah. He was looking at the ground.

Dinah drew little Michal to her chest and covered Michal's eyes and ears as best she could. Jotham was on the ground beside his mother. "Is she dead?" he asked quietly, stroking Meshullemeth's brow.

"She died!" Jedidah cried. "She died right here. We were just standing here, crying together, with our arms around each other and she slipped to the ground. She had just told us what to do with Michal if she dies; she asked us to care for her and to tell her. . . ."

Meshullemeth's lips parted as her hand gently patted Jedidah's back. "I fainted, dear, I fainted. I'm not dead." Startled, as if Meshullemeth had risen from the dead, Jedidah jumped, letting out a little scream. For a moment Jedidah thought she was going to faint from sheer tension and the sudden release of the moment. Sarah burst into tears. She clasped her hands together, using them as an altar for her bowed head.

Dinah lifted Michal into the air and shouted with joy, "Your Imma's all right, Michal, she's all right!" Michal's little eyes brightened up. "Imma! Imma!" she said, stretching out towards her mother. Then drawing back, she put her finger in her mouth and smiled a big smile. Whatever the occasion, Michal knew it required a smile.

The crowd dispersed, eager to tell others the news. It was a delightful story—a new one to be told—unlike so many they had already shared over and over on the journey. Others who passed by looked curiously at Jedidah and Meshullemeth on the ground and then moved on.

Jotham reached over and pulled his blue-eyed friend by the arm. "Imma, Dinah, Sarah, I want you to meet my new friend Josiah. He's just a year older than I am."

Sarah looked at him. "Josiah?"

"Yes," said Josiah. "My father named me after the king—the one who found the word of God after it had been lost in the house of God."

Sarah smiled and patted him on the arm. "What an appropriate name. He was a godly man, and I think you must be also."

Josiah looked at Sarah, then Dinah, and then at the ground. Dinah blushed; he was handsome. She had never seen eyes that were so blue. She wondered if he was an Israelite.

"I've already met Josiah," Sarah said appreciatively. "He came to my rescue when Hannah was trapped under a threshold. I wondered if I would ever see you again, Josiah. I've been looking for you all through this journey and now that it's almost over, I've found you. I am so thrilled you survived . . . that you were destined for captivity and not the sword."

"I am too." Josiah shuffled his feet. Sarah hadn't realized how shy he was. "My father also survived."

"And mother?"

"No. That's why I was so angry and wouldn't help you at first. I had just seen a soldier murder her. He threw her out of a window. I think she broke her neck. She just lay there motionless, smiling at me. Then she died."

Sarah took Josiah into her arms. "I'm sorry, Josiah; so very sorry. Was your Abba with you?"

"Abba was out looking for food. I found him shortly after we started on this journey. I just kept looking. I was determined to look at every man's face before I gave up hope. On the second day of travel, I found him," Josiah's eyes brightened as he told his story. "We were so excited to have each other. He misses my Imma terribly. He's so sad and lonely—even with me. Would you like to meet him? He's not very far. He said he'd head back this way."

Jotham took a few steps and beckoned to Josiah. "Let's go get him."

"Jotham, help your Imma up first," said Jedidah. "I'm still weak from all this. And hurry right back; I'm going to need your help."

Josiah waved and shouted over his shoulder, "I'll help too, as soon as I get my Abba."

"Jedidah," said Sarah, "I'm afraid we'll draw the attention of one of the guards if we don't get Meshullemeth on her feet and walking."

"You're right, Sarah. Meshullemeth, can you get up?"

"I can try. I still feel so weak. I'm sorry, but will you help me?"

"Will we help you?" Jedidah's hands were on her hips. "What have we been doing all this time? Is now the time to stop just because you gave us a scare?" she said with a smile.

Sarah bent down and put her arms under Meshullemeth's. Meshullemeth made a valiant attempt to stand but her legs would not hold her. Then Jedidah and Sarah both tried to get themselves under Meshullemeth's shoulders and prop her up on her feet. As they struggled they both began laughing as they recounted the whole incident.

"I wish . . . I wish. . . ." Sarah stammered as she laughed heartily about the expression on Jedidah's face when Meshullemeth's lips began to move. "I wish you . . . could have. . . ." Sarah's face came down upon Meshullemeth's frail shoulder, her body in spasms. She could hardly stand up. "I wish you could have seen the . . . look . . . on your face when her lips . . . her lips. . . ."

Sarah's laughter made Jedidah laugh even harder. It felt so good to laugh! *When had they last laughed?* Sarah could not remember. Meshullemeth joined in. Weak as she was, she couldn't help it. It was contagious.

Then without warning Meshullemeth felt herself slipping, and neither Sarah nor Jedidah had the strength to keep her on her feet. As Meshullemeth crumpled downward she suddenly felt the strong arms of a man lifting her into the air. *You're huge*, she thought as she looked at him. Then her eyes closed as she slipped again into unconsciousness.

Josiah's father, Nadab, carried Meshullemeth until it was time to stop for the night. She slept all the way, a smile of contentment on her face. Every now and then Nadab would look at her fragile little frame, the long eyelashes sealing her eyes, and the straight dark hair hanging limply and freely over his arm. "She's so frail she's almost weightless," said Nadab.

"It's because you are so big and so strong, Abba," said Josiah. "That's why she feels weightless."

Sarah looked at Nadab. "She wasn't weightless to us! This is the first time during this journey that one of us hasn't had to support Meshullemeth. What a blessing you are to us! I was laughing so hard I couldn't do a thing!"

"It was good, Sarah, to hear you laugh," said Jedidah as she patted Sarah's back.

"And the same for you, my friend. I've never heard you laugh."

Jedidah smiled. "We hadn't been friends until just before the captivity. And I wouldn't say we were friends then, would you?"

"No," Sarah responded, "we were just miserable lonely women who needed to sit with someone. I didn't know anything about you at the time, and I am sorry to say I didn't care to know. I didn't even know you were a widow and had been one for six years."

Dinah looked at Josiah, who was carrying Michal. "And what about your bundle? Does it seem weightless or do you want me to carry her for awhile?"

"I can carry her. Besides, look at her. Does she seem unhappy?"

Without thinking, Dinah put her hand on Josiah's arm to peek at Michal, who was sleeping contentedly in his arms. She looked up at Josiah's face, blushed, and quickly removed her hand. Josiah blushed also. Her hand, soft and warm, had made his skin tingle.

Chapter 12

*T*he Euphrates River led the captives right up to the renowned walls of the Chaldean capital. As they neared the tall gates of Babylon, which glittered boastfully in the sun, the daughter of Zion held her head high. But she could not check the tears of remorse as she remembered the walls of her Jerusalem. Sarah watched with shame as her conquerors paraded before them the remnants of the house of the Lord. There were baskets and baskets of gold and silver dishes, bowls, and other articles— over five thousand treasures from the temple. *Never, never did I think this would happen to me!* Sarah felt angry, indignant, and scared. What awaited her in this land?

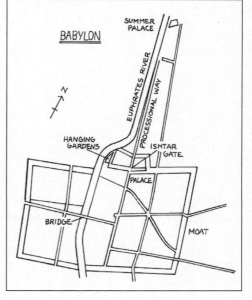

Jedidah stood with her arms around her children, Jotham and Dinah. Jotham's eyes widened at the sight and wonder of it all. Little Michal stood at Dinah's feet pointing at the parade. They experienced conflicting feelings: joy at seeing their sacred vessels, and shame at seeing them in the hands of their conquerors—conquerors who worshiped idols. The entrance to Babylon testified of their idolatry.

Josiah stood next to his Abba biting his lip to hold back the tears. Why exactly he was teary he didn't know. Maybe it was the thought of growing up in a strange land with a fierce and brutal army. Josiah reached for his Abba's shoulder.

Nadab was tall and had a huge frame. His coarse features were appropriate for his size and build. He looked like a high stone tower—a rugged tower belonging in the fields rather than a smooth pillar belonging in a palace. Yet for all his strength, his eyes—with their stubby eyelashes—were gentle. And now, they were not quite so sad as they had been. His was the heart of a shepherd and he had found a little lost lamb who needed his care. A shepherd needed a lamb.

Meshullemeth was that lamb. She stood by his side, holding his arm. Josiah looked upon her without resentment. Now that Josiah had met Dinah, he thought he might understand what his father was feeling for Meshullemeth. And it was all right. His mother could not return to the land of the living.

In a show of pride the returning conquerors took the lampstands, pots, shovels, and vessels from the temple and hoisted them above their heads. Turning in circles, they displayed the spoils of Judah and Jerusalem. Sarah rushed to Josiah's side and whispered, "Tell your Abba to watch carefully for the ark of the covenant. He's tall and can see better than I can. And you watch too, Josiah. I must know if you see it."

Dinah and Jotham, released from their mother's arms, went over to see what Sarah was whispering to Josiah. Dinah just wanted to be closer to Josiah. She had Michal by the hand. Josiah reached down, caught Michal between his hands, and with a whirl—much to her delight—had her on his shoulders. She leaned on his head and put her little hands on his face. Here on her tower she could watch the pomp and ceremony. Josiah looked at Dinah and just grinned, not saying anything except with his eyes.

Sarah distracted Dinah's attention away from Josiah by asking her to watch for the ark as well. Jedidah joined them but was too fascinated by all the revelry to pay attention to what Sarah was saying. Jedidah also wanted to see the famous hanging gardens Nebuchadnezzar had made for his homesick wife. Stories of Babylon's glory abounded, and the captives were about to see it all with their own eyes.

Further along in the procession were carts slowly drawn by large white oxen. They carried the bronze sea from the temple and the twelve bronze bulls that were under the sea.

Sarah stood on tiptoe searching anxiously for the ark of the covenant. Had the priests succeeded in hiding it or had it been discovered? Sarah along with hundreds more watched cautiously. Next came the pillars from the temple—eighteen cubits in height, twelve in circumference, and four fingers in thickness. They were deemed magnificent enough to be brought on carts all the way from Jerusalem. Each had a capital of bronze, five cubits in height, with pomegranates interwoven all around it. All this was Babylon's reward for sending their sons to war; they were trophies of victory preserved by Nebuchadnezzar and his army when they melted Solomon's magnificent temple to the ground and carried away its gold. And yet, with sweet relief, as far as Sarah could see, her conquerors missed the prize of prizes—the most holy of all, the ark of the covenant.

To Israel, the ark was as the throne of God. There the Almighty met with his people in the glory of his presence—a cloud that led them by day, which at night became a pillar of fire. The cloud had been present in the tabernacle and had rested over the Holy of Holies in Solomon's temple. The lid that covered this sacred ark was called the mercy seat—and no wonder, for once a year, on the Day of Atonement, the priest was allowed to enter the Holy of Holies and place the blood of the sacrifices on the mercy seat. First he placed upon it blood for his own sins, then the blood of a goat for the sins of the people. And for another year, there was a covering for their sin.

While the ark was a blessing and protection for Israel, it became a scourge and a plague to her enemies when they took it to one of their villages. The ark housed the sacred tables of the Law and Aaron's rod that budded when the Almighty defended his holy priesthood. It also housed the pot of manna—manna that had sustained their lives as they wandered, in judgment, through the wilderness for forty years.

As the Israelites lined up behind the treasures, those who were helping Sarah look for the ark confirmed her deepest hope. No one had seen the ark of the covenant. Sarah smiled, thinking to herself, *If they had the ark, they certainly would have made a great show of it. Of all that was in the temple, nothing was more significant. The ark would have testified of the total magnitude of their conquest!*

The spoils of victory were taken through the Ishtar Gate, known for its brilliant azure color, and up the slight incline of Processional Way past the infamous Ziggurat tower, the North Castle, and the wondrous Hanging Gardens that were known throughout the world. Proceeding into the inner city they passed the temple of Marduk, which stood among the other principal temples. The Babylonians rejoiced. They had a fitting tribute for the gods—spoils from the temple of the one whom Israel proclaimed to be the only true and living God!

Following the procession through the Ishtar Gate, Sarah noticed the enameled yellow-and-white brick lions, bulls, and dragons decorating its walls—and she thought again of Meshach. He had sought to educate her about other gods so she wouldn't remain so bigoted. Sarah readily recognized the bulls, which represented the god Bel, and the dragon, which represented Marduk. Both were the preeminent gods of Babylon.

But it was the lions representing Ishtar that heightened her sense of captivity, for the animal portrayed on Judah's banner was also a lion. *Judah has become a lamb for the slaughter, and I am among that flock. What will happen to me now? What will my life be like?* Sarah looked at her little circle of friends and suddenly felt alone. Each had a loved one; Sarah had no one. She had left her husband and she didn't know the whereabouts of her remaining two children. She knew only about the one with the blue-green eyes.

As Sarah walked behind the spoils of war up Processional Way she bowed her head. Where Meshach was—whether he was still alive or not—she did not know. She only knew she did not want to see him in her present condition. She looked pitiful. Her skin was dry, parched from the sun and the journey. Her clothes were worn. Her beautiful olive feet were calloused and cracked. In utter shame, Sarah covered her face with her tattered veil. She hung her head as she heard the cheering and jeers of the crowd watching the procession. So this was what it was like to be displayed as a spoil of war! Sarah never conceived her humiliation could run so deep.

When the celebrating came to an end, Sarah and the others walked some distance to join the exiles who had already settled by the Chebar River. They had arrived at their destination, and now the reality of captivity set in. *Where will I live? How will I survive? Do we have any responsibilities? Restrictions? Freedoms?*

Dinah panicked. "Imma, what are we going to do? Where are we going to live?"

"I don't know," Jedidah replied with concern. She looked around and noticed Sarah was missing. "Sarah?" she called. "Sarah? Where did Sarah go?"

"She's gone down to sit by the river," said Meshullemeth. "I think something's on her mind and she wants to be alone."

"I don't like it, Meshullemeth. Something's wrong. . . ."

Sarah desperately needed to be alone. She was holding a cup from which she was forced to drink. A cup—wide and deep—of her husband's judgment. *Why didn't I listen? Why didn't I believe? How could I live with my husband so long and not really know him? Why did I think this would never happen when his word has always proven to be true?* These were questions Sarah needed to sort through and to deal with. She should have seen this coming; after all, they weren't the first Israelites Nebuchadnezzar had taken captive. After passing through the Ishtar Gate, Sarah thought she saw the king standing on the balcony of his royal palace looking down on the procession. It was a degrading experience to one of Sarah's status.

The most recent siege had been Nebuchadnezzar's third against Jerusalem. Ten thousand captives, along with Ezekiel the prophet, had been taken to Babylon when he besieged Jerusalem the second time. By now, more than a decade later, those exiles were scattered to the wind throughout the kingdom of Babylon.

Sarah sat down by the river and stared into the slow-moving waters. She was surrounded by an incredibly fertile and well-irrigated plain. It was so different from her land. Yet as beautiful and impressive as Babylon was, Sarah longed for home. And now, forsaken of her lovers, she remembered she was a mother. She had children. Sarah wept and wept.

It had been such a long time since she thought of her son and daughter. Now she *longed* for them. But what would she do if she found them among the exiles? What would she say? How would they respond to her? Would they scorn her? For a moment she thought with envy of Jedidah and Meshullemeth and their relationships with their children. Sarah felt ashamed. Her cheeks flamed as she remembered how Meshullemeth had given up her food for her children while Sarah had put her desire for lovers above her children and her husband.

For so long Sarah had denied her motherhood. She wanted to be free, to pursue her happiness—or what she thought would make her happy. Sarah had desired a lover, and what lover wanted a woman with children hanging on her? A woman who had suckled little ones at her breast? A woman whose womb had carried another man's offspring? Who wanted to take a mother as a lover? Rape her, yes, but be her lover? Hardly! At least not in Sarah's thinking. And so, wanting a man more than the children of her womb, Sarah had pretended to be what she was not—a woman free to roam. Sarah began to sob, her tears watering the seeds of repentance taking root in her heart.

The settlement alongside the Chebar River became Sarah's refuge. Or was it escape? Relieved of the responsibility of caring for Meshullemeth and Michal—Nadab had taken that role now—Sarah found herself slipping into depression. She stayed by herself. Her days were unproductive. She began to sleep more and more. Sleeping was better than being awake, for her dreams, for the most part, were pleasant. Even the ones she had about her husband.

Sarah wondered why she dreamed of their romance—of their betrothal and how she had followed him through the wilderness. Other times she dreamed of when she was a woman of renown, sought because of her beauty and her wealth. In those dreams she saw herself looking down on a ruined Babylon and Nebuchadnezzar crawling around eating grass like an animal. Sometimes she dreamed of Meshach. They were together again and happy, living in Jerusalem. While Sarah's dreams were her release, they revealed the shallowness of her tangled relationships much like the sun illuminates the translucent fragility of a deadly spider web.

But Sarah's dreams weren't always pleasant; sometimes she had nightmares. There were long, dark fearful nights when she tossed, fought, and screamed. Oftentimes she saw a strange Chaldean hovering above her, leering at her with perverted contempt and lecherous delight. On those nights, Sarah would wake up in a cold sweat. She'd find herself trembling, feeling so desperately alone . . . and stained.

Occasionally Sarah dreamed of her son with the blue-green eyes. On those nights, she would wake up sobbing.

Life went on for the others. But for Sarah, it stood still by the River of Chebar.

Chapter 13

*S*arah was disgusted with herself. She had rationalized that because it was the Sabbath she could just stay on the couch, which also served as her bed. She hadn't gotten dressed. Now Meshullemeth and Nadab were chastening her.

"Sarah, this must come to an end," said Meshullemeth. "You can't just sit around wishing life was different. It's not! This is life now and we must live it. You can choose to live in misery or you can live with hope. You can say, 'It's no use' and it will be so. And you will become useless. Or, my friend, you can determine to believe you have survived for some purpose and discover what that purpose might be."

Sarah looked up at the happy couple before her and responded in her thoughts: *It's easy for you to talk that way. You have someone to love you and loved ones to care for.* Then she felt a rush of guilt. Sarah knew she was deceiving herself. For when everything had become so horrific for Meshullemeth, she had faced life without flinching. If anyone had a right to give in to depression it would have been Meshullemeth!

"You know what Jeremiah told us to do," Meshullemeth continued, frustration edging into her voice. She was greatly concerned. If Sarah fainted in the day of adversity, what kind of an example would that be to those who loved and knew her?

Sarah looked at Meshullemeth. She was finally putting on some weight and regaining her strength. And so was little Michal! The little girl had so much energy it was hard to keep up with her. But Meshullemeth had an advantage—Dinah, who continued to adore Michal and wanted to take care of her. *And Meshullemeth had Nadab! I have no one.*

"What did Jeremiah tell us to do?" asked Sarah somewhat listlessly.

"Now really, Sarah," Meshullemeth responded, her patience wearing thin.

Nadab looked at Sarah with a twinkle in his eye. "What he told us to do is what Meshullemeth and I are going to do. He said we are to build houses and dwell in them. We are to plant gardens and eat the fruit of them. *And,*" Nadab drew out that last word, "take wives and beget sons and daughters."

"Are you telling me you are going to have sons and daughters, or just get married?" Sarah retorted with a grin.

Meshullemeth came back just as quickly. "If you will keep grinning, it *will* be worth it to have children! Do you know how long it's been since I've seen you smile? Probably not since the day you thought I had died!"

"Sarah, get up and get dressed. You are going to synagogue with us." Nadab's words were firm, almost a command.

Sarah looked over at Nadab. He was so tall, so big and . . . so kind. She was happy for Meshullemeth—and a little envious. Not because of Nadab, but because Meshullemeth had a man in her life. Sarah moved to the edge of the couch. She had found this little house of two rooms and, such as it was, called it home. But it was an empty, lifeless home.

"Don't tell me they finally decided to have a synagogue!" exclaimed Sarah. "This I have to see! I can't believe they finally came to a consensus of what it is to be!" she said as she moved into the other room to get dressed.

Meshullemeth patted Nadab's arm. "I love the way you just take charge. Thank you for telling her to get up and get ready." She smiled adoringly at him. How she loved him! On the long journey to Babylon Meshullemeth had despaired of even surviving. Then from the multitude of exiles came this man who swept her up in his arms. Not only did he carry her to Babylon but he had watched over and provided for her since. In addition, Nadab had found employment and they would soon be married. How often she praised the goodness of the Almighty in letting her live and giving her a husband and son to replace those she had lost. And now with her daughter Michal doing so well, her cup was running over.

As Sarah dressed she thought of the times when Jedidah and Meshullemeth had managed to get her out of her house to join the endless discussions among the exiles, who on their holy days carried on long debates about how to celebrate the feasts without a temple. Everyone, it seemed, had a different opinion. Sarah wondered at times if the people took opposing sides just for the purpose of debate.

Sarah knew, however, there was one thing upon which they all agreed: They could no longer offer sacrifices. Not without the temple! *The temple, the temple!* Everything centered on the temple. Three times every year the men of Israel and Judah were to come to the temple in Jerusalem to celebrate the feasts. The feast that would be the hardest to celebrate without the temple was the Day of Atonement. That was the one day in the year when their sins as a nation were confessed and carried on the head of a goat into the wilderness. At the same time, the sacrificial blood of a second goat was put on the mercy seat covering the ark of the covenant.

At these discussions the elders would cry, "Where is the ark with its mercy seat? How can our sins be covered without the blood of bulls and goats? Has not Moses written that without the shedding of blood there is no remission of sins?"

Then the elders and the people would wail. There seemed to be comfort in their wailing. And when they finished wailing, they'd give thanks to the Almighty that the ark of the covenant was not in Babylon. Of that they were convinced! No one had seen it among the spoils. Where it had gone they did not know, but they were certain of one thing: It wasn't in Babylon. Some swore it was hidden in a chamber underneath the Mount where the temple once stood—probably close to the Holy of Holies. The other alternative they didn't want to consider was the possibility that it had burned with the temple. Such a thought was too much to bear!

Sarah slipped on her sandals and began to brush her hair. Its luster was returning. As she caught her reflection in the mirror, she gave a sigh of relief. She was also regaining her beauty. When she was done brushing, she began plaiting her hair.

"Do I have to rush?" she called to her friends.

"No, no. Do what is necessary but don't take too long," Meshullemeth shouted back.

They are probably pleased to have this time to themselves without children around, Sarah thought. As she plaited her hair her thoughts turned back to the exiles and their dilemma. Captivity had hidden their ark but opened their eyes. As the Israelites watched their heathen rulers, they saw the darkness of worshiping idols. They also knew enough of the word of the Lord to recognize that their idolatry had brought this fate upon them.

Was not this warning written in the last book of Moses? Sarah's husband had given this final message before Moses climbed Mount Nebo to look over the Jordan River at the land that had been promised to Abraham, Isaac, and Jacob for an everlasting possession. Hadn't Moses himself been denied this land because he had not treated the Almighty as holy when, in front of the Israelites, he smote the rock a second time rather than speaking to it as the Almighty commanded? Moses was judged by the Mighty One of Israel and denied entrance into the land. And like their revered leader, the people were now being judged and denied the land because they had not treated the Almighty as holy, but rather had worshiped foreign gods.

Whenever idolatry entered the discussion, many of the exiles became strangely quiet. Guilt clipped their tongues. Sarah understood this silence as she sat among them and became even more depressed as she recounted her own sins.

But not all was lost for the exiles. Someone had managed to rescue a scroll with the Torah, and other scrolls with the writings of the prophets and psalmists. These they carried all the way to Babylon, choosing to leave lesser treasures behind. Now there was a renewed interest in these words, for had they not come to pass?

Eagerly a group of the exiles began to pore over the huge but no longer cumbersome scrolls. Hungrily they devoured the words, giving heed to every yodh, iota, and serif, or projection of a letter. This to them was now a sure word of prophecy—a light that shone in the darkness of their captivity.

Cut off from their temple, the elders decided they needed a *beit-knesset*—a meeting house, a synagogue—where the Torah could be studied and a service of worship conducted, even without a priest. Most of the priests had not survived Jerusalem's destruction; therefore, the elders agreed that if they could have a *minyan*—a quorum of ten or more males over the age of thirteen—they could say prayers and hold services in the synagogue. There they would also carry on their *b'rith mila*—circumcising their male offspring on the eighth day of life. There they would celebrate their feasts, make decisions that affected their community, and come together every week without fail to celebrate the Sabbath.

"Sarah!" Nadab's voice interrupted her thoughts.

It must be time to leave, she thought. "I'm ready! I'm sorry; I should have been up and dressed a long time ago," Sarah said as she came out of the room.

As they walked to the synagogue that night, their conversation focused on their new place of worship. "You know, I believe the synagogue will become the center of our lives," said Nadab. "It will be a place that reminds us no matter where we are, we are still the chosen people of the Almighty. I believe it will keep us from being absorbed by the culture in the land of our dispersion."

When they arrived, Sarah and Meshullemeth went to sit with the women. Nadab left to sit with the men. A gray-haired and long-bearded elder who had been taken in the first captivity opened the scroll and read from the Psalms, a Maskil of the sons of Korah. It was just the psalm Sarah needed.

> As the hart panteth after the water brooks, so panteth my soul after thee, O God.
>
> My soul thirsteth for God, for the living God: when shall I come and appear before God?
>
> My tears have been my meat day and night, while they continually say unto me, Where is thy God?
>
> When I remember these things, I pour out my soul in me: for I had gone with the multitude, I went with them to the house of God, with the voice of joy and praise, with a multitude that kept holyday.
>
> Why art thou cast down, O my soul? And why are thou disquieted in me? Hope thou in God: for I shall yet praise him for the help of his countenance.
>
> O my God, my soul is cast down within me: therefore will I remember thee from the land of Jordan, and of the Hermonites, from the hill Mizar.
>
> Deep calleth unto deep at the noise of thy waterspouts: all thy waves and thy billows are gone over me.
>
> Yet the Lord will command his lovingkindness in the daytime, and in the night his song shall be with me, and my prayer unto the God of my life.

I will say unto God my rock, Why hast thou forgotten me? Why go I mourning because of the oppression of the enemy?

As with a sword in my bones, mine enemies reproach me; while they say daily unto me, Where is thy God?

Why art thou cast down, O my soul? And why art thou disquieted within me? Hope thou in God: for I shall yet praise him, who is the health of my countenance, and my God.

Sarah reached over and took Meshullemeth's hand and squeezed it. Then, leaning close to her ear, she whispered, "Thank you. Thank you for coming to get me and bringing me with you to the synagogue. I'm going to slip out now. I need to walk home by myself. But don't worry; I'll be all right."

Sarah kissed Meshullemeth lightly on the cheek and rose to her feet. Whispering apologies, she excused herself as she stepped in front of some of the women. While passing them she felt a tug on her dress. She turned and saw Jedidah sitting with Dinah. Sarah smiled and patted Jedidah as she slid past her. Then she slipped out of the synagogue to walk in the quiet of the Sabbath night.

There was a reverent hush in the neighborhood, a sense of awe. Tonight with a joyous heart Sarah welcomed the Sabbath as her mind and heart turned to the promise her husband had given to Solomon on the day Solomon's temple was dedicated. It was a promise given for such a time as this—when they found themselves captives in a foreign land: "If . . . My people who are called by My name humble themselves and pray, and seek My face and turn from their wicked ways, then I will hear from heaven, will forgive their sin, and will heal their land. Now My eyes shall be open and My ears attentive to the prayer offered in this place."

Sarah set her face toward home. Upon arriving she determined which wall of her small dwelling faced west toward Jerusalem. Then she turned to pray . . . vowing that three times a day without fail she would turn toward Jerusalem and claim the promise her husband had so graciously given them.

Maybe her prayers would be heard. Maybe her land would be healed. And maybe she would be healed as well. Maybe someday she would not have a care in the world. Maybe someday life would be without discordant notes, like the melody of the birds who sang so joyfully each morning and awakened her with their delight over another day—a day without concern because they lived in total dependence on their Creator.

As Sarah hung a reminder on the wall facing Jerusalem, she heard a bird singing in the night. If she could have taken wing like her feathered friend, she would have darted across the city and flitted among the trees of the fragrant hanging gardens. She would have flown above the palace of the king to perch on the white baluster of a small balcony facing west. She would have gazed on a wise and kindly old man by the name of Daniel, who also stood in prayer at that very hour with his head bowed towards Jerusalem. She would have sung her song to this prophet who would give her a divine peek at her very certain future.

Indeed, Sarah's prayers would be answered and in the fullness of time she would be healed as would her land. But not before she walked through a fiery oven burning with incomprehensible horror, the last and worst of several more yet to come. And not before her heart of stone cracked and she was given a new heart—a heart of flesh, which she so desperately needed.

Sarah stood praying to the west. A gentle breeze of hope blew across the embers of the love that had once burned brightly for her husband. *Can that fire be rekindled?* she wondered. *Will its flame remove the chill from the chambers of my heart?*

Sarah slept less and less. Instead she walked and thought about her affliction and wandering—the bitter pain of it all. And as she did, she recalled that her husband's lovingkindnesses never ceased. Her soul would not be cast down any longer; she would hope in him and the promise that his compassions never fail and his mercies are new every morning. She remembered that his gifts and calling of her were irrevocable. *After all, he even engraved my name on the palms of his hands.*

A cleansing and nourishing took place. Each day as his words became her very bread of life, Sarah found new strength, new vigor…and with it came a new beauty.

Chapter 14

The city was crowded. A festive spirit filled the air. Belshazzar, the king of Babylon, was throwing a great feast for a thousand of his nobles. Sarah found it almost impossible to walk the city streets without being pushed or shoved by man or horse. The people were so enamored by all that was happening they weren't watching where they were going. They had come to view the nobles, and the nobles had come to be seen—especially by the young ladies who unabashedly gazed on them with great admiration. These ladies hoped to find an escort to Belshazzar's banquet, where wine would flow like water and every kind of food imaginable would be supplied in abundance, all extravagantly arranged and served on ornate silver trays by tall Nubian slaves.

Men from all over the empire were dressed in their finest, and they put on a parade of sorts as they maneuvered their well-groomed steeds through the streets. The horses' polished coats had been combed and curried to perfection—befitting the grooming of their riders, who towered majestically above the ordinary citizens. Unless they were flirting, the nobles held their heads aloofly erect as if to silhouette their chiseled profiles against the backdrop of the temples looming in the distance. Were they competing with the gods? Some of the giggling young ladies thought so!

I wish I'd chosen another day, Sarah thought as a horse's tail whipped across her face. She backed away. *I'm thankful your groomsman didn't braid your tail all the way to the end. Otherwise I'd have a bruise on my face.* Sarah brushed her fingers over her cheeks. It felt like the horse had left one of its coarse hairs on her.

This is impossible, Sarah thought as she stood on tiptoe trying to get her bearings. She had been in this part of the city very few times during the years of her captivity. Did she avoid it for fear of seeing Meshach? Whatever the reason, nothing would stop her today. She had a compelling desire to visit a man she'd heard so much about—a man by the name of Daniel.

From what Sarah understood, Daniel, now an old man, came to Babylon at the age of fifteen with the first group of exiles from Judah. He'd served as one of Nebuchadnezzar's counselors almost since Nebuchadnezzar's father, Nabopolassar, died unexpectedly. It was then, after conquering Judah, that Nebuchadnezzar had rushed across the desert from Jerusalem to claim his father's throne.

"If it weren't for meeting you, Daniel," Sarah murmured as she turned off the main road and made her way toward the royal palace, "I'd turn around and walk back to my settlement as quickly as possible."

Unsure of where she was going, Sarah stopped to check the map drawn for her on a small piece of parchment. Tracing her path with her finger, from the Marduk Gate and the second wall, Sarah looked for a moment to get her bearings. Looking again at her map, she grumbled to herself, *They say because of your widely buttressed walls you're an impregnable city. But I also think if anyone did break in they'd never find their way to the palace.*

When Sarah finally figured out the map, she smiled with relief. She was closer than she thought.

With just a few more turns, she found herself looking up at a balcony with a white baluster. Surely the baluster was there as a protection for the kind-looking old man leaning on it while he gazed into the western sky. He seemed to be talking to himself. Although the sun directly overhead shadowed some of the features of his face, Sarah could see enough to think that he might have been a handsome man at one time.

"Excuse me!" Sarah called. "Excuse me!"

He must be hard-of-hearing, Sarah thought as the man continued to move his lips while staring toward the west.

Sarah shouted again, a little louder. "Excuse me!"

This time the man looked at her, but as if waking from a dream.

At least his lips stopped moving, Sarah thought. She wondered if they jittered that way because of age.

The man simply looked at Sarah and smiled as if he was waiting for her to say something. He looked at her so kindly that Sarah felt she must beg his pardon again. "Excuse me. I am looking for the home of a man named Daniel."

"You have found him, my friend. I am Daniel. May I help you?"

Sarah shielded her eyes; the sun was blinding. "May I talk with you, my lord? I'm one of the exiles deported from Jerusalem when the temple and city were destroyed."

"I am not your lord, but you certainly may talk with me. In fact, I have a feeling we are supposed to do just that!" Daniel turned to leave his balcony only to return immediately. "Oh, do forgive me for leaving you looking up into this noonday sun. Come in, come in and have a seat," he said as he leaned over the baluster and motioned her in with his hand. "I am coming right down."

Sarah stepped inside from the glaring sun and waited as her eyes adjusted to the pleasant light filtering in from the garden. The sweet perfume of flowers blooming in a profusion of color delicately scented the room.

Hearing the sound of Daniel's feet on the marble steps, Sarah waited quietly at the doorway and surveyed the simple elegance of the room. The home reflected the taste of a man of position. She saw no evidence of a woman's touch, yet the room was classically furnished; it was quiet and orderly.

"My servants are gone. I sent them to help at the palace. There's a feast tonight, you know."

Sarah nodded. "The streets are crowded beyond belief. I almost despaired of getting here."

Sarah loved Daniel's smile. He was tall and slender except for a little round stomach stretching his long brown robe. He wore a simply cut tunic with an edging of gold embroidered around the neck and the hem, which reached to his sandaled feet. His receding hairline gave him a distinguished look. His gray-black hair was combed straight back and his beard was edged sharply in a fashionable way that set off his strong jaw. His eyebrows were heavy and his eyes deep-set and kind.

"Yes, they say over a thousand nobles have come for this feast."

"Are you going?"

"No," Daniel sighed almost as if he were relieved. "I am no longer in the service of the king. In fact, I'm not sure if King Belshazzar even knows I live in Babylon. Or that I served in the palace until his forefather Nebuchadnezzar died." Daniel motioned with his hand. "But enough of my history, Sarah. Sit down, sit down."

Sarah put her hand on the edge of the chair, never taking her eyes off him. She was a little stunned. *I didn't tell him my name. I'm sure I didn't.*

"Did I tell you my name?" she asked haltingly.

Daniel's eyes grew soft as they looked straight into hers. He spoke with a gentle smile on his face.

"Sarah, I know about you. . . ."

Sarah drew back and blushed, unconsciously bringing her hand to the neck of her plain, soft teal dress. No ornamentation of any sort competed with her beauty; it would have been useless.

Daniel, known for his wisdom, understanding, and almost divine discretion in dealing with people, went on, carefully choosing his words: "I know your husband, Sarah, and I know he loves you with an unfailing love. And that, my dear, is all I need to know. Your husband and I have spoken of the future—his and yours."

Sarah leaned forward not wanting to miss a word. She was taken aback by Daniel's reference to their future. "Uh, I'm sorry, but I don't have much time. Perhaps I can come back—later—that is, if it's all right. . . ."

"Yes, yes, of course. I am an old man, leading a quiet life," Daniel said, putting his hands on his knees as if to get up.

Sarah put her hand out to stop him. "No! I didn't mean I had to leave immediately; just shortly. It took so much longer to get here than I thought it would. I'd really like to know about your conversation with my husband. You know, about his and my. . . ." Sarah found herself stammering. "Would you . . . could you tell me what you spoke about?"

Is it excitement or fear that has me tripping over my tongue? Sarah wondered.

"You mean the future?" asked Daniel.

"Yes, yes. That's it." Sarah stopped and looked at him, her eyes full of pleading as if for her life. Her next words came slowly: "Am . . . I . . . in . . . it?"

"In what?"

"In his future?"

"Oh, my dear, yes!" There was such compassion in Daniel's voice that it touched Sarah's heart. "You *are* his future. It centers on you, Sarah, but. . ." Daniel's voice became firm, "for his glory, Sarah, because of who and what he is!"

Daniel's words sounded like a proclamation. He paused for a moment, then leaned forward and looked her straight in the eyes. "You understand that, don't you? Because of who your husband is—by that I mean what he is like, the position he holds, and the power that belongs to him—it's his glory we must be concerned about. Do you understand?"

Sarah felt like a little girl being called to account by a stern and reverenced tutor. She responded with a nod and her brown eyes opened wider.

"Now, then, let me tell you about a dream King Nebuchadnezzar had in the second year of his reign. It was given to him so that he could know the future, and it has to do with you, Sarah."

Sarah leaned forward in anticipation as Daniel continued. "Nebuchadnezzar saw a great statue of a man. The statue had a head of gold, a chest of silver, a belly of bronze, legs of iron, and the feet and toes were iron mingled with clay. These parts represented four kingdoms that would have power over the earth. The head of gold represented Nebuchadnezzar. The four different metals—gold, silver, bronze and iron—showed that power would pass from one kingdom to the other, until a stone, cut without hands, crushed the feet of the statue. That stone, in turn, will become the fifth and final kingdom—a kingdom that will endure forever."

Daniel paused until Sarah's eyes were fixed on his. Then he said, "*This* kingdom is your husband's, Sarah."

Sarah's hand flew to her mouth. *Will I be there?* she wondered. Sarah wanted to know but she didn't want to ask.

Daniel observed Sarah's response but continued. "That is not all I have to tell you. For you see, Sarah, the details of these kingdoms were not given to King Nebuchadnezzar. All he received was this brief explanation of the statue. That was all the king and I understood until the first year of the reign of our present king, Belshazzar."

Now Daniel leaned forward, his face almost glowing. "Sarah, I had a dream one night on my bed."

He leaned back; deep creases formed just above the bridge of his nose. "I don't understand all that I saw or what it means. But I know I am to tell you how it was shown and explained to me. Then, Sarah, you must leave. I've kept you too long. Besides, what I tell you is all you are to know for now."

"How do you know that, Daniel?"

Daniel smiled patiently. He caught the edge of indignation in her voice. He could tell she was used to being in charge. "I just know, Sarah; I just know. And you will know that I knew—when it comes to pass."

Sarah knew that Daniel knew, and that she wasn't to question him any further. "What were your visions about? How did they add details to Nebuchadnezzar's dream? Or, at least, I'm assuming that is what you meant—"

"You have assumed rightly. The king, in his dream, saw a statue of four parts. In my dream I saw four great beasts coming out of the sea. It was explained to me that the four beasts, like the four parts of the statue, were four kingdoms."

Daniel paused, wanting to make sure Sarah was following him carefully.

"Remember that the statue will be destroyed by a stone cut without hands. It will be crushed by your husband's kingdom, which will come last and will endure forever. There was a parallel with the fourth beast in my visions. After the destruction of the fourth beast, your husband's kingdom will rule the entire world. Did you hear me, Sarah? *The entire world!*"

"And," Daniel paused, speaking louder for effect, "this vision of the beasts showed that *you* will rule with him!"

Sarah leaned back on the cushions of the couch for support. Then she swallowed hard and closed her eyes. Tears followed, freely coursing down her face. She didn't brush them away. She began sobbing softly; they were sobs of relief.

Sarah never questioned how Daniel knew. She simply knew that he knew. Understand it or not, she had heard truth. Pure, unadulterated truth from the lips of an exile acknowledged as a genuine prophet of God.

Daniel waited until Sarah opened her eyes and looked at him. After wiping her face with the back of her right hand, she ran the tips of her fingers gently under her eyes. Then Daniel continued.

"Now I am about to tell you something that I do not fully understand. However, you are to know it. It is complicated and has to do with the fourth beast in my vision, so please be patient. In the last time, times, and half a time of the fourth beast's reign, a little horn will come up. As you know, Sarah, time, times, and half a time is a reference to a period of 1,260 days, or three-and-one-half years. It is during this period that the horn rises up to rule over the fourth kingdom. This horn begins little and grows large. The horn is a king who treads down the whole earth."

Again Daniel paused. "Listen carefully, Sarah. This horn will speak out against your husband and will wear down you and your people. But, when the time, times, and half a time is over, the horn's dominion will be taken away and he will be done away with forever."

"And we," Sarah leaned forward, her face intent, her words precise, "will have a kingdom that will never again be destroyed? A kingdom just like the one begun by the stone in Nebuchadnezzar's dream of the statue?"

"Exactly!" Daniel leaned back and slapped his thighs. For a moment he looked like a young man—a tutor who had succeeded with his student!

"When will all this take place?" Sarah asked.

"I don't know. I do know, however, the next two kingdoms that will rule after Babylon. I know because in the third year of Belshazzar's reign I had another vision of the two kingdoms that follow Nebuchadnezzar's. The Medes and the Persians are the second kingdom after Babylon. The Greeks are the third. What the fourth kingdom is I don't know. I was not told. I only know that it is a dreadful and terrifying kingdom. This is the kingdom with the little horn that I just told you about. But that's enough. Right now we are still in the days of the head of gold. Just remember that both the king's dream and mine had four kingdoms before ours!

She smiled. "You are a true Israelite, aren't you? After all these years in Babylon in the service of the king you've never forgotten that you are from Judah, have you?"

"No, Sarah. Even at fifteen years of age when they made me a eunuch in the king's service I determined that I would never defile myself with anything of this kingdom—and I haven't!"

Slapping his hands on his thighs with a sense of finality, Daniel rose from his seat. "Well, it's time, isn't it, for you to go." It was a statement, not a question.

He held out his arms opened wide. "May I?"

Saying nothing, she went into his arms. As she felt them wrap around her, she felt strangely safe. Protected. Secure. It had been so long since she had felt a pure embrace such as this.

As she leaned on his chest, Daniel commented a little sadly, "We might never talk again, face to face. . . ."

For a moment they stood motionless as if both were lost in their own thoughts. Sarah felt like a child resting in the security of her Abba's arms. Then, gently pushing her away and holding her at arm's length, Daniel placed his hands on her shoulders and looked her full in the face. "Don't forget, Sarah, what I have told you today. The vision of the horn and your kingdom is for the latter days. Therefore, no matter what happens, remember how it all ends. And live accordingly, Sarah."

Sarah leaned over, slightly on tiptoe, and kissed his cheek. Then she turned and, without a word, walked out the door. She needed to hear no more. She had enough to remember. *They* would have a kingdom!

Chapter 15

The thoughts in Sarah's mind were as crowded as the streets. Over and over she rehearsed what Daniel had told her, repeating it quietly under her breath. She wanted to commit these things to memory.

As Sarah came to the corner of Enlil Street she turned to the right, presuming this would help her avoid the impossible crowds on Processional Way. At once she realized she was turned around and going north instead of south. Confused and still walking with her head down, she turned around and almost ran into a horse and rider before her. Startled, she let out an involuntary cry.

"If you'd raise that pretty head of yours and watch where you're going. . . ."

Sarah quickly pulled her veil over her head and hurried off in the opposite direction. She knew that voice so well. . . .

Sarah could hear the man's playful laughter as he continued on his way. Although she longed to, Sarah knew she dare not look back.

Suddenly the rider stopped. Apparently he recognized her. "Sarah! Sarah! Could that be you?" Meshach whipped his horse around. In an instant he had dismounted, pulled her into his arms, and was laughing with delight. "It is you! It's really you! I can't believe it!"

Sarah stood there speechless. The next thing she knew Meshach was kissing her. Her arm naturally started to circle his back. Her body gave sway to his, and for an ever-so-brief moment she was lost in the wonder of feelings that had lay dormant for so long. Sarah felt dizzy. Then she realized what was happening. With all the strength she could muster, she tore her lips from his and pushed him away.

Meschach was oblivious to Sarah's anger. He stood looking at her like a happy little boy who had just found a favorite toy he had lost. Grinning from ear to ear, he said, "Oh by the gods, am I glad to see you!"

Sarah winced. The memory of Pellopia flashed before her eyes. Suddenly she empathized with her servant and wished she had never slapped her. Sarah's mind drifted to another time, another place. *I wonder what happened to Pellopia. . . .*

"Sarah, are you listening to me?"

Sarah turned her eyes back to Meshach's still-handsome face. She hadn't said one word to him yet, but he didn't seem to notice. He just kept talking. "I didn't know whether you survived the ransacking of Jerusalem or not! I thought I might not see you again."

Meshach reached for her arm and, using his left hand to pull his horse by the reins, began to steer Sarah through the crowd. He talked excitedly and loudly—too loudly—as they went.

He's speaking words I once longed to hear—words I've thought about so many times. Words that I wondered if I'd ever hear again . . . from this man, whom I thought I loved and needed, Sarah thought.

Her mind was racing, as was her heart. She was stunned. She came into the city to see Daniel the prophet and she ran into Meshach—literally!

"Come, we must talk. We must," he grinned, "make love. You've never been more beautiful. By the gods, captivity, of all things, has become you!" His horse still in tow and his arm around her waist, he directed her back towards the Greek Theatre and its lovely garden.

Suddenly Meshach stopped and looked at her. "You haven't said a word!"

"I haven't been able to! You haven't stopped talking since I nearly collided with your horse." Sarah couldn't help laughing.

Meshach continued talking. "Where have they settled you? Let's go get your things. You're coming home with me. Then we can talk and talk again, making love in between. . . ."

"I'm at the settlement by the Chebar River."

"Oh!" exclaimed Meshach, slapping his hand against his forehead. "By the way, I'm going to Belshazzar's feast tonight. I'm one of his nobles." He grinned. She knew he was proud of himself. Meshach was an ambitious man and apparently his ambition had paid off.

"Congratulations. That's quite an honor. When did that happen?" Sarah wanted to talk about anything but the two of them and their past.

"It began when I left Jerusalem." Meshach's countenance became somber and his voice quiet. "Sarah, I heard it was indescribably horrible. It always is when we conquer an enemy." His eyes searched hers as if he was trying to read her thoughts. "How was it for you?"

Sarah's voice was controlled and her words tart. "Let's just say I experienced what your enemies usually experience—in its fullness."

Meshach registered slight alarm. "You weren't . . . violated, were you?"

Sarah looked him straight in the eyes, keeping her own eyes devoid of emotion. "I survived. I didn't die obviously." She straightened herself. "The past is past." She smiled confidently. "I have a future, Meshach."

He misread her words and thought she was talking about her future with him. Sarah noticed an almost imperceptible change in his eyes and countenance as he thought to himself, *She didn't say, but she must have been raped. She wants me, and that's why she didn't tell me. She thought I would reject her.* Then his thoughts became twisted. He found himself despising her. Angry because she had left him for an Egyptian. Angry because one of his fellow soldiers had taken her. Then a new thought crossed his mind: *What if the soldier who raped her happens to see her with me? I have a reputation to protect now that I am a noble. Besides, I can have any woman I want. Why sleep with a Jew? And, at that, a woman soiled by a man probably beneath my rank. She's nothing more than a captive. Would I want someone to think I'm her captive emotionally and physically? No!*

In his contorted reasoning Meshach knew Sarah would never satisfy him again. Yet like a cat he wanted to play with the mouse between his paws—tease it, wound it, release it, and then catch it again—before he put it to death and walked away without even tasting his prey. He wanted to hear Sarah beg one last time just to prove to himself he was her preference. He would let her think they had a future. Then he would walk away.

Meshach smiled. "And what do you think *our* future will be like in my land, Sarah—in the land of *your* captivity?" Sarah caught the emphasis of his words—the play on her captivity, her role. It brought sparks and boldness as she remembered Daniel's words.

"Meshach," Sarah said looking him right in the eyes. "You and I have no future. You are not included in my destiny. I will not remain a captive forever."

Meshach glared at her in disbelief. He gnawed on his cheek as he waited to hear whatever else she might say. Were these Jews planning some sort of uprising? Was Sarah unknowingly giving away information?

"Jerusalem is my future. My husband is my future." Meshach didn't like the confidence in Sarah's voice. "We have a future and someday *the* city—the very city the Babylonians destroyed—will be the praise of all the earth. Someday the temple your people destroyed will be rebuilt and the nations will stream to it. Every kingdom on the face of this earth, including yours, Meshach, will do homage to my husband and to me."

Her words slapped him in the face, stunning him. Babylon the Great bow to the Israelites? To the *Jews*? It was the last thing Meshach expected to hear. He clenched his fist. He wanted to hit her and send her sprawling to the ground. She belonged at his feet. But *nobles* did not hit women in public places.

Sarah hadn't ended the story right. He wanted to write his own ending!

Meshach snarled, keeping his voice low. "You harlot! You whore! You *Jew!* How dare you talk to your captor, a noble of Babylon, that way! Babylon will *never*—do you hear me?—*never* pay homage to Israel!"

"Meshach, you have a feast you must attend. And I have a country to which I must return. There's a temple to rebuild. There's an ark your army missed. . . ."

With that, Sarah walked away. She didn't know where she was going, but she kept walking anyway. She would figure out where she was later. She never looked back. She had been confident—brash, really—but she hurt. Inside she was shaking. His snarling words, filled with hate and disparagement still echoed in her mind. *Jew* was a new word for her, and it had been spoken in disdain the first time she heard it.

Covering his embarrassment at Sarah's abrupt departure, Meshach mounted his horse and headed for Processional Way. There he would be admired and appreciated by the young maidens caught up in the festivities preceding Belshazzar's feast.

That night one of the hopeful young ladies from the crowded streets had her dream come true. She found an escort—a very handsome one at that! At the party, Meshach got blindly, senselessly drunk. He wanted to obliterate the unforeseen events of his afternoon. Lying on a couch not far from the king's, he nibbled on the neck of his giggling companion. Then he rolled her over, buried his head in her breast, and thought, *Who cares anyway? I know she wanted me. I could tell when I kissed her. I could feel her longing, her passion. She'll prober . . . probberrly. . . ."* Meschach couldn't think coherently, but that didn't matter. This was a feast!

Right at that moment the blare of trumpets arrested everyone's attention, quieting the clamor created by too much wine. With great pomp, tall and graceful Nubian slaves entered the banquet hall. Their gleaming dark arms, stretched high above their turbaned heads, bore gold and silver vessels on massive, ornately designed silver platters. A brazen smile crossed Belshazzar's face as he rose to his feet with a golden goblet in his hand. "These are the vessels taken by the great king Nebuchadnezzar from the Temple, the house of God in Jerusalem. Tonight we will use them to toast our gods!"

People began to laugh and cheer. Belshazzar was going to serve them wine in these vessels! These spoils of war proved that Babylon's gods were indeed greater than the God of the Israelites.

Somehow Meshach got to his feet. *Babylon will rule forever . . . Babylon the Great! I must be the first to toast the king and our gods with wine from the cups that once belonged to the Jews' Most High God.* That would be his vengeance on Sarah for rewriting the end to his story. Taking one of the golden cups from her temple, Meshach toasted his king and his kingdom: "Long live Babylon forever! And long live the king—king above all the kings on earth—forever and ever!"

Meshach lifted the cup to his lips, gulped the wine, then immediately raised the cup again, crudely shaking it to make sure he had not missed a single drop of wine dedicated to Babylon's future. *We'll see whose kingdom endures! We'll see who lives and who dies.*

Then Meshach fell into a stupor...missing the commotion sparked by the sudden appearance of a disembodied hand inscribing a message on the wall: MENE, MENE, TEKEL, UPHARSIN.

Panic seized King Belshazzar, draining the color from his wine-reddened face. As the king's face grew pale, his hips went slack and his knees began knocking together. The banquet hall erupted in confusion as the king cried aloud with trembling voice for someone—anyone—who could read the handwriting on the wall.

When no conjurer, diviner, or wise man of Babylon could interpret the message, the queen entered the banquet hall and told the king about the man named Daniel, an exile from Judah who had interpreted dreams and visions for King Nebuchadnezzar.

Even though Meshach was close enough to touch the hem of Daniel's robe, he was so drunk he didn't hear Daniel interpret the mysterious message on the wall.

"MENE—God has numbered your kingdom and put an end to it. TEKEL—you have been weighed on the scales and found deficient. PERES—your kingdom has been divided and given over to the Medes and Persians."

The last thing Meshach ever saw was the merciless glare of a Medo-Persian soldier standing above him with a sword in his hand.

That night, Darius the Mede conquered Babylon and almost immediately after that, Cyrus, the Persian king over the Medo-Persian empire, sent a decree throughout the land of Babylon:

> The LORD, the God of heaven, has given me all the kingdoms
> of the earth, and He has appointed me to build Him a house in
> Jerusalem, which is in Judah.
> Whoever there is among you of all His people, may the LORD
> his God be with him, and let him go up!

In a sovereign twist of history, which had been prophesied by Isaiah, the Jews were released from their captivity. It was just as Jeremiah, the prophet whom so few people believed, had foretold.

Sarah was going back to Jerusalem to rebuild her temple—a temple that she assumed would never be destroyed again.

Chapter 16

*T*he journey back to Jerusalem was long and tedious. The seemingly interminable hours, days, and months passed in almost ceaseless conversation. The returning exiles talked most about the past as they walked their way along the ancient trade route into their future. A sight, a smell, a sound would cause them to remember something more they could talk about.

Sarah thought about those whom she left behind. Jedidah, her children, Meshullemeth, and Nadab were not among the exiles returning to rebuild Jerusalem. Cyrus' decree permitting them to return came unexpectedly. Although it had been foretold in the scroll of Isaiah, they hadn't understood the prophecy. It was as if a veil had covered their eyes when they read the scrolls.

Leaving those loved ones behind had been a hard decision for Sarah. All but Sarah chose to stay in Babylon. Someday they might return to Jerusalem, but now was not the time. Meshullemeth was pregnant. Michal would have a brother or sister. Everyone was ecstatic about that. And Dinah and Josiah were soon to be married. Of course, Jedidah felt she should stay with her daughter. After all, who knew when she might become a *safta*—a grandmother! Jotham and Josiah were learning a trade. They hoped to have a business of their own.

For these reasons and more, Sarah's friends decided to stay in Babylon. Besides, life had gone well for all of them in the land of their captivity once they heeded Jeremiah's words. They were faring much better than those who were left in Jerusalem after the destruction or those who defied Jeremiah's clear admonition not to go down to Egypt. Also, the exiles had increased in the land of their captivity. And they now lived under Cyrus...a king who respected the Israelites and treated them better than the Babylonians had. Yet Sarah's friends knew in their hearts that because of who she was, Sarah needed to leave.

No matter how much they loved Sarah and would miss her, no one tried to persuade her to remain in Babylon. They sensed Sarah's mission and respected her for it. In fact, Sarah's respect and influence among the exiles had grown during her time in Babylon. Captivity had changed her. She was returning to the character and stature befitting her calling.

Sheshbazzar, a man of good repute among the elders, was in charge of bringing the vessels back to Jerusalem. He and Sarah had become good friends. Although Sheshbazzar's appearance was not impressive, his character was. He was a short man with a long beard that made him seem even shorter. His eyebrows grew so close together they were almost one, which sometimes helped to shade his keen eyes—eyes that reflected his wisdom.

As they approached the city of Aleppo, the prized ancient cypress trees and tall pines turned Sarah's thoughts back to Babylon. "Do you recall, Sheshbazzar, how we sat at the rivers of Babylon and wept as we remembered Zion? We hung our harps on the willow trees and vowed never to sing in the land of our captors."

"Yes, Sarah, I remember. I also remember how the Babylonians demanded songs. But who could sing, Sarah? Who could sing?"

"Why did they want to hear the songs of Zion?" Sarah asked.

"I don't know," Sheshbazzar responded. "Maybe they were curious. Maybe because they knew the history of our people. Or, maybe they simply wanted to increase our misery and make us more aware of our status as captives. Who knows? All I know is that when they taunted us, I asked myself, *How can I sing the Lord's song in a foreign land?*"

"They wanted us to sing but they hadn't sat where we sat! Things have changed now." Sarah's voice took on a little cynicism. "At least our people no longer have to sing their songs for the Medo-Persians."

They walked in silence for awhile, both thinking about the way the Medo-Persian army took Babylon. The Babylonians had been convinced they would never be captured. With the triple-wall system of defense—walls wide enough for a four-horse chariot at the top, the moat, and the canal—they assumed their city was impregnable. Foolishly they had relaxed their guard. Who would have thought that the river running through the city, which provided water to sustain life, would become their means of death?

The Medo-Persians, working under the cover of night, had cleverly diverted the water of the Euphrates River and come right up through the city's water system into the palace itself. The smug Babylonians were caught absolutely unaware! Many said the downfall came because Belshazzar exalted himself, like Nebuchadnezzar before him, against the Most High. He went too far in toasting his gods with holy vessels taken from the temple of the Almighty One of Israel.

The stories of that historic night had floated through the city's populace like feathers released in a wind. A rumor had circulated among the people that when Daniel was called upon to read the mysterious handwriting on the wall, he told the king the party was over.

Sarah longed to see Daniel again before she left Babylon, but that was impossible. When the government changed, Daniel was appointed as one of 120 satraps over the kingdom. Sarah was glad, then, that she had committed Daniel's prophetic dreams to memory, for the Medo-Persian victory over Babylon affirmed to Sarah the accuracy of his visions. This meant that, according to Daniel, there were two kingdoms accounted for and two yet to come. *If Daniel is right, someday the Medes and Persians will be conquered by the Greeks. I don't know anything about the Greeks, so they can't be a significant power. And he never told me the name of the fourth kingdom; that's even more mysterious. How all this will happen I don't know. But...if Daniel's prophecy holds true, it will be our turn! Only time will tell.* For now, Sarah only knew she was most grateful for the decree of King Cyrus. She was going home.

Noticing a small yellow flower beside the road, Sarah stopped to pick it and then ran to catch up with Sheshbazzar. Handing it to him with a smile, she said, "By the way, my friend, I think Cyrus made a wise decision when he put you in charge of all the vessels he's returning for the temple in Jerusalem."

"You are gracious, Sarah. Coming from a woman who belongs to the Almighty that is quite a compliment. However, I'm concerned because even with all the funds Cyrus has given us and all the gifts from our own people who stayed behind, we will still find that rebuilding the temple is not an easy task. Only a little more than forty-two thousand of us are returning." Sheshbazzar paused. "Well, almost fifty thousand, if you add the male and female servants. But a mere fifty thousand will never fill the cities of Israel. And remember, Sarah," he added, "while we've been gone, others have occupied our land. I don't think they'll be pleased to see us. You and I know whose land it is, but don't think for a moment the people who are living there now will agree."

Sheshbazzar took a deep breath. "It will be a battle, Sarah. Are you ready for it?"

"I made up a little song while we were in Babylon, Sheshbazzar. Let me teach it to you; we can sing it the rest of the way to Zion!"

If I forget you, O Jerusalem, may my right hand forget her skill.
May my tongue cleave to the roof of my mouth
if I do not remember you,
if I do not exalt Jerusalem above my chief joy.

Sarah's song became the people's refrain as month after month they trudged on to their city of promise. The people sang, but Sarah couldn't. Her dreams became nightmares filled with anxiety, guilt, and fear. Would her husband be there? How could she face him? Sarah was again fighting depression. At times she thought she'd never be able to climb out of its black hole.

Two assurances became her lifeline. First, she knew her husband did not lie. He had assured her over and over of his unfailing love even when she was in the deepest of sin. Second, Daniel was convinced that she had a future—a future that included her husband. Where her husband was Sarah didn't know; she only knew he was! These assurances were what she clung to.

What troubled Sarah most was not knowing how he would receive her. Although she knew that his was an everlasting love, she still had to look him in the face. *What will he say? Not just with his mouth, but with his eyes?* she wondered. *And what will I say? How much should I say?*

Going back and admitting wrong wasn't easy, especially for a woman like Sarah. Being hard—at times even almost callous—came more naturally to her than being sweet, pliable, and submissive. At times she wished she had been the genteel type. But she wasn't. *Stiffnecked* was the word her husband used.

Could she again be one with her husband when she had been with so many others? Would she ever be completely his? Would she always battle the memories and affections she occasionally felt for other men when her mind and heart as well as her body should belong solely to her husband? Sarah wasn't sure she fully understood the emotional consequences of adultery, especially when she was returning to one who kept himself undefiled. He had done no wrong; the guilt was all hers. How was she to live with that? Were guilt and shame to be her lot forever?

Sarah also struggled knowing she was a mother who had abandoned her children. A mother who didn't even know where they were except for the one with the blue-green eyes. Were they dead? Alive? She hadn't found them in Babylon. Had they gone home? Would they ever come home? And if they did, would they ever speak to her again? Guilt wrenched at her insides, turning over and over, churning in her bowels.

Sarah withdrew, talking less and less to Sheshbazzar and the other people around her. She chose silence but the conversations went on in her mind. Incessant waves of questions demanded answers she could not give—questions that never would have been asked had she lived righteously as a woman, wife, and mother.

If only I could redeem the years the locusts have eaten. If only I had loved your father the way he should have been loved, then I would have loved you, the fruit of my womb, more than I loved myself. . . .

Many times the cloak that served as Sarah's bed became soaked not only from the dew of the morning, but also her tears at night. On the last night when they camped outside Jerusalem—a half-day's journey away—terror gripped her soul. She wanted to run . . . all the way back to Babylon.

Early in the morning just as the sun was rising, Sarah got up, folded her wet cloak, and turned around. She looked behind her. She knew she could make it back to Babylon. She knew she could find work along the way. Back in Babylon, she would be safe with her small circle of friends. She would be secure in a world she had grown accustomed to during her captivity. There, at least, she knew what to expect.

People looked at her strangely as she walked in the opposite direction. Some called to her and asked what she was doing or where she was going. Rather than respond, Sarah simply looked up, smiled, and waved. She stayed as far away from them as she could.

I can give my earnings for the temple and the welfare of the people in the city. Who knows . . . my support may even help my children if they return. And I won't have to face my husband or the rejection of my children. It's better to die without seeing them than live and be rejected by them. The pain is just not worth . . .

Sarah stopped abruptly and threw her cloak on the ground. No longer aware of the people around her, she looked intently at the new day—a day that had come to dispel the darkness of night. It showed every promise of being beautiful with expansive blue skies and white streaks of clouds stretched across the heavens.

What am I doing? Where am I going? Could I ever live with myself if I never tried to make reconciliation? If I never found out how my husband and my children would respond had I taken the risk?

Sarah bent over, whisked her cloak off the ground, and—throwing it over her shoulder—began to sing her song as she turned back towards Jerusalem.

Chapter 17

$\mathcal{W}$ hen the people arrived they found Jerusalem in shambles. The city was a rubble heap they could enter from any direction they chose. No walls hindered them or hid Jerusalem's present distress. No fortifications protected her inhabitants from the onslaught of any enemy who might come against them. Without walls Jerusalem was defenseless—and shamed! What city worth anything did not have walls?

The magnitude of the devastation stole away their joy. This was not Jerusalem, the city of their remembrance. Either the distress of their captivity had been too great, or, in their pain, they had pushed reality deep into their subconscious. Then they had covered the truth with their daydreams. But now they were back. Where were the walls? The temple? The glory they had remembered in their songs?

The destruction was so great it was hard for Sarah to conceive that Zion could ever be glorious again. The labor of removing the destruction of their multiple transgressions rock by

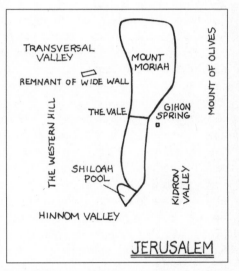

rock and then rebuilding stone by stone was too overwhelming to think about. Why was it that what they longed for was going to cost so much to restore? And, would it be worth it? *If only my husband would wave his hand and make everything the way it was before.*

For a moment everyone surveyed the scene in paralyzed silence. Each wondered if the others were dealing with the same doubt. What would it cost? Were they absolute fools to try?

As Sarah and Sheshbazzar looked over the Temple Mount, he turned to state the obvious. "Sarah, we'll have to start literally from the ground up. Lay an entirely new foundation. And Sarah," Sheshbazzar paused, hating to verbalize what he was about to say next, "the silver, gold, and freewill offerings that Cyrus and our people gave us are generous but not nearly generous enough to ever build a temple equal to Solomon's. I wonder if our people want the temple enough to give it the attention it needs? And, are they prepared to accept a temple less glorious than Solomon's?"

"I don't know, Sheshbazzar. I think we'll have to wait and see which has priority—the houses they want to build for themselves, or the temple." Right now the temple was Sarah's priority, but then she and the others had just arrived. Uppermost in their minds, then, would be their need for a place to live.

Sarah couldn't help but notice that it was the seventh month, the month of Succott, the Feast of Tabernacles. "It's ironic, isn't it, Sheshbazzar, that we are beginning our building at this time? When we are to build booths from the branches of the trees and live in them for seven days to commemorate our exodus from Egypt? This time our exodus is from Babylon!"

Sheshbazzar quipped, "I'm thankful no Pharaoh is chasing at our heels. I much prefer the benevolent Cyrus. Now we must first build our altar for the sacrifices. It is a good place to begin, Sarah, for rebuilding the temple and the walls will require sacrifice."

Hard labor didn't allow Sarah much time to think! It dropped her into bed each night too exhausted for anything but to groan and fall asleep immediately. Sarah toiled right along with everyone else preparing the Temple Mount for the foundation of the temple. Yet she was frequently distracted. Every time she heard someone coming up behind her, she expected to be taken into her husband's arms. She expected him to come and carry her away and tell her that such work was too hard, too much for her. She wanted him to step in, take her place, and send her home to be loved, pampered, coddled. How long had it been?

Sarah waited, hoping against hope that he would come to her. Within a day of their arrival in Jerusalem she went to find the home that once was theirs, but to no avail. It was gone. And so, it seemed, was her husband. The rumor among the people was that he had departed before the Babylonians had scaled the walls. Sarah refused to accept such a terrible thought. It was inconceivable that he would abandon Jerusalem, his temple, and his wife when he knew that tragedy was at hand. She was sure it was nothing more than idle gossip!

I know you are somewhere. And you've got to come to my rescue. You've got to. "Do you hear me?" Sarah shouted as she rose from her bent-over position. She angrily flung a rock and then reached around to press her hand against her aching back. Sarah wondered if she'd ever be able to straighten up again.

"You have to be somewhere! This is *your* temple too, you know! I can't do all this by myself!" Sarah screamed into the wind; maybe it would carry her plight to his ears.

Day in and day out the people labored. Finally the foundation was finished. So was Sarah, and so were the people! They had laid the foundation under great duress.

The usurpers occupying the land did everything they could to discourage the returned exiles from rebuilding the temple. They tried to frighten them. They fought them. They wrote letters of accusation to the governing powers in an attempt to stop the construction of the temple. They played political games accusing the Jews of wrong motives. And all their tactics worked. The building stopped. Sarah and the other Israelites gave in. If her husband wasn't going to come to her aid, she would quit. And that is exactly what she did.

It just isn't the right time to rebuild the temple, Sarah rationalized. So she hired men and sent them to the mountains to get wood for the house she would build for herself. Yet after her house was built she still wasn't satisfied.

Life became harder and harder. It was a struggle simply to exist. *My purse must have holes,* she thought. *I'm always running out of money!* But money wasn't all that she ran out of; food was short in supply as well. Even if she had the money, there wasn't sufficient food to keep people well-fed. The crops just weren't producing as they should. *I'm hungry, I'm poor, and I'm cold. I don't even have enough clothes to keep me warm!*

In the midst of this ever-growing anguish, it never occurred to Sarah that her poverty might be the consequence of improper priorities. But that changed when she met Haggai the prophet.

Sheshbazzar introduced them. In fact, he set up a meeting that included Zerubbabel, the governor, and Joshua, the high priest. Sarah knew Zerubbabel and Joshua, but not Haggai.

At the meeting, Sarah's first impression of Haggai was his stark contrast to Jeremiah. He was a slight man of average height—very ordinary looking. Sarah could not help but wonder if he was a *true* prophet.

Everyone had barely greeted one another when Haggai turned to Sarah and said, "Sarah, I won't keep all of you long. I simply wondered if you were aware of the people's attitude toward the temple."

His voice doesn't have the thunder of Jeremiah, thought Sarah. *He sounds rather normal.* "What do you mean, Haggai?"

Sheshbazzar interrupted, "What he means to say is have you heard the general talk among our people? That is, their rationalization for not finishing the temple."

Sarah had heard, but she didn't want to answer. She felt the same way the people did. So she answered the question with another question to keep from incriminating herself. "What are they saying? Maybe Zerubbabel knows . . . or Joshua?"

Zerubbabel and Joshua shook their heads.

Haggai scanned their faces and made eye contact with them all, one at a time. Then he stood up and slowly paced the room, his hands behind his back. "They are saying this is not the time to build the temple." Then he turned and looked at each one of them again. "Is it time to build the temple? Sarah, is it time?"

Sarah was not going to be maneuvered by this man; she didn't even know him. She looked at Sheshbazzar, who turned away. Then she looked at Zerubbabel and Joshua.

Zerubbabel lowered his eyes to the floor. "They say it's just too hard to go all the way to the mountains to get wood to build the temple."

"Sarah?" Haggai questioned.

Sarah thought, *Here he goes again, singling me out—the only woman in the room!* She looked at him coldly, "Yes, Haggai?"

"Sarah, did you find it too hard to go to the mountains to get wood to build *your* house?"

Joshua bowed his head and rested it on his hands. He sighed, but said nothing.

Sarah felt convicted. She would not flinch from a well-deserved rebuke. "Your point is well made, Haggai. I did manage to build my own home while allowing the temple to lie unfinished. I am as guilty as the rest of the people. I've excused myself, and I have no excuse."

Joshua raised his head and dropped his hands. "And I have no excuse—"

"Nor do I," replied Zerubbabel. "What should we do, Haggai?"

Haggai gazed at them appreciatively. "We must call the people together and tell them to consider their ways. We must help them see the reason that they are harvesting so little, that they are never full nor satisfied, that they aren't warm enough, and that their purses seem to have holes is because they have let the temple of the Almighty lie desolate."

Sarah wiped away a tear trickling down her cheek. She stood to her feet, looked at the men, and said, "Thank you for confronting us . . . and me. Now, gentlemen, if you will excuse me," she smiled wryly, "I must get to bed so I'll be ready to work in the morning."

Within a matter of days, the work on the temple resumed. This time, the people didn't stop until it was completed. Yet in the midst of the great rejoicing that took place at its completion, some people wept because it was not as glorious as Solomon's temple. Sarah was among those who wept.

It may not have the glory of Solomon's temple, Sarah thought, *but at least it's complete. We finally have our temple.*

They had a temple, but no city walls. The walls of Jerusalem were to be their next project. That's when Nehemiah, the cupbearer of the king of Persia, came to their rescue. Nehemiah traveled all the way from Susa, the capital of the Persian empire, to help rebuild the walls. Once again Sarah's back ached and so did her heart. The wall went up, but not without great conflict.

When will my life ever be without distress? Sarah wondered. She felt she'd gone beyond her ability to keep going; she was dangerously weary and she knew it. She needed to sleep. The pressures that abounded were taking their toll—including the still-unexplained disappearance of her husband. What Sarah faced would have broken any ordinary woman. Yet Sarah knew she was built of granite, although there were many times when she didn't feel like it.

At the end of one particularly tiring day Sarah went home and bolted the door, closed all the shutters, put a pitcher of water beside her bed, and crawled under the covers. She slept soundly. But sometime later that night—she wasn't sure when—she was awakened by the touch of a hand on her shoulder.

Sarah turned over, and in the half-conscious stupor of a deep sleep she looked up, smiled, closed her eyes and murmured, "It's you! I can't believe it's you! You've finally come . . . and I'm so tired, My Beloved—so very tired."

Still half conscious, Sarah put her arm around her husband and rested her head on his chest. Then she slipped back into sleep. He held her that way for hours and stroked her hair as she slept. When she finally woke up, they talked quietly as she lingered in his arms.

Sarah rested her head on his chest so that she wouldn't have to look at his face; the pain of her adultery was carved there. She didn't want him to study her countenance because she felt so awkward. Troubling thoughts invaded her mind: the remembrance of her lovers, her infidelity, the pain she had caused him, and what happened to their children as a result. Theirs was a bittersweet reunion.

They talked very little about the past. His only concern was that she had learned her lesson. He wanted to be more than just a faithful friend who would tap her on the shoulder in the hour of temptation and remind her never to live that way again. He didn't want the past to hang as a rotting corpse tied to her back.

Over and over that night—or was it day? (Sarah didn't know because the shutters were closed and she had drawn the canopy around her bed)—her husband assured her of his unconditional love and his commitment to her.

While Sarah rested, he traced the features of her face with his finger. "Sarah, you cannot take a lover ever again. You must choose to love me and me alone." With his hand he turned her face towards his. "Look at me, my love, and listen." Sarah opened her brown eyes. Her long dark lashes were stuck together from the tears she had shed.

"Love is more than an emotion, Sarah; it's a choice. Emotions follow acquiescence and obedience. I cannot and will not tolerate infidelity. You will not play the adulteress anymore. Do you understand?" His voice was firm, yet his words were couched in gentleness.

Although Sarah did not move her face from his hand, she shut her eyes. She could not bear to see the pain in his face as he continued.

"What has happened, Sarah, has taken its toll—not only on our relationship but also on my reputation. It's been greatly damaged. Many have called me to court in their minds and, without hearing my defense, have convicted me of being a husband who doesn't care. They've passed judgment, Sarah, without fully understanding the whole situation. They've accused me of being calloused and unloving because I did not come to your defense against the Babylonians when, in reality, I was very capable of doing so."

Sarah could see his accusers smugly railing at him with their fists in the air, delighted to find an excuse to accuse him and demean his character. For if they could demean him, then, in their eyes, they could justify their wrong actions. Unrighteous men always delight to find flaws in someone who seems more righteous than they. Sarah felt ashamed that the accusers didn't know that she alone deserved to be stoned in this case.

Sarah turned and buried her head deep into his chest. He could feel warm tears flowing onto his garment. He wanted Sarah to understand the deadly ramifications of her infidelity.

"Rulers of nations have ridiculed me and are holding me in derision. They have wondered where I was and why I abandoned you when I had done so much for you in the past. They have asked whether I've become impotent and unable to defend you. As a result, Sarah, they have become brazenly aggressive toward our land. The fear of me is no longer before their eyes. Each wants to lay claim to the land I bequeathed to you for an everlasting possession. Israel is the center of the world; it is a bridge that the kings of the north and the kings of south would like to control. They are thinking, 'Let's claim these everlasting hills for ourselves and make Jerusalem our city.'"

He reached up to his chest, took her hand in his, and kissed it. "With scorn of soul they want to take your land out of your hand and rule over you." Keeping his hand enclosed with hers, he returned it to its resting place on his chest and continued, "Their ambition is to drive our people into the sea. And because I allowed the Babylonians to waste you, they think they can do the same!"

He turned to his side and propped himself up on his elbow. "My reputation—as well as yours, Beloved—has been defamed. Yet, whether or not others understand, I had to allow you—for *your* own good—to suffer the consequences of your disobedience. It is not healthy for anyone to cross the line between right and wrong and then be allowed to get away with it. When they do, their hearts become fully set to do evil."

Once again he took her chin in his hand. "Beloved, look into my eyes and listen carefully even though I have told you this before." Sometimes he treated Sarah more as his child than his wife, but at times like this she didn't mind. As a woman it made her feel so secure. It was like having a father and husband rolled into one being, both loving her as they should to the fullest of measures. "I cannot and I will not alter who I am. Nor will I ever alter or deviate from my principles and precepts of life just to gain the understanding and approval of the multitudes who are passing judgment on our relationship. I will not be governed by the opinion of others. Do you understand?"

Sarah nodded and slipped her head out of his hand. For a long time she lay there in silence thinking about all that her husband had said. She knew it was all right to be quiet with him; she didn't have to talk all the time.

Without saying a word her husband got up, drew back the curtains around the bed, and opened the window shutters. The first light of dawn could be seen overlooking the hills of Judea. Had he been there for a night, a day and a night? Or just one night? She didn't know.

Sarah sat up and stretched. Her body felt cramped from sleeping so long and her neck stiff from leaning on his chest. She stretched her neck muscles by rolling her head in a circle. Then she breathed deeply. The awful tiredness was gone; the aching of her flesh had stopped. Yet she felt as if she could sleep even more. Once again she nestled between the covers.

He sat on the edge of the bed gazing at her. For a few moments he ran his fingers through her hair, like a comb, ever so gently brushing her hair back from her forehead. She closed her eyes. How she loved to have him do this! Then with his finger and with the lightest of all touches, he again traced her face—her eyebrows, eyes, and nose. Then he stroked across her long eyelashes, over her ears, and then around her mouth. As he did, he thought, *You are altogether lovely, my beloved.*

She didn't want him to stop and said so, barely moving her lips as he traced them again.

He laughed a gentle playful laugh. She loved it. Then with a smile ever so tender, he cupped her face in his hands. As he did, Sarah placed her hands over his. Turning her head to the side she moved his right hand away so she could look at it. Then with her forefinger she gently traced the place where he had engraved her on his palms. Sarah knew he would never forget her . . . nor forsake her.

"I need to tell you something, my love."

The heaviness of his voice caused her to look up. Sarah didn't like what she saw in his eyes. She knew he was preparing to say something that wasn't easy to verbalize. It was not only in his eyes, but also in the tone of his voice and the tautness of his lips. Sarah knew from experience that whatever he was about to say was set. When his mind was made up there would be no reasoning with him—no changing his mind. Whatever he determined would surely come to pass.

She waited for him to speak.

"Just before the Babylonians came, I left Jerusalem. I was at the temple and left by the Eastern Gate. For a moment I stood on the mountain that is east of the city and lingered there, thinking about you and all that had happened."

She looked at him, her eyes wide with incredulity. She was speechless. It wasn't gossip after all! He had purposefully left the temple and Jerusalem—abandoned them before the Babylonians ever took the city!

The gravity of his voice and his countenance frightened her as he continued. "I've come now to reassure you of my love, but also to tell you face to face that I haven't lived in Jerusalem since that time and I'll not live here in Jerusalem again," he paused, "for a very long time. A *long* time, Sarah. Instead, I will reside in the home that was mine before you were born. Before I ever found you in the field."

"But, how can I—" Sarah pled.

He put his fingers on her lips. "Hush, Beloved. What I have purposed will not be altered or changed by anything you say. So listen carefully. I want you to remember my words."

His words were quiet, his voice sad but filled with tenderness. As he spoke he stroked her arm. "I will be gone for many days, but you will never ever be out of my heart *nor* out of my sight."

Sarah dropped her head and closed her eyes, giving no response.

"Do you understand?" he asked as he lifted her chin with his fingers.

Her mournful brown eyes, brimming with tears, nearly broke his heart. She was so lovely, so altogether lovely. Even in her sin and rebellion he had not let her out of his mind. He still cared for her deeply even though his heart hurt when he thought of her with all her lovers—lovers taking what was his! What he had bought, paid for, earned, won! Her life, womanhood, beauty, and wealth! Their son with the blue-green eyes.

"No, I don't understand," she sobbed. "I'm home and you're not going to be here. You haven't been here when I've needed you! Why do you have to go away?" There was alarm in her voice.

"Because, my Beloved, though you won't understand this now, you still have much to learn and you won't learn any other way. You think you've already learned your lessons, but you haven't. Sarah, dear, it's a matter of your heart. You need a new heart."

"I don't need a new heart," Sarah said with a hint of anger. "You don't know my heart. Do you think you can see what it's like? It's my heart, not yours, so how can you know it? How can you judge it? It makes me angry to have *you* tell *me* what *my* heart is like!"

"I know, Beloved, I know. . . ."

"Why don't you stay around and see what my heart is really like?"

"Sarah, the sincerity of your heart—the depth and validity of your love for me—will be seen in how you behave when I'm not here in person. Our time to live together again as husband and wife will come. But it is not yet. Believe me; trust me. Remain faithful. I'll know when the time comes. And when it does, I will return and then. . . ."

She held her breath, biting her lip.

"And then I will come home to our beloved Jerusalem and we'll make our home together here. We have a future, but it is yet future, my love."

Sarah looked at him, her soft brown eyes filled with pleading. She knew she could not change his mind.

"You know, I always keep my word. Listen, then, and keep this in mind when you are tempted to give up and walk away from all I have taught and promised you...when you are tempted to listen to those who say I don't really love you and I'm through with you. Remember this when you begin to wonder if this land really belongs to you for an everlasting possession. Remember, there will come a day when I will not hide my face from you any longer."

His words came like a refreshing waterfall cascading over a rock cliff. She opened her mouth, thirsty for its delightfully fresh, cool water. It vanquished her anxiety as it rushed over her.

"We will live together forever. Our sanctuary, our temple, will be here in Jerusalem—more magnificent in grandeur than you can begin to comprehend! It will be here forever, and so will you. You will be mine; I will be yours. All the nations of the world will know it. No matter what they say to you, how they threaten you, or what they do, you can know that what I have planned will surely come to pass. No man can thwart what I have purposed to do. I am behind the good and beyond the adversity. Nothing in the heavens or on the earth—no angel, no devil, no nation, no individual—will prevent what I have purposed from coming to pass." He paused.

"The more you believe what I say, Sarah, the easier you'll find it to live through the days ahead."

He reached over and embraced her in his arms. She could feel his heartbeat. There was nothing she could say; he knew her better than she knew herself. He knew everything. She didn't want him to leave, but she knew nothing could stop him.

Sarah also realized she deserved no future of any kind. It was all his grace—lavish, extravagant grace. A grace she could not comprehend but which she would embrace.

He leaned down and whispered in her ear, "Cling to me in faith, Beloved, as the waistband clings to the waist of a man. And remember: As surely as day follows night, I will keep my promise to you."

Gently he pulled her arms from him, laid her on the bed, and pulled the covers over her shoulders. Tucking her in with a tender smile, he said, "Rest some more, my Sarah. I give my Beloved sleep."

Sarah didn't plead; she didn't cry. The only movement she made was that of her eyes as she watched him rise from the bed. He walked over to the window and closed the shutters, but not quite all the way. As Sarah watched, she wondered, *Why didn't he close them all the way?* She wanted to ask, but she didn't. Then he walked to the door. As he turned for one last lingering look at her, Sarah could restrain her tears no more. They slipped silently from her eyes; she didn't want to let him out of her sight.

"Sarah. . . ."

"Yes?"

"Listen to Daniel. His prophecy is sure."

When Sarah awoke the next day she wasn't sure if she had dreamed about her encounter with her husband or if he had really come. She noticed that the door was still bolted from the inside, but the shutters were open just enough to see that a new day had dawned.

S

Chapter 18

arah paced the room banging the air with her fists. "Why? Tell me why, Nehemiah, are people always opposing us? How big is our land anyway? Why can't they let us live here in peace!"

Sarah's hands moved to her hips. "I get so tired of all their political maneuvering. Horonite! Ammonite! Arab! All three reporting us to the king! May their names be erased forever."

Sarah took a breath and resumed her walking tirade. "All I want, Nehemiah, is what my husband has given me. Not what they have, but what is rightfully mine!"

Sarah's voice grew louder. "Nothing more," Sarah said, pointing her finger at him, "but nothing less! Absolutely nothing less."

Nehemiah loved Sarah's tenacity. She was a worthy Mistress of Jerusalem in her husband's absence. Although the walls had gone up in fifty-two days, Sarah was still rankled by the opposition of Sanballat the Horonite, Tobiah the Ammonite, and Geshem the Arab.

"Can you imagine," Sarah wasn't finished yet, "rebuilding a wall while carrying a load with one hand and a weapon in the other? Having a sword girded at your side while you work on the wall? I don't know how the workmen managed! I'm thankful you were wise enough not to fall for Sanballat and Tobiah's schemes. I'm certain, Nehemiah, that if you hadn't come from Susa we would never have gotten those walls up."

"I had to come, Sarah. The shame and vulnerability of our city—her walls lying in rubble and her gates burned with fire—made me sick. I mean that literally. I mourned, wept, and prayed. For days I fasted. Fortunately I found favor with the king, or I wouldn't have arrived here with the timber and supplies we needed . . . let alone with permission from the king, who said we could rebuild our walls.

"It was amazing!" Nehemiah continued. "The king could have put me to death or forever banished me from his sight because cupbearers are not permitted to be sad in the king's presence. But I honestly couldn't help it. My anguish showed. When King Artaxerxes asked me why I was sad, I became greatly afraid about what he might do to me."

Sarah smiled. "After watching how you stood up to the opposition while we built the wall, it's hard for me to imagine you being afraid of anyone."

"It may be hard for you to believe, but take my word, Sarah. At that moment I knew I could have lost my life. Kings are kings. Life and death are in their hands."

"Yes, but wasn't it you who, in the face of the threats and accusations from our enemies, stood firm, encouraging our people to not be afraid and fight for their brothers, sons, daughters, wives, and houses? I can still hear your voice, Nehemiah. You were marvelous!"

"Sarah, it is the one we serve who is marvelous. And your compliments embarrass me. So let's change the subject. I have a gift for you."

"A gift? Nehemiah, how thoughtful of you!" Sarah exclaimed.

"It's not from me," Nehemiah's disappointment was apparent. "I am just the bearer of the gift."

"You mean you brought it for someone else? Who?"

"Sarah, this may seem strange, but I don't know who the gift is from. All I know is that as I neared Jerusalem, an old man approached our caravan and asked if I knew who you were. When I told him yes, he asked me to deliver something to you. He told me to tell you it was a very important gift just for you from Babylon via Persia."

Sarah was puzzled. "Don't you have any idea who this man was?"

"No, he came and left quickly. All I know is he appeared to be a man of . . . what shall I say? A man of character, integrity." Nehemiah paused and put his hand to his chin as if trying to recall a forgotten detail. "Oh, yes. I thought I heard someone in his company refer to him as Elieazar, but I can't be sure. We were so eager to get to Jerusalem I didn't pay careful attention."

"Elieazar? I know an Elieazar, but. . . ." Sarah paused and looked at Nehemiah. She decided she didn't want to say anything about Elieazar; if she did, it might open the conversation to personal matters she didn't want to mention. "Do you know what the gift is?"

"A scroll."

"A scroll from Babylon via Persia? Who in Persia would send me a scroll, of all things? And why would a man possibly named Elieazar be delivering it? You *really* have my curiosity aroused now."

"The man said to tell you it was written by someone who served the first Babylonian king who conquered Jeru—"

"Daniel!" Sarah screamed with delight, clapping her hands. "It's a scroll from Daniel the prophet, isn't it?"

Nehemiah was taken aback by her excitement. "Sarah, I don't know who it's from. I only know it's a scroll."

"Where is it, Nehemiah?" Sarah asked excitedly. "I have to see it immediately."

"I left it on the table in the outer chamber."

"You left it! How could you?" Sarah's excitement turned to panic. "Suppose something has happened to it? What if someone took it? Or threw it away? Don't you realize how valuable it is if Daniel—may he forever rest in peace—sent it? It could never be replaced."

"My goodness, Sarah," Nehemiah said as he got up, "I'll get it right away."

In just moments Nehemiah was back with the scroll in hand. With great respect he handed it to Sarah. *Are those tears in her eyes?* he wondered.

"Here it is, Sarah. You became alarmed for no reason. Nothing happened to it."

When Sarah took the scroll from Nehemiah, he noticed that her hands were trembling. She noticed it too and smiled weakly. "I'm sorry, Nehemiah. You cannot imagine what this scroll, if it *is* from Daniel, means to me. Oh, it has to be from Daniel!" she said, becoming excited again. "He was one of our true prophets, you know."

"Sarah, if I had known who it was from and what it would mean to you, I would have delivered it much sooner. But I was so preoccupied with building the walls. . . ."

"Oh, please, it's all right now." Sarah stood. "Forgive me for overreacting. I know you had reason to delay. I've got the scroll now, and I'm going home to read it."

Sarah turned to walk away and then paused. "I once talked with Daniel when he lived in Babylon. In fact, we talked on the very day that Darius the Mede conquered the city. We departed from Babylon soon after that. Later, when I learned that Daniel had died, I grieved bitterly. Somehow I always felt there was more he needed to tell me. Then . . . something else happened recently. Daniel's name was mentioned in a conversation I had with someone very close to me. I was told to listen to Daniel."

Sarah looked at Nehemiah and smiled apologetically. "I hope that explains my anxiety. Again, may I ask you to forgive me? You'll understand if I excuse myself now, won't you?"

With that, Sarah left Nehemiah standing alone. He was a little stunned; she hadn't even waited for his reply.

Little did he know the gravity of the gift he had delivered.

Chapter 19

*S*arah sat on her bed and carefully unrolled the scroll. It was from Daniel! Joy pulsed in Sarah's heart. *It must have been my husband who sent the scroll! When he departed, didn't he say, "Listen to Daniel?" And the man Nehemiah spoke to must have been Elieazar. I know, my husband, this has to be your doing!*

Now her husband's words of exhortation made sense. Sarah's eyes eagerly scanned the length of the scroll. What was she to learn from Daniel? She was tempted to read the end first, for surely that would be the conclusion of the scroll's message. But she knew she had to read it from the beginning to absorb and understand its content. Settling back on her bed, Sarah began to read. . . .

> *Sarah, although I do not know how nor when, I believe someday this scroll will reach your hands.*
>
> *It is yours. I've written it especially for you so that you might under-stand things that pertain to your future. This, Sarah, is a sure word of prophecy to which you need to pay careful attention. It will be a lamp for the dark and confusing times to come. The days ahead will be difficult until the end finally comes, when your kingdom will be the only kingdom.*
>
> *Subsequent to what I shared with you the day we met, I had another vision. It came in the first year of the reign of Darius, the son of Ahasuerus. The Medes made Darius king over Babylon.*
>
> *I had been reading Jeremiah's writings about the desolation of Jeru-salem and consequently felt I needed to spend time in prayer and fasting, for Jeremiah said the captivity would last a total of seventy years.*

Sarah paused for a moment. She leaned back against the pillows on her bed and thought about Jeremiah. *So Jeremiah's influence reached all the way to Daniel in Babylon. I didn't know that!* Sarah felt a little guilty. Upon her return from exile, she had inquired about Jeremiah and learned that he survived the Babylonian invasion. Nebuchadnezzar had instructed that Jeremiah was not to be harmed, and Nebuzardan and his soldiers were to do for Jeremiah whatever he desired.

Sarah did not know where Jeremiah was when he died. She had only heard that he and his scribe, Baruch, were forced to go to Egypt. They had settled in

Taphanhes, a fortress city on the border of lower Egypt, where Jeremiah continued to fulfill his calling as a prophet. He had served faithfully until his death.

Sarah could still see Jeremiah standing below her balcony delivering his
message. *How I wish I had listened to you. You suffered for being faithful, and I suffered
because I was unfaithful. At least you didn't have guilt on your conscience. I wish I didn't
have it on mine.*

Sarah picked up the scroll and continued reading.

*It was at this time that I was given an understanding of the vision and
its message. This is the vision I believe you are to know and keep before you,
and it is related to the other visions I told you about. Although they may seem
like a great mystery to you now, they all pertain to what lies in your future.
More and more as you see the future unfold before you, you will understand
this sure word of prophecy.*

*First, let me give it to you in its entirety. Then we will look at it line
upon line.*

*Bear with me, Sarah. Don't say, "It is too much for me to understand."
First you must know the content of the vision. Eventually you will understand. Just remember: This is your future. As you read it, Sarah, watch for
the references to Messiah.*

Messiah! Sarah's eyes lit up.

*Seventy weeks have been decreed for your people and your holy city,
to finish the transgression, to make an end of sin, to make atonement for
iniquity, to bring in everlasting righteousness, to seal up vision and prophecy,
and to anoint the most holy place.*

*So you are to know and discern that from the issuing of a decree to
restore and rebuild Jerusalem until Messiah the Prince there will be seven
weeks and sixty-two weeks; it will be built again, with plaza and moat, even
in times of distress.*

*Then after the sixty-two weeks the Messiah will be cut off and have
nothing, and the people of the prince who is to come will destroy the city and
the sanctuary. And its end will come with a flood; even to the end there will
be war; desolations are determined.*

*And he will make a firm covenant with the many for one week, but in
the middle of the week he will put a stop to sacrifice and grain offering; and on
the wing of abominations will come one who makes desolate, even until a
complete destruction, one that is decreed, is poured out on the one who
makes desolate.*

Just the mention of Messiah excited Sarah and filled her mind with questions.

Yet she knew if she was going to understand what Daniel had written she needed to be patient; it did seem complicated.

> *Sarah, it is important to see that the vision involves seventy sevens. Look again at the words, "Seventy weeks (or sevens) have been decreed for your people and your holy city." Those seventy sevens are determined upon my people. I am an Israelite. A "Jew," as they are now calling us. And the seventy sevens relate to my people and my holy city, which can be none other than Jerusalem. So this, Sarah, is a vision that pertains to you and the nation of Israel. We must keep that in mind.*
>
> *Now let's see what will happen in those "seventy sevens," or we might say seventy weeks of sevens or 490. . . .*

At this point in the scroll, Daniel's words simply trailed off and started again:

> *In those seventy sevens, six things will be accomplished. Let me list them for you in the order they were given to me:*
> *First, the transgression will be finished.*
> *Next, there will be an end to sin.*

"An end to sin!" Sarah exclaimed aloud. "Can it ever be?"

Then she answered her own question, saying, "This vision says there will be an end to sin for Israel. Our transgression will be finished!" Sarah wanted to shout because she knew her sin—her tendency to wander from her husband's righteous ways—had always been a problem between them.

> *Third, to make atonement for iniquity.*

Sarah paused to ponder these promises in light of her own condition. *Can atonement ever be made for my sin? Every year on the Day of Atonement when the priest sheds the blood of bulls and goats I remember my sins, and I tire of remembering them. It never changes. I want my transgressions blotted out from my memory. But is it blasphemous to wonder how the blood of bulls and goats can take away my sins? To wonder how an innocent animal can make atonement for the sins of a human being?*

Sarah sat for a moment staring at the scroll and thinking, *If all this is true, there will be an end to sin! How wonderful that would be!* Sarah looked down at Daniel's next words.

> *Fourth, to bring in everlasting righteousness.*

This was what her husband wanted! For her to live according to what he deemed right. Yet she could not accomplish that. Sarah thought of all the different ways she had tried to cheat just a little—to redesign what was right for the sake of

111

her own benefit, her own desires, or what was expedient for her. She had been sacrificing the blind and lame members of her flock rather than the perfect and the spotless as she had been commanded. She had rationalized her choices in her mind. *After all, the animals I sacrifice are just going to die anyway, so why not keep the best ones alive?*

Deep inside, Sarah knew what she had been doing wasn't right. She knew it, yet she did it anyway. And others in Israel were doing the same. And the priests tolerated it! *Of course, they are also tolerating divorce—even divorcing their own wives! And,* Sarah sighed, *I and many others are not taking our tithes to the temple.*

Sarah mulled over Daniel's words about an everlasting righteousness. They caused her to stop and do a little self-evaluation. In her husband's absence, her commitment to him was waning. She wondered why she found it so wearisome to serve a husband she'd live with one day, even if it wasn't now. Sarah turned on her side, propped her head on one hand, and continued reading.

Fifth, to seal up vision and prophecy.

"I guess that means we'll understand everything because it will all have been fulfilled," Sarah said aloud to herself.

Sixth, and finally, to anoint the most holy place.

What does that mean? Sarah asked herself. *We have the holy place now! It's part of the temple. Anoint it? And all this will be accomplished in seventy sevens, or 490. . . . Four hundred and ninety what? Days, months, weeks, or even years?* She didn't know. All Sarah knew was that her husband told her to listen to Daniel. She kept reading.

Sarah, I want you to know and discern the events that will occur within this time frame of seventy sevens. From the issuing of a decree to restore and rebuild Jerusalem until Messiah the Prince there will be seven sevens and sixty-two sevens; it will be built again, with plaza and moat, even in times of distress.

Let me draw it out for you; the time frame might be easier to understand that way.

Sarah suddenly sat straight up in her bed. "The decree—that's what just happened! Oh by the gods, I—" Sarah quickly clamped her hand over her mouth. *Why do I still use that expression when I get excited or upset?* Her exhilaration, however, was too great for her to stop and ponder the answer to that question or to feel the guilt she so often felt when those words blurted out of her mouth.

Still excited, Sarah spoke aloud again, "Nehemiah just rebuilt the walls of

Jerusalem by the *decree* of King Artaxerxes!" Sarah leaned back on the pillows, groaned, and then sat up again.

"Jerusalem *has* been rebuilt. The plaza. The moat. And in times of distress. The time has started. The 490 weeks, months, or years have begun!"

Sarah went back to read the scroll again, this time more slowly, glancing at Daniel's sketch.

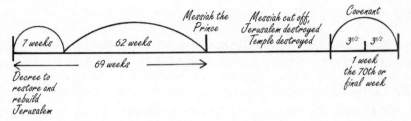

> *From the issuing of a decree to restore and rebuild Jerusalem until Messiah the Prince there will be seven weeks and sixty-two weeks; it will be built again, with plaza and moat, even in times of distress.*

This time Sarah noticed the reference to Messiah. *When is He coming?* she wondered. Sarah leaned over the scroll, puzzled.

She went back to Daniel's diagram. She had not yet paid close attention to it. As she studied it now, she made some calculations. Noticing the mention of Messiah within this time frame made the vision take on an even greater significance than before.

Sarah kept in mind that Daniel had called the seventy weeks the same as seventy sevens. So seven sevens and sixty-two sevens gave her sixty-nine sevens. *Sixty-nine times seven is 483. Is he saying that in four hundred and eighty-three years Messiah will be here? Were the sevens years? They have to be years. Days or months don't seem logical.*

Sarah fell back on the pillows, then turned on her abdomen and tucked one of the smaller pillows under her chin. Her eyes were wide open as she thought about Daniel's words. *I can't believe it! Has Daniel seen when Messiah will come? If so, I'll be here. Daniel assured me that I would be present with my husband when our kingdom reigns over the earth!*

Sarah closed her eyes. This seemed like a sacred moment. After absorbing the impact of Daniel's message, she sat up and read it again. But this time she noticed a different set of words:

> *Then after the sixty-two weeks the Messiah will be cut off and have nothing, and the people of the prince who is to come will destroy the city and the sanctuary.*

"After sixty-two weeks, Messiah is *cut off?*" she blurted. Sarah put down the scroll. She was confused. *If he's Messiah, how can he be cut off?*

Then Sarah looked at the remaining words that puzzled her. *The city and the sanctuary destroyed. I can't believe it. All that we just rebuilt will be destroyed? Again?* Sarah gazed at the scroll in disbelief.

Daniel is mistaken; I know he's mistaken. Sarah got up and slipped out of her dress, washed her face, and put on a gown. Then she got in bed, pulled the covers over her legs, and folded her arms. She remained deep in thought.

Daniel was an old man when he wrote to me. He must have become confused. When Messiah comes, he'll never be cut off. Sarah slid further down into the bed and pulled the covers over her shoulders. She felt cold. Then rolling over, she buried her head in her pillow and closed her eyes. *Jerusalem destroyed? The temple destroyed? That can't be. I can't go through that again. . . .*

But that night Sarah did. She dreamed all night long about the destruction of Jerusalem. The flames, the people screaming and running, a man pushing her to the ground, his leering face and sweaty body—the repulsiveness of it all. All night she tried over and over to get the beam off Hannah but she couldn't. And Hannah died. She saw Jeremiah in the flames and heard his warning. She put her fingers in her ears and ran until she saw more flames, a fire from another time, and she watched with horror as her son with the blue-green eyes walked into them, crying, reaching out for her. She couldn't get him out—he was gone—but she could still hear him cry. Then Sarah walked through the rubble of Jerusalem. She tried to start rebuilding the temple but every time she set a stone into place it fell down. Over and over again it fell down.

When morning finally arrived, Sarah woke up exhausted. Her bed was damp from sweat. She went to her basin, splashed water on her face, then looked out the window shutters. The temple was still standing.

Sarah sighed, relieved. The temple was there. And so was Jerusalem. The sun was shining; there was no sign of fire.

The scroll was on the floor beside Sarah's bed. She rolled it up and put it in a stone jar. Sarah didn't want to read anymore of it. At least not now . . . if ever. How could Jerusalem be destroyed again?

Chapter 20

𝒜 quietness settled over Sarah and over Jerusalem. A wife separated from her husband, a mother estranged from her children, Sarah adjusted as best as she could to life in Israel after the captivity.

Politically, things were at least tolerable. The Medes faded off the scene; rule under the Persians was uneventful. Life was comparatively good . . . until a young Greek general by the name of Alexander the Great overthrew the Persians at the decisive battle of Issus. Now Israel was ruled by a third conqueror, Greece. Anyone sleeping through this rapid wind of change was abruptly awakened by a sound like clashing cymbals as Hellenism collided with the Middle East and with Judaism in particular. Although Alexander died unexpectedly at the age of 33, leaving no heir to his kingdom, the Hellenistic lifestyle he carried to the lands of his conquest survived.

Alexander's kingdom was divided between four of his generals. This was in perfect agreement with Daniel's vision—a vision he recorded before the fact but never had time to explain in detail to Sarah. Yet what Sarah didn't read, she experienced firsthand. Daniel's vision was true, for no man could have brought it to pass even if he had read the script!

Greece was the bronze belly of the statue in Nebuchadnezzar's dream. It was also the third beast that came out of the sea in Daniel's vision. This beast was a leopard with four wings, signifying the swiftness of Greece's conquest; and the leopard also had four heads, which represented the four generals who received rulership of Alexander the Great's kingdom. Two of these generals hellenized the lands to the north and the south of Israel. Seleucus I Nicator took Syria, and Ptolemy I Soter took Egypt.

Israel was the bridge between Syria and Egypt—a bridge eventually crossed by Leah. She was a woman whose life was tainted by the way she coped with the trauma of her childhood. She had been abandoned by the mother who gave birth to her, and Leah opened the resulting wound so many times that she had become hardened by the scar tissue.

Leah hated her mother. So much so that, in a sense, it made her deaf and dumb: She didn't want to talk about her mother, nor did she wish to hear about her. Unless, of course, the news was bad. Leah relished such news because it justified her hatred and self-pity.

Leah was one of many Jews living in Egypt, yet she had not gone unnoticed. Her beauty was surpassed only by her reputation for being intellectually
brilliant and uncommonly clever. Alexandria was the home of her self-imposed
exile. Its famous library was one of her most frequented places. There she discovered a world much larger than the land of her birth and a culture much
broader. There she felt liberated from her roots—roots which, if acknowledged,
required a lifestyle Leah did not want. The library—a treasure house of the writings and philosophies of the world—grafted into her Jewish heritage a new way
of thinking and living.

Leah was content with her existence in Alexandria. But that began to
change when the Bible, the holy book of her people, was translated into Koine
Greek, which had become the common language of all the peoples absorbed by
Alexander the Great's conquests. The Greek translation of the Bible, called the
Septuagint, became the catalyst for a new obsession developing within Leah.
She reasoned that if the Bible could be put into Greek, then Judaism could be
adapted to Hellenism. And that was what her people needed! Something to liberate them so their lives were not rigidly restrained or, even worse, suffocated
by rules and regulations.

*Tuck in the tassels on your prayer shawls and get them out of sight! There's a lot
more to life than what you've been told. Moses put you in bondage; I have come to
deliver you.* These were Leah's thoughts as she arrived in Jerusalem and took up
residence in the City of David. She would begin her campaign in Israel's capital—the wheel hub of a chariot which would roll from Egypt across the bridge
of Israel to Syria and finally make Israel like the nations surrounding her. This,
Leah knew, was her calling in life.

It was a calling made easier because the Ptolemies who dominated Israel
were the same Ptolemies who ruled Egypt. The close contact with these kind
and gracious rulers who favored and protected their Jewish subjects made
Leah's crusade for Hellenism not only palatable but desirable.

Leah was one of two strong Jewish women living in Jerusalem; the other
was Sarah. For a time, both were unaware of the other's presence. One had a
cause, and the other simply wanted peace and quiet.

In fact, life probably became too quiet for Sarah. Maybe that was the reason she felt so lonely. Yet for all her loneliness the thought of having a man
other than her husband was far from her mind. Sarah had learned her lesson—
or so she thought. She gave herself to the routine of life one day at a time.
Everything was done in a perfunctory manner—even her worship at the temple. Routine brought security after all the trauma she had experienced.

From time to time, Sarah thought about her children. Even though she'd
heard no word of them, from the day she left Babylon and set her face toward
Jerusalem, she refused to entertain the thought that they might be dead. *Surely
my children know I am alive. Have they written me off as dead?* When the thoughts

of all her past hurts threatened to disrupt her peace and bring on depression, Sarah buried them.

Though Sarah's life was relatively stable, the world around her was changing rapidly. It seemed as if the whole world was speaking Greek, so Sarah, out of necessity, learned the language. She was not alone; many of the wealthy people in the city learned Greek and made it a priority for their children. This Hellenistic influence at the highest level of society caused Sarah some concern. She was disturbed because the liberality of Hellenism—the licentious lifestyle encouraged by the Greek gods—clashed with the righteousness of Moses' Law with all its holy commandments.

When Sarah heard that their holy writings had been translated into the common Greek language of the day, she wondered if Hellenism was going to overtake the whole world. *It may happen in the rest of the world, but it will never happen here. Not if I can stop it!*

It was at the height of this determination that Sarah's quiet existence was jostled as the balance of power shifted from the kings of the South to the kings of the North. With the shift, Sarah, unaware of Leah and her campaign, felt her Jewishness dangerously threatened for the first time. Matters worsened when Antiochus IV, king of Syria, came into her life. He called himself Epiphanes— "the Illustrious One."

"Excuse me, Mistress, but he's here," said Rizpah, failing to identify the guest.

Just be patient, Sarah thought to herself. *You'll train the girl yet. Someday she'll be the servant you need.*

"Who's here, Rizpah? Does he have a name?"

"Yes."

"Yes what? Rizpah, what is wrong with you? Why are you so beside yourself?"

"I'm sorry, Mistress. It's just that Antiochus—I mean Antiochus the Fourth, Epiphanes—is such an important man . . . a wonderful man."

"Rizpah, look at me and listen carefully." There was a cutting sharpness to Sarah's voice. "Antiochus the Fourth may be an important man, but he certainly is not a wonderful man. Any man who would murder his brother to steal the throne left to him by his father—a father who had just been poisoned—is *not* wonderful. He's a man of intrigue. Intrigue of the worst kind! He has no scruples to restrain him. He's a man—"

"But Sarah," interrupted Rizpah as she crossed her arms. Sarah looked at Rizpah sternly because of her improper address. Rizpah caught the look. "Excuse me, *Mistress*. But I am confused. Antiochus is so nice to me. When he comes into this house, he doesn't treat me like a servant. And I hear he's a generous man who does great favors for his friends. I enjoy talking to him. He's interesting. . . ."

Instantly Sarah recognized what was happening. Rizpah was enamored by Antiochus! *How stupid of me!* thought Sarah. *How very stupid of me, of all people, not to have figured this out sooner! Rizpah is attracted to the man! That's why she continually talks about him and keeps questioning me about him. That's probably why she has been so well groomed lately, dressed in her finest. And why she's defending him now. What exactly has been going on downstairs?*

"Rizpah, that's enough. Tell him I'll be right down. But before you go, please find my sandals for me." Sarah flitted her hand toward her bed. "They're either under the bed or next to the chest."

As Sarah combed her hair, she watched Rizpah in her mirror. Rizpah was young, her figure striking. Her tiny waist accentuated the fullness of her breasts and the slim curve of her firm hips. Her light olive skin was poreless and her eyes were inviting—sometimes dancing with joy and other times moody, but always sensual. *Antiochus would be attracted to her. He's a typical Greek, enamored with beautiful bodies. Besides, he loves to be fawned over; Rizpah is most capable of that! I wish she'd fawn over me a little more. It would certainly make her a better servant.*

"Here are your sandals, Mistress. Should I go tell Antiochus you're coming? I left him standing in the hall."

"Please do, Rizpah, it will take me just a moment."

Rizpah hurried out of the room, talking as she left. "You needn't hurry, Mistress. I'll take good care of him."

I imagine you will, and that's why you don't want me to hurry. How naive can the girl be not to realize I know she's smitten with the man?

As Sarah came down the stairs, she saw Rizpah turn her gaze quickly from the stairway to Antiochus. *She's been watching for me.* Sarah was just in time to see Rizpah's hand leaving his while letting out a restrained little laugh. Sarah, a bit shaken, proceeded down the stairs as naturally as possible.

Antiochus looked up. "Sarah, you are a striking woman! You could compete with our goddesses in Greece."

"Your goddesses in Greece are made of marble, Antiochus. They have ears but do not hear. Like them, I will not be taken in by your flattery."

"Sarah, I know you looked in the mirror before you came down here, so you know I don't lie."

Antiochus grasped Sarah's hand and took charge. "Let's sit over on the couch. I need to talk with you briefly before I go to Egypt."

Antiochus led Sarah to the couch, but she wasn't going to be told where to sit in her own home! Sarah smiled graciously. As the most prominent citizen in Jerusalem, she had to endure his visits to her home. With a sweep of her hand, Sarah said, "You can sit here, Antiochus. I prefer this chair. Now," Sarah smoothed her skirt under her and sat down, "tell me what you want this time, Antiochus."

"I don't want to sit. I want to stand."

"So stand! Stand and tell me why you've come. It *was* to see *me*, wasn't it?"

Sarah couldn't resist letting Antiochus know she wasn't blind to his interest in Rizpah.

Antiochus smiled generously, choosing to ignore her innuendo. He decided to assume it might have been said all in innocence. Besides, he preferred Sarah to Rizpah; Sarah was a much bigger catch. If he had Sarah, then he'd have her influence and power joined to his. Antiochus also preferred older women over the young inexperienced ones. *Maybe she'll come around just out of pure jealousy when she sees what I do for her servant.*

Antiochus decided that today he would be gracious. Charming. Inviting. Walking over to Sarah, he took her hand and softly stroked her palm with his fingers. "Sarah, I came to see you because there is no woman on earth like you. You are desired by so many—"

"Is it me, Antiochus, or the land?" For just a moment, Sarah left her hand in his. His hand was strong and masculine. Her flesh enjoyed the touch though she disliked the man.

"What is the land without you?" Antiochus looked just like the profile cast on the coins bearing his image. The artist was honest. Antiochus' dark hair curled around his face in that famous style adopted by the Greeks. His nose looked like it might have been broken at one time, but even that seemed to add to his masculine appearance. It matched his thick athletic neck and strong jaw. Everything about him spoke of strength—even his eyes. One could see Antiochus was the kind of man who was always determined to get his way no matter what the cost.

Sarah smiled knowingly as she responded, "With me or without me, the land is a bridge between the north and the south. With me, however, it certainly is more passable!"

You're a confident little wench, aren't you? Antiochus thought to himself. He bowed low, brought her hand to his lips, then moved his hand in a gentle caress over her shoulder. "Come now, Sarah, bridges are meant to be crossed by people hand in hand." Catching the flush of her flesh, Antiochus placed her hand back on her lap, his fingers barely touching her thigh. Then he walked across the room and turned to look at her. He would seduce, but he would not plead. And he would reason with her . . . if she could be reasoned with.

"Sarah, you and I could have such a mutually profitable relationship. You know I care for you. If only you could see what we could have together. You have position, but not wealth. Egypt has plenty of wealth for us to share. We could be one people and share one culture."

Now Sarah felt violated by his touch and became angry. "Never, Antiochus, never!"

The resolute tone Sarah spoke with frustrated Antiochus.

"Why do you have to be so stubborn, woman? How can Judaism compare with Hellenism? Why do you resist what so many people in Israel are drawn to? Israel is becoming hellenized, Sarah. Don't fight it."

Sarah knew Antiochus was right. She wished it weren't true, but there were many Jewish people who wanted to be like the Greeks. Not only to dress like them, but also to think and live like them. They even went so far as to imitate their architecture and literature and to give Greek names to their children. She had also recently heard about a Jewish woman from Egypt who was holding literary discussions with some of the prominent women of the city—challenging the narrowness of their Judaistic beliefs and explaining the virtues of gaining a wisdom not to be found in the Septuagint. It was women like these who, with their sensual Grecian dresses, were scandalizing the Jewish women who dressed modestly, keeping with tradition.

Hellenism not only caught the vanity of the women. Jewish men were also lured by the Grecian lifestyle. Some of them, intimidated by the brash boldness of the Greeks and their criticism of the Jewish faith, tried to hide their Jewishness— which became clearly apparent in the Greek gymnasiums where the men walked around naked. Circumcision told it all. Sarah had heard some men were so desperate to be like the Greeks that they had their circumcision reversed.

Sarah shuddered at the thought of the pain. *How could they do it?* Then memories of her past suddenly stood at the door of her mind, as if they had been called home. *I can understand their temptation. But if they only knew where it will lead! The guilt . . . the shame . . . if and when they ever come to their senses.*

Antiochus turned toward Sarah. With a sweep of his hand and a bow he said, "Sarah, I am trying to win you to my side. To make it easy and beneficial for you." Then turning his back to her, he continued talking as he walked across the room, "But, don't forget who is the conqueror! I am on my way to Egypt, and when I am finished there, I'll be back through here. As I said, Israel is becoming quite hellenized. And that is the way I want it to stay."

Turning and looking straight at her, he spoke in a commandeering voice. "Quit preaching at the people, Sarah. This is the world as it is, and you need to conform or get out of the way." His voice took on an adamancy, a fanaticism that made Sarah shudder. "From Greece to Pakistan, from the Black Sea to the Nile and the Euphrates, this is the culture." Antiochus' words matched the set of his jaw and the indignation in his eyes.

Sarah did not turn her eyes away from his. *A storm has blown in. . . .*

"And I will not be resisted by the likes of you, my beautiful serf." Their eyes remained locked. Sarah refused to acknowledge she even heard him call her a serf. When the time came, she'd make her move. Antiochus continued. "Listen carefully. I do not like your narrow, antiquated Mosaic Law. Neither do my soldiers nor many of the people of this land. I don't—"Antiochus paused. "Are you listening? I don't want to be opposed in what I am doing. Do you understand me?"

Sarah continued to meet his gaze. She would not be the first to avert her focus. She kept her eyes void of emotion but inwardly she felt shame. She remembered how at first she, too, was smitten by Antiochus—by his ways and his culture. She hated to think that she had permitted him to hold her hand even for a few moments. Sarah now realized she had let down her guard, and she was alarmed for she knew exactly what was happening inside her.

The frank sensuality of Antiochus' Hellenistic culture was in such stark contrast to the austerity of her husband's ways. The Jews depended on the revelation of the Word of God. The Greeks, however, relied on the reasoning of their mind—an understanding conceived in the finite wisdom of man rather than the infinite wisdom of God. The Greek gods were many and could be seen; her God was one and could not be seen.

"I said, Sarah, do you understand me?"

Sarah didn't say a word. She didn't know what she wanted to say, so she just stared.

"Sar-*ah*! Sar-*ah*!" he yelled, emphasizing the syllables of her name as he did whenever he was angry with her.

The moment Antiochus yelled, Sarah knew she had command of the situation. She would not react. "Epiphanes, you need not scream."

"You called?" Rizpah quickly entered in the room. She couldn't have been too far away.

"No, I didn't, Rizpah. But you can see our guest to the door. He's on his way to Egypt and must be going."

Antiochus walked over to Sarah, took her hand, bent over to kiss it, and looked her straight in the eyes. His voice was gentle again, but the sparks in his eyes made his words more of a threat than a promise. "I'll be back very soon. And when I return, we will pick up this conversation just where we left off."

The fireworks were over as suddenly as they had begun. Then Antiochus turned around. "Rizpah, you are such a lovely woman." There was a sudden change in the tone of his voice when he addressed Rizpah and smiled admiringly at her. It was hard to define the tone. *Gentle and sensual? No . . . subversive! That's it!*

Antiochus turned to Sarah and grinned at her smartly. "How fortunate you are, Sarah, to have such a capable woman to help you." Then turning back to Rizpah, he smiled seductively and said, "Rizpah, please do show me to the door."

As soon as Antiochus and Rizpah stepped out the door, Sarah went upstairs to the room that overlooked the entrance to her house. Standing back just far enough to see them without being seen, she watched, thankful that the shutters had not been closed. She could see Rizpah carelessly look back at all the windows and then grab Antiochus by the hand. They stood talking, his demeanor clearly different from what it had been a few minutes ago. Every now and then Sarah heard Rizpah giggle lightly and saw her look back at the house to make sure they weren't being watched. *Antiochus must be pretty confident of himself if he's being this brazen right in front of my house. Surely he knows I might see them. What is he doing?*

121

Sarah continued to watch. She pondered Antiochus' motives, his strategy. *This is a man highly skilled in intrigue.*

Rizpah laughed louder. Antiochus' hand went to her mouth to quiet her. Then looking beyond her to the house, he put his arms around her small waist and pulled her body to his. Sarah had to walk out of the room; what she had seen awakened desires in her—desires she might enjoy but didn't want. She knew she could have been the one in Antiochus' arms had she so chosen. It wasn't a matter of jealousy. Rather, she was struggling with the cravings of the flesh—cravings that she hoped would go away if she didn't encourage them.

Chapter 21

*A*ntiochus went to Egypt as planned, but his conquest did not turn out the way he expected. He wanted all of Egypt but took only part of it. Although his partial success still brought him great wealth, it was an angry man—a very angry man—who marched across the bridge of Sarah's beautiful land towards Syria.

As Antiochus marched he vented the fury of his disappointment on the Jews. He stormed into the temple, desecrated it, plundered the temple treasury, and continued onward to Syria. He never stopped to talk with Sarah as he had promised, or threatened.

Nor did Antiochus talk with Sarah as he made his way to Egypt again two years later. Apparently he had dismissed her from his thoughts. There were others he could entice to his side by his smooth words. Rizpah was one of them, and he took her to his bed. Why not? She was a servant, but he could make her anything he wanted her to be. All she had to do was curry his favor. And that was easy for Rizpah; she was smitten by him. He rewarded her well as he did all those who were willing to prostitute themselves for the wages of power and position. Antiochus' strategy was to take from those who would not come to his side and give their possessions to those who would.

That was how he had risen to power among his own people and it was the way he planned to win over the Jews. Rob from the rich, give to the greedy. Every man and woman—according to Antiochus—had a price.

Just the prestige of being invited to his bed in his beautiful home was enough in Rizpah's mind. There was quite a story behind the house, which she had longed to see. The house had once belonged to a very wealthy and prominent Jew who was put to death. Why he was put to death no one seemed to know. Nor did they seem to care.

After Rizpah moved out, Sarah never saw her. Nor did she want to; Rizpah had betrayed her.

Antiochus returned from his second trip to Egypt, and again he was an angry man. His plans for further conquest had been thwarted by the Romans, who had sailed to Egypt with a letter from the Roman senate forbidding Antiochus to engage in war with Egypt. When Antiochus asked for time to consider his response, Popillius Laenas, the emissary of Rome, drew a circle around him in the sand and told him he had to give his answer before he stepped out of the circle.

Antiochus had no choice; he was not prepared to take on this upcoming power.

Furious and humiliated, Antiochus marched to Jerusalem to draw his own circle around the city. Then this emissary from hell moved in rabid vengeance. Only those who didn't oppose him were hidden from his misplaced rage. Twenty-two thousand soldiers were ordered to attack the Jews on the Sabbath. They massacred men, women, children, and slaves. Only the apostates were spared. And once again Antiochus desecrated the temple. But this time he took another brazen step forward. He abolished the daily sacrifice and offered an unclean sow on the holy altar.

Antiochus couldn't have Egypt, but no one would stop him from taking Israel. He sent out a decree forbidding all religious practices. No more feasts; no more circumcision. Copies of the Law were burned. Scrolls, parchments of holy Scriptures, and books were confiscated, desecrated with heathen symbols, and then returned to the owner or burned so that all could see and fear. Even observing the Sabbath was forbidden.

Sarah could take no more.

It was night—a clear night illumined by a full moon and a host of stars, their brilliance piercing the cloudless clarity of the cold, crisp atmosphere. Sarah knew where Antiochus would be. She also thought she knew who would be with him: Rizpah.

Sarah grabbed her cloak, flung it around her shoulders, and in a fury strode across the city to Antiochus' house. The strength of her convictions overrode all natural fear. As she approached the residence, her eyes carefully surveyed the scene. There was one room on the second floor that had a light burning. Sarah knew exactly where she was headed; this had been the home of a family friend before Antiochus stole it. Sarah had spent many hours here before her friend was put to death. The memory of Antiochus' greed and unjust actions against her friend fueled her fury.

Sarah pushed open the front door as if she knew it would not be locked and walked quietly but quickly up the stairs. She wanted Antiochus to be caught off guard. It was part of her strategy. As she walked through the hall she could hear voices coming from the room with the light. She paused at the door and listened. They were in conversation. *Good. He's exactly where I thought I would find him.*

Slowly, Sarah turned the handle of the door and gently pushed to make sure it wasn't bolted. Then taking a deep breath, adrenaline igniting her muscles, she threw open the door and charged into the room.

"Antiochus!" she shouted.

Sarah had his attention immediately.

Antiochus was sitting on the bed, propped up against the wall, talking with a woman. Sarah didn't notice the look of astonishment and then anger that crossed the young woman's face. She was hidden in the shadows beyond the reach of the flickering candles on Antiochus' side of the bed. Besides, Sarah had little interest in this woman of whoredoms, who buried her face in a pillow.

For a moment Antiochus froze. He was clearly stunned. Then he quickly pulled up the covers to hide his nakedness. Pounding his fist against the wall behind the bed, he yelled, "Sarah! What are you doing *here?*"

"I am here because I knew I would get an audience with you immediately." Sarah paused for effect.

"Antiochus, I will no longer tolerate what you are doing." Sarah's voice was filled with indignation. "The cries of those whom you have mutilated, strangled, or crucified with their circumcised children hung on their necks *will not* be silenced! When you forbid circumcision you are commanding us to go against a covenant. But covenants cannot be broken! Circumcision is the very identification of who we are!"

By now, Sarah was roaring. She hadn't intended that, but she couldn't hold it in. Nothing could stop her anguished soul from bringing to birth the anger that swelled within her.

Antiochus was livid—absolutely livid. Crimson. But Sarah did not stop. She knew this might be her last opportunity. And she was sure he wouldn't get out of bed in his present state of undress.

"We can't do that! Do you hear me? We can't ever stop being who we are. And circumcision confirms who we are!" Sarah glared at him. Then she growled. "This will not go unpunished. Your gods do not rule, Antiochus. They do not rule!"

Sarah's voice became more controlled yet very grave. "Antiochus the Fourth, you are not 'Epiphanes' the Illustrious One. You have become 'Epimanes,' the madman."

"Sar-*ah!*" Antiochus' speech was that of restrained fury. "You will see who rules! You will see who stands in your holy temple as God. You—"

Sarah didn't wait to hear Antiochus finish. She abruptly left the bedroom, slammed the door shut, and ran down the stairs and out the door. She was shaking violently. She was weak. Spent. Drained of every last drop of indignation's strength.

Had Sarah heard the words of the young woman who was with Antiochus, she never would have made it home.

The woman lifted her head from the pillow in which she had hidden her face. Propping herself on her elbow, she looked at Antiochus and, with cunning and venom in her voice, said, "The woman you hate is the woman I hate. Sarah happens to be my mother."

Antiochus smiled a sick smile. He leaned over and kissed Leah on the cheek. "We have more in common than I thought, my love. Wouldn't she have been surprised to know it was you who was in my bed?" He leaned back and thought about how Sarah would have reacted. Suddenly he pounced on Leah.

"Why didn't you say something? She never would have recovered! By the gods, I'm sorry you didn't speak up!"

Leah lay on her side, clutching her pillow under her head. She didn't move. Her speech was subdued, controlled. "I know you are sorry. It would have been sweet vengeance for you, wouldn't it? However, I was not prepared to face her tonight. Do you know how long it has been since I have seen my mother? When she left me I wasn't even old enough to know about being in a man's bed. The only arms I wanted were hers." Leah shook her head. "How I wanted those arms . . . how I wanted them. But she preferred the arms of a man, a stranger's, to mine."

Leah burrowed her head into her pillow a little bit more and closed her eyes. "I'm not even sure if the woman knows if I am alive, or if she cares."

Was there a tremor to her voice? Had Antiochus seen tears, or was the candlelight fooling him? He didn't want to know. He didn't want an upset woman on his hands—a sobbing, distraught woman. That wasn't what he wanted from Leah.

All that interested Antiochus was what Leah could do for him physically and politically. Her past was her problem and he wanted no part of it. He didn't want to get into long hours of listening. He wanted to think, to plan. . . .

He broke the silence. "Let's go to sleep. Tonight was a little disruptive. Tomorrow we'll make love."

Antiochus stood up and stretched—proud of his nakedness. Then he leaned over the table to extinguish the candles, spitting on his fingers and listening to the sizzle as he snuffed out their light and condemned them to darkness.

Leah watched. *He likes putting out the candles that way.* She wished she could extinguish the anguish of her heart as easily. She didn't like what seeing her mother had done to her.

Antiochus got into bed, his back to her, and pulled up the covers. With his right hand he reached back, groping in the darkness until he found her hip. He patted her, but Leah wanted more. She wanted to be held, cradled, understood. Sheltered from her feelings, her memories. Leah wanted to cry and cry and cry.

"Good night, Leah."

Good night? What's been good about it? She didn't answer. He didn't care.

For a long time, they both lay there caught up in their own worlds of thought. Had Sarah not burst into the room they would have become one flesh that night, but only in a physical sense. Antiochus was too self-centered.

Finally he heard her breathing become subdued. How long had it been since he had said good night? Two hours? More?

Sleep came for Leah, but not for Antiochus. He didn't want to sleep. His mind was racing. His heart devising. He went over and over his plans until he had everything worked out in his head. He wanted revenge—revenge of the most vicious kind.

Now he knew he had it. Now he could sleep.

Chapter 22

*L*eah woke up feeling groggy. She found it hard to collect her thoughts. *Was last night's encounter a dream or had her mother barged in unannounced and yelled at Antiochus?* Leah turned over to ask Antiochus, but his side of the bed was empty. He was gone, executing his plans—plans as black as the night in which they were devised.

Leah was relieved to be alone. She didn't want to get out of bed. She lay there, her arms behind her head, thinking. She was weary. Weary of life. Weary of pain. Weary of lovers. Weary of going from one man to another. Weary of looking for someone to satisfy her unsatiable loneliness. Weary of coming away from these trysts with a greater awareness of the bottomless void within—a void nothing and no one could fill. *Maybe it would be easier to end it all than to go on.*

Leah had thought of taking her life before. Yet if she were going to die, she would want her mother to know—to taste the pain she had caused in her daughter's life. Leah did not want to die in vain. To take her life without her mother's knowledge would be to die in vain.

If she took her life now, Antiochus might tell Sarah. *He'd probably tell Sarah just to get even with her. But what if he didn't?* She could not risk it. Besides, she could take her life anytime. Why be in a hurry and possibly mess it up?

Leah rolled back on her side and closed her eyes. *Maybe I can go back to sleep.* She tried to stop thinking and drift into unconsciousness. But sleep was merciless, unwilling to come to her aid. So Leah turned onto her back again and thought about last night's incident. She hadn't seen her mother for years. She was still beautiful. Even in all her fury, she was desirable and beautiful.

Suddenly Leah sat up as a new thought entered her mind. *How did mother know where Antiochus' bedroom was? She walked in here as if she knew exactly where she was. Had she slept with him?* The thought nauseated Leah. She found herself wondering what Antiochus thought about her mother as a woman. Did he find her desirable? Did he want her . . . even now? *Is she better than me?* Leah found herself curiously torn between the obscenity of it all and the sudden insecurity brought on by jealousy. She didn't want anyone to like her mother more than they liked her.

These new thoughts caused Leah to remember her father's words about a man uncovering the nakedness of a mother and her daughter. Her father had said that for a man to know both sexually was an abomination worthy of death.

Of course, so is adultery. The thought came into her like a sword drawing blood. Condemned by a conscience not quite yet seared, she retaliated and attempted to justify her immorality. *Sleeping with two from the same family has to be worse than adultery! Father may say that every kind of sexual immorality pollutes the land, but sleeping with a mother and her daughter would have to be inexcusable. How could two women tolerate the thought of one pleasing the man more than the other?*

Leah wondered if Antiochus would be honest if she asked him whether or not he had slept with Sarah. From there her thoughts drifted even further. Had her mother been with any man since she returned from Babylon?

Leah lay back down and stretched her arms toward the ceiling. It felt good to stretch her muscles, spread then curl her fingers, and release the tension. She arched her back, then relaxed it. Then she pulled her knees to her shoulders—first the right knee, then the left. As she attempted to relieve her stress, she kept thinking. *Mother, are you now faithful to my father...or do you still take lovers?*

Leah missed her father, but his absence didn't bother her like her mother's did. It was her mother who had wounded her. Her father was just a very kind person who didn't understand her, insisted he knew more about life than she did, and wanted to manage her life for her. But how could he? In her estimation, he didn't even know what it was to live. All he wanted to do was keep her from enjoying life. She didn't like his rules and regulations. Yet, for all this, Leah knew her father loved her. But her mother? That was a different story. Leah didn't know if Sarah loved her even a little bit or if she'd want her if she showed up at her mother's door.

That thought hurt, and Leah hated that she still experienced the hurt. Because she was lying on her side, a tear ran down the side of her face and into her ear. *I won't think about it. I'll think about her lovers.*

Leah sat up in bed as if to formally dismiss the painful thought from her presence. She put her finger into her ear and wiggled it. The tear tickled.

Leah then leaned back against the wall and again asked the same question. *I wonder if she has a lover or if she is faithful to my father even though he's not around?* Leah had heard in the marketplace—a place with eyes, ears, and a mouth—about her father's brief return and his promise to come back sometime in the future and never leave again. She knew her mother was admonished to be faithful. But was she?

Can you live, Mother, without the attentions of a man? I know you can live without your children. . . . The tears began to pour once again much like an expectant dark cloud pours out its rain. Leah buried her head in her pillow, crying, stuttering. "I . . . I know you . . . you can live without me . . . but can you live without a . . . man?" What Leah wanted to hear her mother say was that she could live without a man but living without her daughter was hell.

Leah cried until sleep came and rescued her like a merciful friend.

Chapter 23

hile Leah slept, Sarah screamed. Jared was pulling her through the streets of Jerusalem towards the temple.

Sarah had been amazed at Jared's meteoric rise to leadership. She had known Jared, this Hebrew who said he was of the tribe of Benjamin, for less than a month. He had arrived in Jerusalem about four months ago and was already distinguished among the people as a leader. His appearance was imposing, awakening respect from others. Although he was tall and attractive in his own right, Sarah knew he was respected for more than his physical appearance. There was something about his demeanor. The way he talked and handled himself with people and his great wisdom and insight provoked reverence rather than commanded it.

Jared's broad shoulders gave his tall frame a look of stability. His features were well defined. His long straight nose and high cheekbones gave him an air of aristocracy. His brown eyes were intense but kind. His face was beardless except for his chin, where Jared kept the hair neatly trimmed, close to his face. Sarah liked it; she thought scraggly beards made men look so unkempt. Jared's appearance was pleasing all the way to his high forehead. Even his receding hairline contributed to his distinguished looks.

Sarah watched the back of Jared's head as he hurriedly led her from her house to the temple. He had awakened her just moments ago with his loud pounding on her door. When she answered, he quickly explained that one of the priests from the temple had asked him to get Sarah and bring her to the temple immediately. The priest had also warned them to be very careful. Jared had waited rather impatiently as she got dressed. Now he was dragging her through the streets. Sarah was breathless and tried shouting at Jared, but he whispered sternly for her to quit talking. He wanted to get her to the Temple Mount and then leave as quickly as he could. Sarah continued to shout. "It's my fault! It's my fault, Jared! I aggravated Antiochus. If I hadn't aggravated him he never would—"

"*Die*, Sarah, die," he said firmly. She appreciated his Hebrew rebuke, "It is enough." But anyone who didn't know Hebrew would have thought he was telling her to die. Sarah wished she could die.

"It's done. Now quit yelling. Do you realize you are yelling at me? Come on! We're almost there."

"I know we are almost there!" Sarah puffed. "Whose city do you think this is?" She paused to catch her breath. "If only I hadn't burst in on Antiochus last night maybe he never—"

"Sarah!" Jared's voice was sharp.

Sarah closed her mouth. She was too tired from running to talk at the same time. She had hoped talking would make her feel better. As if repetition would take care of the problem, bring a solution, remove the consequences, or turn back the shadow of the sundial.

Sarah stopped talking, but she continued to rehearse the events of last night in her mind. Eventually she turned her thoughts to the woman whom she saw in bed with Antiochus.

"Jared, I can't keep running," Sarah shouted again. "I've got to walk." She let go of Jared's hand and slowed to a walking pace.

What was I thinking about? Sarah lost her place in her thoughts. *What was troubling me besides Antiochus? Oh, yes . . . it was that woman. Who was she?* Sarah had expected it to be Rizpah. Rizpah needed a jolt, the little traitor! *But it wasn't Rizpah; her hair was black. This woman's hair was a definite auburn. And her skin was whiter, not olive like Rizpah's. Her eyes—what were her eyes like? Did I ever see them?*

"Sarah, stay right here out of sight. Don't move until . . . Sarah! Are you listening to me?"

"I'm sorry, Jared. What did you say?" Sarah had been so deep in thought she hadn't heard Jared talking to her.

"Sarah, time is of the essence. You must listen carefully and do what I say. It's not safe here anymore. . . ."

Jared looked at Sarah and sighed. He knew the priest wanted Sarah to see for herself what had happened but he also knew it wasn't safe for Sarah to be seen. He was eager to fulfill his promise to the priest and then take Sarah back home.

"I want you to stay right here, out of sight," Jared snapped. "Don't let anyone see you until I check the temple area and make sure none of Antiochus' soldiers are here. We don't want to jeopardize your life."

"I am not afraid—"

"I know you're not, Sarah. But you should be! You have more than enough reason to be afraid." Jared looked around, put his hands on her shoulders, and moved Sarah slightly to the left. "Now," he said, while anxiously appraising her position, "don't move! I'll be right back."

Sarah looked around her. She could see fires in various parts of the city and hear turmoil. She heard the cries of the frightened and the anguished. Houses were being plundered, and bodies were being pierced through by blood-sated swords. Epimanes the madman had unleashed his greedy, blood-thirsty army, twenty thousand strong on the people of Jerusalem.

"Sarah," Jared whispered. Although her name was said in nothing more than a whisper, this time Sarah was alert and waiting. Jared motioned for her to join him.

"It's at the brazen altar. Follow me, but watch where you are going. Just remember, Sarah, we *must* hurry. Antiochus said they'd be back, and I don't want you here when he returns with his men. Not under any circumstances. Who knows what that madman will do?"

Despite Jared's admonition, the moment Sarah stepped onto the Temple Mount, her pace slowed. Painful memories returned to her. This temple—the work of the hands of a small remnant—was but a shadow of its former glory.

"Sarah. Watch where you're going—and hurry," Jared said in a low voice.

"I'm coming, Jared. I'm coming," Sarah whispered, unable to conceal her irritation. She was in her temple, where everything said, "Holy to the Lord." *It isn't right to rush across this holy mount. . . .*

There was an aura about the temple which evoked a reverential awe in her breast. *There can't be any place like this in the whole world,* Sarah thought as her eyes swept across the sacred ground.

The temple building now stood straight in front of Sarah. In it was the Holy Place with the table of shewbread on the right. The menorah on the left, with its seven branches, provided the only light in the temple. This was where the priests ministered daily.

In front of the veil that separated the Holy Place from the Holy of Holies was the altar of incense. The veil was a masterpiece of intricately woven linen—blue, purple, and scarlet. Only the high priest was allowed beyond the veil into the Holy of Holies, and at that, only one day of the year, the Day of Atonement.

On that day, the priest entered, in a sense, at the risk of his life. If he ever came into the Holy of Holies without the blood of bulls and goats—blood to cover his sin and the sin of the people—he would be struck dead. If that happened, who would pull him out? No one, for two men could never be in the most holy chamber at one time, even if one was dead. Therefore the other priests had to use a hook to snag the dead priest's garments and drag his body out.

Until recently the high priest had been Jason. He had bought the high priesthood from Antiochus, and for that Sarah held him in disdain. *If Jason had ever gone into the Holy of Holies, surely they would have dragged him out!* She recalled that he had usurped the priesthood from his own brother Onias. And if that wasn't enough to condemn Jason, his support of the Greek gymnasium that overshadowed the temple was!

What has happened to us as a people? Hellenism and compromise are destroying us! We're to be different than the nations, not like them! Now Menelaus has supplanted Jason as high priest. Anyone can buy the priesthood from Antiochus if he has the money and Antiochus' favor! The politics, greed, lust for power, and the prostitution of the priesthood—all those things sickened Sarah as she thought about them.

Sarah's thoughts slowed her pace even more. She permitted herself to venture mentally where she never would be allowed physically as a woman—beyond the veil. The veil was the "door" into the Holy of Holies, which at one time had been the sanctuary for the ark of the covenant.

Now the Holy of Holies was empty. Sarah's countenance clouded as she remembered the ark. For many months the people had searched for it, but to no avail. They knew the ark wasn't in Babylon, but that didn't help them. And no temple priests had survived the Babylonian invasion to tell where the ark was hidden. Sarah felt in her bones it must have been buried somewhere on the Temple Mount—hidden in some secret place prepared by those who knew the Babylonians were coming.

As Sarah walked through the temple she felt a keen sense of the void left by the absence of her husband. Up ahead, Jared was waiting for her. When she reached him he simply directed her eyes with his finger.

Sarah looked, and her hand flew to her mouth. A whimper made its way from the depths of her soul. Then another followed . . . and another. For a moment or two she spoke no words. Then they came, encased in pain, spilling out in unbelief. "No! No! No! How could he? How could anyone be so . . . so despicable? This. . . ." Sarah pointed to the brazen altar, at a loss for words. A statue of Zeus, the god of the Greeks, stood above the altar. "This is . . . ah . . . an abomination! All of it! All this," she said with a broad sweep of her hand, "is an abomination of desolation!" Anger bubbled from her like a boiling spring.

Sarah threw back her head, raised her fists, and cried, "No, Antiochus. No! You shall not get away with this; it will not go unpunished! You will pay. You will pay!"

Sarah screamed to the wind, and the wind carried her voice to the ears of heaven. . . .

Chapter 24

The cold morning air brought relief to Sarah. Usually she found it invigorating, but right now she wasn't sure if anything could be invigorating. Not after having awakened in a sweat several times during the night.

The heat of the flames raging in Sarah's dreams was all too real. Seeing Jerusalem—"Antioch of Jerusalem" as Antiochus had named it—in flames again was almost too much. When Sarah had gone to bed she couldn't stop thinking about what she had seen earlier that day. The temple and the altar of Zeus charged around and around in her head, like chariots competing in a race. When sleep finally came, relief was only temporary, for that's when the dreams came. Sarah groaned and wept. She winced from the heat of the lashing flames. Sometimes she'd awaken and sit upright on the bed until the chill of the room brought her back to the present. Then she'd wrap herself in the covers she had thrown off in the torment of her dreams. Sometimes it was her own voice groaning, "No, Antiochus. Nooooo!" that woke her.

Sarah had to see Antiochus.

This time she would not scream or raise her voice. This time she would not barge in unannounced. *This time I will appeal to him. Try to bring him to his senses. Reason with him. If only he could understand that he was destroying a city, a land, a people he already ruled over! Why destroy what is already yours?*

Sarah hoped in spite of his anger Antiochus could still be appeased. Maybe he would see the folly of it all. Perhaps she could appeal to his deranged ego without compromising her own principles. *Maybe if I humble myself and apologize.* Sarah's mind was full of maybes. No matter what happened, Sarah knew she had to try. *If reasoning doesn't work, then we'll have to take more drastic measures.*

As Sarah approached Antiochus' home, she noticed the devastation in the surrounding neighborhood. However, soldiers had left the houses immediately around Antiochus' home untouched. *No sense in setting a fire where it might spread to places it shouldn't go.*

Sarah knocked and waited. She shuddered. Was it from fear, or the cold air? She knew Antiochus could put her to death or take her prisoner. Jared and others had warned her to stay out of sight. They had heard that when Sarah was mentioned, his rage bordered on the edge of insanity.

As Sarah waited for someone to come to the door, she shuffled from one foot to the other. She decided it was the chilly air that was making her tremble. After all, it was the month of Tebeth. Deep in her heart, Sarah heard again an echo of her husband's words, "You shall not die; you shall live." *It might be Gehenna, as torturous as hell, but I'll survive*, thought Sarah as she rubbed her arms for warmth.

Just as Sarah poised to knock again, the front door opened. The woman with the long almost-auburn hair—whom she had seen in Antiochus' bed the other night—stood before her. Sarah was struck by her eyes. They were a rich brown, accompanied by thick long lashes. Sarah felt like she was looking into a mirror and seeing her own eyes, *Only there's a bitterness there—a darkness*, she thought.

Leah was startled. After so many years she was finally face to face with her mother. Leah scrutinized Sarah's eyes and watched for any hint of recognition. "Yes?" she asked Sarah.

Instantly Sarah made a decision: In no way would she let this woman know she had seen her in Antiochus' bed. She would act as if she did not recognize her. *This woman is not my reason for coming.*

"Excuse me for calling so early in the morning, but I must see Antiochus immed—"

"He's not here," Leah interrupted insolently. "He won't be back until two Sabbaths from now."

When the word *Sabbaths* came out of Leah's mouth she quickly regretted saying it. She could tell by Sarah's expression it had not gone unnoticed.

Sarah looked at her. *This woman is a Jew! A Jew sleeping with a Greek! A Jew won over to Antiochus' side.* Sarah wondered if the woman knew what her lover had done to their city and their people during the night. *If she knew*, Sarah wondered, *would she still be in his house?*

For a moment both were silent. The silence slipped by unnoticed. Each was occupied in her own thoughts. Leah felt confused and caught off guard. She had intended to see her mother at some time to confront her and spew out her pain, hurt, and anger. But this wasn't the way Leah planned it. *What do I do? If I tell you I am your daughter, what will you do?* Leah's stomach hurt. She was cramped by fear—fear that if her mother discovered who she was, she would walk away. At that moment Leah was sorry she had come to Jerusalem. Yet all these turbulent emotions within were masked by a demeanor of cold indifference.

Sarah shook her head involuntarily—as if that were a reflex to bring her back to the issue at hand. The purpose of her visit was Antiochus, not a Jewish woman who was sleeping with her enemy.

Sarah had been convinced Antiochus would be home. Jared had told her Antiochus was coming back. Sarah had dressed carefully for the occasion and planned what she would say. She even rehearsed how she would conduct herself in accordance with the various responses she might encounter. But Antiochus wasn't here! Sarah was frustrated. Disappointed. And it showed.

The woman was staring at her. Looking more deeply than Sarah wanted. Her eyes seemed to be searching for something, wanting something from her.

Sarah felt uncomfortable. "Forgive me; I just assumed he'd be here. It's so important that—"

"Assumptions can be very destructive." Leah's eyes never left Sarah's.

Leah's words and the tone of her voice flustered Sarah. They were void of any emotion, yet almost cutting. *Why? Does she recognize me? Does she know I'm the woman who barged into their bedroom? Is she trying to get rid of me as quickly as possible? What is this woman saying?*

Sarah didn't want to know. She simply wanted to leave as quickly as possible. If she couldn't talk with Antiochus, she'd have to take a different tack. Her thoughts became occupied with what she should do next. Absentmindedly, Sarah said, "Thank you" and walked away, disquieted by this unexpected turn of events.

Leah stood ambivalent, trying to decide what she should do. Her hand went out towards her mother, but Sarah never saw it. Sarah was unaware of the one whom she had once again, unwittingly, turned her back on.

Very slowly, Leah reached out to close the door. Her tear-filled eyes riveted on her mother's back.

Sarah sighed as she hurried to get away from the house. *Why does that woman trouble me so?* Sarah didn't look back.

"Imma!"

Sarah stopped. The word stabbed her in the back.

"Imma!" There was pathos in Leah's voice . . . a pathos tinged with anger.

Sarah spun around. She looked at Leah for a moment and then cried in astonishment. "Leah! Oh Leah, it's you! It's you—" Sarah's words broke as they spilled from her.

In a moment Leah found herself engulfed in Sarah's arms. Leah's tears belied the unresponsive rigidity of her body. She bit her lip; she didn't want Sarah to see her tears.

Sarah was half laughing, half crying—forgetting at that moment this was the Israelite who loved those she should have hated. Hugging her daughter, she exclaimed, "I was afraid I'd never see you again . . . that you'd never come home." Tears streamed unabashedly down Sarah's face. She cupped Leah's face in her hands, and gazed at her in obvious delight.

But Leah's next words lanced the joy that filled her heart. "*You* were the one who left home, not I . . . *Imma*." The appellation *Imma* was soaked with sarcasm.

Sarah stepped back and dropped her hands from Leah's face. It was as if Leah had pierced her heart with a hidden dagger. In shock, Sarah's hand went to her chest. Joy drained from her face. Her eyes widened, searching Leah's eyes in unbelief.

For a moment neither spoke. Their eyes remained interlocked. Sarah stepped back again.

"You're . . . you're right, Leah. It wasn't I . . . no, no, excuse me. It wasn't you, my daughter, who left home. . . ." Sarah's words came haltingly. She was confused. "It was me. . . . I was the one—I was the one who left home."

Leah felt herself softening. She was taken back by Sarah's response, her confession. She had expected Sarah to defend herself. To rationalize. To get angry. To do something other than what she was doing. Anything but this.

There was no color left in Sarah's face. Beads of sweat dotted her brow as she raised a trembling hand to her forehead. It was too much: A night of torment, the disappointment of being unable to see Antiochus, and now the shock of seeing her daughter. The delight; the pain. Sarah felt as if the ground was moving and she began to sway.

Afraid that her mother was going to faint, Leah reached for Sarah's arm. "You'd better come in and sit down. Have you eaten anything this morning?"

Sarah shook her head as her daughter helped her into the house. Sarah felt incapable of opening her mouth to utter even a simple, "No." She was afraid that if she did she might throw up.

"You better rest a moment. Lay on the couch. I'll get you something to drink. A touch of honey should give you strength." Leah looked at Sarah, smiled, and said, "Remember when King David was revived by the stick dipped in honey? You used to tell me the story whe—"

Leah stopped in midsentence. She was remembering her childhood. Tears filled her eyes as she hurried out of the room. As she left, she called over her shoulder, "Just rest. Close your eyes and keep your head down. I'll get you something. I'll be back in a moment."

Sarah's head was spinning. She closed her eyes but it didn't help. She opened them again, trying to focus on one object in the room that wouldn't move. But everything moved. She closed her eyes again and forced herself to take long, slow, deep breaths while she held her head as if to steady it. *Oh, my husband, where are you? Why aren't you here? How am I going to handle this? What am I to say? It's my daughter . . . our daughter. She's alive. She's come home and you aren't here.* Sarah thought about the accusatory tone of Leah's voice when she uttered the word *Imma*.

I don't want to drive her away or hurt her again. . . .

"Here's some hot water with honey and a biscuit. It's all I have right now but maybe it will help." Leah's speech was controlled. Once again her words were devoid of all emotion. Sarah sat up to take the cup from her hand. She watched Leah's every move as she placed the plate on the table beside the couch.

Leah avoided all eye contact. She didn't want to feel even a twinge of sympathy for her mother. Her hands were trembling a little. Leah wondered if her mother had noticed.

"Leah, please sit down." Sarah patted the couch next to her. "I want us to talk."

Leah walked away from the couch and sat down in the chair next to it. Saying nothing, she leaned back and crossed her legs. Resting one arm on another, Leah put her right hand on her chin in a pensive manner and covered her mouth with her fingers. For a brief moment Leah closed her eyes, opened them again and gave Sarah a sullen look.

Sarah knew she should be the first to speak. She leaned forward, patted Leah's knee, and smiled weakly. Leah deliberately moved her knee out of reach. She never took her eyes off of Sarah.

"Leah," Sarah paused, discomforted by the coldness of Leah's eyes. "Never did I dream I would see you under these circumstances. That today, of all days, you and I would see each other face to face after all these years. I—I didn't even know you were here in Israel, let alone alive or dead. . . ."

"Would it have mattered?"

"What, Leah?"

Leah uncrossed her legs and leaned forward, resting her elbows on her knees and her chin on her hands. "Whether I was alive or dead!"

Leah's words were somewhat flippant.

"How can you ask that, Leah? You are my child."

"Imma," Leah said with sarcasm. Having adopted the Greek language as her own, Leah would have said *mother* rather than *Imma*. "*You* abandoned *your* child. Why, then, would it matter if I were alive or dead? If you could so easily walk away and leave me, apparently it didn't matter to you whether I even existed."

"I was wrong, Leah. I was wrong. I never should have left you. I wasn't thinking clearly. I was self-centered. I was . . . I . . . ." Sarah groped for words, "I was drawn away from you—from your father—by my . . . my lusts." Sarah's eyes glistened with tears. "Please, please believe me. I did love you. I do love you. You're my daughter, Leah."

Leah leaned back and purposefully turned her head to the side. Speaking without looking at Sarah, Leah fought back tears as she said, "It's too late, Imma. Too late for me to believe that you love me. If you had truly loved me you wouldn't have left me. You wouldn't have placed your desires above my needs. Not if you really loved me. Love doesn't walk away and leave you to cry all night. Night after night after night. If you loved me, you would have searched for me until I was found. I waited and I—"

"You're right, Leah. You are right. I loved me more than you. What you say is true. But I do care; I do love you. Not as I should have, but . . . oh Leah, I'm sorry, so sorry. . . ."

Sarah was now kneeling at Leah's feet and sobbing. Then she pleaded, "Please, please forgive me. I was wrong. Horribly wrong. I never should have done what I did to you. The years are gone, wasted—years I can never make up for. But will you please forgive me? I need mercy, Leah, mercy."

Leah rose from her chair and moved out of Sarah's reach. Sarah looked up at Leah with tears coming down her face. As Sarah wiped her cheeks with the back of her hand, her eyes searched Leah's countenance for any hint of response.

"Leah, I can't undo the past. I wish I could. But all I can do is work on the future."

Leah whipped back at Sarah. "You talk of a future. I have no future because of what you—my own…mother—did to me." Sarah winced, feeling the lash of Leah's tongue. "I can't think of the future until I figure out the past. It's the past that torments me!" Leah was yelling. "Straighten it out, Imma. Undo it!" The yelling subsided. "Undo it. Loose me from it. Untie me and—"

"Leah, the past is past." Sarah's words were weighted with gentleness. "There is no undoing it, or I would have undone it long ago. Not just for you, but also for your father. And for me, too. We can try to live in the past, talk about it, try to figure it out, but nothing—absolutely nothing—will undo it. Nothing will ever change it. All we can do is ask forgiveness and determine that we will learn from it. We must glean the harvest from the rubble and then put it behind us and move forward."

"And you're off the bema seat—the judgment seat—aren't you, Imma? No judgment! With a simple 'Please forgive me' it's all gone! All is well? No, Imma, no. You've got to pay!"

"Leah, what can I pay? What can I do that will erase the past? Tell me. Believe me, if I could pay, I would gladly do whatever is needed to obliterate the past. I've thought about that over and over again. If we take another person's possession, we can make restitution—we can give an eye for an eye, a tooth for a tooth, a life for a life. But, even with that, we can never undo the past. We cannot return the eye, the tooth, the life that was taken. All we can do is to ask for forgiveness and then try not to repeat the mistakes of the past."

Sarah blinked, wiping her tears again, "My child—my dear daughter—my heart is broken and my spirit is grieved. I beg your forgiveness for failing as your Imma, for not being all I could have been or should have been. Forgive me for abandoning you. I was so wrong. I sinned against you. Yet all I can offer now is to give you my love from this moment onward. I am pleading for your forgiveness, Leah—begging for it."

Leah looked down on Sarah, who was still kneeling on the floor. "I will not forgive you. I can't. I can't send away what you have done to me. You've left me with a great void. It refuses to be filled; I've tried. You've ruined my life! You've deprived me of what every child needs and deserves—a mother who cares more for her child than for herself. A mother who truly loves, not just with her lips but with her life."

Sarah slowly rose up from the floor and sat in the chair. She felt weary. And old. She clasped her hands together and rested her head on them for a moment, pausing as if in thought.

"Leah, I may not have loved you the way I should have. But your father has. He has never failed. He has never taken his hand off you. . . ."

"Curse him, Imma!" Sarah's head flew up. Anger gripped her lips. Leah noted her response but didn't stop. "He didn't keep *you* in line! Nor has he always done things the way they ought to be done. At least in my estimation. With all his power, all his influence. . . ." Leah threw her arm in the air, punctuating each *all*, ". . . he could have made life easier for us. But *he's* not the point. It's you I am talking about. Not my father. You are the one who ruined my life."

Sarah stood up. She could see their conversation was fruitless. Her heart felt as if it had been clawed raw by Leah's words.

"What can I do, Leah?"

"You've done it, Imma, and it can't be undone. You've lost. . . ."

Tears rolled unchecked down Sarah's face. "I'm so sorry I've lost. So sorry. More than anything—except what I have done to your father—I have regretted what I did to my children. To you, to Benjamin, to Saul. You are right; I have lost. Not just once with you, but today, a second time. And the pain seems greater than I can endure."

A sick smile of triumph emerged across Leah's lips. Even though Leah was convinced her mother would never comprehend the magnitude of her pain, she wanted her Imma to hurt—to taste her anguish.

"My pain is greater now, Leah, with this second loss. I always held the hope of reconciliation if we ever found one another again." Sarah was struggling, doing everything she could to keep herself from breaking down into uncontrollable sobbing. "Now my hope is shattered. And you are the only one who can restore it. . . ."

The dam broke. Sarah could no longer hold back the pressure. Her words rode the crest of her sobbing: "Oh, Leah, I'm asking for mercy! Please," Sarah reached towards Leah, "please let me make up to you the years the locusts have eaten—"

Leah's arm went straight out. She held up her hand, five fingers opened wide—a barricade stopping Sarah with a jolt. Sarah's arms dropped to her sides.

Leah had heard her mother beg. She had seen her cry. Now she was in control of the situation; that was the way she wanted it. *You've kept me waiting all these years, wondering if you would really want me once you saw me. Now, Mother dear, it is your turn to wait and wonder. You are not going anywhere, and neither am I. I'm going to stay around to make you pay for the years the locusts consumed. And when your debt is paid, and I am ready, then I'll forgive you.*

"Imma, give up. Believe me when I tell you you've lost. You waited too long to put your arms around me and tell me this."

"But, Leah, my arms are here now, longing to—"

"It's time for you to leave. I have other things to do . . . mother." Leah purposely said "mother" rather than "Imma." Sarah had noticed.

"I'll go," said Sarah. "But, Leah, you must not stay here. You cannot live with Antiochus."

"I can't live with Antiochus?" Leah retorted. "How can a mother who abandoned me tell me where I can and can't live? I'll live wherever I want!"

"Leah, Antiochus is our enemy. He is an enemy of our nation, our people. He opposes all that your father stands for—"

"Imma, Antiochus is *your* enemy."

"No, Leah, you're an Israelite. It is *our* city, *our* sanctuary that he has destroyed. And he's forcing people to make sacrifices to—"

Leah interrupted again. "I'm not listening, Imma. I'm going to *our* bedroom. You can show yourself out. It's obvious you know your way around this house."

With that, Leah headed toward the hall. Then she stopped abruptly in the archway and whipped around. Her words were cutting: "Imma, how did you know where Antiochus' bedroom was? Have you slept in his bed?"

Sarah stood dumbfounded. Before she recovered enough to answer, Leah was gone. A moment later, Sarah heard a door close.

She prayed it would not remain shut forever.

Chapter 25

$\mathcal{A}$ntiochus' soldiers moved throughout Jerusalem and its environs setting up altars and demanding that the people offer sacrifices on them. Then, as if to add abomination upon abomination, his soldiers were instructed to force the Jews to eat the flesh of swine—an animal deemed unclean and forbidden under Jewish law. Although Sarah didn't know Antiochus' whereabouts, it was clear he hadn't disassociated himself from her land.

Jerusalem was again in shambles; it had been ravaged by fire. Houses were being leveled to the ground. Even portions of the walls were torn down by Antiochus' army. Each time Sarah saw Jerusalem's down-trodden walls she was painfully reminded of the insurmountable wall Leah had erected between them.

Sarah had tried to scale the wall to dismantle it stone by stone, but without success. And she was not Leah's enemy! She wanted to bring healing, not destruction. *If only Jerusalem's walls had stood as strong against the forces of Antiochus!* Sarah thought.

For Sarah, walls came to be synonymous with unrelenting pain. She had labored hard to rebuild Jerusalem's walls, which were now being destroyed. But no matter how hard she tried to tear down Leah's wall, it couldn't be demolished!

Sarah spent hours writing to Leah, weeping over her words. She wrote scrolls reassuring Leah of her love and acknowledging the gravity of her sin and confessing her guilt. Never once did Sarah come to her own defense. She felt compelled to put her thoughts in writing with the prayer that Leah would read them again and again until she was convinced of her sincerity.

As she wrote, Sarah acknowledged to Leah that even if Leah granted her forgiveness, healing would take time. As would rebuilding Leah's trust towards her. Sarah pled for that time . . . for the opportunity to prove herself again.

In one letter, she simply asked if they could meet. And in still another, the most recent one, Sarah felt led to warn Leah of the danger of her actions. She begged her to consider the repercussions of her behavior. Sarah warned Leah that her alliance with Antiochus, her absorption with the debauchery of Hellenism, and her forsaking her father's covenant would bring terrible consequences.

Although one of the scrolls was returned with its seal unbroken, the last scroll, the scroll of warning, was not returned. Sarah fasted and prayed night and day that her words would melt Leah's heart of iron.

Ominous reports reached Sarah's ears that Leah was slipping ever deeper into the pit she was digging with her own hands. She was participating in licentious behaviors and rituals being practiced *in the temple,* of all places! Sarah was reluctant to believe the information, but the credibility of her sources affirmed it was more than gossip.

At one point Sarah had gone back to Antiochus' home in the hopes of talking to her daughter. Shame enveloped Sarah when she was denied entrance on orders from the "mistress" of the house. Leah let it be known that she indeed was home yet she refused to see Sarah. Remembering the rejection and embarrassment of that last visit, it was all Sarah could do to force herself to go to the house again. But things were taking a turn for the worse in Jerusalem, and she needed to do something about it. She was convinced that she had to go to Antiochus' house one more time.

Sarah's stomach churned as she knocked on the door. She was shocked to find herself praying that no one would answer. Most of the shutters were closed and no sounds came from the house. When no one responded, Sarah turned and walked away, ashamed at her sense of relief. The continuous rejection had taken its toll.

Sarah drank deeply of her daughter's pain. She now knew how Leah must have felt when she abandoned her. How satisfied Leah would have been if only she had known! Sarah would have gladly shared Leah's great pain and revealed the intensity of her own if only Leah had been willing to give her a chance.

Sarah returned home feeling as though everything was lost. The enemy had triumphed on so many fronts. But what was most heartbreaking was that her own daughter was living in the enemy's camp, sleeping in her enemy's bed, going against everything her father had taught her.

Afternoon or not, I have to rest. Sarah lay down on her couch. Her energy was gone; her arms and legs were drained of all their strength. She closed her eyes. A little bird just outside the house was singing joyfully. *You have no concerns, have you? Every day what you need is provided, and so you sing. How I would love to sing with you—to have no cares.*

Sarah thought about her cares: Jerusalem, the walls, the apostasy of the people, and Leah. *I can rebuild Jerusalem and the walls, but I cannot rebuild my relationship with my daughter.* Sarah then turned on her side, tucked the pillow under her head, and pulled her veil over her shoulders. Maybe she could sleep.

"Sarah? Sarah! It's Jared. Are you home? Sarah!" Jared was yelling and knocking at the same time. The bird flew away.

Sarah had just fallen into a deep sleep. Disoriented and unsure of what was happening or what time of day it was, she was slow to respond.

"Sarah!" Jared yelled again.

"I'm coming," Sarah murmured as she raised herself from her pillow, yawned, and sat for a moment trying to get her bearings.

"Sarah!"

When Sarah finally opened the door, she saw Jared walking away. From the way his shoulders fell forward, she could tell he was disappointed.

"Jared! Jared, is that you?"

Jared turned around, looked at Sarah, and smiled his wonderful smile. "Sarah! How thankful I am to find you at home. You are going to be relieved when you hear what—"

"Is it Leah?" she interjected.

"No." Jared's smile faded. He knew Sarah's heartache. He had even tried talking with Leah, but Leah refused to see him. Jared told Sarah that Leah was trying to punish her, but that didn't seem to ease Sarah's pain.

"Were you asleep?" asked Jared. "You look like it."

Sarah looked at Jared with unveiled disappointment. "I was. I am absolutely drained. Emotionally and physically worn out. So if it's not about Leah, would you mind waiting? Could you—"

"Come back another time?"

Sarah smiled weakly. "Yes."

"Sarah, when you hear what I have to tell you, you won't be tired anymore. This isn't about Leah, but it is good news. This is the next best thing. It would be the best thing if you weren't hurting so much over your daughter."

"Antiochus—he's dead!"

Jared smiled. "That would be nice, but he's not dead. Yet the news is related to him," Jared said with great enthusiasm. "We're not alone. There are others who are rising up against this madman. Not everyone has turned their back on the Law or the covenants. There are some people who haven't sided with Antiochus for personal gain. There are some who are willing to fight, stand for what is right, take action. Wait until you hear—"

"I *am* waiting," said Sarah, who was wide awake now and back in the land of the living. She was eager to hear what Jared had to say. "Come in and sit down, but don't stop talking."

"I can't sit. You know that Antiochus sent his men to the villages outside Jerusalem to set up altars and force the people to make sacrifices to Zeus. Well, listen to this," Jared said excitedly. "When they arrived at the village of Modin, some of the officials under Antiochus went to the home of the most respected man in the village—a priest by the name of Mattathias. He is an old man with five sons. Anyway, they took him to the altar they had set up and ordered him to make a sacrifice to Zeus. The old man refused! He refused, Sarah!"

Jared slapped his hands together. "At that point, another Jew stepped up and pushed the old man away. He wanted to win the favor of the soldier. So he started to offer the sacrifice. This so infuriated Mattathias that he pulled out a knife and killed both the Jewish traitor and Antiochus' officer! In an instant, his five sons were standing at his side, knives in hand," Jared said with a grin.

Sarah's hands flew to her mouth and her brown eyes opened wide in anticipation.

Jared's body language kept pace with his account. "As Mattathias overturned the pagan altar, he cried, 'Whoever is zealous for the laws of our country and the worship of God, let him follow me.' And with that, Mattathias and his five sons made their way to some caves. They've declared war against Antiochus. War, Sarah, war!"

Sarah clenched her hands together, drew them to her chin, leaned her head back, and closed her eyes. For a moment, tears trickled through the shuttered windows of her soul.

Then, when Sarah finished visualizing Jared's story again in her mind, she clapped her hands together, jumped to her feet, and said, "We're not alone, Jared! We are not alone!"

"No, we're not. And a group of us is planning to join them."

"I wish I were a man. I'd go with you."

"I know you would. You'd make a good soldier, Sarah, now that you're in the right camp. Just make sure you stay there. . . ."

"I will," Sarah said with confidence. "I've learned my lesson the hard way."

Jared's voice became firm. "Antiochus has caused enough horror. He's flung truth to the ground. He's trampled the holy place and the Almighty's host too long. His mornings and evenings are coming to a close. We're going to take our temple back, Sarah!"

Chapter 26

*J*ared and a growing number of objectors, including a group known as the Hasidim, "the pious ones," joined the revolt against Antiochus. The zealots grew to be about 6,000 strong. Although Antiochus' troops were better armed, better trained, and greater in number than Mattathias' supporters, Mattathias and his sons were a serious force to be reckoned with.

Not long into the conflict, Mattathias died. Yet the people were not left without a leader. The sons of Mattathias moved to the forefront of the action. Simeon assumed the political leadership of the uprising, while Judas, the one deemed strong and brave even from his youth, took command of what became known as the Maccabean revolt. Judas Maccabeas—the "Hammerer"—would hit the Syrian forces whenever and wherever they least expected it. Using surprise tactics and wisely avoiding open combat, his strategy succeeded.

Even in seemingly impossible situations like the battle of Beth-Horon, their courage and tactics brought them uncanny victories. And with these victories came stories of heroism and deliverance, which served to fuel their determination to win at all costs. Beth-Horon, which was the main approach route to Jerusalem from the coastal plain, was a strategic piece of ground the Hammerer wanted to secure. Yet when Judas and a small band of his men saw Seron and his army coming from the lower region of Beth-Horon, they knew they were overwhelmingly outnumbered.

Judas' men wanted to flee, but Judas challenged them to victory with the power of his tongue. By the time Judas finished his speech, the men had not only changed their minds; they were ready to charge into battle. Outwitting Seron's great army, Judas and his band caught their opponents off-guard and killed eight hundred of them.

The news of the victory at Beth-Horon reached Sarah's ears just when she most needed the encouragement. Things were not going well on Sarah's battle-field. As much as she wished to avoid it, she found herself in a raging war with Leah—a struggle that had continued for some time now. Although Antiochus had left Jerusalem to prepare for a campaign against the Parthians in the east, Leah still lived in his house and continued to wreak havoc among the Jews living in Jerusalem.

Leah was on a crusade; she was determined to win every Jew she could to

Hellenism. With great persuasion Leah assured them that Antiochus would be generous—even magnanimous—to those who would see things his way. Leah's main objective was to reach the women. Her goal was to persuade them to accept compromise rather than be destroyed.

Even though she lived in a male-dominated culture, Leah was convinced that if she could reach the women then they, in turn, would influence the men. She knew women wielded a subtle covert power. Sons are raised by their mothers, especially when the fathers are at war.

A convincing and captivating orator, Leah moved throughout the city making speeches wherever she could gather a crowd. One of the means Leah used to capture people's attention was to let them know who her father was. Once that relationship was established, she would boldly desecrate a sacred scroll or offer a pig on an altar to Zeus and then eat its flesh.

On other occasions Leah went to the marketplace, where she sought to persuade the women that if they truly loved their sons they would not endanger their lives by circumcising them. Leah also reminded the women that to do so was to put their own lives at risk. "Do you want your child thrust through with a sword simply because you cut off his foreskin? Do you think the Almighty would demand such obedience when it might mean your circumcised sons will be murdered then tied around your neck? That's how Antiochus' soldiers will parade you and your husband through the streets! Of what value would that be? Certainly my father will understand!"

Such speeches threw the people into confusion as they questioned what Leah said and compared her words with the Torah. "What about the time the Almighty almost killed Moses because he had not circumcised his son?" they queried.

On other occasions Leah explained the beauty of the human body and why it was acceptable for men to carry out wrestling matches unclothed. She also advocated that men should have their circumcision reversed. "Zeus, while he asks for the place of preeminence," said Leah, "is not so narrow in his ways. He is the chief of gods and is benevolent enough to allow other gods to rule under him. Why worship one God when you can have so many? Wouldn't you rather have many come to your aid? Besides, who is it that reigns? The nation who believes in only one God is now living under the dominion of a culture whose gods are more magnanimous."

On and on went this unceasing conflict until the month of Kislev. The weather was bitterly cold, as it usually is in Kislev, but Sarah felt compelled to go to the market one day. She had heard that Leah would be there. Although this wasn't the only time Sarah had heard her daughter calling people to forsake the holy covenant, it was the first time Leah saw her mother listening in the crowd. The minute Leah recognized her, she became more venomous in her speech. Her words took on a heightened adamancy as she called to her listeners:

"Forsake the holy covenant. Make your sacrifice to gods who will allow you to live as they live—in wanton abandonment to pleasure! Why should you bind yourself to a restrictive code that denies you the right to follow the desires of your heart? To be, in a sense, your own god so that you might know and experience not only good but evil." Occasionally Leah glanced in her mother's direction. Both were cognizant of the other's presence. Leah continued her speech, lacerating her mother with her words. Sarah could feel her soul being cut to ribbons . . . the silent hemorrhaging of the wounds in her innermost being.

The tautness of Sarah's mouth and the use of her veil to wipe away the tears affirmed to Leah her skill in flailing another person with her tongue. Leah became more brazen in her declarations as she assessed the crowd. She wished it were larger, especially today. Sarah listened to her daughter and thought, *You are loud, brash, cruel, my daughter, because you know I'm here. But why? Why do you allow your bitterness to defile so many people and to destroy your own life?*

At times Sarah's body recoiled involuntarily at Leah's words. But when Leah took a Torah scroll, those sacred books of Moses, and grasped a torch from the friend accompanying her, Sarah cringed. She knew Leah was about to set fire to the Torah. Sarah covered her face with both hands and turned away.

As the Torah ignited, Leah yelled, holding it high. "The law is—"

At that instant, a Hasidim bounded out of the crowd. Grabbing Leah by her braided hair, he whirled her around until his knee was in her back. He pushed, forcing her spine into an arch. The excruciating pain piercing Leah's back made her drop the burning scroll. Leah's eyes widened in horror as the man pulled her head back even further. Through clenched teeth, he spit out, "You spiritual *whore!*" Leah's eyes widened in horror as she saw the dagger in his hand.

The sudden commotion and screaming caused Sarah to spin around instantly. She saw what was happening and pushed her way through the crowd toward her daughter, crying, "Leah! Leah!"

Before Sarah could reach her, the man dropped Leah to the ground like a sack of grain and darted away. Blood spurted from around the dagger. Sarah kneeled next to Leah and gently pulled the knife from her throat. She lifted Leah from the dirt and cradled her daughter in her bosom. "I love you, my daughter, I love you. . . ."

Sarah felt Leah's warm blood soaking her dress, seeping between the breasts that once nourished her daughter with their life-sustaining milk.

Leah's eyes were open wide; she was looking up at her mother. Her lips were moving, trying hard to form words. Sarah leaned forward, bending as closely as she could without suffocating her. She strained, trying to hear what her child was saying. Against the gurgling of blood and air, Sarah heard, "Im—"

Leah's eyes were filled with frightful determination. She formed her lips again, her body jerking. Sarah could feel the effort as Leah gave one final push to force out what she was trying to say.

"Im. . .ma."

Leah's head rolled back as her body convulsed one last time, her arms and legs surrendering to death. Still cradling her daughter, Sarah rocked her with a gentle sway. She remembered the first day she held Leah that way—years ago. Or was it an eternity? Sarah used her free hand to push back the bloody strands of Leah's auburn hair. She gently pulled Leah's body closer to bestow the kisses she'd held in trust since the day she and Leah talked at Antiochus' house.

Sarah continued rocking Leah, washing her face with tears—tears of wounded sorrow, of anguished grief, and of regret. But Sarah had no tears of guilt. As the droplets from Sarah's lashes spilled onto Leah's ashen face, Sarah used them to wipe away the dirt from her daughter's cheeks and forehead. In the midst of unequalled grief, Sarah felt relief from the knowledge that she had done everything she could to bring about reconciliation. Leaning down, she again kissed Leah's forehead. Her only regret was the time stolen by a fractured past for which she'd sought forgiveness.

Despite the loss and horror of the moment, a strange peace shrouded Sarah as she sat on the ground. Oblivious to those watching in muted silence around her, Sarah leaned down and whispered in her daughter's now deafened ear, "The war is finally over. It didn't end the way I wanted it to, my precious child, but it is over. How thankful I am I came to the marketplace today . . . that I was given this one last time to hold you in my arms, to have you hear me say one last 'I love you.'"

As someone reached to lift Leah from Sarah's arms, commotion again stirred those in the marketplace. A man ran through the crowd, shouting, "The temple! The temple! Judas Maccabeas has retaken the temple! They've thrown down the statue of Zeus!"

Chapter 27

*I*t was the eighth day of Chanukah. Unwelcome tears silently invaded Sarah's eyes as she lifted a lit candle from its holder. Separating it from the ornate brass menorah, she began lighting the other candles, gracefully displayed just for this one season of the year. Sarah counted the candles as she lit them: ". . . six, seven, eight." Then bringing the ninth candle close to her lips, she gently blew it out, said a prayer, and put it back on the menorah. *Must I cry every time I celebrate this holiday?*

Chanukah was a joyous occasion for her people. A time to remember the dedication of the temple after its desecration by Antiochus. A time to recount the miraculous provision of the oil for the temple menorah. Yet with each celebration, Sarah remembered there had been no miracle to keep Leah alive . . . no miraculous provision of oil for her spirit.

No matter how poor, every Jewish family devised some sort of menorah. Some people even used hollowed-out potatoes to hold the Chanukah candles. Each evening at dusk, families would gather to light another candle until, on the final day,

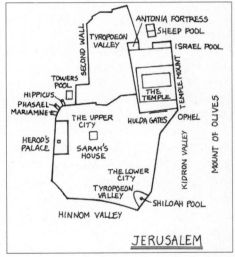

all eight burned brightly. Everyone, young and old alike, knew the story. When the temple was retaken by the Maccabees and the abominable statue of Zeus removed, the priests then set about cleansing the temple. To their dismay they discovered there was only enough oil to light the menorah for one day. For seven days the holy place would have to sit in darkness, for the law required eight days for the consecration of new oil. Yet miraculously the one day's supply of oil lasted for the duration of the eight days they needed!

For a moment Sarah continued to face the menorah, waiting for the tears to vanish undetected while she enjoyed the warmth of the flames. It was cold in the house.

"Sarah."

"Yes?"

"Sarah, turn around. Look at me."

Sarah turned to face Jared. There was nothing about him that could even compete with her husband, yet she enjoyed his company. He was a trusted friend and advisor—a friend born for the day of adversity. Little by little Sarah had opened her life to Jared, sharing the good, the bad, and eventually some of the ugly. The pieces of information about her did not alter his unconditional acceptance of her. To Jared, Sarah was a person of value, and she knew it. She felt safe with him. They were like iron sharpening iron, keeping each other alive, thinking, challenging, and staving off loneliness.

Although tears glistened in Sarah's eyes whenever she felt things deeply, Jared never looked at her as being emotionally weak. She never took on the mold of her circumstances; rather, she shaped them. He liked that; he liked strong women. Thankful that his attraction to her wasn't sexual, Jared simply enjoyed Sarah as a friend.

Right now, Jared could see his friend was hurting. "You're remembering Leah, aren't you?"

"Yes," Sarah paused. Then forcing a smile, she nodded her head, "After all this time, you'd think I could light the candles without crying, wouldn't you?"

"Yes, I guess I would. At least from a man's standpoint. But I wasn't Leah's mother, and I didn't hold her as she died."

"I think it's hard because Leah died the very day the temple was taken back."

Sarah turned back to the menorah again. Lifting her finger, she caught the melting wax from the eighth candle. Her words were almost inaudible. "A destroyed temple was restored . . . and my restored daughter was destroyed."

Sarah gripped the edge of the table that held the menorah and turned again towards Jared. "The two events are so intertwined. When I light the candles, I remember the restoration of the temple. But when I blow out the one I use to light the others, I remember the light going out in Leah's eyes. And then—" Sarah's voice grew more pensive, "sometimes I remember the blue-green eyes of—"

Sarah stopped in midsentence. Jared waited and watched as Sarah stared into the past. She had mentioned blue-green eyes before. They had been words that slipped out of her mouth then, as they had now. Yet he never felt the freedom to ask why there seemed to be pain connected with the thought of them. He wondered if today he would discover to whom those eyes belonged.

Finally he asked, "Of?"

Jared's inquiry brought Sarah back to the present. Ignoring his question, she smiled and said, "Let's go to the rooftop. From there we can see the Festival of Lights as they celebrate Chanukah in the temple court. That is, unless you want to go to the temple and join in the celebration. Please, don't feel you have to stay here with me."

"I don't feel compelled to do anything, Sarah. We've been friends too long for that. Get a warm wrap—it will be quite cool on the roof."

As they climbed the final steps and stood on the flat roof, Sarah pulled her wool cloak tightly about her and flung the corner of it over her shoulder. Tucking her arms snugly underneath, she hugged her body for further warmth. She then tilted her head back and looked at the sky. Even with Jared beside her, she felt lonely. Or was it empty? Life had become less stressful, but it was not without difficulties. Sarah sighed. *There's always something to deal with.* For a brief moment, Sarah wished Jared had gone to the temple for the lighting of the lamps. She might have liked to be alone.

Jared broke the silence. "I can't get over what an ideal location you have. There is Herod's palace to your back, and the Temple Mount is within walking distance below you. If I remember correctly that's Katros' house, isn't it," Jared pointed to his right, "there, two houses from yours?"

Sarah, somewhat disinterested, looked to where he was pointing and answered, "Yes. Do you know him?"

"No. You know I don't keep company with wealthy priests."

Sarah wanted to be quiet, to think. But if Jared wanted to talk, she'd talk. Jared looked at Katros' house and then to the Temple Mount. "This priest has an ideal view of the temple he serves, doesn't he? Just a short walk through the valley to the lower city and the gate where he enters the temple."

Jared walked to the edge of the roof and looked to the east. "I love this panoramic view from the upper city. You can see the whole Temple Mount from here! Look at the lights, Sarah—notice how they play off the gold columns. They say it's a magnificent sight to stand there when the whole women's court is lit for Chanukah."

"Don't get too close to the edge," said Sarah.

Jared stood for a few moments saying nothing, then he turned back to Sarah. The torches lighting Hippicus, Phasael, and Miriamne—the three towers of Herod's palace, which were named for Herod's friend, brother, and wife—illumined Sarah's stately form in the night, but her face remained shrouded in the shadows.

Jared couldn't tell whether Sarah's tears were gone. He didn't want her thinking about Leah tonight. He knew she probably preferred to be alone, but tonight he wasn't going to let Sarah have her way. "When Herod raised the Temple Mount and rebuilt the temple, he made the Kidron Valley seem even deeper, didn't he?"

Sarah went to her chair and sat down as she answered, "You don't realize how deep it seems until you stand at the pinnacle of the temple. Didn't they say the height of the temple platform has to be about fifteen to twenty fathoms?"

"Forty-five," Jared answered. "He's not called 'Herod the Great' for nothing! He doesn't like to build anything small. Look at what he's done at Masada and Herodium. Those fortresses are incredible. But the temple and its platform has to be the greatest of his feats. They say some—at least one—of the stones he used were over five fathoms long and might have weighed over one hundred tons! When Herod builds something, his workmanship shows. Every one of his stones—even the bedrock on which he built the Temple Mount—is edged in the same way. Unless you look carefully, you can't see where the temple bedrock ends and the cut stones begin!"

"Herod has imitated the Roman overlords," Sarah rebuffed. "He wants to be the greatest patron of architecture in the eastern Roman Empire! I don't care what he did for our temple; he's an egotistical maniac. I don't like the man. In fact, I abhor him. I don't even like to acknowledge that he built the temple."

"That's a pretty strong case of dislike, isn't it, Sarah? This temple is a worthy rival of Solomon's. It's certainly far greater than our own rebuilding efforts!"

"It may be a worthy rival, Jared, but Solomon's temple wasn't built with bloody hands. Solomon was a man of peace. He had clean hands. Herod's are stained. Don't let yourself think for one moment that our temple was rebuilt by that man out of any motive other than pride and an attempt to win our loyalty —to prove his so-called Jewishness. Remember, the man is an Idumean! He wasn't born a Jew. You know that the Idumeans were given the choice of either converting to Judaism or being put to death! I wish Herod hadn't converted."

Sarah rose from her chair and crossed her arms underneath her wrap. She began pacing the roof. "Herod the Great? No, Jared, he is Herod the Gory!"

"You're right. He is also a hypocrite," said Jared. "He wears his Jewish mask when he's on stage with the Jews, and he switches to his Roman face when he deals with Rome."

"That's an apt description!" Sarah replied. "No true Jew would do as this upstart foreigner has done. He not only built our temple, he also built temples to pagan gods! He even dedicated some of them to Octavian, who declared himself, of all things, *Augustus* Caesar! Herod knows how to elicit the favor of Rome. He does it by keeping things quiet in Judea, taxing us to death, giving Rome its stipend, building monuments, and then naming them after the Romans! It makes me angry. Even our port city—their 'Roman playground' on *our* soil—is named Caesarea!"

"How do you feel, Sarah, with Herod's citadel and the Tower of Mariamne overshadowing your home? Do you think Herod really thought that marrying Mariamne would make him more acceptable to us? All because she is from the house of the old priest Mattathias?"

"You know, of course, the reason he is so despised by many," Sarah said, her voice beginning to rise. "It's not because he's a despicable ruler. It's because of his half-hearted attitude towards Judaism and his brutality towards his own family. How can a man kill his own friends? His own flesh and blood? His *wife*? Mariamne—or Miriam—whichever you want to call her—was the one and only woman he truly loved. Yet he killed her out of jealousy!"

Sarah was angry now, her voice projecting a little louder. "And according to all reports, he had not found her unfaithful but only feared she would be! Can you imagine? Jared, the man is insane. He's had ten wives. He can't find a woman to fill the void Mariamne left. His emotions range from the brightness of noonday to the darkness of a starless night. He even keeps vacillating over which of his sons is to be his successor. For a while it's Alexander and Aristobulus, Mariamne's sons. Then it's Antipater, the son of his first wife Doris."

"I think Herod's remorse over killing Mariamne made him ill," Jared interjected.

"That, and his heavy drinking. Of course, the drinking started after he murdered Mariamne. How many of his family members and friends has he put to death?"

"I don't know. Who knows what happened to those who were taken to his fortress in the Judean wilderness? None of them have ever been seen or heard from again."

For a moment, they both paused in silence, almost spent by their indignation. Sarah stepped over to the side of the roof and looked at the three towers rising above Herod's palace. They rose like sentinels of the night keeping guard over her city, not so much to protect it as to keep it subservient to Rome. Sarah was still and again the conquered—the vassal of now another power. If she had taken time to think about it, she would have recognized Rome as the fourth power, the fourth kingdom—just as Daniel foretold. Instead, she busied herself with thoughts about the course of events since the Maccabean revolt.

The reign of the Maccabees, or the Hasmoneans as they were called, came to an end because of power and greed. The conflict between Hyrcanus and Aristobulus for the Hasmonean lands had given Pompey, the Roman general, the excuse he needed to take Jerusalem because both Hyrcanus and Aristobulus turned to Rome for help in overpowering the other.

Rome had chosen to side with Hyrcanus, the weaker of the two. His weakness made him easier to handle. When Pompey entered Jerusalem, Aristobulus fled to the temple, which at the time was built like a fortress. Aristobulus had possession of the temple for only three months before Pompey seized it. Out of pure curiosity Pompey had walked right into the Holy of Holies. Although he didn't touch a thing, Sarah found it hard to forgive his sacrilege and Rome's invasion of her land.

The carnage that resulted from Pompey's invasion of Jerusalem was sickening. About 12,000 people had died, yet not all of them at the hands of this pompous general and the infamous short two-edged swords of the Romans.

Some were killed by their fellow Jews and others took their own lives by throwing themselves off the high temple wall. After Pompey, Herod became the ruler over the Jewish people and eventually came to bear the title Herod, King of the Jews.

Even though they had fared better under Herod than they had under the corrupt Hasmoneans, Sarah still abhorred Herod.

Jared watched as the lights on the Temple Mount were extinguished. "Happy Chanukah, Sarah."

As Sarah walked down the stairway to go back into the house, she whispered under her breath, "Hardly, Jared, hardly. And I don't know if it ever will be any different."

Unbeknownst to Sarah, there was another who had been born near Jerusalem who bore the title King of the Jews. It was yet another king who would bring her great grief . . . and a stigma that would become a curse wherever she went.

Chapter 28

*T*he day was magnificent! The earth was dressed in cheerfulness as the sun unabashedly spilled her glory on grass, flowers, and trees. Its brilliance heightened the senses and delighted the eyes. Against heaven's backdrop of crystal-blue sky the waving leaves on the trees looked like silver as the wind shook them with gentle playfulness. Red and purple flowers cloistered together in random patches across the fresh green carpet thrown over the hills surrounding Bethlehem Ephrathah. Every now and then, one would see the flowers dancing with the wind.

Sarah was glad to be out of Jerusalem and away from the Roman architecture as well as the Roman soldiers. She wanted to forget the golden eagle Herod had mounted on the temple. For a few hours, maybe days, if Rachel would let her, Sarah could have a respite from this cosmopolitan city of intrigue.

The songs of the birds, songs without lyrics, were soothing. They were a pleasant change from the shrill, clucking tongues of Jerusalem's hens scratching through the latest gossip and pecking at any tidbit of news. The women of the city loved to speculate about Herod. *Why did he do this? Why did he do that? Who will take Herod's place should he not recover, but die? What will happen to his sister? His mother?* And so on.

By now Sarah had arrived at the outskirts of her destination. *What a perfect day to come to Bethlehem!* She hugged herself in delight and then reached down and patted her faithful donkey. "Aren't you glad we came alone? We have been able to travel in silence without me having to scream at you because of people talking, talking, *talking* all the way to Bethlehem."

Sarah could feel the tension leaving her muscles. The sun not only made everything pretty, it also warmed and relaxed her. Every now and then she'd slip down from the donkey and walk a distance. Stretching her legs. Feeling good.

Oh Rachel, please be home! Don't run away on this beautiful day as I have done. I need companionship, my friend—I need it desperately. And I want to hold your new son. I need to hold a baby in my arms.

As soon as Sarah had received word that her distant cousin, Rachel, had given birth to a baby boy, she began making plans to come and visit. Although they didn't see each other often and Rachel was quite a few years younger, there was a special bond between them. When Rachel and Sarah saw each other, it didn't matter how much time had passed; they took up right where they left off.

There was no hesitation, no awkward feeling of adjustment.

Sarah and Rachel never had need to explain themselves. Nor was there any resentment because too much time had passed since the last visit. The women simply enjoyed each other's company. Whenever. Wherever. They were always on equal ground. Status, possessions, female pettiness which brought schisms among many so-called friends had no place in their relationship.

Judging from the angle of the sun, it was mid-afternoon when Sarah arrived in Bethlehem—a village close enough to Jerusalem that sometimes, on a clear night, Sarah could see its lights from the mountains surrounding the city. Bethlehem was a nondescript but friendly little village inhabited by innkeepers, a few enterprising merchants, and shepherds. Countless sheep etched an account of their wanderings in the contours of the hillsides as they grazed the lands surrounding the town.

Although Bethlehem was little and seemingly insignificant, it was the city of David. Her inhabitants were proud of this designation. In David rested the hope of the ages; according to Micah the prophet, someday Messiah would be born here and rule the earth from Zion. No longer would their nation be the tail ruled over by the nations! And it seemed that as the oppression of Rome grew, so also did the talk of Messiah's coming.

That Messiah would spring forth from Bethlehem sparked an added pride in the Bethlehemites. It also helped the discerning listener evaluate the validity of the claims being made by an ever-increasing number of self-proclaimed messiahs moving throughout the land.

As Sarah made her way into the village, she spotted Rachel talking with some other women. Rachel was slight of build compared to Sarah—a bubbly little woman, happy with life, delightful to be with, and easy to look at. Her eyes danced with joy. No matter what the situation, Rachel always seemed to find something of redemptive value.

People enjoyed being around Rachel. She was pretty and neat. Her long brown hair was woven into a single braid. According to Rachel, this made it easier to care for and easier to keep clean, especially when the winds from the Judean desert blew sand their way. When that happened, everything was blanketed with dust!

As Sarah came up behind Rachel, she could see the wiggly little baby on her shoulder. *It must be Joseph!*

Eager to see them both, Sarah called out, "Rachel! Rachel!"

Rachel turned and frowned, squinting from the sun. "Yes?" she replied quizzically as she shaded her eyes with her free hand.

"Rachel, it's me. . . ."

Before Sarah could even say her name, Rachel recognized her visitor and called out with great joy, "Sarah! Sarah, of all people! What are you doing here?" Rachel walked toward Sarah as quickly as she could.

Sarah's veil dropped from around her head as she cupped her friend's face in her hands and kissed her on each cheek. Tears splashed with joy from Sarah and Rachel's eyes. Half laughing and half crying, they were oblivious to the chatter of the two women Rachel had been talking with.

"Let me have him," Sarah said as she wrinkled her nose at the baby and wiggled her fingers, beckoning him to come to her. Although Joseph had just dozed off in the warmth of the sun and the security of his mother's arms, he obligingly broke out in a toothless grin. Squinching his little eyes, his chunky arms and legs went into spastic contortions as he tried desperately to squeeze some audible expression of delight out of his tiny, pursed lips.

"Here, take him. You've won him already. You always did have a charming way with men, and I can see he's taken with you." Rachel passed her bundle to Sarah, then turned to her friends, who were waiting a little distance away and seemed too shy to join Rachel and Sarah. "I'm coming, I'm coming," she called.

Sarah raised her head abruptly and looked at the women still standing where Rachel had left them. "Oh, I'm sorry! I didn't realize I had taken you from your friends. I'll be fine with the baby; you go on and talk to them." Sarah looked back at Joseph, who by now was contentedly cuddled in her arms. Rachel hurried back to her friends to explain who Sarah was.

With Joseph in her arms, Sarah became lost in memories of years past. Buried memories. Memories that had, up to now, remained unearthed.

In a moment, Rachel was back at Sarah's side. "Forgive me, Sarah. I just wanted to tell them who you are. That my distant cousin, whom I adore, has granted me the favor of a visit."

Rachel put her arm around Sarah's waist and leaned her head on Sarah's shoulder. "I can't believe you're here!" It was then that Rachel noticed Sarah wasn't paying attention—as if she had been transported somewhere else, leaving her earthly shell behind. "Sarah? Where are you, my friend? Are you all right?"

Sarah shook her head as if to bring herself back to the present. "Yes, yes, I'm fine. It's just that—well, I was so shocked when I turned Joseph away from the blinding glare of the sun and saw his eyes. . . ."

"Can you believe it? We were shocked, too. Reuben says there must have been someone in our lineage that had blue-green eyes." Rachel slipped her arm through Sarah's and continued talking without missing a beat. "Come on, let's go in. I'll fix us something to eat. I just made some fresh bread, and Reuben brought home a honeycomb yesterday. It's good! Chewy and sweet. Are you tired?"

"A little, but it's a good feeling—a refreshing kind of tired."

Rachel stopped and looked at Sarah. "Do you want me to take Joseph out of your arms? He's a heavy little sack of barley!"

"Do you mind if I hold him just a little while longer? He's sound asleep." Sarah took her finger and ever so lightly stroked his hairline. Joseph never moved.

"Fine with me. I'll pour us a little wine to go with our bread and honey. Will you be all right here in the courtyard?"

"Of course. I'll just sit here and close my eyes for a little while."

Rachel talked all the way into the kitchen. "That's fine. Get your rest while you can. We have much to talk about, my friend. Wait until you hear about what happened, right here in Bethlehem around the same time Joseph was born. This little village really got stirred up!"

Sarah looked at her surroundings as Rachel busied herself. Rachel and Reuben lived very simple lives, yet she could see Rachel's love of beauty everywhere. Two sides of the courtyard were closed in by walls: one in front and one to the left side of the doorway. The other two sides were bordered by rooms: two on the right side of the doorway for living and sleeping, then a long narrow room (their kitchen and storage area) at the far end of the courtyard opposite the entrance. Everything except for one of the walls was connected by a covered walkway to protect the family as they moved from room to room during the former and latter rains.

Clay pots, some spilling over with flowers and others filled with fragrant herbs, and a small grape arbor overhead made Sarah feel like she had found her own little Garden of Eden.

The early evening sunlight streamed through the leaves and gayly bathed the flowers and pots in a golden glow. Somewhere nearby, a happy bird was singing to its heart's content.

Sarah drew Joseph tighter to her breast. She closed her eyes, leaned back, and for a moment chose to forget that Joseph wasn't hers. And that her husband, who fathered their son with the blue-green eyes, wouldn't be coming home that night. . . .

Chapter 29

*T*he crowing of an exuberant rooster somewhere in the village succeeded in waking Sarah long enough for her to roll over on her mat. She raised her head for a moment to listen for anyone moving about. Hearing nothing, she covered her head and went back to sleep. She was tired, for she had stayed up talking with Rachel long after Reuben had gone to bed.

Rachel woke up with Reuben and fed Joseph. Then, wrapping Joseph nice and tight so he'd feel secure, Rachel tucked him close to her side and drifted back to sleep. How much more she slept, she didn't know. Judging from the sunlight in the courtyard, it was well into the morning when she awoke again and carefully slipped off the bedding so she wouldn't wake her contented son. Rachel wanted time to talk more with Sarah; she sensed there was something Sarah needed to tell her—something about one of her children.

Sarah felt someone stroking her hair. The light touch felt so good that she almost purred like a cat. She loved having someone run their fingers through her hair. Opening one eye, she saw Rachel and thought, *My gentle, delightful friend! Why have I stayed away so long? I need the companionship of a woman like you—secure and content in yourself and with yourself.*

"I think we better get up, my friend, and enjoy another beautiful sunny day. If you get up now, Sarah, I promise we'll go to bed earlier tonight. At least if Reuben has his way," Rachel laughed. "He likes to go to sleep with me in his arms. I'm his pillow."

Sarah turned on her back and stretched. "Was he upset when you didn't come to bed right away?"

"No, not upset," Rachel answered, "just lonely. He's a dear, really. It's just that he knows what it takes for me to get everything done each day. And with Joseph now—"

"It takes even longer, doesn't it?" Sarah yawned and stretched again. Then she rolled onto her abdomen and propped her chin on her hands. "Rachel, for all our talking last night, you forgot to tell me what happened in Bethlehem when Joseph was born. I remembered that right after you went to bed. I was tempted to get you to come back and tell me, but I was afraid I'd wake Reuben. I didn't want him sending me back to Jerusalem. I love this quiet little village."

"I did forget to tell you about the excitement we had in Bethlehem, didn't I?" Rachel tossed her head back, causing her braid to drop into a straight line between her small shoulders. Although the long braid didn't seem to go with her petite frame, the little curls clustered at her temples and the nape of her neck offset its severity and gave a sense of soft femininity that complimented her gentle spirit. "Believe me, I didn't intend to forget. Quiet little Bethlehem was all astir. . . ."

Sarah sat up, drew her knees to her chest, and wrapped her arms around her legs. Resting her chin on her knees, she looked at Rachel.

Rachel continued, "Remember when Caesar Augustus sent out the decree that he wanted a census of all the inhabited earth?"

"Yes, I remember. It was the first census taken when Quirinius was governor of Syria."

Rachel frowned. "I don't remember about Quirinius. Anyway, a baby was born here in Bethlehem during the time of the census. The birth of this little one stirred up a lot of excitement. Shepherds came in from the fields saying they had seen angels who told them that . . . uh, I know this is going to sound crazy, but that this baby was the Messiah!"

"You don't believe that, do you Rachel? Reuben doesn't believe it, does he?" Sarah lowered her knees, tucked her feet underneath her, and came to full attention. "It couldn't have been the Messiah. Surely I would have known about that."

"Sarah, we don't believe the baby was the Messiah any more than we believe our Joseph is the Messiah."

"That's what I thought. And if you'd been convinced, I know you would have let me know immediately. At least I hope you would have."

"I would have. Anyway," Rachel continued, "it was just a day or so around the time Joseph was born. I don't remember exactly because it happened months ago. Also, I had a hard time giving birth; Joseph was so big he wore me out. But that's not the whole tale. Just a number of days ago—maybe ten days, something like that—some men from the East showed up. Magi, they called themselves. Right here in Bethlehem! Asking where they could find the one who was born 'King of the Jews.'"

"Rachel," Sarah hesitated. "The news about the arrival of those wise men spread across Jerusalem like a field of dry grain caught fire. They visited Jerusalem—perhaps before they ever came here. They were looking for someone they called the King of the Jews. Of course, Herod was on that bit of news immediately because *he* is the King of the Jews."

"Yes," said Rachel. "The word of someone else laying claim to Herod's title was quite disturbing to him. The man is insanely jealous and suspicious when it comes to his position. That's why I simply dismissed it all. There are so many self-proclaimed messiahs around these days we could have our pick. But I wouldn't choose any of them. The ones I've seen aren't capable enough to establish any kingdom. Anyway, I heard that Herod asked to see them . . . the Magi, not the Messiah."

Sarah couldn't help smiling at Rachel's last remark. "Did the Magi find this baby? Did you see the Magi?"

"Only from a distance. I don't know if they saw the baby or not. All I know is the men left Bethlehem, and so did the parents and the baby. Where the family went I don't know. Some people said they went to Egypt, but I'm not sure anyone really knows. The visit from the Magi stirred a lot of excitement. Things like that usually happen in Jerusalem, not here."

Rachel paused and looked off into the distance. Then she spoke again, this time more slowly, "It was exciting, but I have to admit it was also a little unsettling. What do you think, Sarah?"

"I think I hear Joseph," Sarah said, rising up to stand. "And I think I better get some relief."

Rachel blushed and was on her feet immediately. "Oh, I'm so sorry! Please forgive me. I'll get Joseph. You know where. . . ." Rachel trailed off.

Sarah smiled and nodded.

Rachel went to pick up Joseph and called back to Sarah, "When you're ready I'll have some bread and cheese and olives for us in the courtyard." Rachel had to raise her voice to be heard over the squirming little bundle perched on her shoulder. Joseph's whimpering became more pronounced as he fought to get his fist in his mouth. "I'll feed this starving one while you eat. Although you aren't letting it be known like Joseph, I'm sure you must be hungry."

"You're right; I am." Sarah slipped on her sandals. "I'll be right back to help you."

"What did you say? I can't hear you," Rachel shouted from the kitchen.

Within a moment Sarah arrived at the doorway of the cooking room. Her presence went unnoticed and for a moment Sarah enjoyed watching her friend as she moved about her little domain. Rachel was humming softly as she kneeled on the floor before the stone and clay stove. Two blackened pots sat on the stove; under them, the embers of the fire barely glowed. By now Joseph had finally found his fist and had contented himself with sucking on what looked like three of his pudgy little fingers.

With Joseph still on her shoulder, Rachel eased her freshly baked bread out of the cylindrical clay oven sitting on the back of the stove. The fire in the oven had given the bread a nice brown crust, which Sarah could hardly wait to coat with honey. Meanwhile she inhaled the fragrant aroma of baked bread, which by now had filled the room. Sarah noticed that to the left of the oven there were a number of clay jugs leaning against the wall. In the midst of them was a clay pot with a lush green vine adorned by red and purple flowers that gave the room a bright, cheery look.

Remembering that Rachel hadn't heard her last words, Sarah began to repeat, "I said—"

"Oh!" Rachel shrieked, turning around quickly. She hadn't realized that Sarah was watching.

Sarah covered her mouth with her hand, trying to suppress a laugh. "I'm sorry. . . ."

"You should be!" Rachel said, her heart still beating quickly. "You know I scare easily."

"Yes, I know, but it's been so long that I forgot. Forgive me. I was just enjoying watching you be a mother and a keeper of your home."

"You're forgiven," Rachel said as she rose from the floor. "Here, take Joseph for a minute while I take care of the bread. I put it in the oven when I got up with Reuben this morning."

"Good, I've been longing to hold him again," said Sarah as Rachel handed Joseph to her. "Come here, you precious one!" Sarah lifted him high and rocked him back and forth. She loved to watch his lips move from a trembling little pout to a smile and see his blue-green eyes light up with delight. Finally unable to resist the urge, Sarah smothered Joseph in her bosom as she hugged him tightly. "I could squeeze and squeeze and squeeze you and kiss and kiss and kiss you!"

Joseph cooed and giggled as Sarah kissed and played with him while she walked around the cooking room. Then, still holding Joseph, Sarah peered into various pots and ran her fingers over the stone mortarium where Rachel crushed the grain into flour. Joseph's chubby hands flailed in the air until he caught some of her hair and tried to put it into his mouth.

"Sarah, I can't get over your infatuation with Joseph. It's funny, but I don't remember you being especially excited about babies."

"I'm changing, Rachel, I'm changing. . . ."

The sudden pounding on the door caused both of them to jump in alarm. They recovered quickly and laughed. Sarah, pointing her finger at Rachel, said, "I'm as bad as you, Rachel! Why don't I go see who's at the door while you finish getting things ready."

Joseph started crying. Sarah pulled him closer to her, patted his back, kissed his soft little cheek, and talked to him as she walked across the courtyard. "There, there, precious one, there's nothing to be frightened about. You're safe right here in your Aunt's arms. That's what you're going to call me—Aunt Sarah. We're going to play some more, in just a moment."

"Bring the tray out here," Sarah shouted to Rachel over the loud pounding.

Sarah was startled when she opened the door. The Roman soldier filling the entryway was the last thing she had expected to see. He stood poised to knock again. Because Sarah's mood had been so gay and lighthearted, she almost laughed. Now she knew why the knocking was loud and impatient.

The man standing before her looked as strong as his knocking—and as irritable. The eyes peering from beneath his Roman helmet were sullen and cold. As Sarah glanced into them for but a moment, she became frightened. There was a foreboding air about him.

Sarah, who didn't usually get intimidated, broke off her gaze and, looking for refuge, turned her eyes to the floor, taking in his leather breastplate, short skirt, and sandaled feet. When she looked at his feet, she involuntarily let out a little scream. Her left hand quickly flew to her mouth as she took a step back. At the same moment, from somewhere unknown, Sarah heard another scream—a heart-wrenching scream filled with terror and magnified a hundred times louder than hers.

Instantly, Sarah lifted her head upward. The scream hadn't come from behind her. Where did it come from? She couldn't see past the barrier of flesh blocking the door. *What's happening?* Fright filled Sarah's eyes as they returned to the soldier's feet, taking in again what seemed like blood spattered in the dirt.

Sarah then moved her gaze up the soldier's left side, where she saw a blood-covered two-edged sword hanging in his hand. The hair on the calf of his leather-laced leg was red. His grip on the sword was so firm that his white knuckles looked like snowcapped mountains jutting from rivers of engorged blue veins.

Is he in pain? Has he been injured? Does he need help? Is that why he's here? For a brief moment Sarah's questions calmed her fear. But then her eyes darted to his face again. *No, he's all right. He's just horribly angry.* Sarah drew back, bracing herself with her free hand on the door.

"Is your baby a boy?" The soldier snarled.

"Yes, he's a boy, but—but he's not mine," Sarah stammered.

This time the soldier barked loud enough for anyone in the house to hear. "Are there any other male children under two years in this house?" More screams from somewhere in the neighborhood caused Sarah's heart to pound. Then Joseph began to wail. Sarah wanted to stuff her fingers in Joseph's mouth, cover him up, cause him to disappear. *Surely my heart's going to burst through my chest!* Was she going to faint? *I mustn't faint. I can't faint. I'll drop Joseph.*

Suddenly Rachel was behind her, the smell of bread still on her hands. She yelled at the soldier, crying, "What do you want? What are you doing here? Get out! Get out!"

Rachel gently pulled Joseph from Sarah's arms. Shielding him from the visitor, she pushed against the soldier's leather breastplate. "Get out, I said!"

The soldier didn't budge as this little woman shoved against him. He simply yelled back at her above all the other noise. "Where are the rest of your children?" He could feel himself getting hotter. He *gave* orders to civilians; he didn't take them. He wanted to blow on this feather of a woman and send her flying through the air. To slap the other woman and send her spinning to the ground.

To shut them up. He'd had enough screaming women for one day. He was trained to fight men, who usually died silently, valiantly. Besides, he was hungry, and when he was hungry he was always more irritable.

Sensing her impotence, Rachel began screaming hysterically. "Get out of here. Get out of here! There are no children in this home—"

"What do you call this?" he said as he grabbed Joseph's arm, wrenching him from the shelter of his mother's side, pulling him out of his wrap.

The little cloth tucked between Joseph's legs fell to the ground of the courtyard as his soft, dimpled body dangled in the air.

"A Jew boy! A little circumcised Jew baby!" exclaimed the soldier. Laughing, he threw little Joseph into the air. Sarah saw the little child's blue-green eyes pop wide open in terror. Just as Sarah emitted another scream and lunged to catch Joseph, the soldier's hairy hand reached up and grabbed the baby by the nape of his neck—as if he were a kitten.

"Death to every male two years and under by order of Herod, King of the Jews," said the soldier without emotion.

As he brought up his sword toward Joseph's heart, Rachel grabbed the soldier's arm, dug in her heels, and pulled with all her might. She screamed at the top of her lungs, "Reuben! No! No!" Rachel's diminutive form was no match for this trained Roman arm that had manned heavy battering rams.

Sarah watched in patent terror as the short sword went straight through Joseph's soft little body and the light went out in his blue-green eyes. "Benjamin!" she screamed. "Benjamin!"

The last thing Sarah remembered seeing before she passed out was blue-green eyes staring at her through flames.

The soldier callously, deliberately opened his fingers and dropped Joseph's body to the ground. Having freed his hand, he backhanded Rachel, knocking her out. Rachel's fingers loosened their grip and slowly slid from his arm as she fell to the floor. Stepping over her, the soldier of Rome walked into the kitchen. His sword remained in his left hand, leaving a trail of bright clear infant blood. He picked up the bread, took a large bite of it, threw the rest down, picked up the cheese, and walked out.

All over Bethlehem that day rose the sound of Rachel "bitterly weeping for her children"—just as Jeremiah the prophet had foretold.

Chapter 30

*T*he atmosphere was charged. People jostled their way into Jerusalem to celebrate the Passover. The talk was not of family, friends, business, nor the holiday, but of the death of Herod, the King of the Jews.

"I wish we'd chosen a different time to leave Bethlehem," Rachel said as she watched Reuben maneuver their cart through the clusters of people who had suddenly stopped to loudly debate some issue. Reuben had been hit several times already by gesticulating arms waving wildly in the air to make a point. All their temporal possessions were in the cart. *How gladly I would abandon them all, Rachel thought, just to see my Joseph happily perched in this cart.*

Emotions ran high on the crowded road. All but Reuben and Rachel's. They felt only exhaustion as they trudged into Jerusalem. Reuben was sullen, silent. He had a rope tied around himself like a harness, taking the place of the mule he had sold. Rachel followed at the back of the cart, pushing. She bent her head low, hoping to hide the tears that came as she recounted how she and Reuben had tenderly washed the hardened blood from their son's ashen body. They had covered him with kisses, rinsing his precious little form in their tears. Then they had wrapped his little body and lovingly placed it in a small stone sarcophagus . . . and somewhere in Joseph's graveclothes, their hearts were lost and buried as well.

Although Reuben walked in silence and would not allow himself to be drawn into conversation, he forced himself to listen to what was being said by others who were journeying to Jerusalem. It helped take his mind off Joseph. How many times had he recalled coming upon Rachel stumbling through the village with Joseph in her arms . . . soaked with blood, weeping in despair, calling out his name? Reuben had already dropped his tools and was running toward home panicked because he had heard the sound of wailing from so many different houses in the village. The two had met each other halfway between their home and the shop where he worked.

The talk of Herod's death continued. "They say Herod's son Archelaus put his father's body on a real golden bier and carried him all the way to Herodium where he put his father to rest. It was quite a spectacle."

Reuben looked at the intent old man with a pinched face as he described the magnificence of Herod's funeral and thought to himself, *If Archelaus gave his father that kind of a funeral, then it was only right I should pay whatever money it took to put our Joseph in a proper sarcophagus.* Because the burial had taken more money than they could afford, he and Rachel had quite a discussion about it.

Reuben wanted Rachel to accept that he was right in doing what he did— spending money they really didn't have. He needed her assurance that some of his decisions were right. He felt burdened by the guilt he had imposed upon himself for being away when the soldier came to the door. Reuben believed he could have spared Joseph's life. He just knew Joseph would still be alive had he been there. He shouldn't have gone to work that day. He should have stayed home with Rachel and Sarah.

Reuben's thinking, of course, was irrational, and Rachel would have gladly told him so. But Reuben never shared his pain with Rachel. He found that it took too much effort to talk.

Ahead in the distance, they could see the temple. The sight of it spurred discussions about Herod's infamous act of mounting a golden eagle on the temple's main gate. Every Jew walking through the gate was rankled by the sight of this graven image hovering above their holy precinct. Especially troubled were two distinguished-looking rabbis in the crowd, who would not let the matter drop!

"I'm telling you, it's not the rabbis' fault. They are teachers; they are leaders of the righteous. They have a right to call upon their students to tear down the eagle!" As he spoke, the young man tapped his own chest as if to strengthen his point as he fired out his defense. "I'd be worried if my rabbi just sat around saying nothing about this abomination, not calling us to take a stand. It's an idol! The eagle is an idol! Rome's idol. Didn't Moses write in the Torah that we're not to make any graven image of *anything* in the heavens above, the earth beneath, or under the earth?"

"I know, I know, but to risk their lives—" the pinched little man replied.

"But," the young one retorted, exasperated with the old man because he didn't seem to understand, "the rabbis thought Herod was about to die! They didn't know he was going to live long enough to burn them alive!"

A third man spoke. His speech was thicker than the others. Reuben didn't know who it was. Nor would he turn his head to see. It took too much effort. Besides, he didn't want to be drawn into the conversation. "Herod didn't burn them all. Some were allowed to live. I think only the rabbis and the students who actually climbed to the roof of the temple, dismantled the eagle, and threw it to the ground were burned."

"Didn't he also burn those who hacked the golden eagle to pieces?" the young man asked.

The man with the thick speech answered, "I don't know. All I know is if Herod had been a true Jew, a Jew in his heart, he never would have put such an abominable thing on the gate to our holy place. It was probably worth dying for, because the eagle wasn't put back up."

"And," the young man chimed in, "if Herod our so-called 'king' had really cared about us, he wouldn't have burned them alive."

"Herod care!" The man with the pinched face spat on the ground. "If he cared, he would have gone ahead and died. Instead, despite the gravity of his illness, he deposed the high priest and condemned others to be burned alive. That was on March thirteenth. Then what does the man do? He goes to seek relief from his own pain in the warm springs across the Jordan. Concerned about his own pain, but not the pain of others! Give me Messiah!"

Reuben turned to his left to see what Rachel was doing; he didn't want her hearing all this. It was on the thirteenth of March that they had decided they couldn't stay in Bethlehem any longer. The sight of the other mothers and fathers whose children had been murdered was too much. Whenever they met the parents of a murdered son, they lived and relived the event—with all its "if onlys." They could not bear to relive it again. Nor could they bear, one more time, to hear that the little baby whom Herod so wanted to destroy had been taken down to Egypt before the soldiers ever arrived in Bethlehem. Over and over they asked each other why Herod hadn't sent a search party to find the baby before he sought to blindly purge Bethlehem of the one who supposedly contested his title King of the Jews.

"Did you know that only five days before his death, Herod changed his will to divide his realm between his sons Antipas, Philip, and Archelaus as well as to order the death of his son Antipater?" The young man walked backwards as he questioned the others.

Reuben wondered if this young man was close to the age of any of the sons Herod had killed. In vexation, he shook his head. *How could any man kill his own son? How could a person who was about to die wish death on one who had not even begun to live? How could any man willfully snuff out the life of his son . . . his friends . . . his wife?* Reuben looked back and caught Rachel's eye. She was at the rear of the cart, pushing with both hands as she talked with a woman holding a baby. He motioned to her with his head to join him.

As she came up beside him, he reached over and took Rachel's hand. Drawing her to his side, he sheltered her under his arm and whispered, "I love you, Rachel. We'll have another child. Not to replace our Joseph, but to add to our family."

Rachel stopped, halting Reuben at the same time. Standing on tiptoe, she looked around to make sure no one was watching them. Then she kissed Reuben just above his beard on the tip of his right cheekbone and quietly said, "Maybe it will be a son . . . another with blue-green eyes." Then with her hand she turned his face towards hers and, not letting go, looked directly into his brown, almost black eyes. She whispered, "It would give me great comfort if we would begin tonight. I've missed your arms . . . my head between your shoulders. We've not drawn close to each other for too long in our sorrow, my husband."

Chapter 31

*S*arah was adamant, determined to have her way. "Reuben, I really want you and Rachel to move in with me. I don't want you to give me a thing except the joy of your presence. I won't have it any other way!"

"But Sarah. . . ." Reuben protested.

Jared smiled as he watched Sarah in action. He knew Reuben's resistance would be useless. Jared had never met a stronger, more determined woman.

"Reuben, it doesn't have to be a permanent arrangement. Just stay with me . . . while we all get over what happened. We need each other. Besides, it would be so wonderful to have a man around the house."

"But what if your husband should return?"

"I wish he would, but from what I understand, he won't be coming back for a while. And if he does show up, then you and Rachel can make arrangements to move to another place. But, of course, not until you've found just the right place. You needn't worry."

"I'm not worried about—"

"Besides, Reuben," Sarah wasn't going to give up, "you don't know Jerusalem that well. You're just getting settled; you're starting anew more or less. Please," Sarah clasped her hands together, "please let me help you in this way, and you will help me by staying here and keeping me company. I'll give you privacy. . . ."

Reuben looked at Jared sitting in the corner on the couch and shrugged his shoulders in a man-to-man sort of way. Jared liked this stocky young man with the black hair and deep-set dark eyes shaded by heavy brows.

Sarah said Reuben's eyes were a greenish black, but Jared didn't see any green in them. He noted that Reuben was taller than Rachel, but about the same height as Sarah. His face was full—*broad, that was it!*—giving the impression it had been roughly chiseled out of granite. Everything about his face spoke of strength: prominent cheekbones, a strong square chin, his beard trimmed short to match the contour of his face. With his curly black hair cropped closely to his head, Reuben would have passed for a Roman soldier had he donned a uniform. Except Reuben didn't project the calloused demeanor of a hardened soldier; rather, his personality seemed to pleasantly match his wife's—in a much quieter version.

From all that Jared had heard from Sarah and from what he'd seen with his own eyes, Reuben and Rachel appeared to be a kind and caring young couple. Sarah hadn't told Jared much about the day their son was thrust through by a Roman sword. It was still too hard for any of them to talk about it. Sarah could feel hysteria rising inside her when she did. Each time she spoke about little Joseph she mentioned his blue-green eyes. But when Sarah came to that point at which the tragedy occurred, she never went any further. Jared would lose her somewhere in time. He usually left then, knowing she had nothing more to say. Sarah simply wanted to be alone and Jared respected that—he left her alone.

Reuben turned and looked at Rachel. "Rachel?"

"I would like to, Reuben, if that's what you want. Maybe until we have another child." Rachel looked at Reuben and winked. Her wink and smile took Reuben by surprise. Rachel had been so somber since Joseph's death. *Maybe this is what she needs—what we all need. O, how I need the wisdom of the Almighty. . . .*

"It would help not to be alone all day long, and. . . ." Rachel walked over to Sarah, gazing at her fondly. Slipping a hand around Sarah's arm, she continued, "Sarah and I have a special friendship but it's one we've never really been able to enjoy as we would have liked. Am I right, Sarah?"

"Yes," Sarah answered, "we haven't—"

Jared interrupted. "I'm from outside the family; I'm just a friend. An advisor, Sarah calls me. But believe me, Reuben, Sarah really wants you. And she needs you, even though she's a strong woman. Please don't think I mean that in the wrong way." Jared looked at Sarah and grinned. "She'll respect your masculinity, Reuben. It's just that the lady is resilient. She's been through a lot—as you probably know—and she's survived. She'll survive now whether or not you live here. It's just that at this time, she told me, having you both around would mean so much to her. As you can see from the house, there's adequate room for the two of you."

Reuben had, in fact, been looking around. He'd never been in a house this nice or large before. The thought of living in such a home and neighborhood was a little overwhelming. He didn't want Rachel to get used to it and become spoiled if he didn't succeed in finding a way to provide enough for them to have a similar home after they left Sarah. Reuben's dream had been to live in lower Jerusalem rather than outside the city walls. But the Upper City, where Sarah lived, had never crossed his mind.

Reuben had been born and raised in Bethlehem. The only time he left his village was when he, along with every other male, as required by the law, traveled to Jerusalem for the feasts of Passover, Pentecost, and Tabernacles. He had never even visited Jerusalem's Upper City!

Reuben liked Jared and felt he could trust him. "Sarah, you have a fine friend and advisor in Jared. And I appreciate the encouragement from you two as well as Rachel. Let me discuss it with Rachel a little more fully tonight. Then I'll give you my decision in the morning, if I may."

Sarah was surprised by Reuben's willingness to even consult Rachel in the matter. Joseph's death *had* changed him. Sarah saw a new respect, an appreciation, a valuing of Rachel, which was unusual among Jewish men. Most Jewish men, especially those who were Pharisees, gave thanks in their prayers that they weren't born as dogs or women. And, it seemed to Sarah, they often treated women accordingly, especially in the rare moments when they were in mixed company.

"Look, Reuben," Jared interrupted, "you and I need to leave right away if you're going to talk to my friend about an apprenticeship. I don't want to walk across the city and not find him at home."

"I'm ready," Reuben answered.

"Please be careful," Sarah's voice was filled with concern. "Watch carefully what you say and whom you talk with. Archelaus may be far from us in Rome securing his position as Herod's successor, but the man has eyes and ears everywhere. There's still much unrest in Jerusalem. I often wonder why we say 'Shalom' when there is so little peace in our city. I'm sure we're going to see that our new ruler Archelaus has all of his father's vices."

"Reuben, do you think you'd better. . . . ?" Rachel moved toward Reuben with extended arms, and as she did so she was struck by her painful memories. She hesitated and buried her face in her hands. Reuben nodded to Sarah with a look that said, *Please take care of her.* "I'll be fine, Rachel. Sarah, please convince her of that."

Sarah moved toward Rachel and embraced her as Reuben hurried out the door.

Reuben still wasn't sure about how to comfort Rachel. *What should I say when she is hurting? How can I soothe her when she is distraught?* That was the reason every night since Joseph's death—except the very first, when they sat huddled weeping in the courtyard—Reuben pretended not to hear her soft cries. Each night when Rachel slid into bed beside him, he lay motionless in an effort to convince her he'd already fallen asleep. It was easier this way, but only for Reuben. He wasn't a talker.

Sarah stood holding Rachel, gently stroking and soothing her. Both women suffered silently for a moment; Rachel was overwhelmed with grief, and Sarah with helplessness. Neither spoke a word. Then Sarah suggested, "Let's go sit on the roof. I could use some sunshine—a change of scenery."

Rachel looked at Sarah pleadingly and said, "Can we talk, Sarah? I need to talk. I don't like feeling this way."

"Of course we can. The men won't be back for a long time," Sarah said as she gently escorted Rachel up the stairs to the roof.

Rachel moved slowly, talking as she climbed. "Reuben won't talk. He just buries it all. But I was there, Sarah. I saw it all from the beginning to the end. If I bury it inside me, the stench of it will make me an angry and bitter woman. It's not good, Sarah, to bury something, to lock it up inside your soul, to hold it captive in leg-irons. If you do you're never free. You're always haunted by its presence."

"Come. Don't stop talking, but sit here."

"No, Sarah. If you don't mind, I need to stand and move. I can't sit right now."

"I don't mind. Please continue. I want to hear what you are saying."

"Where was I?" Rachel asked, a little dazed.

"You were saying that if you kept what happened to Joseph buried inside you, you'd never be free. You'd always be haunted by its presence."

"Yes! You *were* listening, weren't you? Poor Reuben; he just walks away. He wants to *not* discuss it. To forget it. But he doesn't forget, Sarah. He doesn't forget." Rachel paused for a moment and looked at Sarah. "Thank you for listening. Thank you so much, my friend!"

"I'm a friend born for the day of adversity—"

"And Sarah, I am the same kind of friend. I love you. Remember where the Scriptures tell of the love Jonathan had for David? A covenant love that protected and cared...." Rachel paused again. Her eyes searched Sarah's, almost studying her. Then, as if she had made a decision, Rachel walked over to Sarah, knelt before her, and gently placed her hand on Sarah's knee.

"Sarah, you know that I have that kind of love for you, don't you? I care, Sarah, and I feel . . ." Rachel hesitated, then started again. "I feel you need me to care, just as you are caring for me now in my sorrow. You need someone to talk to and to share with. There's something you've buried, isn't there? Something that you've determined not to share with anyone."

Sarah stared at Rachel for a minute. Surprised by the sudden turn of their conversation, she searched Rachel's eyes, looking for trust.

"Sarah," Rachel's words came cautiously, "why were you so fascinated with Joseph's blue-green eyes? Why did you love him so . . . so quickly?"

Sarah didn't say a word. She didn't blink. She kept looking into Rachel's eyes, probing deeply.

Rachel waited.

"His eyes reminded me of someone," Sarah whispered.

"Sarah," Rachel said with great tenderness so as not to scare this little bird sitting before her, head cocked to one side, looking curiously at her, "did you have a son with blue-green eyes?"

Sarah nodded slowly, never taking her eyes away from Rachel's.

"How old was he when he died, Sarah?"

"Two. Two years and nine months and three days. . . ."

"What happened?"

Sarah didn't answer right away. "Rachel, I've never talked about this with anyone—not even my husband." For the first time, Sarah's eyes left Rachel's as she tipped her head back and looked up at the white billowy clouds cozily clumped together in the blue, blue sky. It was a beautiful day. *But should it be beautiful today?* Sarah wondered.

"Rachel, I am not sure if I can tell you. You see, I vowed I'd never tell anyone. That what happened would be forever lost, covered in the sands of time. . . ." Sarah paused.

Rachel waited. Sarah laced her hands together. Resting her chin on them, she drew a mournful sigh. Her eyes were empty, focusing on nothing. Rachel slid off her knees and tucked her feet behind her. This time, Sarah's pause was longer.

Finally Sarah spoke. "Like you said, I'm . . . I'm never free of it. I never know when the memory will come flooding back. When I see his eyes—eyes that never left me until mine deserted his. . . ."

Sarah's chest began to shake. She pursed her lips together tightly. Rachel could hear the air rushing into Sarah's lungs with each spasm of her chest. Her timorous eyes once again searched Rachel's. Rachel wanted to take Sarah into her arms, but she couldn't. Rachel knew she couldn't do anything lest Sarah keep her secret imprisoned in her heart.

Tears filled Sarah's brown, doe-like eyes. They spilled onto her lower lashes and weighed them down until they clung together in her sorrow. The racking, almost silent sobbing increased. Then the dam burst and crashed through the silence with a torrent of words, catching Rachel in their current.

"I offered my son to the gods—to Molech. The priest took him by the hand and walked him up the long stone ramp. He was dressed in a pure white robe I had slipped over his head. The priest took him. I nodded at him and told my son it was all right—not to make a sound, to be strong, to go with the nice man, that he had something he wanted to show him on that big round stone altar. That he was going to see . . . to see . . . to—"

Sarah threw her head back as if to keep the teardrops from falling from her eyes. Then she looked at Rachel again. The tears slipped down her face more rapidly as she asked loudly, "How can I tell you? How can I say it?"

Rachel reached up and gently put her hand over Sarah's pounding fist. "You must say it, Sarah, you must. What was he going to see?"

"The fire!" Sarah shouted. "The pretty fire. . . . Oh Rachel, when the soldier thrust his sword through your Joseph and I saw the life go out of his little blue-green eyes, I saw the flames—*flames!* The flames, Rachel. Benjamin's eyes were wide with fright. He couldn't conceive of what was about to happen. But he trusted me. His Imma was there. . . ." Sarah paused.

"He didn't know the priest who took him by the hand; he didn't know where he was being taken. But he trusted me. He didn't scream. His little lips trembled, but he didn't utter a word. Not a word, Rachel. Not as long as I looked at him," Sarah's words were drawn out slowly as she trembled with anger.

"But then, Rachel . . . I—I turned away! I wanted to run—to get him—to snatch him out of the hands of the priest. But I had sworn by Molech and everyone was watching to see if I would keep my vow. And instead of screaming, instead of stopping it, I turned away."

Sarah's hand grabbed Rachel's and squeezed it tightly, holding it in hers, pounding her lap with it as if to emphasize every word. "Rachel, *I* turned away from my *own* child, my *own* flesh and blood. And the minute I turned my eyes away Benjamin could no longer stand it. He screamed, 'Imma! Imma! Come and get me, Imma!' Then there was silence. Chilling, deadly silence. When I turned back, it was too late. Too late, Rachel. He was in the fire. I saw his blue-green eyes crying in the flames. I know I did. I know I did. . . ."

Rachel gently pulled Sarah into her arms and held her like a little child, rocking her, pushing back the wet hair clinging to her face. Sarah sobbed and sobbed, her tears running down like a fountain. Rachel wept silently with her. Sarah's pain was greater than Rachel's, and Rachel knew it. Joseph had been torn from her side and taken to death against her will. But Benjamin had been offered up to death by the willful consent of his mother.

Sarah stayed in Rachel's arms and continued to weep. Then, seemingly from nowhere, a small dark cloud poured out its grief as the sun crept behind it in sympathy. The rain was warm and gentle, befitting their heartache. For awhile they sat in it. Then when both the cloud and Sarah had shed all the tears they could shed, Sarah rose to her feet and looked at Rachel. She offered her hands to Rachel and reaching down she helped her up, then put her arms around her and held her tight for a long moment. Together they descended the stairs into the house; the only audible sound they heard was that of their long robes quietly dropping onto each step as they descended.

Sarah took Rachel's hand and led her into a bedroom. "This is where you and Reuben can sleep."

Rachel looked up at Sarah as she sat down on the bed. "Thank you for trusting me," Rachel said quietly, gently.

"No . . . thank *you*, my friend, for helping me uncover the ugliness I buried. . . ."

"Sarah, can I ask just one more question?"

"You may ask anything you like. You've heard the worst."

"What did your husband say?"

"Rachel, I've never told him. I couldn't. . . . I stayed away up in the region of Megiddo for days. Then when I came home I told him Benjamin was dead—that someone had captured him and carried him off as a human sacrifice and that he had been burned in a fire."

"Did he believe you?"

"I don't think he did. He questioned me. He urged me to tell the truth and assured me that nothing—absolutely nothing—could keep him from loving me. But I held to my story. All he had was my word. I lied, Rachel! I lied because I could not bear to tell him the truth—to confess my sin, to have him know what really happened, and to risk enduring what the consequence might be even though he said he loved me unconditionally. He wept for days and grieved for years. Sometimes I think it was as much for me as it was for Benjamin, whom he loved so very much."

For a long moment Sarah said nothing more. Then she reached over to caress Rachel's face. "Thank you for loving me unconditionally. I'm certainly not worth it."

"Sarah, it's not a matter of worth. It's a matter of pardon. Of forgiveness for your crime."

"Thank you for calling it what it was—a crime. Intentional murder born out of idolatry. I deserved to die."

"Yes, you did. But you are alive and you are going to live."

Sarah turned and walked towards the door. "Yes, I'll live, but only by my husband's grace."

Sarah paused for a moment, her hand on the latch as she looked back at Rachel. "I only wish I had confessed my sin to my husband and thrown myself on his mercy. I know it would have changed our relationship over the years, and maybe I never would have walked away from him into the arms of another man, and another, and another. And I would have been a better mother. Even Leah might still be alive. But I've sown to the wind, Rachel, and justly reaped a whirlwind. Yet I will survive. My husband promised me . . . that things will not always be this way."

Chapter 32

ith Reuben and Rachel living in her home, Sarah's life took on a new semblance of order and a deeper dimension. Not only were there people to talk with, but things to talk about. The fact that Reuben was working with a devout Pharisee who loved to discuss the Talmud gave much stimulus and a lively energy to their conversations in the evenings—conversations which, on occasions, became heated debates. With all this came a renewed interest in the Scriptures on Sarah's part.

Jared came over frequently; he enjoyed the company of Reuben and Rachel almost as much as Sarah. But what was more intriguing—unusual, really—was that Rabbi Katros, a neighbor several houses away, would join them and listen to Sarah boldly debate life in the light of the oral Law. It was unprecedented for men to allow women to participate in such weighty discussions. Yet the men, under the security and cover of Sarah's home, seemed to relish these occasions. Although the rabbi and Reuben would never openly confess how much they were invigorated by these meetings, Jared was his own man and he didn't care what others thought.

He appreciated Sarah and was thoroughly entertained in her presence. She was feisty when it came to the 613 statutes which, according to many, dictated how the Torah, the first five books of Moses, was to be lived out in their day-by-day existence. For example, what were they to do if they found coins scattered in the street? Could they rightly keep them? Must they be handled the same way as if they were found in a little bag? They never ran out of issues to investigate.

Once Jared came to know the rabbi better, he was fascinated with the man. Jared had never been in close company with devoutly religious men—especially men who were also involved in politics. Jared figured the reason the rabbi had become a friend (and consequently, a more frequent visitor) was because he felt more comfortable visiting Sarah now that Reuben and Rachel had moved in with her.

Rabbi Katros was a tall, stately man with dark, deeply set eyes and a long, hooked nose. He exuded an air of confidence—that is, until he became upset. Then his tone became one of controlled panic. Jared wondered if Katros' confidence came from the sheer force of his personality or if his wealth and position encouraged it. His robes were woven of the finest and most costly material. But then, the rabbi's house was also costly. Jared had heard there were two mikvahs in it. It wasn't every priest who had a private pool of water for purification, let alone two! There was no need for Rabbi Katros to use the mikvahs at the Temple Mount.

Katros, being part of the sect known as the Sadducees, was more liberal in his religious practices and beliefs than Reuben. All day long, when the shop where Reuben worked wasn't busy, Reuben and his employer hammered out the issues of the oral Law—the traditions supported by the Pharisees, which they said were equal to the written law, the Torah.

But the rabbi? Well, that was another matter. The rabbi rejected the oral Law, holding rigidly to the Mosaic code. Rabbi Katros insisted there was no resurrection. Reuben argued that there was. When Reuben and the rabbi started going round and round, Jared would just lean into the corner of the couch and watch. He very rarely took sides. He wasn't one to get caught up in the letter of the Law; he simply knew the Law was *the law*, and he'd try to obey it as best he could.

But Sarah? She would *fly* into the discussions. Her comments often caused great consternation amongst the men because sometimes she sided with the rabbi and at other times with Reuben. Unless of course, Sarah didn't agree with either one. Then she'd just take a stubborn stand on her own ground.

During the discussions Rachel would often slip into the reception room, sitting at the end closest to the courtyard, and listen with wide-eyed fascination. But she seldom said much. If she did, she'd usually see a look of frustration cast a cloud over Reuben's face. She didn't like that, so she usually remained quiet. Of course, having to be quiet didn't frustrate Rachel like it would have Sarah. Rachel was content to swallow her opinions and hold her peace. She enjoyed seeing her otherwise quiet husband debating the issues—oftentimes with much passion.

When Rabbi Katros came to the house—most of the time without his wife, Martha—his conversation often focused on the latest dealings of the Sanhedrin. Katros was a part of this seventy-one-member council that was directly responsible for the affairs of the Jewish people, who continued to chafe under Roman rule.

The little band enjoyed hearing of the Jewish revolts and their various leaders and the latest accounts of the self-proclaimed messiahs, including the rabbi from Nazareth. However, the topic Katros brought up most often was the politics connected with Herod Antipas and the fairly new prefect of Judea, Pontius Pilate. Pilate was not a favorite among the Sanhedrin. The good news was that except for the annual feasts of the Jews, Pilate, thankfully, stayed in Caesarea, where the climate and the scenery were more pleasant for him. And Jerusalem was more pleasant in his absence!

It was two days before the Passover Feast when Rabbi Katros came over just as everyone was finishing their evening meal. Jared was with them. Rising from his mat at the tricillum—he loved lounging at this low U-shaped table Sarah had acquired—Jared went into the central courtyard to greet the rabbi, who came through the door and announced his arrival.

"Peace be on this house."

"Thank you, rabbi, but it looks like it needs to be on your face," Jared smiled as he put a comforting hand on Katros' shoulder and steered him through the courtyard to where everyone was dining.

"There cannot be peace on a man's face when there is no peace in his heart, Jared. Pilate and that man Jesus of Nazareth—whom I hate to call a rabbi because no *good* rabbi would teach what he teaches or break the Sabbath as he does—are going to be the death of all of us! It's not easy, Jared. It's not easy serving on the council," Simeon Katros said as Jared ushered him into the reception room.

"Peace to you all," said the rabbi. He lifted his hand as if bestowing a blessing, greeted Reuben and Rachel, then continued his conversation with Jared. "Just the other day we heard that Jesus, while riding on a donkey down the Mount of Olives—"

At that moment Sarah walked into the room bearing a large glass bowl of freshly washed grapes.

"Look what I have from Hebron!"

"Sarah," Rachel rose to take the grapes, "Rabbi Katros is here."

"Rabbi," Sarah's smile welcomed Katros.

"And peace to you, Sarah. Peace be on this house and on this city; we certainly need it. May the Almighty hear our cry. . . ."

"Come and recline with us at the table," said Sarah.

Reuben intervened. "I'm sure Rabbi Katros would like to wash first." Having studied with the rabbi, Reuben wanted everyone to perform this ritual before eating.

"Of course, of course. Excuse me," Sarah said as she stretched out on the cushion.

The rabbi walked to the three-legged table to the left of the triclinium, lifted the pitcher and poured the water, first over his left hand seven times and then over his right seven times as he murmured his prayer. Then, without giving any thought to it, Katros took the place where the guest of honor would normally recline. He was used to taking the best of seats. Strangely, on that evening, Sarah had not designated the place for anyone.

The rabbi sighed deeply and mourned, "There will never be peace. We will never have peace until Messiah comes. This Jesus of Nazareth has proclaimed the destruction of Jerusalem. He made this announcement as he descended the Mount of Olives. It had the people in a stir again! May it not be true. May it not be true. May it not be true," Katros proclaimed his wish three times as if to declare it so.

Taking a cluster of grapes he shoved them into his mouth, chewing and commiserating at the same time. "Why, oh why does our Messiah delay? Can't he see we cannot continue to survive and keep our sanity under the hateful rule of Rome? I love my luxuries, the niceties of life, but I am outdone by the licentious greed of the Romans. They've expanded on all the worst of Hellenism! And their inhumanity to mankind, especially to the *Jews* is intolerable!" Katros waved his hand through the air. "Intolerable! One would think Pilate would have enough sense to honor our laws and not be so flagrant about breaking them!"

"What happened?" Rachel asked quickly before she realized what she had done. Very rarely did she ever address the rabbi directly. Hers was to serve and listen, and with this Rachel was content. Unless, of course, she forgot herself and was carried away in the intensity of the moment. Sarah, however, could get by with treating the rabbi as an equal because of who her husband was. And, this was her house. Besides, her husband was away . . . not present to frown at her like Reuben.

Yet at that particular moment everyone was so absorbed in Katros' news that no one noticed it was Rachel who asked the question.

"First Pilate tried to sneak those Roman standards with the images of the emperor on them into Jerusalem—an emperor the Romans acclaim god—and as a result got his palace in Caesarea besieged for five days by our outraged populace. Then Pilate caused a riot by taking money from the temple treasury to construct another aqueduct for Jerusalem. The Almighty One knows how we need water in Jerusalem, but Pilate shouldn't try to pay for it with temple funds!"

"And," Katros' face was turning red, "just days ago Pilate dressed his soldiers like Jews so they wouldn't be recognized in the crowds as he rode into Jerusalem in all his flagrant *pomposity!* That's what I call it—pomposity! It was evident he had the whole event carefully planned, for when the demonstrators expressed their outrage, Pilate gave a signal and the soldiers attacked the crowd with clubs. They *killed* some of our people!" Katros took a gulp of wine, set the glass down with a bang, and wiped his mouth with the back of his hand. The genteel man was clearly upset.

Jared, with concern in his voice, said, "I understand the Antonia fortress is filled with Roman troops. Are they expecting trouble during the Passover feast?"

"Yes, and so are we. Between those Galilean followers of this Jesus, whom they are calling the King of the Jews, and—"

Rachel let out a little gasp before her hand covered her lips. Wide-eyed she looked first at Reuben and then at Sarah. The rabbi stopped in midsentence and looked at Rachel. Reuben subtly shook his head, signaling his disapproval to his wife.

Sarah observed the scene, aware of Reuben's nonverbal message to Rachel. She quickly stepped into the conversation, saying, "No feast will ever be without trouble until the Gentiles stop trampling down our land. Never! I wish my husband were here. *He* would put a stop to it all."

"I can't figure out, Sarah, why your husband doesn't do it now . . ." the words rushed out of Jared's mouth before his thoughts could stop them. He paused momentarily, then finished rather weakly, "Especially when he has the power to do so."

The rabbi spoke up. "Well, I don't know your husband personally. But if he has such power, why doesn't he use it? It would be good if he'd return home and take care of that man called Jesus, who's trying to pass himself off as the Messiah, and then rid our land of these Romans who say their emperor is *god!*"

"Sarah? Simeon Katros?" the woman's voice called out the names as if in urgency.

Sarah jumped up, relieved at the interruption. "Rabbi, it sounds like your wife—"

"Why would Martha be coming here?"

Before Sarah could get to the courtyard door a breathless Martha entered the room.

"Simeon! Simeon, excuse me, but some people just came to our home. They want you to go to the house of Caiaphas for a special meeting of the Sanhedrin—the council."

"Now?" the rabbi asked, rather exasperated.

Martha nodded, smiling weakly. "They said it's very important. . . ."

The evening was over; everyone knew it. Quietly each said goodnight. At the door, Jared turned to Sarah with an apologetic look on his face. "I didn't mean. . . ."

"Jared, you needn't apologize. I understand. Sometimes I, too, wonder how my husband can stay away and let me—us—go through such tribulation when, with a word, he could bring it to an end."

Sarah reached up and put her hand on Jared's shoulder—something she never would have done to the rabbi, whom she never touched. "Shalom, Jared. Shalom."

Sarah extinguished the oil lamps, carefully blowing them out and putting them back on their little perches on the walls. She went to her room. Closing the door, she lit the lampstands beside her bed. Sarah was troubled in her heart. The rabbi's words about this supposed Messiah had shaken her. Had Daniel said something about the destruction of Jerusalem, or had she merely dreamed it? Sarah couldn't remember, but she had to find out. Taking a lamp with her, Sarah walked to the large stone jar near the window. She set the oil lamp on the floor beside her, broke the seal on the jar, removed the lid, and reached into the cool stone vessel. For a moment Sarah hesitated. What if she hadn't dreamed it?

What if Daniel did say Jerusalem and the temple would be destroyed again? Did she really want to know? What difference would it make if she knew for sure? Sarah pulled Daniel's scroll from the jar. The moonlight slid around the corner of the window and wrapped its brilliant beams around Sarah's shoulders, joining the little oil lamp in casting its light on the aging parchment. Embraced in its aura, Sarah carefully unrolled the scroll and began to read.

> *Seventy weeks have been decreed for your people and your holy city, to finish the transgression, to make an end of sin, to make atonement for iniquity, to bring in everlasting righteousness, to seal up vision and prophecy, and to anoint the most holy place.*
>
> *So you are to know and discern that from the issuing of a decree to restore and rebuild Jerusalem until Messiah the Prince there will be seven weeks and sixty-two weeks; it will be built again, with plaza and moat, even in times of distress.*
>
> *Then after the sixty-two weeks the Messiah will be cut off and have nothing, and the people of the prince who is to come will destroy the city and the sanctuary.*

There it was! *The destruction of Jerusalem and the temple. Rabbi Katros said the man named Jesus had spoken of that as well! Had the rabbi from Nazareth read Daniel's scroll?*

Sarah rolled up the scroll and stood to her feet. For a moment she gazed out her window into the midnight blue of the heavens. *What will I do if Jerusalem is destroyed? If the temple is torn down again?* Sarah's mind raced back to the first destruction of her beloved Zion. She could almost smell the smoke of its burning.

Turning from the window, Sarah deposited the sacred scroll in the security of its stone vault and went to her couch. She felt drained, yet as she lay upon her bed her mind would not rest. All she could do was think—think and puzzle about the Torah, the scrolls of the prophets, of Isaiah, of the promises of the Messiah, of Messiah's rule on earth. Her mind returned to the words now tucked in the stone jar. *How can Messiah come and then be cut off? I don't understand it. Maybe Daniel was only right up to a certain point. But why, then, would my husband tell me to listen to Daniel?*

Sarah turned from her right side to her left and found herself thinking of the prophet Ezekiel and how he lay on his side for many days as a witness to Israel's sin and the judgment the people deserved. Judgment of which Moses also warned just before he died. *Is the coming destruction of Jerusalem and our temple yet another judgment?* Restless, Sarah turned on her back. There she imagined the statue Daniel described to her: the gold, the silver, the bronze, and the iron eventually mixed with clay. Then she envisioned the four beasts rising from the sea. *Both visions have four elements,* she thought. *Daniel may have been right about the four kingdoms that would rule over us. We're under a fourth kingdom right now. But surely Daniel couldn't have been right about Messiah, could he? If Messiah is Messiah, then he can't be cut off. And why would he let Jerusalem and the temple be destroyed after he came?*

Sarah turned onto her stomach and buried her face on her couch. *I'm just a woman. What do I know about these things? All I know is that I want my husband.*

Turning onto her back again, Sarah recalled Solomon's words in the Song of Songs. "I adjure you, O daughters of Jerusalem, if you find my beloved...if you find my beloved....Where...where has your beloved gone?"

Sarah began to weep. She felt incredibly sad. *Oh Beloved, where have you gone? When are you coming back? Come back . . . rescue me . . . rescue our Jerusalem and return to your Temple. Come back and be here for Messiah. Come, Beloved, please come. . . .*

Chapter 88

*S*amuel, I don't want you following after this Simeon Bar . . . Bar. . . ."

"Bar-Giora, Imma," said Samuel with a controlled voice as he shifted his weight to his other foot. He was disgusted with himself for not getting out of the courtyard door before his Imma caught him, but he wasn't going to let it show on his face. Samuel determined that he'd hear out his Imma.

Samuel had been rightly named. He was asked of God, a son to fill the dark empty cavern left in Reuben and Rachel's hearts when little Joseph's life was snuffed out. Samuel loved both of his parents deeply, but it was his Imma he felt the closest to. They talked more.

Samuel caught Sarah's eyes as they searched his countenance. He smiled. Sarah was his aunt, and he loved her dearly even though right now it was clear Sarah was going to support Rachel. Samuel didn't mind; he could see the admiration in Aunt Sarah's eyes. *She's such a fighter, a survivor. I'm sure when she hears me out she will understand even better than Imma why I want to join Simeon Bar-Giora.*

Simeon Bar-Giora, along with a large band of followers, had just devastated Idumea and moved into Jerusalem in an attempt to overthrow the Romans. He was a formidable leader of immense size and iron-like

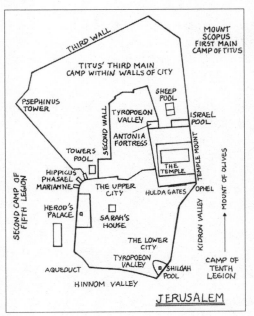

strength. One whom Vespasian, now the Caesar of Rome, wanted quelled along with all the Zealots. This was the task Vespasian gave his son, Titus. He was to subdue the Zealots of Jerusalem who, with others, were determined to break Rome's yoke from Israel's neck.

Sarah and Rachel were not uninformed. Word had it that Titus had returned from Greece for the express purpose of tightening the noose he'd thrown around Jerusalem. The legions of Rome already had the city by the neck. They would strangle the Jews' Zion by cutting it off from all possible outside support. Only the fortresses of Masada, Machaerus, and Herodium had been able to hold out against Titus' legions.

As Sarah surveyed Samuel she knew any leader would be glad to have him for a follower. Samuel was the apple of Sarah's eye, as well as Rachel's and Reuben's. The tunics he wore, with the customary contrasting stripes over his broad shoulders, gave witness of his favor with the Imma who had devotedly woven them for her son. Taller than his parents and slimmer in build, Samuel resembled his father more than his mother. His black curly hair, closely cropped, set off his strong chin and pensive eyes—eyes like his father's, eyes that often looked like they were someplace else, lost in deep and weighty matters.

Samuel was a capable young man who knew how to harness his many talents. In fact, Sarah didn't think there was anything Samuel could not do because he had an uncanny ability to rein in his talents and passions with a wisdom and temperance beyond his years.

The man had grown up under their feet. He had been loved, gently disciplined, prayed for. Even as a young boy Samuel would sit for hours at the low dining table rolling the marbles from his mill game, back and forth, while listening to the lengthy adult discussions of the holy Scriptures and the latest political ongoings.

Often at night, Sarah would go into his room, sit on his bed, tell him a story, and sometimes reminisce about her husband—what he was like, how he dealt with people, the things he had tried to teach her, and how badly she wished she had listened to him.

Then as Samuel grew older, without sharing the details of her sin, Sarah told him the consequences of her disobedience. As she did, the tears in her eyes did not go unnoticed. Samuel was convinced Aunt Sarah wished she had listened and obeyed. That might have been the reason Samuel learned, even as a young man, to listen. And why he was willing to listen now and to hear out his Imma before he tried to reason with her. Even though Samuel was anxious to get going, Sarah knew he would not be rude nor disrespectful to his Imma.

As Sarah watched Samuel grow into manhood she permitted herself to think more and more of her own son. Having dealt with her sacrifice of Benjamin and finding relief through confession, Sarah felt she was ready to resurrect the memory of her other son and confront her final failure as a mother. She wondered where Saul was, if he was alive, and why she had not looked in Egypt for her rebellious runaway son. Would he someday unexpectedly reappear in her life as Leah had? And if he did, how would he respond to her? Would she be able to keep Saul or would he run away again? Or...and the thought was devastating...maybe he wasn't even alive. Had she lost the last of her children to death? To think of such a possibility overwhelmed her.

"Simeon Bar-Giora is a Zealot!" asked Rachel.

"Excuse me, Imma, but Bar-Giora is not one of the Zealots—"

Rachel was far less patient than usual with her son today. Her anxiety was evident as she interrupted him, talking rapidly. "But he has to be! The Zealots split into two factions. I'm sure it was Simeon Bar-Giora who split from John of Gischala. And such a split is only going to bring a greater confusion, mind you, *and* the destruction of our city from within. Samuel, these factions are burning each other's food! Burning warehouses and the corn they gathered to withstand the siege! These men are trying to destroy each other and they'll destroy us all in the process. Then what will be left for you to defend, my son? Think! Think!"

Rachel knew of these events because she had listened carefully to the conversations of the men as they analyzed the status of the city and discussed what they would do should the Romans succeed. Panic began to creep into her voice, raising it higher. Rachel felt she was fighting for the life of her son.

"What if these tenacious Romans are able to keep up the siege on our city while the Fifth Legion levels the whole valley between Mount Scopus and the city walls? We'll never be able to stand against these legions! You know it's their dogged tenacity—the fact that they won't accept defeat—which makes them so formidable!"

Rachel looked briefly at Sarah for confirmation, then quickly turned her gaze back to Samuel as she continued.

"Your Abba says the Tenth Legion has come up from Jericho and is on the Mount of Olives. The Temple wall will never withstand the Roman's battering rams—if they get the rams that far."

Samuel started to speak, but his mother pointed her hand into the air. "And I know, Samuel, I know everyone's convinced Messiah's going to come and rescue us. But what if he doesn't? I don't want to die, but even more, I don't want *you* to die. And—and if you run off after this Zealot—"

Samuel nodded, confirming her words. "Imma, you are amazingly informed. You are right in all you said except for one thing. Simeon Bar-Giora is not a Zealot, and he did not break off from John of Gischala. It was Eliazar—the leader of the Zealots before John of Gischala took over. He was the one who broke off. And you are right. The Zealots will destroy us if they don't stop fighting between themselves and trying to destroy one another. Even now some of them are looting the houses of the people and it is wrong—horribly wrong. They are desperate and in need of better leadership."

Samuel sensed that now was the right time to make his plea. "That is why I want to help Simeon Bar-Giora. We've already had to abandon the northern suburbs and withdraw to our second line of walls. And now Titus has another camp on the upper side of the city. That's *our* side, Imma . . . our side!" Samuel's voice grew louder. "You can see the camp from our roof. Simeon Bar-Giora feels that if we could join Eliazar's followers there would be about eight thousand more of us to hold the eastern defenses."

Samuel paused momentarily. "Imma, I'd rather join the Zealots under Simeon Bar-Giora's leadership and die defending our holy city and the temple than hole up like the Essenes in the Judean desert setting up a library! Preparing a battle manual they call *The War of the Sons of Light and the Sons of Darkness.*" There was an uncharacteristic sarcasm in Samuel's voice as he almost mockingly gave the full title of the Essenes' scroll. "The war is now! *We* are the sons of light." Samuel evidenced his passion by pacing the room.

"Well," Rachel retorted, "I am sorry to say that I'd rather have you in the Judean desert with the Essenes alive for Israel than dead here. You say you are eight thousand strong. What is that, I ask you, against Titus and his *eighty* thousand men?"

"But Imma," Samuel pleaded as he continued his efforts to reason with his mother, "if all of us banded together in this city there would be twenty-four or maybe twenty-five thousand! That's a little less than three to one. King David wrote of one man putting a thousand men to fight. That's why, Imma, I *must* join them—"

Sarah interrupted. Her curiosity was piqued, and it was a good time to change the subject. She knew she would have to side with Samuel if he asked her, for she, too, would rather fight than hole up. "Samuel, who is this man going through our city day and night crying 'Woe to thee, Jerusalem'?"

"It's Jesus."

Rachel's cheeks turned ashen as she turned to Samuel, her voice filled with alarm. "They said he was raised from the dead!"

Samuel interrupted, a smile tugging at the corners of his mouth. He was happy to set his Imma straight on this one. "No, Imma. This is a different Jesus. Not the Jesus of Nazareth whom Pilate condemned to death. This is Jesus, son of Ananias."

Rachel's hand thudded lightly against her chest as she cried, "Oh!" in relief.

"This Jesus, son of Ananias is the man Rabbi Katros told us about. The one the Sanhedrin ordered flogged. And when that didn't do any good, the governor had him scourged to the bone and then released. They declared the man insane!"

"But," Sarah interjected, "none of the Sanhedrin's threats worked. He's still out there demoralizing everyone with his dire predictions—his constant cry, 'Woe to thee, Jerusalem!' What do you think this—"

Samuel interrupted, compassion in his voice. "It's over, Aunt Sarah. Jesus, son of Ananias will never cry again. Yesterday he was struck and killed by a stone from a Roman catapult."

"Where?" both women asked at the same time. Rachel turned to Sarah and let out a little laugh of relief. "We've lived together so long that we think alike!"

Sarah laughed with her, happy to see Rachel's tension lessen a bit. "It's wonderful, isn't it? Now excuse us, Samuel—could you tell us where it happened, and how?"

"It was on the Temple Mount. At first anyone bothering to look could easily see and dodge the stones the Romans were launching. Their light color against the dark backdrop of the Mount of Olives made them clearly visible until the Romans got wise and darkened the stones." Samuel's voice dropped a notch. "The prophet of doom never had a chance."

"It's strange, isn't it?" Rachel mused. "His prophecy about the destruction of Jerusalem was the same as that of Jesus of Nazareth, and they both had the same name."

"Imma, there are many men with the name of Jesus."

"Yes, yes. . . ." Rachel's thoughts turned back to her son. "What if we are destroyed by Rome?" she asked, but didn't wait for an answer. "That's why I do not want you following Simeon Bar . . . Bar. . . ."

"Giora."

"Bar-Giora," Rachel repeated his name slowly. She wanted to remember it lest there be two Simeons. "I want you to wait until we talk with your Abba and Jared. Please, Samuel. . . ."

Samuel lowered his eyes to the floor, shifting from one foot to the other, almost rocking. Rachel could tell he was struggling between his Imma's desire and his will. Waiting, shifting his feet, looking at the floor was Samuel's way of gaining control, of bringing himself into submission—a pattern he followed since childhood. Finally he looked up. Disappointment clouded his eyes, his mouth, and the line of his chin. "I will wait, Imma, because you asked. But can we talk about it as soon as Abba comes in?"

"If he's willing, then we'll talk."

"Will you try to persuade him if he's not?"

"I don't want to, but I will because I appreciate your obedience, Samuel. Just remember we asked God for you and we don't want to lose you."

"I understand, Imma," Samuel paused. "But we must also remember life and death are not in our hands. Ours is only to believe, obey, and reap the blessing or to disobey and reap the curse. I want to honor you as I'm supposed to."

"You know," Sarah said coming out of her own thoughts, "I fear we're going to go into captivity again. . . ."

"But Aunt Sarah, if you believed that, why didn't you leave here when Vespasian became Caesar, made his way back to Rome, and turned over Judea to Titus? You can't leave here now, but you could have then. Why—"

"I don't know why I stayed, Samuel," Sarah responded, a frown on her face. "I don't know. I only wish I had left. I wish we'd all left."

Chapter 34

The city was no longer safe. Jared and Reuben weren't happy to be taking Rachel and Sarah with them but they had no peace leaving them alone in the house. While the Romans camped outside the city walls, famine stalked Jerusalem's streets.

Revolutionaries were tormented as they remembered burning the food supplies of the warring factions who now fought side by side with them against the Romans. Their supplies depleted, the Zealots roamed the city like mad dogs, breaking into houses and ravaging for food. Some of them, when they found no morsel to quell their gnawing hunger, would vent their unreasoning rage by torturing their victims or even killing them. Strangers who caught the smell of cooking flesh drifting through closed shutters would break into those homes and demand a portion of the one the homeowner had killed and was now cooking. All over the city, the insanity brought on by famine crazed the minds of a people who once had highly valued the life of another.

The foursome had each taken a small bag, filled it with food, and hung it around their waists under their tunics. Reuben and Jared then draped themselves with lightweight cloaks bordered in the common gamma pattern of the day. Both carried unsheathed knives that were gripped tightly and concealed by the folds of their cloaks.

Sarah and Rachel each hung another small bag of food around their necks and covered them with their veils. Hearing that the followers of John Gischala and Simeon Bar-Giora had no food, they determined to find Samuel and share with him what little they had.

With great reluctance, Reuben and Rachel had given Samuel permission to join Simeon Bar-Giora, knowing they could not attempt to keep him at home while others were laying down their lives for the safety of Jerusalem. According to ancient law, once a battering ram began hammering the wall of a city, it signaled a point of no return. Surrender could be nothing but unconditional.

Ancient law notwithstanding, Rome's policy was to never allow anything but unconditional surrender once they set up siege against a city. Resistance was futile, yet the stubborn Jews resisted. The issue now, however, was not surrender but survival. The battering ram had already bludgeoned Jerusalem's wall.

Of all the lands Rome had conquered, none had given her more grief than Israel. From the beginning, the Jews had been an open and festering wound in this great empire's side. An incurable wound. They had been conquered, yet not mastered. They were an impossible and, for the most part, uncompromising people—thorns in the sides and eyes of the Romans. Thorns that had to be removed! There would be no mercy.

As Reuben led the small group past the north end of the Citadel, they saw the massive towers of Phasael, Hippicus, and Miriamne. That the towers were still intact strengthened their hope. Up to now the fighting had centered in the Lower City; they were thankful that Samuel had been posted in the Upper City on the western side. Presently the battle was raging in the northeastern region of the city at the Antonia Fortress and along the eastern wall of the Temple Mount.

Rome believed that as long as the temple stood, peace with the Jews was unattainable. A rigid monotheism and a tolerant polytheism—the former demanding righteousness, the latter lusting for the licentious—were incompatible. Rome and Israel could never cohabitate in peace.

A voice shattered the silence. It came from below, on the other side of the wall where they were walking. "Wise and noble Jews, hear my voice; heed my wisdom. Resistance is futile. In a matter of days your city will be taken, and you will be dead from starvation or the sword. But if you will surrender to mighty Rome. . . ."

Jared stopped. It was the voice of a *Jew*—not a Roman!

What Jew could safely walk the other side of this wall and survive with Titus' camp but a stone's throw away? Jared wondered. *Every time a deserter is found, or some poor starving soul escapes the city to forage for food, they are scourged and crucified in front of the walls—in full view of the inhabitants of Jerusalem!*

Jared turned to Reuben. "How could a Jew be outside the city making all that noise and still remain alive? It doesn't make sense. If that man hadn't been planted there by the Romans, he wouldn't live in the time of a cock's crow."

With his free hand, Reuben took Rachel by the arm and steered her toward the wall. "I don't know, but we're going to see." Jared and Sarah followed Reuben.

"Who is it?" Jared asked.

Amazed at the thought, Reuben turned to Jared, "Have you ever heard of Josephus, the traitor? It could be him paying his dues to Rome!"

"I've heard of Josephus the historian," Jared replied, "the one who's written much about our history."

"That's who I mean," said Reuben.

Disbelief crossed Jared's face as Reuben continued, "Do you realize that man could very well be and in fact probably is Josephus! You know, don't you, how Josephus saved his own neck when Vespasian besieged Jotapata and leveled it? When he couldn't convince the people of Jotapata that he was more valuable to the cause outside the besieged city rather than inside it, he maneuvered an escape with forty of the city's leading citizens. They hid in a cave but were discovered. Rumor has it that Josephus wanted to surrender when they were discovered, but the others decided it was more noble to take their own lives. So Josephus pretended to go along with them, volunteering to be among the last to die. But after the others killed themselves, Josephus surrendered to the Romans. Then, to save his neck, he prophesied that Vespasian would someday become the emperor of Rome. Vespasian fell for it. That's why I think this man is probably Josephus. It all seems to fit, doesn't it! One thing for certain: Josephus is no Mordecai; he has bowed to the enemy. May the Almighty give us men who won't bow!"

"He has, Reuben," Jared replied. "You've raised him."

Reuben smiled. "Samuel is an uncompromising young man, isn't he!"

The group suddenly became distracted by another sound. They all turned to see Rachel retching. She was bent over double, trying to turn her back to her companions. Sarah reached over to help Rachel, using her free hand to fumble around under Rachel's veil in an effort to find the small bag of food hanging from her neck and hold it out of the way as Rachel vomited. The sight of the bodies hanging on the crosses just outside the city wall was too much for her.

Freeing herself from Sarah's grasp, Rachel distanced herself from the other three. As she did, Sarah nodded and motioned with her head in the direction beyond the wall. "I'm sure it's the sight of those crucified bodies in all those grotesque positions. . . ."

Jared leaned forward and in a whisper just loud enough for Sarah and Reuben to hear, said, "The Roman soldiers get bored. So to amuse themselves they take the escapees they catch and nail them to these crosses, dreaming up all sorts of twisted positions. The poor souls ventured outside the walls to find some roots or grass—anything to keep themselves alive—and in doing so condemned themselves to a death more torturous than famine. I've heard that the soldiers think the crucifixions will be a deterrent that keeps the Jews within the walls, but apparently the craving for food wins out. Yet I still don't understand how one human being can do that to another." Jared shook his head. "I guess the Romans have become so hardened by the carnage of war that they don't think anything of it. They've become inhuman. They're insensitive to anything or anyone except themselves and their insatiable appetites for some new and varied entertainment."

Jared wasn't going to repeat it, but he'd also heard that some Roman soldiers had caught a deserter who was retrieving the gold he'd swallowed. They had gone wild as the rumor that the deserters were filled with gold spread among the soldiers like a fire. From that time on, when deserters were found, the soldiers often ripped them open and searched their bowels for gold and other swallowed treasure.

Rachel straightened up and turned around to walk back to the other three. Her face was flush from nauseous convulsions; and her eyes were moist with tears. "Forgive me. The sight of those people threw my stomach into an uproar. All I could remember was the day I saw the Rabbi from Nazareth hanging beside the road," Rachel wiped her sweaty forehead with her hand, "near Golgatha—the place of the skull. A sign that said 'King of the Jews' was nailed above his head. When I remembered the sign, without any warning our little Joseph flashed before my eyes and the soldier with the sword . . . and I . . . well, you know."

Rachel looked at Reuben, who was biting his lip. His eyes were clamped shut.

Jared glanced nervously from one to the other. "We'd better find Samuel and get back to our house before someone breaks in and ransacks it."

"I can't go back, Reuben. Please don't make me. We've got to find Samuel. If I can just see him and just know he's all right. . . ." Rachel pleaded, her eyes entreating him.

They continued their search until the men insisted they return home. "Perhaps Samuel has gone home," Reuben reasoned with his wife. "We need to make sure he is not there waiting for us. And if he's not there, then maybe we can try to find him from the roof before it gets dark." With this new ray of hope reviving their fainting hearts, Sarah and Rachel acquiesced and they all returned home. Much to their disappointment, however, the house was empty. Feeling their grief, Jared said, "I'll go to the roof; you rest here." But the others had to go with him—to make sure, to know for themselves that the streets had been carefully searched by their own eyes.

But their eyes were to be greeted by another sight they hadn't expected. As they arrived at the top of the stairs they saw billowing smoke and red flames lashing the sky. The Temple Mount was ablaze! Sarah turned away, her head bending lower and lower.

The burden of what Sarah saw weighted heavily on her back until her chest caved in and her shoulders slumped in defeat. Anguish eroded the porcelain smoothness of her face as she covered her ears with her hands. She wanted to shut out the message roaring in the wind. The cry of tumult, of war, and of defeat—like leaves caught in a dust storm—swirled from the Temple Mount and screamed across the valley to her rooftop in the Upper City.

Finally, slowly, Sarah turned around and straightened her back and looked again at the Temple Mount. Had she and the others been vultures hovering above the city, they would have seen the Romans bursting through the inner courts of the temple and driving the Zealots into the sanctuary as the outer rooms exploded in flames. They also would have discovered the reason they hadn't found Samuel. He had left the relative safety of the Upper City, having been dispatched to the Temple Mount.

As Samuel's loved ones surveyed the fire and destruction from their distant roof, Samuel found himself in the very midst of it. The temple platform was strewn with bodies covering it like an obscene carpet. Some lay motionless while others writhed and groaned in pain as the horses of the Roman Cavalry gingerly yet sometimes unsuccessfully tried to wedge their hoofs between the scattered limbs. Samuel gaped in mute horror as the Romans carried in their standards and offered a sheep, a pig, and an ox to their gods—gods whom they thought had brought them victory.

Jared, Reuben, and Rachel stood paralyzed. Sarah, somewhat in front of them, was frozen in disbelief. The group looked like stone statues—like the towers of Herod's palace looming in the background. Sarah, standing closer to the edge of the roof than the others, turned to face them and with incredulity cried, "It's Tisha B'av! The same day and month that the Babylonians destroyed our temple! How can we build another temple?"

In the month of Sivan, Sarah thought to herself, *the Romans breached the wall. Late in Tammuz they took the Antonia Fortress away from the Zealots. Now it's Tisha B'av and the same things have happened in the city that happened when the Babylonians destroyed Solomon's temple. Where are you, my husband? Why, at least, didn't you send Messiah? Was that asking too much?*

Sarah couldn't cry. The hurt ran too deep, beyond emotion.

They stood silently, respectfully—mourning a Judaism which ceased that day with the destruction of their temple. Jared approached Sarah and took her by the hand. "Reuben, we must get the women out of here. The Romans will soon invade the Upper City."

"No, Reuben, no!" Rachel whirled toward Reuben. "I am not leaving without Samuel!" Rachel was trembling and her words loud, filled with determination, seeping out of taut lips and clenched teeth. "I am not leaving without our son. We've got to find him! We've got to . . . Sarah! Sarah!" she began screaming, obviously panic-stricken.

Sarah turned to Jared, her crestfallen eyes imploring his as she spoke. "What if Samuel comes back and we're not here?"

Chapter 35

The haggard expression on his face and deadened look in his eyes immediately alerted them. Something was wrong! Reuben was out of breath or out of strength. They didn't know which, but Rachel and Sarah both anxiously awaited Reuben's first words as he entered the house.

"John of Gischala escaped from the temple and then joined Simeon Bar-Giora to try to bargain with Titus. All they wanted to do was take their followers and go to the desert, but Titus refused. It was nonnegotiable. Only unconditional surrender would do."

Rachel and Sarah searched Reuben's eyes, looking to see if there was any hint of Samuel's whereabouts. They suspected Reuben didn't have good news, or he would have told them immediately. He would have burst through the door into the courtyard shouting, "Our son lives!"

Unable to wait any longer and willing to know even the worst, Rachel spoke. "Reuben, have you any news about Samuel? Tell me whatever you must. I cannot wait any longer to hear. I must hear—"

"It's not bad news, my wife."

Sarah leaned back, finally able to breathe. Rachel leaned forward. Her sad eyes looked relieved, but not at peace as they searched Reuben's. Something was wrong, but Rachel didn't know what. She only knew something was very, very wrong. "Is he wounded?"

"I don't know, Rachel," Reuben sounded weary. Totally spent. "No one knows. I don't have one bit of news about Samuel—not even a thread. Nothing. Absolutely nothing."

Sarah leaned forward, her body taut, a tone of determination in her voice. "But surely someone somewhere has seen him. He couldn't have simply disappeared."

Reuben's whole demeanor—his countenance, his speech, his body language—seemed that of a defeated man. There was an edge to his voice. "Sarah, I don't know what more there is to be done. I have walked for hours, dodged Roman soldiers who are looting and burning the Lower City. I have turned over so many corpses with short-cropped black hair that I don't think I can look death in the face one more time. I have retched my guts out. The sights, the sounds, the smells. I have stopped any Jew who looked like he might have fought in the battle, and there are very few of them around. Most were killed or have gone into tunnels beneath the city."

Rachel leaned over and took Reuben's hand in hers, her eyes full of empathy. Reuben hardly seemed to notice. She wanted to tell him he didn't have to say any more, but she knew that for his own benefit as well as theirs he needed to tell them all he had done to try to find their son.

"I have looked at old people too weak from starvation to move. I have heard the screams, the pleading of those about to die by a Roman sword. I have listened to the groans of the dying, the labored breathing of those gurgling in their own blood. People have cried for me to save them, and others, to kill them. I could do neither. I have skirted fires, and I—" Reuben clenched his teeth and his fists, pounding the air, his knuckles almost white from the intensity of his grip. He began sobbing, "I have resisted the temptation to kill Romans with my bare hands as they rape our women before killing them and ravage our city without even a shred of conscience. And in this, Rachel, I have found in my heart that I, too, could be a murderer. I've walked through Sheol, Rachel, and *still I have not found our son!*"

"Reuben, you've done all you can. . . ." Sarah's words were quiet.

"But it's not enough, is it, Sarah?" Sarah detected a note of bitterness, of self-pity in Reuben's voice. When she saw Rachel jerk up her head in astonishment, she was convinced. Sarah didn't like what she heard. And it wasn't what Rachel needed, nor Reuben, for that matter. "I still don't know a thing about our son!" Reuben began to sob uncontrollably. Neither of them had ever seen him like this.

Sarah continued, "But it is enough, Reuben, because it is everything *you* could do. The matter is now out of your hands. And if you are going to be any good to any of us, you must let it go. You must recognize and live with your impotence; you must walk in faith. There is a time to die. And if it isn't Samuel's time, then he is somewhere—"

"But where?" Reuben jumped to his feet and turned on her. "Where, Sarah, where? Where?" He was losing control. Reuben knew it and so did Sarah. However, Reuben wasn't sure he cared. *Why not give in? Let it go? Let my emotions have full control? After all, don't I have a valid reason?*

"I don't know *where*. None of us do." Sarah's words were hard and seemingly unfeeling. She knew her voice was cold, but she had to bring Reuben back to reality, to responsibility. "But we know where *we* are. *We* are here, and *we* are responsible for this minute, for what *we* do with what *we* have, with what *we* know. And if Samuel is dead, you cannot bring him to life. You do not have that power. However, if he is alive you know that he will do everything he can to find you. Therefore, it is *your* responsibility to do everything you can to make sure he can find you—alive, well, and in your right mind. Not destroyed, Reuben, by this incomprehensibly horrible but *not devastating* circumstance of life."

Sarah stopped briefly to catch her breath. "Sometimes we are not masters over our circumstances, but we can always master our response. That choice is ours, Reuben. Yours. No one on earth can take it from us unless we allow it. And then it is not a matter of one taking it; rather, it is a matter of our giving it away. Now, Reuben, what are you going to do?"

Reuben looked at Sarah, absolutely stunned. In that instant he recalled what Rachel had told him of Sarah's life—of Benjamin, her marriage, the death of Leah, her failures, the consequences to her and to them and their nation. He remembered, and wondered. *How can Sarah live with herself? How can she continue to function . . . to find even a morsel of joy, of happiness—ever? How can she keep her sanity? How could she emerge from that kind of past and be the seemingly healthy and stable woman she is?* Now Reuben knew. And with that realization, he knew he had a choice to make: What would he do with the opportunity before him?

The silence was heavy and uncomfortable. No one spoke. Then suddenly the door crashed open and Jared rushed in not even stopping to knock. "Sarah! Reu—" he said with urgency. "Oh, you're all here!" he cried with relief. He was out of breath. "If we are to have any hope of survival, we must leave the city immediately. They've just captured Simeon and John. The Roman ramps will soon reach the walls of the Upper City. . . ."

Instantly Jared stopped, noting the silence around him. "What's going on? Did I—? Is it Samuel? Is he. . . ."

Reuben looked at him. "We were just talking about Samuel and what we need to do."

"Is Samuel all right?" Jared asked with concern.

Reuben responded, "We don't know, Jared. I can't find out anything— not one thing. At least we haven't any evidence of his death, which, of course, leaves us with hope." By now Reuben had reined in his emotions.

Sarah looked at Rachel and noted the relief in her eyes . . . and the pride. Rachel smiled weakly. Sarah's words had also been for her. Rachel knew she must leave the city without Samuel and learn to live in the hope that someday, if Samuel survived, he would find them. She knew Jerusalem would be their point of contact. It was their home, their land. If Rachel survived, Jerusalem was where she would be if it were in her human power to do so. If Samuel survived, she knew her son wouldn't rest until he returned here.

"Reuben," Rachel looked at her husband, her smile gentle, filled with confidence, "what do you want me to do?"

Jared interrupted, adamant. "We have to leave—*all* of us!" His emphasis was on the *all;* Jared wasn't sure if they were thinking of waiting for Samuel. But if they did wait, he knew they would lose their lives.

Reuben looked at Jared. "We're going with you and Sarah. If Samuel is alive, he'll find us if we survive."

At that moment, the words Sarah's husband had spoken echoed in her heart: *You will not die—you will live.* Resolute, she straightened her back, clenching her teeth with determination as they prepared for their exodus. Sarah knew she would return. *This land is mine, and I will possess it.*

Chapter 36

Soundlessly they made their escape, thankful for the cover of night. The darkness not only gave them greater protection, it also kept them from seeing the carnage of the day. Reuben led the way across the valley, through the Lower City, over the rubble of the wall, and down into the Kidron Valley. Having seized the Temple Mount, the Romans now unleashed their destruction upon the Upper City.

Reuben and Jared planned to slip between Titus' encampments on Mount Scopus and the Mount of Olives and then head for the Judean desert and eventually Edom. They made their way through the ruined city in silence, dressed in the darkest garments they could find. Rachel had remembered what Samuel said about the Romans darkening the catapult stones so they couldn't be seen against the backdrop of the Mount of Olives, and suggested that they wear dark clothing. That would make them harder to detect.

Cautiously the band of four wove their way around the graves of those laid to rest in the Valley of Jehoshaphat. Many had been buried here in the belief that those in this valley would be the first to be resurrected. As they reached the bottom of the Valley of Jehoshaphat—the Kidron Valley—they stopped to catch their breath.

Jared released a sigh of relief. "At least we made it this far. Maybe there's hope for our survival." Sarah did not respond as she turned for one last look at the Eastern Gate. In the darkness of the night it looked like a disjointed skeleton—a set of dry bones—dancing in the flames that were still burning on the Temple Mount. *Is the gate moving, or is it me?* Sarah started to sway. Jared and Reuben, both seeing her at the same time, rushed to her side. Catching her by her arms, they forced her to sit on one of the tombs.

"Sarah, you must eat." Rachel thrust a hunk of bread into her hands. "Take this, and some cheese."

"But I—" Sarah protested.

"'No' is not your choice," Rachel said. "I watched you; you didn't eat as the rest of us did before we left."

"I wanted to fast."

Jared whispered indignantly, "Now is not the time. You need your strength for the journey. Wh-what do you think you are anyway? Someone exempt. . . ."

Sarah put the bread and cheese into her mouth. She chewed the food slowly, relishing every swallow. As she sat there regaining her strength and her equilibrium, the valley was so peaceful she—

Then, from nowhere, a stone came rolling down the hill. A collective gasp escaped their mouths. With bated breath they waited, terror tightly gripping their hearts. Jared turned as a hostile voice pierced the silence. "You'd better come with us. If you break to run, or try to fight, we'll kill you on the spot." The soldier laughed a little, enjoying their dismay. He motioned with his spear for Sarah to get up. Their hearts were in their mouths . . . throbbing, pounding, choking them with fear.

There were only four soldiers. Apparently a patrol—a stealthy one. The soldier continued, "We want slaves, but only slaves who know how to obey their masters. It's your key to survival. And we are not desperate; there are more slaves here than we need."

Rachel reached for Reuben's hand. The spear came crashing down between them. Rachel jerked her hand away, but not before the ragged edge of the spearhead hit her. Wincing with pain but saying nothing, she reached up and pulled her other hand along the edge of cloth draped over her head. Finding the end of her veil, she whipped it around her wound several times and pulled the material tight in hopes of stopping the bleeding. All the while Rachel was careful to hide her wound from Reuben, fearing that he might foolishly try to defend her.

The soldier snarled contemptuously. "No touching, no talking if you want to live. *And. . . .*" he drew out the word *and* for effect, "no helping one another. If you are not strong enough to make it on your own, you are not strong enough to be a slave."

Sarah was glad she had taken the bread and cheese. Now she lowered her voice to an uncharacteristically submissive tone, saying, "Slaves, I know, are not allowed to speak without permission from their masters. Therefore, will you permit me to ask you a question, my lord?"

The soldier was caught off guard by Sarah's response. He liked the sound of her voice. Come daylight, he would see what she looked like. "You have my permission."

"Where are we to be taken as slaves?"

"I don't know—probably scattered to different parts of the Roman Empire. I just know I am to bring you to the ship. There your destination will be determined by the ship you travel on. It's a long way to the port. You had better save your strength." For a moment the soldier caught himself being civil and *liking it.* Then remembering who he was and why he was here, he barked out, "No more questions."

Joining up with other survivors, they walked a great distance that night before they ever stopped. Those who fell by the roadside and cried that they could go no further were either thrust through the heart with a spear or had their throats slashed. Quickly. Expertly. It was a warm, quiet death . . . as the life of the victim gently seeped away, leaving a crimson trail, staining the earth, crying from the ground.

❧❧❧

The sun heralded the breaking of day. Rachel waited until the guard had passed by her, then she sat up and stretched. For a moment she looked to her left, watching the rising sun smile its promise of a clear and sunny day. Although the land was denuded of trees, a bird sang happily perched on a scrubby bush. The Romans had carved deep into the countryside in order to gather enough timber to build their siege ramps and weapons of war.

As Rachel turned from the blinding brightness of the sun, she was shocked to see a large group of men marching by silently almost in unison. They were a human chain, tied together by their feet. Their cadence amazed Rachel even more as she noticed that each man's arms were tied in front of him instead of swinging freely for balance.

Soldiers, mounted on magnificent steeds, guarded the marchers. Famine hadn't touched the horses. The captives, bound together by ropes, focused their eyes straight ahead. They appeared to give no heed to the people sleeping to the right of them as they headed north just a short distance from the road.

Something about the group captured Rachel's attention, but for a moment she didn't know what it was. Then it struck her. *There's not one short man among the group. Nor have I yet to see an ugly one. They're all magnificent specimens of manhood—in the prime of their masculinity, strong. No wonder they are tied together. Unleashed they'd be formidable.* Their profiles were aglow in the gold light of the morning sun. Not one of them looked anywhere but straight ahead. *I wonder who they are? Where they're being taken?*

Rachel surveyed her surroundings to locate the positions of the guards when suddenly her leg cramped. The agony was terrible—she wanted to cry out, to kick, to stretch it, to grab it, do *anything* to relieve the spasm! Desperately she tried to change her position without disturbing those sleeping about her.

She crawled up on her knees, pushing the toes of her right foot to the ground to get some relief. She must be able to walk that day or they'd kill her. Yet she knew if she tried to walk at that moment, she'd fall to the ground. Panic seized her. Her leg felt gnarled. Breaking into a cold sweat, Rachel twisted her body, seeking relief. She pushed her injured hand into the ground trying to balance herself. Blood trickled from her lower lip as she fought to keep from crying out.

A young man among the captives, not far from the rear of the ranks, noticed from the side of his eye a writhing figure in the foreground. Because of the sun, it was hard to make out exactly what was happening. All he could discern was that it was a woman because there was a veil over her head.

Forbidden to speak or look to the right or the left, he was tired of staring at a forest of broad olive necks moving in unison before him. He was also tired of silence. Tired of body. They had walked all night. He was especially tired of following the black head of hair rigidly set on a neck that looked like it was cast in iron. *If I had to fight him in an amphitheater, I'd surely lose.*

He was among seven hundred men chosen because they were tall and handsome, thus rescued from immediate death. Judging from the height of the majority of the men, he must have barely qualified. They were to be shipped back to Rome and paraded through the streets as Titus and his legions returned triumphantly with their spoils of war. What awaited the captives after this, they did not know.

Cleverly, the young man had devised a scheme to amuse himself and divert his thoughts from the tiredness of his body. Throughout the journey he had been picking out some point of interest to focus on in the distance. Then in his mind he would calculate how many steps it would be before the focal point was out of his peripheral vision. They were forbidden to look any direction but straight ahead. It was a forced march. They had a ship waiting for them. Titus was anxious to return home. The soldiers didn't want their stride broken, thus the order. Any look to the right or the left, if caught, brought an excruciating blow from a Roman spear to the head of the violator.

The young man figured he only had about ten, maybe twelve, steps before the woman would move to the forbidden range. He hoped another person would sit up after her. It was hard to focus on sleeping bodies. *One.* He began counting off the steps. *Two. Why are they sleeping when it's daylight? Three. I wish we'd had a chance to sleep. Four. I wonder if some of them are dead? Five. Woman, what are you doing?*

As a result of her squirming, Rachel got tangled up in her cloak, tunic, and the belt that hung from her waist, which normally kept everything in place. Bound by her garments, all she could do was stare at the ground trying to figure out how to free herself. Finally, in desperation, keeping the suffering leg straight so it wouldn't spasm again, Rachel put one hand on the ground and pushed herself up to loosen her clothes.

Reuben raised his head slightly. Squinting because of the sun shining directly in his eyes, he whispered to Rachel, "What are you doing?"

Rachel never looked at Reuben. She was trying to determine how to get herself out of the bind she was in, and she didn't want to bring attention to Reuben and endanger him in any way. She had seen enough beatings on this journey.

Six. Her head's down. What's she looking at? Seven. Please look up; I need to see a kind face! Eight. Besides the face of a soldier who hates me. Nine. Good-bye, little woman. . . . Ten.

"I'm caught," Rachel's whisper was as strained as all of her pulling. "But don't touch me. Please don't, I'll . . . I'll—" Then with one final jerk, she threw herself off balance and landed square on her bottom with a heavy thud. As her head whipped back, Rachel found herself looking straight at the parade of captives. She couldn't believe her eyes. Without thinking she cried out, "Samuel! Sam—"

Reuben quickly thrust his hand over Rachel's mouth and brought her to the ground. Her eyes were wide, never leaving Samuel as she struggled to free herself from Reuben's grasp and turn on her stomach so she would not lose sight of her son.

Samuel's head whipped to the side for just an instant, then quickly his eyes were once again fixed on the olive necks before him. Although he had just passed her, Rachel heard it—a coarse whisper, the word she wondered if she'd ever hear again: "Imma."

Reuben heard it, too. Releasing Rachel, he jerked around to look, biting his lip lest he too cry out and get them all in trouble. Joy and fear wrestled in his heart. As his eyes followed his son, they caught the soldier riding toward them from the far side of the column of captives. *Have we been heard? Oh Elohim no, please, no....*

"Are you going to sleep all day?" shouted a stern voice from behind Reuben. "Get on your feet! We have a long way to go. . . ."

Immediately Rachel was on her feet for one last look at her son—a look she would have to treasure in her heart for longer than she wanted to know. The soldier on the horse sat motionless, looking puzzled. Then he reined in his horse, turned to the left, and moved toward the front of the column of captives.

Bending down, supposedly to fix her sandal, Rachel whispered to Sarah, "Our son lives."

Sarah looked at Rachel as she stood up, and with tears in her eyes, she moved her lips without uttering a sound. "And so do we. . . ."

It shall come about that as the LORD delighted over you to prosper you, and multiply you, so the LORD will delight over you to make you perish and destroy you; and you shall be torn from the land where you are entering to possess it.

Morever, the LORD will scatter you among all peoples, from one end of the earth to the other end of the earth; and there you shall serve other gods, wood and stone, which you or your fathers have not known.

And among those nations you shall find no rest, and there shall be no resting place for the sole of your foot; but there the LORD will give you a trembling heart, failing of eyes, and despair of soul.

So your life shall hang in doubt before you; and you shall be in dread night and day, and shall have no assurance of your life.

In the morning you shall say, "Would that it were evening!" And at evening you shall say, "Would that it were morning!" because of the dread of your heart which you dread, and for the sight of your eyes which you shall see.

—DEUTERONOMY 28:63-67

ope! I'll survive because I have hope! The quick glimpse of his mother, the remembrance of her calling his name, his loud whisper "Imma," the hope his mother had heard him, the incredible timing of the unexpected interchange, the soldier ordering those beside the road to get up on their feet, and the fact he survived all this without detection, that he wasn't beaten, that he was still alive . . . these things Samuel recalled to mind during the remainder of his journey. *I have hope!*

And with the hope came new strength for his journey. Samuel determined in his mind that he would not succumb to despair. He would not believe the rumor that once the captives had been paraded through the streets of Rome they would all be destined for death. Instead, he would live in the hope of life until he came face to face with death itself.

The long and arduous march to the port city of Caesarea became easier as Samuel pondered the sustaining power of hope—the vigor and motivation it brought to life. He resolved to never lose hope—not as long as breath was left in his body. And when death did come, he would release life in hope of the *resurrection*. Like Daniel, the prophet his Aunt Sarah had told him about, Samuel determined to become a man of insight, a man who stood firm and did exploits for the Almighty One of Israel.

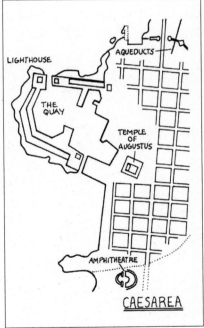

Though the days were long and the landscape often boring as they trudged the Via Maris to waiting Roman ships, Samuel stopped his practice of picking out landmarks and counting steps. Instead he contemplated life and the hope of one day seeing his Imma and Abba again. Surely that was his father's hand that had covered his mother's mouth!

Samuel also thought of Jared. Jared had been a friend to him; he had helped persuade Samuel's father to let him join Simeon Bar-Giora. Even though Samuel now had ropes around his ankles and wrists, he was proud that he had fought for his people and his Jerusalem. He had no reason to hang his head in shame.

Samuel then thought of his Aunt Sarah. As he walked, he kept cadence in his mind with his treasured memories. One of those was what his aunt told him about Daniel. He relived the nights Sarah sat upon his bed telling him stories, talking about life and her husband. Sometimes Sarah would go to her room and come back with the scroll Daniel had written. As she read Daniel's words to him, though he didn't really understand them, he remembered his sense of awe that a man like Daniel would write to his aunt.

Finally, the walls of Caesarea loomed before them. Finally, they were permitted to move their heads and look about them. Finally, in a mysterious act of mercy, their hands were untied. However, the command of silence was not revoked; they were not allowed to speak to one another.

Samuel's eyes peered through the forest of heads on his left, widening as he saw the panoramic Roman theater facing the sparkling emerald waters along the shoreline of the Mediterranean. The breeze from the sea, the beauty of the day, the sight of trees, the smell of ocean air, and the singing of the birds delighted Samuel's senses, resurging his passion for life. This was the city built by Herod the Great! It was Herod's window to the Greco-Roman world he loved and wished to duplicate on this side of the sea.

Caesarea is more resplendent than I imagined. No wonder the Romans love this city! Samuel, awestruck with the scenery, didn't notice the stir they created as they marched down the bustling, narrow street in a single column.

The Gentile citizens of Caesarea gaped openly at them as they passed— appreciating the beauty of their height and form and excited at the thought of these prisoners fighting to their deaths with wild beasts or gladiators in the Roman amphitheaters.

The captives were driven straight through the city, past the pretentious building that housed the public baths in the middle of Caesarea. There they entered the port area itself. The dazzling sunlight made a breathtaking sight as it played off the white marble of the Temple of Augustus and then danced on the crystal blue-green Mediterranean. Herod had imported the marble all the way from Rome.

Walls and towers on broad quays guarded the harbor. The single northern entrance protected incoming ships and the harbor itself from the prevailing southwest wind. The port was teeming with sailors.

At about three fathoms from the edge of the sea the Roman hostages were brought to a halt. To Samuel's left stood the Temple of Augustus facing the sea, and to his right was a huge open plaza and the right side of the quay, where several ships were tied up. For the moment they stood taking in the excitement and mystery one finds in a harbor where sea meets land and sailors from far-away places are freed from the confines of being under sail.

As the prisoners waited for their next command, Samuel determined to do all he could to escape. To him, risking his life in an attempt at freedom was better than passively being led like a lamb to the slaughter. He was not a trophy of Rome! He was a Jew of the tribe of Judah. Israel was his heritage; it was where he belonged, not Rome.

The port was crowded, noisy, confusing. Surveying the situation, Samuel deduced that if somehow he could get free he might just be able to lose himself in the crowds and find his way to freedom. First, however, he'd have to free his left ankle from the rope.

As the captives waited, staring at the crowds who were staring back at them, Samuel carefully lifted his right foot. He coughed to provide a distraction while he bowed his head and then reached down. With his finger, he caught the thong of his sandal and pulled it off. He then began his search for a sharp stone, a piece of glass, maybe a bone someone had tossed on the ground after eating lunch—*anything* that might be used to sever the rope binding his ankle. He prayed as he carefully moved his bare toes over the limited space of marble pavement allotted him. Suddenly he winced as pain pierced the ball of his foot. Whatever it was, he had come down on it too hard. Yet Samuel knew that if it had been sharp enough to cause him pain, then it might also be his key to freedom.

Balancing himself, he delicately felt out the shape of his find with his toes. One end of it was sharp, and the other was smooth but thick. It was quite long. *Probably a fish hook. If it is, I'll probably tear myself up in the process. But if it works, it will be worth the pain.* Patiently he maneuvered his find between his toes and then lifted it to begin working on the rope.

From time to time he'd catch his flesh. All his self-control was summoned forth to keep from crying out or groaning as the flesh was torn from his leg along with strands of the rope. At times he dropped the hook and panicked inwardly until he had it in his grip again.

Twice Samuel lost his balance and bumped against his comrades, but no one paid him any attention except to slam an elbow into his ribs. The freedom to look about, the change of scenery, the busyness of the port let his maneuvering go unnoticed. And because the prisoners were crowded together, the blood trickling onto the marble stones went unobserved as well.

As Samuel balanced himself, trying to hurry the process, it suddenly occurred to him that in freeing himself he was also, to a degree, freeing the man in front of him and the one behind. Eventually his fellow captives would miss the tension they felt from being tied to one another!

Although Samuel was sickened by the thought that freeing the others might increase his chance of getting caught, he continued tearing at the rope while he tried to figure out what to do. *How will the men react once they sense that lack of tension? Maybe it won't be noticed now, with us all crowded together, but what about when they board the ship?* Surely his fellow prisoners would not tell on him. Or would they? And if they didn't, for certain the guards or the sailors watching the gangplank would notice. *And they will search me out.* The Romans were that way. What a fool he was! *Maybe I should stop.* Just as that thought crossed his mind the rope broke. It was too late.

A wave of nausea came over Samuel. *How stupid of me not to think this through before I cut the rope.* Then an idea came to Samuel. They were packed together and no one could move but a few inches. *I'm nauseated; why not vomit? No one's going to go anyplace. No one's going to come to my aid.* Samuel began retching, forcing his meager rations out of his stomach. He knew no one would look, nor would they want to be close to him. Fortunately they couldn't move.

He continued regurgitating as he crouched to the ground. There he groaned quietly, keeping up the pretense of intermittent vomiting as he frantically searched for the ends of the rope. Once they were in his hands, acting as if he was supporting himself, he found the calf of the man in front of him. With another retch Samuel pulled on the man's leg, causing him to stumble slightly backwards. *Thank you, kind sir, your sandal is a little messy but it gives me exactly the extra slack I needed.*

The man turned his head to the side and let out a whispered curse. Samuel patted him twice on his back. Then, grateful they were packed so closely together, he tied a knot that he prayed would not come undone.

Wiping his mouth with his hands, Samuel stood up. The odor of his breath and the smell rising from the ground gave an authentic air to his actions. As Samuel looked around, appraising his surroundings, a cold sweat broke out on his brow. Like it or not, his course was set. If he didn't try to escape now, he'd be discovered. The knot was tied.

There were two large ships in the harbor bearing Roman standards. One was nestled to the right almost in the corner of the quay. The second, which seemed larger, was anchored on the left of the quay as one faced the sea. Was the ship to the right the one they would board? If so, Samuel knew his plans were futile. There was no way to break away in the open plaza without running, and if he had to run, there was only the sea or the plaza. Both would mean detection and certain death.

"Let's move!" yelled a soldier as he tightened the reins on his horse, which pranced nervously in place. The soldier motioned with his head that they were to board the ship on the left of the quay. Samuel smiled. He had a chance. They would have to walk around the Temple of Augustus—behind it, down the side to the left, almost circling it to get to the ship.

As the men fell into line, Samuel knew his only hope was to somehow slip between the marble pillars that formed the four-sided portico of the temple before the group moved too far away. He figured that once he was inside the temple he would cross to its right, survey the large open plaza, and when it looked crowded enough he would walk to its entrance facing the sea and lose himself in the crowd. He knew he couldn't go back through the city the way they'd come into the port, for there was the danger that he might meet Titus himself or other prisoners being brought into the city. Therefore he had to go north, get out of the city, and then make his way south to the city of Yavne. *But how? How?*

The chain of captives turned around and began marching toward the back of the temple, which was now on Samuel's right. But Samuel was not in the line of men closest to the temple. They were two deep between him and the portico of the temple. *Two rows of men tied together, and I am supposed to be tied with them! Think! Think!*

They rounded the corner and were now walking alongside the back of the temple to get to the other side of the quay. Hemmed in by the fairly narrow space between the temple and the port wall, they were jammed together. In just a moment they'd be rounding the next corner of the temple. Panic hit him. He remembered he'd seen a small plaza on the other side just before they came to the quay. *There will be more room; surely they'll spread out and put more distance between me and the temple. That will lessen my chances of getting away.* In a flash Samuel knew what he had to do.

Swinging his left leg behind the man to his left, he caught the leg of a man in the next row. Putting his hand on his right thigh to brace himself, he jerked with all his strength, at the same time letting out a low groan. Two rows of men to his left stumbled, some falling to the ground and taking others with them. A number of them uttered cries of shock and oaths. The men behind Samuel staggered and pushed against him. It was the first time in all their journey that anyone had fallen. Soldiers shouted, cursing the clumsiness of the prisoners. Confusion reigned.

With all the attention directed to the tangled jumble of bodies and ropes on the left side of the column, no one noticed that one man was free to make his way to the edge of the temple. Samuel had two lines of ropes to hurdle, and he made it without tripping. In the tumult of it all, everyone felt free to talk to one another. That gave him his chance. Samuel leaped to the temple porch and stepped behind the massive Corinthian pillars.

Now Samuel had to cross the temple and survey the plaza on the right side of the quay. As he walked to the other side, he saw that the temple was deserted except for two people standing at the entrance.

Another ship had just passed the huge tower at the harbor's entrance, thus capturing everyone's attention. It, too, bore a Roman eagle. Samuel decided to go to the side porch, ascertain the situation in the plaza, and then plan the path he would take. Maybe by then the two people in the temple would leave and he could walk out without passing anyone. He didn't want to be seen, for his tunic was dirty and one foot was without a sandal. His ankle was crusted with blood. If someone stopped to look at him carefully it would be easy to surmise he was a runaway slave.

Just as Samuel reached the other side of the temple, he saw Roman soldiers filling the center of the plaza and barking orders. Contemptuously they spit out the word *Jew* at the exhausted, straggly herd. Samuel stepped back deeper into the shadow of the pillars and began a systematic survey of the crowd, looking for his loved ones.

He didn't want his loved ones to see him; it might endanger their lives and his. His mission was to live, not die. Just a look would be enough to sustain him. And at least he would know they had made it this far—to the ships. Which ship and what destination he could not know, but he would know they were alive and not buried in Israel's soil.

Samuel carefully scanned the portion of the group he could see from where he stood. Not finding his parents or Sarah or Jared, he moved back between the next two pillars and again surveyed the crowd. Hearing the orders that the prisoners were to move, panic invaded his heart. The systematic search had to end; there was no time. His eyes darted back and forth.

The prisoners moved forward to the edge of the water. *Were they going to board now?* A soldier moved through the group randomly dividing people— some to the right, others to the left. Samuel stepped closer to the edge of the porch and watched in pain as the soldier on his horse eased his way through the slow-moving mass of Jews.

Samuel stretched upward and stood on tiptoe trying to see beyond the horse and its rider. Frustrated, he glowered at the soldier, who was bringing down his spear to separate two women who were holding hands. Although Samuel could only see their backs, he could tell they were resisting.

The woman on the right appeared to be pleading with the soldier, but the spear held. Although Samuel couldn't hear what the soldier was saying, he knew from his countenance the answer was a firm no. A man who had his arm around the shoulders of the woman on the left pulled her to him. Her trembling shoulders told Samuel she was crying. His heart ached. Had these Romans no compassion? What difference would it have made whether the prisoners were separated or allowed to stay together? None. The soldier's action was simply a display of the hardness of men's hearts.

The woman on the right was prodded onward by the soldier's spear at her back. At that moment she turned around for one last look back. Samuel recognized her immediately, and his thoughts screamed, *It's Aunt Sarah! He must be separating Aunt Sarah from Abba and Imma! But where is Jared? Why isn't he with Sarah?*

Frantically Samuel's eyes searched the people around Sarah. *Surely Jared would be at Sarah's side, protecting her even as Abba was protecting Imma.* Finally Samuel saw Jared's head beside the horse, and he wished he hadn't. The soldier was now separating Sarah from Jared and laughing at their apparent pleading as once again his spear became a rod of separation. Sarah stood all alone in the middle, cut off from her loved ones. Samuel watched his aunt grow taller right before his eyes as she straightened her back and walked on, head lifted high. *Aunt Sarah will survive.*

Samuel smiled wryly. *And I'll be here when you return. . . .*

"You found them all? You're pleased?" The voice behind was cloaked in kindness.

Samuel's heart was in his mouth. A sweat broke out on his brow as he turned to see who had been watching. A young woman stood behind him, slightly shorter than he was. Unsure of her intentions, he searched her face. For a moment she allowed him to look into her eyes, then her gaze moved instantly to his feet. He watched as she winced. Samuel could see pain in her eyes. Then she took in his dirty, weathered clothes, the dust that powdered his skin and made it look older, and the oiliness of his hair. She smiled winsomely. For the first time, he noticed there was no belt around her waist; her tunic hung straight from her shoulders. There was no cloth draped around her and tucked in at the waist. Rather, the cloth was folded over her arm, which she extended towards him along with her belt draped on top. She spoke with compassion. "Here, put this over you quickly and tie it with the belt. I will walk you across the plaza to—to—which way are you going?"

Again his eyes searched hers. They were a beautiful blue, clear like the sea. "I'd like to tell, but I can't. I hope you—"

"I understand. I believe you are right. It would probably be safer for both of us. You must hurry."

As Samuel tied the belt around his waist, he looked at her again. She smiled, not embarrassed in the least. She was statuesque, classic. Her blond hair rested on her shoulders, nestled softly around her long neck. A braid encircled her face, giving her a dignity complementing the straightness of her posture. Her complexion was fair, unmarred. The sun, about to settle into its bed in the sea, first leaned down to kiss her on the head and on her shoulders. The golden rays shone in a way that they gave her almost an angelic appearance. *Beautiful!* If Samuel hadn't known angels always appeared as men, he would have thought she was an angel sent to deliver him. He smiled broadly, and she grinned.

"Why?" he asked with a puzzled look, wondering why she had chosen to help him.

"I really don't know. It's just that when I saw you come into the temple, look my way, and then walk to the pillars, I felt you needed help. And that you needed to live. For you to die would seem like such a waste. . . ."

Chapter 38

*A*cross the sea from Herod's window, Titus marched alone under the wooden and stucco arch that had been made for his triumphal entry into the breathtaking glories of Rome. None but the recipient of this honor could pass under this arch, which would forever bear testimony to the greatness of his conquest.

At a later date, the wood portion of the hastily assembled arch would be replaced by stone and marble, and the top crowned with a chariot and four bronze horses. On one of the arch's sides would be a relief of the Romans bearing on their shoulders Judah's massive, ornately carved menorah—one of the spoils of war taken from the temple in Jerusalem. The relief of the seven-branched candlestick would include no flames, for the Romans had extinguished the light of Israel forever. Or so they thought.

On the same relief would also be Roman figures triumphantly blowing silver horns—the same horns that had been used in the Jewish worship services to assemble the people and commemorate their sacred feasts. These assemblies and feasts were now no more, for the temple, the axle of the wheel carrying Judaism from one year to another through the cycle of holy feast days, had been destroyed. How could there be sacrifices without a temple? And without sacrifices how could the God of the Jews be propitiated? Surely, with Israel's temple destroyed their worship would cease, their fanaticism would give way to reason, and their people would be absorbed by the culture of mighty, invincible Rome!

It was a day of triumph. Vespasian and his son, Titus, celebrated it properly by striking a new coin with the inscription *Judea Capta*. Again Judah was taken into captivity, her survivors scattered to the four winds. And although Israel may not have known it, according to the Law and the prophets, it would be for a long time, but *the last time*. Eventually, many would return to their land never to leave again until Messiah came!

Little did Titus or other Romans realize that one of the human spoils of war they left behind would again become a thorn in the side of Rome along with almost a half-million other people. The Romans might have carried away the menorah, but the light of Judaism did not go out. Before the destruction of Jerusalem, Ben Zakkai, then an old man, was secreted out of the earthly Zion in a coffin. On the coast near Joppa, with (of all things) the permission of the Romans, he established a religious school, the forerunner of all yeshivot, or schools of learning, which would keep the torch of Judaism burning. Rome thought a little school of learning far from Jerusalem would keep the Jewish people satisfied and out of trouble now that the temple was destroyed. The school was in Yavne, the town that Samuel had fled to when he escaped Caesarea.

There Samuel sat at the feet of men who were to shape, try, and test his thinking, one of whom he would eventually follow to the Judean desert.

"But Messiah will come at any moment. Why must we fight again?" Levi asked Samuel with exasperation and incredulity.

Samuel looked at his new friend Levi. A friend he admired, a friend he was very fond of. A friend who believed with all his heart Messiah was coming . . . soon. This was because Levi, like Aunt Sarah, was troubled by some of Daniel's writings. Based on Daniel and Isaiah, Levi figured out that Messiah's coming should be anytime now. Levi had his pinched nose in the sacred scrolls all the time and was constantly involved in discussions about the Mishnah, or the oral Law.

Samuel admired Levi's diligence when it came to spiritual matters, but Samuel thought he was too caught up in the endless debatings and codifying of the Mishnah. Rabbi Judah Hanasi, upset with the way the people were inter-preting the scriptures in the light of new circumstances, had ordered that the Mishnah be written down in a definitive form; however, Samuel had his own opinions about that. He felt all their study of the Mishnah kept them from the Bible itself. On this Samuel stood alone, and while Levi did not agree with Samuel, they still enjoyed a rare and special kind of friendship.

When Samuel thought of his friendship with Levi, he wondered if it could be likened to how Jonathan and David felt about one another. *Well, maybe not exactly. Levi can be awfully exasperating at times. Besides, Jonathan was willing to fight alongside David whenever he needed support. Levi isn't willing to fight with me. Or, maybe he is. . . .* Samuel decided he wouldn't give up.

"We must fight, Levi," Samuel reasoned patiently, "because Hadrian, the new emperor, has banned circumcision and instruction in the Law. These are the very lifeblood of Judaism. Don't you see? They took our temple. Are we going to let them take these, too? Think, Levi, think! Rabbi ben Zakkai too believed Messiah would come, but don't you remember what he said? 'If you are holding a seedling in your hand and the coming of Messiah is announced, first plant your seedling, then go out to greet the Messiah.'"

"Yes, Samuel, I know. I know what the rabbi said, yet I also know he was against any kind of violent resistance. Don't forget that! Don't forget that, Samuel." Levi jumped to his feet, pointed at Samuel with his finger, then imme-diately sat down again and pounded the table. "He also said disaster follows open rebellion. You can go follow Bar Koseba or Bar Kochba—'son of the star,' as Rabbi Akiva calls him—but I'm not going. Despite his name, Samuel, I'm convinced he is not Messiah, nor his forerunner. I am *not* going, Samuel. I'm not." Levi shook his head adamantly. His pinched nose seemed even more shriveled with his thin lips tautly stretched over his gritted teeth. Levi was a small but wiry young man with plenty of mettle.

"Well, Levi," said Samuel as he reached across the table and banged his hand in front of Levi, "I am going to plant my seedling. And if Messiah comes, then I won't have to stay in the battle. He'll bring it to an immediate end."

Samuel stood up. He knew the discussion was over and that he'd have to go to Rabbi Akiva by himself. "Maybe Messiah will see our zeal and reward us by coming," Samuel said. "And if not, I'd rather die than see Hadrian build a temple to Jupiter on the ruins of our Temple Mount and change the name of our beloved Jerusalem to Aelia Capitolina as he says he is going to do."

"You might die, Samuel. You might die." Levi's nodding head gave affirmation to his words.

"Besides," Samuel wanted to leave Levi with one last point just to support his argument, "if our people aren't circumcised, then they are breaking the covenant. Moses almost got killed for that. I'd rather get killed for defending the sign of our covenant with the Almighty!"

"What a shame if you do. You should live, Samuel; you should live."

Samuel left Yavne immediately. His confidence was in Rabbi Akiva. After all, the rabbi was the foremost spiritual leader of the day. If Rabbi Akiva supported Simeon bar Koseba, surely the man was worthy to be followed. Samuel thought of what people were saying about Simeon bar Koseba—that the Torah had a prophecy in the book of Numbers, B'midbar, which was being fulfilled in him. Samuel reasoned as he walked. *Maybe B'midbar does refer to Bar Koseba when it says, "There shall step forth a star—kokhav—out of Jacob." Maybe he is Messiah! That was why Rabbi Akiva renamed Bar Koseba to Bar Kochba—son of the star! If he is Messiah, how awful it would be if I did not follow him into battle.*

Samuel kicked stones and remained deep in thought all the way from Yavne to Joppa. He'd had enough of studies; now it was time to live like a Jew! Yet he wished he didn't have to do it alone. He missed Levi. Samuel had never had a brother except the one he never knew.

When Samuel arrived at Joppa, he stood looking at the sea and for a moment permitted himself to think of the beautiful Gentile with golden hair who had come to his rescue. Samuel didn't allow his thoughts to last long, for he could never marry a Gentile. They were considered unclean. Even to go into their homes was forbidden. He was almost sure that was in the oral Law somewhere. At least that was what he had been told. That was why Samuel never asked her name when they met. He didn't want her to have a name. Remembering her face and her concern for him was distracting enough.

Samuel sat at the edge of the sea watching the sun say its good-byes to the day. In evening's last hour, against the backdrop of an intense blue heaven, the sun first draped the billowy clouds in brilliant reds, then dressed them in pinks that reminded Samuel of the flowers Aunt Sarah often brought home from the fields. Eventually the pink softened into shades of coral and then gray, until the scattered iron-gray clouds were all alone in the black of night—just like him. It was lonely, colorless. Samuel lay back on the grass. Maybe he needed to sleep awhile before he went any further.

"Samuel. . . ."

Samuel sat up and looked around. He couldn't see anyone, but he was sure he heard his name being called, even though the sound was no louder than a whisper. Frightened, he sat very still, listening intently.

Then after what seemed a long time, the whisper came again. "Samuel . . . Samuel . . . Samuel." Three times!

Samuel turned, peering into the darkness on his right and then his left. Seeing nothing, he slowly rose to his feet and then quickly turned around full circle. He saw no one. Moments later he heard his name being called again in a distant ghostlike voice.

"Samuel . . . Samuel. Don't go to war without Levi. . . ."

Samuel shouted with great relief, "Levi! Levi! Where are you? Get out here."

Levi came walking out of the dark laughing; he was clearly pleased with himself. "Did you think it was the Almighty One of Israel calling you like Samuel of old? Oh man of little faith, why didn't you say, 'Speak Lord, for thy servant hears?'"

As soon as he saw Levi, Samuel ran and grabbed him. Lifting his friend's slight frame and bobbing him up and down in the air, he cried out, "I'm so glad to see you—so glad!" The weakness Samuel had felt was now replaced by joy.

"I want you to know, Samuel, that you are wrong, you are wrong, you are wrong. When you say it three times, it makes it true. You are wrong, but I couldn't let you go to war by yourself. You're like a brother, Samuel, the only brother I have, and I have to keep you alive."

Instantly Samuel's loneliness was gone. He no longer thought of the Gentile girl; he had a Jewish brother born for the day of adversity in the near tomorrows.

Chapter 39

$\mathcal{S}$amuel and Levi were careful to stay off the roads as Rome poured more soldiers into the land to quell the revolt led by Simeon bar Kochba. Israel had become an albatross around Rome's neck. Hadrian summoned Severus, his most brilliant general, from Britain to take command of the legions. They were facing a Jewish army five to six hundred thousand strong, employing tactics different from a centralized insurrection. The Jews were fighting on a number of fronts in a surge-and-attack mode.

By the time Samuel and Levi arrived in Jerusalem to join Simeon bar Kochba, Samuel's hero had overwhelmed the Roman legions in the south and liberated Jerusalem. Samuel jingled the newly cast coins in his hand. It gave him a sense of pride to be associated with such a strong leader.

"Look, Levi. Our very own coins. No more Roman coins for Israel."

"You look, Samuel. Bar Kochba is your hero, not mine."

"Why must you be that way, Levi?" Samuel was walking with his head down studying the coins in his hand.

"I am what I am, Samuel. You either like it or you don't. At least I am here with you to keep you alive."

"You can't keep me alive if I am appointed to die." Pointing to the coins, Samuel said, "Look. This denarius has a three-stringed lyre with the inscription, 'For the freedom of Jerusalem,' and Simeon bar Kochba has liberated Jerusalem! His name Simeon is on the other side."

"No, Samuel, no! We the people of this land have liberated Jerusalem, not your Bar Kochba."

Samuel ignored Levi's retort. He would not allow Levi to diminish his joy at seeing Jewish coins for the first time. "Look, here. On this bronze coin. It's the newest one. It says, 'First Year of the Redemption of Israel' and on the other side it says, 'Simeon, Nasi of Israel.'"

"Ah, he's liberated Jerusalem, and now he's nasi, a prince! Now he's a prince." There was sarcasm in Levi's voice.

"One thing about you, Levi, is I don't miss a thing you say. You never say something just once!"

"You know, Samuel, when Rabbi Akiva saw Bar Koseba, he cried out, 'This is the king Messiah!' and Rabbi Yohanan ben Torta came back with 'Akkiva, grass will grow in your jawbones, and he still will not have come.' I am telling you, this man is not Messiah, so don't believe it. Not everything one hears about the man is good. It isn't good."

"Simeon bar Kochba may not be Messiah, and that's all right. But don't forget that he just liberated Jerusalem, he just *liberated* Jerusalem, he just liberated *Jerusalem!*"

⊰∾⊱∾⊰

At dawn, Samuel was standing his watch in the Citadel at Betar, about a two-hour walk southwest of Jerusalem. The morning was serene, regally quiet, majestic. Samuel didn't want to move, to breathe, to make a sound lest he spoil the solemnity of it all. In reverential awe he peered down into the deep ravines surrounding Betar's nest on this steep hill. There were deep chasms on every side but the south. Samuel felt like a raven spreading its wings and riding quietly, effortlessly on the wind. He could see the wall and its semicircular tower, which defended the city. Although things were not going well in their fight against the Romans, Samuel still felt secure. He was with his hero, whom he had come to know well. So well that he now called him Simeon.

Samuel's reverie was abruptly broken by the sound of rushing footsteps and Levi's voice shouting at him.

"Samuel, Samuel! Hurry, we've got to leave," Levi said with urgency.

Samuel turned to Levi, looking rather disgusted. "I can't go with you. Can't you see I am on duty in this tower? I am to watch for the Romans. I can't leave my post. What are you doing here, anyway?"

"Samuel, do you think I don't know what you are doing? Do you think I would call you to leave if I hadn't been summoned to do so? Now, hurry—it's urgent. They're sending someone to take your place. They have another assignment for us. Come on, come on!"

"I'm coming, I'm coming. . . ."

As they speedily descended the steps from the tower Samuel called to Levi, who was outdistancing him. "Where are we going?"

"I don't know. They are going to tell us right now." Reaching their destination, Levi said, "Here—in here," as he pointed to a small room where Simeon sat with a scroll spread out before him.

Samuel was breathless but not Levi. Levi's skinny little body could run and run without being out of breath. He was much stronger than he looked.

Bar Kochba was just signing his name to the scroll—*Dictated by Simeon bar Kochba.* The Prince of Israel looked haggard to Samuel. Or was he worried? Concern was mixed with admiration as Samuel gazed at the man. There was nothing Samuel would not do for this strong and powerful leader.

Simeon looked at Levi and Samuel, wishing he were young again. The revolt was losing ground; the tide was turning. Simeon believed his time was running out. "I want you two to carry these scrolls to the leaders of the revolt in

Ein Gedi. I've received word that the Romans are headed our way. When they come they will set up a siege around Betar even as they did around Jerusalem and Masada. Pray that they will not succeed."

"Maybe it is time for Messiah to come," Levi volunteered.

"Maybe he will, Levi, maybe he will. Heaven knows Messiah is our only hope." Simeon's smile was faint and weary, but Levi beamed from ear to ear. His pinched nose crinkled with joy as he realized that Simeon didn't think he was the Messiah. From that moment on Levi had a new appreciation for this valiant Nasi of Israel who was willing to lay down his life to liberate the land from the oppression of Rome.

"Under no circumstances are the two of you to try returning to Betar if you see Roman camps around this place. If we die, we die. But I want no one dying needlessly. I want you to live for Israel—for the coming of Messiah."

Simeon did not have to ask if they understood. Their vigorous nodding reassured him they had heard and would respect his wishes.

"Now, be gone! And don't forget the Scriptures say there is no retirement in the time of war. Be valiant soldiers. Remember the Shema, 'Hear, O Israel! The Lord—'" Levi and Samuel joined in unison with Simeon, "'is our God, the Lord is one.'"

Levi and Samuel were gone almost as quickly as they descended the top of the Citadel. Levi was elated. Those few minutes with Simeon had changed his whole perspective. He could talk of nothing else on their long journey to Ein Gedi except the insights he had gained about Messiah in his studies of the prophets.

"I've been thinking, Samuel, about the last chapters of D'varim—Deuteronomy—in the Torah, and I believe what we are enduring is part of the Almighty's judgment."

Samuel shook his head in disagreement. "I don't believe that, Levi. You must be reading it wrong. How could the Almighty allow his own people to suffer so? You're mistaken."

"I tell you, Samuel, we deserve what is happening. We didn't listen to the Almighty. We don't live by his book, the Bible. We pick and choose what we want to believe and obey. We think that because we're his chosen people judgment will not come on us. We're wrong, Samuel. We are wrong and are going to be dead if we don't change. The prophet Isaiah said we would be paid back double for all our sins. Double, Samuel! Double!"

Samuel didn't say anything more. He just listened all the way to Ein Gedi.

By the time they finally arrived, exhaustion set in and they slept the sun around. Then for the next several weeks they worked under the command of the leaders at Ein Gedi. Their favorite commander was Jacob, a big burly man born with a scowl on his face. He had a warm heart for his fellow Jews, but he loathed the Romans.

In the late afternoons when they were permitted time to themselves, Samuel and Levi would go exploring. They recounted and relived as much as they could remember of the lives of King David and King Saul, of the books of Samuel the prophet, and of David's times of hiding from Saul in the region of Ein Gedi. They also talked about Saul's son, Jonathan, and the covenant he made with David. Then they both shared what they thought about David and Jonathan's relationship.

It was late one afternoon when Samuel and Levi decided to cut a covenant together, just as David and Jonathan had done. Understanding a covenant to be a solemn and binding agreement, broken only at the cost of their lives, Levi and Samuel stood opposite one another in the sands of the Judean wilderness. Each removed his robe and handed it to the other. Then as each put on the other's robe, Levi, then Samuel, said, "You are putting on me. Everything I am and everything I have is yours." Then the two men exchanged their belts and their swords, vowing with their strength to protect and defend one another all the days of their lives. And, if necessary, to lay down their lives for each other. From that moment on, Levi and Samuel were blood brothers.

Making a covenant was such a solemn occasion—a sacred moment—that they didn't converse much except to make their pledges. As they walked back to rejoin the group, their arms on each other's shoulder, Samuel and Levi walked a little taller in the knowledge that, indeed, each now had a real brother.

When they returned to the cave where their two leaders slept, they sensed something was seriously wrong. Some of the men gathered around the fire were downcast. Since neither of them recognized the man who was speaking, Samuel and Levi sat down on the rock floor of the cave to listen. "The battle at Betar—"

Jacob leaned over to Samuel and whispered in his ear, "This man just rode in and is bringing us news of the siege of Betar. He just started talking about it. You haven't missed anything, but be prepared. He's already warned us the news is not good. In fact—"

Levi interrupted, putting his forefinger over his mouth and then pointing to the stranger who was now speaking. He didn't want to miss a word the man was saying.

"The siege wall the Romans built was just like those they built at Jerusalem and then Masada," the stranger continued.

Levi leaned over to Samuel. "Remember, Simeon said it would be—"

The man continued, "The battle was fierce. Rabbi Akiva is dead, and . . . and . . ." the man put his head in his hands, shook it, then pulled his hands back to his ears and let them slide down his neck while he said the words they all dreaded to hear. "Simeon bar Kochba, the Prince of Israel, is dead. He died valiantly."

Tears came to Samuel's eyes. He didn't bother to wipe them away. He was not ashamed of crying at news like that.

The bearer of bad news looked at them solemnly. "Betar fell because of treachery—"

"Who?" the men asked almost in unison.

"I don't know his name."

"Rabbi Akiva," Samuel asked, "was he at Betar?"

The man responded immediately. "I'm . . . I'm not sure."

Samuel turned to Levi. "He wasn't there when we were there, was he, Levi?"

"No, if he had been I would have been sitting at his feet the entire time questioning him and discussing the Torah. No, he wasn't there then, not then."

Samuel turned to the man again. "Well, did he die there or not?"

"I . . . I don't really know. I'm tired from my journey. Shaken by the events. You understand, I'm sure. I need some sleep. Aren't you tired?"

"But you said he was dead before you told us about Bar Kochba." Levi's voice was uncharacteristically smooth; he asked his question as if he was trying to draw something out of the man.

"Well," Samuel asked, "if you don't know that, then tell me, do you know anything about his death?" Samuel seemed a little irritated with the man and the man sensed it. He looked at Samuel for a moment, as if he was trying to figure out how to answer him.

"How," Samuel asked in a way that showed the man he intended to hear the truth, "did the rabbi die?"

"He . . . the rabbi . . . was captured and tortured. At least that's what I heard." The man's eyes searched the eyes of the men in the cave. Levi watched him. "Reports have it he was flayed alive and then torn to death by metal combs."

Everyone in the cave sat in silence for some time. Then one by one they filed out, saying nothing. Finally, Jacob hollered, "Tomorrow we'll talk about what we do next!"

It was dark as the men went to the corners of the caves where they slept.

Samuel and Levi went out and sat in the darkness for a while. *I wonder,* Samuel thought, *if we're all thinking what it would be like to be flayed alive?* Samuel had seen a burnt offering flayed, but at the time the animal had been killed first.

"What are we going to do, Samuel, now that Bar Kochba is dead?" asked Levi.

"I don't know. I suppose in the morning our leaders will tell us where we fight next."

Levi looked around and asked Samuel, "Where's the man who brought us the bad news? And why didn't he tell us his name?"

Samuel motioned with his head toward the cave where they'd had the meeting. Then realizing that Levi might not be able to see the movement of his head, Samuel said, "In the cave. Isn't that him putting dirt on the fire?"

Levi looked and for a few moments didn't say anything. Then they rose and headed for their cave, still saying nothing until Levi asked, "Why is the man putting dirt on the fire? It'll be pitch black in there." Levi paused, then spoke again. "Samuel, I don't like the man. I don't trust him. Have you ever thought he might not be telling the truth? He just might not be telling the truth."

"Well," Samuel responded, "why would he come all this distance to tell us something like that if it weren't true?"

"I don't know, Samuel, I don't know. And it could very well be true, but I don't trust the man. Maybe—maybe he's the betrayer," Levi mused as they entered their cave. "Maybe he is telling the truth, but maybe he came to win our confidence and then trick us—maybe take us somewhere we shouldn't go."

"Levi—go to sleep, go to sleep. Your mind is working overtime."

Levi reached over and slapped Samuel on the back as he laughed, "I'm going, I'm going."

Samuel went right to sleep. His breathing was heavy. But Levi couldn't sleep. He was restless. *How did the man know all the details of Rabbi Akkiva's death but not know where he died? It doesn't make sense. . . .*

Levi got up and walked outside. It was a dark night with very few stars in the sky. The moon was hiding behind some wispy clouds. It was cold, but even as skinny as he was Levi still liked the cold. He looked toward the other caves. He noticed a figure moving stealthily, it seemed, from the cave where the leaders slept to another cave nearby. The caves were almost in a row. His and Samuel's was the third one, almost around a curve.

If someone is just leaving the leaders' cave then they must still be awake. I'm going to go talk to them—unless that stranger is still awake, too. Levi headed for the cave. *If he is, I'll just ask Jacob to come out and talk to me in private. If the man is indeed the betrayer, then we have to find out before he learns about our plans. And if he's not, then I'm the fool.*

Levi walked into the cave. He was pleased the clouds had abandoned the company of the moon, for that gave him a little more light. He carefully made his way in the dark to the place where Jacob slept. Seeing the dim outline of Jacob's form, Levi whispered, "Jacob . . . Jacob." Getting no response, Levi stooped down and began shaking Jacob gently on the shoulder. As he did, he felt something warm and wet on his hand. Unable to tell what it was but suddenly suspicious, Levi brought his hand to his mouth and licked it. It was *blood!*

Levi stumbled his way to the other side of the cave, where Asher slept. Unable to rouse him, he grabbed him by the feet and pulled him out of the cave into the moonlight. *Asher's dead! Jacob and Asher! Oh my soul, my soul! Samuel, Samuel—*

Levi scrambled from the cave, slid down its hilly incline, and ran, stumbling through the dark. Afraid to cry aloud not knowing where the betrayer was, Levi prayed he would get to Samuel before it was too late. As he ran, darting through the shrubs and rocks, questions ran with him in his mind. *How did he kill them? Why didn't they scream? Why didn't I hear something? I was awake, but I didn't hear a thing.*

Levi clawed the dirt as he climbed up the entrance to his cave. Just as he rose to his feet he saw the shadowy form of a man bent over Samuel. The man had one hand holding something over Samuel's mouth. His other hand was poised with what Levi supposed was a knife. Samuel's legs were thrashing the air. Levi dove low, straight for the man's midsection. Hitting him like a battering ram, the man doubled over, crashing into the rough stone wall of the cave. His head made a dull cracking sound as it whipped back, and his upper body fell forward, trapping Levi in the fold of his body. Samuel pulled Levi free. Scrambling to his feet, he said, "You saved my life, Levi! You, *you* saved my life!"

Levi wiped the blood from his mouth with the back of his skinny hand. Smiling weakly, he said, "That's why I came Samuel; that's why I came." With that, Levi passed out. His pinched nose was broken.

Chapter 40

ut listen for just a minute," Sarah said as she leaned across the table and smiled broadly at the old rabbi who bore a long, soft, snowy white beard. Although Rabbi Solomon ben Asher was politely shunned by the other two rabbis in their community because of his lack of reverence for the Talmud, Sarah adored this short, stooped-over little man and enjoyed his visits at her house. His intent but often impish eyes danced with glee when he pointed out (to whomever would listen) the sufficiency of the Scriptures over the Talmud. Rabbi Solomon was the only leader in their community who didn't live by the dictates of the Talmud.

"Sarah, I *am* listening," the old rabbi gently remonstrated. "What would I do, living here in Cologne, without you? What a lonely and discouraged old man I would be, dwelling here so far away from Jerusalem in the Rhineland. Who would speak to me about the things of the Almighty One and the holy books, Sarah, if it weren't for you?"

"I don't like the Talmud," the rabbi continued. "And you know, I really don't think what the Talmud has become is what Rabbi Judah ha-Nasi intended when he codified the oral Law. First it's the oral Law. Then the Mishnah—the teachings—are combined with the discussions on the teachings, or the Gemara, and the two are called the oral Law!" The rabbi threw up his wrinkled hands, which were always trembling. "And all this makes up the Talmud!" Rabbi Solomon shook his head.

"It is too much. Too much, Sarah. I'm a simple man, a simple rabbi. All I need to have and to know is in one book—the Bible. From it I can figure out how to live. It is there in principle. The Almighty's precepts are enough!"

Rabbi Solomon leaned forward, his posture taking on the intensity of his speech. "Why do I need man's interpretations? Are they inspired? No! Look at all the different interpretations. The schools of this rabbi, that rabbi, the Jerusalem Talmud, the Babylonian Talmud. *I* can figure out how to obey the Almighty, Sarah, if I know the holy book. If . . . if . . . did you hear my if, Sarah?" His beard bobbed upward following the thrust of his chin. "*If* I know the Holy Bible."

"So the others think I'm a heretic!" Solomon raised his right hand in the air as if to dismiss the others. "They don't want to talk to me about the Bible. But thanks be to the Almighty One, he put you in this city. If you had to leave

Israel, Sarah—if you had to go into captivity—at least you came here for me. It's hard to have to live with Dusia, my dear daughter—may a blessing be upon her—in a city where no one wants to listen to me! So I'm listening, Sarah, I'm listening. What do you want to say?"

Sarah grinned appreciatively at the old man as she moved to the edge of her chair. "I believe I've seen something that fits with the writings of Daniel," she said. "Daniel said he wanted me to know and to remember Nebuchadnezzar's dream. You know, the one of the statue of gold, silver, bronze, and iron, which later became iron and clay. Remember?"

Rabbi Solomon nodded his head affirmatively as Sarah continued. "That statue collapses when a huge stone cut without hands crushes the feet. The stone then becomes a great mountain. Of course, you know Daniel wrote that the four parts of the statue represent four kingdoms, and the stone represents Messiah's coming to rule the whole earth. Finally, rabbi, finally, we will have a kingdom that can never be destroyed."

"So, Sarah. So we both know this." His trembling hand was in the air helping him with his question. "What do you want to say, Sarah?"

"Rabbi," Sarah leaned across the table again, eager to hear his thoughts, "Do you think the division of the Roman Empire into two parts was symbolized in the two legs of the statue? You know, the eastern part of the empire became the Byzantine, and the western part the Latin. Remember that the chest of the statue had two arms and it represented the Medo-Persian Empire—two empires combined. Do you think the two legs symbolize the Byzantine and Latin empires?"

Rabbi Solomon leaned back in the chair, closed his eyes, and pulled on his beard for a moment or two. Then he began stroking it. "You're a thinking woman, Sarah—a thinking woman." Solomon opened his eyes and looked at her. Sarah thought she saw in them a glint of admiration. The rabbi's hand became motionless, resting on his beard. "You could be right, Sarah." He nodded his head and closed his eyes again to think. "You could be right."

Delighted that he didn't dismiss her thought immediately, Sarah waited patiently, studying his face while his eyes were shut. Once again, his hand stroked his beard. The rabbi always took a while to get to the question at hand. Sarah had become accustomed to this; she didn't mind just sitting and waiting. This was what made Rabbi Solomon special! Besides, Sarah felt that caring for him and being a friend in his loneliness was one of her duties—a kindness to be shown, a good deed.

"Have you gone to sleep on me, rabbi?" Sarah's laugh was playful.

"Do you hear my snoring? If you don't hear me snoring, I'm not asleep! I was thinking, Sarah, thinking. You know Daniel is very hard to understand."

"Why is it so hard if we simply let the words say what they say and don't add our own complicated interpretations or mysticism? I have to believe the

Bible was written so anyone who cared to could understand it—even a woman! It's not for just an elite group of *Tennaim*, teachers. If Daniel says, 'These are four kings—four kingdoms—who shall rule the earth and the name of the first is Babylon,' then that is what he meant. The interpretation is given in the text. Now, reason with me as you so often challenge me to do. Anyone who can count and who knows our history knows that Daniel named the first three kingdoms, but not the fourth. After Babylon came the Medo-Persian Empire, then the Grecian Empire, and what followed Greece? What was next?" Sarah leaned forward. "Rome! Rome has to be the fourth and final world empire!"

The rabbi's eyes were wide open and twinkling. "You are right, my friend . . . hmmmm. Very interesting. Rome divided. Two legs . . . hmmmm. My, how we have suffered as a people under Rome." The rabbi was off on a little side tangent again. "Oh, sometimes Rome has been good, but most of the time it has been bad, Sarah, so bad."

The rabbi continued. "The Romans have broken into our homes and synagogues and plundered our property. They've driven us from villages. I know you already know that. It is all because we are Jews. . . ." The rabbi's voice was filled with sadness. "All because we are Jews. A Jew's a Jew! Just like a Moslem's a Moslem, a Roman's a Roman! But we're always treated worse, aren't we, Sarah? First the emperors of Rome persecuted us, then they persecuted the Christians. Then when Constantine made Christianity the official religion it grew worse for us. In Constantine's edict of Milan we are *religio licita*—legal. Then the next moment anyone found preaching Judaism to Christians is burned alive. And what did the Emperor Justinian do in our beloved Israel?"

Solomon stopped and looked Sarah straight in the eyes. "I don't like it that they are calling Israel 'Palestine' now!"

Solomon paused. His statement about Palestine made him forget for a moment where he was in his conversation. Then his eyes brightened. "What did the emperor do? He forbade all Jews entrance into Jerusalem except one day a year—the ninth of Av, Tisha B'av—when we remember the destruction of our temple. Interesting, Sarah, interesting."

The rabbi was stroking his beard again, but this time his eyes were open. "First the temple is destroyed by the Babylonians on Tisha B'av. They were the head of gold on Daniel's statue. Then the temple was ravaged again on Tisha B'av, but this time by Rome—the fourth kingdom, the iron. The last kingdom before the stone comes." He paused for a moment. "Interesting, interesting. Daniel definitely says it's in the days of the ten toes when the stone will crush all the other kingdoms and set up a kingdom that will never be destroyed."

The rabbi paused again for a moment, his eyes closed. Sarah waited; she knew he was thinking. Then his eyes reopened. He had an intent expression on his face, with furrows between his bushy brows. "Sarah, if the legs are the division of the Roman Empire into east and west, what are the ten toes?"

"I don't know." Sarah leaned back, propping her elbow on the back of her chair and resting her chin on her hand. For a moment they were both silent, deep in thought.

"Sarah, if Daniel says the stone crushes the statue on the feet of iron and clay and he says, 'In the days of those kings,' maybe someday Rome will no longer be in two divisions, but ten."

"Rabbi," Sarah raised her chin off her hand as she sat up straight, "do you realize what you're saying? Think with me," Sarah said excitedly. "If that is correct, Messiah won't come and we won't rule with him until somehow there's a tenfold division—ten kings or ten whatever. . . ."

"Sarah, be careful with whom you discuss this. The church doesn't want to hear about the Jews having a kingdom and ruling with Messiah. The church doesn't favor the Jews. Even Saint John Chrysostom—the patriarch of Constantinople and great Father of the Orthodox church—condemned us, saying we were responsible for the death of Jesus, whom they call the Christ. He told the church we were worthy of persecution."

The rabbi shook his head sadly. Sarah could see the pain in his eyes as he continued, "It's there, Sarah—a hatred for the Jews encouraged by the church. And Saint John was a man known for his charity and ascetic lifestyle!

"It's a mystery, Sarah. They cannot understand why we don't convert, and when we don't convert they try to force us. What blindness! How can one man dictate what another believes? Pouring water over the head in baptism isn't going to change the way a man thinks. It only makes him wet on the head. Or maybe I should say in the head." The impish gleam twinkled in his eyes. "True belief must come from the heart, from the mind. It must be inward, not merely outward."

"Rabbi, do you know Emperor Justinian has forbidden the study of the Talmud and other commentaries on the Scriptures? And he has placed Imperial Guards in some synagogues to make sure that when we intone the Shema we no longer say, 'Hear, O Israel! The Lord is our God, the Lord is one.'" Sarah raised her voice. "We cannot even say 'The Lord is one.'"

The rabbi nodded. "The church doesn't know the Scriptures. They profess belief in the Old Testament—what we call the Bible—but they forbid us to quote D'varim, Deuteronomy 6:4. I'm telling you, Sarah, we are in trouble. We are in trouble because people don't know the Bible! In here, my friend," the rabbi was pointing to his heart, "there is a feeling that things will get worse for us just because we're Jews and—"

"Sarah!" Dusia's hard pounding on the door and her loud voice matched her body. The door came flying open before Sarah could even respond. "Sarah! Abba!"

"We're here, Dusia, having a little glass of wine and a good discussion."

Every time Dusia came charging into the house, Sarah wondered if she would take the doorposts with her.

"You're discussing and I'm in the kitchen cooking and cooking! Peeling, chopping, and cutting and no one to help me. The Sabbath is a day of rest because a woman needs to rest from getting ready for it! And where is Abba?" Dusia swept her hand in the air toward Rabbi Solomon. "Talking about the Holy Bible, which says man is to labor six days and then rest. And where should you be today, Abba? In the synagogue." Dusia held up her hand as if to silence him. "I know, Abba, I know. They don't want you in the synagogue. But I want you in the kitchen! It's still the sixth day, and I need help before three stars appear in the sky."

Dusia had said all that with one breath.

Sarah looked at the rabbi. Dusia's scolding didn't bother him; he was used to it. Dusia nagged and complained, but she gave him a place to live. And he knew it wasn't easy for her. The families of the other two rabbis had respect from the community, and Dusia? Well, Dusia suffered because of her Abba's rejection of the Talmud and his stubborn adherence to his belief in the total sufficiency of the Bible. So whatever Dusia said to him was fine with him. He had a roof over his head and very good meals; Dusia cooked well because she loved to eat.

Rabbi Solomon slowly rose to his feet, pulling himself up with the help of the table. "Old men shouldn't sit still so long. . . ."

"Old men should be helping their daughters," Dusia retorted. She took her right hand off her hip to wave at Sarah as she headed back toward the door, calling out, "Shalom, Sarah. Don't be late for our Shabbat dinner."

"Dusia, Dusia. . . ." Rabbi Solomon shook his head as he stood, his short frame still somewhat bent over. "Shabbat shalom, Sarah—"

"Hurry, Abba," Dusia nagged as she paused in the doorway. "You can wish Sarah a proper Shabbat shalom at our Sabbath table."

The rabbi stopped for a moment. Straightening his back with the help of his hand, he said, "I must get me a walking stick. You are coming to dinner with us, Sarah?"

"I am coming to dinner."

"Good, good," the rabbi's eyes brightened, "then it will be a good meal."

"Dusia's meals are always good."

"I meant good because we'll have good food for thought. We can discuss the Bible some more. I'll read from Sh'mot—Exodus—since we'll celebrate Passover in just a few days and we'll—"

"Abba!" Dusia's head was back in the doorway.

"Run on, Rabbi Solomon. I'll be there soon."

"Run? I wish I could run. It's not so good to be so old. Nothing moves right," the rabbi murmured as he made his way out the door.

231

Sarah watched in amazement as Dusia lit the Sabbath candles. The perspiration and the anxious frown were gone, as was the haranguing. The work was done; there were no more orders to give. The loaves of bread made especially for Shabbat were set next to the wine on a table covered with Dusia's finest linen.

Everything was in place, including Dusia. Black lace covered Dusia's powdered face. The candlelight softened her large nose set between the peaks of her fat cheeks. The flickering lights kindly shadowed the two furrows above her nose and added a silver sheen to the gray at her temples. The dowager empress of the home was ready to welcome the Sabbath, which would, for a day, bring rest from Dusia's domineering ways. The Sabbath transformed Dusia and her family loved it.

Dusia's daughter Miriam sat next to Sarah, and Dusia's son Aaron sat next to his Saba, his beloved old grandpa. Both children wiggled in anticipation of the evening meal. Dusia's husband Gershom rose to his feet and turned to Aaron. "May God make you like Ephraim and Menashe." Then as he turned to his daughter, Miriam, she gave him a big smile. Gershom noticed her front tooth had finally come out today. He grinned. "May God make you like Sarah, Rebecca, and Rachel."

Dusia looked at her children, beaming with the blessing of their father. Then Gershom turned to Dusia. Looking at her endearingly, he blessed his wife. "An accomplished woman who can find? Far beyond pearls is her value. Her husband's heart relies on her, and he shall lack no fortune. She repays him good, but never harm, all the days of her life. . . ."

As Sarah watched Gershom, she thought, *Oh, husband, how I long to hear you give me this Shabbat blessing, even as Gershom is blessing his wife.* Dusia's head was bowed slightly, yet Sarah could see her eyes glisten. Dusia lived to hear these words so tenderly spoken each Shabbat in the presence of her Abba and her children. Tonight, Gershom would hold her, love her . . . it was written in the Talmud. The Sabbath was her day, her night. The reward for her six days of grueling labor.

"Blessed art thou, O Lord our God, King of the Universe, who creates the fruit. . . ." As Gershom said kiddush, Sarah found herself longing for her own home, with her husband at the end of the table where Gershom was saying kiddush. Her mind wandered to Benjamin and Leah. *There would be two empty seats at our table, but maybe Saul would be there.*

Sarah's thoughts were arrested as the door burst open and banged loudly against the wall. Dusia jumped to her feet and screamed. Miriam ran into her arms as Aaron clutched his Saba.

Gershom whipped around as a man dressed in a black robe with a huge crucifix dangling from a thick gold chain yelled, "You have broken the edict of Justinian, the Emperor, you Jew!" The cleric spit out the word *Jew* with venom.

"No murderer of Christ is to celebrate the Passover when the Christians are about to celebrate the resurrection of the one *you* crucified!"

"But we're not celebrating Passover," Gershom retorted in dismay. "It's Shabbat. . . ."

Looking a little nervous, the cleric hesitated a moment. Had he made a mistake? *What does it matter,* he reasoned to himself. *I'm here and they deserve to be punished anyway for killing the Christ.* Regaining his confidence he growled, "I say you are desecrating the Lord's death!"

In an instant the candles, dishes, bread, and wine went crashing to the floor as one of the two men accompanying the cleric pulled the tablecloth off the table.

Pushing back his chair, Rabbi Solomon stood and, raising his trembling hands above his head, cried out, "Hear, O Israel! The Lord is our God, the Lord is one!"

"Blasphemer!" the second man shouted. Summoning all his strength, he backhanded the old rabbi, sending him crashing against the wall. Rabbi Solomon's head hit with an awful thud, and his neck whipped forward with a snapping sound.

The man who hit the rabbi looked on in disbelief, visibly shaken by this unexpected turn of events. What if he'd killed the old man? Quickly he turned and talked to the rabbi as if he were alive, "You're also forbidden to deny the Trinity. The Lord is not *one,* you old blaspheming Jew!"

Sarah watched Rabbi Solomon slide to the floor. His eyes rolled back in his head and blood trickled from his mouth. Sarah knew he was dead.

Incensed, Sarah bent down, picked up a candlestick, and walked toward the stunned cleric with fire in her eyes. "I am a guest in this home, a witness, and you have just killed a man who was not celebrating the Passover. Do you hear me? *Not* celebrating the Passover. You don't even know the difference between the Sabbath and the Passover, and it is going to cost you! It is you who has broken the law of Justinian, the very emperor who codified the Roman law!"

With that Sarah thrust the candlestick upward into the air for emphasis. Then she waved it in the cleric's face as one of his companions pulled on his cassock. "Do you think *you* will escape?" Bewildered by Sarah's bold threats, the men retreated, backing to the door step by step as she advanced toward them.

Sarah's yelling stopped as abruptly as it began. Then in the most authoritative voice she could evoke, she looked each of the men in the eyes and said, "I have influence in high places, and I am going to report you to the Bishop! Now I command you to give me your name and the name of your—"

By this time the men were already out the door.

Sarah turned. Dusia was on the floor, holding her Abba in her arms, rocking him, weeping, kissing his ashen face. Miriam was hanging onto her mother's arm, crying softly. Gershom and Aaron stood dumbfounded, gazing at Sarah, unable to speak.

Weakly Sarah walked over to the table, put down the candlestick, and turned to go to Dusia and her beloved rabbi. But just as she turned, she fainted.

Little did Sarah conceive of the strength she would need for the future. The feeling her rabbi held in his now-still heart was right. Life would go much differently for her and her people in the years ahead.

Chapter 41

"Can you imagine? They're actually going to let us into Jerusalem!" Samuel's eyes danced with delight. "Tonight, we'll be there."

"Samuel, you're the dreamer. I'm the skeptic. We're walking from Tiberius to Jerusalem for nothing except to have our hopes dashed again. I can't believe it. I can't believe it." Levi stopped right in the middle of the road while Samuel kept walking.

Samuel looked over his shoulder at his friend. Levi couldn't talk without moving his arms, holding his head, or hitting his head with his hand. And when Levi became intense or excited he sometimes would stop walking. "Levi, if you keep stopping to talk we will never get there before the sun goes down."

"I know, Samuel, I know. And believe me, it's for nothing. For nothing!" Levi threw up his hands in resignation and began walking again. He had been chastising himself for leaving the relative peace of Galilee and the intellectual stimulation he found in discussing the *Responsa of the Geonim* (excellencies).

Being dispersed had brought all sorts of problems and questions to the Jews. However, with the help and scholarship of the Geonim—the heads of the academies of Sura and Pumbeditha in Mesopotamia—they were gaining a greater understanding of the Babylonian Talmud. And Levi didn't want to miss any of the discussions.

According to the reports of those coming from other Jewish communities, the *Responsa*—the scholars' responses to their questions of interpretation—was bringing an inner cohesion and a new vitality to their faith. Levi loved that, and though he wanted to walk inside the walls of Jerusalem again, he longed even more to stay with the scholars in the Galilee. That's where he and Samuel had moved with the Sanhedrin after the Bar Kochba defeat, and except for annual trips on Tisha B'av, they had not gone to Jerusalem.

"Levi, sometimes I don't understand you. Why can't you believe we're finally going to walk Jerusalem's streets again?"

Levi ran to catch up with Samuel. "Do you have to walk so fast? Jerusalem will be there when we get there." Levi was a little breathless. Sitting with the scholars had not only expanded his mind, it had also expanded his waistline. Samuel reached over and teasingly hit Levi in his midsection. It was a little soft and it showed.

"That's why you're out of breath. Too much sitting! Now that you've taken care of your mind, you need to take care of your body. This walk will be good for you. Besides, if you would learn to walk while you talk, you wouldn't have to catch up with me."

"All right, Samuel, all right. Enough said. Enough said." A half-crooked smile came across Levi's lips. "I'm here, I'm here."

They walked for a while in silence, munching on some fruit and barley bread they had brought with them. They had mutually agreed to save the dried fish, olives, and cheese for later, in case they couldn't find food in Jerusalem. The silence didn't bother either of them, but Samuel savored it the most. He was enjoying the change in scenery from the Galilee as they walked up to Jerusalem. And it was *up!* He felt the pull on his legs. Thinking he'd try a change of stride, Samuel turned around and walked backwards. As he looked behind them, he saw Mount Gerizim and Mount Ebal in the distance, now on the other side of Samaria.

Samuel's thoughts went back to the Nevi'im—to Joshua, who had led the children of Israel over the Jordan to possess the land given to them by the Almighty One of Israel. At those two mountains they had recited the blessings and cursings recorded in Deuteronomy. According to the Bible, this land belonged to them. It was theirs. An everlasting possession.

It distressed Samuel to hear people call their land Palestine. *Palestine! Not once is it referred to as Palestine in our Bible! Who, then, has a right to call it Palestine?*

The Romans were to blame. After Bar Kochba was killed, they renamed the land Syria-Palestina out of vengeance, banning the name Judea. Bar Kochba's defeat still brought pain to Samuel's heart—especially when he remembered the men, women, and children who had hidden in the caves south of Qumran. They had chosen to die of starvation rather than surrender to the two Roman camps who turned their caves into tombs. Samuel knew he would have been buried there with them if Levi hadn't adamantly refused to accompany Samuel to the caves.

Samuel stretched both of his arms out wide as if to embrace the life given to him. Again he vowed to live his life to the fullest for the cause of the Almighty and his people.

Levi broke the silence. "You know, Samuel, I don't know which I hate worse. What Hadrian did to Jerusalem, naming it Aelia Capitolina, and building that abominable temple to Jupiter on the Temple Mount," Levi spit to show his disgust at the sacrilege, "or what Constantine allowed his mother, Queen Helena, to do—build churches all over Jerusalem. Whose land does she think this is?" Levi's words reeked with sarcasm. "Restore *her* holy places?" He laughed. "They said she discovered many of these sites in her dreams."

"Don't fret, Levi, don't fret," said Samuel. "Now that the Moslems have freed Jerusalem from the Byzantines, we'll build beautiful synagogues there. Maybe like the one we built in Capernaum."

"The beauty also comes from the setting, Samuel. Capernaum is set by the sea." Levi put his hands over his heart and assumed a look of mourning. "We've only been gone a few days and already you are making me more homesick. I want the Galilee. Let's go back, Samuel. Please, let's go back."

Samuel gave Levi a hard push on his shoulder—a little too hard. It sent Levi spinning, and he caught his foot on a rock and ended up on the ground. Shocked, he looked up at Samuel, trying to read his face. Samuel laughed and offered Levi his hand.

For a moment Levi hesitated. Samuel's smile was a little too cocky for Levi.

"I'm sorry, I didn't mean to push you so hard. With all that new weight on you I didn't think a little push would topple you. Come on, take my hand," Samuel urged as he reached down toward his friend.

Reaching up, Levi took a strong grip on Samuel's hand, and jerked him to the ground. The next thing Samuel knew Levi was sitting astride his chest, bouncing up and down. "See how heavy I am! See how heavy I—"

Samuel gave Levi a hard push and sent him tumbling. "See how strong I am!" said Samuel with a cheerful smile. Levi scrambled to his feet and headed for Samuel, looking like he was ready for a wrestling match.

Samuel held out his arm as if to stop him. "If we keep this up, we won't get to Jerusalem before dark and we'll be exhausted. Let's call it a truce. What do you say?"

Inwardly Levi was grateful. He knew he'd been sitting in too many synagogues and schools doing nothing but talking and listening and talking. He was out of shape. The fact that Samuel was calling off the match allowed Levi to look like a possible contender for a victor's wreath. It was a matter of ego. "I will," he responded graciously, lifting his hand in the air. "But for your sake, you ought to be glad. You ought to be glad."

Levi brushed off the dust and vegetation that had become attached to him. "Now what was it we were saying about Jerusalem, the city of peace?" he asked, deliberately emphasizing the irony.

Samuel responded, "You know, I'm glad that when the Moslems came the Byzantines surrendered peacefully, or Jerusalem would have been destroyed again."

"Right! But what have we got now? Mosques all over the place. We have simply exchanged the cross for a crescent!" Levi threw up his hands in disgust. "A cross for a crescent!"

"You are right," said Samuel, "but at least life is better for us under the Moslems than under the Christians. At least the Moslems are tolerant of both Jews and Christians because they are monotheistic like we are. Moslems also claim to believe in the one and only true God. You can't fault them for that. They let us have our separate communities, our *millets* as they call them. They aren't forcing us to convert as so many of the Christians wanted us to do. And, the Moslems allow us to enter Jerusalem. I tell you, Levi, we're far more secure now than we were. And Moslems aren't seen decorating or painting anything with the figures of humans or animals. No graven images for them!"

Levi stopped again and looked at Samuel quizzically. "How do you know all these things?"

Samuel grinned. It pleased him to be able to tell Levi something he didn't know. "I get out and talk to people and listen to them. I find out what's going on. You should try it, Levi. Do you know Islam has religious schools too, like ours? In these *Madrasa,* as these schools are called, they have scholarly debates as they go over their *shariya*—religious law. They even have their scholars' interpretation, just like our *Responsa.* Sounds like they have copied what we do, doesn't it?"

Samuel continued, enjoying every moment of sharing what he knew. It felt good to be doing the talking for a change. Usually it was Levi. "It's good to know what's going on around you. And if you know what you believe, I mean really know it, you don't have to be threatened by what others believe. It's the people who don't know what they believe or why they believe what they do who are in danger. You are safe, Levi. You know the Bible for yourself. You're a thinking man."

Levi stopped again and looked at Samuel with panic in his eyes. "You're not going to read their holy book, are you? The Koran?"

"No, I don't have one. But I wouldn't be afraid because I know the Bible. I've heard the Bible taught in the synagogues and the schools of the Torah all my life. If the Koran didn't agree with our Bible, I would know it was wrong, for the Bible is unadulterated truth. Truth sets you free, Levi, unless you turn your back on it. And if you do turn your back on it, I guess you're worse off. You've turned away from what is true and therefore what is right. You've exchanged truth for a lie!"

Levi looked troubled. "I don't think the rabbis in the Galilee would allow you to read the Koran, Samuel. They wouldn't be pleased."

I'm sure you're right, Levi. And I told you I am not going to read the Koran, so let it go. But I want you to know I am not afraid of it. Those who have read the Koran—and they are reliable sources, Levi—tell me that much of the Koran was taken from the Bible and some of the Christians' New Testament writings. Mohammed's teaching is their substitute for the Bible; it's their way of trying to bring their people to an ethical monotheism that fits their ways. And when the Jews didn't come around to Mohammed's version of God and adapt to his teachings, the Sabbath was changed to Friday, the prayers were to face Mecca instead of Jerusalem, and they came up with a date different from ours for their principle feast. And somewhere, sometime, Jesus Christ—the Christians' so-called Messiah—was incorporated into the Koran. The Koran proclaims Jesus Christ a prophet and includes some of his teachings." Samuel paused briefly. "From what I understand, if you didn't know the Bible, you could easily be swayed by the Koran."

Samuel looked up ahead and put his hand on Levi's shoulder. "Come on, let's hurry. There's the Damascus Gate. We can go down the Decumanus to the Temple Mount. Before we go anyplace else, let's go pray for the peace of Jerusalem."

As Levi and Samuel entered the gate their eyes darted from one person to another in utter fascination. Intrigued by the varied clothing, the cacophony of sounds and languages, the donkeys and carts, and the people haggling over prices, Samuel inadvertently took the main cardo—taking them through the very heart of the city. Unexpectedly and unhappily they found themselves in front of the Church of the Holy Sepulcher, where, according to Queen Helena, Jesus of Nazareth had supposedly been buried and raised from the dead.

Levi's skin crawled at the sight before him. He grabbed Samuel's arm and whispered angrily, "Why did you bring us this way?"

"I—I don't know," Samuel stammered, looking first in one direction and then another. His agitation unnerved Levi. "I don't know, Levi. I'm confused. I'm—"

"Christ killers! Look, Christ killers!" someone screamed.

Fear gripped Samuel's heart as he looked to see who had screamed the words and who were the objects of this sudden and seemingly insane accusation.

"Infidels! Death to the infidels!" Others took up the chant.

"This is our land," someone else shouted. "It belongs to the holy Catholic church! To the Christ! To the holy Mother of our Lord! Rid the land of the infidels! Spill their blood as they spilled our Lord's blood!"

Without warning the incited mob began running towards Levi and Samuel. A few people had sticks in their hands. Samuel became alarmed. *Where did they come from? What was happening? What had he and Levi done?*

Samuel grabbed Levi's hand and cried, "Run!"

"Where, Samuel? I don't know where I am!" Levi's face was deathly pale; his hand was cold and sweaty. "Elohim!" he shouted. "Elohim!"

"Hang on to me—don't let go!" Samuel ordered as he jerked Levi off his feet, turned from the mob, and headed across the stone court back the way he thought they had come.

"I'm going to be sick," Levi screamed as Samuel pulled him along.

"You can't," Samuel shouted back. Then he stopped abruptly, almost causing Levi to fall over him. "Oh Levi, there's more coming from over there. We're blocked in!"

"Elohim! Elohim! Help us!" Levi cried.

Samuel assessed the situation instantly. There was no place to go but into the church itself. He noted that the whole complex was surrounded by a high wall. *Maybe we can get lost in its maze of columns,* he thought. The angry mob would have a hard time staying together in there.

"Stop them . . . stop them!" shouted one of the men, seeing the direction Samuel and Levi were going and realizing their plan. "Stop them!"

Levi screamed as a man reached out and grabbed his tunic. Samuel instantly grabbed Levi's wrist and pulled him away with a strong jerk. Samuel didn't know where he got his strength and sense of direction, but he utilized it, choosing a flight of stairs and then going through the first of three doors in the precinct wall. He found himself in a colonnaded atrium. With hinds' feet, he ran between the columns. On the far side of the courtyard he spotted a triple set of doors that appeared to lead to the basilica itself. Samuel headed in that direction with Levi in tow, breathlessly muttering, "Elohim—save us—"

Samuel whispered back, "Don't stop praying . . . he's answering."

For a moment or so the noise of the mob seemed to lessen a little— maybe it was out of reverence for where they were, or maybe the people had broken up. Samuel didn't want to slow down; he wasn't going to take any chances.

Just then, Samuel stopped.

"Wha—"

Samuel clamped his hand over Levi's mouth and pointed. Coming out of the basilica was a man in a long black robe of sorts with a huge cross hanging on a gold chain around his neck. He had long black hair, a bushy black beard streaked with some gray, and an odd-shaped hat on his head which looked as if it was sitting on his heavy eyebrows. His hands were awkwardly positioned as he held before him an enormous gold cross with the figure of a man hanging on it. Following him were some younger-looking men who also wore black robes.

"Are they coming for us?" Levi whispered, his eyes wide with fascination. He had never seen anything like this, nor had Samuel.

"I don't think so," Samuel whispered, his eyes never leaving the procession. One of the men was swinging an ornate metal pot on a chain. Smoke was coming out of it. "I don't know what they are doing. But as soon as they move away from the door, we'll go down this colonnade and slip into where they just came from. And whatever you do, don't make a—"

Samuel's instructions were interrupted by a man's angry shout. "Some of you go down this side. I'll take the right; they've got to be in—"

"Silence! Silence!" The man with the cross ordered loudly. "Have you no respect for the house of God?"

"But holy Father—"

"Silence!"

For the first time, Samuel released his grip on Levi's wrist. Leaning over and cupping his hand over Levi's left ear, he whispered, "Elohim has heard. Follow me very quietly. We are about to go into a church."

"But—" Levi blurted out just a little too loud before Samuel's hand clamped his mouth. Samuel leaned over again and whispered, "There's no other way, believe me, or I would take it. You called on his name. Follow me. . . ."

Just as Samuel slipped through the door, he turned and saw a few men, each down on one knee before the priest and his cross, and using one hand to make a motion from their head to their chest and from one shoulder to the other.

Quietly Samuel and Levi made their way through the basilica, cautiously trying one door after another, until to their utter amazement they found themselves on the street again. This time instead of fighting the crowd, they gladly lost themselves in the maze of people and animals. Finally they made their way to what they thought would be sacred ground—the Temple Mount.

They had been told about the Dome of the Rock. However, because they had never seen it, in their minds it didn't seem as bad, as large, as imposing, as permanent as it was. But they were stunned by what they saw before them. Caliph Abd el-Malik had enclosed the el-Sagra—the Stone of the Foundation, where Abraham had offered Isaac—with the Dome of the Rock!

Samuel and Levi had heard that mosques had been built in Jerusalem, but it never occurred to them that the Almighty One of Israel would ever allow an Islamic sanctuary to be built on their sacred ground—where his temple itself once stood in all its holy majesty.

Weary and spent from the emotions of the day, their bodies gave way. Samuel and Levi sat and wept like little children. All they could think was, *Our temple should be here! Our temple should be here! Our temple should be here!* If only saying that three times would make it so. But it didn't.

Two days later another caliph, Caliph al-Hakim of Egypt, ordered the destruction of the Church of the Holy Sepulcher. It was as if lightning had hit a stone and sent sparks flying across the Mediterranean—sparks carried by the wind into Europe. There the sparks settled on a dead tree and set it ablaze. Then another gust of wind ignited the whole forest, inflaming men's hearts with an unholy fanaticism to free the Holy Land from the grip of the infidels. Not only Moslem infidels, but Jewish ones also! And while the crusaders were purging the land, would it not be justifiable to seize a spoil for themselves?

The pilgrims who traveled from Europe to Jerusalem were the spark; they carried back tales of the infidels' occupation and desecration of the Holy Land. And in France stood the dead tree outside the walls of Clermont, where Pope Urban II issued his mandate: "Go to Jerusalem, the center of the world, the jewel of that Holy Land which has been made forever sacred by our Savior . . . Jerusalem is now held prisoner by our godless enemies . . . seize back the land taken by pagans! Do not be afraid. Those who die on the journey will have their sins immediately forgiven. I pledge this by the power God has vested in me."

The intense brutality of the first crusader attack on Jerusalem two years later was unrivaled. Even the earlier Moslem invasion of Jerusalem could not be compared with the severity of this Crusade. Without even bothering to identify anyone—Christian, Jew, or Moslem—the third wave of these crusaders descended upon Israel and wasted Jerusalem. Men, women, and children were hacked to death with swords in such brutality and violence that mounds of heads, hands, and feet were seen throughout the city. As one crusader walked through the carnage of bodies and limbs, he was heard to say, "What an apt punishment."

What more could Samuel and Levi and the Jewish people endure? More . . . much more . . . far more than they ever dreamed. The Crusades had just begun.

Chapter 42

Sarah stood at her doorway looking at Aaron and wishing Rabbi Solomon ben Asher was still alive and leaning on his grandson for support. Sometimes Sarah sat at the table weeping, other times she smiled as she recounted the hours they spent discussing the Bible. Sarah often recalled how the dear old man had valiantly stood to his feet in defense of truth. It was the rabbi's courageous stance and the cleric's senseless cruelty that had infused Sarah with the courage to take her own bold stand when the cleric sent her rabbi crashing into a wall to his death.

But her beloved rabbi wasn't the only one Sarah missed. She also missed Dusia and all her flurry. Dusia's visits had grown more infrequent since the rabbi's passing because every time she stepped in the door of Sarah's house she'd burst into tears. So if Sarah wanted to see the family, she had to go to their house—which made her feel uncomfortable because they never failed to welcome her like a heroine!

Yet life went on. It always did. Sometimes in joy, sometimes in sorrow, but it went on. The Jewish people had a will to survive and their close-knit communities with their distinctively Jewish way of life was the glue that kept them from falling apart and being absorbed in the lands of their dispersion.

Aaron spoke, interrupting Sarah's thoughts. "Aunt Sarah, may I come in and have a glass of wine with you like Saba did? We can discuss the Torah. I think about you often and wonder who will teach you now that Saba's dead. You can't go to Torah school like I do because you're a woman." Aaron's unexpected sensitivity and childlike reasoning undid Sarah. Going quickly to the heavy mahogany cabinet, Sarah took out a little glass to fill with grape juice, pausing for a moment to get control of herself. With a wipe of her hand she banished the tears threatening to trickle down her cheeks.

"How very kind of you, Aaron," Sarah flashed a tender smile. "If you will sit at the table, I'll pour your drink into the glass Saba always used and cut you a piece of my kuchen, which I just took out of the oven. It's a sweet cake you'll like. Then you can teach me what you have learned at Torah school."

Aaron smiled, pleased with himself. Imma was wrong; Aunt Sarah did need him to teach her. He could tell by her voice. Aaron sat down and unfolded a precious scrap of paper on which he had written his notes. Bowing his head he studied it. Taking Saba's place would be a big responsibility. But someone had to.

Abba was too busy and his sister Miriam couldn't because she was a girl. All she knew to do was work around the house. But then, that's what women and girls were to do so the men could study. Unless, of course, they had to work, like Abba.

Sarah took out special plates for the kuchen. She wanted to make this a memorable occasion for Aaron. Seeing him at the table made Sarah long for Samuel and once again she became lost in her thoughts. *Where are you, Samuel? Where did they take you?* Sarah could see her hand caressing Samuel's cheek. *Are you well, Samuel? Maybe in your distant land you'll meet my son, my Saul. Maybe someday you and Saul and I shall sit together at my table in Jerusalem, and your Abba and Imma and Jared will be there, and my husband will say kiddush. Then maybe Elijah will come and fill his chair and tell us the good news that Messiah has come. . . .* Sarah sniffed loudly, wiping the runaway tears that escaped down her cheeks to her chin. With a sigh, she forced herself back to the present.

"Are you all right, Aunt Sarah?" Aaron called from the table.

"Yes, I'm all right. Why do you ask?"

"It sounds like you might be getting a cold."

"I'm not getting a cold, Aaron. I'm fine. But thank you for asking. You are such a considerate young man. I hope you never change."

"I won't, Aunt Sarah. I don't ever want to get in trouble like Aaron in the Bible did when he and Moses struck the rock a second time. Do you know they couldn't go into the Promised Land? I want to see the Promised Land. Abba says someday we'll go there."

Sarah looked at Aaron bent over the table, staring intently at his piece of paper, his legs curled around the legs of the chairs. His heavy shoes and wool socks were good protection against the cold. The Rhineland could be so very cold. "I want to go there, too, Aaron." As Sarah set Saba's glass on the table she rubbed Aaron's head carefully so as to not loosen his yarmulke. She wanted to hold him tightly in her arms, but that was hardly appropriate behavior towards one's teacher.

"Here's your drink, Aaron."

"Is this wine like Saba drank, Aunt Sarah?"

"Not exactly, Aaron. But it's the same color and tastes almost the same. And I poured it in the very glass Saba drank from every time he came over. Now, Aaron, it is to be your glass."

"Will you save it so no one else but me can drink from it?"

"I will save it just for you."

Sarah pulled up her chair, opposite Aaron, the place she always sat when she and Rabbi Solomon discussed the Bible. She froze when Aaron gazed straight into her eyes and in all innocence asked, "What are crusades, and why are they bad?"

Regaining her composure and groping for wisdom, Sarah said, "Why do you ask?"

"Don't you want to answer me either, Aunt Sarah?"

"What do you mean, Aaron?"

"Well, when I asked Abba and Imma what they were whispering about—you know, about crusades—they told me I was too young to have to know about them."

Sarah looked at this little man sitting at her table. His brown hair was so silky and soft it was hard for him to keep his yarmulke in place. His dark brown eyes framed by long, thick eyelashes looked at her so trustingly that she found herself torn between wanting to answer his question and yet, like his parents, not wanting to give him a burden too heavy for his young shoulders.

Aaron looked at her quizzically. "Why are they bad, Aunt Sarah?"

"How do you know they're bad? Did someone tell you that?"

"No, but the other boys and I in Torah school talked about it. We decided they must be bad because a lot of our parents—especially our Immas—cry when they talk about them. And sometimes Abba has to hold Imma and tell her everything will be all right. My friends' parents won't tell them either. But we decided if they make people cry, they have to be bad."

"But sometimes people cry when they are happy," Sarah proffered.

"I know. Imma cries sometimes when Abba says the kiddush to her on Shabbat, but this is different."

Sarah reached across the table and patted the hand swishing the paper back and forth on the tabletop. Aaron's right elbow rested on the table, supporting his chin in his hand. "Aaron, I can't answer your question because you've let me know Abba and Imma don't feel it is best for you to know. But I can tell you this: Your Abba and Imma love you. Whatever they think you need to know, they will tell you. Now, what is my lesson for today? I can't wait to hear what you have to tell me."

Aaron sat up very straight, assuming the position of teacher. "Well, there was a famous rabbi—Rabbi Solomon, just like Saba's name, only his last name was ben Isaac—like Isaac in the Bible. Isaac was the son of Abraham. Abraham had two wives, you know, only one wasn't really supposed to be his wife. They had a baby named Ishmael, but Ishmael wasn't the son the Almighty One promised Abraham and Sarah. Sarah was Abraham's real wife. Her name is the same as yours. Their son Isaac is the one the promise came through. We're the people of Abraham, Isaac, and Jacob. Jacob's name was changed to Israel. Did you know that?"

"Yes, Aaron, I did. Saba was a good teacher just like you are. Did you know Israel means 'he who strives with God'?"

"I'm not finished, Aunt Sarah."

"Of course not, Aaron, but have a taste of my kuchen. It's especially good today."

Aaron took a gulp of his juice and stuffed his mouth with kuchen. With crumbs from the cake falling from his lips, Aaron continued the lesson. "Rabbi Solomon ben Isaac lived in France but he studied in our country." Aaron seemed proud of that point. "The rabbis at school are excited about what he's written and say someday Jews all around the world are going to study what he says. They call him Rashi."

Sarah looked at Aaron in astonishment. "Are you studying Rashi's work?"

"No, but I thought you needed to know about him because everybody thinks he's important, and you need to know that if someone tells you his name." With that, Aaron folded his scrap of paper. "Well, I've got to go." He slid out of his chair, picked up his cloak, and wrapped it around him, saying, "Imma said I had to get home before it got dark. She worries, you know."

Sarah got up and took her dark cloak and a heavier scarf for her head from the hook near the door. Throwing it over her shoulders, she said, "Aaron, let me walk you home. I'd like to visit with your Abba and Imma and see Miriam. I've missed seeing your family."

Aaron chatted as they walked towards the edge of the Jewish quarter. Sarah didn't like to go this way into the Christian section anymore, but because of the configuration of the area, it was the closest way to the family's home, which was above Gershom's shop.

"Imma doesn't like to come to your house, Aunt Sarah, because it makes her think of Saba, and she cries. That's why we had to move 'cause Imma didn't want to eat in the dining room anymore. She said she could still see Saba leaning against the wall. I don't like to remember that, do—"

Suddenly an angry shout ricocheted through the air. "Vengeance for—!"

Sarah pulled Aaron tightly to her side and wrapped her arm over his ear, seeking to shield him from the menacing voice piercing the evening. Aaron thrust up his head in dismay as Sarah put her finger over her mouth, instructing him to be quiet. His eyes dilated in wonder and confusion.

"—the crucified one upon those of his enemies who live here in our midst. Vengeance for the crucified one!"

Sarah's eyes darted frantically, looking for a way to escape. *It must be the monk, Radulf,* she thought as she stepped into the doorway of a nearby shop and peered into its windows. Radulf was a monk who traveled from city to city inciting the local Gentiles to take vengeance for the death of the rabbi from Nazareth. Stories abounded of the massacres of Jews following in his wake. Although the bishops of Regensburg, Mainz, Worms, and even other cities tried to shelter the Jews, they were often no match for the easily ignited passions of the prejudiced.

Sarah could feel Aaron's little body trembling with hers as she pressed her face against the window of the shop. *Where am I? Whose shop is this?* Sarah leaned her head on the cold pane. *I've got to think—where are we? Why wasn't I paying attention?*

"Oh!" she shrieked in surprise and fear.

Sarah felt herself being pulled through the open door. Her heart galloped out of control. Suddenly she was staring into the face of a man she didn't know. Taken totally unawares, her hand fumbled back, catching Aaron's woolen cloak. For a moment fear immobilized Aaron's tongue, but his eyes told the story. He was terrified. Then Sarah heard his trembling whisper, "Are they going to baptize us, Aunt Sarah? Abba said he'd have to die first. Do—" Aaron's whisper turned to a scream as two strong arms lifted him from his feet and hoisted him over a broad shoulder. "Do I have to die, Aunt Sarah?"

When the man had bent over to pick up Aaron, Sarah noticed there was no yarmulke on his head. His face was unbearded. Was he an enemy? Sarah tried to catch his eyes to read her fate, but his back was to her as he again grabbed her wrist and pulled her after him.

"Quiet! Not a word," the man said with a voice that sounded as strong as his appearance. Knowing the danger behind her, Sarah decided not to fight him—yet. She nodded weakly at Aaron, affirming the man's instructions. Aaron's stomach was almost on the man's shoulder; he wondered if he was going to be sick. Stricken with fear, he wanted to cry.

The man pulled Sarah through upright bolts of heavy damask material and then around wooden crates as they skirted a mammoth oak table and headed toward a door at what she surmised to be the back of his store. Then just as quickly as he had picked up Aaron, he set the boy on the floor again. Then he looked at Sarah, who breathed a sigh of relief. The man's eyes were a strange mixture of sternness and compassion.

"Listen to me carefully," he said. "You cannot go home under any circumstance—I don't care where you live. You don't know who's a friend or who's an enemy. You must leave Cologne immediately. There's going to be a bloodbath for all Jews who refuse to be baptized. Take the yarmulke off the boy's head, cover his head with a shawl if it has to be covered, and go into Bohemia. Don't go down the Rhine; the crusaders are headed that way along with old Radulf. One feeds off the other. You're not safe here or in France."

"But the boy's family . . . I'm not the mother—"

"Where does he live?"

"In the Jewish quarter. He's the tailor."

"Is his name Gershom? The tailor who used to have the large shop on the main street of Cologne until Jews were forbidden to do business with anyone but other Jews?"

Sarah answered cautiously, wondering whether she was wise to say anything or not. "Ye-yes. He is this young man's father." She nodded slowly in affirmation as she drew Aaron closer to her.

"Is his house above his shop now that he's living in the Jewish quarter?"

Sarah looked at the man without responding. How did he know Gershom still had a shop and there was a house above it? What were his eyes telling her?

"You're afraid to trust me, aren't you? It's all right. Every now and then, I've gone to his shop. No one can cut cloth better than Gershom ben Moses."

Sarah stood still with her eyes looking straight into his, but saying nothing.

"I understand." His voice was suddenly filled with tenderness. "I'm sorry. But you have to realize that some of us don't blame you for killing Jesus Christ. He had to die. It was God's plan; we're *all* sinners. If what's happening to the Jews doesn't prove that, what does? Even the pope is a sinner, or he never would have instigated these crusades in the pretense of liberating the Holy Land. He was tired of these lords and princes warring among themselves. Not everyone who is joining the effort to liberate the Holy Land has pure motives. That's why the crusaders have stopped in Cologne. While they kill your people along the way, many of them also get rich dividing your booty among them."

His words stunned her. Sarah wanted to agree with him; he was right. However, all she could believe—though she didn't want to—was that he was luring her into some sort of a trap. If she agreed with what he said about the pope, then he could bear witness against her. Quietly, mustering up all the confidence she could, she said, "I'm sorry. I'm afraid to trust you. May we go out the back way?"

"I'm begging you—don't go anyplace but out of the city. For God's sake, believe me. Just trust me." His voice was filled with urgency. "There are plans to massacre every Jew who won't submit to baptism tonight, and somehow I don't think you would—"

"You are right. I'd die first." Her eyes would not let go of his. Sarah felt strange looking at eyes as blue as the summer sky when the night was so clouded with terror.

He continued to plead. "Then you and the boy must take the road through the woods and spend the night there. If you will just trust me, I will try to get to the boy's house, warn the family, and bring them to meet you."

"I'm afraid you'll—"

Suddenly there was a loud pounding on the door of the shop. A man was yelling something about Jews.

"It's all right. It's just because our shop is right on the edge of the Jewish quarter. They want to make sure no Jews are hiding in here. The door's bolted with an iron bolt. But you must go. They've determined there won't be a Jew left alive in this city unless they're baptized. Even then, who knows what they will do after they baptize you. The stories coming from other cities are horrifying. Many of your people have simply chosen to take their own lives."

A wide-eyed Aaron who hadn't missed a word spoke up timorously. "My Abba and Imma said they would die if someone tried to make them be baptized. What's baptism, Aunt Sarah?"

The man stooped down and looked Aaron right in the eyes. "It's a sacrament of the church, and the church says it makes you a Christian."

Aaron liked the man's eyes. "Are you a Christian?"

"Yes."

Aaron drew back until he bumped into Sarah. He looked up at her, fear flickering in his eyes. Sarah patted his head, put her arm around him, and turned again to look at the man.

"You needn't be afraid," the man said gently. "I'm not going to hurt you, nor am I going to try to make you a Christian. Baptism can't do that. And I can't. It's ridiculous to think that sprinkling holy water on someone's head makes him a Christian. Besides, I read once in our Bible about a man who was willing to lay down his life for the Jews, not kill them. You are God's chosen people." As he stood to his full height, his gaze turned to Sarah. "Now, we have to get you out of here. Will you tell me where his—"

"I can't. I just can't. I've never heard anyone talk like you before," Sarah said as she took Aaron's yarmulke from his head. "I want to trust you, but I can't. Thank you for pulling me inside, and for your concern." Sarah put her hand on the latch. The man pushed the door open and patted Aaron on the head as they walked out.

"May his angels watch over you," he said with a sad, troubled voice.

With her cloak half covering Aaron, Sarah hurried down the path behind the man's shop and then turned right toward the street that led to Gershom's shop. Seeing two men standing on the corner, Sarah crossed to the other side of the street, trying to disappear in the darkness. Aaron could feel her body trembling.

"Are you cold, Aunt Sarah?"

"Hush, Aaron." In her fear Sarah spoke louder than she meant to. Her voice cut through the cold night air, carrying the sound farther than she wanted.

"There's one! Get her!" Sarah let out an involuntary scream as one of the men accosted her, grabbing her by the arm. Jerking her arm from his, Sarah broke into a run, dragging Aaron with her. Then Sarah heard another shout from a different direction.

"Curse you, woman! I've caught you!" A shadowy figure with a vaguely familiar voice lunged at her from seemingly out of nowhere. He grabbed her and spun her around, nearly yanking her arm out of its socket as he dragged her back the way she had come. If Sarah hadn't held onto Aaron she would have fallen. The man continued yelling bitterly, "Curse you, Kristine! What are you doing with these men? I'm sick of your infidelity. I don't want to hear a word from you. You're coming home with me right now, or I'm going to beat you and the boy right here on the street."

"Hey, what are you doing?" yelled one of the men who had accosted Sarah.

The man who had Sarah in tow turned and for a brief moment glared and threateningly raised his fist at the one who dared to question him. Then he turned to proceed rapidly down the street, yelling over his shoulder, "If you want to live, you'll never see *my* wife again!" His words were filled with venom.

The man in the street cupped his hands around his mouth and yelled back, "We thought she was a Jew."

Sarah's rescuer drew her around the corner. Aaron was sobbing. Finally the man stopped. "Now do you believe me?"

Sarah was crying, her whole body trembling with fear. "But—where—where did you come from? How did you know?" Sarah looked in relieved disbelief at the man who had pulled her inside his store earlier.

"I was afraid something like this would happen. After you left I had a feeling I needed to go to Gershom's. And just as I rounded the corner I saw the two men gesturing toward you so I started running and tried to figure out what to say so they'd let you go. Now, please, uh . . . what's your name?"

"Sarah."

"Sarah, do you think you can trust me now?"

"Yes! Oh yes! Forgive me. Please, I wish I'd listened. . . ."

"I do too. We have no time to spare. If you'll do what I say, I'll try to reach Gershom and have him meet you in the forest just before the next village. I'll get you on the right road, but then I must leave you. I'm sorry, but if I don't hurry. . . ." The man looked down at Aaron knowingly.

Sarah caught his meaning.

"Aunt Sarah, where are we going?"

"Hopefully to safety for now, Aaron. But someday we're going to the land my husband promised us as an everlasting possession. We'll be safe there."

Or so Sarah thought.

Chapter 48

achel, listen to what I heard the other day. I wrote it down because I wanted to share it with you. It sounds just like you: 'I am at the tip of the Western world, but my heart is in the East.'"

Rachel put down her mending and looked at Reuben. The sight of him still quickened her heart. This quiet but strong man never ceased to amaze her. *Who would ever have thought that this simple man from the city of Bethlehem would have become such a successful tradesman, learn to speak fluent Arabic, and be respected by both Jews and Gentiles! And who would have thought that I would live in such comparable luxury in such a golden age as this?*

"Who said that, Reuben?"

"Judah ben Samuel ha-Levi."

"Where is he from?" Rachel queried.

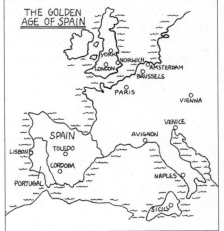

"Imma! Don't you know who he is?" exclaimed Rachel's daughter Rebecca. Rachel couldn't tell whether it was amazement, amusement, or a slight note of disdain in Rebecca's voice. Rebecca's countenance didn't give her the answer. "No, Rebecca, I don't know who Judah ben-whatever-his-name is."

"Judah ben Samuel ha-Levi, Imma."

Rachel smiled. She could tell from Rebecca's voice that she wasn't demeaning her. Rachel wanted her daughter to be a woman who honored God, respectful to him and to her parents at all times. Sometimes she worried though. She wasn't always pleased with some of the friends Rebecca chose.

"He's a poet, Imma. He writes in Arabic and Hebrew. He's the one from Toledo—"

"From our city! Then why have I never heard of him?" Rachel interrupted.

"Well, he was born in Toledo but studied at Lucena. He wrote the controversial poems on Solomon's Song of Songs," Rebecca responded.

"What made them controversial?"

Reuben interrupted. He preferred that Rachel hear the answer from him rather than their daughter. "He brought out the uh . . . the . . . sexual themes in the Song of Songs."

"Reuben! How can you—" Rachel gave her husband a disapproving look, shifting her gaze rapidly from him to Rebecca and back. Then lowering her eyes quickly to her mending, maybe to hide the blush on her face, she muttered, "I'm glad the man left Toledo—scholar or no, lover of Zion or not. I'm grateful he's not here writing such things."

Rebecca looked at her father and smiled. She hadn't missed her Imma's interchange with Abba. She knew it was time to change the subject. Why had she brought it up anyway? Sometimes Rebecca was shocked at her own lack of discretion. Her Imma was having a hard time realizing that her daughter was now a young woman almost of marriageable age.

"Imma, what Abba wrote down reminds me of you as well. Even with all that we have and all the blessings we as Jewish people enjoy in Spain, your heart is still in the land of Israel."

"Yes, daughter, my heart is there. It should be. Not only because it is our land and where we belong, but somehow I believe in my heart that your brother, Samuel, is still there. And I want to see our land; I want to find our son." Rachel turned and looked at Reuben. He nodded. He wanted Rachel to see her son; the cheerful, sunny disposition that once attracted Reuben to Rachel had been covered by a hazy cloud from the time she had been separated from their sons. The brightness that once shone from her had dimmed when Joseph was taken by death and then Samuel by war.

"And I, Imma, would like to see the brother I have never seen. But I wish he would come here." A pout crossed Rebecca's lips. "I don't want to leave Spain." She pounded her knee for emphasis. "I have my friends, our community, my school, and I want to live here, get married here, and stay here for the rest of my life. Maybe Samuel will find out about us and come here. I don't want to go to the Promised Land. I don't know anything about it. I'm happy here."

"I'm glad you are happy here, my daughter. And maybe Samuel will find us if he is still alive," said Reuben.

"He is still alive, Reuben. I know he is still alive. I saw him alive and I know. A mother knows these things."

"I pray to God he is still alive, Rachel. And if he is, then maybe he will find us and come here. But Rebecca, your Imma still wants to go to the land of Israel. Like ben Samuel ha-Levi, her heart is there."

"The heart of *every* Jew should be there," Rachel added. "Even yours, Rebecca—even yours. What have I done, where have I failed, that my one and only daughter, my gift from the Almighty, does not love his land and does not want to be in his land? In our land? It's our possession. Should we not possess it? Should we tell the Almighty One of Israel, 'Never mind, I'll take Spain?' Did he give us Spain? Does the Torah tell us it is Spain he gave to Abraham, Isaac, and Jacob and the children of Israel? What do they teach you in school?"

"Oh Imma," Rebecca rose up from the stool on which she was sitting and rushed across the room to her mother's chair, "Imma, I am sorry. It's just that—that—oh, what can I say?" Rebecca stomped her foot in frustration and went back and plopped on her stool, propping up her chin with her hands.

Reuben watched them both, thinking, *I wonder if you two know how alike you are?* He looked at Rebecca and remembered how, after they arrived in Spain, Rachel told him she was with child again. He had suspected it, but had waited patiently for her to tell him. That night he wept tears of gratitude as he thanked the Almighty for hearing his prayers and giving them a child to help fill the void left by Samuel. And it was a girl! That was good—not a substitute for Samuel, but a sister.

Reuben also never ceased to thank the Almighty that he had allowed them to see Samuel as they journeyed to Caesarea and boarded the ship that was to bring them to Spain. Just to know he was alive brought great hope! Every day when Reuben said his prayers, he prayed that Rachel was right about Samuel being alive. So many Jews had died in Israel and around the world, and Reuben had been told their people were not faring as well in other countries as they were in Spain. So for the sake of his Rachel, he never assumed Samuel was alive. Better his wife should be surprised by the Almighty than be disillusioned.

As he sat thinking about all this, he began to wonder about what had happened to Sarah. And Jared. Were they alive? And if so, where were they? Were they faring well, or suffering like so many he heard about? Would they be surprised to hear that he and Rachel had a beautiful daughter, soon of marriageable age?

Reuben knew it was by the providence of the Almighty that they were taken to Spain. Why they had been so blessed he didn't know. They were living in the golden age of Arab civilization—a golden age attributable, in large degree, to the incredible influence of the Jews living throughout the Islamic world. *This really is the golden age of Spanish Jewry*, Reuben thought.

In Spain, the Jews were respected and appreciated. Many of them moved in high places. Hasdai ibn Shaprut served as physician and minister to Caliph Abd-ar-Raham III, traveling on delicate diplomatic missions. When Reuben considered the number of gifted and acclaimed Jewish poets, scholars, and even doctors living in Spain, he felt proud to be a Jew. Although Maimonides, the brilliant scholar and doctor, had been forced to flee Cordoba because of persecution from the fanatical Muslim Almohads, even then, by the providence of the Almighty, he ended up in Cairo as the court physician to Saladin. There he was able to help rich and poor alike. Life under Moslem rule in Spain had not been difficult.

"Reuben! Reuben!"

"Yes, Rachel?"

"Where were you?"

"I was thinking. . . ."

"About?"

"About us, the Almighty, and his providence. About Sarah and Jared."

"I want to meet them, Abba." Rebecca addressed her remarks to her father, because at the moment she was frustrated with her mother.

"Maybe someday we'll all be in Israel together," said Rachel. "What do you think, Reuben?"

Still somewhat immersed in his thoughts, Reuben answered, "It would be the Almighty, Rachel, the Almighty. Only by his providence. . . ."

Chapter 44

'm telling you, I was there. I heard it with my own ears." Jared's face was red. He was frustrated by the mental blindness of the men sitting around Jurnet's dining room table. All the men, with the exception of Jurnet (whom Jared always addressed by his surname), and Enoch, Jared's young friend and business partner, were scholars of the Talmud—scholars whom Jurnet patronized. Two of the scholars were also involved in trade on the side. Or was it the Talmud on the side? Jared didn't know.

The Jurnet family had lived in Norwich for several generations and were probably one of the wealthiest families in the city. And Jews at that! Financing was Jurnet's profession. That was how he and Jared became acquainted. Jurnet had business partners in London, he traveled a lot, and he had a large-scale operation that handled huge sums of money. Jared was in the moneylending business also. Many Jews in England were.

With most opportunities of earning a dignified living being closed to Jared because he was a Jew, he found that he could do what the Christians could not do—be involved in usury. The Third Lateran Council forbade all Roman Catholics to lend money at interest, threatening that those who did so would receive a non-Christian burial. But moneylending was vital for the economy, and so was survival for the Jews. Since the Talmud said that the preservation of life was a holy act, the Jews chose to save their lives by becoming moneylenders. Dealing fairly and justly and following the laws of the Talmud in respect to commercial transactions, the Jews thrived as merchants and moneylenders. They became the bankers of Europe. Yet even this vocation was not without cost, for the monarchs bled them in taxes and levies. And then when a monarch found himself too deep in debt, he merely expelled the Jews and confiscated all they owned.

Moneylending had made Jared a wealthy man in his own right—but not a blind one, like he considered most of the men around the table to be. Jared looked over at Enoch. "You tell them."

Enoch shrugged his shoulders and lifted his hands in a display of helplessness. "Jared's concern is valid. I, too, have heard firsthand accounts."

Jurnet took quick inventory of the men sitting at the table. Their close-mindedness embarrassed him. "Gentlemen, gentlemen," he intervened, "please, it is our duty to listen. Not to agree, but at least to give our brother a fair hearing instead of constantly interrupting and shaking our heads in disapproval before we have heard the whole story. I know such conversation isn't pleasant; it's more tantalizing to debate the Law. But tonight, let's reason with our friend. I have invited him here as my guest because I believe he bears listening to. Now if you gentlemen would do me the courtesy. . . ."

Jared watched as their moods changed once the old man graciously commanded their attention. Jared understood why he was so successful. Even Jurnet's appearance gave credence to his character. His tall stately form, always well groomed, his white hair and beard neatly trimmed, and his simple but dignified well-tailored clothes set him apart as the gentleman he truly was. Even his grand stone house on King Street looked like Jurnet. The man was always discreet, always in control of the situation—never controlled by it.

He's always calm, Jared thought as he rubbed his face. His face felt like fire and he knew it was glowing. But Jurnet's face never turned red. *Mine doesn't often, either, but when it does, everyone can see it. I wish I could learn his secret.*

The youngest of the group, Abel, feeling responsible to shoulder the blame in order to help save the older men from embarrassment, spoke up as the rest of the scholars adjusted themselves in their chairs—some taking another drink of their wine or reaching for a biscuit with downcast eyes. "Forgive me, Jared, for not giving you the opportunity to be heard."

"Uhm . . . yes. . . ." A few of the men muffled their assents.

Jared began, "Thank you, Jurnet. Gentlemen, your host invited me to share with you what—in the light of a number of events—I believe is the future of the Jews in England. Events which undoubtedly, by their very nature, will bring about the extinction of the Jewish communities throughout England."

"But we've been here since William the Conqueror," a man at the other end of the table interjected.

"And," a man with a long skinny face spoke up, "what would the king do without our money?" *He must be one of the tradesmen. I should have written down his name,* Jared thought as he cast a pleading glance at Jurnet.

Jurnet spoke again. "Remember, gentlemen, we cannot wisely debate the issue until we have heard it. I am sure Jared has much more to say, after which I am quite confident he would be most interested in hearing your insights and evaluations of his concerns. Now, Jared, would you so kindly proceed?"

"Ah...Jared?"

Jared had been so taken with Jurnet's diplomacy, making mental notes, that for a moment he forgot his purpose and didn't hear that it was his opportunity to speak—hopefully without interruption. "Oh . . . yes. The events . . .yes, the events in Norwich and York I believe were simply harbingers of worse things to come. Monks around Europe have picked up the Norwich case and are spreading it like seed on the fertile soil of anti-Jewish sentiments aroused by the Crusades."

"Excuse me," Abel interrupted, "but since I am young and new in Norwich, I don't know what you are referring to when you speak of the Norwich case."

"Thank you, Abel, for being so humble as to ask. Would one of you gentlemen, who may be even more familiar with it than I, be willing to share with Abel?" Jared smiled, pleased with the new strategy he had just conceived. Maybe if he could get the men themselves to talk about what happened in Norwich it would open their eyes.

A frail old rabbi pushed back his chair and slowly rose to his feet. His bony hand shook as he spoke. Why the rabbi stood Jared didn't know, unless it was because he was so short and he felt lost in the chair as he sat at the massive dining room table.

"I was there at the trial. You see, Abel, just before Passover—and the Gentiles' Easter—a young boy by the name of William disappeared. He was the son of a substantial farmer here in Norwich, and an apprentice to a skinner. Well, according to the accounts he was last seen going into the home of a Jew. That was March twentieth if I remember correctly. . . ." The rabbi looked about the table for affirmation, his head bobbing almost as much as his hand. Jared wondered how his yarmulke stayed on his head with all that motion and his white hair being so sparse and stringy. They had all left their ridiculous conical hats in the foyer, despising what they were forced to wear as Jews.

"That's right, the twentieth of March, rebbe," one of the scholars chimed in.

"Two days later," the rabbi resumed his account, "on the Wednesday of the Christian's holy week, the boy's body was found east of the city in Thorpe Wood. His head had been shaved and his body stabbed many times. Little William's mother and a local priest by the name of Godwin said the boy was killed by the Jews as a re-enactment of Christ's passion." The old man put his trembling hand on the back of his chair to steady himself and started to sit down.

Abel spoke. "Did it come to court? You called it the Norwich case."

"May . . . may I. . . ." the old rabbi straightened his legs and, holding on to the edge of the chair, brought himself again to his full yet diminutive height. His head bobbing he asked, "May I answer that?"

"Please do, rabbi. I so appreciate your speaking up," Jared replied. His heart went out in compassion to the old man.

"At an ecclesiastical court meeting they accused some Jews of this sacrilege. Why, they even had two little Christian maidservants who worked for these Jews who claim to have witnessed all this through a crack in the door. These little maids testified that after the synagogue service they had seen the boy being gagged, tied with cords, and then having his head pierced with thorns. After which," the rabbi sighed, "they said the Jews bound him on a cross, and nailed his left hand . . .left hand?" the rabbi queried himself, raising his left hand and looking at it. "Yes, it was his left hand and foot. And they pierced his side and then poured scalding water over his body."

The rabbi paused and, with his trembling hand, wiped his reddened eyes. They looked weak and frail, as if they had shed many tears. Everyone watched silently, waiting respectfully. As Jared looked around the table he saw he wasn't the only one who loved this old man.

"Excuse me," said the rabbi his voice trembling even more. "It grieves my heart to think anyone would believe that Jews—who so honor, so value, and so treasure life—would do such a barbaric thing, or that these young ladies would tell such a gruesome lie. There were no marks on William's body that supported their tale, but they were believed. Not by the authorities, but by the common folk. The local magistrate wouldn't allow the people or the priest to do anything to the Jews. He refused to allow them to stand trial, saying they were the king's property. But the damage had been done. And it continues to be done, for now the people are attributing all sorts of miracles to this boy's body. They—they have canonized him as a saint! William of Norwich, they call him." Once again with trembling hands the rabbi began his descent into his chair.

"May I add one more thing?" asked Thomas ben David, a man of middle age with heavyset eyebrows, a bulbous nose, and thick lips. Jared nodded. "This Norwich case set a precedent for accusing Jews of two things. I have heard from my cousin in Bristol, who heard from another person in Gloucester—and even as far away as France and the Rhineland—that Jews are now being accused of what are called ritual murders. And listen to me on this one: They are also accusing Jews of what they call blood libel."

"What's blood libel?" Abel blurted out, his eyes widening.

"Tell him, Thomas," said Jared, pleased with the dynamics of the conversation. They were telling each other what he wanted them to remember and take serious note of!

Thomas grinned ever so slightly. "Well, it's like this. Now you have to follow me carefully. If you do you'll understand what we're up against. Because the whole thing of ritual murders and blood libel had its beginnings in Norwich, England—right in the city in which we live. They say the day that William was found dead was the second day of Passover." The men nodded their heads. "Well, superstition has it that Jews all have hemorrhoids—that is, ever since we cried out to Pilate at Jesus' trial, 'His blood be upon us and upon our children.' Now, they claim our sages have told us these hemorrhoids can only be cured through 'the blood of Christ'—in other words, by embracing Christianity. But they also claim that the Jews took the sages' word literally, thinking that if we wanted to be cured we must kill a Christ-substitute each year."

"And if I may interrupt you for a moment, Thomas," Jared interjected with a smile at Thomas, who returned his smile and nodded his assent. Jared couldn't believe how well the meeting was going and that this was even the same group of men he had faced a few moments ago. "The pope has now declared that the host—that's the bread-like wafer used in their communion service—is actually Christ's body. Consequently they are accusing Jews of stealing the host and torturing it, making it relive the sufferings of Jesus Christ. They say we afflict the host in the same way as these allegedly stolen children are being tortured. Some accounts even say that sometimes the host flies into the air, becomes a butterfly, causes earthquakes, or—this is their most common story—screams in pain or cries like a child."

Jared paused for a moment. "Now, Thomas, please continue. . . ."

"What is so scary is that the lie begun here has spread all over Europe. The charges have become epidemic. In Deggendorf, Bavaria, they massacred the whole Jewish community for profaning the host. They burned their bodies and divided their property. In France a Jewish community of twenty-one men and seventeen women was accused of murdering a Christian boy. They were all put to trial by water—if they said they believed but refused the water of baptism then they were burned alive at a huge stake. In Paris, a Jewish couple accused of pricking the host was sentenced to death. They were burned at the stake. And the church in the Rue des Billettes, where the so-called desecrated host was exposed, is now a place of pilgrimage for Christians. Every Christian who goes there carries home the story of the Jews' desecration. The crusaders called us Christ-killers, and in their eyes, that's what we continue to be."

"But surely," Jurnet spoke up, "the authorities don't believe such nonsense —especially when there is no valid, concrete evidence. We have English law . . . why, even our Talmudic law has had an impact on England. Some of our laws, the commercial ones I know, are actually part of the guarantees of rights and privileges granted by King John in the Magna Carta."

Enoch answered, "You are right, Jurnet. We have English law, and ecclesiastical law. And the law is fine when it is to men's benefit. But if it's not, men will do everything they can to get around it. Men become blind to the law where emotions, prejudice, or money is concerned, and all three are concerned here. Besides, it's the populace that is being persuaded of the nonsense, not those sitting in genuine ecclesiastical inquiries. When our cases have progressed that far, we've been given fair trials. Our problem is that the populace is spurred on by the monks, including the Dominicans and the Franciscans, who at the Fourth Lateran Council were especially mandated to put down heresy. At first they didn't see us as heretics, but something has happened and they have become our enemies."

Jared smiled at Enoch, who had become like a son to him. He was proud of the way this young man was expressing himself. "The masses become so incited by the prejudices, stories, and fantasies they hear that the majority of the Jews never get a genuine ecclesiastical inquiry. The mob becomes judge, jury, and executioner. Look at what happened in York on Shabbat Hagadol. Because this Sabbath preceding Passover coincided with the Christian Holy Saturday, the Jews had to take refuge in Clifford's Tower—the tower of the royal castle! And could they escape and live? No! They chose to die at each other's hands rather than fall into the hands of an angry mob." Enoch avoided looking at Jared as he spoke of this last incident, recalling the tremendous pain it brought to both of them.

Enoch went on, "A mob which, by the way, under our king Richard the Lionhearted, caught the crusade fever. Let's face it. We are hated, not trusted—simply because we are Jews. Have you seen those caricatures? The drawings of Jews sucking on the teats of swine, embracing their hindquarters, and eating . . . uh, eating. . . ."

Tears formed in Enoch's eyes. He couldn't say it. It was too demeaning, too crude. The men stared sullenly at the surface of the table and slowly nodded their heads in sympathetic agreement. They understood. They had seen the caricature.

Enoch cleared his throat, regained his composure, and continued, "Then there are the statutes in the churches of France and Germany—the carvings, on Bible covers, of two women: *Ecclesia et Synagoga*. Ecclesia, the church, stands tall and triumphant, a crown on her head and the host and wine in her hand; while Synagoga is blindfolded with a crown falling from her head. In one hand she holds the tables of the Law turned upside down and in the other a broken scepter. What does that image say as it is circulated near and far?"

Jared noticed the elderly rabbi wiping his eyes again. Jared had said very little up to this point. Now he prayed for wisdom; he knew his turn was coming and he felt their very lives and the Jewish communities and synagogues were at stake. So much so that at that moment he wanted to scoop the old rabbi into his arms and carry him to safety—safety which he knew was not in England. But where? Spain?

Enoch paused for a moment, then continued. "And finally there's the issue of money. People, as a rule, are blinded by money. And consequently they are seldom rational or objective or fair when their economic status is at stake. Greed unfortunately prevails. We who are moneylenders can speak to that. But remember, because we are the moneylenders, if they wipe us out, they also wipe out their debt! When they can accuse and condemn us, then our booty becomes theirs.

"Do you know what they did at York? The mob destroyed all the Jewish records and burned the promissory notes of Christian debtors—notes which were deposited in the local churches. And this brought a loss to the royal treasury. So what did King Richard do? He began the Exchequer of the Jews. Now all our transactions as Jews have to be registered and recorded. Do you think he was protecting us? No! Rather, his own coffers! Remember what is written in the law: 'The Jews themselves and all their chattels are the king's . . . if anyone detains them or their money the king may claim them, if he so desires as his own.' Watch! I warn you. What has become our livelihood will become the cause of our poverty and maybe the loss of our lives."

Enoch leaned back. "I've talked enough." Jared smiled inwardly as he thought to himself, *Enoch, you may not be able to quote the Talmud, but you can quote the king's law of the land.*

Jurnet wiped his forehead and looked at Jared. Thomas reached over and patted Jared on the back. Thomas, having made his contibution, became a listener—a sympathetic one.

Jared sensed that it was time for him to speak. "With all this persecution has come our economic degradation. Travel for Jews is no longer safe. Christians have organized merchant guilds, which are monopolizing trade. Some countries are already isolating Jews from other peoples by requiring that they live in select areas separate from the rest of a town or city. They are forbidding us to do business with anyone outside our newly walled-in communities, and I believe we will see more and more of this in the future. There are boycotts, of Jewish businesses, even right here in England."

Jurnet nodded, affirming Jared's words. The nodding did not go unnoticed, for Jurnet sat at the head of the table with Jared to his immediate right.

Jared continued. "At one time we were secure in England because we could be moneylenders while Christians were forbidden such a role. But with the flood of anti-Jewish sentiments and the changing business and trade conditions that I have just stated, we are seeing even monarchs demand impossible tributes, levies, and taxes. And the king is getting deeper in debt to his moneylenders. I believe, gentlemen, we will soon find ourselves expelled from England, our property confiscated, and we left as paupers . . . if we are left with our lives. I am saying this to warn you to get your families out of England while there is still time."

"But it's not right!" Abel blurted out indignantly.

Thomas leaned back and drummed his thick hairy fingers on the table. "It's not right. It's not fair. But is it ever? After all, we're just Jews. What recourse do we have?"

The old rabbi leaned forward. Clasping his trembling hands on the table, he lifted his shaking head heavenward and said, "We have the Almighty." Then he lowered his head and made eye contact with every man sitting around the table. "We have the Almighty One of Israel. What more do we need? I am an old man. Soon I will be in the grave. I will not have to go through what many of you will go through. But let me leave you with this assurance. While you may not understand his ways, what the Almighty has purposed will come to pass. What he has planned no man can thwart. Isaiah recorded that truth for us. We need to listen to the prophets. They give us the whole story. You are living in only one part of the story now. There is a blessed ending. However, not until we receive back double for all our sins. Isaiah says this also. These are not my words."

Once again, bracing himself with one hand on the edge of his chair, the rabbi struggled to stand. As he did so, he said, "The Almighty never leaves his throne."

Then, placing both hands on the table and almost gripping its edge, the old rabbi quoted from the prophet Habakkuk in a strong but trembling voice that matched his bobbing head: "I heard and my inward parts trembled; at the sound my lips quivered. Decay enters my bones, and in my place I tremble. Because I must wait quietly for the day of distress, for the people to arise who will invade us. Though the fig tree should not blossom, and there be no fruit on the vines, though the yield of the olive should fail, and the fields produce no food, though the flock would be cut off from the fold, and there be no cattle in the stalls, yet I will exult in the Lord, I will rejoice in the God of my salvation. The Lord God is my strength, and He has made my feet like hinds' feet, and makes me walk on my high places."

❧~❧~❧

The next day Jared and Enoch left England on pretense of business, but not before they went to the home of the old rabbi. Jared wanted to persuade him to join them on their trip to Spain. If necessary, he would have gladly gathered the man in his arms and carried him all the way to Spain. But the rabbi couldn't go. As the housekeeper let Jared and Enoch into his house, she informed them that he had died in his sleep that very night.

Jared was relieved. The rabbi he had known and loved for but a day was gone. He thought of Isaiah, whom he had heard the rabbi quote: *The righteous man perishes, and no man takes it to heart; and devout men are taken away, while no one understands. For the righteous man is taken away from evil . . . he enters into peace; they rest in their beds, each one who walked in his upright way. . . .*

As Jared looked at the rabbi's now lifeless form, he did what he wanted to do the day before. Leaning over the bed, he gently picked up the rabbi and cradled him in his arms. The head that bobbed incessantly now lay quietly on his chest. The tremoring hands were at rest and his tears were finished. Jared bent down, pressed his lips to the old man's forehead, and laid him gently back on the bed. "Shalom, dear rebbe. Shalom."

Then straightening himself, Jared performed k'riah, tearing his shirt.

The housekeeper stood in the corner, captivated by the stranger's tenderness for the rabbi she had devotedly served all these years. She was not surprised that although this man knew him for only a day, he had grown to love him.

As she handed Jared his cloak, she reached up and patted him on the cheek. She said nothing; her eyes said it all. As Jared fastened his cloak and took one last look at the rabbi, he wondered what death he himself would die and if someone would be there to tear his garment in mourning for him.

Chapter 45

"*W*hy do we have to be Jews?"

"What did you say?"

"You heard me, Imma," Rebecca's voice was curt. "I said exactly what I said. Why do we have to be Jews?"

"How can you ask such a question? Why would you ask such a question? Reuben! Reuben!"

Rebecca watched her mother carefully. Rachel had been totally discomfited by her question. Rebecca was now sorry she had asked. It just came out as she was helping her mother clean up the kitchen.

"Reuben!" Rachel shouted.

"Imma, you needn't call for Abba. You can answer this—"

"Yes, Rachel, I'm here," said Reuben, stepping into the kitchen. "You don't need to shout. What do you want?"

"Why didn't you come when I first called you?" Rachel retorted sharply.

"I was coming, Rachel. I told you I was coming, but apparently you didn't hear me. Maybe you and Rebecca were talking or making noise." Reuben smiled and put his arm around Rachel's shoulders. "I will always come when you call. What is it that you want, my love?"

Rachel was unresponsive to Reuben's touch; her response told him that something was not right in the kitchen. "We have a problem, Reuben." Rachel was wringing a towel in her hands.

"Oh, Imma, aren't you carrying this a little too far?" Rebecca asked sarcastically as she vigorously scrubbed a table that, to Reuben, already looked clean.

"Too far? Too far? When my daughter asks a question like that?"

Reuben turned to Rebecca. "Rebecca dear, what question did you ask your mother?"

Rebecca never raised her head but kept on scrubbing the table. "It was just something that came into my mind, Abba."

Reuben reached over to the table and gently put his hand on Rebecca's, stopping her scrubbing. "What came into your mind, my daughter? It's all right to say it. If it's in your mind then it needs to be discussed, thought out, understood."

Rebecca lifted her eyes from the table and for a moment said nothing while she searched her father's eyes. Reuben smiled tenderly, letting her glimpse the unconditional love and acceptance residing in him. Rebecca was of marriageable age, and he would not have her very long. Soon a marriage would be arranged. He wanted to give her the example of a good parent; she would be the mother of his grandchildren.

After a moment she said, "I should have asked you, Abba."

"Asked me what?" His words were gentle.

Rebecca watched his eyes carefully to see his reaction as she answered his question. "I asked, Abba, why do we have to be Jews?"

With that Rachel sat in the chair at the kitchen table and began to fan herself while she muttered, "Why do we have to be Jews, she asks! We were born Jews!"

Reuben reached over and patted Rachel's arm as if to quiet her. He loved these two women and didn't want to be caught between them. He knew it could easily happen if he weren't careful in the way he handled this situation. Although he wouldn't permit himself to react, he, too, was quite concerned about Rebecca's question and wanted to know what prompted it.

"Rachel, if our daughter asks a question like this, then there has to be a reason." Reuben then turned to his daughter. "Rebecca, you are a thinking woman. I know and admire that—women should think. Now tell me, what was it that caused you to think about a question like that? I know that you know we are born what we are born. So why this question?"

Rebecca continued to stare at her father, wondering how honest she should be.

"Come, come . . . let's sit at the table and talk about it. It's an interesting question. Rachel, why don't you warm some milk for us."

"Something to drink! We just finished our supper!"

"I know, I know. But if you don't mind, I would like something. You can listen to Rebecca's reason for her question while you fix it. And let's have some biscuits as well."

"Biscu—"

"I know," he said, lifting his hand as if to stop her comment, "we just ate. But I like biscuits when I drink something warm. Now, Rebecca, tell us what prompted your question."

"I asked the question because I—because I—oh Abba," Rebecca cried, tears filling her eyes, "how honest can I be with you?"

Rachel looked stunned at Rebecca's outburst. She suddenly realized they were dealing with something very grave and if she wanted to find out what it was, she must follow her husband's example and not be reactive. Rebecca could become quite testy and stubborn with her mother, and Rachel knew it. She and Reuben had often discussed it.

As Reuben looked at his daughter, he cried out in his heart to the Almighty for wisdom—grateful that Rachel had called him into the kitchen.

He loved his daughter, and he was gripped with fear, a very real fear, that he might lose her.

"I want you to be totally honest with me, Rebecca. I've—we've told you over and over that we love you unconditionally and always will. You are our gift from God, an answer to my prayers. I want to know exactly what you are thinking. Nothing less than the truth. And I don't want you to be afraid of hurting me. You may be as honest with me as you will be—or care to be—and I hope that means you will be totally honest."

"All right, then." Rebecca looked at her mother, who was putting the biscuits on the plates.

"Mother?"

"My heart is the same as yours, Abba," Rachel's hand went to her chest as if to emphasize what she said, "and I'm sorry I reacted as I did. It was just that...that you took me by surprise. We want you to be honest with us, Rebecca. That's what we want."

"All right, then, you asked. I—I—" Rebecca took a deep breath and blurted it out—so loudly it surprised her. "I don't like being a Jew, and I want to change."

Rachel turned toward the cupboard where she was attempting to pour milk into the pot. She didn't want Rebecca to see her face. A wave of nausea surged inside her. *Am I going to be sick? Or faint?* Gripping the end of the cupboard with her left hand, her right hand trembled as she tried to pour the warm milk into the pot. Some of it missed the pot altogether.

For a moment no one spoke. Then, with a controlled voice, Reuben asked, "Rebecca, why don't you want to be a Jew? How do you think you can change what you are?"

"Can we all sit down . . . Abba? Imma?"

"Yes, yes, of course. . ." Rachel was relieved to sit. "Reuben, why don't you fill our cups?"

Reuben jumped up to get the pot and glasses and saucers, relieved to be able to do something. He had never expected to hear his daughter say she wanted to change from being a Jew. *What does she mean? How can one change being a Jew?* And then suddenly it hit him. *No! No!* his mind screamed. *Oh Almighty God, it couldn't be! It couldn't be. . . .*

Limply he set the pot on the table. His shaking hands rattled the glasses on their plates a little as he set them down.

"Rebecca, please tell us what you mean." Reuben filled the glasses.

Rachel noticed his hand was shaking. She searched her husband's face. What was he thinking? Why was he shaking? She blew into her glass and took a sip of the steaming milk. She needed strength.

"I can't stand being different any longer. We are different. We eat differently, we believe differently, we worship differently, we live differently! Everything about us is different. And I'm tired of being different. And I'm scared.

Why do I have to wear something—this yellow badge—that tells people around me that I'm a Jew? I can't stand it. I just can't stand it anymore. I'm a woman. I have feelings like a woman. Like every woman—"

"Rebecca," Rachel asked, panic clutching at her heart, "are you in love with a Gentile?"

"No, Imma, I'm not in love with a Gentile. Do you think a Gentile would choose a Jew? No, it is more than that."

"More? More what?"

"More than being in love with a Gentile. I want to *be* a Gentile."

"How can you be a Gentile? You are a Jew!"

"I'm a girl . . . a woman. I live in Spain. I want to live like a true Spaniard. Like the others live, not like we live."

Reuben reached over and took hold of his daughter's hand. "Rebecca, is there something wrong with the way we live?"

"No, Abba, no. It's just that *I* don't want to live this way. It's all right for you and Imma, but I *don't* want to live this way. I *don't* want to be *a Jew*. I'll never go anywhere in Spain as a Jew."

"But, Rebecca, look at the heights many of the Jews in Spain have attained to. Look at our contribution to the world of scholarship, poetry, medicine, the arts, the royal court. . . ."

"Abba, I know. But we are marked as Jews. We are forced to wear this badge, which labels me a Jew." Rebecca began pleading, "Abba, you move outside Jewish circles. You know what is happening to people just because they are Jews. You know that more and more we are being limited. Jews were even accused of causing the Black Death, a plague that they say has killed one-fourth to one-half the population of Europe. This accusation caused so terribly many of our people to be massacred. It's ridiculous! We, the Jews, are always the scapegoats. And many times, we are the goat of sacrifice! Here, even in Spain, we don't have the freedom, the acceptance we once had. You are not blind, Abba. You know this, don't you!" It was more of a statement than a question. "Be honest with me, Abba, be honest. I'm right, aren't I?"

Reuben sighed. He felt tired. Incredibly tired. "You are right; things are not good now for the Jews. Not good in the world, and not as good as they once were here in Spain, but that doesn't mean things will get worse or that they won't get better."

"Has it gotten any better in other parts of Europe, Abba? You know the answer is no. It has become worse and worse."

"But, Rebecca, it has always been good here in Spain—better for us here than in any other place in the world, even in Jerusalem."

"Right," Rebecca replied, "but not anymore. Spain is going the way the world has gone. Being a Jew will always be painful. The world doesn't like us, Abba. Face it—the world does not like us!" She screamed.

"Rebecca! Don't scream," Rachel's words came as a command. A mother's instant rebuke.

Reuben was weary. "It is not necessary, Rebecca. It's not good."

"I'm sorry, Abba, but I feel like shouting. I don't want to be hated. I don't want to be marked because I am a Jew. I am a woman—a woman like every other woman in the world. I have feelings like other women. Desires like other women. Emotions like other women. I hurt, I cry, I laugh, and I—I—want to be happy like any other woman. I want to be married, to have children. And I don't want them marked because they are Jewish! And don't tell me not to raise my voice, because I've got to raise my voice. I don't want to be a Jew!" She pounded her hand on the table. "I want to change. I want to change!"

"Change how, Rebecca?" Rachel leaned forward and rubbed her daughter's back, her voice now steeped in warmth, just like the milk.

"I want to become a converso."

For a moment Reuben rubbed his eyes with his hands. Then he looked up into space. It was what he feared she was going to say when she mentioned wanting to change. *A converso!* He felt sick—terribly sick. His heart was pounding. *Will it pound right out of my chest?*

Rachel reacted. She couldn't help it. "A converso! You can't! You can't!"

"Imma," Rebecca's tone was very firm, her words almost threatening, "you promised you would listen. That I could be honest. I am being honest. I can, and I will be a converso."

"Reuben! Reuben!" Rachel pleaded. "Do something. Say something!"

Reuben turned to his daughter and, with all the courage and self-control he could muster, he asked, "How, my daughter, can you give up your Jewish faith? Do you believe in Jesus Christ? Do you think he is truly Messiah?"

"Abba, who knows who is Messiah? Who knows when Messiah will come? Has he come? Will he still come? I don't know what the Bible says. I don't have my own copy. I cannot read it for myself. I only know what I hear the rabbis say in synagogue. Even they do not always agree. But it does not matter. No, I do not believe Jesus is the Messiah."

Both Reuben and Rachel let out sighs of relief as their daughter continued. "I don't even know that much about him except that people say we, the Jews, killed him. But, I don't have to believe that Jesus is Messiah to become a converso. All I must do is be baptized and go to their church. I can believe what I want to believe. I can still keep the Law; many conversos do. I will just do it secretly. Nobody needs to know what I believe. That is between me and the Almighty."

"But the Almighty wants us to live the way *we believe*. And don't forget, Rebecca, we are the Almighty's chosen people!"

"Chosen for what, Abba? Chosen to suffer? To be marked for the rest of our lives? To live differently than others live and to be persecuted for it? Chosen to be the object of man's ridicule, suspicion, persecution? Man's whims? One minute people like us because of what they can get out of us, and the next they hate us and mistreat us simply because we are Jews. Are we not human beings with the same feelings, rights, desires, ambitions? If this is what it means to be chosen, I wish the Almighty had chosen someone else! I want to live, Abba. Live without fear, live with hope. I don't want to be different—marked for life! I want a good life, and that's what I see the conversos having. Many of them have not given up their faith; they have merely subdued it."

"Is it a good life, Rebecca?"

"Answer that for yourself, Abba, Look at what they have. They have acceptance, rights, privileges . . . favor that you and Imma do not have. You have some business acquaintances who have become conversos. Who's in danger? You or them? Who has it better? You or them?"

"It all depends on what you call better."

"Better, Abba, is the way they live. They have life as it should be lived!"

"Rebecca," Reuben pleaded gently, "life is not what takes place on the outside, but on the inside."

"But the outside affects the inside!"

"No, my child, it is the opposite. You cannot always control the outside, but you can control the inside. Therefore, what goes on inside affects how you deal with the outside. Rebecca, dear, you are looking at the world apart from faith. You are looking at today. A truly righteous man—a righteous woman—knows there is a tomorrow because there is God. The righteous look not at today alone but at the tomorrows, which the Almighty holds in His hand."

"Abba, I *am* looking at tomorrow. And tomorrow I want to live in Spain with all the privileges and hope a Gentile has. And I can have that as a converso. Thousands in Spain—I'm sure tens of thousands—have become conversos. Why, there are even conversos holding prominent places in King Ferdinand's court."

"Don't forget," Reuben countered, "there is also a Jew—not a converso—Don Isaac Abrabanel. You've heard of him. The great scholar-statesman who administers the finances of the kingdom and who wields considerable influence with Queen Isabella and King Ferdinand. He's living proof that Jews can reach prominence without becoming conversos."

"Abba, I have already thought it through, and I want to convert!" Rebecca turned to her mother. "Imma, I don't want to hurt you or Abba, but at my age, I must do what I must do. If I am old enough to get married, I am old enough to do what I believe is right and best for me."

Reuben responded, "That is true, but let's reason together as father and daughter for a moment. Think with me and consider my questions. If you convert, will you believe Mary is the mother of God? Can God have a mother? And will you go through Mary to get to the Almighty? Will you now believe that the pope speaks for the Almighty and his words are as reliable as the Almighty's?"

"Abba, how do you know these things?" Rebecca asked, surprised at what she was hearing.

"I am exposed to everything and anything through my business. I listen. I want to know and understand what goes on in our world, so I ask questions. And I listen carefully. I am asking you very valid questions."

"I believe you, Abba."

"Good. Now let me ask you some more. Would the Almighty turn against his chosen people and make them wear clothing that marks them as Jews? Would the Almighty say we become his people simply by being baptized with water? Would we truly become his children if that baptism is forced on us? Would the Almighty declare that those who refuse baptism and are Jews should be beaten, tortured, burned, and pitilessly murdered? Would the Almighty say that once unbelievers are murdered it is permissible to steal their property? Would the Almighty order the church, if it is truly his representative, to march to the land of Israel and drive the Jews from the land he promised to Abraham, Isaac, and Jacob for an everlasting possession? Does the Almighty go back on his word, or does he watch over it to perform it?

"Think about it, Rebecca. Are these things in accord with what you know about the Almighty? Are the character and actions of this church, which professes to be the embodiment of truth and the only way to salvation, in accord with what the Bible proclaims about the Almighty?"

Rachel listened in utter amazement to her husband. She didn't know he knew all these things. *But then*, she reasoned, *Reuben's in touch with the world through his trade, and I live cloistered in the walls of our community.* Then Rachel began to wonder how Rebecca got outside those walls. Where had she as a mother failed? Or had she?

Reuben reached over and took his daughter's hand in his and looked her straight in the eyes. "Rebecca, dear, is what you wish to do in accord with the Bible, our holy Book? Can you truly follow men like Vincent Ferrer, who sweep through Spain bringing conversions by intimidation? Or Tomas de Torquemada, confessor to Queen Isabella, who hates not only Jews but also conversos, whom he calls *marranos*—swine? Or Alfonso de Spina, who in his book *Fortalitium Fidei* charges Jews with ritual murders, blood libel, and advocates not only the expulsion of Jews from Spain but also an inquisition against all conversos to see if their conversions are genuine? Don't forget—conversos are being called marranos by the very people who hate the Jews!"

Rebecca pulled her hand from her father's and rested her chin upon it as she propped her elbow on the table. She stared off into space.

"Rebecca, should there be an inquisition, would you pass the test? Can you lie about your beliefs? What if you didn't pass the test? Are you willing to suffer the consequences? After all, if they kill Jews, will they spare those who profess to be conversos but in their hearts remain Jews?"

Reuben put his hand under her chin and gently turned her face towards his. "Think beyond today. Beyond the external. You must live with what you are on the inside. And think beyond the temporal. Consider the eternal. Most of all, Rebecca, ask yourself, Can my reason be justified by the Bible? For to both Jews and Christians it is the Holy Book. Granted, the Christians add the New Testament, but both claim the Old Testament as the word of God. Does what you wish to do—does the church you wish to join—measure up to the Almighty's plumbline of truth?"

Reuben tilted Rebecca's head back and looked into her downcast eyes. "Do what is right—what is according to truth, my daughter. That is all I ask."

Rebecca's eyes were filled with tears and her voice with frustration. "But, Abba, I don't *know* what the Bible says. I only know what others tell me it says, so I must go by what is in my heart."

"No, Rebecca, no. The Almighty tells us that our hearts are deceitful and desperately wicked. You cannot trust your heart. You must be guided by his Word. Give me time, Rebecca, please, I beg of you. Give me time, and I will get you a Bible. I will go to the synagogue and beg for the scrolls. Or, maybe I can get a Bible for your very own. Not too long ago the Bible was printed on what is called a printing press. I will begin inquiring among the tradesmen coming from Germany tomorrow. Just please promise me that before you do anything you will read the Bible—the Old Testament—for yourself. Then you can compare what you see in the Christians' lives with the word of the Almighty. Then you can ask yourself if, before God, you can follow their ways. A man's ways reveal what he really believes. Will you do that for an Abba and Imma who love you and only want your very best? Will you promise me just this one thing?"

Rebecca looked at him, tears spilling down her face. Her lashes were stuck together. Her long dark brown hair, which cascaded onto her shoulders, slid up and down as she vigorously nodded her assent. She still looked like a little girl to Reuben. It was hard for him to believe she was now old enough to marry. Jews wedded their children too young to suit Reuben.

"It may take you several months to read it, but you will, won't you? After all, becoming a converso is a life-changing decision."

Rebecca rose from the chair and threw her arms around her father's neck and sobbed. He pulled her to his lap and held her tight, rocking her in his arms like he had when she was a little girl. Rebecca did not resist. He had allowed her to be honest, and she would still be his little girl—for now.

Rachel stood, feeling weak and frightened. She enveloped Reuben and Rebecca in her arms and kissed them both. How she wished they all were tucked away safely in Jerusalem and that her beloved Samuel could be part of their circle of love. That was her wish, yet she couldn't help but wonder. *Will it ever happen? What will we do if Rebecca becomes a converso?*

Chapter 46

"Jared, I've met a girl." Enoch's words were solemn, but spoken with a hint of excitement.

"Is she Jewish?" Jared asked without looking up. He was reading Rashi's commentary on the Talmud, which he had just purchased. He wanted the book because it was the first Jewish book printed on the new printing presses.

"Uh . . ." Enoch hesitated but for a second, "yes."

"Are you sure?" Jared laid down his book and looked at Enoch. Enoch seemed a little nervous; he appeared to be making little progress with the letter he was writing. He had sat motionless for a long time at the desk, not even raising his head in response to Jared's question.

Jared studied Enoch. His hair was a sandy color. From whom Enoch had inherited it, Jared didn't know. Certainly not from his mother, whose hair was the color of black silk. Enoch was nice looking; he was tall but a little slight in build. His warm, gentle brown eyes made him appear friendly, but he couldn't be described as decidedly handsome. Jared smiled; he loved this fatherless young man. In Jared's eyes, Enoch was a gift—the son he could not father because he had chosen not to marry. Enoch filled the void Samuel left; Samuel had been like a nephew to Jared.

Jared missed Samuel a great deal. Losing track of Samuel's whereabouts because of the Roman siege, then being separated from Reuben and Rachel, as well as his good friend Sarah, left him totally adrift—alone on the sea of humanity, tossed by the waves of history. History he could not control. Then Jared met Elisheba and fell in love. He fell in love with both the widow and her son Enoch. In them Jared found his moorings. Then . . . then . . . the thought of what had happened afterward filled Jared's eyes with tears. If Enoch was falling in love, Jared understood. *And if the girl is Jewish and righteous, I will do everything I can to help him get married. Enoch should get married while he can . . . before it is too late. Life as a Jew is too uncertain; it must be lived while it can be lived.*

Jared had a hard time forgiving himself for waiting to marry Elisheba, but then it had been a mutual decision. They had wanted to give Enoch time—time to adjust to the idea of having a new father. Enoch had so loved his father that his death was quite a traumatic experience for him. They didn't want their marriage to add to this trauma. So Elisheba and Jared agreed to wait. *We waited too long. Oh Elisheba, my love, why did I ever let you travel to York to visit your mother on Passover? If only I had known! If only I had insisted that you wait until after the Christians' Easter. If only I had not listened to your uncle's assurances that he would take good care of you. If only I had gone with you. If only....*

When Elisheba didn't come home, Jared became concerned and went himself to York. He discovered that under duress and accusations from the Christians, the local Jews had fled to Clifford's Tower. There, with no hope of escape, they all took their lives.

Over and over, Jared's mind pictured Elisheba dying—dying alone, dying without him. First, undoubtedly, putting her mother to death, and then her uncle. Or would her uncle have insisted that he die last? He was a righteous man...strong. Jared's only comfort was knowing that at least Elisheba had been with her mother and her maternal uncle. She hadn't been totally alone.

Jared shook his head. He must not let the past spoil Enoch's joy.

"To whom are you writing?"

"Her."

"Her?"

"The young woman I've met."

"Why are you writing to her? Can't you talk with her?"

"Sometimes."

"Where do you see her?" Jared asked. "I know it's not in the synagogue. Or at least, from what I can tell, no young woman there has caught your attention. But I know you've caught the eyes of some of the young women."

Enoch put down his quill and turned from the desk to stretch his long legs, which had been confined too long. He smiled bashfully. "How do you know I've caught the attention of some of the young women?"

"I watch them point and whisper and walk your way. And if you happen to glance in their direction, they look down."

"You are quite observant, Jared. Quite observant." Enoch grinned.

"Tell me where you met this young woman. I do assume she is young!"

"She is young . . . and beautiful. But not commonly beautiful. Her beauty is a different kind of beauty."

"Oh?"

"Her beauty comes alive when she talks—when she tries to make a point or persuade you of something." Enoch's eyes lit up as he talked about her.

"She must be a thinking young woman."

"Yes. She thinks, she reads, she questions. She's ambitious. She wants to live. . . ."

Jared's brows wrinkled to a puzzled expression. "Where did you meet a woman like this?"

"In the library."

"I see. You've been going to the library for more than a month now. Has she been there that long?"

Enoch grinned sheepishly and laughed. "Yes."

"Well, that answers one question I've had—why you've spent so much time at the library. It's not typical to find young Jewish women in libraries. You are sure she's Jewish, aren't you?"

At that moment Enoch hoped that perhaps they could avoid getting into the question of her Jewishness. Fortunately, Jared continued. "I'm surprised her parents allow her to go to the library. You have to admit it's not the typical place to find a young, single Jewish woman. When am I going to meet her? Or can I? Maybe there is a marriage contract—"

"No. I've already asked. Her parents haven't found anyone suitable yet, she says."

"Would they find you suitable, do you think?"

"I don't know. I don't know what value they place on Talmudic scholarship. Besides, Jared, I don't know if she would find me suitable."

"Ah, I see. You only know that you are attracted to her."

"Yes, Jared, and I know you understand. You can remember—" Enoch hesitated. "I remember you and Imma. . . ."

"I do too, Enoch," said Jared. "I do too. No need to talk about the memories." Jared stood up. He didn't want to think about Elisheba anymore today. It still hurt too much. As he stretched he wondered if it would always hurt too much. "We must retire for the night. I have to think about how I'll build my connections here in Spain. It's not going to be as easy as I thought it would be, but I am still pleased we came. My heart aches for all those who were expelled from England. There's not a single Jew left in that country."

As they walked down the hall to their respective bedrooms, Jared put his arm around Enoch and asked, "Now tell me, what is the young lady reading in the library?"

"The Bible."

"That's a good but *large* book to read."

"They just received some Bibles that were made on what's called a printing press. They were printed in Germany."

Jared nodded, then paused for a moment in the hall. "Oh, Enoch," he said with concern in his voice. "You better go to the library as much as you can. The situation is getting serious here in Spain. Rumor has it that the Jewish issue is no longer in the hands of the pope or the populace. Alfonso's program is to make it the official business of the government and the church of Spain. So we may not remain in Spain very long. The papacy has objected to the inquisitions because they are outside their papal power, but that hasn't stopped Alfonso, nor the Dominican Prior, Tomas de Torquemada. Torquemada, by the way, is determined to hunt out every *converso* and either put them all to death or isolate

273

them so the Christians of Spain will not be contaminated. I am not sure if you know who the man is, but Torquemada is Queen Isabella's confessor. He wields a tremendous influence with the queen. And he's burned many conversos—marranos, he calls them—swine." Jared sighed. "Those Jews who became conversos are going to live to regret it—that is, if they live."

Jared paused again. "Goodnight, my son." He reached up, put his hand on the back of Enoch's neck and pulled the tall young man down for a fatherly kiss on his forehead. Then, after turning toward the door to his own room, he asked, "You feel sweaty, Enoch. Are you all right? You're not getting sick, are you? Besides lovesick, I mean?"

"No . . . no, I'm fine." But as Enoch walked to his room he was thinking, *No. No, I'm not fine. You've frightened me because she's thinking about becoming a converso—and I don't want to lose her the way we lost Imma!*

Enoch and Jared both dreamed all night about the women they loved . . . and they both slept fitfully.

Chapter 47

Enoch paced in front of the library rubbing his hands together. He was cold. *I must have left my cloak on the chair when I wrote my note to Jared.* Enoch had left early while Jared was still in his room, so he left a note telling Jared he had followed his advice. Enoch was going to the library and might not be home until late that night.

Enoch had been awake before the sun, his mood concurring with the darkness outside. He was exhausted. He hadn't slept much, and when he did sleep, his dreams weren't pleasant. He could see Rebecca tied at a stake and Torquemada laughing and crying out, "Morranos! Morranos!" as he bent to kindle the wood with the flaming torch in his hand. Enoch's mother was also at the stake saying she didn't want to die; she wanted to live, to love. Jared and Enoch struggled to pull the torch from Torquemada's hands while he laughed. But he was too strong for them. Neither could they loosen the ropes that held their women captive. It seemed to Enoch that he cried, struggled, and pleaded all night.

Now he waited, looking anxiously in every direction. He walked from the street to the library, back and forth, again and again, just in case Rebecca had somehow slipped in unnoticed. Fear gripped his heart. *What if someone overheard what Rebecca is thinking of doing? What if someone told on her? What if she's been found out and they've come to take her before the courts? Suppose . . .*

The "what ifs" were agonizing. For the first time, Enoch began to sense the depth of pain and torment Jared went through when Imma didn't return from York and he later learned that she had died.

Enoch wanted something to drink, to put something in his stomach, but he was afraid to leave the library and go around the corner even for a quick nourishment. What frustrated him more was that he didn't know where Rebecca lived or how to reach her. All he knew was that every day she came to the library, and—this gave him some comfort—she said she would continue to come until she finished reading the Old Testament. How Enoch prayed nothing would deter Rebecca from her goal!

An hour passed, and then another. Enoch became so weak he feared he would faint if he didn't get some sort of nourishment into his body soon. Finally, leaving instructions with the man at the desk and pleading with him not to let Rebecca enter or leave without his note, Enoch hurried around the corner to get a cake.

Just as Enoch entered the tavern, he heard someone call out, "Enoch . . . Enoch."

As he turned in the direction of the voice and saw who had called him, tears flooded his eyes. The sight of Rebecca seated safely in the corner—wrapped in a long, deep-red velvet cape with a black lace scarf draped loosely around her neck—broke the dam. She was alive. She was free. She was *beautiful!*

"What are you doing here so early in the morning? I thought you weren't coming to the library until the afternoon!" Rebecca was all smiles, obviously delighted to see him and oblivious of the torment she had caused him.

Enoch wanted to take her in his arms and cry. It was all he could do to keep from breaking down and sobbing. He fell into the chair opposite her and reached across the small highly polished table. Taking her hand, he brought it to his lips as he looked her in the eyes. Then he gently folded her hand in both of his.

"Enoch, why are there tears in your eyes?" Her voice was soft, filled with concern. "Is everything all right?" His reaction to seeing her this morning stunned her. She knew he liked her—more than liked her. However, he had never touched her except when he placed her cloak on her shoulders. Sometimes his hands would rest for a delightful second, but nothing more than that. And now suddenly it was as though they had already spoken of love.

"Everything is all right now that I know you're all right."

"Of course I'm—" Rebecca stammered. She was more shaken than she thought by his kiss on her hand and the feeling of his firm hands surrounding hers. "—I'm all right. Why wouldn't I be?"

"Haven't you heard?"

"Heard what?"

"What is happening in the royal court with the king and queen. The pressure Tomas de Torquemada is putting on Ferdinand and Isabella to expel the Jews?"

"Expel us? From where?" Rebecca queried.

"From the country. From Spain."

"But they can't!" Rebecca drew her hand from his. Confusion crossed her countenance. "This is our country . . . this is where we've lived all our lives. Look at what we have contributed to Spain! The positions we've held! You must be mistaken, Enoch. Your information must be wrong. They wouldn't—"

"I am not wrong," interrupted Enoch. "I wish I were. I wish it with all my being. I have lived in three different nations. I lost my father in the first one because he was a Jew. My mother in the second one because she was a Jew. And now, Spain will be the third country I've had to leave because I am a Jew."

"See, Enoch?" Rebecca brightened up. "Now do you see why I want to become a converso?"

"Rebecca, please," Enoch leaned over the table and whispered, "don't use that word in public."

"But," Rebecca leaned towards him, lowering her voice and smiling as if she had tricked him, "if I become a converso, I will be *one of them*, and they won't make me leave."

"Oh, but you don't have the complete scenario, my dear. Surely you know about the inquisitions, don't you?"

"I've heard about them. I know the pope is upset with some of the abuses connected with them. But they aren't going on here in Toledo. At least I don't think they are."

"Rebecca, where have you been? Don't you know what is going on around you?"

"Enoch, don't forget I live in a Jewish community. They would die if they saw me in this tavern, eating in a place they would consider unclean. The Jews don't talk about the conversos. Such a thing is an abomination—a reproach against Judaism. A converso to them is like a marrano—a swine, an unclean animal."

"Well, my dear," Enoch used the word *dear* again and noticed that Rebecca didn't seem to mind. "You need to understand that you would not be safer nor more secure in Spain as a converso than as a Jew." Enoch then lowered his voice, relieved that the tavern was almost deserted. "In fact, right now I believe the conversos are in far more danger than the Jews. That is what the inquisition is all about—to root out the conversos who, in their hearts, never really converted. To root them out and annihilate them."

"How are they finding out they're not truly converted?" Her eyes widened in fear.

"I will answer your question but first I need something to eat. Let me order us something." Enoch started to get up.

"I'm really not hungry, Enoch, but something to drink would be wonderful, if you don't mind."

Mind! he thought. *Mind a drink? I'd lay down my life for you, my lady. What is this small request?* Enoch smiled, rose from the table, and went to tell the proprietor what they wanted to eat and drink.

As he walked back to the table, Enoch beseeched the Almighty to help him convince Rebecca of the seriousness and danger of her quest.

"Now then, do you know about the three hundred conversos who were burned at the stake in Seville? Of the others rotting away in prisons? Do you know the infamous Tomas de Torquemada is now the Inquisitor General, a man determined to search out and try every converso? He considers conversos 'hidden dangers' because so many pose as converts when truly they are not. And even if he finds them to be genuine converts his desire still is to isolate them in walled-in communities where they cannot possibly contaminate, pollute, or influence Spanish Christians in any way.

"Alfonso de Espina compiled a volume, *Fortalitium Fidei*, in which he lists twenty-five 'transgressions' by which unbelieving conversos can be identified. Rebecca, stop and think. If they caught you in even one of those twenty-five transgressions—that is, if you refused to attend Mass, didn't make the sign of the cross, or never mentioned Jesus or Mary—then that could be evidence enough to burn you at the stake or throw you into a prison. We're not talking about hiding your Jewish acts, but about failing to do Christian acts."

Rebecca motioned with her head, trying to warn Enoch that the woman was bringing their food. But he was so intent he missed her signal. She then put her hand over his just as he said, "Rebecca, the queen's secretary—a converso—has just been demoted. I—"

Rebecca quickly interrupted, deliberately raising her voice. "Enoch, here's the woman with our cakes."

The woman smiled at them, revealing a missing tooth that left a gaping hole right at the front of her mouth. As she bent over to set their food before them, the large gold crucifix hanging from her neck swung back and forth in midair, dangling the form of Jesus before their eyes.

Enoch was thankful neither of them had on the badges that marked them as Jews. In the whole two months they had spent together in the library, Enoch had never seen Rebecca wear her distinguishing mark.

They stopped talking until the woman finished. She grinned at them knowingly, looking at Rebecca's hand on Enoch's and walked away. Rebecca hadn't withdrawn her hand after trying to get his attention, and Enoch hadn't moved. He didn't want to.

"May I tell you one last story?" asked Enoch.

"If it's not too sad." Rebecca moved her hand as she took a sip of her drink. Enoch missed its warmth, the thrill of its presence.

"It is sad, but sometimes we need to hear sad things so we can learn from them. Unpleasant things don't go away just because we close our eyes or choose to remain ignorant of them. It doesn't alter their reality. But an awareness of them can help us to be wiser and more prudent in our behavior. So, please, let me tell you the story, even though it is sad."

Enoch drank in her uncommon beauty as he began. "The richest converso in the city of Sancho de Cuidad bought a boat and sought to escape with his family, but it was all to no avail. The winds drove them back here, where they were brought into our city and burned to death—mother, father, and children. All were tied and burned together. Can you imagine? They were shown no mercy. They would not let them flee. They would not spare their lives. Instead the inquisitors killed them simply because they refused to listen to their pleading or to believe they were truly converted."

Unexpectedly, Rebecca rose to her feet. "Enoch, I must go now. I have to go. I have to think. I must make sure things really are as bad as you say. As I read through the Bible—I'm almost finished, you know—one thing I saw was the importance of two or three witnesses. I want to see if there are others as alarmed or fanatical as you are. Or, if for some reason, you just don't want *me* to be a converso."

Enoch stood up. He knew this wasn't the time to say anything more. It was obvious their discussion had ended. "Rebecca, would you mind if I called on you in your home? I would like your parents to get to know me, and I would like you to meet the man who is like a father to me. May I call on you?"

"I would be honored," she said, then paused as if she were thinking. "But you must promise me one thing."

"What must I promise?"

"That you will not tell my parents what you just told me unless I give you permission in our conversation to do so."

Enoch looked at Rebecca for a long moment before answering. Then almost grudgingly he responded, "If this is your wish, I will honor it."

"Good." Rebecca was in control, and she was comfortable with that. "Now, can you come for a light meal tomorrow?"

"Not today?"

"Not today. I want to think and to find out what I can. I am still not convinced. . . ."

There was a slight flippancy in her voice. Enoch didn't like it, especially after he had anguished all night over her very life. Perhaps that was the reason for the edge in his voice when he replied, "I'm not lying, Rebecca. Nor am I exaggerating. But, then, you will discover that what I have spoken is confirmed in the mouth of two or three reliable witnesses. So, tomorrow it shall be."

"Two o'clock?" Rebecca's eyes searched his. She knew they had been sparring, and that she had started it. *Have I offended him?* she wondered.

"Two." Enoch turned to walk away.

"Wait," she laughed. "You need to know where you are coming, don't you?" Reaching into her drawstring purse, Rebecca pulled out a little card and handed it to Enoch. "My Imma always makes me carry this in case I am run over by a horse or something. Please be sure to give it back to me tomorrow."

Enoch watched Rebecca as she wrapped her lace scarf around her head and turned up the collar of her cape. His heart ached, caught in a whirlpool of joy and pain. And in the heartache of that moment, realization implanted the knowledge that if their relationship progressed, his heart would pain him even more. The questions tumbled through his mind: *Do I want it? Can I bear it?*

Chapter 48

I'm not sure we approve of what you have done, Rebecca. This is not customary. It is the parents, the matchmakers, who arrange for families to meet."

Consternation was written all over Reuben's face. These past two months had taken their toll on Reuben and Rachel as they talked long into many a night. At times their relations became strained as they discussed and re-discussed the way they had raised their daughter—the only child they had *now*. Their one opportunity to succeed! What had they done that their daughter would come to a decision like this? A converso! Now she had invited a perfect stranger to their home! A young man who obviously had intentions on their daughter.

"This young man has no family for us to meet? Who is he—Melchizedek? No mother, no father, no genealogy, Rebecca!"

"Abba," Rebecca's eyes lit up for she knew who Melchizedek was, "that's a poor illustration. I should say 'Yes, Abba, like Melchizedek,' and then like our father Abraham you would have to pay tithes to Enoch!"

Rebecca laughed, proud of herself.

Reuben was amazed by his daughter. *What Jewish girl knows who Melchizedek is?* The illustration had merely popped into his head, yet his daughter—*his daughter*—could correct him! *She's too smart! She thinks too much and wants to figure out too many things! She's a woman. She should be married. But to a man whom we don't know? Never!*

Rebecca was grinning from ear to ear. These past two months of reading the Bible had opened a whole new world for her. She had loved reading about Sarah, the beautiful wife of Abraham who was desired by kings! Deborah, the fearless judge who went to battle and delivered their people from the oppression of Sisera! Huldah the prophetess, who told King Josiah what God was going to do! That's why her visits to the library took her so long. Hours each day, day in and day out. Rebecca wanted to absorb what she read. Meditate on it. She found herself fascinated with God and his ways. With men and women and what happened when they obeyed and disobeyed. She began to understand their history as Jewish people and why they were suffering the way they were. It seemed that the Almighty *did* watch over his word to perform it!

If only I hadn't taken her to the library. Then she never would have met this man, Reuben reasoned in his heart. But what could he do? The rabbis had forbidden Reuben to bring his daughter to their yeshiva, where she could sit with the Holy Scrolls. "It wasn't proper," they had told him.

Of course, Reuben would not tell them why he was so desperate. He just let them think he was a man who had lost his senses. He didn't tell the rabbis or anyone else about Rebecca's desire to become a converso. He was afraid they would not understand—that they would react, maybe fly into outrage, condemn his Rebecca publicly in the synagogue, and ostracize her in the community. He feared they might destroy any possibility of helping and restoring his daughter.

Reuben bore his burden alone, but he bore it.

He had cried out to the Almighty. He had prayed and prayed. He had searched and searched for a Bible, and no Bible could be found. Then one day it came into his mind. *Or was it a message from the Almighty that the Gentiles might have a Bible in their library?* Yet that presented another problem. The Gentiles' Bible contained the forbidden New Testament! The fact that the Gentiles' Bible was translated into Latin posed no difficulty, for Rebecca had learned Latin as a child. Her tutor knew Latin, and Rebecca was brilliant when it came to languages. But the New Testament? Reuben's dilemma was resolved when Rebecca, under oath, promised her father she would not read it. She would stop with the book of Malachi.

"Reuben, the young man is coming," Rachel threw up her hands in despair. "There is nothing we can do about it. We don't know where he lives. We cannot contact him. All we can do when he gets here is tell him we are sorry but he cannot come in, and that we forbid him to see Rebecca anymore."

"Imma!" Rebecca stomped her foot in anger. "Imma!"

Rachel held up her hand as if to silence her daughter. Anger flashed from her eyes to Rebecca's, giving greater impetus to the tone of her voice. "Rebecca . . . honor your father and your mother!"

Rebecca stormed to her room, shouting like a spoiled, hateful child. "Now do you understand why I am going to become a converso?"

She wanted to wound her parents. And she had. She knew what she had done, and she knew it was wrong. But she stayed in her room and refused to talk to them.

Reuben slumped into a chair. In a moment, Rachel was on her knees in front of her husband, lifting his chin ever so gently. Looking into his troubled eyes, she said, "Reuben, we must set limits somewhere. Rebecca is a young woman now. We cannot make all her choices for her. We can instruct her, warn her, and admonish her. But ultimately she must make the decision and then bear the responsibility of her choices."

Reuben leaned back more until his head rested on the back of the chair. His legs and feet were so extended that his body was almost flat. He was staring at the ceiling but he was listening. His hand reached over, blindly searching for Rachel's head. When he found it, he stroked her hair gently.

Rachel continued, "You have done everything you can possibly do. Now we must put it into the hands of the Almighty."

Everyone in the house wondered when two o'clock would finally come. Rebecca stayed in her room until just before the time for Enoch to arrive. Then she washed her face, changed her clothes, brushed her hair, and went downstairs to sit silently.

Rachel went to the kitchen to set out some plates and glasses just in case there was a turn of events. Rachel liked to be prepared for any sort of contingency. Besides, after this was over, she planned to have her husband and daughter sit down, eat something, and talk. She would not endure this hostile silence much longer. This was her home, and she would not put up with having a tense atmosphere. The glasses banged on their saucers as she set out the dishes.

Reuben went upstairs for nothing and then came down again, going over and over in his mind what he would say to the young man when he came to the door with his friend. *I forgot he was bringing his friend. Who is the friend? What did Rebecca tell me?*

Reuben walked into the parlor and, acting as if nothing was wrong, asked, "Rebecca, who did you say this young man's friend was?"

These were the first words spoken to Rebecca since she had gone running to her room. Their first communication since the banged door. It felt good. Normal. Words spoken respectfully. It warmed the atmosphere.

"He's the man who's befriended him since his father and mother died."

"They died?"

"Didn't I tell you they died?"

"I don't know; maybe you did. All I remember is that you told me he didn't live with his parents and that you didn't know who they were. How did they die?"

"Both were killed because they were Jews. First his father, which left only his mother. Then when they fled to England, his mother was taken. Remember the Jews who died in York in the tower on Shabbat Hagadol? She was one of them."

"Where was Enoch?"

"With his friend. His friend loved his mother and was going to marry her."

"How sad. . . . The young man has had a sad life, hasn't he?"

"Yes he has, Abba, very sad."

At that moment, they heard the sound of someone ringing the bell hanging outside their door.

"Reuben, you answer the door," said Rachel.

"The door?"

"Yes, it must be the young man and his friend."

Enoch stood waiting at the door, nervous and a little disconcerted. Jared was standing quite some distance behind him at the gate. Reuben and Rachel hadn't been the only ones who were unhappy about this meeting; Jared was not pleased that the young woman had invited them to her home without first consulting with her parents. "Something like this needs to be more formal, Enoch. There needs to be a written invitation. This is Spain. These are Spanish Jews, and they have a culture just like we did in England. Things must be done with propriety."

Jared had nearly refused to come with Enoch, but at the last minute relented. They agreed that Enoch would go to the door and apologize for his unpropitious behavior. Jared would be there for support, but only Enoch would go to the door. He had to do this alone. It would be a good lesson for him.

Just as Enoch was preparing to knock a second time he noticed the bell hanging beside the door and pulled its chain. He had overlooked it when he first knocked lightly on the door. It wasn't until he rocked first on one foot and then on the other, nervously looking around, that he spotted the bell.

In just moments, all too quickly for Enoch, the door swung open.

The men stood face to face—both feeling awkward, but neither aware of the other's discomfort. Reuben began.

"Good afternoon." Just as he said it, Reuben no longer desired to do what he had planned. Not since Rebecca had told him about Enoch's sad life. *The young man probably doesn't know any better—not having a father or mother, and being from England.* Reuben then wondered where the young man's friend was. At that moment Enoch shifted his feet, and Reuben caught a glimpse of a man shadowed by the gate.

"I'm Enoch, sir."

"Yes, yes, I know. Rebecca told us you were coming. You see, uh, we . . . we don't know you . . . didn't know you were coming, and well . . . ."

"Sir, I've come to apologize. I realize now that what I encouraged Rebecca to do was improper." Enoch wanted to make sure he would get all the blame. "I mean, improper in that you were not consulted first—that there was no formal invitation."

Enoch had removed his hat when he began speaking. Now he was backing away, holding his hat in his hand, bowing, and wanting to run. "Please forgive me, sir. Perhaps another time. . . . That is, if you so desire. Good day, sir."

With that, Enoch's hat was back on his head as he hurried out the gate, his swinging cloak emphasizing his hasty exit.

Reuben, surprised, raised his hand in the air to bid Enoch farewell. "Thank you, thank you—very kind of you. . . ."

Reuben closed the door and turned to face his two women. Rachel and

Rebecca had properly kept their places in the parlor. Wishing they could have witnessed the exchange between the two men, they eagerly waited to hear what had happened.

Chapter 49

hat happened, Reuben? You look pale."
Rachel's hand was on Reuben's face. "Did he get angry? Was he unkind to you?
Did he say something to you under his breath?"

"Was he hurt, Abba?" Rebecca tugged at his arm. "Could you tell if he was
terribly offended? Do you think I will ever see . . ."

Reuben put one hand to his head and ran his fingers through his hair. "I
liked him. I liked him. I didn't want him to go. He was such a gentlemen, so
polite, so apologetic. I feel terrible. He seemed so . . . so alone."

"Where was his friend?" Rachel asked. "His friend was supposed to come
with him."

"He stayed back at the gate—"

"Was he nice?" Rachel continued her interrogation.

"I don't know. I couldn't even see the man."

"I . . . I feel bad. Very bad—like I should go and get them. They both
came all the way here just to apologize. He was so nice. He didn't even ask to
come in to see you, Rebecca. He just held his hat in his hand and apologized for
being improper."

"What could he know about being proper if he doesn't have a mother?
Reuben, go—go quickly! Get the young man. I've got the dishes out. We'll offer
him something to eat."

Rebecca looked at her mother, stunned at this turn of events. *The dishes
out? Was Imma going to have them in? It was her decision to tell them they couldn't
come in!*

"Should I?" Reuben asked. "Wouldn't it seem strange?"

"No, no. Go—"

"Go, Abba, go!" Rebecca clapped her hands. She knew Enoch had to be
dismayed; he had been so eager to come.

Rachel headed for the kitchen, calling over her shoulder, "I feel you
should go, Reuben. I don't know why, but go get them."

Rachel had listened from the door of the kitchen with a twinge of guilt
and compassion as Rebecca told her father about Enoch's sad family situation.
Now as she arranged cakes on the plates, she muttered, "Poor young man . . .
mother, father killed. Having to leave England, living with a man, not knowing
what is proper. . . ."

Rebecca rushed into the kitchen. "Imma, look at me," said Rebecca, grabbing Rachel's hand as she was reaching for the dishes. "Stop for a moment and look into my eyes. Imma, I am sorry—truly sorry. Even if you didn't want Abba to get Enoch, I would still be sorry. I was wrong. I said what I said about becoming a converso because I wanted to hurt you, to make you pay for not doing things my way, Imma. Will you forgive me?"

Rachel pulled her hand from her daughter's, taking Rebecca's face in both her hands, nodding, crying, sniffing. "I forgive you. I forgive you. It's *so* hard, Rebecca, *so* hard to be a mother. Especially when you are my last chance—my last child I have to raise. It is so unsettling. I don't want to lose you. I don't want you to make mistakes. I don't want to drive you away. But I can't just let you have your way because I am afraid I'll lose you. It's hard to raise children. Someday, the Almighty willing, you will know. Over and over I have to remind myself that I can't make you be the woman you should be. Only you, my daughter, only you can do that. I am responsible to do what I should do, but you are responsible for how you react, for what you do, and—like it or not—for what you become. . . ."

"Oh Imma, I love you!" Then Rebecca said it again, like a pronouncement of fact, "I do love you. I know I fuss with you and, as the children of Israel tested the Almighty, I test you. And it's not right. I'm sorry, Imma. I *do* love you."

They were in each other's arms, reconciled for one sweet moment, understanding each other's frustrations. It was a moment Rachel treasured even more than Rebecca, for Rebecca was not yet a mother.

As Enoch rounded the gate, Jared put his hand on his shoulder and patted him. He had heard what Enoch said to Rebecca's father and he was proud. He could feel Enoch's long frame trembling.

Jared stepped in front of Enoch, stopped him in the pathway, and held him at arm's length, facing the gate through which Enoch had so gallantly walked. Jared looked at Enoch's tear-filled eyes and then put his arms around this God-given son. He was facing the gate, his hand thumping Enoch's back as Reuben abruptly rounded the corner and found himself face to face with Jared. Reuben stopped instantly, disbelief overwhelming him. "Jared! Jared? Is that you?"

Enoch felt himself thrown aside as Jared bounded toward Reuben. Suddenly the two men were in one another's arms, pounding each other's backs with tears, shouts, and exclamations all tangled up in "Reuben" and "Jared" and "by the Almighty," "I can't believe it," "where," and "how. . . ."

"Rachel! Rachel, come here!" Reuben shouted, then turned back to Jared. "Sarah—any word about Sarah? I can't believe it's you, Jared. I just can't believe it!"

Stunned and ignored in the confusion of the moment, Enoch followed them into the house and walked over to Rebecca; both stood dumbfounded, wondering what was behind all the excitement and Rachel's happy sobs.

Afternoon turned to evening. Day turned to night. Laughter turned to tears as the three adults recounted the days of the past while Enoch sat close to Rebecca on the couch, enjoying her nearness as they listened intently to things they had never heard from their parents. As far as Enoch was concerned, Jared *was* his father.

Minutes turned to hours, and the conversation turned from the past to the present—to news Jared had not even shared with Enoch, news that had come from reliable sources even that day. News Jared was compelled to share.

"Our Catholic king and queen, Ferdinand and Isabella, signed a decree today requiring all professing Jews to leave their dominion within four months. We have four months to leave, either by land or by sea. If we don't—if we refuse to leave—we must either die or be baptized."

Enoch looked at Rebecca, searching her eyes for some sort of response. His hand groped for hers. When he found it, she squeezed his hand and smiled. Enoch knew at this moment what he felt all along: Rebecca would not convert. She couldn't. She did not really believe the Catholics' teaching, and she couldn't risk her life for something she didn't believe. Enoch sighed as the burden tumbled from his shoulders.

Jared continued. "They say we can dispose of our property if someone will buy it, and we can take anything with us except gold, silver, minted gold, and any other object of which export is prohibited."

"In other words," Reuben said, seeing the irony of the situation, "we must leave all our wealth—all that we've worked for and earned in our lifetime—to fill the coffers of the king and queen. We sell our property for nothing. And the nothing we get for it, we must leave. The buyers are advantaged to steal what they have not earned and to call it not stealing, but purchasing. No trips to the confessionals are required in this instance!"

"As I understand," Jared continued, "the king and queen used the Jews—their contributions both administratively and financially—until they could take Granada, the last Moslem stronghold on Spanish soil, and unite Spain. Now that it has been accomplished—three months ago—they are finished with us except to deprive us of all our possessions, which, to their greedy delight, will replenish their depleted money chests."

"But," Rachel interjected adamantly, "surely someone can persuade them of the foolishness of their actions. Think what we as a people have contributed and will continue to contribute to the welfare and wealth of Spain!"

Jared turned to Rachel. "Don Isaac Abrabanel, even with his standing with the king and queen and his great reputation as a financial advisor, was not able to persuade them against such an action. They say he begged the king and queen to change their minds, even offering thirty thousand gold ducats. Someone said that King Ferdinand almost wavered. Then, in a dramatic and decisive move, Torquemada threw a crucifix at the king's feet and shouted,

'Judas sold his master for thirty pieces of silver, and you want to sell him for thirty thousand pieces of gold? Take him and sell him!' The king bowed to Torquemada's intimidation. The decree for our expulsion stands; we must be gone in four months."

"Is there no other recourse, Jared?" Rebecca asked.

"Only one, Rebecca—only one. Baptism." Jared paused. "Now let me ask you a question. Would you, a young Jewish woman, do that to save what you can always lose? Or would you lose your material possessions to save what can never be taken—your faith in the Almighty and the gift of loving him above all else?"

Rachel and Reuben waited; they were stunned by Jared's boldness. Enoch was equally surprised. He had said nothing to Jared about Rebecca wanting to become a converso. But Jared had figured it out for himself. On the first night he and Enoch talked about Rebecca, Jared had deduced something was amiss when Enoch hesitated in response to Jared's question about Rebecca's Jewishness.

And now, Jared's opportunity to intervene had arrived. He knew this was the time to draw a line and help Rebecca determine on exactly which side she stood. He would not pass this opportunity by; the young woman had asked the question about any possible recourse, and Jared knew his response was reasonable and appropriate.

As Rebecca looked straight into Jared's eyes, she remembered Joshua's words to the children of Israel and how they pierced her heart as she read them in the Bible: "Choose for yourselves today whom you will serve." She also remembered reading of Elijah's confrontation with the Israelites as he challenged the prophets of Baal: "How long will you halt between two opinions? If the Lord is God, follow him."

Only Enoch was relaxed as Rebecca spoke. She chose her words carefully, determined to speak honestly. "I don't know if you knew this, but I was thinking of becoming a converso. I love Spain, and I wanted to stay here for the rest of my life, enjoying all the privileges and benefits that could be mine, and to do so without fear, by converting to the Holy Catholic Church.

"However, as I have read the Bible these past two months I have watched how the majority of the Catholics in Spain live while professing to believe in God and in their Holy Bible, which, of course, is both the Old and New Testaments."

At that moment Rebecca stopped and looked at her Abba. "Although I do not know what is written in the New Testament; out of obedience to my Abba, I have not read it. Anyway, as I was saying, I can now say with confidence that the majority of Catholics do not live in accordance with what I have observed about God. And to be honest, neither do many Jews. Therefore, in all honesty, I cannot embrace their Christian faith."

Enoch squeezed Rebecca's hand. Reuben and Rachel reached for one another as a peaceful calm released the tension in their faces. Rachel had been gritting her teeth.

Rebecca continued, "In addition, as you put it so well, Jared, I will ask, 'What will a man give in exchange for his soul?' I would not trade my soul for Spain. In fact, as a result of reading the Bible, I desire to live in Israel, not in Spain. Israel is where Messiah will come."

"And where Samuel is!" Rachel exclaimed as tears of sweet relief tumbled from her eyes.

Reuben walked across the room, bent down, took Rebecca's face in his hands, kissed her and said, "And Israel is where we will go." Then looking up at Jared, he asked, "Jared?"

Jared nodded. "That's where we'll go. Enoch?"

Enoch pressed Rebecca's hand into the couch. "Yes, that's where we will all go—to the land given to us by the Almighty as an everlasting possession!"

Rachel sat up, her voice weak as she choked through her tears, "And we'll look for Sarah. She must still be alive. She *has* to be alive!"

Jared smiled. "Sarah will live forever. . . ."

That very night they made their plans to leave Spain. Fifty thousand Jews remained and were baptized. But Rebecca was not numbered among them. Instead, she cast her lot with the almost one hundred thousand who left.

In that same year, Christopher Columbus sailed from Spain to find a new world. On all his letters he inscribed a strange cipher at the head of every page—a cipher bearing strong resemblance to the Hebrew initials used to abbreviate the phrase *in God's name*. Religious Jews prefaced their documents with those same Hebrew initials.

Chapter 50

*S*amuel leaned against the gnarled trunk of an enormous olive tree on the Mount of Olives. It was a tree whose roots were probably more than a thousand years old. From there Samuel looked across the Kidron Valley to the walls Suleiman had erected around Jerusalem. *I must admit Suleiman's walls are impressive and so is the new facing he added to the Dome of the Rock. But I don't like it. It makes the Dome look even more striking, more appealing.* The Iznik tiles, in their many shades of blue and turquoise, caught the sunlight, making the structure seem almost of another world. Looking at it depressed Samuel. *That's where I wish I were—in another world instead of in mine,* Samuel thought. He threw an olive. *People shouldn't call Suleiman magnificent. Only the Almighty is magnificent. Men always want to take his glory for themselves!*

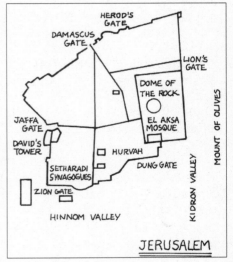

Samuel ate olives and threw the pits at a big rock. Nothing pleased him today. He felt sad, alone, angry. *Where are you, Levi? I'm tired of waiting for you.* Levi sent a message for Samuel to wait for him on the Mount of Olives. He and Eliyahu, Levi's new friend, were journeying from the school at Safed in the northern Galilee to Jerusalem.

Samuel thought meeting Levi here was pointless, but there had been no way of telling him that. So here he sat, and he was tiring of waiting.

As he waited, Samuel reviewed the course of events that had brought them to Jerusalem and the house in which they now lived. Or rather, in which *he* lived. *Levi spends more time in Safed studying that mystical Kabbalah than he does in Jerusalem. He's been gone for months!*

After the crusaders were defeated by Saladin and the Moslems once again occupied Jerusalem, the Jews were allowed to return and again take up residence in the earthly Zion. Samuel and Levi, after a big debate and a near split-up, had finally moved to the Holy City. Their David/Jonathan relationship had been on shaky ground for awhile.

The reason for their near split-up was because Levi, the incurable scholar, didn't want to leave the Galilee, where sages congregated. He was an incessant debater and found many of his own kind in the Galilee. At times it grated on Samuel. Samuel genuinely loved Levi—even as, he thought, King David must have loved Jonathan. And just as the king owed Jonathan his life, so also did Samuel feel he owed his life to Levi. However, Samuel insisted on living in Jerusalem. It was the city of David, and it was Samuel's turn to determine where they should live! Samuel stood up pacing the hillside as his mind kept turning. *What else was there to do?*

For a while they lived together in one room behind the broken semblance of Jerusalem's desecrated walls. There they found enough work on which to subsist. However, after the Mamluks came to power, Samuel and Levi found a ruined house with pillars of marble and a beautiful dome. This they converted into a synagogue, and finally Samuel was satisfied. He was building something he believed in—in his Jerusalem. It was the most ruined of all cities, yet it was a city Samuel loved almost more than life itself. As he watched Jerusalem being restored to life, Samuel could now, to some degree, appreciate Suleiman's walls.

Samuel pulled at the loaf of bread he had purchased from a street vendor. It was no longer warm but tasted good with the hunk of cheese he brought for his breakfast.

Lost in the turmoil of his thoughts, his back against the tree, Samuel was startled to hear the voice behind him. "SAMUEL! SAMUEL! THE MESSIAH'S COME!"

Samuel whipped around, dumbfounded at this announcement as Levi slid down the stony ground. He could tell from the sound of Levi's voice that Levi was convinced Messiah had come! Eliyahu followed Levi, nodding his head, beaming from ear to ear. "He has, Samuel! He has come!"

Samuel jumped to his feet. "Where? How do you know?" Samuel had longed for Messiah to come.

Levi's eyes were wide with excitement—almost hysteria. He could hardly talk. "He's here! Messiah's in Jerusalem!"

"See," Samuel said gleefully, "see, Levi, I told you! We should be in Jerusalem, not in the Galilee! Aren't you thankful you're not in Safed right now studying the Kabbalah? You'd miss the Messiah!"

Samuel threw up his arms and began to dance, motioning to the trees, "Trees, clap your hands. Mountains," he shouted, sweeping his arm to the mountains, "sing with joy, for the Redeemer has come to Zion! Zion, the city of David!"

Levi and Eliyahu threw their arms around Samuel and laughed with joy as Samuel continued his accolade of praise, "Bow, Suleiman! Bow to the One more magnificent than you! Down, you Dome of the Rock! Messiah has come to rebuild his temple!"

The trio danced in circles on the mount until they collapsed on the ground, out of breath.

"Now," Samuel said, "tell me where we find him."

Levi looked at Samuel and said, "We don't know."

"You don't know?" Samuel shouted and jumped to his feet. "Messiah is here, and you don't know where he is? Don't tell me you are playing a trick on me. I will slaughter you like a red heifer on this mount and your ashes will not be saved—nor holy!"

Eliyahu pulled on Samuel's baggy trousers. "Calm down, calm down. I promise you; I swear by the throne of the Almighty—"

Levi punched Eliyahu on the arm. "You're not supposed to do that. You shouldn't swear by the Almighty's throne."

Eliyahu jerked his shoulder away from Levi. "I was only making a point," Eliyahu's tone was solemn. "Samuel, we *are* telling you the truth. Messiah *is* here, right here in Jerusalem, even though we don't know exactly where he is."

"Nathan of Gaza, a scholar of the Kabbalah," Levi smiled, "has sent letters all over the Diaspora telling everyone that Messiah is here. Messiah is going to save the Diaspora from terrible persecutions, especially the one taking place in Poland since the death of Sigismund II."

"Wait! Wait!" Samuel waved his hands at his friends. He was alarmed, yet he hoped they would prove his anxious thoughts wrong. "Are you telling me you *think* Messiah has come because a scholar of the Kabbalah has declared him Messiah?" Samuel was very wary of the Kabbalah, although the movement had many followers, of which Levi was one.

Samuel was anything but a mystic, and Kabbalism was mysticism—taken from the Sefer ha-Zohar, *The Book of Splendor*. The *Zohar*, as it was called, was written by a Moses de Leon, a Spanish Jew. The Kabbalah center now in Safed had its start in Spain. Samuel wasn't sure where Kabbalah, "a thing received," originated. However, he knew it wasn't in line with the clear teaching of the Scriptures. The Kabbalah was at the root of the conflict between Samuel and Levi and was why Levi had stayed away so long.

Levi looked at Samuel. "Must you always be the skeptic? Can't your mind be open to new things? New interpretations?"

Samuel looked up. The air seemed chillier. Had the sun gone behind a cloud?

"What are you looking at, Samuel?" Eliyahu asked.

"Nothing. . . ." Then Samuel began thinking aloud, "When Messiah comes, aren't things supposed to be different than they are right now? Doesn't Ezekiel the prophet say something about us being gathered to Jerusalem out of the graves of other nations before Messiah can come? I don't see many Jews around here. There are more Turks here than Jews!"

Levi jumped to his feet. "That's the problem with you, Samuel. That's the problem! Everything has to be written in the Book. Written in *the* Book. Don't you know that behind those biblical words are hidden meanings? That . . . that only certain people—spiritual people or the enlightened—can receive?"

Disgust registered in Samuel's eyes as he asked, with a tinge of sarcasm in his voice, "Are you enlightened? Are you one of the *special* ones?"

"Samuel, Samuel, let's not quarrel again. I—"

Now Samuel was on his feet, facing Levi. "Levi, I am not quarreling. It's just that I happen to believe that truth is truth. The Almighty wants *all* of us to understand the Bible and know his ways. Not just a few, or an elite group! Now tell me, *who* is this Messiah?"

Eliyahu looked up and said, "Sit down, both of you. Let's talk like sensible people."

As Levi collapsed on the ground, his legs naturally folding up under him, he looked knowingly at Eliyahu as if to say, "I told you it might be this way." Then Levi turned to Samuel and said, "His name is Sabbatai Zevi."

"Where is he from?" Samuel's voice was calm. He seated himself on a rock.

"He's from Turkey—Smyrna." Eliyahu volunteered. "And Samuel, people *everywhere* are excited about him. Jews all over the world are preparing for judgment day. They are selling their possessions, converting their wealth, and buying goods and food for their journey to Jerusalem when the call comes."

"How long has he been here in Jerusalem?" Samuel inquired.

"We don't know, Samuel," Levi slurred Samuel's name, making a hissing sound. His voice was taut as he asked, "Is this an inquisition?"

Samuel responded in the demeanor of an older brother, "Not of you, my friend, but of this one who claims to be Messiah."

Levi shook his head. "How could you have been so excited in one moment and now so doubting in the next? I just don't understand you. I just don't understand—"

"Because I believed you. In your excitement, I became excited until my mind caught up with my emotions and I realized I needed to ask questions and examine the facts rather than being carried away on the wind of your excitement. It's all right, Levi. We just have to be sure this really is the Messiah and that he is in line with the prophecies—all the prophecies of Scripture—before we get others aroused and following the man. We don't want to lead them astray."

Levi was on his feet again. "Are you saying I am leading you astray?"

Samuel pulled Levi's tunic. "Sit down, Levi. Don't get upset. I know you wouldn't intentionally lead me astray." Levi sat down as Samuel continued his questioning. "What do the rabbis say about this . . . this uh . . . I cannot remember his first name. . . ."

"Well, if he is Messiah, Samuel, you better get his name straight. It is Sabbatai Zevi." Levi's tone was caustic; he was still smarting.

Samuel had hurt his friend and he was sorry, but he wasn't going to back down. This was too critical an issue. "Let me ask again: What do the rabbis say about Sabbatai Zevi?"

Eliyahu spoke up. "Some don't like him."

"They don't?" Samuel asked quizzically.

"They're jealous, Samuel," Levi responded quickly. "They're just jealous."

"Is that all?" Samuel asked. Neither answered. Finally Samuel said, "Look, let's go into Jerusalem and see if we can find him. Then we can talk to him and decide for ourselves."

"We're tired," Eliyahu said to Samuel. "We've walked all the way from Safed just to meet you here and tell you the news. If we can't find him right away tonight, can we do it tomorrow?"

"You can go rest now if you want, but I want to settle it in my mind tonight. If he's Messiah, I want to know and not waste a moment following him. But if he's not, then I have to find out or I'll never be able to sleep."

The three of them started down the slope of the mount. As they did so, Samuel asked, "How long has Sabbatai Zevi been in Jerusalem?"

"They say he's been here quite some time. He was here earlier, then left. Now he's returned."

"Well," Samuel mused, "it seems strange that, if he is the real Messiah, the whole city is not aware of it. After all, Messiah is Messiah. The prophets say when he comes everyone will know it. In fact, not until just now did I remember that Zechariah the prophet tells us his feet will stand on the Mount of Olives and split it from east to west. The same Mount of Olives we've just walked down. And as we can see that hasn't happened yet."

"Samuel," Eliyahu asked, "how do you know all these things?"

"I read the Bible. I go to our Synagogue and read the Bible."

"And?"

"What do you mean, 'and'?"

"And what other books do you read? The Talmud? The Zohar? The—"

Samuel interrupted Eliyahu, "No other books; just the Bible. It's enough for me."

Eliyahu asked, "Are you a Karaite?" Eliyahu knew the Karaites were a sect that had been around for a long time; they based their beliefs and practices wholly on the Bible.

"No, but they are smart to stay with the Scriptures."

Levi didn't say anything. He was angry at himself for not asking the questions Samuel was asking. He wished he'd been more prudent before he so rashly proclaimed Messiah was here.

When they entered the city, Samuel suggested they go immediately to the synagogue and see if anyone there could tell them how to find this supposed Messiah.

Levi saw the rabbi first and went up to him. "Rabbi ben Haim, may we ask you a question please?"

The nearly toothless rabbi smiled. He spent virtually all of his time at the synagogue now, and since the death of his wife, nothing made him happier than for someone to talk to him. His tiny room had become too lonely and quiet since his chatty little Sofia was gone. "Come, come, sit down. We are waiting for a minyan, so we can have prayer. Maybe you can stay. There'll be three of you and we'll only need seven more. Then we'll have ten—our minyan!"

"Six more, rabbi. Four plus six—that will give us our ten," Samuel smiled, hoping he hadn't offended the rabbi.

"That's right, that's right," he said with great enthusiasm. "I forgot to count me! That's good! Just six more. We won't have to wait so long. Now tell me, what do you wish to ask?"

Samuel looked at Levi. "Levi?"

Levi, still downcast, motioned with his hand for Samuel to speak.

"Rabbi ben Haim, we hear there is a man whom some believe to be Messiah."

"Ah, yes, yes." The rabbi's hand moved animatedly through the air with the proclamation of each yes. Then with one final thrust of his hand, he said, "I know who you are talking about, but he isn't Messiah," and with a sense of finality he pounded his knee with his hand.

"How do you know?" Eliyahu leaned forward as if to receive a secret. Levi lowered his eyes to the ground and watched his feet as he nervously moved them back and forth.

"He left! Didn't you hear? When the rabbis in Jerusalem threatened to excommunicate him, he left. Hmmm," the rabbi sat shaking his head, "some weeks ago, I believe. . . ."

Levi looked up at the rabbi. "Weeks ago? Before we even left Safed to come here?" Levi felt deceived. Deceived and foolish.

"Oh yes! Yes! It was a scholar of the Kabbalah who wrote letters saying Messiah had come. Sad, isn't it?" The rabbi rubbed his fingers on his lip. "Sad. So many were hopeful, but what has happened is even worse."

"What happened?" Samuel and Eliyahu asked, almost in unison.

"Oh, they had hardly been on the sea—or maybe they had landed, I'm not exactly sure. Anyway, the Turkish authorities intercepted the ship, or met his ship, and put him in chains to take him to Adrianople. Sabbatai Zevi was given the choice of converting to Islam or being put to death. He converted to Islam. Yes . . . yes . . . quite sad. So many have been deceived. Some people even sold their possessions in preparation to come to Jerusalem and be with Messiah! Sad," the rabbi was rubbing his lip again, "sad. . . ."

"Rabbi," Samuel said, "my friends have walked all the way from Safed and they are very tired. Would you mind if we didn't stay for prayers? If we see any other men on our way home, we'll tell them you need a minyan so you can pray."

"Go—go—" the rabbi stood to his feet and smiled. "I understand. I remember when I was young and got so tired. Go get some rest!"

As they walked out, Levi put his hand on Samuel's shoulder. "I'm sorry, Samuel. I am truly sorry. I'll learn. I need to get back into the Bible and see again what it says without reading things into it. Maybe that will keep me from being deceived. I don't want to be deceived, Samuel . . . especially about Messiah!"

Chapter 51

$\mathcal{S}$arah's heart was heavy as she listened to the Baal T'fila, the leader in prayer. She was thankful he didn't lead their weekly Shabbat services. He had come from the Jewish community in Kiev just for the feast. Although the chanting voice befitted their annual Yom Kippur service, Sarah would have dreaded hearing him week in and week out. When he spoke, it was always in a monotone.

How different this is, celebrating our day of atonement in this humble little home rather than in our temple in Jerusalem, Sarah thought, surveying the surroundings.

Through the opening from the kitchen to the large room which today served as the village synagogue, Sarah could catch just a glimpse of Aaron and Gershom, their heads covered with their talliot—matching prayer shawls with bands of blue.

The bands of blue on a tallit served as a reminder that they belonged to the Almighty and were to live accordingly as a separate people. *Separate we are,* thought Sarah, *and it is our holy feast days, such as this and our Shabbat, which hold us together. They keep us a distinctive people on the face of the earth—distinctive though scattered to the four winds.*

A slight smile crossed her lips on this somber holy day as she looked at Aaron. Just weeks ago, Aaron made his Bar Mitzvah. Now he had his own tefillin bound around his arm and head, just as Gershom and the other men in the large room had their phylacteries bound around their arms and heads. Aaron sat tall and straight, listening soberly to the service. This was his first Yom Kippur since entering into manhood. It was obvious from the look on his face he was taking it most seriously.

Sarah looked at the tzitzit on Aaron's woolen tallit. The fringes lovingly knotted by Gershom were now somewhat grayed with age. The tallit Aaron wore was the same one Gershom wrapped Aaron in when he was three and took him to the cheder the first time—the Hebrew school in the Rhineland.

The night the family fled the Rhineland, the Christian Gentile who rescued Sarah and Aaron told Gershom and Dusia to take only the barest essentials with them, for they had little time to meet Sarah and Aaron in the woods. Considering Aaron's tallit a bare essential, Dusia wrapped it with Gershom's, praying her son would live to wear it for his Bar Mitzvah. Little did Dusia—or any of them—realize then that they would be celebrating Aaron's coming to manhood in a little village just outside Kiev!

How different were their lives in this little shtetl—a town so small that Gershom and Dusia's home was all the Jewish community had for a synagogue. A home that the couple now lovingly shared with Sarah, grateful that she once again had been instrumental in saving their lives. Word had come to them after their flight from Rhineland that all the Jews in Cologne who refused baptism were put to death.

As the Baal T'fila turned to face east towards Jerusalem, Sarah could see the ark. Behind the ark's blue curtain, embroidered in loving handiwork with the Star of David, were the sacred scrolls—another treasure they had carried with them all the way from Cologne. The man who rescued Sarah and Aaron had run into the synagogue as the people were fleeing and boldly took the scrolls from their resting place in the ark. Gershom was shocked at the brazenness of this Gentile friend; however, now he saw the hand of the Almighty in his friend's act. Had the scrolls stayed in the synagogue, they would have gone up in flames. These were the only scrolls in the whole shtetl. That was why Gershom's home became the synagogue. That, and the fact that it had one of the largest rooms among the few Jewish homes in the little town.

The ark sat upon a table made just for this purpose by a carpenter in the village. The table was his contribution, a gift for the Almighty. It was intricately carved with a vine bearing grapes twining about its front legs and along its apron to the middle of the table, where the ends of the vine joined with a Davidic star. The vine, he said, was to remind them of Isaiah the prophet's words that Israel was a special planting of the Almighty.

The women sat in the kitchen on benches at a long narrow table—separate from the men. Sarah was thankful for the straw spread over the cold earthen floors. On Yom Kippur no one was allowed to wear leather shoes. The straw kept the cold from penetrating her heavy woolen stockings, as did the coal-burning stove in the corner of the kitchen.

As Sarah's eyes surveyed the straw she saw drops of blood from the kapore, the sacrificial fowls brought by the women to Gershom and Dusia's farm for the slaughter. Again a smile crept across her face. Sarah could still see Miriam's wide-eyed fascination as her mother swung a live chicken over their heads while they said their prayer of repentance. The chicken served as a substitute for the scapegoat.

Throwing all her weight into the ceremony, Dusia had nearly frightened the chicken to death! Just the force of the chicken being swung by Dusia caused the bird to shed some of its feathers out of sheer panic. As with the ritual on Yom Kippur when the temple was still standing, the scapegoat was released into the wilderness, while the kapore, the other goat, was sacrificed for the sins of the people. This chicken didn't know it was the scapegoat and not the kapore!

Looking at this little band of Jews worshiping, Sarah recounted again their various stories—many relived by the women as they sat with Dusia and Sarah at their kitchen table plucking geese and duck feathers during the winter evenings. The feathers became feather beds and pillows, the birds' tails became pastry brushes, their wings became feather dusters, and the stories? Well, they became their history books. The history of the wandering Jew, as the Gentiles derogatorily called them. A term derived from a legend conceived in a twisted, prejudiced mind. The legend stated that a Jew who had laughed at Jesus on the cross was condemned to wander the earth forever. This legend was passed along and with time there developed many different versions of it.

One of the women at the table, Malka, had fled from what was now being called Germany. She had gone to Poland. Then came the first persecution of the Jews in Poland. A rabbi in Posen and thirteen elders were charged with the theft and desecration of church property. They were tortured, then burned alive. This had terrified Malka and her family. But it was the anti-Jewish riots in Cracow that caused Malka and Manasseh to leave Poland and flee to the village near Kiev. What they didn't know was that anti-Jewish violence had already spread its reign of terror even in Kiev.

Another couple, Hendrich and Pola, wrapped their son in a blanket and fled Austria just before the Jews were expelled and their property confiscated. After Duke Albrecht of Austria accused the Jews of supporting the Protestant reformer Jon Huss, Jewish children were stolen from their parents and baptized, while adults were burned at the stake. Sarah remembered Hendrich telling his and Pola's story as they all sat at the kitchen table one cold evening eating Dusia's potato latkes.

That was the time Dusia stood at the stove the entire evening frying the potato pancakes on the huge iron sheet on top of the stove. Because she fried them in oil that night—which was very scarce—and added just the right amount of crushed garlic, the pancakes were devoured almost the moment she proudly set them on the table. In their little Jewish community, there was none who could equal Dusia when it came to cooking! No one could rival Dusia's latkes, no matter how hard the women tried. Eventually they gave up. Dusia was crowned the latke queen.

While everyone was devouring their latkes, Hendrich shared his concerns. "At first we thought Luther, the German reformer, would become our ally, for he spoke favorably of us as God's chosen people. Some said he thought that once he'd exposed the corruption in the Catholic church we would all convert to Christianity and come flocking to their baptismal fonts. However, when the Jews didn't respond as he expected, he turned on us. He—"

"Excuse me," Gershom interrupted, "but wasn't Luther the one who wrote the pamphlet against . . . ah . . . what did he call us?"

Without thinking, Pola answered, "Sabbathists." Then she blushed. It was the men who were to carry the conversation. In fact, it was a rare and unusual treat for the women to be included on an occasion like this. Usually the women talked with women and men with men. Even at their weddings, the men danced with men and women with women. Such a rare treat like this must have been because of Dusia's potato latkes!

Hendrich resumed talking. "It was called 'The Letter Against the Sabbathists.' But what was far more damaging was the one which followed, which he called 'The Jews and Their Lies.'"

Dusia turned from the stove and, taking her eyes off her cooking for a moment, asked, "Lies? What lies?" With all her hard work at the stove, Dusia felt she had earned the right to be a part of the conversation.

Hendrich took another quick bite of hot latke. Tossing it around in his mouth until he could get a gulp of their homemade beer, he muttered, "The same lies of which they have accused us down through the ages—blood libel, ritual murders, poisoning of wells, desecration of the host. . . ."

Sarah entered the conversation, indignant. "How can people like that ever expect us to accept their religion? Who wants to associate with people who are not only prejudiced in their thinking but totally unloving to their enemies? People who steal children and force them to be baptized? Who torture and burn their parents? If this is what *their* Christ tells them to do, I have no desire to be associated with him in any way."

Pola looked at Hendrich. "Tell them about Italy."

"What about Italy?" Dusia shouted from the stove.

"Well, Pola and I were going to go to Italy. We thought we might be safe there. Why we thought that—"

"*You* thought it, Hendrich," the words flew out of Pola's mouth again before she could catch herself.

Hendrich frowned and continued, "The pope put out some kind of order ..."

Gershom helped him. "A bull."

"Yes, that's it! A bull," Hendrich smiled. "Thanks, Gershom."

Pola thought to herself, *It is a man's world, this Jewish society of ours!*

Hendrich moved on, "In this bull, he directed that ghettos be built throughout Catholic Europe—especially in the German-speaking cities. But also in Italy. At first they weren't referred to as *ghettos*. Rather we were just to be penned up in specific areas in the cities. The first place this happened was in a gun factory called La Gheta in Venice. Some people believe that's where the term *ghetto* originated. Others say it came from the word *borghetto*, which in Italian means little town or suburb. Anyway, when Pola and I heard that the ghettos in Italy were surrounded by walls with only one gate that was kept locked from dusk to dawn, we decided we'd better go to Poland or Russia."

Hendrich stood up, looked at Dusia, and patted his stomach. "I probably would be slimmer had we gone to Italy, but then I would have missed your latkes and wouldn't have really lived! You have retained your crown! You are still the potato latke queen!"

Sarah watched Dusia's fat little body bustle with pride. It pleased Sarah to hear Dusia complimented, for her friend had labored hard all evening.

Having lost herself in the recollection of the stories of the people gathered for the Yom Kippur service, Sarah had not paid attention to the rest of the service. Now she was abruptly brought back to the present as the women rose almost of one accord from the table. They had fasted since sundown the night before; it was time to go home and feed their families.

That night the large room resumed its role as Sarah's bedroom. As she pulled the covers over her shoulders and turned her eyes to the ark, she thought of the words from the book of Psalms—words written on the scrolls tucked away behind the curtain. "O God, thou has cast us off, thou has scattered us, thou hast been displeased; O turn thyself to us again."

Sarah closed her eyes, and whispered softly, "I miss you, my husband. . . ."

Chapter 52

*G*ershom sent Miriam and Aaron to the barn to thresh the wheat. It was a task the children disliked and did not want to do. However, since they had been forced into farming by their circumstances, the whole family, including Sarah, did many chores they did not like to do just to keep body and soul together. Yet farming did have its benefits. Dusia always had food of some sort to place on their table, though many times the food was potatoes, in one form or another. And they always managed to fill the stomachs of those who periodically fell upon hard times. Dusia took great comfort in that.

Theirs was a rather poor Jewish community. Fortunately, everyone contributed what they could, so they all survived. Many of the women assisted their husbands through creative hundling—trading what could be traded, hopefully for money. And if money was not available, they bartered their work. That was the reason Dusia refused to sit at the table doing nothing while she listened to Gershom, even though Gershom was urging her to rest.

"I have to make my challot. The women are waiting for their challot! What are they going to do if they don't have this bread for Shabbat? Do you think they are going to welcome in the Sabbath Queen with ordinary bread! Talk, Gershom. Talk. I'm listening."

Dusia fussed as Gershom pleaded with her to sit down. She was irritated; he didn't seem to understand that she labored in order to provide the necessities of life that the farm could not produce—such as well-sewn clothes. While Dusia excelled in the kitchen, sewing was too quiet and physically confining a discipline for her. She had to be able to move, to hustle, to bustle.

The tension of the moment was evident as she braided the sweet dough. The braid was too tight. Pulling it apart, she started again, hoping she hadn't ruined this loaf by handling the dough too much. She had a reputation to maintain!

"Dusia, I just want to make sure the children don't come in unexpectedly and hear what I am saying," explained Gershom, his patience a little strained because Dusia kept working while he talked. *The woman can't sit still!*

"Sarah, watch for the children for me," said Dusia. "And shell the peas while you sit there." Dusia motioned with her hand. "Sit on the other side of the table so you can see the door or your neck will be stiff from turning around all the time."

Sarah smiled as she moved to the other side of the table. Those who sat in this kitchen came under Dusia's command. Even Gershom knew the kitchen was Dusia's domain. The woman frustrated him, but he loved her. Getting ready for Shabbat always created a tension—a tension that didn't fly out the window until the Shabbat candles were lit. There was no rest until Dusia dropped proudly at her table arrayed in the best of her shabby clothes, her veil covering her head as she waited to receive Gershom's blessing. Not only was the food the best for Shabbat, but so also was Dusia. She was bathed and perfumed, ready for *their* night. The Talmud commanded husbands to love their wives on Shabbat, and she was still eager to see Gershom fulfill this heavenly command.

Right now, however, Dusia was so upset with Gershom's pressuring her to sit down and with the possibility of a ruined challah that she wondered if she really wanted Gershom to touch her—Shabbat or not!

Sarah broke the tension. "Gershom, are you worried about the children because you don't want them to hear you talk about the Cossacks?" Gershom looked at Sarah, surprised. "How did you know?"

"Cossacks? The Cossacks are in Poland, not Kiev!" Dusia retorted without looking up as she carefully braided another loaf of bread.

Gershom could read the concern on Sarah's face as she responded to his question. "Malka was telling me what Manasseh has heard . . . something about the Tsar and the Ukrainian Bohdan Chmielnicki?"

"That's right," Gershom responded, looking over his shoulder at the door. "Alexei Mikhailovich is not happy being merely the Tsar of Russia; he plans to seize Poland. Apparently he thinks aligning himself with Chmielnicki and his Cossack band of murderers is the way to accomplish this.

"Chmielnicki has a grudge against the Polish-Catholic estate owners because they ruthlessly exploited the orthodox peasants. But instead of going after the estate owners, Chmielnicki spared their lives as well as the orthodox priests and went after the Jews. The Tatars from the Crimea and the Russians living in Poland joined the Cossacks and went through Volhynia and Podolia slaughtering any Jew who refused to convert to Christianity. That is, if they even made the effort to find out whether our people were willing to convert. It seems the Cossacks just wanted to massacre them. It is said their brutality is incomprehensible. They have killed more than one hundred thousand Jews!"

Dusia stopped braiding her bread. Her hands began trembling. In her mind she could see her Abba lying against the wall, his neck broken, his eyes darkened—paralyzed in death. Dusia put both her hands on the bread board and leaned on them hard.

Gershom noticed Dusia's reaction and was immediately at her side, holding her with both of his hands on her waist. He was afraid Dusia would faint. Gently he put his arm on her shoulder, turned her around, and led her to the table. "We'll help you with your bread. It will be ready for Shabbat. But for now, please sit with us and rest yourself." As he set Dusia delicately on the bench, he leaned down and kissed her cheek.

Gershom's unexpected tenderness touched his wife. As weak as she was, she decided she was glad after all that this was her night. Then and there, Dusia determined she would never miss a Shabbat. *Who knows how many of them we will have together.*

Sarah looked away, granting them a moment of privacy. The very sight of them brought pain to Sarah's heart. Her husband was not here to comfort her or kiss her on the cheek. Sarah looked out at the sunshine. She could see the tall stalks of oats waving gaily in the gentle wind, showing off their golden heads as they danced in the ripening warmth of the sun. The bright green grass bordering the edge of the field along the road heightened the yellow coloring of the oats. Soon it would be time for harvest. Harvesting was hard work. But it was also rewarding when the sun shone brightly as it did today. *How is the world so beautiful when man is so ugly and cruel?* Sarah wondered. *One hundred thousand Jews! And all dead simply because they were Jews!* The thought staggered her mind.

Gershom spoke, "We must make plans to leave."

Sarah turned from the window and looked at Gershom. "Gershom, did you notice the oats?" Then Gershom's words suddenly registered in her mind. "Excuse me, what did you say?" She couldn't believe what she had heard.

"I said we must make plans to leave here. I fear for our lives."

Dusia looked at her husband, her voice trembling as she asked him, "Do you really think the Cossacks would come to a shtetl as insignificant as ours?" Her mind raced back again to the night they fled Cologne—to the panic she had thought would rupture her heart if she didn't quiet it. Then she remembered how all her best efforts could not make her heart beat slower. . . .

Sarah looked at Gershom. "To where will we run? If what Manasseh heard was accurate, then the Cossacks are coming this way even now. How can we possibly outrun their horses?"

Chapter 53

That night, Gershom called the men of their Jewish community to a meeting in their home. Dusia stationed herself in the kitchen preparing something for them to eat. Crisis or not, she would live up to her reputation. Miriam and Aaron were sent to Pola's. The excuse Dusia gave them was that Pola needed them to help care for her little one so she could finish some sewing. Miriam was thrilled, but not Aaron. He knew his father wanted him out of the house. He was upset. After all, he had already had his Bar Mitzvah! Now that he was a man, shouldn't he be allowed to meet with the men? Aaron sensed something was wrong from the way his father and mother were behaving. Both seemed nervous, unsettled. Although he tried to pry infor-

mation out of Aunt Sarah, his efforts were futile. Aaron kicked the dirt as he walked to Pola's. *I'll be the only man left in Pola's house. It just isn't right!*

Sarah was given the task of opening the door for the men. Upon entering the house they congregated in the far corner of the large room, joining in the talking and gesturing typical of their group.

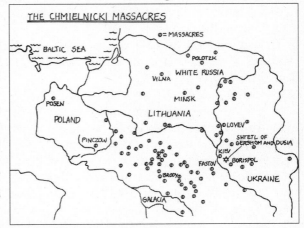

Only tonight there was more animation and excitement than usual, with Gershom in the middle. Each man was dressed in his *kapote*, a long black coat tied with a string at the waist. Each also had on his *shtreimel*, a black hat distinctive to their Jewish community with its wide brim covered with mink tails. The shtreimels were trimmed in rather skimpy wild mink tails, except for Hendrich's. His was trimmed in tails from specially raised minks. No part of the black brim on Hendrich's hat could be seen because the mink was so luxurious. The men's ambition was to someday afford a hat like Hendrich's. All except Gershom, who didn't care. The hat was not important to him. Tonight Gershom was hatless except for his yarmulke.

Sarah stepped into the kitchen to help Dusia, who was working as quietly as possible so she could overhear what the men were discussing. It was hard, though, to understand what was being said. Sometimes two or three of the men talked at the same time. Their voices, fluctuating from loud and passionate to very low, hushed tones, sounded more like murmuring than conversation.

Finally, when the food was ready, Sarah and Dusia sat down with a cup of barley tea and waited to be summoned.

"It's the children, Sarah, that I'm so concerned about." Dusia was wringing the towel she had absentmindedly carried to the table with her.

Sarah reached over and patted Dusia's nervous hands. "I know, I know."

"It isn't like my children haven't been through this before. For a long time after Abba's death they suffered with nightmares. What will *this* do to them?"

"Maybe, Dusia, the men will—"

"Dusia! Dusia!" Gershom shouted from the large room.

Dusia sprang up from the bench and hurried to the door. She could easily have shouted back her response but she wanted to see what they were doing. "Yes, Gershom?"

Gershom looked at her and smiled. She was relieved. She could tell by her husband's expression the men had a plan that pleased him. "Have you something for the men to eat, wife?"

Dusia thought, *What a question! Have I, Dusia, something for the men to eat? Why does he think the men are so willing to come to a meeting on the night before Shabbat!*

"It's nothing much, really, but it's ready. . . ."

Gershom knew that wasn't true. So did the others as they gathered eagerly around the kitchen table. Dusia had made *kreplach*—delicious cheese-filled dumplings. Although these were a treat she usually saved for the holidays, Dusia had decided tonight they needed something special. Who knew what the future held? Who knew when and where they would again eat kreplach?

The men were delighted; Gershom was proud. He slipped from the table, patted Dusia on the back, whispered something in her ear, and sat down again. *Who knows how long we will have together like this,* Gershom thought. Gershom's and Dusia's thoughts were the same, but they never shared them. These kinds of thoughts a person was to carry alone . . . or so they believed.

As Dusia and Sarah served the men, they were told the plan.

Gershom spoke first. "I am convinced the Almighty has given us this plan. If we ran from the Cossacks, to where would we run? And how could we outdistance their horses? To hide is better than to run."

"But," Manasseh interjected, "it's only better, I believe, because of the way we are hiding. I'm sure hiding in attics wouldn't be safe, but to dig holes in the ground and then cover ourselves with dirt and straw—that to me seems the safest. It is a splendid idea, Gershom, a splendid idea."

Gershom nodded. He was not finished. He was concerned that they choose the right place to bury themselves. "You must make sure not to bury yourselves where a horse can step on you! That is critical. Choose your places carefully, for if one person is discovered, then they will look for others. A parent should be close to the younger children. However, if you have a very young child—like you, Moshe—then you should put the child in the hole with you and be ready to cover his mouth if necessary. Just tell the children that if they will be very quiet, then they will have to do it this one time only. The Cossacks massacre and then they move on, sweeping rapidly from one town to another. They don't return. And as we agreed, we will take turns watching for their approach from the attics in Moshe and Manasseh's houses. Their windows face the road coming into and going away from our shtetl. We all must practice and practice. Everyone in your family must practice running and hiding in their hole—covering themselves with dirt, straw, or whatever so as not to panic when they get in the hole for a real emergency."

Sarah spoke up as she filled the men's plates with more kreplach. "Excuse me, but have you thought of the houses? They—"

Hendrich interrupted. "We haven't talked about the houses, except that some of us could dig our holes in our houses. Is that what you mean?"

"No," Sarah answered, "what I mean is that if none of us are here, then it has to look like we have run away, or they will start to search for us."

One of the men banged the table with his fist. "Sarah is right! It can't look like we're still here! Our houses must look emptied. We must hide our things. But where will—"

Dusia retorted immediately, "In our attics. We must store things in our attics and live with but the barest of necessities in our houses. We'd never have enough time to get our belongings into our attics and our families into our graves once we knew the Cossacks were coming."

The men listened respectfully.

Hendrich turned to Sarah. "Sarah, can you gather the women early in the morning and explain what they must do?"

Dusia, feeling slighted, turned toward her samovar and busied herself with making tea. She hated the tears that came unwelcome to her eyes. *I must be tired...or tense,* she thought.

Although Sarah never looked Dusia's way, she knew Dusia would be hurt. Her response was immediate: "I would be glad to help Dusia do whatever she wants me to do. Her idea is a wonderful one."

Dusia stood staring at the samovar, gazing at it while she regained her composure. The samovar was her pride and joy. She had done a lot of hundling to save enough money to buy it. Although Dusia wanted Gershom to have a shtreimel with the finest of mink tails, she had rationalized that this samovar was needed more because they hosted so many visitors. A samovar was essential for making great quantities of hot drinks. She smiled as she looked at the tall brass pot with its skillfully curved and graceful handles on each side, its shiny spigot in front, and the top crowned with a little holder made especially with a container for the tea. She had spent a little extra money to get one that was hand-painted in enamel with bright and colorful flowers. It was so pretty that it looked as though it belonged in the home of a wealthy Russian. Dusia quickly touched its side to make sure enough hot coals were in the center compartment to keep the water in the belly of the samovar nice and hot.

"Thank you, Sarah," Dusia turned from the samovar. "Now, would any of you like more tea?"

For twelve days they took turns keeping watch, first praying that Bohdan Chmielnicki and his cruel Cossacks would not come until their graves were dug. They decided to call them graves, for it would be a resurrection unto life if these holes protected them from the Cossacks. Then, once the graves were dug, they prayed that the Cossacks would miraculously bypass their shtetl. Yet they practiced and practiced—the lookout running to the first house, and then one from that house running to the next, and so on. They would run to their graves and remain there until Gershom, Hendrich, or one of the men had inspected them, making sure their covering was adequate. The men had another reason for these practice sessions, which they didn't mention to the women or children. They wanted everyone to get used to lying in their graves for longer and longer periods of time.

Then it happened. The day arrived. The door burst open. Moshe's oldest son, Asa, stood before them, his eyes wide with fear, not speaking a word. Aaron looked at him. "Cossacks?" Asa nodded and ran out the door, never saying a word. Aaron shouted, "Cossacks! Cossacks! Miriam, the Cossacks! Run and tell Abba; he's in the field. I'll run to Zevi's house and be right back."

As Miriam flew into the kitchen, Sarah, who had heard the announcement, said, "Miriam, you go with Imma. I'll run and get your Abba."

Miriam hung her head. "But I want to get Abba. . . ."

Sarah's voice was stern as she reached for Miriam's chin, turning it upward until she was looking her straight in the eyes. "Miriam, you must do what I say. If you obey, you could save our lives. Dusia—"

Dusia was coming out of her room with the talliot. She wanted them with her in her grave.

Sarah ran out the door as fast as she could. Gershom had promised to stay close to the house. "Gershom! Gershom! It's time—they're coming!"

Gershom dropped his scythe, acknowledged that he understood, and ran for the barn. That's where their graves were dug. As he ran he prayed the Cossacks wouldn't set fire to the barn—a possibility he hadn't considered until two days ago. Gershom was told Chmielnicki's wrath knew no restraints and his cruelty no limits. This thought perturbed him, but it was too late now to change his plans.

Aaron was back. The women were already in their graves. Remaining silent as they had agreed, they simply began covering their bodies with the pile of dirt next to them. Dirt that had been in and out of that grave over and over again, day in and day out. Aaron threw straw on Aunt Sarah while Gershom covered Dusia and Miriam, who had insisted on sharing a grave. Then Aaron stood to his full height and looked at his Abba. "Abba, please, please let me cover you. I'm a man, Abba. Let me. I love you. I love you . . . please."

Gershom was unprepared for this sudden outburst from his son. He'd never heard Aaron express such passion, such love before. His eyes flooded with tears as he stood for a moment gazing into the eyes of his firstborn.

"You are a man, my son! A man I am very proud of. Bury me, son. But you be the first to be resurrected!"

When Aaron finished covering Gershom, he dropped into his own grave and began to move the dirt over his legs and trunk as he had done several times a day for the past ten or eleven days. How many times he had done this he couldn't remember right now. As Aaron covered himself, carefully piling the straw around his nose so that he could breath, he could feel the ground trembling. At first he wondered if his trembling body was shaking the ground. But, as he grew quiet, he realized that it was the Cossack horses that were shaking the earth as they galloped ever closer. Aaron commanded his body to lie still, but every now and then, as if to defy him, it trembled in disobedience.

Like a thunderous wave crashing over the earth, the Cossacks arrived. Some of them rode right into the barn, and the ground rumbled even more. Aaron prayed Miriam would not become frightened and start to cry. He had talked to his sister over and over, every night, rehearsing with her how crucial it was that she not cry, move, or utter a sound, no matter how frightened she became. He stressed the danger she could bring to them all—to herself, Imma, Abba, Aunt Sarah, and finally him, her brother. Challenging her imaginative spirit, Aaron told his sister she could be a heroine and someday be able to tell all her friends the story of how she and the Almighty saved the lives of their family.

"Jews!" Some man screamed. "Jews! You better come out of this barn—out of your hiding places—or we'll burn you alive."

Gershom's stomach churned within him. Why hadn't he thought that they would burn the barn? It was only logical! All he could think was that the barn seemed the best place to hide his family. *Should I get up? Should I tell the family to come out of their graves?* It had been his implicit instruction that he was the only one who could tell them when they were to come out of their graves, and no matter what happened, they were not to move without his orders. *Elohim, Elohim, what do I do?*

Just then the sound of more horses coming into the barn rumbled through the ground. Someone was shouting orders, then one voice rose above the others, "What did you find, Bohdan? Every house we entered looked deserted. Nothing even worth taking."

Aaron opened his right eye and peeked through the tiny window of straw he had made so he could see what was happening. A horse stood to the right of his grave. The rider was fat and somewhat short, and his eyes appeared dark and cruel. His long straight nose came to an abrupt stop at the tip of a black mustache curving over the corners of his mouth and hanging just below his jawline. A funny-looking hat rested on his head, covering it almost like hair. The hat was trimmed in fur, and at its very center just above his thin eyebrows, two tall feathers rose straight up out of the fur. In one hand he carried what looked like an iron mace. It was long and decorated with what appeared to be a molded brass design. It was topped by a large, round ball that had little metal spikes protruding from its whole circumference. Aaron wondered if it was used to crush the skulls of men. The rider kept a tight rein on his horse, who pranced the ground, causing Aaron's head to ache. The man appeared to be surveying the area carefully as if he was looking for something.

Then Aaron saw a flash of fire. Was it a torch?

"Bohdan," Aaron thought it was the same voice that had spoken just a moment ago, "what did you find?"

Suddenly Aaron's thoughts connected. He realized the identity of the fat man on the horse. "Chmielnicki!" Aaron said before he could stop himself.

"Nothing," Chmielnicki yelled back at the same time Aaron uttered his name. "Not a thing. Not a living soul! I knew we should have gone straight to Kiev." The voice was angry. "They must have heard we were coming and run for their lives!"

The men, in mockery, mimicked what their intended victims might have said. "The Cossacks! The Cossacks are coming!" Then another shouted crudely, "Hide your circumcised boys! Run, you old men and women! Flee, you men who have become boys, and lay down, you maidens! The Cossacks are here!" The men broke into scornful laughter.

The noise crescendoed to deafening levels as all the Cossacks took up the shout, "The Cossacks are coming! The Cossacks are coming!" The rafters trembled as did the Jewish bodies secreted in the graves.

Aaron saw Chmielnicki flip his horse's reins as he bellowed above his rowdy men, "Let's run the Jews down! Run them into the bowels of hell!" Chmielnicki then charged from the barn. Again the men took up the shout, "The Cossacks are coming! The Cossacks are coming!" leaving the taunt to echo in the hearts of all those listening beneath them, shielded only by dirt, straw, and divine providence.

In the distance they could hear one man shout, "I forgot to burn the barn!"

Another man laughingly shouted back, "Then burn the field—it's closer!"

Gershom closed his eyes. His body became like Dusia's pudding. For a few moments he lay pondering the great persecution that would precede Messiah's coming. Then he began to quietly recite the words of Maimonides, words written in their prayer book. "I believe with complete faith in the coming of Messiah, and even though he may delay, nevertheless I anticipate every day that he will come."

Gershom repeated the words over and over, his voice growing increasingly louder. Then two more voices joined with his. "I believe with complete faith that there will be a resuscitation of the dead whenever the wish emanates from the Creator. Blessed is his name and exalted is his mention."

Sarah lay motionless, listening. Tears coursed down the sides of her face as she joined in with the others. "Forever and for all eternity. For your salvation I do long, Hashem. I do long, Hashem, for your salvation. Hashem, for your salvation I do long."

Aaron rose first from his grave, just as his father had said he could. Then he went to his father and uncovered him. Throwing himself into Gershom's arms, he sobbed. Together they wept, and again repeated, "I believe with complete faith in the coming of Messiah, and even though he may delay, nevertheless I anticipate every day that he will come."

Chapter 54

"Sit down, Hendrich; please sit down. I'll have Aaron fetch Gershom. Aaron, get your Abba." Dusia dismissed Aaron with a wave of her hand and turned back to Hendrich, motioning him to a chair in the large room. "It's late. Gershom needs to stop working anyway. That man! How hard he works!"

Dusia, too, had been working hard. So hard she didn't even feel like making a cup of tea for Hendrich, so she kept him out of the kitchen. Dusia figured he would stay only a few minutes anyway. She had labored in the kitchen all day making special cakes for some Gentile women in the shtetl next to theirs. She wanted to buy Gershom a new shtreimel with beautiful mink tails.

"So you have been in Kiev?"

"Yes, I just returned. Stopped in to tell Pola I was home, then came right over here," Hendrich said.

"Your news isn't good news, is it, Hendrich?"

Hendrich studied his neighbor's plump little face. Dusia looked like she loved cooking. She also looked like she sampled everything several times before it was served. He was glad Pola preferred sewing to cooking!

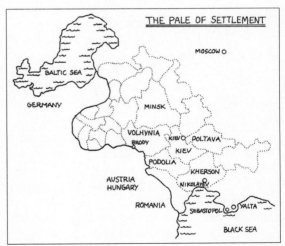

Hendrich paused a moment. He didn't want to answer Dusia's question, but he knew he could do nothing else.

"No, Dusia, the news is not good. I was hoping to wait until—"

"Shalom, Hendrich, shalom!" Gershom had rushed in from the field. Hendrich had promised to come over as soon as he got home from Kiev. Recently a man had passed through their shtetl bearing disconcerting news, and Hendrich would either confirm or disprove what the man had told them based on what information he received during his trip to Kiev.

Aaron was right behind his Abba. The young man was growing all at once, seemingly right before their eyes. He would be a tall one.

"What did you hear, Hendrich?" Gershom asking before he even sat down. Aaron remained standing.

Hendrich glanced quickly at Aaron and asked, "You want me to tell you now?"

Gershom motioned for Aaron to sit down. "It's all right, Hendrich. My son is a man now. He needs to know what is happening. I want him to learn to make wise decisions. Excuse me, Hendrich," Gershom turned to Dusia. "Dusia, please call Sarah. She stopped to pick some flowers; I want her to hear this also. Gershom called to Dusia as she left through the kitchen. And where is Miriam?"

Dusia shouted over her shoulder, "Miriam's helping over at Pola's. Sarah!"

"I'm right here, Dusia," Sarah said as she entered, causing Dusia to jump. "Look at the bouquet I picked for us! Aren't the flowers beautiful this spring?"

"Gershom is talking with Hendrich and he wants us to join them. Hendrich has come back from Kiev. His news isn't good," Dusia said as she put Sarah's bouquet in a large red enameled pitcher.

"What is the news?" Sarah asked.

"Dusia! Sarah!" Gershom called to the women, pleading. "Please come. Hendrich can't be kept waiting."

"Coming, Gershom, coming," Dusia answered. Then she said to Sarah, "I don't know the news yet; I just know it isn't good."

Sarah sighed heavily. *What will we hear next? Can't it ever be good news?*

As the women sat down, Aaron smiled. *Women were so different from men. Would a man be picking a bouquet and putting it in a vase at a time like this?* he thought to himself.

Gershom leaned forward in his chair, his hands clasped together in front of him as he rested his arms on his legs. "Now, what did you hear in Kiev? Are there really pogroms going on?" Aaron too leaned forward, eager to hear, happy to be included. Ever since their "resurrection day," a new love and greater appreciation had emerged between father and son. From that day forward Gershom treated Aaron like a grown man—an equal. And Aaron never took advantage of that. He received the honor with humility of heart. He truly loved his Abba.

Hendrich's countenance was sober. His face looked tight. "It's the Cossacks again. Only this time they are called the Black Hundreds. And now they have the backing of the Tsar. They call their attacks pogroms because they come like thunder. But now in a way it's worse than what happened in Kiev when the Cossacks rampaged through the countryside abusing and massacring the populace. Now they are censoring all Jewish books, banning us from wearing our traditional Jewish clothes, making the Hassidim cut off their side-locks, and then expelling Jews to the Pale of Settlement."

Hendrich leaned forward, lowering his voice almost as if he were going to tell them a secret. "When the Black Hundreds sweep through Jewish shtetls and communities raping, looting, slaughtering and burning, the authorities—the *authorities*, mind you—are told not to intervene until the third day of the incident!" Hendrich leaned back and threw up his hands in disgust and amazement. "*Three* days! Three days they wait before they stop all the harm. They shut their eyes and wait while all this is done to our people. Do you realize what that means? All this is under the control of the authorities! It is planned! Permitted! They come into villages and take away our children, conscripting them even as young as eight years of age! Can you imagine your child being taken away at age eight—to-to only Elohim knows where—and never seeing him again? And now they are coming into the villages and doing even worse! If anything *can* be worse. And they're doing it for one reason only. One reason. . . ."

Hendrich's voice became louder, more indignant, yet no one flinched for on the inside they screamed with him. "We're Jews! That's all—just Jews! In Kishinev there was a pogrom on the eve of Passover in which the attackers destroyed fifteen hundred Jewish homes, hurt some six hundred people, and killed nearly fifty. Wasn't it enough that Chmielnicki and his Cossacks killed over five hundred thousand Jews in eight years? That's more than the number that have been killed since our temple was destroyed and the Holy City ruined by the Romans! And now they are either killing us or rounding us up and moving us into the Pale of Settlement."

Hendrich had been using his hands to emphasize what he was saying. He now spread them apart and began moving them closer together as if he was trying to condense a large object down to a smaller size. "They are squeezing us, confining us into a small stretch of land—the Pale of Settlement—so we won't contaminate the populace. Shutting us up to appalling poverty because we can't come out of the settlement to earn our living. They tell us we cannot speak Yiddish, and that no Jew can hold public office even within the pale! Not even a rabbi in his own community, unless he has perfect command of the language of the people ruling over them." Hendrich's face was crimson.

Aaron waited until Hendrich finished; then he spoke. "I think it all has been exacerbated by an article that appeared in a Russian newspaper. It was called *The Protocols of the Learned Elders of Zion*."

"I haven't heard of that, Aaron," Sarah said. "What is it about?"

"It's an anti-Jewish work. It's about a mythical council of Jews who plan to take over the whole world. There are now so many Jews in Russia—especially since Catherine the Great annexed most of eastern Poland and the Ukraine—that people feel threatened by us. Of course, the annexation was many years ago, but it increased the number of Jews in Russia. It is said there are more than four million Jews in the Pale of Settlement right now, but—"

Hendrich interjected, "And there will be more." He paused, wondering how to say what was coming next. Then, deciding there was no delicate way, Hendrich continued, "Our shtetl will be part of the Pale."

Gershom jumped on Hendrich's words immediately. "Are you sure?"

Dusia froze, her body trembling slightly, tears silently but profusely pouring down her cheeks. She had learned to cry without making a sound; she simply sobbed and cried aloud somewhere inside herself.

No one could see Sarah's eyes; she had leaned her head forward and covered her face with her hands as if deep in thought.

All the color drained from Aaron's face. He felt sick at heart. He had such high hopes of going to school and someday becoming a writer like Mendele Moscher Sforim. He had read Sforim's book *Mendele, the Bookseller*. It was the first book ever to be published in Yiddish, the language of the Jewish secular culture in Eastern Europe . . . and in the ghettos.

Yiddish was a unique mix of Hebrew and German. But Aaron's secret dream was for his people to someday speak their own language, the one spoken by Moses and the prophets—pure Hebrew. Aaron wanted not only to speak Hebrew but to teach and write it. And he dreamed of doing it in Israel, the land promised to the descendants of Abraham, Isaac, and Jacob by the Almighty. For now Yiddish was fine, but someday if Aaron could have his way it would be Hebrew!

At that moment, Aaron's dream came crashing down, shattering into a hundred little pieces with Hendrich's news. *They're forcing us to live in the Pale!* Aaron felt as though he had just been sentenced to prison. For surely, prison is what it would mean to live in the Pale of Settlement.

Hendrich looked at Gershom. He hated to confirm it. It made him sad . . . and angry. "I am sure. It is a cold, hard fact. Everyone in our community will be part of the Pale. The Pale will encompass us. It was confirmed to me today when I was in Kiev."

Gershom rose to his feet. There was nothing more to discuss with Hendrich tonight. Tomorrow, the men of the community would gather together again to talk about what they would do this time. He thanked Hendrich for coming.

After Hendrich left, Gershom crossed the room to put his arms around Dusia. He wanted to hold his wife for a moment. Sarah went into the kitchen, put hot coals into the samovar, and poured in the water. She put the tea container on the top. Sarah had something she'd been wanting to discuss with the family for quite some time, and she knew tonight was the night.

Aaron followed Sarah into the kitchen so his parents could have a moment of privacy. Sitting down at the table, he became lost in his thoughts. Neither spoke until the cups were on the table and the tea was ready.

"Aaron, would you please ask your parents to come and have tea? I need to talk with them and you."

Aaron looked at his aunt. At that moment he knew in his heart that Sarah was leaving. He didn't want her to go; she had always been so special to him. He laughed to himself as he remembered how, as a little boy, he went to her house to become her teacher! As if a little boy could take his Saba's place!

Aaron stood up, walked into the large room, and looked around. *I wonder why we always call it the large room? It looks so small now.* His eyes went to the ark. He remembered how they made a box and buried the scrolls in the ground when they knew the Cossacks were coming. The scrolls were now back where they belonged—behind the curtain of the ark. Some of the words on the holy scrolls were inscribed upon his heart. It was times like these that made him want to read and study the scrolls more—especially the *Nevi'im,* the prophets. Aaron wanted to see for himself what the Nevi'im said about Messiah and his coming.

With the increasing persecution came a greater anticipation of Messiah's coming. Many people were saying the persecution that they as Jews were now enduring was a sign that Messiah's coming was near.

"Abba! Imma! Aunt Sarah would like you to have tea. She wants to talk with you both . . . and with me also. If that is all right with you?"

Dusia dried her eyes. She didn't like to cry in front of her loved ones. She was glad Miriam was still at Pola's.

Sarah poured the tea and began talking. "I know you are tired; I'm sorry to bring this up now. But because we don't know how soon they'll come to make us part of the Pale and our situation is so uncertain, I feel we must discuss this tonight."

Sarah looked at the faces of her loved ones. It was hard to tell them what she felt she must do. "You are so very dear to me. You have been my family. But it has been in my heart for quite some time now that I must go to Germany to try to find my son and then go on to Israel. Somehow I believe Saul may be in Germany, and I cannot rest until I know for sure. If I can't find him there, then I know I am to return to Israel." Sarah saw Aaron's eyes light up at the mention of Israel. "Although I love each of you dearly, it is time now for me to go home."

Aaron looked at his aunt, excitement in his eyes and his voice. "Germany? Then Israel? You know Aunt Sarah, when we were talking with Hendrich and he interrupted me, I was about to mention that many in the Pale are talking of returning to Israel. They say if Jews must be shut up in the Pale of Settlement, then we would be better off in our very own country."

"Also, there's a man in Vienna who writes for a newspaper," Aaron continued. "I think his name is Herzl. Anyway, I heard from someone that he held a conference to talk to our people about becoming Zionists and returning to the land that is rightfully ours. He even wrote an essay called, 'Der Judenstaat'—the Jewish State. They say the essay is very powerful. I want to get a copy of it, but I can't find one anywhere. I asked Hendrich to see if anyone in the Jewish community in Kiev had a copy I could borrow. I guess he forgot to ask about it when he heard the news about the Pale. I think I would like to become a Zionist. I believe—"

"Son, your aunt hasn't finished talking. We want to hear what you have to say, but now isn't the appropriate time." Gershom's rebuke was gentle.

"I don't mind, Gershom," said Sarah. "I'm glad that's how Aaron feels. Aaron, my heart rejoices to hear what is dear to you. Our hearts are one! And we will talk about this more, but first let me say again that I feel it is best for me to leave you. With the situation as it will be in the Pale, you don't need another mouth to feed or body to house. . . ."

They looked at her, stunned. Then Dusia said, "Sarah! How can you say that? You don't know what it has meant to us—"

"Oh yes, Dusia, I know and I appreciate it. You need not say any more. But that is not my reason for leaving. Please forgive me for mentioning it, as I know you gladly share everything you have. Really, I am leaving because I feel compelled to search for my son. I cannot explain why, but, as I just said, I believe Saul may be in Germany. Anyway," Sarah paused for a moment, then her next words spilled out. "I would like to offer to take Aaron with me. That is, with your permission, and if he wants to go."

Color flushed Aaron's cheeks. He became so excited his words stumbled over themselves. "Abba, Imma! May I go—please?" Then Aaron saw the cloud of pain shadowing his father's face.

How can I give up this son whom I love so much? The answer sprang up as quickly as the question had. *Because, Aaron, I love you so much and this is best for you, my first.*

Aaron instantly regretted his request. Looking unflinchingly into his father's eyes, he forced his words to be strong. "Abba, I won't go. It is all right. I didn't mean to hurt you. I got carried away. It's all right, Abba; I will stay with you and Imma."

Gershom returned his son's gaze. Tears welled up in his eyes, yet a gentle smile of contentment graced his lips. He was willing to sacrifice his own desires to please the one he loved. Gershom thought of how Abraham had offered up Isaac, and how God gave Isaac back to him. *Elohim, I ask only one thing: someday, restore my son to me. . . .*

Chapter 55

*L*isten to me!" the young man shouted from the Hamburg street corner. "Listen to me." The zealous orator waved his arm to draw the passers-by to the marble rim of the statue that served as his platform.

Aaron studied the young man. He guessed that most likely the man was a university student, for there was a scholarly air about him. Everything about his dress and demeanor spoke of discipline and confidence. Aaron's day was free, so he decided to listen to what the man had to say. Aunt Sarah was meeting with some leaders from the Jewish community in Hamburg. She would not be done for a while, and Aaron had nothing else to do except return to the library he enjoyed so much. But he was tired of reading. He wanted to stretch his legs, enjoy the sunshine of this autumn day, and see more of this German city before they were on the move again. Unless, of course, Aunt Sarah happened to find Saul.

Aaron drew closer and listened. "It is Christianity, with its emphasis on mercy and forgiveness, that has made Germany weak. These sentiments stand in the way of the greater virtues of control and power. Compassion makes a state weak; unbridled power makes us strong. It is not the meek who will inherit the earth, but the strong—the master race Germany will produce. If Christ was divine, it is only because we all are. Man must replace God as the center of art, philosophy, and history. Listen to Nietzsche—the man Adolph Hitler, our new Fuhrer, reads—and you will be in proper company. Nietzsche said, 'Do we not hear anything yet of the noise of the grave diggers who are burying God? Do we not smell anything yet of God's decomposition? Gods, too, decompose. God is dead and we have killed him. The churches are the tombs and sepulchers of God.'"

Aaron looked at the crowd to see their response. He was surprised at how many people stayed and listened. Wasn't this a Christian nation? The place of the reformation? It seemed incongruous to Aaron that they would stand listening without some expression of passion. *Do they believe what they are hearing? Are they merely curious? Or*, Aaron's next thought scared him, *do they want to believe what the man is saying?* No one in the crowd opposed, jeered, or even showed agreement with his views. They simply stood listening. Aaron saw no indication of anyone's emotion or reaction.

The young man, on the other hand, was quite passionate and articulate. Aaron wondered if the concepts he spoke of were being taught in university classes. By now, Aaron was convinced this man was a student.

He decided to move on. The Almighty wasn't dead, and no one would ever bury him. Rather, from what Aaron had read of the Bible, the opposite was true. God was going to bury multitudes when he unleashed his wrath upon the earth. Aaron wondered what it would be like for Nietzsche, who was now dead, when he stood before the Almighty at the resurrection.

As Aaron lingered at the corner wondering which way to walk, he found himself continuing to think about Nietzsche. *Nietzsche was insane for the last eleven years of his life—probably because he tried to bury God.*

The young orator continued to draw more people as Aaron tried to decide whether to go back to the library or continue his walk. He was ready to step off the curb when he heard the speaker say, "We must protect the Aryan race from the Jews who plot to take over this world. Have you not read *The Protocols of the Learned Elders of Zion?* Do you not realize—"

Aaron turned around. He knew now that he would stay. He waited to hear what this bold speaker believed and was publicly proclaiming about the Jewish people.

By now the crowd had grown. No longer were they dispassionate listeners. Aaron could hear shouts of affirmation from some of those around him. Aaron didn't want to stand among them; he didn't know whether it was fear or anger that made him want to keep his distance. But where could he stand?

As he looked about, he saw a tall man who seemed to be listening intently. His arms were crossed. One hand propped against his chin, his fingers almost hiding his small, neatly trimmed black beard.

The man was well dressed, distinguished looking. His black overcoat, made of fine wool, had been tailored to fit his broad shoulders and medium frame.

As Aaron moved so he could see the expression on the man's face, he looked closely at the dark eyes set above high cheekbones and made more prominent by a high forehead and the hairline receding over his temples. Aaron could tell he was grieved by what he heard. As if he sensed that Aaron was staring at him, the man quickly cast his eyes in Aaron's direction, smiled kindly, and then returned his attention to the speaker.

Listening, Aaron continued to draw closer toward the concerned gentleman. The impassioned orator was trying to convince his listeners to embrace his beliefs. "I challenge you to read Chamberlain's book, *The Foundations of the Nineteenth Century.* You will see that it was the Jews who destroyed the ancient world and who are even now corrupting Europe and tainting the Aryan races with their Semitic blood."

Aaron turned abruptly as he heard, in a voice barely more than a whisper,

"Sh'ma Yisroel, Adonai, Elohenu, Adonai ehad!" His eyes locked with the dark eyes of the gentleman, whose hand was still against his chin and almost covering his mouth. Slowly searching the man's eyes, Aaron repeated the man's words, but not in Hebrew. "Hear, O Israel! The Lord our God, the Lord is one!" The man responded with a smile. Quietly he whispered to Aaron, "I think it might be best for us to leave this crowd right now. Just in case our Jewish heritage shows."

The man took Aaron by the elbow, steering him through the crowd, which by now was consumed in the fire of the speaker's burning hatred. When they came to the street corner, the man's hand was still on Aaron's elbow. After they crossed the street and were a safe distance from the crowd, the gentleman spoke. "I'd be interested in hearing your impressions of that young man's speech. You didn't by any chance attend the same university? The one right up this street?"

"No, sir. You see, I am not from Germany. As a child I lived in Cologne but then we were forced to flee for our lives. After that I lived in a shtetl near Kiev until I returned here recently with my aunt."

"Shtetl? That's Yiddish."

"Yes, sir. We are Ashkenazi Jews. You sound like a Sephardic. Are you?"

"Yes, you might say that. It's strange, isn't it, that we identify those from Spain as Sephardic Jews and those from Europe as Ashkenazi." The man laughed. "I don't know what to call you. What is your name?"

"Aaron. And yours, sir?"

"Jared. Jared Seforim."

"It's very nice to meet you. Since my aunt had some business to attend, I have the day free. Say, are you from Hamburg?"

The men continued walking, neither taking thought of where they were going.

"No, I'm not. In fact, I will be leaving Hamburg tonight. I am going to Israel while I can still get there."

Aaron stopped and turned toward Jared. "Israel!" he exclaimed. "That's where I long to be!"

Jared playfully hit Aaron on the elbow. "Well, then come with me! You're old enough!"

Excited about the prospect of going to Israel yet at the same time aware of his present obligations, Aaron looked at his feet as if contemplating what he should say. Then, lifting his head, he said, "I would love to . . . more than anything else. But right now I have to stay with my aunt. Yet I would love to hear what you know about Israel. What is it like there now?"

Jared reached under his lapel and pulled a pocket watch from his vest. He studied the time for a moment, then said, "I still have a little over half an hour before I must pack and board my train. Would you like to have something to eat? Or maybe something to drink? There's a coffee house right here."

Aaron shrugged his shoulders and said, "Yes, gladly. I have nothing else to do. And I can think of nothing I would enjoy more than talking to a man who is going to Israel."

The coffee house was dark inside; the furnishings and decor appeared to be made of dark oak. They removed their coats and sat in a booth facing one another over a heavy table. The dreary atmosphere was soon brightened by a woman wearing a red apron embroidered with flowers of yellow and blue. The apron was tied over a white blouse with puffy sleeves and a blue embroidered skirt. She was blonde-haired, blue-eyed, and sturdily built, and she arrived ready to take their order with true German efficiency. For a moment she stood poised with pencil in hand looking at them skeptically. "Juden?" she asked, to which Jared immediately replied indignantly, "Nein. Nein." He then proceeded to place their order in flawless, fluent German.

As soon as their server walked away, Jared said, "Forgive me for denying our Jewishness, but I don't have time for us to look for another place to eat and talk. Because this coffee house is virtually empty, I think we might as well stay. Just watch for the woman. When you see her coming, nod to me and we'll change the conversation. Now, Aaron, tell me about yourself."

"If you don't mind, sir, since our time is so limited and I already know about me, I'd rather hear what you have to say about Israel. What is going on there? What do you do there? Do you mind talking about Israel?"

"No! Of course not," Jared said, somewhat amused. He found himself drawn to this young man's zeal.

Aaron posed his first question. "Have you ever heard of a man named Theodor Herzl?"

"Yes. You see, I am a Zionist at heart. Herzl is the father of Zionism."

"I've tried to read everything I can about him. I would have loved to attend the first World Zionist Conference he set up."

Jared smiled, nodding his head in agreement. "I was there, Aaron. It was really something. I remember Herzl made us all dress up for the occasion. Black ties and tails. He wanted the world to sit up and take notice. Herzl even rented formal attire for those who couldn't afford it. Anyway, that's how I became involved in the Zionist movement. I was already headed for Israel from Spain with some friends and a young man who is like a son to me. But our ship had to land in Genoa because of a problem, so I decided that before leaving for Israel I would try to find a woman I know. And that is how I ended up in Germany. I thought she might be here."

"My aunt came to Germany to—" Aaron abruptly stopped speaking and leaned forward. In a low voice, he said, "Here comes the woman with our food. Time to change the subject."

Jared immediately launched into a dissertation on the German economy and how it was on the upswing just as the woman arrived to place their sandwiches and drinks on the table. She lingered longer than necessary, and Aaron wished she would leave. He wondered if she was intrigued by Jared's soliloquy on the declining value of the mark, which had been valued at four marks to one American dollar, then 75 to one, then 400 to one. The mark's worth then plummeted to seven thousand to one dollar, and finally bottomed out to four billion to one. Worthless!

That's when the woman interjected how Hitler's rule had changed all that. Workers now had job security, health service, and a way to enjoy a free holiday and learn more about the Third Reich at the same time. It was obvious to Jared and Aaron that this woman was in agreement with whatever their new Fuhrer did as long as she was well cared for.

By the time she left their table, they had forgotten what they had been discussing before her presence interrupted their conversation. Time was passing too quickly. Aaron leaned across the table and said, "I am impressed that you know so much about the German mark."

"Money has been my business for a long time, Aaron. In fact, that's the reason I became involved in the Jewish Colonial Trust." Jared noted from Aaron's frown that he didn't know about the Trust, so he continued. "The Jewish Colonial Trust was Herzl's way of trying to get funds when independent Jewish financiers couldn't be won over to the cause of Zionism. Anyway, I've been involved in helping raise those funds. But things are getting bad in Germany, and I have a feeling that if I don't leave the country right away I may not get to Israel. Even now, getting to Israel is not all that easy. The British make it hard on us—but that is another story. When you arrive in Israel, you will experience this firsthand."

Jared pulled out his watch. "You better drink up, my friend. I don't want to leave you in a place where Jews are forbidden."

Jared rose from the table, paid the bill, and they went out on the street. Aaron couldn't believe their time had run out. He felt as though he was losing a friend. He felt a strange ache inside him, mingled with fear.

Once outside, they donned their coats. Jared turned to say good-bye. Reaching into his suit pocket, he pulled out a gold calling-card case. Aaron noticed the elaborately engraved initials on it. Jared took out a card, handed it to Aaron, and instructed him, "Don't lose this. It has my Jerusalem address on it. I want you to promise you will look me up when you get to Israel. If you need a place to stay, you may stay with me—and I do mean that. You seem like a fine young man—a true son of Israel who will be an asset to the re-establishment of our nation. May the Almighty watch over you."

Jared's eyes moistened as he noticed the tears sitting on the edges of Aaron's eyelids. Quickly Jared embraced him and turned to leave. Aaron watched him walk away. Before Jared took more than a few steps, he turned around and looked intently into Aaron's eyes. "Remember, Aaron, ideas do have consequences. The belief that God is dead frees men to do whatever they deem right. The young man we heard speaking today is Germany. Take your aunt and leave this country as quickly as you can. If you are coming to Israel, the time is now. Shalom, son of Israel."

Aaron's eyes followed Jared's form until he was out of sight. He kept wishing Jared would change his mind and come back. He wanted to take him to meet Aunt Sarah. Little did Aaron know, however, just how wonderful a meeting that would have been...a meeting that would have spared Sarah the most horrendous of horrors.

Chapter 56

*W*hat a pleasant November evening! Aaron decided to walk rather than take the trolley to the synagogue where he was to meet Aunt Sarah. It wouldn't take too long to reach the neighborhood where the majority of the Jews in Hamburg resided. Aaron had heard it said that between nineteen and twenty thousand Jews were living in Hamburg. This was where Sarah had gone to inquire about Saul.

Aaron hoped Sarah had heard some word about Saul. They had traveled through Germany, from one city to another, until he lost count. Finally, in Berlin, someone said Saul might be living in Hamburg. That excited Sarah; finally, she had confirmation her son might be alive. Aaron couldn't bear the thought of her not finding him and being disappointed again.

The day had been quite eventful. Aaron had much to think about as he walked. He was anxious to tell his aunt about his meeting with Jared. Every now and then, Aaron pulled Jared's card from his coat pocket and reread the address to make certain he had memorized it correctly. Having talked with Jared, Aaron wanted more than ever to get out of Germany and be on the way to Israel. If Saul were found, they could leave immediately. But if not . . . Aaron didn't want to think about that! He only knew, from his time with Jared, Germany probably wouldn't be safe for them much longer.

Aaron thought of the many things he had seen with his own eyes and what he had heard as they traveled through Germany—sights and stories testifying to the increasing hostility shown to the Jewish people. He remembered hearing about Karl Valentin being sent to a concentration camp as a dissenter because he had imitated Hitler and his mannerisms in a nightclub act. Then in the library Aaron read of the Nuremberg Laws of 1935, which reduced Jews to the status of second-class citizens and made it illegal for them to visit certain public places and cafes.

Aaron grinned as he remembered how smoothly Jared had handled their waitress when she asked if they were Jews. The man was marvelous; he was so calm about it all. Aaron could grin now, but not then. At the time it scared him. Having read of the Nuremberg Laws, he now understood why he had seen Nazis pushing a woman down the street in Berlin with a placard around her neck stating "I slept with a Jew." He could still remember vividly the anguish and shame on her face.

By now it was becoming dark outside. Aaron passed a Jewish shop on the edge of the neighborhood where he was to meet Aunt Sarah. In the window was a sign that read *Kauff nicht bei Juden*—Don't buy from Jews. German swastikas and stars of David plastered the windows. He walked on. Suddenly people were shouting in the streets. Or were they screaming? The sound of breaking glass shattered the atmosphere. Instantly the street filled with people. In the distance beyond the shops of the Jewish quarter, flames ignited the evening sky.

The synagogue was burning! "The synagogue!" Aaron shouted as he broke into a run, propelling himself faster and faster, panic surging adrenaline through every vein and artery. *Aunt Sarah! Where are you?* Loneliness haunted him as he ran. He longed for Jared to run beside him, to help him search for his aunt. He needed Jared's calm confidence. Aaron wanted to cry, run away—to hide, but he knew he couldn't. *I'm a man—the only man Aunt Sarah has right now—and I must take care of her.*

People were racing down the street in all directions. Aaron could feel glass crunching under his feet. People were smashing windows and reaching through the broken glass, looting merchandise once beautifully displayed. Dangling price tags evidenced the value of the stolen goods. Shop owners who had not yet closed up for the night were fending off attackers with brooms or whatever else they could find to use as weapons. Yet frequently their weapons were wrenched from their hands and then turned ferociously against them.

Cries of pain hung in the air, piercing Aaron's eardrums, grieving his heart. The broken glass strewn on the street around the synagogue glowed in the light of the fire, giving the deceitful appearance of crystal. *Where are you, Aunt Sarah? Where are you? Elohim! Elohim!* Aaron's eyes scanned the mass of human turmoil.

Then Aaron saw her. There standing on the other side of the blazing synagogue! Its surreal majesty was still intact, and its beauty for a short time was etched in golden light against the ever-darkening sky. This edifice of Judaism would not disintegrate into charred anonymity so easily.

Sarah's mind ran in all directions. She wanted to run through the madness searching until she found Aaron. She wanted to snatch him up and drag him away from this place, even as she had that night in Cologne. But reason told her that if she left the place where they had planned to meet she might never find him. The heat emanating from the burning synagogue was scorching. *Where are you, Aaron? Why aren't you here? Why are you late? My husband, where are you? I need help—*

"Aunt Sarah! Aunt Sarah!"

At the moment Sarah heard Aaron's voice, she felt herself being pushed further away from him. Men wearing brown shirts and carrying sticks and clubs were pushing the crowd back from the fiery house of worship. *Why aren't they helping the people whose stores are being destroyed, those whose merchandise is being carried off? Why are they pushing me?*

As Aaron frantically tried to push through the people and the line of brown-shirted men, a man turned around and, swearing in German, clubbed Aaron, sending him sliding into the glass-littered street. Sarah screamed and rushed toward Aaron only to be repelled by another wooden club. The swastika on the Brown Shirt's sleeve seemed to glow in the light of the burning synagogue.

Aaron struggled to get his footing in the shards of glass littering the street. He winced in pain. Slivers of glass pierced his hands. Blood streamed from a cut over his ear. Once again, Aaron hastily scanned the line of Brown Shirts, looking to see where it ended, searching for Sarah. Spotting her, he cried out, "Aunt Sarah! Go that way!" motioning with his hand for her to meet him at the end of the Brown Shirt barricade.

Sarah shoved and stumbled through the weeping throng of Jews who stood in horror mourning their synagogue, the glory of their neighborhood, the testimony of their Jewishness. As the flames devoured the building, the holy scrolls—made of lamb's skin—curled in the heat, dying in ashes.

Finally, Sarah reached Aaron. Kissing him, she wiped the blood from his ear. Then, taking his hands, she turned his palms up and began removing the remaining bits of glass.

Sarah and Aaron made their way to the rooms they had rented, all the while choking on the smoke they had inhaled. While Aaron cleaned up, Sarah made tea. The hot tea helped soothe the fear chilling them deeper than their bones. For a few minutes they sat in silence. Then, having recovered somewhat, they talked of the nightmare their people had just endured.

"I believe, Aaron, this night of broken glass will be blamed on the citizens of Hamburg. But this was not a spontaneous uprising. To me, it has the elements of a pogrom. The newspapers will say it was an act of retribution against the Jews by citizens indignant over the killing of Ernst von Rath at the German Embassy, but it will be a lie. The killing of van Roth is merely a propitious excuse to instigate tonight's riots."

"Who killed him?" Aaron asked his aunt.

"A Jew. A young, impulsive, hurting Polish Jew. His parents were waiting at a border transit camp, stranded in that no-man's land as they were being expelled from Germany. I am certain this is the excuse the Nazis needed and will use to come against us. They want people to turn on us. Why would those Brown Shirts be there, holding us back from our burning synagogue, while allowing the citizenry to plunder the Jewish shops? I believe we'll soon hear that what happened in Hamburg was repeated in cities all over Germany this very night. Think, Aaron. We've got to think. Things are not always as they appear."

With those words, Aaron suddenly remembered his encounter with Jared earlier that day. Jumping up, he ran to get his coat.

Sarah looked up at Aaron, confused. "What's the matter, Aaron? Where are you going?"

Feeling Jared's card in his coat pocket, he began to laugh with joy. He had not lost it! Then he laughed at the ludicrous thought that must have crossed Sarah's mind as he ran for his coat. His was a laughter unwarranted by the events, springing from fragile emotions bound by a tension that needed unraveling—laughter that bordered on weeping. "You thought I was . . . was go . . . going somewhere!" Aaron laughed.

Then Sarah began laughing simply because Aaron was laughing. She didn't try to stop until her laughter turned to sobs. Aaron wrapped his arms around her with Jared's card still in his hand. "Aunt Sarah, how thankful I am you and I are together and we are both all right. I was so scared! I ran so hard, crying to Elohim, praying you would be all right. You are all right, Aunt Sarah. You are all right. And I'm all right." Aaron held her until their tears subsided. Then he sat down across from her.

Sarah looked at Aaron, her eyes red and puffy from the tears, the heat of the flames, and the smoke. "Why did you get your coat?" she asked him, rubbing her eyes.

Aaron grinned and held up the card. "This! This is what I was getting. It was in my coat pocket and for a minute I panicked because I thought maybe I lost it when I was knocked down in the street."

"What is it?"

"It's a calling card."

"A calling card!" Sarah exclaimed. "You were that concerned about a calling card? Whose card is it?"

"It's from a man I met today. You'd like him a lot if you met him. His name is Jared Seforim, and—"

"Jared! Jared!" Sarah interrupted, crying. "You met Jared! Where is he? Why didn't he come with you?"

"You know him, Aunt Sarah?"

"Oh yes, yes, Aaron! He is one of my dearest friends and trusted advisors! I didn't even know if he was alive or dead. I haven't seen him for such a long time. Didn't he tell you?"

"He doesn't even know about you, Aunt Sarah. I never mentioned your name. I started to, but we were interrupted. And our time was so short. . . ." Aaron was upset with himself. "Why didn't I mention your name? I started to, but the waitress...oh, I'm so sorry." Aaron saw the disappointment on her face. "So sorry. . . ."

"Aaron, it's all right." Sarah said, smiling weakly. "There was no way you could have known we knew each other." Sarah got up from her chair and headed toward the coat rack. "You can put on your coat now," Sarah said, laughing again, but this time from joy. "We'll go surprise him together. I can't wait to see his—"

Sarah stopped in midsentence. Aaron was sitting on the edge of his chair, his face buried in his hands. Mystified, she asked, "What's wrong, Aaron? Are you all right?"

Sarah hurried to his side, sitting on the arm of his chair. Finally, Aaron looked up, recovered enough to talk. "He's gone, Aunt Sarah. He left today for Israel. The card has the address where we can reach him in Israel. We can't go see him now."

Aaron dropped his eyes to the floor. "I'm so sorry, Aunt Sarah. I started to mention that you, too, were looking for someone, and then the waitress came, and . . . and . . . oh Sarah! You must be the woman Jared was trying to find. He was sailing from Spain to Israel but his ship had problems and they landed in Genoa. He felt he was to come to Germany to look for a woman. I didn't ask who he was talking about, but it must have been you!"

Sarah returned to her chair and sat down. She felt drained. "I'm sure it was me he was seeking; that is so like Jared. He is a friend, Aaron, who has been closer than a brother. A friend who would lay down his life for me." Sarah nestled a little deeper into the chair cushion and closed her eyes. Aaron could tell she was thinking. He watched her silently, every now and then closing his eyes and reliving his day.

Finally Sarah spoke. "I think it was better, Aaron, that Jared did not know. I really do." Sarah straightened up in her chair and looked at Aaron. "Aaron, I found out more about Saul. He is in one of two places—either in Holland or in Israel. I need to go to Holland first and contact the Jewish communities to make certain he isn't there. And if he's not, then I will go to Israel."

"When do we leave for Holland, Aunt Sarah? Jared said we must leave Germany immediately."

"Jared is right. He is a very astute man. Now, listen to me carefully. I have already thought this through and talked it over with some wise men in this community who know the state of Germany's affairs. I am going to Holland alone—"

"No, Aunt Sarah," Aaron interrupted. "No! Abba would never forgive me if something happened to you."

"Aaron, Abba isn't here, and he does not know the situation. He would want what is best and wisest for both of us." Sarah raised her hand to silence his objections. "Listen to me. I know what I am doing is right. You cannot go to Holland with me. It isn't safe. Besides, after your encounter with Jared tonight, I know it is right for you to go to Israel. I want you to go and join Jared. You can tell him that I'm all right and I've gone to Holland. Let him know that I will come to Israel very soon. Jared will care for you as if you are my son. And I will rest easier just knowing Jared is alive and that he will be in Israel waiting for you. Who knows—maybe you will meet him on the way."

Aaron sat looking at his aunt. He felt torn. Torn between duty and concern . . . and the overwhelming desire to be in Israel working side by side with Jared for the creation of their Jewish state. Maybe it would become a reality before his aunt ever got to Israel.

"Now, Aaron, the men I spoke with are arranging for your departure early in the morning. You must pack. And so must I. I, too, must leave in the morning—for Holland." Sarah rose to her feet, stretched, then walked over to Aaron, who was now out of his chair. Cupping his face in her hands, she said, "And after Holland, I go home." Standing on her tiptoes, she lowered Aaron's head down as she had done so often in the past and kissed him on the forehead. "Next year, Aaron . . . next year in Jerusalem."

That was what Sarah wanted, what she believed...but it wasn't to be, not for a long time.

Chapter 57

t was the day after Tisha B'av. Rachel was concerned about Rebecca. "Are you sure you're not too weak? I don't want you fainting during the wedding ceremony. You've been fasting two days now—first for Tisha B'av and now for your wedding. Why," Rachel asked, "did you and Enoch insist on getting married the day after Tisha B'av?"

Rebecca didn't answer right away; she was wondering if Enoch would mind if she explained the reason they had chosen this particular day. It was their special offering to the Almighty. Although the family had protested their timing, Rebecca and Enoch gave no defense for choosing for this date except to say it was the best day for the kibbutz on which they lived to have a wedding...and the best time for all their friends to attend. But up to this day, their true reason had not been shared.

"Imma," Rebecca said, then paused. There was a burning in Rebecca's eyes which went beyond a bride's passion on her wedding day. As Rachel looked at her daughter, she thought, *It's like a holy consecration. This daughter of mine has never been the same since she read the Bible through. How wise Reuben was—how wise.*

"Imma," Rebecca sighed, hesitating. Her eyes searched her mother's, as if trying to make a decision. Then, feeling freedom in her spirit, Rebecca decided to disclose their secret. "We chose this day after Tisha B'av—the anniversary of the two destructions of Jerusalem—because we wanted our marriage to be used, no matter what it costs, for the rebuilding of Jerusalem in preparation for Messiah's coming. I know that may sound preposterous, but just as our nation went into captivity because of our sin, so do we want to live righteously in this land to bring back the Almighty's favor upon us rather than his wrath. We haven't shared this reason with anyone because most of the people on the kibbutz believe that Israel's rebirth as a nation *is* Messiah. But Enoch and I believe differently."

Rachel took Rebecca's lovely face in her hands and kissed her daughter's lips—lips that, to her, had uttered beautiful words. Now she was glad the children had chosen this day. How well she remembered the night of Tisha B'av, when she, Reuben, Jared, and Sarah fled the destruction of Jerusalem. Rachel's eyes filled with tears not only because she was touched by Rebecca's words but also because she missed Jared and Sarah more than her heart could tell.

With a sigh, Rachel gave words to her longing. "How I wish Jared and Sarah could be here for your wedding! That they, too, could hear with their own ears why you and Enoch chose to marry on the tenth of Av. I know it would bring tears to their eyes just as it does to mine. May I share that with your father?" Rachel asked as she rearranged the flowers in Rebecca's hair. "He will be so proud. Such a gift you are! And such a gift from the Almighty that we should be here in Israel and that our Samuel should be with us! My dream is fulfilled; my prayers are answered. Well, almost. When Jared and Sarah are here, we will be complete again."

"Enoch longs to see Jared, Imma. He's the only father Enoch has. Just think—Enoch has no mother, no father. Both are dead simply because they were born Jews. This is why Enoch and I believe so adamantly in a homeland for our people—a land where Jews no longer must live in fear just because they are Abraham's children by promise."

"Our Jewish heritage bears a price, my daughter, but also a blessing," said Rachel. "Enoch has the Almighty! He is one of the Almighty's chosen people. We must not forget that. Now," Rachel beamed, "this is your wedding day. A day of rejoicing! The fasting is about to end, and we will soon feast. As our tradition says, you have fasted as a couple about to be married, your sins are forgiven, and you start anew!"

Rebecca laughed, "It's tradition, Imma! But it's not in the Bible. If it were, I would have married sooner!"

Chana, one of Rebecca's friends from the kibbutz, hurried into the room. "What are you two doing? Everyone is waiting! Enoch has signed the ketubbah; your marriage contract has been witnessed. Your friends are waiting to escort you to your throne. Queen for a day!" Chana laughed. "Just remember, my friend, it is for *one* day only. Tomorrow it's back to the life of the kibbutzim! This land of ours gives us no rest—only the Almighty on Shabbat!"

Rachel glowed as she accompanied Rebecca to her wedding throne next to the chuppah. The little tent under which the ceremony would take place was the work of Rachel's hands. The chair serving this regal function was clothed in a white sheet, tied with ribbons, and crowned with fragrant white flowers and delicate pink roses. Everything required to celebrate this special occasion had come from the kibbutz. The residents of this collective group lived communal lives, owning nothing and sharing everything as they sought to redeem their land from its years of desolation. Rebecca breathed deeply; her throne was encircled with her favorite flowers, which had been chosen simply because of their fragrance.

Rachel took her place in a chair with the other guests sitting in front of the chuppah, facing her daughter's throne. To Rachel, Rebecca had never looked more beautiful. Her long black hair loosely pinned on her head was encircled by a simple garland of flowers and grape leaves set over exquisite lace mantilla brought from Spain. The white mantilla softly draped itself over her hair, caressed the contours of her radiant face, and then cascaded over her shoulders and the simple long white dress which barely touched her ankles.

As Enoch's friends happily ushered him to his waiting bride, the men sang a psalm of joy: "As the bridegroom coming out of this tent rejoices to run the race." Rebecca looked with anticipation at Enoch. This was a psalm they had chosen for their ceremony. Enoch took Rebecca's hand and led her to the chuppah, supported by four poles. There, Enoch entered first, and then waited for Rebecca to join him under this symbol of his house.

Rachel watched Reuben with pride as he accompanied his new son-in-law to the chuppah. Standing next to Reuben was Samuel. Although Rachel had promised herself she would not cry during the ceremony, the sight of Samuel and Reuben together stirred her emotions greatly. Tears coursed unrestrained down her cheeks as she remembered the many years they had been separated from their son.

Samuel was still the same in heart, yet different. His character had not changed, but a new intensity drove his life. His thoughts were of nothing else but of Jerusalem belonging solely to the Jews. He longed for the holy city to be under Jewish rule without the domination of foreign powers, who, in Samuel's eyes, were usurpers of what the Almighty had deemed Israel's earthly Zion forever.

Rachel watched as Reuben fulfilled the role of the groom's father, draping a white kitel, also worn on Yom Kippur, over Enoch's head and shoulders. Rachel gazed in awe at her husband as he came to take his place in a chair next to hers. When she married Reuben in Bethlehem, little did she realize the greatness of the man hidden beneath his placid exterior. Then she had only known him for his kind and gentle ways. Reuben patted Rachel's hand as he sat down, beaming from ear to ear. Samuel and Levi took their stations beside the back two poles of the chuppah.

As Enoch stood under the chuppah, Rebecca began gracefully walking around her bridegroom. She was to encircle him seven times—this tall, young lover who had captured her heart not with his handsome features but with his spirit and his mind. As she walked, her eyes beheld him adoringly, and his eyes conveyed a longing older than hers—a longing that reached all the way back to the day he first saw her at the library in Toledo, Spain. Enoch had waited patiently for a long time to know his virgin bride.

Reuben, stroking Rachel's hand, whispered, "You did an outstanding job of making the chuppah. I am so pleased you chose to make it in the design of a simple tallit. It is befitting the essence of this union—a work of the Almighty, an answer to prayer for our Rebecca." Then Reuben joyfully declared, "Someday our grandchildren will be married under it!"

Rachel smiled. Her husband had always been careful to praise her. As Rebecca finished her seventh circle around Enoch, everyone began to sing:

He who is strong above all else
He who is blessed above all else
He who is great above all else
    May he bless the bridegroom and the bride. . . .

The rabbi put his hand over the cup of wine and recited the blessing: "Blessed are you, Lord our God, who has made us holy through your commandments and has commanded us concerning marriages that are forbidden and those that are permitted when carried out under the canopy and with the sacred wedding ceremonies. Blessed are you, Lord our God, who makes your people Israel holy through this rite of the canopy and the sacred bond of marriage."

As Enoch and Rebecca drank from the goblet of wine, Reuben gazed up at the star-studded night and thought, *How fitting it is for this marriage to take place under the Almighty's canopy of the heavens. May your children, my Rebecca and Enoch, be as the stars of the heavens,* he thought.

With love radiating from his eyes, Enoch slipped the solid gold band on Rebecca's index finger. He smiled. Now whenever she pointed with this finger— as Rebecca so often did when emphasizing her words—people would know she belonged to one man . . . him! Holding Rebecca's delicate hand in his, Enoch recalled the day he first held it in Spain, hoping that someday she would become his. Smiling, he said, "Behold, you are consecrated to me with this ring according to the Law of Moses and Israel."

Enoch picked up the ketubbah—the marriage contract—and read it loudly for all to hear and witness. Intent on his reading, Enoch did not notice the stir among those who were standing at the back of the crowd. There, a man whom no one recognized was pushing his way through the people.

A note of apprehension struck the minds of some of the men, yet they did not know what to do. So many recent incidents of violence had occurred on kibbutzim throughout the land that people were sometimes overly cautious. There were many people living in Israel who did not want the Jews returning to what they now considered to be *their* land—not the Jews'. Those jostled by the stranger determined to monitor the man carefully, yet in their minds was a gentle reassurance that those on watch tonight had not abandoned their posts. Had they known a second stranger freely lingered in the background, leaning against a tree behind them, they most likely would have stopped the man, even if it meant disturbing the ceremony.

The guests listened intently as Enoch read the marriage contract. "The groom and the bride have also promised each other to strive throughout their lives together to achieve an openness which will enable them to share their thoughts, their feelings, and their experiences."

Enoch paused. Looking up, his eyes could see only Rebecca. Everyone else became a blur through his tears. Unaware of the man who by now had stopped momentarily in the midst of the people and stood on tiptoe to survey his surroundings, Enoch continued, "To be sensitive at all times to each other's needs, to attain mutual intellectual, emotional, physical, and spiritual fulfillment. . . ."

The man moved forward, slid his hand into his coat pocket, and then into the pocket of his pants. ". . . to work for the perpetuation of Judaism and of the Jewish people in their home, in their family life, and," the next words were unexpected, "for the establishment of the state of Israel." The stranger halted, focusing intently on Enoch.

Just as the rabbi called for the recitation of the seven blessings, Enoch turned his gaze from Rebecca, interrupting the rabbi and the ceremony. Rebecca alone knew what Enoch was about to say. She had agreed to his plan, and now gave him her full attention as he said, "In addition to Rebecca's parents, Rebecca and I wanted to have four others witness our marriage and our consecration to the formation of the State of Israel in preparation for the coming of Messiah. We wanted these four people, who hold a special place in our hearts and the hearts of Rebecca's parents, to hold the four poles of the chuppah."

The man moved closer. The hand in his pocket now firmly grasped what he had been searching for. Watching Enoch and Rebecca closely, the man continued to scan the crowd carefully, especially those nearest the canopy, as if he were looking for a specific person.

Enoch continued, "As you will notice, only two people presently stand holding the poles. One is Rebecca's brother, Samuel, whom she had never seen until she came to Israel, but whom she now loves as if they had grown up together." Samuel leaned over and patted Rebecca on the shoulder, missing the movement of the man coming up on his right. Enoch then turned toward Levi on his left, causing Samuel to lean even closer to Rebecca so he could see Levi. "In all the years of the family's separation from Samuel, the Almighty did not leave Samuel without a friend—a covenant partner. Just as David had Jonathan and Jonathan had David, so also did the Almighty give Samuel a dear friend in Levi."

The man froze in the shadows as a cloud crossed in front of the moon. His companion, whom he left standing unnoticed behind a tree, now moved in to the outer edge of the wedding guests. Everyone's attention was focused on the chuppah, the aura of the flickering candles adding to the solemnity of the joyful occasion.

Enoch glanced from Levi, to the two unattended poles, then to Rebecca's parents. His eyes again became moist. "Rebecca and I so wanted the other two poles to be held by a man and a woman. A woman I have never met, but who took Rebecca's parents under her wing, saving their lives and enabling them to give birth to my bride. Her name is Sarah. The man whom I longed to have here is one who has been a father to me since the death of my parents—a man I have come to love even as my own father, the father I hoped to have here for my wedding."

The man pulled his hand from his pocket, stepped out of the dark shadows, and moved toward Enoch. Wiping his tears, he walked to his pole, his eyes fixed on Enoch.

Then Jared spoke, his voice quivering. "By the grace of the Almighty, I am here, my son. May I speak the first blessing. . . ."

Enoch gasped. Slipping his trembling arm around Rebecca, he drew her close, never taking his eyes off Jared. Jared fought to keep his composure as he pronounced the blessing: "You abound in blessings, Lord our God, source of all creation, who created man and woman in your image that they might live, love, and so perpetuate life. You abound in blessings, Lord, Creator of human beings," Jared paused briefly and then added these words to the traditional blessing, "who did give this eunuch a son."

This blessing, of the seven that were planned, was the only one spoken in the ceremony. After Jared's, no other blessing was needed. His words embodied the essence of the rest and were enough. At long last, Jared had returned home—and father and son were reunited in their land of promise.

Jared stepped away from his pole. He took the handkerchief he had searched for in his pockets and handed it to Enoch. Enoch, in turn, gave a corner of it to the rabbi. With the holding of the handkerchief, the ketubbah was now considered binding. Jared would be the first to record his name as a witness.

Following tradition, Enoch lifted the goblet, eager to smash it and bring the ceremony to a close. But Jared quickly grabbed the glass from Enoch's hand. Then he lifted it up and saluted Reuben and Rachel, who sat in silent awe with tears streaming from their eyes as they marvelled at the wonder of the whole event.

Jared smiled and spoke as he handed the glass back to Enoch. "Before Enoch smashes the glass in memory of the destructions of our beloved Jerusalem, I'd like to ask the young man who accompanied me from Germany to come and stand at the fourth pole in Sarah's stead—for Sarah lives!"

Rachel, stunned by Jared's announcement, gasped in disbelief. Then she exclaimed, "Elohim! Elohim! Sarah lives! She lives!"

Reuben turned to watch Aaron make his way through the guests and take his place at the empty pole. Upon reaching the pole, Aaron made eye contact with Samuel, the other young man his aunt loved so dearly. They smiled at each other. Instantly Aaron knew he had a friend. Then Aaron turned toward Rachel, Reuben, and the guests and said, "Sarah lives. Physically she is now in Germany or Holland, but her heart is here in Eretz Israel."

With a jubilant shout, Enoch threw the goblet to the ground and crushed it with his heel. Aaron surveyed the shattered glass and remembered Kristallnacht. It had been as Aunt Sarah said—a night of planned destruction, a pogrom all across Germany. *Aunt Sarah, do you still live? Are you safe? Did you make it to Holland? Come home, Aunt Sarah . . . the land is empty without you.*

Chapter 58

abbi Moses Uri Halevi sat shaking his head, saying nothing. His long white beard swept his chest with every movement. His son, Aaron, was also silent. Sarah watched the two—father and son, both rabbis, both imprisoned by the Dutch authorities for circumcising a group of marranos who had fled Spain. Rabbi Moses' son, Aaron, reminded her a bit of *her* Aaron. She prayed her Aaron had found Jared and was safely on his way to Israel.

Sarah greatly valued the counsel of this wise father and son. She was willing to wait while the old rabbi shook his head. *If these two men could convince the Dutch authorities that the presence of Jews in Holland would advance the commerce of the country and that their city would benefit from the Jewish presence, then surely they can tell me what I must do to reach Israel.*

"I'm thinking, Sarah. Thinking. Give me some time. And while I think, you be thinking also."

His voice was raspy, worn with age. As Sarah observed the old man whose eyelids now closed over his bulging eyes, she thought about her people. *We have been persecuted for almost a millennium in the lands of our dispersion. The persecution has made us impotent. We negotiate, pay, plead, cajole, try to earn favor, make ourselves useful, indispensable—we do everything. Everything but fight. In our ghettos, the Judenrate—the compliant, fearful, and sometimes sycophantic leadership of the Jewish councils—compile all the information on births, deaths, the records of who we are, what we are, where we are, what we have. Then the Germans take the lists and use them to systematically gather us, cram us into rail cars, and ship us off to the concentration camps. To Sobibor, Treblinka, Chelmno, Belzec, Maianek, and Auschwitz. We believe that all persecutions—no matter how severe—will come to an end, and so we endure . . . to save the remnant. But if someone doesn't do something— take some action, intervene—there won't be a remnant.*

Sarah screamed inside herself. *Hitler doesn't want some of our property; he wants it all! He doesn't want to exterminate some of our people; he wants to annihilate every Jew from the face of Europe! And will America be next after Europe?*

Sarah thought of the Jews in America. Anti-Semitism was also there. That was the reason American politicians only allowed a tenth of the quota of Jews to immigrate. Yet, Sarah sighed, *our people have fared better in America than anywhere else.*

The Jews in America were separated by a wide ocean from the atrocities of Hitler—an ocean that kept their eyes from seeing the human ash darkening the heavens, reminding those drenched in its rain that humanity is but dust. The geographical distance, along with material prosperity, gave many American Jews a callousness Sarah did not like. *And I, even I, am weary of struggling to exist—of struggling to return to the land given me by my husband. At times I'm too weary to think of all that it will take to fight the nations and establish a homeland where our people are not persecuted any longer simply because they are Jews.*

Sarah reached up unthinkingly and felt the band encircling her arm with the yellow Star of David. Never, never did she dream she would be made to wear such a thing. To be set apart by her husband's laws and commandments was one thing, but to be set apart and marked by an enemy was another!

"Sarah."

The old rabbi's eyes were open again. His eyelids were like window shades that would roll only halfway up.

"Yes, Rabbi Moses."

"We must look for a place to hide you. You must become a *diver.*"

"Rabbi Moses, forgive me, but I don't know what a diver is."

Aaron spoke. "A diver, Sarah, is a person who goes into hiding."

"But rabbi, I cannot go into hiding. I *must* get back to Israel. I can't find Saul. I've tried—you know I have. You and your son Aaron have tried; Jews all over Germany have tried. Now I must go home. There must be a way, there has to—" Sarah broke off abruptly. She realized she was going on and on while they listened patiently.

"Sarah," Rabbi Moses sat up in the tattered old chair covered with heavy green damask and faded with the years just like the man who sat on it, "I know it is not your nature to hide, but if you ever intend to return to Israel, you must hide! You must dive out of sight. Hide in the storm cellar until the tornado passes. We, too—my son and I—are going to be divers. In fact, we are so thankful you came now. Had it been two days later, we would not have been here. And no one would be able to tell you where we went."

Sarah, now docile, listened. She was worn out. Getting out of Germany had been an ordeal beyond her limits of comprehension. She was so thankful she had sent Aaron on to Israel. That is, *if* he had made it. And now she wondered about the whole idea of hiding because of her experience in fleeing Germany. Sarah's nerves were fragile, her emotions volatile. And she didn't like it. It scared her to be this way. Now she wished she had abandoned the search for Saul sooner and left Holland when the borders were still open into Belgium. Or that she had crossed the sea to England; at least the British were offering some resistance to Hitler. Churchill finally had seen the madness in the leader of the Third Reich.

Sarah knew Winston Churchill had to be incredibly embarrassed that he had once heralded Hitler's accomplishments as being among the most remarkable in the history of the world. Now Churchill wanted to bomb the German concentration camps where Jews by the thousands were being exterminated each day. But no one would listen to him. Not England, not America. Had Sarah been in England, she would have stormed the Parliament, agreeing with Churchill and saying, "Do it; do not delay!" Then she would have departed for Israel. But not without first taking the British to task for their traitorous White Papers.

These White Papers contradicted the Balfour Declaration, which expressed approval on the part of the British for the establishment of a national home for Jewish people in Palestine. The White Papers, which restricted the immigration of the Jewish people, were written just to placate the Arabs. All because the Arabs assisted England in World War I in exchange for a piece of Sarah's land! Just thinking about it made Sarah furious! And being furious made her even more emotional...and tired.

The rabbi talked on. Sarah stood up. Resigning herself to the fact that the situation demanded she must become a diver, she determined she would learn how.

Aaron rose also. His father continued to ramble, but then, it was his age...and the wear and tear of years of negotiating for the rights and recognition of Jewish people in Holland. Rights that the Jews in Holland had enjoyed for a long time.

The Dutch could not have been kinder to the Jews. Holland had been a wonderful place for them to live. This was, in part, because of his father's wisdom and perseverance. But now that Hitler had taken Holland, life would be different. Terribly different. Yet Aaron knew the hearts of the Dutch people. Many would help the divers, including many in the church. The Dutch were different than the Germans.

"We'll be in touch with you tomorrow evening, Sarah, to give you instructions," said Rabbi Moses. "In fact, can you come at five o'clock? Then we shall all dive."

Assuring them that she would be there, Sarah pulled on her heavy coat, donned her beret, and left hurriedly. Frightened by her fragile emotions, she had one objective—to get home as quickly as possible. The sound of her heels clicking on the cobblestones scared her. Sarah glanced nervously over her shoulder almost continuously as she made her way to the house she'd rented upon arriving in Amsterdam. Fear seized her mind each time footsteps echoed behind her. She wanted to run, but forced herself to walk. Every time someone approached from the opposite direction, she dropped her head. When Sarah finally reached her house, she hurried in, bolted the door, and pulled all the shades. There she sat motionless in the dark for what seemed to be hours.

Is the punishment for my years—our years—of disobedience not enough? Are there yet more dregs to be consumed as I drink from my husband's chalice of judgment?

Indeed, the cup would be tipped yet higher. But it was a cup not without purpose. The hands that had given her the cup bore the brand marks of a covenant he had made and would never revoke.

Chapter 59

*F*illed with anxiety, Sarah stepped out the door. The sun's bright radiance made her wince. It was a little after four, and there were no clouds in the sky to filter the sun. The only clouds were in Sarah's heart. After she had arrived home last night she had locked and hidden herself in the house, and since then not a shade had been lifted nor a curtain moved. If Sarah hadn't been out of food, she would not have ventured out even now. Instead she would have run straight to Rabbis Moses and Aaron and then right back home until she went diving, as the rabbis called it. Even the thought of diving terrified her. Whom could she trust? What Gentile would risk his life and security for a Jew?

Sarah kept her head down. She was afraid to look up or be noticed. She had heard tales of Jewish women being snatched off the streets by lust-filled soldiers who dragged their victims into alleys and played with, tormented, and humiliated them. Despite their cries for help, no one dared to come to their rescue. Sarah knew Germans were forbidden to know Jews sexually; Aryan blood was not to be tainted. But no regulation existed to keep them from sadistically making sport of Jewish women.

"Look, I said!" a man shouted coldly, tauntingly. "Look at him!"

Sarah froze, her body shaking. At first she thought the command had been directed at her. Fearfully she raised her eyes, and then her head. The voice was so loud, so intrusive, she was surprised to find that the one giving the orders was standing some meters away.

"Look at him and laugh," he screamed, his voice reaching an unnatural pitch, "or you will be doing the same thing!" He then let out a string of profanities.

About fifty meters away, Sarah saw a German officer with his back toward her, waving his gun in the air. He was screaming at a group of terrified onlookers, all of whom wore arm bands bearing the yellow Star of David. It was obvious they didn't want to look at the spectacle before them.

Sarah looked and saw an old rabbi on his hands and knees sweeping the street with his long white beard. *Rabbi Moses!* Sarah thought with alarm. Nausea and fear swept over her.

"Laugh! Or I'll kill you and give this rabbi your blood to help him mop the street!"

With that, the officer pointed his gun at an elderly woman standing to his right and fired just above her head.

Two of the women in the group screamed involuntarily as the gun went off. Forcing out unnatural sounds, the people feigned laughter. Weakly. Nervously. Guiltily. But there were also tears. Their laughter disintegrated into sobs.

"If that doesn't make you Jewish swine laugh, what about this?" the officer put his polished boot on Rabbi Moses' rear and, with a violent push, sent him sprawling on the ground. The rabbi's face scraped against the rough cobblestones, tearing his frail skin. Then the officer raised his foot again, intending to bring it down on top of the old rabbi's hatless head. Sarah could stand it no longer. She darted toward the soldier.

A hand firmly grasped her left arm, propelling her to the right, down an alley. Her captor then wrapped an arm around her shoulders and covered her mouth with a hand. Stunned into submission, Sarah kept walking. Sarah couldn't see her abductor, whose face was covered with a scarf. The abductor leaned near Sarah's face as if they were close friends having a confidential talk. The woman's voice was low. "You can do nothing but get yourself killed. Rabbi Moses would not want that. Don't say a word. Just listen! You are to come with me. You can *not* go home. They are searching for you. You left your house just in time. I was coming to Rabbi Moses' home to take you diving. I know your name is Sarah."

As they walked the woman periodically glanced from side to side, but in a natural way. "As much as you are able, you must trust me. Otherwise you will not be safe."

"But the rabbi—"

"No talking now! In a moment we're going to stop very quickly. You must be absolutely still. I have to be certain no one is following us. When we stop, don't speak. Just listen carefully. If you hear anything—anything at all—nod your head."

"Now," the woman said tersely.

They stopped in unison, like a drill team, and waited. There was silence. Blessed silence.

Then just as quickly the woman ordered Sarah to resume walking. They turned down a side street lined with trees.

"Look to your right. Do you see anyone?"

"No one," Sarah could barely get out the words.

"This is it. We're almost there." For the first time, the abductor looked Sarah full in the face. She smiled as she reached up, removed the scarf from her head, and draped it casually over Sarah's shoulder, covering the Star of David on her coat. "Now, you must walk straight through the front door of the house where I am taking you. Climb the staircase in front of you just as if you owned the place. When you reach the top of the stairs, at the second landing, enter through the first door on your right. Do *not* stop to talk to anyone. And walk with your head up! Act as if you are totally familiar with your surroundings. Make yourself comfortable. This will be your home until I can find a way to get you out of Holland."

Out of Holland! For the first time since leaving Rabbi Moses' home last night, hope stirred somewhere deep within Sarah. "But I thought Rabbi Moses said—"

"We can't talk now, Sarah. I must get you off the streets immediately. After you go to your room and I make sure everything is safe inside the house and that we have no unexpected visitors, we will talk. Now, let's go up these stairs into the house. Casually, but quickly."

The woman breathed heavily as they walked up the steep steps on the front of the tall brick rowhouse. She was short of breath from talking. "Remember," she whispered, "second landing, first door on the right."

The moment they entered the house, the woman turned to the left. Opening the tall wooden doors, she shouted, "I'm home . . . and I'm starving. Do we have company or may we eat?"

Sarah proceeded to climb the steps, looking straight ahead just as she had been told to do. She thought she heard Ruth sigh when a woman's voice from inside the house answered back, "We're alone."

Sarah wondered, as she turned to ascend the second flight of stairs, if they were speaking in some kind of a code to one another. When she reached the second landing, she entered the first door on the right. Once she was in the room, she suddenly realized how very spent she was. She hadn't slept more than one or two hours the night before. Feeling her strength ebbing, Sarah sat down on the bed. She remembered the woman's encouragement that she make herself comfortable. Giving in to her weariness, Sarah decided to lie down for a few minutes.

The woman woke her two hours later. "I am so sorry to wake you but you must eat something now." She paused. "And I know I haven't introduced myself to you yet. My name is Ruth."

Sarah sat up on the bed. A tantalizing smell drifted up from the small tureen containing potato and leek soup. Slices of warm, soft brown bread with a large chunk of butter covered a blue and white plate of the same design as the tureen. The food was invitingly arranged on a silver tray placed on her bedside table. Three pale peach tulips in a blue and white vase graced the tray. Next to the vase was another silver tray bearing a china teapot hidden by the cozy coverlet designed to keep it warm. On the lace doily sat a smaller teapot filled with hot water and a delicately shaped teacup decorated with dainty flowers that looked like they had been gathered from an old English garden.

Sarah sat for a moment without speaking—drinking in the pleasures, beauty, and decorum of a life gone by, a life lost to her. A life she almost forgot had ever existed. Sarah lifted the pretty china tea strainer and, placing it over her cup, poured herself some tea. She felt as if she had been transported to another country and another time. Then Sarah remembered she had no friend to share all this with. She was all alone. Cut off. None of her loved ones knew where she was or whether she was alive.

Sarah studied Ruth. Was this some hideous plot by a Gentile who wanted to lure her into Hitler's snare? Ruth was an ideal Aryan. Her eyes were blue, almost the same blue as that painted on the china. Her hair was a lovely blond. Her skin was fair, smooth, poreless. Why would an attractive woman who lived in a house like this—with all the amenities anyone could desire—risk her freedom and possibly her life to rescue a Jew? Sarah was puzzled.

Ruth placed the silver tray on a walnut washstand next to the wall opposite the bed. Then, sitting on the foot of the bed, Ruth folded her slender hands together. Looking gently at Sarah, she asked, "May we talk for a few minutes? I should first explain where you will spend the night. Because the Nazis are known for invading people's homes any time they please, especially if they think we might be sympathetic to the Jews, you cannot sleep in an ordinary bed. They know the only two people who live here are my blind mother and myself. As of yet, our house is not set up for emergency drills and other precautions like some of the other hiding places are. In fact, you are the first diver we've taken in. As soon as we are prepared, we'll have more of your people living in our home. But that requires time and a great deal of covert construction. However, Sarah—may I call you Sarah?"

"Of course. And may I call you Ruth? I like the name. It is in our Bible."

"I know. My mother specifically chose the name for me from the book of Ruth. Mother believes that names are significant. That is why the Lord named people the way he did, like changing Abram to Abraham, and Sarai to Sarah."

Sarah looked at Ruth quizzically. "Excuse me, but you appear to be pure Aryan. I was wondering why you would risk your life for one Jew. Now I understand."

"Understand what?"

"That you have Jewish blood in you. That you are part Jew and that's why you're helping me."

Hands still folded, Ruth looked at Sarah. Bending her head to one side she looked up at the ceiling for a moment. Then she looked at Sarah again, a smile radiating through her eyes as well as on the gentle turn of her lips. Impishly she told Sarah, "I am pure Aryan, but I have a love—a deep love—and obligation to the Jews. I am willing to risk my life, as you say, for one Jew because one Jew gave his life for me."

Then looking Sarah straight in the eyes, Ruth's words suddenly became very sober. "I am a Christian, Sarah. A true Christian. Not like those who over the years professed Christianity while killing Jews. I am one who knows the Word of God—your Bible and mine." Ruth hesitated for a moment, wondering how to explain herself without giving Sarah the impression she was sheltering her for the purpose of proselytizing her. "I don't want to offend you," Ruth noticed Sarah stiffening, "but I want you to understand where my heart is. When someone claims to believe Jesus is the Christ, or Messiah, as you would say, and accepts him as such, then that person has an obligation to love and care for God's chosen people, the Jews. How can one say, 'I love God' and not love the people God loves?"

Sarah swung her legs over the side of the bed and stood up. "You took me in to try and convert me, didn't you?" she said sharply. "I would think Rabbi Moses would have used more discernment in his screening process. I don't mean to be rude, but—"

Sarah stopped when she saw that Ruth's head was bowed. Sarah watched her intently, almost angrily. She could see Ruth tighten her lips, then, after a long moment, let them relax again. Sarah felt betrayed, yet she was also confused by this woman's sacrifice. And embarrassed because of her quick retort. Sarah felt a strange mix of feelings inside her, but more than anything else, she felt awkward.

"I am sorry, Ruth. I don't mean to be rude, but I don't belong here. Maybe there is someone else you can help."

Ruth's silence made Sarah uncomfortable. She wished Ruth would say something. Awkwardly, she started to walk past Ruth toward the bedroom door, wondering where she should go.

Ruth looked up with teary eyes and gently placed her hand on Sarah's arm. "Sarah, wait. Please wait. Please forgive me. This was not a subject I intended to address unless it came up naturally. My prayer, my fervent prayer, is that I might simply be used of God to—to—" Ruth was trying to control her voice but she was having trouble quelling the emotions rising inside her so she could get the words out. "I want to be used of God . . . to do this unto the Christ I believe in, for—for—" Ruth was choking as she spoke, "for he said if I did it unto you, a Jew, then I—I—was doing it—to him."

Sarah could see the deep blue of Ruth's eyes churning beneath the surface of her tears.

Ruth continued, "You—you asked. Don't you understand? You asked, Sarah. Or I wouldn't have brought this up. . . ."

Ruth covered her eyes with her hands. Her body racked convulsively as she tried to suppress her sobbing. "I've—I've failed! My very first time, and I've failed. Rabbi Moses . . . he trusted me. But he wa-was concerned—because I didn't have any—" Ruth kept swallowing, laboring to talk, "experience. But things were so—bad. And he—he couldn't find any—any—"

Bitterly ashamed of herself, Sarah reached over and pulled Ruth's heaving form to her chest. Instantly Ruth's arms returned Sarah's embrace as she continued crying. Sarah couldn't explain why, but now she felt at peace. She knew she could stay. She had peered into the windows of Ruth's soul, and she trusted what she saw. Sarah had never met a woman like Ruth before.

As Sarah held her rescuer, she began to realize the strain Ruth must be under—taking so great a risk for her as well as caring for a blind mother.

Then Sarah's thoughts went to another Gentile, also named Ruth—a woman who long ago had pleaded with another Jewish woman, "Do not urge me to leave you or turn back from following you; for where you go, I will go, and where you lodge, I will lodge. Your people shall be my people, and your God, my God. Where you die, I will die."

Sarah patted Ruth's head, attempting to comfort her. Then in a sudden, inexplicable surge of love, Sarah drew Ruth closer. *I wonder, Ruth—will you die because of me?*

Chapter 60

*T*hey were wonderful, delightful days of respite. An oasis in a desert of the shifting sands of Jewish exploitation and anti-Semitism. Sarah and Ruth became the best of friends. They were like two young girls at a slumber party who practiced their game of hide-and-seek every day.

Sarah received immediate affirmation of Ruth's sincerity when, on the morning following her arrival, they quietly made their way downstairs for breakfast and Sarah saw a kosher kitchen. There were two sinks, two sets of dishes and two sets of silverware. Of course one set was in the kitchen and the other was in the dining room so as to not draw suspicion. *Besides,* Sarah thought as she walked cautiously through the house, *in a house this grand and so beautifully furnished one could expect more than one sink. A second sink in the pantry could easily be explained to inquiring authorities, as well as the extra silver and china.*

Even after Sarah had been with Ruth and her mother for two weeks, she never tired of entering the parlor and basking in the aura of its elegance. The rich, heavy damask draperies provided a suspicionless cover for the long narrow windows. Sarah looked about her as she stood surrounded by beautiful antiques. A fireplace with a high mantel was crowned by a painting that looked as if it had been done by one of the old masters.

In her mind, Sarah stepped back into another world—a world she had forgotten. A world described to her by the wealthier, more successful Jews who had won acclaim through their great achievements in business, finance, literature, philosophy, science, the arts, and sometimes politics. Sarah had not moved in such realms of luxury since the day she rebelliously shook her fist in her husband's face, closed her ears against his words, and walked down the road to meet her Chaldean lover. *What a great cost! What a tragic, painful, awful cost!*

"Sarah? Sarah!" Ruth's mother called out softly. "Are you in here, my dear?"

"Yes, Mrs. Vandermer. I'm here, enjoying the beauty of your home."

The dear old lady, elegantly dressed, stood with her hand on the walnut threshold of the parlor, looking around the room as if her blind eyes could still see everything. "It is beautiful, isn't it? It's etched in my memory. The Lord blessed my husband greatly in both the jewelry and the clock business. Two businesses! My, how they kept him busy! It seemed everyone wanted our jewelry and our clocks. He employed mostly Jews, you know." Mrs. Vandermer extended her hand in Sarah's direction. "Excuse me if I offend you using the word Jew. It is said so wickedly these days I find myself wanting to find another word that will show my respect for you. Shall I call you Israelites?"

"No, ma'am. You are kind, but to refer to us as Jews is acceptable to me. I know what I am and I know the term was coined simply to identify us as those taken from Judea in the captivity. But I do appreciate your sensitivity, Mrs. Vandermer. Thank you."

What a gracious lady! Sarah thought. *She must have been a beauty in her younger days, for she is still beautiful now despite her age.* The skin gracefully draping her face was delicately soft, almost transparent. Her hair was a pure, soft white. A single strand of lustrous pearls encircled her neck. The soft, blue-gray color of her dress was accented with a broach and earrings fashioned from richly colored amethysts surrounded by tiny seed pearls.

"Oh dear!" Mrs Vandermer said in slight self-disgust. "I was to tell you to come upstairs immediately. Ruth says you must not linger downstairs. You need to be close to the bed in case anyone comes. Now, we're not going to do so well with this little project if I don't do what I am supposed to do, are we?"

Sarah smiled, forgetting that Mrs. Vandermer was blind.

"Now hurry, dear, hurry. Or you will get me in trouble!"

And with that Mrs. Vandermer walked over to the long walnut stairway. The wide steps were covered with a Karastan runner, and each step had a brass rod that helped to hold the carpet tight. The runner muffled the sound of people's footsteps, which could be either good or bad—depending on who was listening. Ruth had told Sarah she was praying about whether she should take up the carpet or leave it down. She didn't want her mother to slip on the wooden steps, but then if soldiers unexpectedly raided the house, she wanted to be able to hear them coming up the stairs.

"Sarah," Mrs. Vandermer began, then stopped. "Oh, there I go again. They told me for your safety I'm not supposed to call you by name. Will I ever learn? Forgive me, dear, forgive me," Mrs. Vandermer muttered.

Sarah patted Mrs. Vandermer on the back as she passed her on the way up the stairs. "Don't worry. For now it is just me. You'll learn."

Sarah climbed about five more steps then turned around. "Mrs. Vandermer, what will you do if you get caught?"

Without hesitation the older woman answered, "Sarah, you know the Almighty does according to his will in the army of heaven and among the inhabitants of the earth. None can stop his hand or say to him, 'What are you doing?' That is written in the book of Daniel, and I believe it. Now, run upstairs before I get in trouble with Ruth."

Sarah paused as she opened the door to Ruth's bedroom. Never had she been in a more beautiful bedroom in all her life. She loved it—from the lace curtains bordering the windows to the carved dresser with its triple mirrors to the massive but majestic four-poster bed with its elegant carvings and plush mattress suspended high off the floor. The high legs of the bed and its wooden skirt were covered with two layers of dust ruffles. A little walnut stool stood beside it, ready to assist those who would crawl up into the bed and its world of mammoth pillows covered in skillfully embroidered linen cutwork. Some of the pillows were large enough to lean on, others were small, edged in delicate lace or tatting, simply there to delight the eyes. Everything was white linen and lace, giving the aura of sitting in a garden of baby's breath.

"Where have you been, Sarah?" Ruth's voice was strained. "Haven't I told you that you must come up immediately after we eat? As it is, we are already taking a chance. I know you think you can hide deep in the pantry if necessary, but I just don't think it is safe. I'm nervous. Informers are everywhere. Some divers were discovered last night. And, if the Germans came to the front door, you would be trapped down there."

"Ruth, they aren't going to see anything through those heavy velvet curtains over the windows and the front door. And you know how quickly I can get up these stairs."

"But what if you slip or fall? I would never forgive myself for not being more vigilant."

"Wait a minute," Sarah snapped. "I don't want you to say that again. Our agreement is if we are caught, we are caught. We did the best we could."

"But," Ruth was edgy, "if you don't cooperate, then we haven't done the best *we* could."

"You are right, but let's not get sidetracked. I want to be sure we both understand. We may not agree on who Messiah is, but we both agree that no one can thwart what the Almighty plans. I am not going to die, Ruth; I just know I am not going to die. I have a future."

Ruth smiled and pointed to the bed. "Right now your immediate future is under that bed. Now get to it. We have to practice. See if you can beat yesterday's time." Ruth had her father's pocket watch in her hand. "Ready, set, go!" she said, injecting a tone of urgency in her voice.

Sarah fell to the floor and slid under the lace and linen dust ruffles to the center of the bed, feeling for the flat sliding door. Slipping it open, she reached up, grabbed an iron bar, and pulled herself up into the wooden box. This wasn't one of her favorite drills; she hated being confined into such a small place. Sarah thought the idea ingenious and was impressed with the carpenter's work, but she felt like she was in a coffin buried under Ruth's mattress with its linen sheets and down comforter. At least the box was deep, so she did have room to turn. At night she often found herself sleeping on her stomach, her nose in one of the breathing holes.

Just when Sarah thought it would be safe to come out again the doorbell chimed. Ruth jumped. Falling quickly to the floor, she lifted the dust ruffles as if Sarah could see her and said, "I'm not expecting anyone. Don't move. Stay there until I tell you everything is all right."

The chimes sounded again, followed by rapid, furious pounding. Ruth could hear shouting. She ran to the window and peered out the lace curtain. A car marked with a swastika was parked at the curb. The engine was still running, and a German soldier was sitting at the wheel. Ruth couldn't see the front door from her window because the inset of the front door obscured her view. Rushing to the bed she dropped to the floor and whispered loudly, "It's the Germans! Pray! I love you, Sarah; you're like a sister to me. I love you."

Ruth scrambled to her feet and walked slowly, purposefully to the door of her bedroom. The front door chimes rang incessantly. Ruth paused. Taking a deep breath to bring herself under control, she murmured, "They'll never find her in that bed. Never! I know they won't."

As Ruth descended the stairs to the front door, she knew her mother was in the kitchen, praying. Ruth had forbidden her to go to the door; she didn't want some Nazi smashing her against the wall in anger or frustration. Taking another deep breath, Ruth ran her fingers through her hair as if combing it, smiled, and opened the door.

Ruth clutched to the doorknob for support. For a moment, she thought she would faint from fear. Two tall, irate German soldiers nearly filled the doorway. Both were officers, as evidenced by the epaulets on their well-tailored uniforms with brass buttons. Hatred glowered at her from beneath the visors of hats brandishing the German emblem. But what made Ruth's blood rush to the knot in her stomach was the man standing behind them. It was Rolf, the carpenter who had made the bed.

Rolf's face was black and blue with an angry red puffiness under his left eye, which was swollen shut. Blood still oozed from the cut on his head near his hairline. His left ear was badly swollen and his nose looked broken, as did the fingers of his right hand, which he cradled gingerly with his left hand. Ruth wondered if his shoulder or right arm was also broken.

The officer on Ruth's left reached behind him, never removing his eyes from Ruth's. Grabbing Rolf by the collar of his wool coat he threw him into the foyer. "This man has some fine carpentry work to show us," said the officer in a voice laden with sarcasm. "If a terrible accident had not broken his hand so that he can no longer hold his tools, we might—after seeing his work—have asked him to make something for us."

"Show us your work!" The same officer who had grabbed him by the collar pushed Rolf towards the stairs. Then he turned around. Jerking Ruth by the arm, he pushed her into Rolf. "You will come too. We want to see your beautiful bed."

The other officer remained behind as they walked up the stairs. Patting what looked like a rubber truncheon in his hand and never speaking a word, he walked to his right and looked in the parlor. Then turning slowly—almost pensively—to his left, he walked into the dining room, and surveyed his surroundings as if inspecting the house.

Ruth caught herself on the banister as she was thrown into Rolf. For a moment their eyes met. Neither said a word. Rolf's bloodshot right eye, the only one he could open, was shrouded in remorse. Ruth comforted him with a slight smile, trying to make her eyes speak the words, "I understand."

Rolf stumbled to Ruth's bedroom door and stood mutely before it, his head lowered towards the floor. Bowing his head made his eye throb more, but even so, in his shame he could not bear to look anywhere but down. He did not want to see anyone's face or look into anyone's eyes. He had broken down under torture—he had given in—because he could not bear to see them beat his wife and son anymore with their hard rubber truncheons.

The officer leaned forward, opened the bedroom door, and called over his shoulder as he walked into the room. "Wagner, get up here! You did not make your bed!" His laugh was cruel. He was pleased with his joke.

At that moment, Sarah knew her hiding place was known to these officers. She determined not to resist. The minute her suspicions were confirmed in another way, she would come out from hiding. She did not want to be taken away with broken bones because a bed came crashing in on her, nor did she want to endanger Ruth and her mother even more. Quietly, slowly, inch by inch, Sarah slid the trap door open.

Wagner yelled back, "In just a minute. I have to get the axe."

Ruth could hear Wagner shouting something out the front door. She supposed he was calling to their driver to bring the axe in.

The officer looked around. "What a beautiful room you have." As he walked to the bed, he removed his glove and felt the border of one of the large pillows. Leaning over to look at it more closely, he said, "Linen. Very fine linen. Belgium...or maybe Swiss? Beautiful cutwork. Expensive. This was very costly." He set his truncheon on the bed and put his leather glove back on. Then, picking up the truncheon and slapping it into his other hand, he crossed the room and looked out the lace curtain. "Fine lace. Ah, he's coming with the axe." Ruth didn't say a word; Rolf's face was still cast to the floor.

The officer walked back towards the bed and stopped. He was in no hurry; he was enjoying tormenting his prey. "This bed is an antique, is it not?" He ran his gloved hand over the carved posts. "I have never seen one quite like this. Was it specially made for you?"

Ruth did not answer.

"Maybe you didn't hear me." His voice became louder as he asked again, "Was it specially made for you?"

Ruth wondered how Wagner was treating her mother. She hadn't heard a sound. At least she didn't hear any crying. "My parents left it to me," Ruth answered carefully just in case her mother had somehow managed to escape detection. Ruth prayed fervently that she had. Although she longed for a peaceful death for her eighty-year-old mother, both mother and daughter realized their new venture would make that unlikely.

Just then the soldier who'd been waiting in the car entered the room, axe in hand. "Colonel Wagner told me to bring it up. He's still looking to make sure no one else is in the house."

"Then, Dedrick," the officer's voice was strained as he pulled on the mattress, sending pillows, comforter, and linens sliding with it to the floor, "break it open, and let's see what treasure has been hidden under this mattress."

Dedrick raised the axe above his head. Rolf dropped his chin further into his chest. The light from the window etched his beaten, defeated silhouette, illuminating the tears falling from his eyes.

As Ruth opened her mouth to shout, "No!" She saw Sarah sliding undetected from beneath the bed. Quickly, to distract the officer, Ruth moved to the end of the bed, grabbed the post, and screamed into his face, "Why do you have to ruin a perfectly beautiful antique bed, you—you—" Ruth groped for a word that would turn his attention to her as the stunned soldier still held the axe questioningly above his head. "You swine! You Nazi swine!" Ruth screamed the words with all the force she could muster as Sarah slithered on her stomach towards the open door.

Furious, the German officer swung his truncheon at Ruth, pinning her head against the massive bedpost. For a brief moment her blue eyes flashed open, then closed slowly as she slipped to the floor, leaving a trail of blood on the white linen duvet at her feet.

Sarah was down the carpeted stairs in a flash, her hand sliding down the banister. The front door was open. She prayed the car was empty. Dedrick was upstairs with his axe; maybe there were no other soldiers.

Just as Sarah hit the bottom stair, Wagner emerged from the parlor he had been admiring. As he walked he was tapping his truncheon in his hand just as he did with his riding stick. It was a habit. The instant he saw Sarah, he moved with the reflex of a well-trained soldier, caught Sarah's long black hair, and clubbed her with the truncheon. Sarah dropped to the floor, unconscious. "I got her," he yelled.

The axe fell on the bed. A gun fired. The bone-chilling sound echoed . . . just once. The officer and Dedrick walked out of Ruth's bedroom and down the stairs with deadly detachment. For a moment the Nazis paused in front of Sarah's form while the officer examined his uniform to see if any blood had gotten on it. Looking at Wagner, he said, "Any others?"

"No, they must have been alone."

"I shot the carpenter. Dedrick, drag this Jewish whore to the car. We'll take her with us."

Dedrick grabbed Sarah's arms and dragged her down the rough brick stairs outside, scraping her legs and back. As Dedrick struggled to lift her dead weight into the car, he became angry. He knew what the officers were doing; he had to do all the work while they scrutinized their victim's treasures, determining which they wanted to add to their private collections.

Wagner closed the door to the house. The two men, backs ramrod straight, clipped down the steps with a pompous attitude of self-importance. "Where will this one go?" Wagner asked, pointing to Sarah with his truncheon.

The officer opened the car door and slid into the front seat opposite Dedrick, motioning him to drive on. As he closed the door, he answered, "If she lives, most likely she will be sent to Auschwitz."

Chapter 61

*T*he rigidly fixed order of day and night remained. But Sarah could not remember what day it was. *Was today the sixth, or the fifth of the month?* Sarah watched the morning light peeking through the slats of the wooden prison transporting her by rail across Germany to . . . where? The Germans called the cattle cars *waggonen*. Keeping time with the rhythmic clicking of the train wheels, Sarah's mind repeated Jeremiah's words regarding the order of day and night: *If this fixed order departs from before me, declares the Lord, then the offspring of Israel also shall cease from being a nation before me.* Recalling her husband's promises helped Sarah fend off the overwhelming despair crushing her spirit as she considered the improbability of emerging from the rail car alive.

Three days—maybe four—had passed since she'd had any water. Her lips were cracked and hard; her throat was swollen almost shut. Her tongue now filled her mouth. Sarah wished it would rain again. The rain made them damp and chilly, but it also brought a blessed wetness through the slats, cracks, and the little windows in the roof. The rain had been the very life of many of the captives. To others it was the hastening of death—the nudge their fevered bodies needed to push them out life's door.

Thankfully, Sarah was positioned in the corner of the boxcar. She had licked the damp wood where a leak in the top corner sent a tiny rivulet of life-sustaining water down the side of the car. Unlike the others, she had no baggage for exile, no small bundle of treasures, no necessities—not even a coat. She had nothing to use as a pillow, a wedge of comfort between her head and the slats of the car. She longed for something to hold, to possess. All she had were the same clothes that covered her the day the German officer clubbed her on the head and dragged her from Ruth's home.

What became of Ruth and her mother Sarah didn't know. Each time she asked, the SS officer struck her with his hand and screamed, *"Blode lumpen"*— idiotic whore. Finally, Sarah stopped asking. With deep sadness in her heart, she knew she would never have the opportunity to thank Ruth one last time for risking her own life to save Sarah's. *Did you lose your life, Ruth, while mine has yet been spared?* Sarah closed her eyes, remembering again the night they first met. *Do not urge me to leave you . . . your people shall be my people . . . your God, my God . . . where you die. . . .*

Sarah had eaten nothing since her last delightful breakfast with Ruth and Mrs. Vandermer. For several days after her incarceration, Sarah savored that breakfast over and over again in her mind, trying to remember just how the eggs, bread, jam, and orange juice tasted. Now Sarah wondered if she even had the strength to lift food to her mouth if something were to be given to her.

The stench in the boxcar was becoming unbearable. All about Sarah the living were sleeping with the dead. *Maybe the Germans will have mercy on us,* she thought. *Maybe they will stop the train and let us walk and stretch legs that feel as if they might never move again. And maybe they will remove the dead.*

How many people had been packed into their car? Was it eighty-five? Or had they pushed in more—ninety, ninety-five? What had the soldiers said when they shoved everyone through the opening and then slammed the rolling door shut? Sarah tried to remember. She could still hear the echo of the lock being snapped. Then came the endless hours of sitting and waiting for the train to get underway. The atmosphere had become stifling hot. The air refused to move—just like the bodies that were too tightly packed into the boxcar.

Bad became worse as the stench of diarrhea reeked in the air. Everyone shared the humiliation of losing their privacy in caring for the normal functions of their bodies. All human dignity had been stripped from them. What were they to do? Then a resourceful woman thought to donate the cooking pot she had brought with her, and a rabbi made an encouraging speech about the natural, God-given functions of the body. He said they must not be ashamed.

When the train finally began moving, the pot was emptied through the little window at the top of the wagon. An elderly man began intoning the shema and the others joined him. *"Sh'ma Yisroel, Adonai, Elohenu, Adonai ehad!"* Hear, O Israel! The Lord is our God, the Lord is one!

After seemingly endless days, the train finally reached its destination. Before the lock could be removed from the door, a boy who had hoisted himself to the window cried out, "Auschwitz! The sign says Auschwitz!"

Some people in the boxcar were convinced he was mistaken, and told him so. "We are Dutch and German Jews. The Germans wouldn't take us all the way to Poland—to Auschwitz! That's where the Poles are taken!" Some began to cry. Others clutched their children close about them, speaking soothing assurances. Some optimistically gathered their remaining earthly treasures, prodding their children to not leave anything behind. They would need all they had brought.

Then the door slid open. Men in striped suits with little striped caps resting on heads almost devoid of hair reached in with emaciated arms to pull them out. Some of the striped suits jumped into the boxcar to push them out. A mother with a tiny baby over her shoulder tried frantically to crawl back into the boxcar as a striped suit pulled her back. "But I forgot the diapers! I have no diapers!" she shrieked.

For just a moment grief flickered across the eyes of the striped suit. Then he growled, "Leave them. You won't need them."

"But I must have them," she argued. "My baby—"

With a hard shove, he pushed her into the mass of confused, broken humanity crowding the platform in front of Auschwitz.

All ages. All sizes. All shapes. All from different walks of life. Some strong, some weak, some so infirm they could hardly put one foot in front of the other. Some rich and well-dressed—even in coats of fur—bearing an air of dignity as they held suitcases deemed proper for the journey. Others were pitiful looking, scroungy, poor, coatless. They carried their possessions in sacks of their own devising. Yet all now stood on a common platform melded into one class—the miserable.

Sarah stood in the boxcar surveying the scene before her. She was the last to leave it, as she had been first to board. German soldiers and officers milled about, viewing their new arrivals with disinterest. Vicious dogs, German shepherds, strained against their leashes, struggling to break free. The dogs snarled and drooled, showing long, pointed teeth. Now and again a threatening bark sent a child fleeing to the dark safety of a mother's coat.

Sarah looked in front of her as a striped suit lifted his hand to help a young girl by the name of Rivkah out of the car. As he did, he whispered, "You are sixteen." Rivkah smiled, flattered. "I'm just tall. Only thirteen, almost fourteen."

"You are sixteen. Only sixteen-year-olds live," he said quietly through his teeth.

Rivkah had made the journey alone. Separated from her mother at the train station, she had wept for days afterward until there were no more tears left in her dehydrated body. Sarah had watched her huddling in the opposite corner of the boxcar. Whenever Sarah had been able to catch Rivkah's eye, she sent her a loving smile.

As Sarah's feet hit the platform she saw that the women were being separated from the men and herded into a line just for females. Sarah stared, horrified, as sons were ripped from their mother's arms and husbands and wives tearfully called to one another. Those who attempted to secure one last embrace, one last goodbye, were struck to the ground.

Unable to hold his anger, a husband leaped at an SS officer who was mercilessly beating his wife across her face with a walking cane while she screamed and squirmed on the ground in an attempt to shield their baby. The officer promptly shot him.

Sarah pushed her way towards Rivkah. Putting her arm around her shoulders, she whispered, "I will help you look for your mother later. You must not break line, dear. It could cost your life . . . or your mother's. Remember now, if anyone asks your age, you are sixteen."

A German officer stood at the head of the women's line. He was flanked by two soldiers holding snarling black doberman pinschers on short leashes. The dogs clawed the air, straining to be loosed. One by one, in a dispassionate manner, the SS officer divided the women using the black leather riding stick in his hand. Sarah watched carefully. Mothers with babies or children went to the left, along with the old women and those who were extremely weak or infirm. Whenever the women being separated tried to cling to each other, the officer became enraged. Yet at other times when women pleaded to go with their sick ones, he smugly acquiesced, apparently amused at some dark secret he possessed. Inflated with his power over life and death, his own mortality was now forgotten. What these compassionate and grateful women did not know was that the privilege he had so generously granted them was their destruction in the gas chambers of Auschwitz.

In less than an hour, they would trample one another screaming, crying as they pushed and clawed for their final breath of life. In a matter of minutes mothers would rock their children, pulling them to their breast to quiet and shelter them from the gas pouring from the shower heads above. Before long, all those directed to the left would be dead. But Sarah did not know this . . . then. She simply watched and wondered what their destiny held.

Rivkah looked at the officer and hesitated as she said, "I'm—I'm—"

Sarah interrupted. "Sixteen."

Rivkah said, "That's right. Sixteen." She didn't want this nice woman to get in trouble for telling a lie.

The officer questioned Sarah, pushing his riding stick against her chest. "Her mother?"

"No, her aunt."

Pointing his riding stick in the direction they were to take, he announced his verdict. "To the right."

Sarah knew from what the striped shirt had said and from the girl standing just in front of Rivkah that those going to the right would live. The young girl standing in front of Rivkah had said, "Fourteen." She was sentenced to the left.

Sarah's eyes went to the sinister motto hanging above the gate to Auschwitz. *Arbeit macht frei!*—Work makes free.

As Sarah passed through the gate into Hitler's Gehenna she heard her husband's voice: *You shall live, not die.* The words descended on her ears as if spoken from somewhere above. Sarah looked up. A gray ash floated down from the heavens. A strange odor hung in the air. Her mind went back to the destruction of Jerusalem and the smell of boiling human flesh. Sarah turned up her palm. The ash floated onto her hand. Never had she seen anything like it.

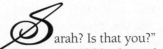

Chapter 62

"Sarah? Is that you?"

Seated on the ground outside her tunnel-like barrack, Sarah raised her hand to shield her eyes from the sun. It was difficult to see the two women standing in front of her; the sun was at their backs. For a moment she paused to study them. Her right eye was swollen almost shut. It hurt to look up, especially into the sun.

Sarah was in pain. Yesterday when she dropped a rock that her work detail was passing up the hill, the kapos had hit her. That was all it took. Just the rolling of one clumsily dropped rock, and Jacko, the overseer of their commando, was on her in a matter of seconds. His response maintained his reputation. Jacko was known as one of the most volatile and vicious of the kapos. With one blow from Jacko's hand Sarah had been sent plunging headlong down the hill. She couldn't tell whether the swelling came from the impact of his hand or from the rock on which she landed.

Who are these women? Sarah frowned. She had never seen them in her barracks. *Of course,* she reasoned, *there are endless rows of barracks in each block, and each has tiers of bunks reaching all the way to the ceiling. Maybe they're new, or maybe I missed seeing them.* Then Sarah thought about *zahlappell*—roll call. She hadn't seen them at roll call either.

Sarah was cautious. A revolt was in the making and she was part of it. Before she spoke, she wanted first to know whom she was addressing. She didn't want to endanger anyone's life, nor did she want to be found out. Too much was at stake. Too many lives.

Without answering their question, Sarah rose to her feet as she said, "The sun is blinding me. It's hard to see your faces. I've never seen you before. What are your names?" Sarah brushed the dirt off her long drab gray prison dress. The tattoo on her left arm, A-16750, was clearly visible. After what she estimated to be about three years at Auschwitz, she looked like a flat board. Her protruding bones resembled nails hammered almost through the surface of wood. Her breasts were gone, as were those of all the women detained in Auschwitz for any length of time. Famine saw to that.

The rations in the women's camp at Auschwitz consisted of a cup of black coffee in the morning, then a bowl of thick green slime—if one wasn't at the end of the line—and a daily ration of bread. Sarah was now but a shadow of the woman she had been, a skeleton covered tautly with skin and two haunting eyes peering out from their bony sockets.

Sarah waited for a response. Terribly disappointed and somewhat intimidated by this woman they had heard about and believed to be Sarah, the older woman of the two spoke in a trembling voice, "We're sorry. We just thought—"

Suddenly recognition flashed across Sarah's face. "Dusia! Dusia! Oh, my friend it is you! I can't believe it is really you!"

Falling into each other's arms, they wept in disbelief and gratitude. They had been reunited in Auschwitz, of all places! Sarah pushed Dusia back and looked at her. Laughing, she spread her arms wide. "Look at us! Is it any wonder we don't recognize each other? I haven't seen my face in a mirror for three years, but I can feel. I know there isn't a bit of fat left on my body. Nor is there on yours."

"Oh, Sarah! When you frowned at us and didn't respond, I was so disappointed. I thought my heart would break."

"Dusia, where's Miriam? She's not . . . ? She is alive, isn't she?"

"Aunt Sarah," the other woman spoke, almost indignantly. "I'm Miriam. You know me, Aunt Sarah!" Hurt was in Miriam's voice.

Sarah could sense Miriam's hurt and was horrified. Miriam looked much beyond her age but Sarah knew she couldn't let her know. "Miriam, dear, you've grown up—into womanhood! Please forgive me. I was so excited about seeing your Imma I didn't take a good look at you."

"I haven't seen myself in a mirror for two years." Miriam tried to smile, but doing so hurt her swollen, cracked lips too much. A huge sore at one corner of her mouth oozed brown liquid. Sores from the sun were scattered throughout her scalp, and her short hair was grouped in patches.

Sarah would never have recognized Dusia if she hadn't been able to see her eyes. Her once-plump little friend who so loved to cook and to eat was nothing but skin and bones. Sarah was amazed at how small her bones were.

Taking Sarah's hand and gripping it almost too tightly, Dusia asked, "I must know the truth about my Aaron. Is he here in Auschwitz? We were transferred here not too long ago, but we can't find out anything about him." Her voice trembled and her hand shook as she squeezed Sarah's even tighter. Dusia's eyes locked onto Sarah's, not letting them go. Dusia had to know the truth, no matter what it was. "Is he alive?" she asked again.

Sarah beamed the largest smile that had crossed her lips since she had been sheltered in Ruth's home in Holland. "Dusia and Miriam, I was with Aaron on *Kristallnacht* and sent him the next morning to Israel!"

Dusia covered her face and wept as Sarah continued, "And although I have not heard, I have every reason to believe that Aaron is there in the safekeeping of a close friend. As you know, your son's dream was to be in Israel. That is where I sent him as I went to Holland. It was in Holland that I was arrested, and from there I was brought here. So Aaron was spared all this."

Dusia looked up, fear creeping into her eyes. "Saul?"

"I still don't know where Saul is. But I had word that he is alive. Now, tell me about Gershom. Do you know where he is?"

"We know Abba's alive," said Miriam as she looked at Dusia. "Imma, can I tell Aunt Sarah how we know?" Miriam was trying to smile.

"Of course, of course." Dusia hungered to see Miriam experience any kind of emotion. The simple task of survival consumed all their energies. Dusia had seen how the naked horror of life in the camps left them void of emotion and passion. Each captive tended to move into her own world—a world of one, where she lived intent on her own preservation. Unless the care and responsibility of a loved one provided a sense of purpose outside herself, it was insidiously easy to become emotionally detached from every other human being.

Dusia was also relieved to have found Sarah, for now if something happened to her, then Miriam would have Sarah. Although their barracks were a distance apart, the three of them were back together, in a sense. *Maybe there's a way we can change barracks with someone,* Dusia thought.

Miriam launched into her story. "Some of us had the idea of taking scraps of paper wherever we found them and writing names and notes on them. Then we tied them to rocks and threw them across the fence to the men's camp. Well, we put Abba's name on a list and threw it over. We just found out that he is alive here at Auschwitz! He's with us, Aunt Sarah. He's working in the Sonder-Kammando. We don't know which commando that is because there isn't one like it here in the women's camp. But we are told Sonder-Kammandos get plenty of food."

Sarah felt sick, but she forced a smile. She was glad they didn't know what the Sonder-Kammandos did. The news would have devastated them. If Sarah's information was correct, those in the Sonder-Kammando were fed well because they were periodically executed. That is, if they didn't commit suicide first. They were the strong men who were well-fed and preserved so they could clear away the bodies from the gas chambers. Theirs was the most inhumane of all the tasks at Auschwitz. After the people were executed in the showers, the Sonder-Kammandos went in to search the bodies for hidden gold and jewels. When that was done they had to carry the dead to the ovens. Almost without fail, as they did their work they would come across family, friends, neighbors—and the guilt that came from surviving while so many died was too much for them to bear. Those who didn't commit suicide often went insane. Eventually they were all exterminated one way or another…or so Sarah heard.

"Sarah," Dusia asked, "do you know about the Sonder-Kammando?"

Sarah smiled weakly. "I am so thankful you found out that Gershom is alive. And I believe I just heard the bell for zahlappell. We'd better hurry so we can stand in line for three or four hours for a roll call that will take only minutes,"

Sarah said sarcastically. "And they do this twice a day! If they'd only give us that time to rest, we could do so much more work for them. They are madmen! Insane!"

Cupping their skeletal faces in her hands, Sarah kissed both of them. Then, looking into their eyes, she said, "Be strong and courageous!" With that she turned and walked away, trying to hide her tears. Sarah knew that because of the revolt, which was tomorrow, she would not see them again unless she was caught. If that happened, she'd probably be killed.

As she walked to roll call, Sarah thought about the revolt. *If the Allies won't bomb the crematoriums, I'll do it. And, like Esther of old, if I perish, I perish. But if I am to survive, I will survive. And the odds are on Daniels' side! I cannot be a slave to the fear of death.* As Sarah rounded a neighboring barrack, she halted dead in her tracks. *Is Gershom one of the Sonder-Kammandos involved in this revolt?*

❧❧❧

Four days later when Dusia and Miriam were finally able to return to Sarah's section of the camp, Sarah was nowhere to be found. Dusia was puzzled; her heart was crushed.

Miriam wept but said nothing. Her Imma was all she had. If anything happened to her mother, Miriam knew she would be totally on her own.

The more Dusia inquired about Sarah, the more frightened she became. Yet, for Miriam's sake, she tried to quell her fear. No one had any news of Sarah; no one wanted to talk. There were no clues except for one that Dusia chose to ignore. When asked of Sarah's whereabouts, one of the women from Sarah's barracks simply rolled her stark, bulging eyes upward and asked, "Did you know that Crematorium III was blown up?"

Dusia knew there had been an explosion, but nothing more. *What did Crematorium III have to do with Sarah?* She wondered. *Why would the woman mention the crematorium without any provocation whatsoever?* Dusia asked the questions and then barred from her mind any answer that might rob her hope. That was, until several weeks later.

The day they heard of the revolt, Dusia and Miriam were standing in their line of five for zahlappell. The revolt was the whispered talk of roll call because of the hanging scheduled for the next day. They learned that the explosion of Crematorium III was not accidental! Jews working in a Krupp plant had smuggled in explosives. Some of the skilled Soviet prisoners had turned the explosives into grenades and bombs. These were then smuggled to the Sonder-Kommandos of Crematoriums III and IV, who used them to destroy Crematorium III. Twenty-seven Jews escaped and three SS men were killed. In retaliation, two hundred and fifty Jews were then massacred by the guards. And four Jewish women who had helped smuggle in the explosives were caught. They had been undergoing torture these past several weeks. In the process, two had died. Tomorrow, the other two would be hanged. Every prisoner without exception was required to watch the hanging—eyes open wide.

When the news reached Dusia's ears she thought she was going to faint. *Sarah, were you part of this revolt? Am I going to have to watch. . . .* Dusia put her hand to her forehead as she began to sway. . . *watch them hang you?* Then she crumpled to the ground, bumping into Miriam.

"Imma! Get up. Get up quickly, Imma. Pleeease!" Miriam was on the ground, kissing her mother and shaking her bony frame. Afraid that soldiers would come and take her mother away, she looked up at the woman standing next to her and cried, "Help me! Please help me. She's got to stand up; they're coming for roll call!"

"Help yourself! Who has the strength to help anyone else?" The woman's voice was cold, as from the grave, void of life, without hope, without strength. Miriam looked around. She felt as if she was in a forest of dead trees standing like sticks shorn of their branches, hollow inside, unable to sway with the wind. No one moved. No one bent down to help.

"Imma! Imma!" Now anger rose in Miriam's voice. "How dare you do this to me?" She shook her mother again—hard. Then she slapped her face. A torrent of tears broke through the walls of her heart, gushing from her eyes as she screamed through clenched teeth, "You can't leave me! You can't! Get up!" Miriam lifted up Dusia's head, convinced this ground would become her mother's grave. "What will I do if they beat you? If they take you away from me? If they kill you?"

Miriam laid her head on her mother's chest as she cradled her mother in her arms. How could she live without her mother? Miriam's tears ran down Dusia's face and around her neck. Miriam looked at her mother again, rocking her, sobbing, and pleading, "Imma! Imma! They're coming for zahlappell. Please get up!"

Dusia opened her eyes just as two bony arms reached down and pulled her to her feet. Miriam looked up in surprise. The bony arms belonged to the woman whom she had asked for help. Tears glistened in the woman's eyes. "I'm sorry. My mother died here in Auschwitz. I've been on my own too long, just trying to make sure I survive no matter what. Forgive me. I'm angry and bitter—because no one helped me with my mother. I forgot...I forgot I was a human . . . my brother's keeper."

The next day Dusia and Miriam stood with the other women prisoners of Auschwitz to witness the hanging of the two women who had been caught participating in the revolt. It was a command performance of the SS. The women had their warning: If they closed their eyes or looked away even for a second, they would be shot on the spot.

Dusia strained to see the faces of the two women as the kapos put ropes around their necks. Their bodies, except for the broken bones, looked like every other woman's in the camp—skeletons covered with dry, bleached leather. Only their faces might tell who they were. Yet as Dusia searched the faces to identify Sarah she could see her search was in vain. Neither of the women were recognizable. The torture had disfigured their features.

The order was given, and the chair the first of the two women stood on was kicked from beneath her. Her body dropped with barely a jolt. She weighed so little and the rope was so big that it took a little longer for her to suffocate. Then as the chair was kicked from beneath the second woman, her fellow prisoners heard her cry with all the strength she could muster, "Revenge!" No one moved. Outwardly no one responded. They simply stared. The woman's body jerked, causing her legs to sway as her face turned heavenward. Her eyes remained open as if in determined defiance.

"Revenge." Was it said again? Or was it the echo carried by the hearts of those who cried with her?

Dusia knew it was something her spirited friend would cry, but was it Sarah's voice?

Dusia didn't want to know.

Chapter 68

"*W*ho is she?"

Yael knew he was exasperated with her, but what could she do? "I am telling you, Dr. Ben Judah, I do not know who she is. I'm the night nurse, the one in charge. What will I say to the day shift? I have a patient under my care but I don't know who she is or how she got here?"

"Look, Yael, it has been a long night. I had to do surgery on some poor fellow from the Stern Gang. He was preparing a bomb for an Arab, and it blew up in his hand. I operated on him for most of the night. And it is still night! I need to go home. I need rest, Yael. Rest! She's *your* patient. You find out who she is!" Dr. Saul Ben Judah threw up his hands. He headed toward the door shaking his head and muttering under his breath, "If you hadn't stopped me, I could have been home by now, ready to hit the bed."

"Ben!" Although Yael addressed him by his nickname, her voice was sharp. "We are *all* tired. *All* overworked. These conflicts with the Arabs and the casualties they bring wear on all of us—not just you. Go on home. But remember, doctor, what you have seen and what I told you. A woman is lying in this bed and she was not here when I made my rounds two hours ago!"

Yael sounded like a general—loud, commanding. Her frustration was evident. "Absolutely no one in this hospital can tell me how she got here or where she came from. And she's in a coma, so *she* can't tell me. She has no doctor. What if there's some pressure that needs relieving under that pitiful-looking skull of hers? I asked you because you are the only doctor in this hospital at this present moment. And when it comes to neurology, Ben, you are the best!" Then she became sarcastic. "But go to bed, Ben. Pleasant dreams!"

Ben was standing with his hand on the door to the room, wishing he didn't feel so tired. He tried to get his perspective. *What was my reason for studying medicine?* he asked himself. *Why did I come to this God-forsaken land anyway? Why did I become part of this Yishuv, this Jewish community, when I could have stayed at Henry Ford Hospital? I came because I'm a Jew and because I want a land for our people. But also because I want people for our land. I came to take care of our people! Abba, how calloused can I get?*

Dr. Saul Ben Judah walked back to the bed. The woman looked bad enough for him to simply pull the white sheet covering her over her face and pronounce her dead. The sheet lay flat and stiff over a formless body. The woman was completely motionless, barely breathing. He stared down at her for a moment. One couldn't forget a face that pitiful. Her short black hair stuck out of a scalp covered with red, oozing sores.

Ben leaned over and looked at her face. Then he drew back and looked again as if to focus his eyes. Ben had the feeling he had seen her face before. He knew he hadn't, yet she reminded him of something...someone. He couldn't remember who or what; his almost photographic memory failed him tonight. He was just too tired. Ben sat on the edge of the bed.

Then like a flash of light hitting him, Ben knew. He couldn't explain how or why, but he knew. Ben threw back the sheet and reached for the woman's left arm. There it was: A-16750! He looked at Yael. "Why didn't you tell me she was from Auschwitz!"

Yael was stunned. "I didn't know! I haven't touched her! This is just the way I found her—with a sheet pulled over her body!"

"Yael, this is why I left the United States and came to Israel," Ben said excitedly. Seeing the tattoo had rejuvenated him. "I fled Germany while I could still get out. I left behind everything I had achieved in medicine. Then in America, I had it all once again. But when I saw the photographs—the black and white evidence of what had been done to six million of our people as well as the myriad of Gentiles they didn't count, when I looked at the faces of people just like her, and when I read about the medical experiments done by perverted, twisted, demonic minds passing themselves off as doctors—I left again. I left America to come here and take care of my people. I don't know who this woman is, but she is the reason I'm here."

Now his adrenaline was flowing. Ben's tiredness was suddenly overridden by the remembrance of his mission, or as he would say, his calling.

"Yael, see if there's anyone in the lab who can run some blood work for me. Then I need to set her up for radiology. I will examine her now, and—"

A smile played at the corner of Yael's lips as she remarked, "You certainly don't seem tired. You're just going to make the rest of us tired with all these orders, aren't you?" Her tone was playful; she was relieved to feel the tension lift. "By the way, Ben, when they ask the patient's name, what am I going to say? Madame X?"

Ben was leaning over the woman, looking into her right eye while holding up her eyelid against the jutting bone of her eyesocket. Dropping her eyelid, Ben straightened up and studied her frail form for a long moment. Then with a compassionate smile, he said, "Nothing about this woman looks anything like a Madame. Let's just call her . . . ah . . . Israel!"

Ben's eyes glistened as he gently stroked her face. "That is her name— Israel. She is the Israel that survived Hitler's extermination camp." Once again he opened her eye. Peering through his ophthalmoscope and turning his head to check all the angles, he murmured, "Israel, you'll not always look this bad."

Somewhere deep in her consciousness Sarah heard voices. But she couldn't reach them; she couldn't communicate with them. She tried to move, to speak, to open her eyes, to say "I'm here. My name is Sarah." But she couldn't. They were just too far away. If she couldn't reach the doctor, maybe the doctor could reach her. Maybe. . . .

Deep inside Sarah puzzled over the same question the woman's voice had asked. *How did I get here? To a hospital in Israel? What do I remember? What? Yes, I remember. They were auctioning me off. No one wanted me. They saw my naked ugliness. No one wanted me!*

"Who will give twenty shekels of silver and a homer and half of barley?"

No! He must be mistaken. That's the price of a slave! Wait! Wait! He can't hear me. Don't sell me yet! Maybe I'm worth more—more than twenty shekels of silver and a homer and half of barley!

"Sold! I see your hand. Sold for twenty shekels of silver and a homer and half of barley."

I'll turn my head away. I won't look at the people who came from all the nations to see what bargain can be found in my naked, homeless, hopeless flesh.

Someone's coming through the crowd. Is this the one who bought me? If he paid only the price of a slave for me, will I become his slave? I don't want to be a slave! I'm so tired—so tired of serving the nations. So tired.

I'll close my eyes. I won't look. I'm too tired. I can't be your slave. I'm too tired. I ran and ran; Gershom helped me escape. We escaped together! Gershom will come and buy me. Gershom, get up! Get up; you can't die! Gershom, the crematorium is gone now. It is gone. Gershom, we blew it up! Get up, run! We must hide. We must get up. Gershom will buy me.

My eyes. He's making me open my eyes! I can't. I won't. Please, I don't want to see who bought me.

"Beloved?" It was his voice—my husband's. Am I dreaming? Is it the voice of my beloved calling to me? I must open my eyes and make sure I'm not dreaming. I must open my eyes.

"Beloved, it is I. Open your eyes."

"Yael! Yael! Israel has opened her eyes!" Ben straightened up and stroked Israel's face. He looked around to see why Yael hadn't responded. She was gone. Looking down at his patient, he smiled. "She didn't hear the good news. Your eyes are open! Israel, you're going to be all right. You're going to live, not die." Ben patted her on the shoulder and then left the room muttering to himself, "Now, first I'm going to. . . ."

Her body began to heave, her chest rising and falling slowly, restrained almost as if she were afraid to breathe. Her mouth was tightly shut, biting her lip, muffling her sobs.

"I'm here, Beloved. I bought you out of the slave market, and you are mine."

He lifted me into his arms and began making his way through the crowd. As he reached the middle of the mass of curious onlookers, he said, "I'm taking her home."

I saw their faces. Some watched in silent awe, but others jeered and made cat-calls. Some were disinterested. It does not matter you nations, you people. I am in my husband's arms. He has not forgotten me. I played the harlot and had many lovers, but he has not forgotten me. Do you see? Look, look, he's carrying me!

"*Are you taking me home, my Beloved?*"

"*I am taking you home.*"

"*And you will stay with me, my Beloved, won't you?*"

"*No, not for many days. Your loyalty to me is still like a morning cloud—like the dew that goes away early. There is yet one more sieve of destruction, Sarah, that you must walk through. And then...then, Beloved, we will set up our kingdom, and then all these nations will know.*"

"*Know what?*"

"Israel, open your eyes. Open your eyes one more time so Yael can see them before we go home and get some rest. Open them, dear Israel, hurry! Hurry, we're tired."

Yael patted Ben on the back. "You're a good man, Ben. Besides being an outstanding doctor, you are a good man. Now go home. If you say she opened her eyes, then she opened them. We'll see when she does it again."

"*Don't leave me! Please, my Beloved, don't leave me. . . .*"

"*I'm not far away. And when the time is right—when it is time for the end—*"

Two young men rolled a stretcher into the room. "Lady, it's time to take you to X-ray."

"She's in a coma, don't you remember?" said one of the attendants. "She can't talk or move. We have to lift her onto the stretcher by ourselves. But from the looks of her, one of us could do it. Like the saying goes, the woman's just a bag of bones and a hank of hair!"

"Hush! Don't you know that people in a coma can sometimes hear what's being said?" said the second attendant.

"Nah," said the first one as they rolled the sheet under her, using it as a sling to slide her onto the stretcher.

"Uh-huh. It's true; they can. It's been proven."

"*Did you know, my husband, that Daniel talked about the end time?*"

"*Yes, I know. I sent his scroll to you, remember? You should read it again.*"

"*But I lost it.*"

"*It is in the Bible. You'll find it. Sarah, rebuild the waste places, inhabit the cities. For I am going to increase the flock of our people on this land and eventually, my Beloved, I will bring all our people home, just as I promised you years ago. The lands of their dispersions have been as graves to them, but I am going to open up those graves and bring them to the land that is theirs for an everlasting possession. And when they all have come home, then they will know that I am the one who has done it.*"

There was a pause, then Sarah heard her husband again.

"*I must leave you for now, for a time. I have placed you in good hands. You will be nursed back to health. And soon you will be more beautiful than ever before."*

"But when? When are you coming back?"

"When you come trembling to me and my goodness. On that day in the end time you will call me Ishi, my husband, and will no longer call me Baali, my master."

"I can't understand it, Yael. I can't find anything that is wrong. Yet Israel stays in her coma. I've read the newspapers to her. I've played the radio for her. How many people in Israel have a radio? All these stimuli. She's heard the good, the bad, and the ugly of all that is happening in our nation. I've talked to her about it all. And still she won't wake up. I know, Yael, I *know* she opened her eyes! Elohim! How I wish you had been here, Yael, just to confirm it!"

"Ben," Yael's voice reflected her concern, "why don't you let go of Israel? Move her to a home for Holocaust victims and let her go. Caring for Israel has become an obsession with you."

"I know. It's strange, isn't it? Very strange. I myself wonder why I can't let her go. But I can't. I don't understand the reason, but I can't. Right now it seems I'm all she's got. Inside, I feel like I must take care of her."

Yael looked at her watch. "Ben, you're about to miss the most important broadcast in our history. Just think—tomorrow the British move out! Today marks the end of the British Mandate. They sure sold us to the Arabs, didn't they? Turning their backs and looking the other way."

Ben looked out the window. "Wouldn't it be wonderful if Theodor Herzl had lived to see this day? You know, in 1897 he wrote a letter in which he said that if he were to predict that there would soon be a Jewish state the reply would be universal laughter. Then he said that in fifty years, everybody would understand such a declaration. He wrote that exactly fifty years ago! You know it was the public humiliation of Alfred Dreyfus, the French Jew falsely accused of espionage, that opened Herzl's eyes to the plight of the Jews and our need for our own homeland. For me, it was the Holocaust."

"It's 3:55, Ben."

"Turn it on. I'll listen to it in here. Maybe this broadcast will wake Israel from her coma and give her the will to fight!" Ben slid into the chair he'd brought from his apartment and placed beside her bed. "Do you want to listen with me?"

"No, I'll leave you and Israel alone. I've got to have a cigarette, and you won't let me smoke it in here. I'll be back as soon as it's safe to leave the radio in the other room and not miss anything historic."

There was a lot of static coming from the radio, but Ben listened anyway. If he ever married and had children, he wanted to be able to tell them what he had heard firsthand at this moment in Israel's history.

The voice of David Ben-Gurion came on the air. "In the land of Israel, the

Jewish people came into being. In this land was shaped their spiritual, religious, and national character. Here they lived in sovereign independence. Here they created a culture of national and universal import, and gave to the world the eternal Book of Books. Exiled from the land of Israel, the Jewish people remained faithful to it in all the countries of their dispersion, never ceasing to pray and hope for their return and the restoration of their national freedom. . . ."

Ben got up from his chair and went to Sarah's bed. "Israel, are you listening? Do you hear? Open your eyes, Israel! Just look at me so I know." Ben paused, sitting on the side of the bed, not wanting to miss Ben-Gurion's words. "By virtue of the natural and historic right of the Jewish people and of the resolution of the general assembly of the United Nations, we hereby proclaim the establishment of the Jewish state in Palestine, to be called Israel."

"There, Israel." Ben's fingers moved back and forth over the tattoo on her arm, his voice choked with emotion. "Ben-Gurion's done it. We've done it. Now the question is, Will the United Nations accept us? Maintaining our state is going to be war, Israel—full-blown, all-out war. The Arab nations will not give us our land without a fight. They want to drive us into the sea."

Ben rose from the side of her bed and went back to his chair to finish listening to the broadcast. Ben-Gurion was laying out the principles that would guide their nation. It was about 4:35, according to Ben's watch. Ben-Gurion was bringing his speech to a close. "With trust in the Almighty, we set our hand to this declaration at this session of the Provisional Council of State . . . in the city of Tel Aviv on the fifth day of Iyar, 5708, the fourteenth day of May, 1948. Let us all stand to adopt the Scroll of the Establishment of the Jewish State."

Ben jumped from his chair to stand to his feet. Tears streamed down his face as a rabbi prayed, ". . . to him who hath kept and sustained us and brought us into this time."

"Your name is not Ben. It is Saul."

Ben spun around, stunned. He looked at Israel. Her eyes were open! Leaning over the bed he looked into her eyes with hopeful anticipation. "What did you say?"

A smile tugged at the corners of her mouth and her eyes moistened. "Your name is not Ben," she said as her bony hand reached up to his face. "When you were born, I named you Saul."

Ben searched Israel's face, her eyes. Although taken back by her words, in that divine moment Dr. Saul Ben Judah knew—innately—why he had not been able to walk away from this woman. His voice was barely a whisper. "I can't believe it. I can't believe that after all these years, we have finally found one another."

Reaching down ever so gently, Ben gathered her into his arms. Bending his head to hers, he rocked her back and forth, whispering over and over again, "Imma, my Imma! Israel...you're my Imma!"

Chapter 64

lthough Sarah didn't want to be late to the Ma'ariv service and miss Kol Nidrei, the opening prayer for Yom Kippur, she was reluctant to bring dinner to a close. It had been a feast. "The feast before famine" she called it as they went from this final meal of the day to the twenty-four hour fast of Yom Kippur. For a moment Sarah's mind drifted back to Auschwitz. Even though the prisoners had desperately needed every bit of food they could get their hands on to sustain their lives for yet another day, many still fasted on Yom Kippur. And no feast preceded their fast in Hitler's death camps!

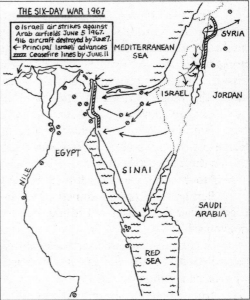

The remaining loaves of bread to her right reminded Sarah that once again she had baked too many challot for the occasion—another aftereffect from Auschwitz. Sarah always prepared more food than was needed.

Sarah looked around the table, appreciating her circle of loved ones one by one. Jared, sitting to her left, was now a member of the K'nesset—the governing body of Israel.

From the time Jared had returned to Israel he had devoted himself to one passion—the establishment of a secure homeland. A nation where he not only would live out the days of his life but also a home where Sarah could return. His dedication to this cause was tested on many and varied fronts: from battling malaria, as he fought to redeem the land itself from the swamps and years of desolation and neglect...all the way to fighting tightfisted investors as he traversed the world securing loans and investments to finance the absorption of Jewish immigrants returning from the four corners of the earth.

However, it wasn't until Sarah returned that Jared moved into the political arena. His entry into politics came at Sarah's unrelenting insistence. Now Jared served Israel under the leadership of Golda Meir, the first woman in Israel to hold the office of prime minister.

When Jared told Sarah that it was she, not Golda, who ought to have been the first woman prime minister, she laughed. Amused at his suggestion, she replied, "I am content, Jared, to wait for my husband's return. Then and only then will we cease to be the derision of the nations. It will be their turn to bow at our feet. Bow or suffer *his* consequences!"

As Sarah's eyes moved from Jared to Enoch and Rebecca she wondered how long it would be until her husband returned. Sarah was weary—weary of war. They had already lived through three wars in the short timespan since declaring their Jewish state!

The first, the War of Independence, came immediately. The day after Ben-Gurion proclaimed the newly founded State of Israel they were attacked by Iraq, Lebanon, Syria, Jordan, and Egypt. And again after this war, Sarah was forbidden entrance to the Old City of Jerusalem, where she once resided.

The loss of lives stemming from the endless conflict between Arab and Jew wearied them all. She recalled the day when Jared told her of Haj Amin el Husseini's call for a holy war. Husseini, a spiritual leader in the Arab world, had urged the Arabs to drive the Jews from Palestine. Hitler was not alone in his hatred of the Jews; it was Husseini's anti-Semitic views that compelled him to seek Nazi support before and during World War II.

Like Hitler, Husseini wanted not only to remove the Jews from Palestine but also to eradicate them from the face of the earth. It galled Sarah that the leaders of the Arab nations would not allow those who occupied Israel during the years of their dispersion to live in peace with them in the land. It wasn't that she wanted them gone; she simply wanted the opportunity to co-exist peacefully. *Why must the Arab leaders always stir up their people and inflame their emotions? Breed conflict and discontent? Feed them lies? Is it too much to ask that this tiny portion of our land—far less than was promised to Abraham, Isaac, and Jacob—be returned to us so we might have one place in this large world where we can live in security? Should not our land be returned, at least in part, to its rightful owner? Are we not willing to share it with them? To live peacefully together?*

Sarah shook her head. She didn't want to think about it—not tonight. It was far more pleasant to continue her visual journey around the table.

Although still childless, Rebecca and Enoch were passionately in love. Not only with each other, but also with Israel. True to their wedding vows, they longed and strived for the day when the nations would beat their swords into plough shares and their spears into pruning hooks. When nation would not lift up sword against nation and neither would they learn war anymore. After serving in the Israeli Defense Force and also finding herself unable to conceive, Rebecca felt she could best serve Israel another way. With great joy she gave herself to the work of absorption, patiently helping Jews who were returning from a multitude of nations and cultures. It was these people who became Rebecca and Enoch's children. In fact, Rebecca always seemed to have some young child or teenager from a foreign country in tow!

Sarah grinned as her eyes moved to Samuel and Levi. Neither of them had changed. They still thrived on their debates and disagreements. Sarah's grin broadened as she remembered hearing the two of them tell about quarreling over which group to join in fighting against the British during the period when Britain had control over their land. That had happened before Sarah ever found herself miraculously transported to Israel, her homeland. Before Israel became a Jewish state.

Samuel had wanted to fight with the Irgun under Menachem Begin, while Levi was convinced they should join the parent group, the Haganah. Of the three groups of the time—the Haganah, the Irgun, and the Stern Gang—the Haganah was the most conservative. The latter two dissident groups were more extreme than the Haganah, favoring stronger repressive measures against the British. The Irgun and Stern Gang were not only angered by the British favoritism shown to the Arabs, but were also fed up with the way the British purposely turned their backs when the Arabs attacked the Israelites. The British watched passively for a time, then were incredibly slow about coming to the aid of the Jews. Weary and worn to their limit with negotiations, the dissident groups wanted to speed up the process. They felt they needed to hit the enemy with swifter and more painful reprisals.

Samuel had been eager to fight, ready for instant and decisive action. Levi, however, had been more cautious, wanting to move slowly...deliberately. He believed careful negotiations would eventually achieve their goals with less hardship for all concerned.

For a while the two were unable to reach an agreement as they continued what they called their "discussions"—a term that made light of the intensity of some of their talks. Finally Samuel suggested they compromise and join the Stern Gang, also known as the Lehi. Lehi was an abbreviation for Lohamei Herut Israel—the Fighters for the Freedom of Israel. When Levi heard this, however, he dug in his heels and suggested they split. The Stern Gang was the most extreme of the three!

Realizing the depth of Levi's feelings, Samuel relented, remembering again their covenant and how Levi had saved his life. Samuel consented to join the Haganah. In the end, both had a good laugh because the Irgun and Haganah joined forces to begin a wave of terrorism against the British. They didn't let up until the British left Palestine. Just the fact that the British still called it Palestine rankled Samuel!

As Sarah listened for a moment to Samuel and Saul discussing the latest threats from Syria and Egypt, she was struck with wonder that Samuel and Levi were still alive. That they had survived these past three wars—the War of Independence; the Sinai Campaign, when Egypt attacked Israel; and the Six-Day War, when the Arab states united against Israel—was a miracle!

The War of Independence, which began with the formation of their Jewish state, was the most perilous for them. Both Samuel and Levi had remained entrenched in Jerusalem during its long siege by the Arabs. As the roads and supplies were cut off to Jerusalem, food and water became so scarce in the Holy City that they had to be rationed. It was the scarcity of food that had turned Samuel's thoughts back to the time when Titus and his Roman army besieged Jerusalem.

When the Arabs eventually took the Old City and mercilessly blew up their synagogue, it was almost more than Samuel could endure. Once again, the Israelis were cut off from their earthly Zion. Every time Samuel approached the new Jordanian border dividing Jerusalem into east and west or stood at the Mandlebaum Gate—forbidding him access to the Old City and his beloved Temple Mount—his soul writhed in torment. How could the nations of the world sanction an action that so clearly went against the Word of God? His torment knew no relief until the Israelis unexpectedly recovered their beloved Jerusalem during the Six-Day War. To Samuel this was a gift from the Almighty, an unseen but divine intervention, for this was a war forced upon them. When the Israeli soldiers took back the Old City, Samuel and Levi stood at the Western Wall of the Temple Mount and wept with unabashed joy.

"Imma, another piece of challah please."

Sarah was oblivious to Saul's request—lost in her thoughts while the conversations at the table continued around her.

"Imma! Imma, are you there?" Saul waved his hand in front of her face.

Startled, Sarah turned to Saul, who was sitting on her right. "What? Did you say something?"

"I did. I asked for more challah but you didn't even respond. I wondered if you were in a coma again!" Saul grinned. They loved to recall their climactic moment—the day Israel was reunited as a nation and they were reunited as mother and son.

"No, I was just thinking. Sorry." Sarah smiled as she handed Saul his bread and watched him immediately rejoin the conversation. Although she didn't know it, Saul was in the middle of making an important point; he and the others were discussing the imminent possibility of another war. Or, as some at the table insisted, *probability*.

Mother and son had shared a home together since the day Saul discharged her from the hospital. What joy it brought her! No longer was Sarah addressed as Aunt in her home. Now she was Imma. The anguish she had suffered at hearing other sons call their mother Imma—one of the dearest words in the Hebrew language—was gone! She and Saul had not only been reunited, but totally reconciled. A reconciliation of which Sarah was confident.

Just after Rosh Hashanah had begun, Sarah had gone to her son one last time to make sure he had forgiven her everything—that he was totally reconciled in his heart. That was the last time Sarah would ever ask her son for his forgiveness. She smiled as she remembered how Saul leaned over, kissed her on the lips, and said, "Your iniquity is taken away." Then, kiddingly, Saul told her if she didn't quit asking for forgiveness he was going to put her into another coma so she could only hear but not talk! Sarah knew Saul was right. Once forgiveness was granted, it was unnecessary to ask for it again.

Reaching over, Sarah tore off a piece of the challah, put it in her mouth, and continued to drift in her reverie. *Maybe I wanted to ask Saul's forgiveness again because of the time of year.* The ten days between Rosh Hashanah and Yom Kippur were deemed days of return and reconciliation. A time when Jews all over the world were admonished to examine their lives and be certain there was nothing between them and another. *Or did I do it because I wouldn't let go of my guilt? Because I didn't feel worthy to be forgiven? To be called Imma?* Sarah sighed. *Why did I think of forgiveness as a matter of worth when it's a matter of grace?* Saul had to remind her!

With an impish impulsiveness, Sarah picked up the rest of the challah and tossed it over her shoulder! Aaron saw it all.

"Aunt Sarah, what are you doing?" Aaron exclaimed as he started to get up and retrieve the bread.

"Sit down, Aaron." Although Sarah smiled, Aaron knew it was a command. "It's all right." Aaron had been eyeing the last piece of challah and determined that if no one asked for more, he would have it. But now it was on the floor!

Sarah never looked to see where the challah landed. She didn't care! Like her transgressions with her son, Sarah put the bread behind her. As the Scriptures said, her sins were behind her back, where they would be remembered no more. Sarah vowed if they ever came to her mind again, even if she had to do it a hundred times in a hundred seconds, she would remember where she tossed the bread—behind her back. And that's where her sins would stay!

"What did you do, Aunt Sarah?" Levi's query turned everyone's attention to Sarah.

"Nothing, Levi, that for you—or the rest of you—is worth interrupting your conversation. Carry on," Sarah said as she turned and winked at Aaron. Aaron wished he hadn't said anything. It was just that he had waited for that piece of bread, and now it was somewhere on the floor. "Aaron, after our meal, would you please pick it up and throw it in the garbage?" Sarah asked.

Curious, Levi leaned over the table toward Sarah and, in almost a whisper, asked, "Pick up what, Aunt Sarah? Pick up what?" Levi wanted to know what was going on.

"Levi," Sarah replied with a touch of sternness, "let it rest and get back in the conversation."

Sarah wasn't finished thinking about Saul. Soon Yom Kippur would begin and they would be admonished to seek reconciliation with the Almighty for their transgressions.

Sarah turned to look at her son. Saul's broad shoulders towered above those of the other people at the table. He was a tall man with thick, shiny black hair and a wonderfully handsome face. Sarah knew it was more than just a mother's pride. Some said Saul was one of the most handsome men they had ever seen. And his looks befitted his character. When looking in Saul's eyes one saw a mixture of tender compassion and mischief. He was a man capable of deep emotion and lighthearted humor. His was an unusual but delightful combination of virtues. He possessed integrity; he was a man faithful to his beliefs and unwavering in his commitment.

Sarah knew boundless joy now that she could share her home with a son nearly lost to her forever. Saul loved his Imma. And missed his Abba terribly. Only his father could fill the void inside him. Yet even with his longing for his father and the memories of what home had been like before his mother walked out, Saul was happy because he was back with Sarah, and back in Jerusalem, his earthly Zion.

Like the others at the table, Saul was absolutely committed to the security of the State of Israel. It was evident by the way he lived. Not only did he serve Israel as a doctor, he also had joined Rebecca and Enoch in the task of absorption, determined that every Jew in the world not only had a place to call home but also ought to come home! In thinking about all this, Sarah recalled how she and Saul had almost missed ever being reconciled. Saul was supposed to have been with a team of doctors and nurses who were ambushed by Arabs in Sheikh Jarrah. Many were roasted alive in their armored vehicles. If Saul had been with them he never would have been at the hospital at the time of Sarah's mysterious arrival. Saul's life had been spared on that fateful day in April because by mere minutes he missed the armed convoy on its way up Mount Scopus. What was more grievous was that the deaths of this illustrious medical team could have been prevented had the British not turned a deaf ear to the Jews' calls for help. A British soldier had given Mohammed Neggar the date and hour of the convoy's passage and assured him that if they attacked the convoy the British would not molest them. The British kept their word.

As Sarah surveyed the men at the table, she knew the security of their people was uppermost in their minds. Security was what those who survived the death camps desired above all else. Otherwise, life held only the terror of an uncertain future. The survivors of the Holocaust had already walked through the fires of Gehenna. Now they needed the still and untroubled waters of the Mediterranean and the Galilee, the healing powers of the Dead Sea, the security of home.

"Like it or not, I believe we are headed for another war!" Reuben's voice was uncharacteristically loud.

War. The word shook Sarah from her reverie, commanding her attention. Now her thoughts were turned from Saul to the men seated around her table.

"I agree it's inevitable," Jared responded. "But Golda is hesitant to call up the Israeli Defense Force even though for some time our intelligence reports have been telling us Syria and Egypt are up to something. Remember, Saul, back in May when we received information about the reinforcement of Egyptian and Syrian troops on the borders?"

Sarah listened intently, trying to bring herself into the context of their conversation. She, Jared, and Saul had talked extensively about the situation with Syria and Egypt. Now the discussion at the table apparently was centering on it. The thought of war clutched at her heart, as it did Rebecca's and Rachel's. Sarah could tell by their expressions. For a moment, Sarah was sorry she had been out of the conversation. Her eyes focused again on the men sitting at the table.

Are these men going to fight again? Will there be still another war for Israel? And if so, will they make it through this one? For how long will we have to endure this endless turmoil—this unrelenting tension?

Like a thief, Sarah's thoughts ransacked her heart, stealing her joy. *Why won't the nations allow us to live in peace? Why, with all the land our neighbors have, do these nations still want ours? Why do they want a piece of land the size of Massachusetts, that tiny state in America? There's no logic to it! It seems as if the conflict between the descendants of Esau and Jacob will never end.*

Sarah was wearied by the conflict. *Over twenty Arab states with vast territories, endless oil, and billions of dollars and the Arabs won't rest until they have our land!* She hated it. And she resented the media for siding with the Arab nations rather than Israel. Just who was the aggressor? Certainly not the Jews! Of course they weren't perfect, and she didn't agree with some of her people's responses and reactions. But they were not the aggressors. The blind bias not only of the media but also of the nations seemed diabolical to Sarah. *When it comes to Israel's defense and welfare, it appears the superpowers and the European socialist nations won't take a stand and speak out on Israel's behalf for choking over the Middle East's oil! Would the fate of small countries like Israel always rest with the superpowers, who had their own interests to guard?*

Jared continued. "Then in September, we had another report of troop buildup in Syria and Egypt. I cannot help but wonder if Golda's getting some advice assuring her there's no threat of imminent war."

Aaron hadn't said much during the meal. As a writer he had learned to listen. Although Aaron had fought in all three wars, the weapon he loved using most was his pen. Fluent in Hebrew, Russian, German, English and Arabic, Aaron was fearless and most persuasive with his pen. Yet what people appreciated the most was Aaron's honesty. He was a man who wrote only truth; he was without guile. Now he felt he had to speak up, for he was troubled by a question that was nagging at his mind. "What if they attacked on Yom Kippur?"

"But," Rachel retorted immediately, "no one would do that to us! It's our most sacred day of the year!"

Enoch added, "It's also our most vulnerable day of the year! No radio, no television, no newspapers, no transportation. The orthodox won't even answer their telephones on Yom Kippur. Our streets are virtually deserted. Everyone's shut inside, fasting. For twenty-four hours nothing is open. We hibernate on our holy day. How would we ever ready our men? And, even worse, how could we fight on two fronts at the same time?"

"If there's any possibility of an attack on us, then why not just make a preemptive strike?" Samuel asked. "It seems obvious to me the Syrians and Egyptians are going to hit us sometime soon. Everyone knows that; they are still smarting over their losses in the Six-Day War. Their wounded egos demand reprisal. Why do we wait for them to hit us first when we know they're massing their troops to drive us into the sea?"

Jared looked around the table. "A preemptive strike would save countless lives, Samuel, and I have the feeling that is exactly what Dado would do if he was given the go-ahead. I know the man!" Everyone in Israel called David Elazar—the minister of defense and the chief of staff—by his nickname Dado.

Saul jumped in. "But you know why we don't do a preemptive strike, Jared. If the Syrians and Egyptians were standing at our borders shouting, 'Ready, aim,' we probably wouldn't fire until they did! Simply because if we did, we'd never get assistance of any kind from anyone. Not now nor probably in the future. At least that's what many believe. We must wait to be attacked. Then we can fight and protect ourselves. But I'm sure most of the other nations don't want us to win; heaven forbid that we should gain back any of the land given us by divine decree and upset our aggressors. I doubt if even the United States would come to our defense if we made a preemptive strike. I say that based on my experience in America during part of Hitler's holocaust! America simply closed her eyes as she did everything she could to limit Jewish immigration. The United States didn't even fill their quota of Jews! I may be wrong, and I hope I am, but I think America is caught up in power, politics, and materialism."

"But surely," Rebecca said wanting to go back to Aaron's earlier statement, "no one would attack us on this day. Everyone knows what we believe. No day of the year is more solemn, more holy than Yom Kippur."

"Rebecca, what do they care about us?" Enoch said intently. "If they are going to plan an attack on two fronts, what better time is there to do it? And because Yom Kippur falls on a Friday this year, all Israel is set for a long weekend! Remember, what is our Israeli Defense Force noted for? What's the IDF's reputation? It's our incredible ability to rapidly mobilize our forces and strike back. Our enemies could not pick a more advantageous time to attack! A time when it's the hardest for us to call our military into action!

"Look at the Six-Day War. It was a war we didn't plan . . . a war forced on us. But we won it in just six days! And not only did we defend ourselves against our aggressors, but we also reunited Jerusalem under Jewish sovereignty for the first time since the Bar Kochba revolt—an astounding feat. That's why we can now sit in Sarah's beautiful house behind the Old City's walls overlooking the kotel." Enoch leaned forward and pointed to the ceiling. "Go to the roof! Look at the kotel, the Western Wall of our Temple Mount, sitting right under the Dome of the Rock. It is teeming with Jews who have anything but war on their mind. Don't you think the Arabs who literally look down on us from the site of their mosque don't know when we are the most vulnerable? Every Arab involved in intelligence knows how we spend this day!"

Aaron spoke up, his tone adamant. "And will the Arabs who live in Jerusalem and in Israel fight with us to protect this land? Or, if given the chance, will they join the Syrians and Egyptians and help them take back Jerusalem?"

"You're right," Saul quipped. "I tell you—and mark my words—the Arabs will never, never rest until they have Jerusalem back under their sovereignty."

Levi leaned forward in his chair, "It will never happen! Not on Yom Kippur! It will never happen!"

"It may not, Levi," Enoch replied soberly, "but if it does you can know it will be over my dead body."

"And mine," Aaron added, remembering the terror of hiding from the Cossacks and the panic he felt when he crossed the German border. Although his military service curtailed his writing, Aaron never resented it. Without the IDF, the Jews would be driven into the Mediterranean. Aaron remembered Kamal Irekat's dubious claim. This man, who commanded the Arab irregulars between Bethlehem and Jerusalem and who was given to much pageantry and prose, proclaimed himself to be the first Arab who publicly vowed to throw the Jews into the sea.

"Aaron! Enoch! I don't like to hear you talking that way. Please," Rebecca pleaded, "can't we change the subject? It's still the time to feast. I'll mourn tomorrow—not today."

It was time to bring this conversation to a close. Sarah stood up. "We are going to miss the opening prayer at the service if we sit here any longer. Go, change your shoes. Remember, no leather on Yom Kippur! We need to leave in no more than ten minutes."

As everyone rose from the table, Rachel looked at Reuben. "Your kitel is on the chair in Sarah's room, freshly prepared for you."

"Good. I'll put it on and be right back." Reuben pushed his chair from the table. "Thanks for such a wonderful meal, Sarah!"

As they walked to the synagogue, intermittently greeting others with the *gemar hatimah tovah*—"May you finally be sealed for good (in the book of life)"—it was hard for Sarah to believe there might be another war. Surely with the swift victory achieved in the Six-Day War their enemies respected the Israelite's ability to defend their land. Not only their ability, also their spirit.

Sarah's prayers and penitence in the synagogue were fervent that night— more fervent that usual. So were the men's, as far as she could tell from her seat in the balcony of the women's section. As she looked down on them covered with their talliot, passionately calling to the Almighty, she wondered if they, too, sensed in their hearts that they would soon be on the battlefield yet again fighting to hold the land given to Abraham, Isaac, and Jacob as an everlasting possession.

After synagogue, they departed for their homes.

As Rebecca and Enoch slipped into bed, Enoch propped his head on his elbow and looked at Rebecca. "Do you know, my wife, how very much I love you?"

Rebecca turned on her side, tucking her pillow more tightly under her head so she could look at Enoch. "Yes, I do, my husband. You have wonderfully demonstrated your love to me and I can't tell you what it means. You were so rightly named Enoch. You are a man who walks with God, even as Enoch of old walked with God. And it shows, my beloved. Your reverence for the Almighty shows in so many ways—in the way you treat me," Rebecca's eyes glistened, "and in the way you honor me as you honor your own flesh. Thank you for not putting me down because I am a woman as some Jewish men do their wives. . . ."

Enoch's hand went to Rebecca's hair. "Your hair is so beautiful. . . ."

Rebecca grinned. "I'm glad we are not Hassidic. I'd have to cut it off and cover myself with a wig." Rebecca propped herself up on her elbow. "You know, Enoch, I never could understand why they still make their wives wear wigs. There's nothing in the Bible about it. It's simply tradition, which to me makes no sense. If the purpose is to keep them unattractive, it doesn't always work. Some of the women look more attractive with their wigs." Rebecca lay back on her pillow, her silky black hair cascading over the crisp white pillowcase. For a moment she gazed at the ceiling, contemplating the life of a Hassidic woman. "If that is what they think is right, then I respect them for it. I'm just thankful I don't have to wear a wig."

Enoch's hand moved from his wife's shoulder down her arm. Longing filled his eyes. Then suddenly he turned on his back and folded his arms across his chest almost as if to restrain himself.

Rebecca turned to her side again, placed her hand on his chin, and turned his face towards her. "Enoch?"

"It's Yom Kippur, Rebecca. We're to abstain—to mortify our flesh—for these twenty-four hours. Yet somehow I feel this may be the last night you and I have together. . . ."

Rebecca withdrew her hand and lay on her back, pulling the covers up over her shoulders. She closed her eyes. She didn't want to think about war. She didn't want to worry about death. She wanted to live and to have a child with Enoch. She wanted sons and daughters who would grow up in peace, not in fear. She wanted them to live in a land where *Jew* was not a dirty word, a word of derision, a word that evoked the scorn and wrath of her fellow man. *Is war the only way to make this possible? Can't peace be negotiated?*

For a while they lay beside each other saying nothing. Each was lost in thought, yet comfortable, allowing the other to choose what to think about in the incredibly quiet hours which so characterize Yom Kippur in their predominately Jewish nation...a holy hush commencing with the appearance of the first star in the silent heavens above.

Rebecca turned to Enoch. "The Bible says nothing about fasting from your husband or wife on Yom Kippur. Our marriage bed is sacred . . . honorable. If I didn't become one with you and this was our last night together for a long time, I don't think I could forget the memory of your words. The memory of failing to say I love you in a way I would never express it to another human being on the face of the earth."

❧❧❧

It was a few minutes after twelve noon the next day. Rebecca was curled under Enoch's arm as he finished reading the last verse of Daniel, Aunt Sarah's favorite book. "But as for you, go your way to the end; then you will enter into rest and rise again for your allotted portion at the end of the age."

Then the air-raid sirens pierced the air—and the hearts of all Israel.

Rebecca bolted upright and looked at Enoch. It was a sound they had not wanted to hear but had anticipated.

"It has happened, hasn't it? It's war!" Fright crept into Rebecca's eyes, followed by tears.

"I don't know, my beloved. I only know something is terribly wrong or the sirens wouldn't be sounding."

Enoch's eyes were moist as he took Rebecca into his arms and held her tight. So tight it almost hurt. Both wondered if they would ever see each other again or if this would be the last time until they rose again from the dead for their allotted portion at the end of the age.

For a few minutes Enoch stroked the long, beautiful hair he loved seeing spread all over the pillow. Then, loosening his grip a little but with her head still on his shoulder, he recited the twenty-seventh Psalm in a hushed tone. "The Lord is my light and my salvation; whom shall I fear? The Lord is the defense of my life; whom shall I dread? When evildoers came upon me to devour my flesh, my adversaries and my enemies, they stumbled and fell. Though a host encamp against me, my heart will not fear; though war arise against me, in spite of this I shall be confident. One thing have I asked from the Lord, that I shall seek: that I may dwell in the house of the Lord all the days of my life, to behold the beauty of the Lord, and to meditate in His temple. . . ."

Enoch then arose and hurriedly dressed for battle while Rebecca remained on the bed silently watching his reflection as it filled the large mirror hanging above their dresser.

Her thirsting eyes were still drinking in every memory of him as he turned and, without moving toward her, said, "I *must* go. I don't want to leave you, but I must. You are my love . . . the darling of my life. My precious Rebecca, whom I have loved since the first day I saw you. When you read your Bible and come to the Song of Songs, remember, 'you are my beloved, and I am yours. . . .'"

Enoch turned to walk out of the room when Rebecca noticed his military tags on the dresser.

"Enoch! You forgot your tags!" she said with alarm as she bound from the bed to get them. "You *have* to wear them. You have to!" she said as she slipped them over his head and tucked them in his shirt. Their self-imposed restraint now lifted as Rebecca put her arms around him and began covering his lips, cheeks, his ear with kisses. "Enoch, where are you going? What will I do? Oh, my beloved, thank you, thank you for obeying your heart last night."

❧~❧~❧

Eight days later, Enoch's tags were brought to Rebecca. Enoch died in a tank, one of the six tanks used to stall the Syrian advance over the Golan Heights. As Rebecca sat *shiva*, the traditional first week of mourning, she looked at Rachel and Sarah at her side and quietly said, "Do you know what an Israeli captain who was fighting on the Golan with Enoch told me? He said he was looking up and saw a great gray hand pressing downward from the heavens, as if it were holding something back. I wonder if that is why our armed forces destroyed all those Syrian tanks and pushed the Syrians back to their original lines?"

The war was over nineteen days after it began. Sarah, Rachel, and Rebecca sat with many other families keeping shiva. And as they did Rebecca often remembered that Yom Kippur day when she reminded Enoch of his tags. How thankful she was that she noticed them lying on the dresser. Aaron had forgotten his. As Sarah and Jared sat shiva for Aaron, Sarah realized they would never know where his body was—even as they would never know the whereabouts of Dusia and Miriam's remains. *Gershom must have fallen somewhere along the route of escape from Auschwitz.* She couldn't quite remember.

On November 11, the agreement for the cease-fire lines was signed by Israel and Egypt. Sarah went to the roof of her home and gazed down upon the kotel, then up to the Dome of the Rock and out to the hills of Judea. The day was as clear as polished glass. Her eyes could glimpse the edge of the Dead Sea, where the heavens met earth and sea.

We lost 2,500 of our people, who fought and fell like lions. Our position after this war is better than it was before, but there is a mourning over the land.

Then, looking towards the heavens, Sarah asked, "How many times must you shake us through the sieve of destruction?"

The word of the LORD came to me saying, "Son of man, set your face toward Gog of the land of Magog, the prince of Rosh, Meshech, and Tubal, and prophesy against him, and say, 'Thus says the Lord GOD, "Behold, I am against you, O Gog, prince of Rosh, Meshech, and Tubal. And I will turn you about, and put hooks into your jaws, and I will bring you out, and all your army, horses and horsemen, all of them splendidly attired, a great company with buckler and shield, all of them wielding swords; Persia, Ethiopia, and Put [Libya] with them, all of them with shield and helmet; Gomer with all its troops; Beth-togarmah from the remote parts of the north with all its troops—many peoples with you. Be prepared, and prepare yourself, you and all your companies that are assembled about you, and be a guard for them.

"After many days you will be summoned; in the latter years you will come into the land that is restored from the sword, whose inhabitants have been gathered from many nations to the mountains of Israel which had been a continual waste; but its people were brought out from the nations, and they are living securely, all of them. And you will go up, you will come like a storm; you will be like a cloud covering the land, you and all your troops, and many peoples with you."

Thus says the Lord GOD, "It will come about on that day, that thoughts will come into your mind, and you will devise an evil plan, and you will say, 'I will go up against the land of unwalled villages. I will go against those who are at rest, that live securely, all of them living without walls, and having no bars or gates, to capture spoil and to seize plunder, to turn your hand against the waste places which are now inhabited, and against the people who are gathered from the nations, who have acquired cattle and goods, who live at the center of the world.'

"…And it will come about on that day, when Gog comes against the land of Israel," declares the Lord GOD, "that My fury will mount up in My anger. And in My zeal and in My blazing wrath I declare that on that day there will surely be a great earthquake in the land of Israel.…all the men who are on the face of the earth will shake at My presence; the mountains also will be thrown down, the steep pathways will collapse, and every wall will fall to the ground.

"And I shall call for a sword against him on all My mountains," declares the Lord GOD. "Every man's sword will be against his brother.…And I shall magnify Myself, sanctify Myself, and make Myself known in the sight of many nations; and they will know that I am the LORD."

—EZEKIEL 38:1-12, 18-21, 23

Then those who inhabit the cities of Israel will go out, and make fires with the weapons and burn them, both shields and bucklers, bows and arrows, war clubs and spears and for seven years they will make fires of them.…And it will come about on that day that I shall give Gog a burial ground there in Israel, the valley of those who pass by east of the sea, and it will block off the passers-by. So they will bury Gog there with all his multitude, and they will call it the valley of Hamon-gog. For seven months the house of Israel will be burying them in order to cleanse the land.

—EZEKIEL 39:9, 11-12

Sarah contemplated the Judean mountains from the rooftop of her home in the Jewish Quarter. The land of Israel no longer stretched barren toward the horizons as a continual waste. The hills and mountains surrounding Jerusalem and the lands clear beyond the Galilee were covered with settlements of Jews who had come out of their graves, so to speak, where they had been buried in nations not their own. Multitudes had returned home from the four corners of the earth. Finally, Sarah and her people felt a semblance of true security. The peace process, it seemed, might work after all.

The cost has been great, Sarah thought, recalling the years since the Six-Day War. *So much has transpired since that time. We have conceded some of the land for peace, but at least I don't feel the way I did when we rebuilt Jerusalem's walls after Nebuchadnezzar's destruction. At that time we couldn't rest without our walls of defense. Now, however, we live like an unwalled city . . . in peace.*

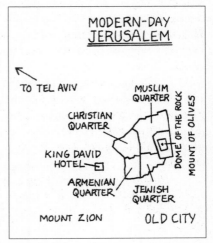

Peace that had come at a great price. The Jews conceded sovereignty to the Palestinians over cities which, according to the biblical record, were deeded to Abraham, Isaac, and Jacob—not to Abraham's son, Ishmael, and his offspring!

The nation of Israel trudged on through the turmoil of Yitzhak Rabin's assassination, one of the darkest hours in Israel's history, when an Israeli citizen was the first to take the life of an Israeli prime minister. They suffered suicide bombings committed by the Hamas, a group of terrorist extremists seeking Israel's demise, not peace. Not a soul living in Israel had been unaffected by the upheaval and violence. The country was so small that every family had someone who was connected in one way or another to a person who had been senselessly murdered. In this storm-tossed nation which valued and treasured every individual life, the blood of her slain brothers cried out from the ground.

But now, Sarah thought, *it is quiet. Finally quiet. Maybe, just maybe this time it will work. Maybe my grandchild will grow up in peace.*

"Imma Sarah? Imma, are you up there?" Rebecca called, climbing the narrow spiral staircase to the roof. Sarah could tell from her voice that Rebecca was winded.

"Yes, dear," Sarah called back happily. "Come on up. Or would you rather I come down?"

"No, no. I'm fine," Rebecca responded, still out of sight. "The exercise will be good for me. Just give me a minute and I will be up. I just didn't want to climb up the stairs only to find you weren't there!"

Sarah's life had taken some totally unpredictable turns. One was Rebecca. Sarah loved Reuben and Rachel's daughter dearly, yet she had never dreamed Rebecca would become her daughter-in-law and that Reuben and Rachel would truly become family, in the sense of bloodline, sharing a grandchild of all things! Everyone was very pleased, and Sarah still couldn't believe all that had transpired over time to bring about these circumstances.

Although shiva, by Jewish custom, lasted but seven days, their mourning over the loss of their loved ones lasted much longer. Upon hearing of Enoch's death, Rebecca said *berakhah*: "Blessed are you, Lord our God, King of the Universe, the true Judge." The words came involuntarily. Although she had uttered berakhah on earlier occasions upon hearing about the death of other people's loved ones, never did she plan to be in the position of having to say it for her beloved Enoch. As she spoke berakhah for her husband, Rebecca remembered the last words they had read together that Yom Kippur morning. Reading Daniel that day had been unusual for them to do, but now she was thankful they had. The closing words of Daniel brought comfort to the finality of Enoch's time on earth: "then you will enter into rest and rise again for your allotted portion at the end of the age."

Rebecca, along with Enoch's loved ones, performed the traditional *keriah*, the tearing of their garments. The act itself was meant to serve as an outlet for the pent-up anguish, an expression of the pain of separation brought on by death. But it was a paltry, inadequate expression of the tearing in her heart. The torn garments were never mended, and at the time of her loss and for several years after, Rebecca wondered if the same would be true of her broken heart.

But there was Saul, with the family, missing Enoch, and grieving with Rebecca. Saul had stood at Rebecca's side as they heard with an air of finality the traditional first spadeful of dirt spilling down onto Enoch's coffin. Then, in great patience and with the healing brought by time, Saul grew to love Rebecca and when the time was right he expressed his desire to marry and have children by her should the Almighty grant it. Children who would be *sabras*—Israelites born on Israeli soil.

"Whew!" Rebecca said, using her hand to push against the middle of her back as pregnant women so often did when heavy with child. "I should have told you to come down instead of trying to show what good condition I'm in by climbing those stairs."

Sarah looked at Rebecca and smiled. Never, ever did she dream Rebecca would call her Imma. Now she was thankful Saul had waited so long to marry. What Rebecca lost in her beloved Enoch she now found in Sarah's Saul. *And I have a daughter—a wonderful daughter. May our relationship be as Naomi and Ruth's,* Sarah thought as she looked at Rebecca. The comparison caused Sarah to wonder again whatever happened to Ruth. Sarah still experienced a bittersweet mixture of love, gratitude, and pain when she remembered the Christian Gentile in Holland who risked her life by hiding her from the hateful Nazis in order that she might live.

For a moment Sarah thought back over the events of her life. For the most part her life had been etched in pain, lived on the edge of death and destruction. *But now, maybe the turmoil has come to an end.* Sarah motioned with her head. "Sit down, Rebecca. Sit down. Every opportunity you have, sit down, my dear. That is no small child you are carrying."

Rebecca patted the little hand or foot, whichever had nudged her at that moment, as the child rearranged his position. "He's getting comfortable. He usually does when I sit down. It seems to be getting a little tight in there. I hope he comes early!" Rebecca leaned her head against the edge of the chair and stiffened her aching back. "Imma Sarah, I came to see if you wanted to walk to the shuk." Rebecca loved the atmosphere of the marketplace, or as they called it, the shuk. The colorful displays of vegetables, fruit, fish . . . the smells, the colors . . . the hawking of wares as people walked through the market . . . all delighted Rebecca's senses. She much preferred the shuk over the Supersol when the time came to get her fruits and vegetables.

"I ate some fresh strawberries dipped in chocolate at the Hilton Hotel the other night. Now I am craving them. I have the chocolate needed to make them, but not the strawberries. Besides, it's such a lovely day to go to the market. Would you like to join me, Imma?"

"Oh, the shuk would be wonderful! I need to get some fresh vegetables and some fish. But are you sure you feel up to it? Don't you want me to drive? It's quite a long walk."

"No, no. Driving the car down these small streets and outside these city walls is so wearing. Besides, Doctor Saul wants me to walk. He says the more that I walk, the easier my delivery will be. And if I was able to make it up these stairs, then the pull up Jaffa Road will be nothing."

"All right. But promise me that on our way back we'll catch a cab instead of walking up to the Jaffa Gate."

"I promise." Rebecca said as she stood, pushing on her back again. "You know, I think you have the best view of the Old City. I can actually see what's happening on the Temple Mount from here. Wouldn't it be awesome to be able to walk up there to our Temple? In all these years since my return my feet have never walked on that sacred ground. All we are able to do is stand at the Western Wall and pray. Of course, I realize the ultraorthodox Jews would be horribly upset if any Jew stepped on top of the mount. Most of them still believe the holy ark of the covenant is buried in some chamber down at the level of Solomon's day."

Sarah gazed at the Temple Mount, remembering the last time she had stood there—just before Rome destroyed her temple and broke down Jerusalem's walls. *So much has happened since then.* Sometimes Sarah thought if the accounts of the Jewish people's lives in the lands of their dispersion were written in books, then those books just might fill the whole world. Sarah wistfully responded, "Maybe someday, Rebecca. Maybe sooner than we think. Maybe soon you and I will walk together on that mount holding the hands of your son."

"The temple is your passion, isn't it, Imma Sarah?"

"Yes, my dear, rebuilding our temple is my passion. And although at this point in time attempting to rebuild it where it belongs—on the Temple Mount —would cause a holy war with the Arabs, the Muslims, I believe it will be rebuilt. And right where is should be. No other place."

Undeniable confidence rang in Sarah's voice as she stood beside her daughter-in-law, rubbing Rebecca's back with her right hand. "All sorts of preparations are under way. You do know, don't you, that we are breeding red heifers right here in Israel? We have to. Without the ashes of the red heifers there is no purification, and the priests could never perform their duties. And speaking of the priests, just two weeks ago I went with my friend Zipporah to watch them weaving her husband's garments for the temple service. My, Zipporah is proud! Many of those who believe themselves to be of the priestly line are doing the same. Quite a number of garments were waiting there to be picked up. I saw the names of them—Levi, Leveneson, Levenstein, Cohen…and others.

"It seems like everyone is involved in some way in preparing all that is necessary to reinstitute the temple worship so that we will be ready as soon as our temple is completed. When the time finally comes to rebuild, they say the construction of the temple will take no time at all. I believe the builders would be willing to work around the clock!" Sarah patted Rachel's back. "But enough for now. If we don't get to the shuk all of the best strawberries will be gone."

Taking her little pull cart, she and Rebecca walked out through the Jaffa Gate. For a moment, Sarah stood surveying the tasteful architecture of David's Village from the high vantage point afforded by this gate. The beautiful condominiums before them were covered with Jerusalem stone and sported smart black domes. The domes themselves were topped with beige caps. The condominiums were graced with balconies adorned with splashes of red and pink geraniums blooming happily in the sun. The King David Hotel, with its distinctive green windows set in Jerusalem stone, stood regally on the hill behind the village, a monument in its own right, from the days of the British occupation.

As her eyes took in the architecture, Sarah was thankful that after the British took Jerusalem from the Turks, the British governor, Sir Ronald Storrs, enacted a bylaw requiring that all Jerusalem's buildings be dressed with natural stone. *I wish the same ordinance had been enacted for Tel Aviv! Tel Aviv would be much more attractive.*

Sarah motioned with her hand. "Oh, Rebecca, I love this scene! I marvel at its beauty every time I leave this gate, but I wouldn't trade my apartment for one of those condominiums—not for all the money in Israel! Nor would I live in Tel Aviv. It may be the cultural center of Israel and the first city Israel built upon becoming a nation, but it is not *my* Zion!"

Patiently they waited at the curb for the symbol of the little green man to appear on the traffic light signalling them to proceed. Traffic was heavy, as always, in Jerusalem, but today it was heavier because it wasn't the rainy season. A line of tourist buses waited for the pedestrians to cross. Unconsciously taking Rebecca's arm, Sarah asked, "Don't you love looking into the faces of those tourists and watching their awe and excitement as they look at the ancient walls of the Old City? Can you imagine what it means to them to come here? Jews, Christians, Muslims! To each one of them, this is their holy city. Which I don't mind," Sarah laughed, "as long as they remember to whom this city is deeded."

Rebecca, mesmerized by the tapestry of faces eagerly emptying from the buses, replied, "Just wait until they get inside and walk through the different quarters—Muslim, Armenian, Christian, and our neighborhood. Their eyes and ears can't take it all in; I've watched them. They are staggered by the realization that they are looking at sights that date back over three thousand years! Saul laughs when he says that in America people get excited about things that are a few hundreds of years old while with us it's millenniums!"

Rebecca felt the pull on her thighs, her calves, and her back as they walked up Jaffa Road to the shuk. She again put her hand in the small of her back. Sarah reached over and rubbed it. "Are you sure you don't want to hop in a taxi?"

"I can't 'hop' anywhere. Besides, I can't give in. Saul will be so proud of me when he comes home from Hadassah Hospital tonight."

Sarah looked about her, remembering what Jerusalem was like after the War of Independence. During that time Jerusalem was divided into east and west. The eastern part, held by the Jordanians, had been forbidden to the Jews. "My, how we've prospered! I think the other countries—even the Arabs—are envious. It's Jewish ingenuity. We've learned how to survive. We've had to. We were well trained in the lands of our dispersion as we worked to carve something out of nothing. Now we have done the same in Jerusalem, only better."

Rebecca noted the pride in Sarah's voice and smiled. "This is home, Rebecca. This is *our* home!"

"A crowded home, Imma Sarah. A big family. And the closer we get to Ben Yehudah, the more crowded it is." At that moment a woman pushed Rebecca out of the way. Rebecca was moving too slowly to please her. Rebecca frowned.

Sarah saw the frown. "Are you sure you're all right? There's a bus coming. We can ride."

"No, I'm fine. I know it sounds a little cowardly, but after witnessing the terrorist bombings of our buses I have decided to walk as much as possible. I frowned because I'm just not used to being shoved, pushed, or barged in front of. We didn't live that way in Spain."

"I know what you mean," said Sarah. "The Sephardi Jews from Spain never lived like the Ashkenazi Jews who came from Germany and Poland then were spread all across Europe. Life was easier for you in Spain; it was more gracious and gentle. But elsewhere our people had to push and shove for everything they got. I don't like it either, but I try to remember what it is that made them that way. These traits seem to have been passed down from generation to generation. Maybe with time life will become more genteel for all of us."

"I hope so. I'm ready for it—anytime."

Sarah had found herself growing more content with the present, better acclimated to the times. Now her thoughts focused more and more on rebuilding her temple.

"How do you think I'd look in a skirt like that one?" Rebecca asked, nodding her head towards the young girl in front of her. The girl's tight skirt, barely covering her bottom, accented her every curve as she sauntered across the street.

Sarah frowned. Sights like that distressed her, as did the increasing immorality of her people. A vast majority thought nothing of premarital sex or divorce. *Before Yitzhak Rabin was assassinated, Simon Peres said he wanted Israel to become more like the rest of the nations. I'm sure this isn't what he had in mind when he said it, but we certainly have become like the nations in regard to our morals! The commandments about adultery and coveting a neighbor's wife are blatantly broken, if even remembered. As a whole our Jewish nation has little regard for the commandments. More and more, children are growing up honoring their parents less and less.* Sarah was thankful Rebecca and Saul were not immoral or disrespectful. She wanted to do all she could to make sure her grandson wouldn't be either!

Breaking out of her thoughts, Sarah quipped, "If you walked through Hassidic Mea Shearim dressed like that, I wouldn't have to say a thing to you! The men with their pe'ot—sidecurls—would stone you," Sarah chuckled as she grabbed Rebecca's arm and squeezed it, "and I might help them!"

As they turned into the shuk they were brought to a sudden halt. Sarah's cart jammed into her ankle, causing her to wince. A mass of people were huddled right inside the shuk's entrance. Turning to a woman, Sarah asked, "What's the—"

Almost in unison, the crowd made a hushing sound.

Everyone was hovered around a radio, bent forward, listening intently. The eerie silence of the shuk was so uncharacteristic it carried its own fear. Rebecca took hold of Sarah's arm as they joined the listening crowd. "We are urging the utmost calm. Return to your homes immediately. Get your gas masks and go to the closest bomb shelter. You will be given further notice what to—"

An air-raid siren interrupted the broadcast, piercing the silence and creating panic in their hearts. Sarah looked up. There was no activity in the skies— no sounds of jets. All she saw were bountiful clouds moving serenely across an azure canvas. Sarah questioned the serenity of the heavens. *How can it look so peaceful when terror storms the strongholds of our hearts?*

"Imma! Saul . . . Imma!" Rebecca's lips were moving. But Sarah couldn't hear what she was saying. Everyone was shouting; the shuk was in bedlam. Some ran to the closest vendors making hurried purchases as the merchants emptied their boxes of money into their pockets and closed their stalls. Some merchants waved people off with a flick of their hand while others wouldn't even acknowledge their presence. People were anxious. Some had begun to panic. Most were pushing to get out of the shuk. Children were either struck dumb or asking a thousand questions as they were dragged along by tense hands gripping them too tightly. Many cried and some screamed as their young minds sensed that something was terribly wrong.

Jaffa Road was total confusion by now. People were scrambling to get home—pushing, shoving, grabbing taxis, jamming traffic. Horns honked impatiently. Everywhere Sarah turned she could hear a chaotic babble of languages. Frightened, many people had reverted to the tongue of their dispersion. At that moment it seemed as if all of the more than one hundred languages spoken in Israel could be heard on Jaffa Road. Men stood on the streets kissing loved ones good-bye while their women clung to them in fear. Couples tenderly whispered what might be the last words they would ever share while others shouted instructions over the din of noise. The Israelis had been trained for times of emergency like this, but in this moment of reality many forgot what they had learned. They had held such high hopes of enduring peace that they were caught off guard by the suddenness of this threat.

Sarah grabbed Rebecca, pulling her towards a telephone and yelling in her ear, "Do you have a phone card? Mine's about used up! I'm going to call Jared. We can't get anyplace in all this chaos anyway. Some of the taxis aren't even stopping to pick up passengers. I've got to find out what is going on."

Rebecca nodded while fumbling around in her purse. She found the phone card just as they came to a phone. "May I call Saul when you finish?"

Sarah nodded while she asked for Jared. "Yanit, this is Sarah. Can I speak to Jared?"

In what seemed like just seconds, Jared was on the line. "Sarah, I need to keep this brief." No shaloms, no pleasantries, Jared gave Sarah a quick rundown of the latest news.

Sarah covered the mouthpiece as she listened to Jared, speaking to Rebecca at the same time, "It must be a real crisis."

"Are you there?" Jared asked.

"Yes, go on."

Jared was shouting into the phone. "A massive army is coming down from the north."

Syria popped into Sarah's mind. Then, just as quickly she dismissed the thought, realizing it was an unreasoned assumption. *Syria's so close they wouldn't be headed here; they would be here already. Overhead right now!*

"From our intelligence reports, it's believed Israel is the target. Also, there are movements in the south. Sarah, it's massive. Our reports indicate they are armed to the hilt. We just can't understand why there's no air strike. All we can figure is that they don't want to destroy the land—just conquer it. Evidently, they must want everything intact. That's all we can surmise."

"Are you sure we're the target? Not Lebanon or Syria?"

"We believe it's Israel they're after. Just a moment—" Jared interrupted himself. Sarah suspected he was talking with someone at the other end of the line.

Again Sarah cupped her hand over the phone. "Jared says it's not an air strike. We're all right for the moment. I'll be off the phone in a minute." Sarah took her hand off the phone to talk to Jared. "Yes, yes . . . I can hear you."

"Sarah, intelligence picked up something from England. The British were just in contact with the troops that are coming against us. It's unclear which country or countries are involved, but the British said that they and the other superpowers will never stand for this attack. They say the army can't plunder our riches and then just walk away. Apparently, America's response was the same. It almost seems like a repeat of Nixon's response when Russia threatened to move unilaterally into Israel. Only this time England and the United States are not calling a red alert like President Nixon did.

"When was that?" Sarah puzzled aloud.

"When Anwar Sadat of Egypt suggested that Russia supervise the cease-fire after the Yom Kippur war."

"Yes, I remember. What about now—did America or England tell them they would defend us if this army, whoever it is, doesn't stop?" Sarah asked.

"No. All they've done is condemn the aggressor's actions, giving them a verbal rebuke. Just a slap on the hand, so to speak."

Sarah sighed in resignation. "We have no real friends, have we, Jared?"

"No, I guess not. Sarah, I hate to hang up, but I have to. I'll call or get back in touch with you as soon as I can. Have you talked with Saul?"

"No. But Rebecca's with me. We walked together to the shuk. She's going to call him now. Before you hang up, may I ask one last question? If there is no air strike, why are they encouraging everyone to go to the shelters?"

"It's precautionary." There was a long pause. "Sarah, don't overreact or say this to anyone else. But this is the most massive affront ever to come against us. It's possible we will not survive the attack. It's a matter of sheer numbers and military force. We're badly outnumbered. I had hoped that our wars were over and that we'd achieved a lasting peace." Jared paused again. "You know, if we do survive this attack, I believe a good many Israelis might just be willing to sell their souls to the devil himself if he could guarantee peace. Sarah, I'm sorry, but someone needs to talk to me. I have to go. Shalom. . . ."

Shalom? Peace? What a strange greeting we Israelis use in a land that knows no peace, Sarah thought as Rebecca quickly called Saul.

After Rebecca hung up the phone, she walked over to Sarah, who was trying to get a taxi. They knew their chances of getting one in these circumstances were extremely slim. But much to their surprise, they didn't have to wait long.

As they shut the doors of the taxi, the driver looked in the rearview mirror and said, "The only reason I picked you up in all this traffic and confusion is because my wife is just as pregnant as you are. All the other taxi drivers are headed for home. But I'd want someone to do this for her. Where did you say you were going in the Old City?"

"The Jewish Quarter—"

"I'll take you as far as the Zion Gate or the Dung Gate," he interrupted. "Whichever I can get to, or at least as close as I can. If the traffic is heavy, I may have to let you off at the Jaffa Gate. But I hate to see you trudge up that steep ascent."

"Fine, fine, wherever you can," Sarah said as she searched through her purse for some shekels. Then she remembered her cart. "My cart! I left my cart!"

"I'll buy you a new one for your birthday, Imma. Let's just get home."

"What did Saul say?"

"He said to come home immediately and to bring you with me. He'll meet us there."

Saul was pacing the floor when they arrived. Assuring her son she would be all right, Sarah left for her house. Jared would call her. Besides, going to a bomb shelter made no sense. If there was to be no air strike, then why go to a shelter crammed with people and sit there doing nothing? Sarah wanted to be on her roof, where she might be able to see what was taking place. She called her roof her "garden watchtower," and that's where she headed immediately upon arriving home, taking her portable phone with her.

Drawing a blanket around her, Sarah surveyed the landscape. The air was crisp, clear. From her vantage point on the roof, Sarah could see every quarter of the Old City. To the east was the Western Wall and the Temple Mount, and to the southeast were the mountains of Judea. Behind her to the west was the old Jerusalem Hilton towering from its hill, its red sign aglow.

Fatigued, Sarah settled down into her lounge chair and covered herself with the blanket, tucking it tightly about her. As she gazed out onto the Temple Mount she relived the moments of the day, reflecting on how in a matter of minutes her hope had come crashing down again. Her peace once more was shattered just when Israel felt so secure in her unwalled cities. Sarah soon fell asleep in her chair, worn out by the day's disappointment.

Sometime later Sarah awoke with a start. She could feel her lounge chair sliding across the roof. Dazed and disoriented, she wondered if she was dreaming. She attempted to rise from the chair, which was now inching precariously close to the edge of the roof, but she fell—unable to keep her balance. Again Sarah tried to stand, but she couldn't get her footing. Her whole house seemed to be moving. For what seemed like minutes she simply knelt in the spot where she had fallen, remaining on her hands and knees, trying desperately to steady herself. In the distance, mortars flamed across the night sky as the sound of war echoed across the Judean mountains. *Is it the sound of war or the groaning of a multitude?* Sarah wondered.

Lightning crackled through the heavens, pursued by bolts of scarlet fire. Bursts of light like falling stars pelted the earth as the lightning charged through the sky. Again Sarah's house swayed. Or was it the whole earth? Then the perpetual flame that burned on top of the synagogue near the Western Wall suddenly went out. Sarah could hear people screaming; everything was draped in a blanket of total darkness.

Once again Sarah tried to get up. Again, it was impossible. Crawling back to the chair that had been sent sliding out of her reach, Sarah pulled the blanket from it and covered herself. Then, still trembling uncontrollably, she laid face down on the cement and wept. This was more than war; it was an earthquake! A great, violent earthquake shaking the whole land of Israel.

After what seemed like an eternity the quaking finally subsided. Too weary and too scared to make her way down the winding staircase in the black of the night, Sarah huddled in her blanket on the roof, napping intermittently until she awakened to the sound of . . . *singing?*

Stiff and sore, Sarah pushed herself to her feet and looked down on the Western Wall. The kotel was jammed with people. Israelis, both orthodox and non-orthodox, were at the wall, praying, shouting, and throwing their hands towards heaven in unrestrained expressions of joy.

"Imma! Imma!" Saul shouted as he climbed the wavering staircase.

"I'm all right, son," Sarah called back. "Be careful on those stairs. The earthquake may have shaken them loose."

Saul looked around as he emerged onto the roof. "Where's Jared?"

"I don't know. I never heard from him."

"I would have died, Imma, had I known you were alone! I couldn't get to you!" Saul paused, then announced, "Imma, last night you had a grandson." Saul's pride was evident as he took a moment to stretch. He was tired. "I delivered him myself right at home! I wish you hadn't missed it. It was just Rebecca and me. Can you imagine—a neurosurgeon delivering a baby? I'm glad for those days in obstetrics during my internship!"

Sarah's hands flew to her mouth. Delight filled her eyes, then a cloud. "Is Rebecca all right? What about the baby?"

"Yes, yes. You wouldn't believe how well she did. She breathed and pushed and delivered our Joshua. He must weigh four to four and one-half kilos. He was a big one. It was a good thing Rebecca didn't go any longer. She must have been farther along than we thought." Saul paused ever so briefly and spoke again with his next breath. "Well, Imma, what do you think about it?"

"About the baby?"

"No! About what happened last night."

"I don't know what happened . . . except that we had an earthquake."

"You mean Jared didn't call you? He called me. Where's your phone? Maybe the batteries ran out. Anyway, the IDF is all astir. I can't believe it, and neither can they. They say it's a miracle. I say my Almighty Father moved! It had to be Abba! There can be no other explanation for it. The armies coming against us from the remotest parts of the north were *destroyed!* Destroyed, Imma! The heavens rained fire and brimstone, and there were torrential rains and hailstones! What we felt were the aftershocks. Aftershocks from an earthquake that literally threw down mountains. Our enemy was completely wasted, and we survived!" Saul was so excited his voice was quivering. "It had to be Abba! It had to be! The armies came down as far as the mountains in northern Israel, then they were inexplicably, supernaturally destroyed! There are even reports that in their confusion the soldiers began killing one another. It will take us months to bury the dead!"

Stunned and speechless, Sarah looked at her son. She was still trying to pull her thoughts together.

"Rebecca had me get the Bible and read to her from Ezekiel. I think it was chapters thirty-eight and . . . and . . . yes, that's it! I am determined not to forget them. It was Ezekiel thirty-eight and thirty-nine. I plan to show them to the staff at the hospital. Rebecca's convinced Messiah is coming. You better get ready to—"

At that moment Saul had turned to look at the Temple Mount and tell Sarah to make preparations to build her temple. What he saw made him stop in midsentence, astounded. "Oh Elohim! Look, Imma! Look! The Dome of the Rock—the earthquake damaged the Dome of the Rock!"

Chapter 66

Sarah took one last look in the mirror before she answered the phone.

"Sarah, this is Jared. Can you meet me at the K'nesset in thirty minutes and no later?"

"Certainly. You sound like you are in a hurry," said Sarah.

"I am. Things are really moving around here. I'm sorry I can't pick you up myself, but I'm needed here. By the way, this is not typical Israel tonight, so dress up."

"I'm already dressed and you won't be ashamed," Sarah laughed. "I just checked the mirror before I answered the phone."

"We'll be going by police escort to the King David from the K'nesset. I've got to run. . . ."

"Run, Jared. Shalom!" Sarah heard the other end of the line click dead as she said, "Shalom." As soon as she laid the receiver back in its cradle, the phone rang again. Sarah was tempted not to answer it; she didn't have much time.

"Shalom—"

"Sarah, this is Rachel. We wondered if you and Jared wanted to come over for coffee after the dinner meeting tonight? We haven't seen you for such a long time."

Sarah looked at her watch. In five minutes she had to be on her way. "Rachel, I'd love to come, but I just talked to Jared. He sounds fatigued. With the recent changes taking place in world governments and this new leader's interest in Israel, Jared hasn't had a minute to call his own. I hope he's not sorry he was elected to the K'nesset. Can I call you later?"

"Of course! Reuben just got home today, and he may have to leave again in two days. We simply wanted to touch base. Plus, Reuben's been very anxious to talk with Jared and to hear about what is happening."

"How is our newborn grandson doing? I heard that Rebecca and little Joshua visited with you today."

"He is absolutely wonderful. Who ever would have thought, Sarah, that you and I would share a grandson with blue-green eyes?"

Sarah smiled. Now when she saw blue-green eyes she *could* smile! "I'm in a hurry. I have to meet Jared at the King David Hotel, but before I hang up, tell me quickly—how is Reuben?"

"Like Jared, he is worn out. He's been in charge of moving all those men throughout our land to mark the bones of the army from the north. He's also been mobilizing another contingency to collect their bones and remove them for burial. That's been a lot of work. Did you know they're burying them in the valley east of the Sea? They call it Hamon-gog. Reuben says it's no easy task. He's also showing signs of fatigue. Plus—"

"Rachel," Sarah tried to interrupt.

"—there's another group that Reuben put in charge of gathering the weapons left lying on the ground."

Sarah looked at her watch. She suspected Rachel hadn't heard her. *She's probably working in the kitchen while she's talking to me on the phone.* Rachel was known for cradling the phone on her shoulder and walking around the house doing her work as she talked. Sarah decided to give her one more minute, and then she'd speak louder to get Rachel's attention.

"Reuben says burying the dead will take about seven months, but we'll benefit from it. The weapons they left will give us fuel for seven years. Amazing, isn't it! Reuben says we've plundered the plunderers!"

"Rachel . . ." said Sarah, more loudly this time.

"What are you wearing tonight? Are there going to be leaders from other countries? I'm so curious . . ."

"Rachel!" Sarah shouted. "What is it you're doing that prevents you from hearing me?"

"Oh! I'm sorry, Sarah. I'm washing the dishes—pots and pans. I'm sorry. I have the phone cradled on my shoulder. You know how I am, always doing two things at once. . . ."

"I understand. But I have to hang up, Rachel. I promised Jared I wouldn't be late."

"Jared's not coming to get you?"

"No, I'll have to take a cab and get there in twenty-five minutes."

"You better hurry. You know what Jerusalem traffic is like when all these leaders come."

"Shalom, Rachel," Sarah put the phone down immediately. She had to hang up. With Rachel, it could take two full minutes to say good-bye.

After Sarah stepped into the cab, she leaned back in the seat for a minute to catch her breath. *What amazing times these are! An army miraculously destroyed, weapons that give us needed fuel for seven years, and ten different governments fusing together into a coalition. And little Israel in the middle of it all! What will happen next, my husband?*

Sarah rested until she heard the taxi driver say, "Fifteen shekels."

She paid the cab driver, got out, and headed for the K'nesset. Jared was waiting for her in front of the building, talking with another man. Both were waving their arms adamantly. Seeing Sarah, Jared broke away and, within a few minutes, they were on their way to the King David Hotel in a motorcade of sorts. Jared slouched next to her and leaned his head back on the seat. "I'm so thankful you could come." He reached over and patted Sarah's hand. Then turning to look at her, he said, "You were right. You are a discerning woman. You look *very* good!"

Sarah smiled. "Thanks. Every woman likes to hear that. And thanks for being such a good friend, Jared, and including me in affairs like this."

"Anthony specifically asked me to invite you."

"Jared, I don't even know the man. And I'm not sure I really want to."

"Well, you better prepare yourself because he wants to meet you."

"Why me?"

"The temple, mainly. I don't think you realize, Sarah how well-known and influential you are in Israel. Everyone knows you are one of the greatest proponents for the rebuilding of the temple. And, even though some orthodox factions may not approve of everything you do, they still support your efforts towards rebuilding the temple. They want their temple too, and frankly, they are tired of waiting for it. Of course, I'm not telling you anything you don't already know, but they are genuinely distressed because our government won't move on this issue. They want the government to give them permission to start building the temple where it belongs."

"Why would the man want to meet me to discuss the temple?" Sarah's heart quickened. Now she was curious. Maybe she wanted to meet Anthony after all if he was truly interested in the temple.

"Anthony knows you are a major player among the orthodox who want to see the temple rebuilt. And I believe Anthony thinks the temple is his key to getting a treaty signed with the State of Israel." Jared sat up for a moment and turned to look Sarah full in the face. "Do you know that the coalition of governments the man represents almost reminds me of the old Roman Empire?!"

Jared settled back again and closed his eyes as he continued talking. "Anyway, Anthony is here because these nations want to make a covenant with Israel. That's the term they are using—covenant! Smart terminology to use when working with people who have made and understood covenants all throughout their history."

Jared opened his eyes for a moment and turned again to look at Sarah. "The man amazes me, Sarah. At times he reminds me of Henry Kissinger. Golda Meir told me years ago that Kissinger had an incredible ability to remember details. When Kissinger helped negotiate the cease-fire arrangements with Syria after the Yom Kippur War, Golda said he knew more about Kuneitra and the positions on the hills surrounding Kuneitra on the Golan than any minister in the Israeli cabinet except the former generals. Anyway, like Kissinger, Anthony knows almost too much about Israel. It's almost scary. And by the way, did you know that Hussein's son, King Feisal, once tried to give Kissinger *The Protocols of the Learned Elders of Zion* to read?"

"Did Kissinger take it?"

"No. And I'm glad. *The Protocols* is probably one of the most destructive pieces of anti-Semitic literature ever produced, especially with its fabrication of the Jews' plan to take over the world. Sometimes, though, when I talk with Anthony, I get the feeling he has read the book. But instead of being concerned about the Jews taking over the world, Anthony seems to be planning to do just that! And I just have the feeling—mind you, at this point it is only a feeling because he is moving very diplomatically—that Anthony would crush anyone who got in his way, including his own mother. I've never met a man—a man . . ." Jared hesitated, groping for the best way to describe Anthony. "How do I say this? Let me put it this way: I've never met a man more skilled in intrigue than Anthony is. He could easily have invented the word. What I find most puzzling is the way Anthony courts both Iraq and Israel at the same time and gets away with it. That defies reason."

"You know Jared, every time I hear someone say 'Iraq,' I want to say 'Babylon.' Babylon once encompassed what is now called Iraq. To me the two are synonymous. Babylon destroyed our temple and took us into captivity. I know that was long ago, but they haven't changed; they are still our enemy. When I read the first mention of Babylon in the Bible's book of Genesis, as the Gentiles call it, I feel as if she is pictured as the mother of the nations. Babylon has to be the mother, for that's where all the different languages—and hence the nations—were born. To me, it seems the mother who birthed the nations passed on to her children her hatred for Israel. We have no true friends, Jared. No trustworthy friends. It's almost as if there's an unearthly, devilish enmity among the nations towards us."

Jared's eyes were closed as he spoke. "I hadn't thought of it like that, Sarah. And when you say we have no friends, you are right! This is why I believe the K'nesset is so open to Anthony's proposal." Jared sighed. "Fighting the K'nesset wears me out."

Jared was tired—very tired of fighting. The K'nesset was divided two to one, and Jared was with the minority. He was the resistant remnant. "The world is changing, Sarah—the balances of power, the coalitions. It is frightening. We're headed quickly in the direction of one global government. And you know what? I wouldn't be a bit surprised if Anthony headed it up. The man is shrewd. Very shrewd. . . ."

Jared paused for a moment. Sarah studied his face. His eyes were closed, but his mind was open and running full speed. "Anyway, Sarah, the man wants to see you after the dinner tonight. He said he wants to talk with you in his suite. It's all right to go; it's set up like an office. Plenty of security. But be careful. Anthony is smooth, and I mean smooth. . . ."

"You will come with me, won't you?"

"I wasn't invited. Anthony may think he will be more successful in persuading you to work with him if he has you to himself. But you don't have to worry about his manners as a gentleman. According to our information, women hold no interest for him. The man is married to power, and power consumes all his energies."

Jared opened his eyes. They were nearing the King David Hotel; he could tell by all the noise. "How I wish we didn't make such a racket every time some head of government comes to town. All those sirens going off and the police on their loudspeakers barking at the people to get out of the way gives the feeling that a major disaster has occurred. Then add all the drivers impatiently leaning on their car horns. What do they think blowing their horns is going to accomplish? Maybe it keeps them from getting ulcers. With all the big hotels here on King David Street I pity the people who live and conduct business here. Their street is perpetually blocked."

It took a few minutes for the motorcade to inch up to the front of the King David. The police stopped all the traffic as the motorcade drove through the circular drive and one by one dropped off their passengers under the hotel's stone-arch portico. As Jared helped Sarah out of the car, he leaned close to her and whispered, "Remember, be cautious. Watch what you say. Anthony's like no other man you've met. He is here to make a seven-year covenant with Israel. I am very opposed to it, and he knows that. He may try to use you as a pawn in his dealings with me."

Sarah glanced to her left as Jared closed the door to the car. She noticed the men standing guard on the roofs of the low shops next to the King David as well as on the four-story building beyond it. Each had a gun in one hand and a radio in the other. Sarah wondered: *Just who was guarding whom? Was Israel guarding Anthony, or was it the other way around?*

After dinner, Jared and Sarah stood at the end of the private dining room just to the right of the lobby. They were saying goodnight to the prime minister and his wife when Sarah caught Anthony approaching them from behind. She caught his reflection in the long, heavily draped beveled-glass mirrors. The mirrors that replaced the original windows when the hotel was expanded were a nice touch, as was the pleasant dining room overlooking the pool.

The man in the mirror was tall, nice looking, and impeccably dressed in a well-tailored suit. He moved with great poise and self-assurance among the small clusters of people who lingered to talk. Smiling, Anthony shook the prime minister's hand and then bowed toward his wife as he said, "It was a good and profitable day. You are a discerning leader, my friend." Then, turning to Jared as the prime minister departed, Anthony smiled heartily. "Jared, I'm sorry we weren't able to sit together at dinner tonight. Ah, and you are Sarah?"

Anthony never paused for an answer. He knew all about Sarah. His files contained several pictures of her. He reached for her hand. "Sarah, I have looked forward to this dinner simply for the pleasure of meeting you." Anthony kept Sarah's hand in his as he turned to Jared. "I believe I am looking at the beauty of Israel embodied in one woman. Why didn't you tell me she was so lovely?"

Jared responded, "You never asked. I thought you were more interested in her sphere of influence than her beauty. However, you are right—she does embody Israel."

Sarah withdrew her hand from Anthony's and, with the utmost of charm and the most disarming of smiles, said, "Gentlemen, that is enough about me. . . ."

A slight smile played at Anthony's lips, his eyes intently focused on Sarah's as he replied with what seemed like deep sincerity, "I don't think there could be enough, Sarah." He paused for just a moment, his eyes still communicating with Sarah's. Then he said, "Jared, would you mind if I take a few minutes with Sarah while you mingle among the other dignitaries? Of course, if it is permissible with you, Sarah."

"Jared mentioned that you wanted to talk about the temple," Sarah laughed delightedly. "Anytime someone wants to talk about our temple in a positive way it certainly is permissible. Where shall we sit and talk?"

"Would you mind coming up to my suite? I have set up my offices there and it is much quieter than here with all these people in the lobby. I requested my particular suite over the presidential suite because it is one of only four with a balcony overlooking the Old City. The view from my balcony is breath-taking."

As Anthony escorted her to the elevator, Sarah said, "If you think the view from the King David takes your breath away, then you should see the view from the roof of my home. From there one can see the top of the Temple Mount with the kottel below. I personally think my roof has the most magnificent view in all the world. And," Sarah said almost coyly, "I don't think there is too much bias in my statement."

Anthony put his hand lightly on Sarah's waist as he ushered her into his suite, nodding at the security man outside the door. It disturbed her how good Anthony's touch felt. It also disturbed her that Anthony seemed to know innately how to draw people to him. "I would love to see your home sometime, Sarah. Maybe on my next visit to Israel. . . ."

"Let me know when you are coming and I'll see if we can arrange it."

"The pleasure will be mine, Sarah," Anthony's voice was almost seductive, "all mine. Please have a seat, and I will fix us a drink. What would you like? I have some wine, scotch—"

"I would enjoy a glass of wine."

"Red or white? The red wine is nice and sweet."

"Something sweet would be perfect. I didn't touch the dessert tonight, although it looked wonderful."

Handing Sarah the wine, Anthony sat down on the edge of the couch opposite hers. Placing his glass of wine on the table between them, Anthony looked straight into her eyes, never breaking his gaze. The way he sat down gave him a commanding appearance. His smile was also strangely commanding yet still charming. His eyes reminded Sarah of the clear blue of the Mediterranean, with a shoreline of long black eyelashes as dark as his hair. His eyes, like his body language, were intense. It was the kind of intensity that created an excitement and anticipation for what he was going to say. The man clearly had a charisma about him which, like the fragrance of his cologne, penetrated the air. His magnetism made a person want to know him. Even Sarah found herself greatly intrigued by the man.

"Sarah, I am sure Jared told you the governments I represent want to make a seven-year treaty with Israel. It's a treaty that will assure you not only peace, but a guarantor of that peace." As Anthony paused to let the words sink in, he scrutinized Sarah, carefully measuring her reaction to his words.

"And the price of this treaty, Anthony? It appears to me that the fate of small countries always seems to rest with the superpowers. Of course, they have their own interest to guard. What interest does this treaty guard, may I ask?"

"Since the negotiations are not complete, let's just say this: I'd like a summer home—a place to 'pitch my tents' on your beautiful holy mountain. As your guest, of course. And when I visit, I'd like very much to spend my time here in peace. We all want peace—peace and safety.

"The coalition of governments I represent," Anthony continued, "is seeking world peace, and we want to bring peace here to the Middle East. With our influence in Iraq, we believe peace is possible. We are prepared to enter what I would like to call a seven-year covenant guaranteeing peace for Israel—a covenant which, because of our combined strength and political clout, we are certainly able to sustain. The purpose of my visit is to explain this covenant to the controlling powers in Israel and work out the details of such an agreement. For this reason I am certain you can understand why I cannot say more. At this point, there has yet to be an affirmation of the covenant."

Anthony edged forward on the couch, close to the front of the cushion and closer to Sarah. His hands were clasped. "Now in the light of all this, I want to talk about your favorite subject, Sarah—the temple." Anthony spoke her name differently this time. It slipped off his tongue in a way that conveyed an unwarranted, almost brazen intimacy. Once again she found herself drawn into his crystal blue eyes. "Sarah, how would you like to start building your temple within, say…a month?" Anthony's eyes never moved, his intensity never wavered. He took in every detail of Sarah's countenance and body language, watching her response to his question.

Sarah wanted to gasp, to cry with delight, but she controlled herself. Something deep within her restrained her spirit, pulling against his eerie seductiveness. Sarah didn't feel attracted *to* the man; rather, she felt attracted *by* the man. *What is it about him. . . ?* she wondered. In an instant Sarah knew. Anthony reminded her of Antiochus Epiphanes! It was as if Antiochus had been reincarnated.

Sarah deliberately forced herself to lean back on the couch, responding slowly, cautiously. Now she understood his seductiveness; it was almost demonic. "Rebuilding the temple has been the hope and dream of multitudes of Jews who believe the temple must be rebuilt before Messiah comes. Yet we have been constrained by the whole political genre in this city." Sarah's voice remained level. "You know as well as I do, Anthony, that Israel cannot and will not build her temple on any location other than the Temple Mount, where it belongs. How then could *you* so maneuver the situation as to bring about its construction within such a short span of time? You know the holy war that would ensue if the State of Israel—notice I said the State of Israel—even talked of erecting a temple on the mount—a mount which the Muslims consider their holy ground dating back to the time they conquered Jerusalem. Think of the conflict we'd have on our hands!"

Anthony reached over and took Sarah's hand. Although his gesture caught Sarah by surprise, she handled it with ease. Sarah was now fully alert to his manipulative intentions. Smiling at him, she pulled her hand back gently and propped her chin on it.

Anthony wasn't pleased with Sarah's response. He was puzzled that she didn't jump on it. And now Sarah had withdrawn her hand from his. What had turned the current from warm to cool? He had underestimated her reaction . . . a mistake he rarely ever made. And he didn't like it. Anthony decided to bring the conversation to a close. He had to have more information. Having Sarah's backing would be nice, but if he had to, he could move ahead without it.

"It wouldn't be your war, Sarah, but mine...ours, the nations backing me. If Israel accepts the covenant terms, it will also be my responsibility to negotiate with the Palestinians about the rebuilding of your temple. They will no longer be Israel's problem, but mine. Mine along with a coalition of ten nations to support me, but a problem that I am well able to handle myself. After all, as I said, I will pitch my tent on your holy mountain. And when I come, I'll want to dwell here in peace."

Sarah stood, smiling lightly and firmly keeping her gaze fixed on Anthony's eyes by sheer force of will. She asked, "Is it a place to pitch your tent, or is it a secure bridge you are looking for? A suspension bridge from north to south? And a Dead Sea worth billions?"

For a fleeting second Sarah saw Anthony's eyes narrow, flickering ever so slightly. Then the fire was extinguished as quickly as it took spark. Anthony rose to his feet, his smooth smile and gracious demeanor belying his inward rage. He had wanted to dismiss Sarah; however, there was one last card—a trump—he had yet to play.

"Remember, with the temple, the Jews could re-institute their sacrifices." Anthony watched Sarah's eyes to see if this announcement really was his trump card. "Thank you for our time, Sarah. I take great pleasure in honoring those who so kindly acknowledge me with their presence and assistance. Please tell your friends and associates that they need to ready themselves to commence building the temple. As soon as the treaty is signed," Anthony paused for effect, "they can begin their sacrifices again!"

Purposefully, with graceful deliberation, Sarah turned her back to Anthony and walked to the door. She could feel the color draining from her face as Daniel's voice resounded almost audibly, "And *he* will make a firm covenant with the many for one week, but in the middle of the week he will put a stop to sacrifice and grain offering." Her body suddenly felt weak. She felt that if she didn't keep moving she might faint. Refusing to display her weakness, she kept her shoulders straight, her head held high.

Sarah knew the covenant would be signed. Her question was, Is Anthony the "he" of Daniel's prophecy? She vowed to herself that if the temple was built, she would count the days, marking them one by one, beginning from the signing of the covenant.

Chapter 67

"Aunt Sarah, can we talk with you?"

Startled, Sarah turned around in her chair. "Samuel! Levi! You surprised me! I didn't hear you coming up the stairs—this is wonderful! I was just wishing someone was here enjoying this view with me."

Sarah rose from her lounge chair, greeted the men with hugs, then put an arm around each one and walked with them to the edge of the roof. "Come, look with me. It's *our* people, on *our* Temple Mount! I doubt I will ever get over the awe of seeing our people in their temple offering sacrifices!"

Sarah slipped her arm from behind Samuel. "Excuse me! I get teary when I talk about it." Sarah laughed a little, wiping her tears. "My cup would surely overflow if our Jerusalem didn't have so many Gentiles milling all over the city. With our temple came compromises and a covenant I still don't trust. But then we dissenters stood in the minority, didn't we? However, we do have our temple, and we have our sacrifices. For that I shall be grateful!" Things had changed so much for the better that Sarah had willfully suppressed any question that surfaced about Anthony's identification with the "he" in Daniel's prophecy.

Samuel, too, had tears in his eyes. "I remember Aunt Sarah, when I watched the Romans destroy the temple. I will never forget walking through the terrible carnage. In fact, sometimes I still dream about it. So, as I look at it today, I can understand your tears."

Levi patted Sarah on the shoulder. "You know, we should just be grateful the temple is here! We did everything we could to get it rebuilt, but we just couldn't make it happen. Then the Premier General steps in and makes a covenant with the K'nesset and opens a way for the rebuilding to begin. And now we've re-instituted our sacrifices! What Anthony—excuse me, the Premier General—did was almost like Messiah showing up!"

"Levi," Samuel retorted, as he looked at his friend in shock, "how on earth can you make such a statement? In no way can they compare! Except that, for all intents and purposes, it looks as if the Premier General is out to rule the world. Don't make such comparisons, Levi! It's . . . it's blasphemous!"

Levi threw up his hands, his voice indignant. "Okay, okay, I'm sorry, I'm sorry! It was a poor comparison—a *bad* comparison. But believe me, I didn't intend it to sound blasphemous."

"Sit down, you two. Can I pour you some lemonade? I made it myself."

"I would love some, Aunt Sarah, and I know Levi would, too."

"Samuel," Levi quipped, "I'm right here. You need not answer for me."

As Sarah poured the lemonade she asked, "Are you two having a disagreement?"

"Just a debate, Sarah, just a debate." Levi took a long drink of the lemonade and immediately shoved his glass toward Sarah for a refill just before Samuel could ask Sarah to pour him some more.

"Samuel thinks the Premier General may be the fulfillment of the king described in the last chapter of Daniel. That's why he responded so indignantly when I inadvertently—did you hear me, Samuel?—*inadvertently* compared the Premier General to the Messiah. You have heard, haven't you, Sarah, that there are several men in our land now claiming to be the Messiah?"

"One of them, Aunt Sarah, says he is Sabbatai Zevi come back to earth." Samuel cast a glance that said, "I told you so" in Levi's direction. Samuel was remembering the time on the Mount of Olives when Levi had come running to tell him that Messiah had come and it was Sabbatai Zevi!

Sarah replied, "The Sabbatean movement never completely died out, did it? I think it's safe for us to say this man is not Messiah. The Sabbatean movement has supported several so-called Messiahs since its inception. Their Messiahs were all delusional and their followers were deluded!"

"Well," Levi asked, "what do you think about the prophet who's creating a stir in Jerusalem as he calls our people to repentance? He says he has come to restore the hearts of the children to the fathers and the fathers to the children. To 'prepare us for the dreadful and awful day of the Lord.'"

Samuel quickly added, "From what I have been hearing about this prophet, he is genuine to the core. He is reputed to have the same power Elijah displayed in the days of the schools of the prophets. Some are even saying it's because of him that terrible things are happening around the world—the blood, the fire, and the columns of smoke in the sky and on the earth. No one can reasonably explain why these natural disasters are happening. Remember that terrifying day we had recently when the sun was turned into darkness? Then the moon turned into what seemed to be blood. A lot of people died from the sheer terror of those events!"

Sarah spoke. "According to the reports on the international news, it's estimated that tens of thousands may have died. It's such a significant number some people are calling for the prophet's death. They are blaming him for the cosmic disasters that have been coming upon us. But if the man were a Gentile instead of a Jew, would they be calling for his destruction? Some are saying he should be beheaded like Iraq is doing to so many. It reminds me of the days when the Jews were blamed for the Black Plague and other disasters and consequently put to death."

Samuel moved to the edge of his chair, his eyes dancing with discovery. "You know that every *Pesach*—Passover—we traditionally leave an empty chair at the table, waiting for Elijah to return. Why? Because the prophet Malachi wrote that Elijah would come before the great and terrible day of the Lord. This man is proclaiming that same message. Maybe this year he will sit in Elijah's chair and—"

"Samuel," Levi retorted, "you and I have already discussed all this! Remember, we want to know what your Aunt Sarah thinks about these things, as well as what she thinks about Daniel. Please, let her talk."

"Well," said Sarah thoughtfully, "all that you say about the man does seem to be in line with Malachi. I too have been watching him carefully. With anticipation, but also with caution. I don't want to be deceived.

"You know," Sarah continued, "I was reading Daniel again last night. For some reason I couldn't sleep. I kept drifting in and out of consciousness—half here and half somewhere else. Anyway, something was tugging at my mind, making me think I needed to read Daniel. I almost felt as if I'd never get to sleep unless I got up and read it. I am ashamed to say that I've let myself get too busy—I know that's a poor excuse—and I haven't read the book in so long.

"Now," Sarah said, looking at Samuel, "tell me what you saw in Daniel that reminded you of Anthony. I'll call him Anthony since that's what I called him before he ever donned the title Premier General." Sarah reached over and picked up her Bible. "If you need a Bible, you can use mine."

Samuel took the Bible from Sarah and flipped the pages until he came to Daniel. "Listen to this, and tell me if it doesn't sound like Anthony. And by the way, you have heard the news today, haven't you? I'm sure it will be in the paper tonight."

"What news? I haven't heard anything. I've been here on the roof all morning reading . . . various portions of Daniel, Ezekiel, and Joel. I haven't even eaten lunch. I felt I needed to fast. Tell me, what was on the news? Was it Iraq, or Babylon, as some are now calling it? Have they massacred more people again?"

Levi interjected, "That is still in the news. People are dying right and left for their faith. Babylon has a vendetta against all other religions—"

"No, Aunt Sarah," Samuel intervened, eager to show them from Scripture why he was convinced Anthony was evil. "The big news today is the Premier General's conquests. Or should I say *attempted* conquests? He tried to conquer Jordan."

Sarah sat upright, shocked. "He tried to . . . ? Did he succeed?"

"No, Jordan escaped out of his hand," Levi answered. "But the Premier General has all but conquered both Syria and Egypt."

Sarah leaned back. For a minute the slightest hint of a smirk played on her lips. She felt a tinge of satisfaction at hearing of Syria and Egypt's demise. These northern and southern neighbors had been barking at her borders for years like wild dogs dying to be loosed to scavenge her land. *At least we are protected by our covenant with the Premier General. He's not attacking us or attempting to take over our country*, she thought. Sarah recalled how, over three years ago, the K'nesset accepted Anthony's covenant proposal. Jared and nearly a third of the others in the K'nesset stood against the majority, dubbing it a "covenant with Sheol." But the covenant was passed in the K'nesset by a margin of two to one.

"Anyway, Aunt Sarah, this is what we came to seek your opinion on because you know so much about Daniel. Levi thinks I'm reading in meanings that are not there. And maybe I am. I don't want to add anything or to misinterpret it. But if I am on target and what I believe is accurate, then we are headed for serious trouble. Listen."

Samuel bent over the Bible and began to read. "Then the king will do as he pleases, and he will exalt and magnify himself above every god, and will speak monstrous things against the God of gods; and he will prosper until the indignation is finished, for that which is decreed will be done. And he will show no regard for the gods of his fathers or for the desire of women, nor will he show regard for any other god; for he will magnify himself above them all."

Levi's exasperation was evident as he asked, "Sarah, do you see my problem? The Premier General *hasn't* magnified himself above other gods! He just doesn't believe in them. . . ."

Samuel glanced at Levi and said, "Levi, please let me finish reading. Then we can all discuss it."

"I'm listening. I'm listening. Read."

Samuel continued, "'But instead he will honor a god of fortresses, a god whom his fathers did not know; he will honor him with gold, silver, costly stones, and treasures.' Now listen to this: 'And he will take action against the strongest of fortresses with the help of a foreign god; he will give great honor to those who acknowledge him, and he will cause them to rule over the many, and will parcel out land for a price.'"

Samuel looked at Sarah. "Doesn't that sound to you like what Anthony is doing?"

Sarah nodded affirmatively as she said, "It does. Read on."

Samuel continued, "And at the end time the king of the South will collide with him, and the king of the North will storm against him with chariots, with horsemen, and with many ships; and he will enter countries, overflow them and pass through."

This time, it was Sarah who interrupted. She couldn't help herself. "That does sound like Anthony! North . . . Syria. South . . . Egypt." Sarah contemplated further. "Of course, in modern-day terms, chariots might be tanks. . . ."

Sarah momentarily gazed off in the distance, pondering what Samuel had read. As she did so, out of the corner of her eye she could see commotion taking place on the Temple Mount. Curious, Sarah leaned forward to focus more intently on the mount. Samuel went on reading, but Sarah couldn't pay attention. The sight in the distance was too captivating. There were crowds of media people and television cameras recording the excitement just outside the temple.

"He will also enter the Beautiful Land, and many countries will fall; but these will be rescued out of his hand: Edom, Moab and the foremost of the sons of Ammon." Samuel paused, staring at the page. Then, pointing at the words without looking up, Samuel slapped the side of his face as he exclaimed, *"Oi-vah-voi!* Anthony just attempted to overtake Jordan. And he *failed!* Think about it: What is modern Jordan? Isn't Jordan the land once known as Edom, Moab, and Ammon?"

Levi jumped to his feet. "You're right! Let me see that." Levi pulled the Bible from Samuel's hands. "Where . . . what verse were you reading?"

Samuel stood up, looked at the Bible over Levi's shoulder, and ran his finger down the page as he tried to find the place. "It's here in the eleventh chapter . . . we started at verse 36 . . . let's see—"

"I got it, I got it!" said Levi. "It's verse forty-one." Levi read it aloud, "'He will also enter the Beautiful Land, and many countries will fall; but these will be rescued out of his hand: Edom, Moab and the foremost of the sons of Ammon.' You may be right, Samuel!" Levi exclaimed. "You may just be on to something. What do you think, Sarah?" asked Levi as his eyes continued scanning the page, reading the verses silently. "Sarah . . . ?"

"What?" asked Sarah, clearly oblivious to the discussion at hand.

"What do you think?" Levi asked Sarah again. Samuel took the Bible from Levi and continued reading silently. He had to tilt the Bible upward as he did so, for now the sun was setting and it was becoming harder to see.

Sarah was still inattentive, mesmerized by the sight across the way.

"Sarah, what are you looking at?" Levi went to stand beside her as Samuel looked up from the Bible.

"Something is happening on the Temple Mount, in front of the temple gate. Look at all the cameras and microphones. What do you suppose it could be?"

Samuel was now at Sarah's side. "Do you want to go see?"

"Yes, but I'll have to change first. Let's run down into the house. I'll be just a minute, and then we can go. It's nearly time for the evening sacrifice anyway."

As they entered her living room, Sarah called to them over her shoulder as she went to change. "Turn on the television. Get channel 2. CNN couldn't possibly be covering it this quickly. I'll be right there. If you're hungry, get yourself something out of the refrigerator. . . ."

No more than a minute had passed before Samuel yelled, "Aunt Sarah! Come here . . . quickly!"

Sarah threw on her robe and ran to the living room. As she did, she heard

Anthony's voice. Samuel's finger was pointing in the direction of the television screen. Without saying a word Sarah dropped into a chair. Anthony's words seemed so loud, so adamant they found it hard to absorb what he was saying. The Premier General stood with the temple in the background, reciting a long list of his accomplishments since his rise to prominence. As his speech continued, he became more animated and boastful—eventually speaking against the Almighty of Israel. Sarah cringed inside at the blasphemous words now pouring out of his mouth. Accusations and defamatory statements were directed at her husband, as Anthony declared him impotent, unable to come to Israel's aid. He called him uncaring, unmerciful, unfaithful, and full of wrath and judgment. Then Anthony pronounced Him *dead*.

Tears filled Samuel's eyes. Levi was stunned. Sarah stared intently at the television screen, her face livid, her chest and arms flushed.

Then Samuel yelled, "Look! Look where he's going!" The cameras followed the Premier General right into the temple itself—a place that no Gentile was permitted to enter. Yet there was the world's Premier General walking beyond the table of shewbread into the very Holy of Holies! Anthony motioned for the cameramen and reporters to follow. Some media personnel hesitated, drawing back, while others practically tripped over themselves trying to get as close to the Premier General as possible.

Then, raising his hand to add emphasis to his demonic boldness, Anthony declared with the fire of a dragon, "The covenant between the World Coalition Government and Israel has come to an end. And an end has come to every sacrifice. There is to be no worship of any god, but one. I *am* god!"

With that edict Sarah sprang to her feet and shot her fist toward the ceiling. Wrath mingled with anguish as her words reverberated off the walls. "Blasphemy!" she shouted. "Blasphemy! An abomination of desolation in our holy temple!"

Sarah's whole body trembled violently as Samuel gently eased her into a chair. Her body began convulsing with silent sobs as she buried her head in her hands. The memory of Antiochus Epiphanes loomed before her mind like an ugly apparition—Antiochus and the unholy statue of Zeus he set up in her temple so long ago. It was truly as if Antiochus had been raised again from the depths of the abyss.

Finally, finding her voice again, Sarah looked into Samuel's anguished eyes, "Please, hand me my Bible. Will you, please?"

Samuel and Levi watched mutely as Sarah turned to the back of the Book and began counting under her breath.

After a few moments had passed, Sarah lifted her eyes from her Bible. The color was gone from her face. "Since the day Anthony and Israel signed their covenant I have marked off all the days, tabulating them week by week. Forty-two months have passed. Forty-two months, by Jewish reckoning, equals one thousand, two hundred and sixty days—exactly three and one-half years. The events are unfolding exactly as Daniel said—Anthony, the Premier General of the World Coalition Government, is the little horn of Daniel chapter seven. And we have been given into his hand for time, times and half a time—another three and one-half years!"

Sarah continued, her voice quiet, devoid of emotion. "According to Daniel, it will be a time of distress such as never occurred since there was a nation until this time."

"Worse—" Samuel asked with trembling voice, "worse than Hitler's holocaust?"

"Worse, Samuel," Sarah's voice was now barely audible. "The prophet Joel said there has never been anything like it, nor shall there be again after it."

Chapter 68

"Yes," Sarah said wearily as she guardedly answered the phone.

"Imma," said Saul, sounding stressed. "We're prepared. Are you ready?"

I'm not leaving, my son, Sarah thought, *and I don't know how to tell you. Your father promised this land to us, and I will not relinquish. Others may sell their souls to this devil, but I will not. You must leave, but not your mother. How lonely I will be without you. And what if . . . what if . . .* Sarah reined in her thoughts, sighing heavily. Her sigh was all Saul heard.

After discussing the matter, Sarah and Jared were convinced their loved ones must flee Jerusalem for the sake of their lives. Yet Sarah was equally convinced she had to stay. Jared, however, would not let her stay alone. He vowed to protect her even if doing so would mean his death. Having reached this agreement, the two of them decided not to break the news to the others until they neared the Judean wilderness. The situation was too tenuous for them to delay their departure while arguing the issue. Sarah would talk with Saul and Rebecca on the trip.

Sarah stood with the telephone still in her hand, lost in thought. Her shoulders felt as if a ton of Jerusalem stone was weighing on them. For a moment her eyes surveyed the decor of the Arab home in which they had found refuge. The reality of her surroundings only compounded her sorrow. Sarah doubted she would ever see or live in her own home again.

"Imma...is that you?" Sarah's lack of response brought greater consternation to Saul's voice. "Imma, are you all right? Is anything wrong?"

"Yes, son, I am all right. Everything is wrong in life right now, but I am all right, and I am ready."

"Are Reuben and Rachel there?"

"Yes, and so is Jared." Saul was troubled. His mother's voice didn't have its usual enduring ring.

Sensing Sarah's weakness, Jared took the phone from her hands. She didn't offer any resistance. "Saul, this is Jared. We're all here, and we're ready."

"Are you sure we'll be traveling light, Jared?" Anxiety peppered Saul's voice. "Imma does understand that we can't take anything more with us, doesn't she? She hasn't packed anything for our trip besides the food, has she?"

"She understands," Jared responded. "Where are Samuel and Levi?"

"They're coming with our transportation. It wasn't easy to get. We'll meet you just as we planned. Jared, be careful. Tell everyone Joshua's doing great. He's excited about the trip; he has his little backpack on and is eager to get started."

A slight smile crossed Jared's face. "He's the only one who's looking forward to this, but I am glad he's excited. We don't want him experiencing fear at this young age." Jared then looked around him before continuing. Turning his back to Sarah and Rachel, he cupped his hand around the mouthpiece of the phone and whispered so softly that Saul could barely hear him. "Saul, I'm concerned about floods."

"I'm concerned too," said Saul, taking precautions to make sure Rebecca wouldn't hear as she passed by him while making last-minute preparations. Saul and Rebecca were staying in the home of another Jewish sympathizer. "We'll talk about it. I'm glad Samuel and Levi know their way around."

It was evident to Jared that Saul, too, was guarding his words. "We'll be there soon, Saul. Shalom." Jared hung up the phone and scratched the stubble of his newly grown beard.

Reuben looked at him quizzically. "Your beard really makes you look different! Is everything ready?"

"You look different too. And yes, everything's ready," Jared said as he bound the black cord around his Arab headdress. Appraising himself in the mirror, he commented, "I always wondered what we'd look like if we had been born Arabs instead of Jews. Now, seeing myself in this Arab headdress, I know! I never thought I'd wear one of these on my head! How do I look?"

Jared turned to Sarah and Rachel, who were looking at him from behind shrouds of black wool veiling everything but their eyes. "Well, you two are certainly, ah, well covered! I am not sure I would know you if I saw you anywhere but here!"

Reuben surveyed Jared, circling around him. "You look *almost* as authentic as I do." Then he looked at Rachel and Sarah. "Remember, we are going out through the Damascus Gate. It's the Arab Quarter. There's to be no talking! If they discover we are Jews, we'll be dead Jews. Sympathetic Arabs would be a rare find—that is, unless they are genuinely Christian. So remember, absolutely no talking. Even though you speak fluent Arabic, Sarah, you still sound like a Hebrew."

Practicing silence, Sarah nodded her head. Rachel and Sarah were resigned to the dark, heavy dresses reaching to their feet and the black woolen headwrap of Arab women. Levi, who could speak flawless Arabic, had bravely purchased their attire the previous night. When he finally returned from the market having escaped detection, they had all felt a tremendous sense of relief.

The marketplace was overflowing with people. Sarah and Rachel, their dark eyes darting from face to face, yet making contact with none, walked in front of the men. Jared and Reuben wanted to keep them in sight.

The atmosphere in the city was dark and foreboding. Few in Jerusalem, even non-Jews, fully understood what would transpire now that the Premier General had declared himself to be higher than the Almighty and called the world to bow at his feet. Uncertainty settled like a heavy morning dampness deep into every nook and cranny of the land. Changes of great proportions were being instituted daily not only in Israel but also throughout the world. Anthony had even set into motion a number of alterations in times and in law. These changes, coupled with the inexplicable and cataclysmic events taking place globally and being viewed on television worldwide, caused men's hands to fall limp and their hearts to melt. In this crucible of anguish men groaned, gripping their thighs like a woman in labor.

Yet others—those who aligned themselves with the new Premier General—experienced a strange, perverted, unearthly euphoria as they plotted the demise of their common enemy—the Jews. Anti-Semitism plummeted to more sinister levels as it baptized men's natural affections into the cesspools of hell. The stench from this suspicion and animosity permeated the air above Jerusalem as the little band of refugees made their way out the Damascus Gate.

Samuel and Levi, each wearing Arab headdress, were waiting with jeeps. Everyone boarded the vehicles and the group motored along in total silence until they were well outside the confines of the city. The ride down the Jericho road toward the Judean wilderness and the Dead Sea was arduous and long. Jared, Reuben, and Rachel rode in Levi's jeep; in Samuel's jeep were Saul and Rebecca, and Sarah with Joshua merrily bouncing on her lap.

"Joshua, a long time ago your Safta took a long journey like you and Imma and Abba are taking now. On my journey I made up a little song and I sang it all the way so I could remember it. The words I sang helped me to be strong and courageous. Do you know what strong and courageous means, Joshua?"

Joshua nodded his head vigorously. "Look, Safta," he said, flexing his little arm and pointing to a muscle that looked big to a boy of three-and-a-half. "See how strong I am? Feel, Safta, feel."

Sarah smiled as she put her fingers around his little arm. "Oh," Sarah cooed, "you *are* strong! Very strong! Now, do you know what courageous means?"

Joshua grinned and shook his head back and forth with all the vigor he could muster. "No, Safta. No!"

"Well, Joshua, to be courageous means to act strong and stay calm even when you're scared and you want to run away."

"I won't do that," Joshua said enthusiastically, looking at his mother. "I'll be . . . be. . . ."

"Courageous," Rebecca interjected.

"Good, Joshua! Good for you! Now, Safta has made up a song for you to sing. Do you want to sing it so you can be strong and courageous too?"

Joshua nodded dramatically as his eyes took in the awesome Judean hills. Painted in varying shades of color depending on the sunlight, the hills bore their own unique beauty—a beauty that went unnoticed by a little boy who was more impressed by size than by color and lighting. "I'm strong now, Safta! See my muscle?" Joshua flexed his arm again.

"Yes, I see."

"Sing, Safta!" Joshua squealed excitedly. "Sing!"

"Okay. Listen carefully and watch what Safta does while she sings. You follow me; that will help you remember the words. Abba and Imma will sing it too. It goes like this:

"We shall not die, (*Sarah dropped her head and closed her eyes, then raising her head again, she popped her eyes open as wide as she could and threw her arms in the air*) but we shall live.

Because we are his chosen, (*she sang as she patted her right cheek*)

His promises will not fail. (*Sarah held up her hands to picture an open Bible*)

Day and (*using her hands, Sarah formed a circle spreading her fingers around her face to depict the sun*)

Night stand, (*quickly she folded her hands and laid her head on them as if she were asleep. Then she stomped her feet—right, then left—on the floor of the jeep*)

And so shall Israel! (*then Sarah raised her arm and flexed her muscle*)

Joshua laughed with delight as he tried to copy Sarah.

"Joshua, this song is about us. It's about you, Abba, Imma, Safta, and all the Jewish people. And it's also about Saba, Safta's husband."

"Saba's in the car!" Joshua said, pointing to the other jeep, where Reuben sat.

"That's right, Joshua. Saba's in the car. But you have two Sabas," Sarah said, holding up two fingers.

"No! One!" Joshua yelled back, holding up one finger and then pointing again to the other jeep.

"No, two! You have two Sabas," Sarah said as she held up two fingers. Although she laughed at Joshua's adamancy, inside she felt a twinge of pain. Joshua had never seen his other Saba, and neither had Sarah for what had been ages. She longed for his rule and for their family to be restored. She longed to see her beloved and to see Joshua with his Saba.

"Where's my other Saba?" Joshua asked inquisitively. "Did he die?"

Wondering why a three-and-a-half-year-old would even think of death, Sarah looked quizzically at Rebecca, who shrugged her shoulders. In almost a whisper, Rebecca said, "He's smart, Imma Sarah. Always asking questions. Several days ago Saul was talking about a patient who died and had to explain to him what that meant! It must be your side of the family; even my Imma said

I was not as precocious as Joshua is!"

"Joshua," said Sarah. Joshua turned to look at her.

"Joshua, look at me and remember what I am saying. Saba's *not* dead. He will never die. He's gone now, but he is coming back very soon." At that moment an idea arose in Sarah's mind. She wondered if Joshua would understand, and decided to give it a try.

"Look at my fingers and count them," Sarah said as she held up three fingers. "How many fingers do you see?"

Joshua looked intently at Sarah's fingers for a moment. "One...two ...three!" Joshua shouted the word *three*. "Three, Safta."

"That's right. Now how many fingers do you see?"

Joshua paused, most likely wondering what Safta was up to. "One that comes back down."

"That's right, Joshua. The bent finger is half a finger, isn't it?"

Joshua nodded his head and looked out the window.

"Joshua, look at Safta just one more time. Then we'll sing and you can look out the windows." Joshua obediently turned his head and, with big trusting eyes, looked at his Safta as she said, "Remember my fingers? In one, two, three and a half years, you are going to see your Saba. When you are just a little past seven years old you will see him. And you are going to love him so much and he's going to be so happy because he already loves you."

Joshua looked at his Safta, whom he already loved so much. "Does he know me?"

"Oh, yes! He has us all engraved on the palms of his hands. He can't forget us. Every time he looks at his hand he sees a mark right here." Sarah took Joshua's soft, chubby little hand in hers and rubbed her thumb in his palm.

"I'm on his psalm?" asked Joshua.

"Palm, Joshua. Palm. Yes, you are. When you see Saba, you ask him to show you his hand—his palm. Now let's sing, Joshua."

"We shall not die, but we shall live.
Because we are his chosen, his promises will not fail
Day and night stand, and so shall Israel!"

Saul had been listening from the front seat of the jeep. Tears coursed down his cheeks as he thought about seeing his Abba. Somehow he sensed his presence in the jeep as they sang their song.

Leaving the Jericho road, Samuel took a little-used dirt trail that would take them deeper into the Judean desert. The desert was full of trails used by Bedouins, caravans, smugglers, and various armies over the years. Their plan was to go as far as they could in the jeeps. Then Samuel and Levi would lead everyone on foot through territory they knew well. Samuel would have preferred to stay in Jerusalem, but no one else knew the territory as he and Levi did. It was for the sake of the others that he was willing to come. This was the desert where he and Levi had fought and hid during the Bar Kochba revolt. As Samuel thought about those days, he became more excited. Maybe they'd even sleep in the cave where Levi saved Samuel's life! *It would be great,* Samuel thought, *to tell Joshua the story, and to show him where Levi and I made our covenant. Besides, I've always wanted to see Petra. Maybe that's where we'll hide—somewhere near ancient Bozrah—after we skirt the Dead Sea and head into Jordan.*

"Well, this is it," Samuel said as he brought the jeep to a halt. "We walk from here on." He slipped from behind the wheel and stretched. His eyes surveyed the stark beauty of the barren Judean hills, which careened from the heavens to the deep valleys and wadis below. An occasional clump of trees and shrubs marked the wadi's course, bearing witness that in an earlier season the ground had been soaked with life-bringing water. The wadis were now as dry as bones bleached in the sun, and were of the same muted off-white color as well.

"Hurry, Imma," said Saul, beckoning to his mother. "We want to get as far as we can before it gets too dark."

"Saul. . . ."

The way Sarah said his name caused Saul to stop instantly. In disbelief he put down the backpack Samuel and Levi had brought for him and walked over to his mother.

"No, Imma. . . no!"

"Saul, listen carefully. I cannot join you," she said as unbidden tears welled up in her eyes.

Saul reached towards her. "Imma. . . ."

Sarah extended her hand, her voice firm. "Please, please listen to me. Nothing you say or could say will change my mind. I must stay in Jerusalem. I will not die; I'll live. Jared will stay with me. If you didn't have a family, I'd have you by my side. But your responsibility is your wife. You leave me and cleave to her. That's what the Bible says, and we have found it is a book to be obeyed. I am putting all my faith in its promises and its prophecies. If Daniel is correct, and so far he has been, then we will be together again in about three and one-half years. He said that those who endure to one thousand, two hundred and ninety days will be blessed. That's thirty days beyond three and one-half years. What Daniel means by that I do not know, but I plan to endure. You do the same. We will endure as a faithful remnant—not like those who have defected to the side of the world's Premier General.

"Now, please, it is getting late and we are behind schedule. Go. Take charge, my son. Don't make me have to persuade everyone. Assure them that they should go on without Jared and me. Lead them to safety; go to Edom. Anthony tried to conquer Jordan and he didn't. Maybe somewhere near ancient Bozrah you can find a place to hide until the day of destruction is over. Maybe Petra."

Saul turned and started toward the little group huddled around Jared. He was frustrated not only because of the fear he felt for his mother, but also because he knew that no one and nothing could change her mind. He knew his mother.

"Saul?" It was barely a whisper, but he heard it. Saul stopped and looked back at the woman who had given birth to him.

"Thank you again for loving me unconditionally. For understanding my heart and sharing my passion for our people and our land. For choosing to suffer with us and being willing to die for what is right and true. It's because there are some things that are more important than life that I hold you in an open hand."

Sarah waited as Saul went over to the group to explain why she and Jared were not going with them. Then she joined the group. No one said anything. As Sarah hugged Rachel and then Rebecca, Jared took Reuben aside. He knew Reuben didn't need to hear what he was about to say, but for his own peace of mind, he said it anyway. "Reuben, you've worked down in this area. You know the danger of flash floods; they can engorge those dry wadi beds in an instant at this time of year. Whatever you do, stay out of the wadis. They're deep and hard to get out of in a hurry. When the waters come, it's like the waters of the Red Sea covering Pharaoh and his armies, drowning everyone caught in its turbulence. Many have lost their lives in these floods. Don't take any chances, okay?" Jared squeezed Reuben's shoulder. "I don't think we could handle not seeing you at the end of these days."

Sarah stooped down in front of Joshua and kissed him. Then, just before getting up, she looked Joshua in the eyes and said, "Now Joshua, be strong and courageous. Remember, Saba is coming. Teach our song to the others. Abba and Imma will help you."

"And Saba has me on his psalms!" Joshua exclaimed as he held up his little hands with his chubby fingers spread wide.

As Sarah stood to her feet, she whispered, "Me, too."

Jared and Sarah stood waving and watched as the group began their descent into the wilderness. *I wonder where Jared and I will hide?* she thought. Then, cupping her hands to her mouth, she shouted with all the strength she had—one word at at time.

"Beloved, it is the day of the Lord and he's hiding you in the day of his anger!"

The echo of her words reverberated through the mountains. *Hiding . . . hiding . . . hiding . . . day . . . day . . . day . . . anger . . . anger . . . anger. . . .*

Chapter 69

"*S*top! Stop!" screamed the Premier General as he let lose a stream of profanities.

The jeep flying the ensign of the Premier General skidded to an immediate but smooth halt. The man at the wheel, Master Sergeant Olson, wanted to hit the brakes hard—so hard it would send the jeep spinning, catapulting the Premier General through the windshield and against the meter-high stone wall just below them. *I'd like to see the guy spread-eagled on those ancient rocks with his brains splattered all over the place. Then if tourists ever came to this ruined city again, the guides could say it was on these ancient remnants of the Babylonian destruction of Jerusalem that the Premier General of the world met his unfortunate and untimely death.* Master Sergeant Olson hated the man sitting in the rear of his jeep.

For a moment Olson permitted himself a glimpse of the Premier General in his rearview mirror. *He probably wouldn't have a scratch on him; he's like the devil himself—you can't get rid of him!* Olson then looked immediately to his left. He didn't want to make eye contact with the Premier General because when he was angry, his eyes took on a sinister glaze.

Olson had no idea about what had roused the Premier General's anger. He wanted to drum his fingers on the steering wheel, but he didn't. Nor did Olson's countenance give a hint of his thoughts. He knew he had to keep his expression as blank as possible, for the Premier General didn't miss a twitching muscle. His eyes took in everything. Sometimes Olson thought the Premier General could read men's minds. But then he knew that couldn't be true. If it was, Olson would have been beheaded a long time ago! Olson didn't say a word as the fuming world leader grabbed the seat in front of him and got out of the jeep. He simply stayed in his seat staring at the low, modern-day wall surrounding the remnant of the ancient stone wall some seven meters below.

Why is he so mad? Olson wondered. *But then, who knows what perturbs the man? It could be anything! One minute the commander in chief can be the most persuasive and likable person on the face of the earth, and then in a second—not a minute, but a second—he can turn into the devil himself!* Olson wished he had never attained the dubious but coveted honor of driving this madman around. But there was no escape now.

He had driven the Premier General around various parts of the world in modes of transportation as varied as limousines and tanks. Olson could drive anything anywhere. In his position as the personal chauffeur of this man, he saw a lot and heard too much. It gave him nightmares. That's why he slept as little as he could—just enough to function. He knew that his job was safe only as long as he never talked about a single thing he heard or saw. Although no one ever said anything to him about keeping his mouth shut, deep inside himself Olson knew if he ever revealed anything it would mean the literal end of him. The perverted viciousness of the Premier General was well known by those in the Premier's inner circles. Anthony had no regard whatsoever for the lives of others.

Once again, Olson glanced in the rearview mirror. He wanted to see where the Premier General was going. Seeing that the General's back was to the jeep, Olson reached up quickly and adjusted the mirror so he could watch what was going on. As he did, he made a mental note to readjust it when the General wasn't looking. This man didn't miss a thing!

I wonder who he's talking to? Olson mused. There was nothing familiar about the couple he observed in the rearview mirror. The Premier General's back was still to the jeep. The woman looked livid; her mouth was closed. Taut. Her hands were on her hips. Olson couldn't see the face of the man, but he knew this wasn't a reunion of old friends. *If the Premier General has friends!*

For a moment Olson's eyes left the mirror as he looked around what was once—about three and a half years ago, he reckoned—called the Jewish Quarter. The place was in a shambles. *What a contrast from the Temple Mount proper!*

They had just come from there. The Premier General wanted to check out *his* temple and make sure it hadn't been damaged when they captured Jerusalem. His order was that it be left standing as a monument of the greatest of his declarations—that he was the one and only god to be worshiped without equivocation. Olson had heard that the Jews called the Premier General the Abomination of Desolation. As he thought about what he had seen in the wake of the Premier General's attack on Jerusalem, he concluded that the Jews had rightly nicknamed him!

Master Sergeant Olson glanced into the rearview mirror again and was astonished to see the woman shaking her fist in the face of the Premier General. Olson longed to turn around and watch the scene; it wasn't often that someone had the courage to defy the General to his face.

Anthony grabbed Sarah's forearm ruthlessly, his fingers almost shutting off the circulation. "Listen here, Mrs. Israel," he snarled in a low and sinister voice. "The only reason I allow you to breathe is because I want to see your torment when I return from Edom with the bodies of your son, his wife, and your grandson. Joshua they named him! God our Savior—ha! There is no savior but me. And rest assured, Sarah," Anthony hissed, "unless you take your own life, I swear to you that you will see their dead bodies with your own eyes. Then I will gouge out your eyes and rip out your tongue. After which, little Jewess, I will flay you alive in front of the world like a burnt offering on my altar!"

Sarah's eyes never flinched in the face of Anthony's threats. Jared watched in stunned amazement at the evil that possessed the man. The whole time, the Premier General never once looked at Jared or acknowledged him. He had headed straight for Sarah and spoke to her as if no one else were present.

"No one, but absolutely no one, contests my rule! As god, I hold the power of life and death," Anthony spat out venomously. Then he threw Sarah's arm into her face, turned around, and walked back to the jeep.

Sarah continued to stare angrily at Anthony as he walked away. Upon swinging himself into the jeep he looked back with contemptuous arrogance and in a sneering laugh said, "I'll be back in a day or two with the carcasses of your beloved ones!"

Paralyzed by anger, Sarah did everything she could to keep from shaking. When the jeep was well out of sight and she could no longer hear the sound of its engine she screamed, fell to the ground, and covered her ears with her hands trying desperately to deafen the threats resounding in her head. A loud crash sounding from the hills surrounding Jerusalem caused her body to jump. Once again she thought she could hear the wailing of the inhabitants of the city. Only this time it seemed like little Joshua's voice was among them, crying, "Safta . . . Safta." Kneeling in the dust of the centuries Sarah rocked back and forth, fighting to keep her wits about her, clutching to her sanity.

Sarah's eyes had never blinked during the encounter with this beast of a man. She had willed them to be as cold and hard as steel. But now she broke. Her spirit was crushed. Reeling back and forth on the ground she wailed from somewhere deep in the bowels of her being. *Auschwitz was nothing compared to this! O my God . . . my husband . . . where are you? Where are you? Have you deceived me? Where are you? Are you going to let your son die? Are you not going to save our Joshua? Is this the end of us instead of the end of time? Have you indeed abandoned us?*

Jared stood nearby like a tree beaten in the wind, boughs broken. He watched Sarah's anguish, feeling completely helpless. He thought they had wept and wailed until no more tears were left. Their strength had dried up like a broken potsherd which had lain in the desert sun for centuries. The mere effort of putting one foot in front of the other seemed to require all their strength and concentration. They were emotionally bankrupt.

Jerusalem had been sacked by the nations. Led by the Premier General, the armies of the earth had stormed her gates, captured the city, plundered the houses, and ravished the women. Jared and Sarah witnessed it all. And now this encounter with Anthony! Jared wondered how much Sarah could endure. Now he saw it. Sarah was broken.

Even though Sarah tried with all her might to squeeze the sight from her eyes, the dashing of the children and the raping of the women played again and again on the screen of her mind. Once again her mind went back in time and she saw the forged iron of the Roman soldier's sword viciously piercing Joseph's little body. The screams and weeping of the women of Jerusalem reminded Sarah of Rachel weeping for her son, and now she was among them weeping for Saul, for Joshua, for every Jewish mother down through the centuries who had lost loved ones simply because they were Jews.

Then another picture flashed through her mind—what she and Jared had seen that very afternoon. Women of Israel hanging their heads in shame, having been ravished by leering men from a multitude of nations. And once again after so very long a time, Sarah could feel the uncleanness in her skirt, the violation of the Babylonian soldier as he forced her into the rubble. Hunching even lower, Sarah tried to bury herself deeper in the bloody dust of their supposedly sacred city. *Oh my husband, can't you hear our blood crying from the ground? Hasn't it reached your ears? Or have you grown deaf?*

After some moments of weeping, Sarah untangled her hand from her hair and moved it under her face to wipe her eyes and nose. As she lay with her face in the dirt, she fought to obliterate Anthony's threats with verses she had marked in her Bible—verses she had wanted to remember about the day of the Lord. *"I will punish the inhabitants of the earth for their iniquity. . . . A day of distress . . . of darkness. There has never been anything like it, nor will there be again after."* Sarah's mind riveted on that last word. *After! After! There is an after!* Then the promise of "after" clashed with Anthony's threats as they resounded again in her ears. *"I will gouge out your eyes . . . flay you like—"* No! No! I will not die! Sarah cried in faith. *My husband said I will live. Daniel said I will rule. It is you Anthony, who will die . . . who will be annihilated forever!*

Jared stood motionless, shifting his eyes back and forth from Sarah to the destruction of what once had been Jerusalem. Although half the population had been exiled, they and others were not cut off from the city. For some strange reason the surviving remnant were free to roam through the ruins. Jared wondered if it was because Anthony wanted them to see what he had done by the power of his might.

By now, Jared thought, *Anthony and his armies must be headed for Jordan, Edom, and Bozrah, searching out those who escaped Jerusalem to save their lives. Will he find our friends and loved ones hiding in the caves? Or had Samuel and Levi been able to take the little band safely to the ruins of Petra and hide them in the city of rock carved in the burnished red mountain? If that is where they are, then maybe they'll be safe,* Jared reasoned. *Safe at least from an overwhelming onslaught. Neither tanks nor a calvary can storm the narrow entrance to that ancient city.*

Even though he knew it was futile, Jared puzzled in his mind for some way to warn Saul and Rebecca . . . to get word to Reuben and Rachel . . . to urge Samuel and Levi to take them and flee. Then his thoughts returned to Anthony's threats about Saul and Joshua and he wondered if sorrow would end up being added upon sorrow to Sarah's already unspeakable grief.

Knowing that warning their friends and loved ones was humanly impossible, Jared's eyes surveyed the almost desolate city, noting how few survivors were left. Men seemed scarcer than gold—scarcer than the gold of Ophir.

For a time, Sarah's body continued moving back and forth in its rhythm of grief. Then her moaning and rocking stopped. With her head still buried in the ground, Sarah felt new strength coursing through her body as she recounted the promises she had read and marked in her Bible. In her mind, Sarah could see the passages she had underlined and thematically marked because they shed light on her future—promises of Messiah's coming and of the subjugation of the nations. Of multitudes in the Valley of Jehoshaphat while her husband sat to judge the nations gathered there. *Gathered there!*

Sarah's heart quickened. The dawn of understanding broke on the horizon, bringing light, expelling the darkness of the night. *They are there now! Now! The nations are there in the Valley of Jehoshaphat! At least those that Anthony hasn't taken with him to Edom and Bozrah!* Sarah's spirit rose like the light that had dawned brightly in her understanding. *I am alive. Jared is alive. Not every Jew is dead. Had a third of Israel survived the fire just as Zechariah promised?*

Jared looked wearily upon Sarah. Unaware of what was taking place under the mass of tangled hair covering her head, he reasoned that he must do something. He could not lose Sarah to the impotence of despair without a fight.

"Get up, Sarah," Jared said sternly. "You cannot surrender to Anthony's threats or abandon yourself to despair. You're alive, Sarah! You are alive, and so am I. It looks as if a number of us, maybe a third of us, have come through this fire! Get up, Sarah . . . now!"

Jared reached down and pulled roughly on Sarah's shoulder, determined to not let go until she was forced to lift her head and meet his eyes. He would not let her slip through his hands to drown in an ocean whose depths of grief knew no measure.

Sarah raised her head and looked up at Jared, tears streaking her dirt-stained face. She brushed the sand from lips which were swollen and bruised. Jared wondered if Sarah had purposely bitten herself in an attempt to keep from screaming. Although she looked physically and emotionally defeated, Sarah's eyes glistened with hope, shining like the morning dew catching the first rays of the sun.

Jared sighed. His tension eased, leaving him weak, almost faint. As he pulled Sarah to her feet, she smiled weakly and began to sing very softly, "We shall not die, but we shall live. Because we are his chosen, his promises will not fail. Day and night stand, and so shall Israel!"

Jared smiled back at her. It was a haggard, weary smile, yet a smile it was. "Now the Sarah I know is back. For a while I thought I had lost you."

"Jared, the armies in the valley—"

Jared didn't notice the excitement in Sarah's voice; he was too distracted by his wounded leg. It was throbbing with pain from standing in one place too long. "Sarah," he interrupted, "let's go back to our cave and rest." Noticing the weariness in his voice, Sarah subdued her passion to tell him of her revelation regarding the nations in the Valley of Jehoshaphat.

Jared continued, "I just don't have the strength to walk any place but back to our cave. We have endured enough trauma for one day—for a lifetime, really. We have to rest. We can come back tomorrow. I have to go back right now, or you are going to have to abandon me or figure out a way to carry me back."

As they began the walk back to their cave, Sarah looked down into the Kidron Valley, a part of the extended Valley of Jehoshaphat. It seemed she could hear the confused babble of the nations gathered in that valley as far as she could see from north to south.

"Jared, I heard these armies are camped as far north as the plain of Megiddo."

Jared nodded affirmatively. He not only lacked the strength to walk, but also to speak.

When they arrived at the cave, Sarah gathered some wood and lit a fire. Seated with her back against the wall of the cave, Sarah watched the fire consume the dried straw that she broke bit by bit and threw into the flames. Her words and mood were contemplative. "This has been a time of distress without equal. In all my life, I never have seen anything that compares." She paused briefly. "I've watched as men, women, and children writhed in agony—an agony beyond the Crusades, the Inquisition, the pogroms. Beyond the horrors of Sobibor, Treblinka, Auschwitz—all the death camps combined. Yet until I saw the unbridled evil in Anthony's eyes this afternoon, my mind couldn't conceive how something so unspeakably horrible could happen to this world. We have experienced an agony beyond any horror the human mind can envision...beyond even Hitler.

"And I have wept, Jared, not only for our people and Jerusalem, but. . . ." Sarah hesitated for a moment, then threw the whole handful of straw into the fire. "But because of what I have seen inside me."

Jared raised his head and looked at Sarah. He had been gazing at the fire, watching Sarah's bits of straw go up instantly in flame and then curl into a golden glow that eventually disintegrated into ashes. He was taken back by Sarah's statement. Although they had never discussed it, he too had wept because of what he had seen in himself.

The greatest grief Jared had to deal with—the most glaring remonstrance he felt—was the many years he spent in the K'nesset seeking to govern the Almighty's chosen nation apart from the Almighty's Word, the Bible. Jared remembered when Prime Minister Rabin was trying to negotiate peace with Arafat and the Palestinians that Rabin said something to the effect of, "It does not matter what the Bible says." Or, was it, Jared mused, "The Bible has nothing to do with it?" And although he disagreed in his heart with Rabin, Peres, and the others, Jared hadn't taken the time to investigate it for himself. *If I believe the Bible is the very word of the Almighty, then I ought to have studied it and governed my private and political life accordingly. If only I had gone beyond the Torah to the prophets, the Nevi' im, I might have seen...and understood what was happening. . . .*

Sarah began speaking again. "I feel I've been refined, purged. And purified. For so long I have not only harbored a deep resentment towards my husband, but at times I've nourished it. It was the Holocaust. I could not understand why he allowed Hitler and his henchmen to do what they did and why he allowed the world to turn its back on our suffering. I couldn't forgive him. He could have stopped it, and he didn't. The Holocaust seemed to me to be the ultimate chastening! Unjustified, inhumane, perverted . . . and unreasonably cruel when so many died with his name upon their lips. I know Daniel spoke of my husband's sovereignty when he wrote, 'None can say to him, what are you doing?' but there is no way I can understand it. I just don't understand! Isaiah wrote that he would pay us back double for all our sins. How I fervently pray that our time of sorrows is over!"

Sarah stood to her feet and took one last look at her clump of straw disintegrating in the fire. For a moment she empathized with the straw. Then she went to the little bundle of treasures she had stored deeper into the cave. This was Sarah's section of the cave. Jared slept close to the front of the cave to ensure Sarah's safety. He always kept a knife at his side as well as a gun with a silencer.

After they had said good-bye to their friends and loved ones in the Judean wilderness, Jared and Sarah had joined a resistance movement that had taken its name, in part, from Daniel chapter seven. The little band called itself The Faithful Remnant, Saints of the Highest One. Convinced that the Premier General was the king described by Daniel as the little horn, the band determined never to bow to Anthony. They would die first, resisting his every attempt to wear them down as they faithfully waited out the time, times, and half a time of Anthony's rule.

Sarah returned from the back of the cave with her Bible. For a moment she sat silently counting the marks she had made on the blank pages at the back of the book. Finally Sarah said, "Although I haven't made any marks for nearly a week now, I believe we have survived almost one thousand, two hundred and sixty days of unadulterated hell since Anthony broke his covenant and desolated our temple."

"Are you sure you counted them right? It seems longer. Much, much longer." Jared rose to put more wood on the fire, to ward off the chill in the cave. They kept the fire small and a good distance from the entrance so it wouldn't be detected. When it became dark, Jared would extinguish the fire for their safety.

"I've marked off the days one week at a time in this little Bible," Sarah said, waving it in the air. "That's forty-two months!"

"All I know is that it's been three-and-a-half years of inconceivable, unrivaled torment." Jared leaned against the cave wall. The cave wasn't a comfortable place to live. *But we are alive and have a roof over our heads,* Jared thought, smiling at the irony of this roof over their heads. He and Sarah had found refuge in all sorts of places since they parted from their friends and loved ones in the Judean wilderness.

"I feel as though the very fires of Gehenna have been lapping at our faces," Jared continued. "I've seen men gnaw their tongues in pain until they were bloody pulps. What we've seen and lived through is incomprehensible… beyond what my mind can absorb."

"It's the day of the Lord, Jared—the dreadful day of the Lord." Sarah rose to her feet, talking louder as she walked to the mouth of the cave. "The ravages of my husband's day of reckoning as he purges not only our nation but the entire world from all its evil. But this is not the end," Sarah said with confidence. "The purging is not the end. That's what I realized when I buried my face in the dirt this afternoon. That realization is what gave me the strength to get up and face the future—a future Anthony will *not* have!"

Jared drew up his wounded leg and tried to rub the stiffness from it. Then, pushing himself to his feet, he joined Sarah at the opening of the cave.

For a moment they looked silently out into the night. The heavens looked like polished ebony studded with diamond-like stars except, Sarah noticed, for an empty area to the north. "Jared, as I understand Daniel's word, this time of distress will not go beyond one thousand, two hundred and ninety days. We can't give up now; we are almost there." Sarah squeezed Jared's arm. "Daniel said we'd be blessed if we waited and endured to one thousand, three hundred and thirty-five days."

"But will we, Sarah? Can we? What if Anthony returns from Edom? What if the remaining armies still camped in the Valley of Jehoshaphat become hostile to the scraggly remnant who survived the attack against Jerusalem? We've been waiting for Messiah ever since the promise was given—I can't even remember how long. My faith is ebbing from me, Sarah. How long can we wait? And—" Jared paused, "what if he does not come this time?"

I shall set My glory among the nations; and all the nations will see My judgment which I have executed, and My hand which I have laid on them. And the house of Israel will know that I am the LORD their God from that day onward. And the nations will know that the house of Israel went into exile for their iniquity because they acted treacherously against Me, and I hid My face from them; so I gave them into the hand of their adversaries, and all of them fell by the sword. According to their uncleanness and according to their transgressions I dealt with them, and I hid My face from them.

Therefore thus says the Lord GOD, "Now I shall restore the fortunes of Jacob, and have mercy on the whole house of Israel; and I shall be jealous for My holy name. And they shall forget their disgrace and all their treachery which they perpetrated against Me, when they live securely on their own land with no one to make them afraid.

"When I bring them back from the peoples and gather them from the lands of their enemies, then I shall be sanctified through them in the sight of the many nations. Then they will know that I am the LORD their God because I made them go into exile among the nations, and then gathered them again to their own land; and I will leave none of them there any longer. And I will not hide my face from them any longer, for I shall have poured out My Spirit on the house of Israel," declares the Lord GOD.

—EZEKIEL 39:21-29

It will come about in that day that I will set about to destroy all the nations that come against Jerusalem. And I will pour out on the house of David and on the inhabitants of Jerusalem, the Spirit of grace and of supplication, so that they will look on Me whom they have pierced; and they will mourn for Him, as one mourns for an only son, and they will weep bitterly over Him, like the bitter weeping over a firstborn.

—ZECHARIAH 12:9-10

The LORD will be king over all the earth; in that day the LORD will be the only one, and His name the only one.

—ZECHARIAH 14:9

Chapter 70

*S*arah!" Jared's voice, barely above a whisper, was tainted with fear as he searched for Sarah's shoulder in the narrow beam of the small penlight he held. "Sarah, wake up! Wake up. . . ."

"Wha . . . what's wrong?" Sarah asked sleepily.

"I don't know, but—"

Sarah dropped her head back on her pillow as she groaned, "Jared, get the light out of my eyes. It's the middle of the night. I'm exhausted . . . please."

"Sarah, it's *not* the middle of the night. It's the middle of the morning!"

Sarah opened her eyes briefly then immediately closed them again. "Jared," she murmured, "it's dark out. It's night."

Finding Sarah's shoulder with his light, Jared shook her rather roughly. "It's dark but it isn't night! It's the middle of the morning! Something strange is happening, Sarah! You have to get up!"

Once again Sarah forced herself to open her eyes. Her eyelids were heavy, nearly swollen shut, waterlogged from so much crying. Turning her face away from Jared she closed her eyes again. Burying her face in the pillow, Sarah grumbled, "You must have been dreaming. Go back to sleep . . . we have to have some rest. It's dark, so it's still night."

Jared directed the flashlight to the face of his wristwatch, checking it again for what seemed to be the hundredth time. He was finding it difficult to believe his watch could be correct. *Is it really midmorning?* Jared was puzzled. A strange darkness filled the heavens and covered the earth. It was as if someone had called a moratorium on night and day—canceling the night, evicting the moon and the stars, but forbidding the sun to come up.

Jared felt so wrung out he could easily have gone right back to sleep. Yet he was convinced there was something eerie and unnatural about the darkness and he was concerned. For more than two hours he had sat at the mouth of the cave watching for the sun to appear on the horizon. According to his watch, it was long overdue. How many times he checked the time and rehearsed and then re-rehearsed the events of the preceding day he didn't know. All he knew was everything before his eyes confirmed that daytime could not have come. Yet his wristwatch staunchly affirmed his reasoned calculations that it must be day. The second hand on his watch was moving. The date had advanced one day, and the time read 10:21 A.M. The moon was gone and the heavens starless, so it couldn't be night. Night had been passing for too long. Finally, Jared concluded it was neither day nor night.

Sitting in the darkness next to Sarah, Jared was perplexed. Something was wrong—terribly wrong. A chill ran through his body, causing him to tremble. *Should I make her get up or let her sleep?*

Without warning, Jared was tossed on his side as the ground shook violently. A rock crashed down from the ceiling of the cave and debris rained from above. Sarah awoke with a start. As she tried to sit up she lost her balance and fell with a thud to the hard floor of the cave. "Jared! Jared!" she screamed in alarm.

Jared struggled to get himself into a crawling position as once again the whole cave shook. His penlight had been knocked from his hand. Frantically he fumbled toward the arrow of light piercing the darkness. Gratitude surged through him when he finally grasped it. Fortunately he hadn't turned off the little flashlight. "Sarah! We have to get out of here! It's another earthquake!"

In the last three-and-a-half years an unprecedented number of earthquakes had occurred with destructive intensity. But until now, none had ever disturbed their cave. This was different! Panic rushed through Jared's heart, causing it to beat wildly.

"Sarah, stay on your hands and knees—even if it hurts! Follow the light!"

Sarah crawled behind Jared, wincing now and then as her hands or knees landed on a sharp rock. Her lethargy was gone, replaced by a surge of adrenaline. By now Sarah had noticed the strange darkness penetrating the cave, and it frightened her.

The cave rocked again, sending Jared sprawling. Again the penlight was knocked from his hand. He could taste blood on his lips as he groped for the flashlight again. Jared prayed the batteries wouldn't fail them. Licking his cut lip, he called behind him, "Sarah . . . are you all right?"

"I'm okay. Just keep going. We've got to get out before this cave becomes our tomb!"

Jared helped Sarah to her feet as they reached the opening of the cave. Just as she stood the shaking stopped. Both gave a sigh of relief. Then a bolt of lightning illuminated the sky. Sarah jumped, letting out a scream. Thunder rolled with an ear-shattering crash from the bass drums of heaven.

Jared reached for Sarah's hand and pulled her back from the opening of the cave. "For some reason, Sarah, I believe we need to go to the Mount of Olives."

"I do, too, Jared," Sarah said with amazement. "That is just what I was about to say!"

As they cautiously made their way from the cave to the Mount of Olives, a calm settled over the land like a blanket. Although no sun could be seen in the heavens, a dim light emerged seemingly from nowhere, giving shape, shadow and form to the trees and landscape before them.

"What time do you have on your watch, Jared?"

Jared shone his penlight on the dial. "Eleven twenty-two."

"That's so hard to believe from the looks of things, isn't it? I wonder if this darkness is related to the destruction of Babylon. The strong winds of these past several days could have carried the smoke of its burning from Iraq."

"I don't know," Jared responded as they began winding their way up the back side of the Mount of Olives. "Yesterday I talked briefly with a man who said he watched the destruction of Babylon on television just before the Premier General and his forces attacked Jerusalem. People everywhere are shocked that a city as powerful and wealthy as Babylon has been completely destroyed. According to this man, the inferno so illuminated the atmosphere that even from this distance he could see Babylon burning! The man said he believed Babylon fell for the slain of Israel . . . for the slain of all the earth."

"What do you think, Jared? Could this darkness be from some sort of atmospheric condition caused by Babylon's destruction?" Sarah asked, lifting her hand into the air.

"I don't know, Sarah. All I know . . . to be perfectly honest with you . . . is what I feel. I hate to admit that while we were in the cave the terror was so overwhelming I thought my heart would fail me for fear."

"You know, don't you, Jared, that Jeremiah—and others—foretold Babylon's destruction. Yet how many times did we court Iraq as if we had to appease them? It's so strange, isn't it?" Sarah rubbed her arms. She missed feeling the sunlight warming her back as it usually did when she climbed the Mount of Olives at this time of day. "It's also a strange feeling to read a prophecy in the Bible and wait with expectation for it to happen. Then time passes and the event still hasn't occurred, so I continue to wait, and still it doesn't come to pass. Eventually I find myself growing complacent in that knowledge, thinking of it as always future. Then suddenly the thing I've waited for comes. When it finally does happen, I find its coming almost impossible to believe!"

Pausing for a moment in their ascent up the mount, Sarah turned and looked to the southeast toward Jordan and Edom. For a few moments she looked longingly into the hazy darkness.

"Sarah. . . ?"

"I'm thinking about Saul...Rebecca...little Joshua. Do you suppose...?"

"Sarah, if I were you, I wouldn't suppose anything that I couldn't see or that hasn't been confirmed as fact. If you dwell on Anthony's threats, you'll be weighted with an anguish that will only debilitate you. Just wait. Wait until you know. Then, Sarah, confront reality with the reserves you've stored up for that day and whatever it holds—relief, joy, or sorrow."

Sarah turned from the darkness behind her and they resumed their ascent up the mount. In several minutes they would be at the top. From there they would be able to look across the Kidron Valley, the Valley of Jehoshaphat, to their ransacked Jerusalem.

Jared stopped and rubbed his leg.

"How's your leg?"

"I'll make it. I just become more aware of it on a climb like this." Jared straightened up. "I wonder if the armies will still be there in the valley. There was no way Anthony could take all of them. I hear they're camped from as far north as the plain of Megiddo all the way into the south as far as—"

A bolt of lightning shattered the sky. Peals of thunder jolted the mountain. Sarah fell into Jared's arms; for a moment they clung to one another in terror. Like the exuberant blare from a full orchestra starting up in a hushed auditorium they heard the clamor of war rising from the valley. People were shouting.

Jared bounded up the remaining distance toward the pinnacle of the mount, pulling Sarah behind him. The other side of the Mount of Olives—the side facing Jerusalem—was peppered with Jews who had survived the attack on Jerusalem. They looked on in disbelief as they watched the armies in the valley turn on one another in fear. Soldiers were killing each other in confusion! Terror reigned. Cries of anguish turned into unearthly screams as again lightning shot low, casting men to the ground in abject fear. The earth shook violently from deep within as the mount shifted beneath them in a destabilizing sway.

Again thunder pealed from the heavens as if heralding the sudden light that shone brightly from the southeast. The light emanated in supernatural brilliance from a majestic figure riding upon a white horse. It was just as in the days of old when a conqueror charged forth mounted on the back of a white steed, declaring his intentions of victory. His whole being glowed in brilliant light. The Jews on the Temple Mount and the Mount of Olives lifted up their hands crying with one voice, "*Baruch ha ba B'shem Adonai. Baruch ha ba B'shem Adonai.* Blessed is he who comes in the name of the Lord." Over and over their cry went up, reaching to the heavens as the trees clapped their hands and the mountains sang for joy.

Messiah! His splendor covering the earth. Messiah! His radiance like the sunlight. Messiah! Majestic in his apparel, marching in the greatness of his strength, coming from Edom, Teman, Bozrah. Every eye beheld him as he progressed through the Valley of Jehoshaphat to the Mount of Olives. In one accord the elect of the Almighty cried out, "Who is this who comes from Edom with garments of glowing colors from Bozrah—this one who is majestic in his apparel and marching in the greatness of his strength?"

A body was draped face-up across the back of the horse, between Messiah and the mane of his magnificent steed. The man's arms and legs dangled lifelessly; his eyes gaped out from their sockets, frozen in the shock of death. A wave of excitement swept through the multitude on the mount. It was Anthony—the man who was known to all as Premier General of the world!

People clapped, cheered, and shouted with joy as Messiah triumphantly ascended the eastern side of the Mount of Olives in front of Jerusalem. His voice rang under the heavens as the sun proudly beamed in the dawn of a new day. "It is I who speak in righteousness, mighty to save! The day of vengeance was in my heart, and my year of redemption has come."

At the sound of his voice and the nearness of his presence a great mourning swept across the multitude as they looked—in full realization and unveiled recognition—upon him whom they had pierced. Falling to their knees, the chosen bowed prostrate before him, their mourning like that of one who mourns for an only son. A train of people were following in Messiah's wake, and the graves on the side of the mount and in the valley below the Eastern Gate began to quake.

When he reached the top of the mount, Messiah turned his horse to survey those remaining in the valley below. A shout of rebellion rose from their lips as defiantly they raised their fists in an outburst of rage. Sarah, Jared, and the other onlookers watched in awe and horror as the flesh of those who had gathered to make war against Jerusalem decomposed on their bodies at that very instant. The eyes of both man and beast camped in the valley rotted in their sockets. Flesh sloughed from their bones. Their tongues rotted in their mouths. The Valley of Jehoshaphat ran with blood, staining the flesh as it melted.

Then Messiah dismounted from his horse. His garments were stained as one who had trod the winepress alone. As his feet touched the Mount of Olives, the earth quaked and a great crack split the mount down the middle from east to west so that half of the mountain moved toward the north and the other half toward the south. A gasp of amazement went forth from the multitude on the Temple Mount. Sarah and Jared stood dumbfounded as the land before them changed into a plain from Geba to Rimmon south of Jerusalem. As a result of the mountain's split, the ancient city, his earthly Zion, seemed to rise taller, more majestic in strength. Jerusalem had remained steadfast, refusing to surrender her God-ordained hill—set there by decree from the days of old.

Then fresh, pure streams of water spilled from beneath the Temple Mount and gushed into the valley as if to cleanse away the blood and corruption desecrating its soil. Its life-giving torrent flowed east to the Dead Sea while another branch flowed west to the Mediterranean.

Messiah turned to face the multitude that had followed in the train of his victory. Sarah's eyes scanned their faces. Where was Saul? Joshua? The others? Had Messiah slain Anthony in time? Sarah gazed at the General's body now truimphantly thrown to the ground. Then she lifted her eyes to search the faces of the many who had fled to Edom and Bozrah, but her loved ones were not among them.

Where are they? Surely they've survived! Oh, please. . . . Panic began to rise inside her. Must she ask Messiah? Standing on tiptoe, Sarah looked for the radiating aura of his glory. Where did Messiah go? She had lost sight of him!

At long last, Sarah's eyes fell to the perimeter of the multitude. Messiah had stooped down and was talking to a young boy standing beside a man who was kneeling on one knee, as together they stroked a lion. Sarah gasped. It was Saul! Her heart raced. *If it is my Saul, then surely the young boy with him must be Joshua!* She could see that the boy was stroking the lion with one hand and petting a lamb with his other. He was oblivious to all else about him, apparently fascinated with the lamb peacefully resting in the company of this docile lion.

Just then, Messiah swept the boy into his arms. He turned toward Sarah. It *was* Joshua! Sarah's hands flew to her mouth in delight as tears of joy and relief sprung in her eyes. Messiah smiled broadly as he walked toward Sarah, carrying Joshua in his arms like a shepherd carrying a lamb from his fold. As Messiah walked, Sarah's eyes remained fixed, never wavering from the sight of him. Speaking to Jared, whom she assumed was still nearby, Sarah whispered, "They live. They live! And we, Jared . . . we have attained! We've attained to the day of his coming. Maybe now my beloved will come. . . ."

Sarah opened her arms to receive her Joshua but was dismayed as she saw that Messiah intended to walk past her! It was as if he hadn't even seen her or he didn't know where Joshua belonged. Yet he continued to smile broadly. Then Sarah noticed that his eyes were focused beyond her as if looking at someone else. *Who? Who is he looking at? Joshua belongs with me!*

Sarah turned to see . . . and there he was! Joy mixed with fear surged through her. Sarah felt as though her heart stopped beating in her chest. *My Beloved! He has come! In all of his glory, he has come!* He stood before her as though he had been there all the time and Sarah just hadn't seen him.

Sarah watched in stunned silence, moved too deeply to utter a word, as Messiah handed Joshua to her husband. "Abba, your lamb is home—delivered safely into your arms."

Sarah waited as her husband took Joshua to himself.

For a moment Joshua simply looked at him in fascinated curiosity. Then quizzically he asked, "Are you my Saba?"

Delight spilled from the Almighty's eyes as he smiled and said, "Yes, Joshua, I am your Saba."

"How do I know you are?"

Sarah's husband held up his mighty hand, fingers spread wide. "Put your finger right there, in my palm. Or as you used to say, Joshua, my psalm."

Joshua grinned and put his finger in the palm of his Saba's hand. Feeling the mark, he promptly wrapped his arms around his Saba's neck and squeezed him hard. Then, leaning back in his Saba's arms, he asked with the deepest voice he could muster, "Do you know how old I am?"

Tears coursed down Sarah's cheeks as she recalled her last instructions to her grandson. He hadn't forgotten that when he was seven, Saba would come.

"Yes, Joshua, you are seven. I've been counting day by day for these last three and a half years so I could come and see you . . . and your Abba . . . and your Safta. It's been so lonely, Joshua, so lonely—especially without your Safta."

Then, putting Joshua down, he walked over and drew his trembling, weeping wife to himself. Sarah wept and wept, overwhelmed with his everlasting love, with his lovingkindness, relieved that her waiting was over. When her tears finally subsided and she became quiet in his arms, he leaned down and whispered in her ear, "Hephzibah"—my wife. Slipping from his arms, Sarah dropped to her knees and bowed at his feet where she belonged. Putting her arms around his legs, she whispered, "Ishi, my husband . . . forgive me. Please, please forgive me!"

For a moment he stood stroking her hair with his hand as he did so long ago in the years of their betrothal, when she followed him so willingly through the wilderness. There on her knees as she bowed at his feet the centuries passed before her . . . and once again Sarah wept as she realized that it was only because of who he was that she had been rescued once and for all from the hands of her enemies . . . and from her sinful heart of stone.

As his engraved hand caressed her hair, he said, "Your iniquities are gone, my Beloved. You are cleansed. The cities will again be inhabited. The waste places will be rebuilt. I shall build a highway of holiness and take the sons of Israel from the nations where they have gone. I will gather them from every side, from the four corners of the earth, and bring them into their own land. All Israel is coming home, Beloved. They are on their way now. And look—look behind me from where you are kneeling. Do you see David? He will reign again. And Abraham, Isaac, and Jacob? Do you see them? We will all be together. And Daniel, your beloved prophet. The end of the age has come, and I have raised him from the dead just as I promised. Look closely at the multitude, Beloved. Jeremiah no longer weeps. Do you see them? Do you see them all coming, bringing their sheaves with them, rejoicing?

"Stand, Beloved—stand on your feet! Let the nations bow down before us, for Messiah, the stone, has come and crushed the statue of gold, silver, bronze, iron, and clay. Our great mountain will fill the earth. The sovereignty, the dominion, and the greatness of all the kingdoms under the whole heaven are now given to our people. Our kingdom will be an everlasting kingdom and all dominions will serve and obey us."

Sarah rose, pulled to her feet by the strong arms of her Lord. "Ishi. . ." she whispered.

Cupping her face in his hands, with tears in his eyes, the Almighty looked at her tenderly and said, "Sarah . . . oh Sarah, to the world you were just a Jew. But now . . . now they know you are Israel, my Beloved."

Jack, Bob, Steve, Jan, Linda…
Carolyn, Bunny, Ettie…
Jane, Yael, Kent…
Danny, Ruthie, Esther…
Moshe, Dov, Ilya, Tommye…
Vladimir, David, Gershom…
Carol, Martha, Abir…

and all those who prayed and those who
labored to free me up—thank you for your
vital and unique contributions in this work
for the Almighty and His beloved Israel.

Glossary

Ashkenazi: German Jews; west, central, and east European Jews.

Bar: "Son of" (Aramaic) in personal names. **Ben** (Hebrew) means the same.

Byzantines: Ruled the eastern portion of the Roman Empire beginning in C.E. 395 until C.E. 711. Strongly supportive of Christianity.

Diaspora: Collective term for the dispersal of Jews and those living outside Eretz Israel.

Eretz Israel: The "real estate" of Israel; the Promised Land; Palestine.

Essenes: A monastic, strictly-regulated Jewish sect; considered themselves priests but differed in fundamental beliefs and practices from the Jerusalem priesthood.

Gehenna: Another term for the Hinnom Valley, used as a synonymous reference to hell.

Gemara: Rulings, etc., of the amorais, supplementing the Mishnah and forming part of the Talmud.

Gomer: Unfaithful wife of the prophet Hosea; the steadfast love of her husband throughout her harlotry is used to represent God's unfailing love for Israel.

Hanukkah (Chanukah): Feast commemorating the victory of the Maccabees over the pagan Greeks.

Hassidim: Followers of devout form of Judaism with strong mystical element, usually in eastern Europe.

Heder (or chedar): Judaic primary school.

Idumean: A people who were forcibly converted to Judaism by the Hasmonean king John Hyrcanus.

Jihad: A term used in reference to an Islamic belief that a necessary and permanent state of war must exist until the entire world submits to Islam.

Kabbalah: Jewish mysticism. "Practical kabbalah" is a form of magic.

Karaites: An eighth-century Jewish sect that rejected the Oral Law or post-biblical rabbinic teaching and adhered to the Bible alone.

Ketubbah: A Jewish marriage contract.

Kibbutz: A Jewish settlement, usually agricultural, in which people own property in common.

Kiddush: Blessing over wine, preceding Sabbath or festival meal.

Koran: A set of "revelations" written by Muhammed, the Islamic prophet; considered the holy book of Islam.

Maskil: Member of the Jewish enlightenment or haskalah.

Mishnah: Codified version of Jewish Oral Law.

Pogroms: Russian word meaning "riot"; used to disguise organized governmental and police actions against Jews as spontaneous outbreaks of indignation; in actuality, Jew-baiting.

Rosh Ha Shanah: Jewish New Year holiday.

Saba: Grandfather.

Safta: Grandmother.

Sephardi: The Jews who settled in Spain and Portugal.

Shema (Sh'ma): Judaic confession of faith (Deuteronomy 6:4).

Sukkot (Succot): Festival of Tabernacles.

Tallit (Talliot): Prayer shawl.

Tefillin: Phylacteries or small leather boxes fixed to the arm or forehead during prayers.

Torah: The Pentateuch, the first five books of the Bible, or scroll thereof; the entire body of Jewish law and teaching.

Yeshivah: A rabbinical academy. The rosh yeshival is head of it.

Yishuv: A settlement; the Jewish community in Eretz Israel before the state was created.

Yom Kippur: Day of Atonement.

Zohar: The principal work of kabbalah, a mystical commentary on the Pentateuch.